Praise for
Curse of the Tahiéra

A powerful all-engrossing epic

Wendy Gillissen's wonderful début novel is a powerful all-engrossing epic, in which love and forgiveness are essential lessons to be learned. The rich history and cultures of the land in which the tale unfolds is entirely convincing, as are the story's well rounded and sympathetic characters. For all it's depth, Wendy has succeeded in writing a thoroughly enjoyable tale which never once becomes heavy going or dull (the curse of many fantasy epics I have endured over the years!).
Tangle Catkin, Fae Nation

Captivating from beginning to end

Curse of the Tahiéra achieves on nearly every level of excitement and entertainment that the genre of fantasy prescribes. It's enlightening in its connection with real world values of love, honour, and camaraderie and on top of that, its great entertainment. Gillissen's take on pixies, beasts, and other common fantasy figures is unique and revitalizing. Fantasy novels are all about the journey, and Gillissen is able to weave several into a single amazing voyage that is captivating from beginning to end.
Eric Jones, Bookreview.com

Brims with imagination

What a marvellous book. This is a coming of age, young adult tale, filled with a deep spiritual understanding, which I am positive has much to do with Wendy Gillissen's experience as a past life therapist, and her specialisation in dream-work. It's been a long time since I've read a fantasy adventure like this and Wendy Gillissen has a style of storytelling that brims with imagination.
Sassy Brit, Alternative-Reads.com

It can be a dangerous thing for a man not to know who he is

Curse of the Tahiéra succeeds on so many levels; the characters have personality, depth and personal history, the fantasy environment is vibrant, detailed and filled with mythic wonder and the storyline is absorbing and well paced from beginning to end. Plain and simple it's one of the most enjoyable fantasy books I've read in a long, long time.

However my highest praise for Ms. Gillissen's book is reserved for the deep, profound spirituality oozing from her written words; her understanding of the nature of dreams, her innate knowledge of the unseen but sometimes felt life force emanating from the world (or worlds?) around us and the way in which she reveals the spiritual underpinnings and karmic destiny that ultimately determine who and what we are.
Brian E. Erland, Amazon top 500 reviewer

Curse

of the

Tahiéra

Aguéri

Curse of the Tahiéra

This paperback edition 2009
Aguéri Publishing
www.agueri.net
Cover design: Wendy Gillissen
www.wendygillissen.com

Contents

Prologue

Dead silence spanned the plain. They came with the failing of the light. Their slender swords gleamed silver in the pale light of the moon. On the other side of the plain young, inexperienced hands clutched their swords, and old men held their breath. A dark horror crept over the battlefield and smothered everything in its path.

A dark figure stood at the top of the cliff. The wind lifted strands of midnight hair. They floated about his head as if they had a life of their own. He steadied himself and drew his sword. His voice was a whisper.

Now.

One
A Journey North

Rom met Yldich on a trip to the North when he was almost twenty years old. He was a slender young man, with hair the colour of crow feathers, and eyes that were almost as dark. He had a temper on him that was like an underground forest fire. It could smoulder undetected for a long time, and consume him from the inside, but a well-aimed spark and sufficient fuel could ignite it and make it blaze like a bonfire.

At an age when most young men had already put down roots and were tending their fields and holding, their young wives raising their first babies, Rom travelled the country alone, buying and selling goods. To the northeast he went in spring, selling precious dyes, spices, silk thread for embroidery, silver needles, buttons of mother of pearl and any other things that were rare to the people of the northeast. Back to the South he travelled in autumn, to stay in the old cottage and buy goods from local farms and holds to sell next spring.

When people from the village started to say Rom should stay on the farm and get married like any honourable young man his age, he ignored them. When people said he was a strange one, always had been, and no good would ever come of him, he ignored that, too. When a migrant farm worker who had sampled a lot of strong local ale one night in the inn referred to him as 'that shady *Tzanatzi*-looking bastard in the corner there', he did not ignore it, and the man ended up with a broken nose and a lost tooth. Rom ended up in the village lockup. It had taken two town guards and a wrathful innkeeper to subdue him.

When the after-effects of the alcohol and a thorough beating had worn off and he regained consciousness, he found himself in an uncomfortable situation. Not only did the numerous hurts and aches vie with each other to get his attention, he also had to find a means to pay both the substantial fine for fighting in a public place as well as the furniture and goods the innkeeper claimed had been damaged in the process. The list included three chairs, a table, ten bottles of wine, two bottles of brandy, a keg of beer, the farmhand's tunic and some other assorted items Rom couldn't remember breaking. But then, he had been reasonably drunk.

Apart from that, to contest the fine would mean demanding justice at Court. He had no taste for that. It was common knowledge that Southern judges did not favour *Tzanatzi* in their rulings. But it meant a substantial portion of his earnings from the trip to the northeast were lost. He would have to set out again as soon as possible, to earn back some of the damage. It would mean travelling in autumn, when the winter snows threatened from the North, instead of waiting for spring in the comfort of the old cottage.

He set out a few days later, on horseback, leading a pony laden with merchandise and supplies for his journey. His ribs were still sore, but the cuts on his face were healing nicely.

The first days of his journey were uneventful. The nights were still warm, so he slept beside his horse, wrapped in his blanket. When the evening air became edged with a chill that hinted at the end of summer, he decided to seek a place indoors to stay the night.

The first wayside inn he stayed in was *The Squealing Pig*. It had a bad reputation as far as food and hygiene were concerned, but it was a good place to start a journey, for lodgings were cheap and as the inn was frequented by both locals and travellers from all over the kingdom, it was a good place to sample the local news. Though Rom was not one to chat with locals, his face was familiar to most frequent lodgers as he had travelled the same route before. So they treated him fairly enough, though they knew better than to try to get him to socialize.

It was down in the common room that evening, while Rom washed down a somewhat dry meat pie with a mug of home brew, that he was warned off the journey north. Not as many people stayed at the inn as was usual that time of year, and a big, ginger-haired traveller in his early forties was obviously looking around for some company. Rom ignored him, but the man took a seat at the same table, across from him.

Unfortunately, as there were no other diners present, he could not pretend the man was not there without insulting him. The incident of the previous week still fresh in his memory, he nodded stiffly. He silently hoped the man would be put off by his grim appearance, the yellow-purple discoloration around his left eye, and the healing cuts, visible remnants of being in a fight. The man seemed to take no notice, however, and introduced himself as Yldich. He spoke with a subtle accent Rom had never heard before.

Yldich did not seem to mind Rom's monosyllabic answers to his questions where he was from ('south,') and where he was going ('north,') either, as he had enough tales of his own to fuel the conversation. He told Rom about his travels, his home, and his experiences on the road, evidently enjoying talking and hearing the sound of his own voice. Despite his tendency to keep to himself, Rom found he actually enjoyed the man's tales. He gave a silent, encouraging nod every once in a while to keep a story going.

Yldich had signalled the serving boy to refill their beer mugs for the third time, when he said: 'Well. This business of yours up north, will it take you through Gardeth Forest?' Rom's head snapped up. He glanced sharply at Yldich. 'I thought as much,' Yldich said. 'You haven't heard about the trouble people have had up there then?'

'I usually go around, because my business is with the villages near the east coast.' Rom turned his mug around in his hands and frowned at his beer. 'I've never gone through the Forest all the way.'

'Better go around again,' Yldich said in a low voice. His eyes narrowed under his heavy brows. 'I've barely been able to get through in one piece myself, this time. And I know the region well. Something's haunting the Forest, something that doesn't like people passing through.'

He set his mug down on the table with an audible thump, and sat back in his chair. 'It started about ten years ago. Well, the Forests have always been dangerous for the unwary to cross, especially in winter. Frozen branches crashing across the paths, horses getting spooked and running off, ropes breaking on you for no apparent reason. Treacherous frozen lakes appear where there hadn't been any before. But last winter it got really bad.'

He leaned over his mug, and fixed Rom with a stare, his grey eyes like ice under an overcast sky. 'Travellers have been disappearing. Their bodies were found at the Forest's edge, frozen solid. They looked as if they died in terror.' He took another draught of beer. 'Now, some say the Forests have been getting worse because they've been stirring up trouble in the mines in the South. Disturbing some sort of balance, something to do with dark spirits or whatnot.' He shook his head and sat back. 'I'm just a simple farmer, I don't have anything to do with that sort of thing. But you mark my words, young man, be careful, or better still, don't be passing through the Forest at all.'

Privately Rom thought Yldich might be a farmer, but whatever he was, he wasn't simple. He wondered also if there could be a specific reason the man wanted to discourage him from travelling through Gardeth, other than warning mere strangers from the goodness of his heart. But he couldn't think of any.

'I've got no choice but to pass through the Forest,' he said. 'It's already late in the year, and I can't afford to waste any more time.' Yldich shook his head in disapproval. He looked concerned, but he did not press the matter further.

'Well, you do as you see fit, lad.' He got up and left a small pile of coins on the table to pay for the beer. 'Sleep well, now.'

'Good night.' Rom watched Yldich leave. He moved surprisingly graciously for a man of his heavy build.

While Yldich had a short talk with the landlord before he went up the stairs, Rom stared at the worn tabletop, lost in thought. Maybe Yldich was trying to warn him off the journey through Gardeth not because of supernatural danger, but a natural one. Rebels? Robbers? But what would be his motive to dissuade him from passing through? Rebels would not take offence at a lone traveller passing through. Robbers would welcome the chance of an easy prey. But if the Forests were home to any kind of illegal activity, why would Yldich not just say so? Why the ghost-stories? It made no sense. Unless the man was the gullible, superstitious kind, and he didn't seem to be, not at all.

When he was finally in his bed, he mentally went over his supplies again. He thought of the small but sharp knife he always had with him on his journeys. It could cut through tough ropes, leather, roots and the like, but it would not be of much use against robbers.

Despite Yldich's warnings, he decided to go directly north and pass through the Forest as quickly as possible. That way he might avoid the worst of the winter weather.

The next morning, after a quick and simple breakfast of stale bread and hot soup, Rom went outside to pack. He was checking on the ropes and leather harness when he heard a short, deliberate cough behind him. He turned around sharply. Yldich carefully stood just a few paces behind him. He grinned through his trimmed rusty beard.

'Good morning to you,' he called. 'Still set on going north?'

'Yes,' Rom said. He wondered what would be next.

'That's just as well. I've decided to go visit my relatives in Hernicke. It's just on the other side of the Forest. I will accompany you.'

Rom felt singularly ill at ease riding through the southern fringes of Gardeth Forest with his new travelling companion. He was not used to having company on the road. In fact, he wasn't used to any kind of company at any time. From a young age he had always taken care to go about his business alone.

Yldich did not seem to share his discomfort. He was humming under his breath, looking around with his bright grey eyes. There was no beginning or end to the cheery tunes, just endless meandering notes.

The older man apparently knew the Forest well. On his journeys to the northeast, Rom had always taken care to follow the well-trodden paths used by farmers and goat herders. But Yldich had chosen a route that took the men straight through the Forest, and ignored the existing paths and trails altogether. What means he had of knowing the way through the trees, which looked all the same to him, Rom could not discern. He seemed to find his way through the foothills and trees effortlessly.

The cheerfulness of the humming contrasted with the sharp vigilance with which Yldich took in his surroundings. Was he on the lookout for signs of trouble? Rom's eyes flitted across the path, but he could discover none. The forest floor looked undisturbed; there were no signs that anyone had camped along the trail recently. He was also concerned about Yldich's motives for travelling with him. First, the man wanted to dissuade him from going north. Then he had insisted on going too. Somehow Rom had been unable to shake him off. He was like a big, stray dog that followed him around and wouldn't go away. Suddenly his mouth pulled in a wry smile. It was the other way around: he was following the dog's lead.

Every once in a while, Yldich pointed out something to him: a lizard basking in the sun, almost invisible against the background because of its bizarre camouflage patterning, a small group of deer in the distance, that threw back their heads and sniffed the morning air, a beautiful large hunting cat that moved noiselessly through the underbrush. Rom wondered at the abundance of life around him. It had never been so apparent to him before. Had it always been there but had he never seen it? In contrast to his stream of talk the evening before in *The Squealing Pig*, Yldich was silent except for his humming and occasional remarks.

When the sun was sinking behind the tall trees, they stopped to make camp in a small clearing. Rom gathered some dry grass and twigs to start a small fire. He had some trouble getting it going. Yldich had seen to the horses and had gone, probably to relieve himself. Rom was busy with the fire for a long time, frowning and concentrating. It was already getting dark.

Just as it caught and he had a small blaze going, he heard the snap of a twig behind him. Without thinking, he threw himself forward and whirled around on the forest floor, putting the fire between him and whatever was behind him. He fumbled for the knife in his belt. He had it out, ready to strike, when he recognized Yldich, who stood there with a dead rabbit hanging from his belt. Yldich lifted an eyebrow at the sight of the sharp knife pointed at him.

'Caught us some supper,' he said. He sat down and proceeded to skin the rabbit with his belt knife. Rom released a breath and got up slowly. He put the knife away and started to feed the fire little twigs. Every once in a while he threw a glance at Yldich. The man deftly pulled the furry skin off the rabbit, taking care not to tear it and spoil it. His face was expressionless.

When the rabbit was roasting on a makeshift spit, Rom said: 'How did you catch the rabbit?'

Yldich grinned. 'I called him.'

'What?' Rom blinked at the man, as if he doubted he'd heard him right.

'I called him. He was ready. He came. I caught him.'

Rom raised his brows in incredulity. 'Just like that?'

'Just like that,' Yldich said softly. 'I would have preferred not to take his life. But we have to be careful of our supplies, we have a long road ahead of us. Bad weather's coming.'

Rom stared at him. The sky had been clear all day. He wondered once more just what kind of man he was travelling with. Was he merely an eccentric, was he mad, was he dangerous? Would he be killed in his sleep tonight?

When they had eaten, Yldich stretched his heavy limbs and sighed. He arranged his blanket around his large frame moving slowly and carefully, as if he was aware of the younger man's misgivings. 'Have you ever heard the tale of Rabbit and the king of the Pixies?' he said. Rom gazed at him through the fire. He shook his head.

'One day, Rabbit was running from his enemies. He was making his way through the Forest, chased by teeth, nails and fangs, and because he had no means to defend himself, all he could do was run. It was dusk, that magical time between night and day, and he was still running, and getting really tired when he crossed the border of the land of the Pixies.

As it happens, the King of the Pixies was having a Feast. All the woodland folk were there: beautiful deer with antlers, adorned with field flowers, field mice with little gems tucked behind their ears, and lots of Pixies having a good time.

"Welcome," said the King of the Pixies. He was the most magnificent of all creatures present. His coat was studded with precious stones and he had a wreath of delicate night-blooming flowers in his hair. His eyes were as bright as peacock feathers. He looked at Rabbit, who was still panting from being chased through the Forest all day and all night. "Well met, young man," he said, and belched discreetly behind his hand, for he was slightly tipsy from the elderberry wine. "Please join us in our merry-making, and know that if your heart desires anything tonight, you shall have it." Being slightly drunk made him generous.

Rabbit thought for a while. He was really tired of being chased. He said: "Your Magnificence, if it's not too much trouble...."

"Not at all," the King of the Pixies said without hearing him out. "Tell us what you would have, and I will see to it that it shall be so."

"I would like to be safe from my enemies," Rabbit said. "I would like to have a coat of armour, and sharp teeth to defend myself with, and sharp nails to hurt my enemies with."

"Eh?" The King said, being temporarily distracted by an attractive pixy lady passing by. "Very well," he said. "Let it be so!" He waved his hand, and spoke a secret spell. And in no time at all, Rabbit was transformed.

Rabbit felt it instantly. For one thing, he was much taller than he used to be. He was heavier too. His hide was thick with scales, from the tip of his nose to the tip of his little tail. His claws had grown to the length of small daggers, and they were very sharp. His teeth had grown into fangs. Rabbit was very pleased.

"Now no-one will bother me ever again," he thought. "Now I will be safe from my enemies." He thanked the King of the Pixies extensively, and went on his way again.

He strode through the Forest, feeling big and strong. A large forest cat had followed his rabbit-smell to the border of the land of the woodland Pixies. When Rabbit came out, she picked up his trail again.

"Ah," she thought, "here's that little bunny-smell again. I'll have a feast tonight." Then she bumped into Rabbit's transformed self. Her yellow eyes went wide. She screeched, and all the hair on her back stood on end. She turned her tail on Rabbit as quick as she could. It was three times the size it had been. And that was the last he saw of her.

Rabbit was very satisfied with the effect of his transformation. He walked home, much at ease and taking his time. Who would bother him now? He hummed as he approached the rabbit hole were he lived with his wife and children.

"I'm home, dear," he sang, but there was something odd about his voice. "Must be my improved girth," Rabbit thought. Mrs. Rabbit came out, with the little rabbit-children behind her. Their eyes went wide when they saw Rabbit standing there, with his scales, his fangs, and his nails. "I'm back, my love," Rabbit began. "And you wouldn't believe what happened," but before he could finish his sentence, Mrs. Rabbit whacked him on the head with a large stick. The little rabbits shrieked and fled down the hole.

"Get away from us, you monster!" Mrs. Rabbit used the stick in an honest attempt to bash his head in.

"No, no, wait, it's me, let me explain!" Rabbit tried to shield his head from the resounding blows. Mrs. Rabbit had a good aim. But the words came out all slurred around the heavy fangs that now occupied his mouth and he didn't recognize his own voice.

"Get you gone," Mrs. Rabbit cried, and after one more painful blow, Rabbit fled.

He walked through the Forest, feeling wretched and alone. After a time, he became hungry. He thought: "I'll feel better when I've had a bite to eat. Then I'll go back to my wife, and explain it all," and he went searching for something to eat. He tried to nibble the grass, but his fangs got in the way. He tried to dig out some roots, but he hurt himself with his long, sharp nails. He tried for a long time to find something he could eat, but it was no use. After a while, he became thirsty.

"I'll have some water, first," he said to himself, and he went to the edge of a small forest lake. He was so tired and hungry, he dropped to the ground at the water's edge, as he moved his head to the water. But he was not used to the heavy bulk of his armoured body, and he toppled over. Rabbit fell into the water, and he couldn't swim, not with the long nails and the heavy scales on his body... so he sank, and the water closed above his head, and that was the end of Rabbit and the gift of the King of the Woodland Pixies.'

After Yldich had finished the story, he fell silent.

'So... what does it mean?' Rom said.

'Mean? Well, with my people, to find meaning in a story is left to the discretion of the listener.' Yldich chuckled softly. Rom stared into the glow of the dying fire, his brows knit. He didn't like riddles. He was about to ask Yldich another question, when he became aware of a soft snoring sound. The man was sound asleep.

The next morning, Rom woke up with a start. The sun had been up for a couple of hours at least. Despite all his intentions to be wary and keep an eye on his companion, he had slept through the night, deeply and without waking once. He cursed himself softly and looked about. Yldich and the horses were gone.

Rom felt a sense of panic build up in his chest. He started to think quickly to push it down. What could have happened? Could there be a reasonable explanation for the absence of both Yldich and the horses? The pony's load was still where he'd left it, at the edge of the clearing. Maybe Yldich had only taken them to the pond they had seen yesterday, to drink.

He looked at the tracks the horses' hooves had left, but they went the other way, deeper into the Forest. What if Yldich had stolen the horses and left him intentionally? He would be alone, on foot, in the middle of Gardeth Forest. He had only the small pack of provisions he had laid aside yesterday. They wouldn't last long, and he had no means to hunt for himself.

He considered quickly stuffing his belongings in his pack and following Yldich's trail, to overtake him and get the horse and pony back. The other man was taller and heavier, but anger and despair might give him the edge he needed. Maybe he could subdue him in a surprise attack.

He was just picturing how to surprise Yldich and throw him off his horse, when the man appeared from the other end of the clearing. He whistled softly and walked as if he were taking a relaxed morning stroll. The horses and the pony followed him obediently at a few paces distance.

'Where did you go?' Rom called, his voice hoarse with anger and relief.

'Oh, there's a patch of herbs the horses like, just a bit to the east.' Yldich smiled cheerfully as he crossed the clearing and walked up to him. 'Will do them good, I thought, so I took them there.' Then he saw the look on Rom's face. 'Why, what did you think?' Rom hesitated. 'I see,' Yldich said. 'You thought I'd gone off with the horses.' He frowned. He started to put the baggage back on the pony and checked the straps. He seemed deep in thought.

Rom waited for him to say something more, but Yldich went about clearing camp and getting ready to travel in silence. He quickly ate some of the leftover bread and cheese, and handed Rom a share without comment. He then hid all traces of their fire. He buried it in the sand and laid some branches over it.

Then he did a strange thing: he went and stood in the middle of the clearing, his eyes closed, and started to sing in a language Rom had never heard before, his hands palm upward. When the chanting had ended, Yldich opened his eyes slowly and kept still. He looked as if he were waiting. An expectant silence seemed to fill the clearing. A blackbird started to sing. Its song rang clear in the morning air. A dragonfly flew across the field in a straight line, its wings an iridescent green. Yldich wasted no time. He strode to his horse and mounted.

'Well, stop standing about then, let's go!' He spurred on his horse. Rom still stood beside his horse, watching him in wonderment. He quickly mounted when Yldich was about to disappear between the trees. He followed him in the direction the dragonfly had gone.

They rode through the Forest in silence. Rom noticed the landscape changing subtly; green, leafy trees were being replaced by tough birches, tall pines, and oaks with gnarly trunks and roots. Yldich was doing his good-humoured humming again. It blended in perfectly with the sounds of forest floor. It removed all need for talk, and Rom was grateful for it.

After a while Yldich stopped humming and turned to Rom. 'Tell me, Rom, what's your horse's name?'

Rom started and looked up. 'Well, I call it *horse.*'

Yldich laughed out loud. A few birds, startled by the sudden booming sound, rose from the bushes and scattered through the air, chattering like affronted old ladies. 'Don't tell me you don't know your horse's name?'

'I bought it off a farmer a couple of years ago. It didn't occur to me to think of a name.'

'And the pony?'

'I call it *pony.*'

Yldich laughed again, shaking his head. Rom didn't know whether to be offended or to laugh with him. His mouth twitched. 'Where I come from, it would be considered very strange behaviour to live with a fellow creature for years, even ride on his back, and not know his name,' Yldich said. 'Now, if you listen closely enough, you can discover your horse's name.'

Rom's eyes widened in incredulity. 'How?'

Yldich laughed again at the expression on his face. 'Just ask him.'

'That's madness. Are you saying horses can speak?'

'Not exactly,' Yldich said. 'What I'm saying is that if you listen closely enough, you can hear what they say. Now,' he said quickly, before Rom could voice his disbelief, 'I don't mean your horse will tell you his name like a human person would. What I'm saying is, that if you take the time, and watch, and *listen*, you might learn more about your horse you might ever have assumed possible. Or any other being, for that matter.'

He motioned at the area behind them. 'For instance, how do you think I knew where to look for the herbs this morning? I don't keep a map of this area in my head. I listened for what the horses wanted, and they directed me to it. It's very simple. Just listen.' Rom sat shaking his head at him in silence. Yldich chuckled. 'By the way,' he said. 'His name is *Skála.*'

At noon, they rested the horses and ate some more of the leftover bread. They sat at the edge of a small dry gully surrounded with bushes.

'I don't understand,' Rom said, while they were eating. 'How can you know the horse's name is Skála, when you tell me they don't use words as humans do?'

'Good question. They don't. What I 'heard', so to speak, was not the exact word, *Skála*, but its meaning. In my language, it means something like *likes to run with the wind.* Did you ever notice Skála being restless in windy weather?'

'Well, yes... but I thought the wind made him nervous.' Yldich shook his head.

'Try and pay attention next time he gets restless. My bet is, when the wind is in the west, he'll want to run with it. You should let him. It's his *érstwae*.'

'It's his what?'

Yldich searched for words. 'It's difficult to translate. Every living being has *érstwae*, men, women, children, horses, even dogs. It can be an element, an animal, a mineral... your *érstwae* depends on the hour on which you are born, and on the signs that accompany your birth. With my people, our names are based on it. But *érstwae* can change over time, as you learn, and grow, and change by new experiences.'

'So what's your *érstwae*?'

Yldich chuckled. 'You could know if you had paid attention. If you're not perceptive enough to see it, I'm not going to tell you. But you might want to find out what *your érstwae* is.'

'How?' Rom said, his interest raised in spite of his scepticism.

'Pay attention. If you want your *érstwae* to come to you, all you have to do is invite it. Then you pay attention. You watch, and wait, and listen.'

When they were moving again, Rom made an attempt to locate his *érstwae* without Yldich noticing. He tried looking around, taking in as much detail of the world around as possible. He tried listening, but all he heard were the familiar sounds of the forest: rustling leaves, the chirruping of birds, the sounds of small creatures in the undergrowth. Yldich saw him work at it, frowning with effort, and laughed.

'It doesn't work that way, lad. You have to feel it in *here*.' He pointed at his chest, at the height of his heart. 'Feel the connection. Feel how you're a part of everything else. Know it. Then your *érstwae* will come to you. Maybe,' he added, a teasing glint in his eyes. Rom stared at him. Yldich sighed. 'You'll work it out.'

That night, when the fire had gone out, Rom fell asleep and found himself standing before the burnt-out fire pit. It was dark, yet he was able to see the forms of the trees before him in a greyish light. He moved his hand in front of his face and saw it clearly. It emanated a subtle silver light. He was strangely unsurprised. He started to walk carefully through the dark forest, his senses tuned into the world around him more sharply than they had been during the day. He heard a small mouse-like creature scurry through the leaves and twigs on the ground in a hurry. An owl flew overhead at its leisure, surveying the ground for prey.

While he made his way through the nightly forest, he became subtly aware of another conscious creature's presence. How he knew this, he could not be sure of. He felt as if someone was watching him. He knew the creature was there before he saw the eyes. They were fluorescent green. The eyes moved towards him. Then he saw the animal that was the owner of the eyes. A large, black hunting cat was stalking him. He froze.

The cat circled him, and Rom sucked in his breath. He hardly dared breathe out again. The cat was big, bigger than the wild cat he had seen the other day, almost as big as a large hound. It circled him three times, without making a sound, and every circle narrower than the last, until it stood face to face with Rom. Rom's breathing was shallow, he felt his heart beat wildly, high up in his chest. He wanted to turn around and flee; he knew that if he did, the cat would be on him in a heartbeat. There was nothing left to do but stand there and stare back into the eyes.

They were beautiful eyes, of a deep, luminescent green. They were different from the cat's eyes he knew from experience. Some house cats did have an uncanny intelligent look in their eyes. But looking into the big hunting cat's eyes, he saw that it truly saw him and *knew* him. He would have been only mildly surprised if it had started to speak. But somehow, he felt human speech would be beneath the magnificent, deadly creature. It would be crude and awkward compared to this knowing silence. All he would want to know was in the creature's eyes.

The cat moved as if to pounce, but instead it set its front paws, the large, razor-sharp claws clearly visible, heavily on Rom's chest. Its big feline head was now nearly level with Rom's. The cat opened its mouth slightly and breathed, as if it wanted to taste the air between them. Rom was frozen by the sight of the animal's large head, the sharp incisor teeth, so close to his face. The cat sniffed and looked straight in the eyes with a piercing stare. It opened its mouth wide and screamed at him. Shocked, Rom stumbled backward. The animal raked his tunic and the skin beneath painfully with its claws as it slid down.

The spell broken, Rom turned and ran as hard as he could. He heard the cry of the cat close behind him. Fear spurred him on faster. Branches scratched his face as he scrambled through the forest in a panic.

He was caught by his shoulders, a sound booming in his ears. He cried out, struggling, and suddenly looked into Yldich's face. The man was shouting at him. Bewildered, he tried to fight him off, but the other man held him in an iron grip against the trunk of the tree he had been sleeping under.

'Let me go,' he yelled, struggling frantically.

'Stop it, Rom,' Yldich shouted, and shook him. Rom blinked, bewildered, and stopped struggling. 'You were screaming in your sleep.' Yldich slowly relaxed the grip on his shoulders. Rom lowered his hands, and Yldich let go. Rom moved his hand across his face. It was damp with cold sweat.

'I... I was having a nightmare.' He wiped the hair out of his eyes.

'So you were.' Yldich moved to the fire pit and got a small fire going again. Then he went to fetch the water skin. He filled the cooking pot and put it on the fire. 'Let's hear it then,' he said in a good-humoured tone.

Rom took his blanket with him to the fire. He sat down and wrapped himself in it. 'You —you want to hear my nightmare?'

'I'm not sleeping anyway after this, and it will be morning soon.' Yldich filled their mugs with some dried herbs from his bag. 'Besides, nightmares are important.'

'I thought they were just... scary dreams.'

'There's dreams, and then there's dreams.' Yldich filled their mugs with hot water and handed one to Rom. He sat back at the other side of the fire. 'My people take dreams very seriously. Nightmares are unfinished dreams. Important ones. Tell me about yours.'

Rom drew a hand across his eyes. 'Well, I was walking through the forest. It was strange, because I could see in the dark. There was this black forest cat. It came to me. No, it stalked me, going around me in circles. Then it came up to me. It screamed at me, and I ran....'

Yldich stared at him with wide eyes. 'A black forest cat? It came up to you?'

Rom nodded. 'It stood with its paws on my chest, and looked me in the face. It screamed at me.' He put his hand on his chest where the claws had scored him. It still burned. 'It raked me with its claws, and I ran as fast as I could—' Yldich put down his mug.

'Let me see.' He reached out to pull aside Rom's tunic. Rom flinched, jerking backwards, away from Yldich and overset his mug. Yldich froze and looked at him sharply. He drew back his hand and sat back. His movements were slow and careful. He gazed at Rom without the usual twinkle of amusement in his eyes. 'What happened to you?'

Rom settled in his place before the fire again. He pulled the blanket closer around him. He was frowning. 'What do you mean?'

'Well,' Yldich reverted to his usual lilting speech, 'ever since I met you, you have reminded me of the pup my daughter took home with her one day.' He smiled grimly. 'It had been beaten and misused, so it was distrustful and anxious. We had to put it away eventually, because it attacked the children when they startled it. When trust is broken early, it's hard to trust people again.' Rom stared at his hands. His face was tense. He didn't speak. 'Some stories can poison a man from the inside, if they're not told,' Yldich said slowly. 'Tell me. What happened to you? Why are you so distrustful?'

Rom's head snapped up. He shook the hair out of his eyes. They had turned black. 'Why did Rabbit ask for a favour of the King of the Pixies?' He clenched his fists. 'I've been running from the past all my life. What good is there in telling about it? It can't be changed.' He looked down and muttered to the ground: 'Why should you care, anyway?'

He stood up brusquely and moved to walk away from the fire. The blanket dropped from his shoulders. The strap of his tunic was loose.

Yldich looked up at him. His eyes widened. 'Rom. Look at your chest.' Rom looked down. There were bloody claw-marks, big ones, crimson against his pale skin.

'This isn't possible. This isn't happening.' Rom tugged at the straps of Skála's harness. The horse whinnied in protest. Rom hurriedly fastened his saddle. The marks on his chest burned, but the rest of his body felt icily cold.

Yldich was urgently talking to his back. 'Rom, wait. Don't run off in a panic. The forest is too dangerous to blunder through like a fool. Wait, now. There's something I should tell you....'

'What now? More about rabbits and pixies?'

'No, indeed. About black hunting cats.'

Rom shuddered and said nothing. He rolled up his blanket and threw it behind the saddle.

Yldich shook his head and sighed. 'Have you any idea what significance the black cat has where I come from? It's the... the *daemo*, the chief Spirit Animal of the *Tzanatzi* people.'

Rom stiffened at the name. He fastened a rope. 'There are no *Tzanatzi*, this far to the north.'

'Not anymore. But once there were. Many of them. They came to the North, when they settled in these lands many years ago. These woods were their battlegrounds.'

Rom shook his head. He felt another story coming on. 'What's that got to do with me?'

Yldich gazed at him, long and deliberately, the dark hair, the dark eyes. 'Well, look at you, lad.'

Rom felt the blood rise in his face. His fingers tightened on the rope. 'What are you implying?'

'Easy, now. There's something I haven't told you. It wasn't a coincidence that I met you in the *Squealing Pig*. I was there on purpose, to meet you, or someone like you.'

Rom spun around. 'I knew it! I thought there was something suspicious about the way you sought me out. And when you were going north too, it was too much of a coincidence.'

'Maybe,' Yldich said with a wry grin. 'But even as your intuition was right, there's a difference between malicious and good intent. I didn't deceive you to bring you harm.'

Rom drew up a brow. 'So why did you deceive me?'

'Rom, I am *Yaever* for my people,' Yldich said, the melodious accent more marked than before. 'It means true-dreamer in our language. It means I have, how does one say in your language, *warning* dreams, dreams that come true. I knew how to find you because I dreamt you.'

Rom's eyes widened. 'You dreamt me?'

'I knew I had to go south, and search the inns along the way for a dark-haired young man with dark eyes,' Yldich said in a chanting tone. Rom guessed he had told this story before, many times. 'He would be travelling on his own, he would be a loner, and he would have great significance for my people, my House, and for the dark powers that are threatening us. I knew so in my dreams. I've dreamt you for over seven years.'

'What—what are you talking about?' Rom said. 'What dark powers?'

'For years, I've had dreams about something dark, something evil, being awakened in the earth. At first, they seemed to be only nightmares.' Yldich shook his head. 'But it's true what I told you at the inn. A balance has been disturbed. A horror is stalking the Forest. One by one my nightmares are coming true. Who knows where it will end?' Rom felt a shiver travel along his skin.

'All I knew,' he heard Yldich continue, 'was that I had to find you, because somehow you may avert the evil that's threatening my people.'

Rom shook his head in uneasy disbelief. 'What about the black cat? What does that mean?'

'That's what I wonder, too. But bearing in mind your appearance, Rom,' Yldich said, choosing his words with care, 'my guess would be you have *Tzanatzi* blood in you. The cat sought you out for a reason. I've never heard of the children of *my* people dreaming a powerful *Tzanatzi daemo* in their first true-dream. It must mean something. It must be important. Maybe it's telling you to tap into your heritage. So you can make a difference somehow.'

Rom scowled. 'I want nothing to do with that—that *filth*. All I want to do is go north, tend to my business, and go home.' He turned brusquely and tied his tunic with fingers that were stiff and cold.

'If you don't stop running from the past and face it,' Yldich said softly, 'it might hunt you down one day.' Rom ignored him. He strode off to the pony to pile on his luggage as quickly as he could. He donned his cloak and mounted the horse. Skála's ears were turned backwards. He sidled, and then moved hesitatingly. Rom spurred him on. He turned to look at Yldich.

'Safe journey,' he muttered. He felt a strange, sinking sensation beneath his anger. He hurried the horse along to escape it. The pony followed. They shot away into the trees.

'*Neachspragae*,' Yldich said softly. 'Until we meet again.'

Two
The Riders

Hours later, when the sun had risen almost to its zenith, Rom looked around for a place to rest the horses. It appeared to be one of those autumn days when nature has one last go at denying the slow death of summer. It was hot. The temperature did nothing to cool Rom's temper. He bit his lip, while he searched the forest floor with his eyes for pitfalls. It wouldn't be long now before the horse, no, Skála, would need to drink and rest. He scowled.

'Wonderful. Now he's in my head.'

He travelled through an area where the trees thinned out and yellow fading grass covered the ground. The welcome increase in light and range of vision was spoilt by the increase in insect life. Rom, Skála and the pony were beset with buzzing insects.

Finally, they came upon a small stream which was running through the Forest. Rom decided to fill the water skin and let Skála and the pony drink, then follow the course of the river for a bit upstream.

There was a small grove of willow-trees and bushes near the stream. He tied Skála and Pony to some trees near the water. They drank thirstily. Rom submerged his head in the icy water. It stung his face with cold. He shook his head like a dog, to shed the water from his hair. It fell back into his eyes. He decided to use his knife on it one of these days to cut it. Shaving would be a good idea as well, he thought, as he felt the two days' growth on his chin. He sat by the side of the stream and scraped his face carefully with the razor-sharp knife. After he filled the water skin, he decided to go for a short walk upstream, to get a view of the terrain to the north and to stretch his legs. They were stiff from the hours of riding.

He followed the stream until he came to a spot where the Forest had moved almost to the water. The stream must have changed course long ago. Bushes lined the river on either side.

He had started to search for berries, when he heard the sound of horses coming from behind. He froze. He had not met any other travellers on the road when travelling with Yldich. He did not know what to think of it. He thought of hiding between the trees, but the riders must have already seen his horse and pony, tied to the willows a little way back.

He heard a shout. Obviously the riders had already seen him. They came straight for him. It was no use to hide. He stood still and tried to remember where he had left his knife after shaving. Then the riders were on him.

The moment he set eyes on them up close, he knew he was in serious trouble. The riders reminded him of the deserters and mercenaries he had seen in the filthiest inns and taverns of the South. Dressed in worn tunics, greasy leather, and bits and pieces of old armour, they looked like the type of men who had nothing to lose. Though some of them had lost some personal items on the way. He saw one missing part of an ear, some missing one or more teeth, a finger or two. They looked even more unkempt then he would after travelling for weeks, no months, sleeping in ditches. Probably they hadn't seen the inside of a house in years.

The riders circled him like wolves. There were at least ten of them. He attempted to ignore the rise of an icy, visceral fear deep in his belly. One of them reigned in his horse and spoke to him.

'You're the one who travels with the *Einache* rebel leader?' It sounded more like a statement than a question.

Rom frowned at him. 'What are you talking about?' The man slid off his horse in a fluid motion. He looked less dilapidated than the others. He was a little older and taller than Rom, with hair the colour of dark honey. He would have looked handsome after a wash and a shave. Three long strides took him right up to Rom. He looked him calmly in the eyes and struck him on the left side of his face.

Rom reeled from the impact and fell back heavily. He was dazed. The young man, his strength greater than one would expect from his build, gripped him by his tunic before he could fall to the ground and held him up. A trickle of blood dripped from Rom's mouth. He coughed, tasting blood, and swallowed with difficulty.

'I'll ask you again, and this time I advice you not to waste my time,' the man said. 'Are you the one travelling with the *Einache* leader?'

'I've no idea what you're talking about,' Rom said truthfully. He started to feel obstinately defiant. It was better than feeling terrified, he decided. The man calmly hit him again, harder, and allowed him to fall this time. Rom passed out before he hit the ground.

When he woke up, he felt slightly sick. It was the only thing he was conscious of for a time. Then he carefully opened his eyes. It was dark; the only light came from a large fire a few feet away. When he looked at it directly, the light seared through his eyes and exploded in the back of his skull. He groaned and closed his eyes again. He tried to get a sense of his situation by touch alone. He was lying with his back against the big roots of a great old tree. His hands were tied in front of him with strips of leather. He heard the riders being busy with the tasks of a small camp.

He heard a high voice. 'Hello? Sir?' It came from somewhere in front of him. He dared to open his eyes once more. It was less bad than the first time. The voice spoke again. 'I—I've brought you some water.' He focused his eyes and a face came into view. It was a young boy's. He didn't look more than ten years old. His face was dirty and his clothes looked worn. They were at least two sizes too small for him.

'Who are you?' Rom said.

'I'm Eald.' The boy pronounced it as 'hay-eld'. His accent reminded Rom of Yldich. 'Here's some water.' He held out an earthenware bowl. It seemed to have been made by a drunken potter. The water wasn't entirely clean, either. But Rom accepted the bowl thankfully, if with difficulty. He drank with care, his tied hands under the bowl, and tried not to drop it in his lap.

'Thank you,' he said. 'I'm Rom.' The boy smiled a nervous half smile and vanished. Rom lay back against the roots of the tree and closed his eyes.

He became aware of someone staring at him. He opened his eyes. The man with the honey-coloured hair sat cross-legged in front of him.

'You're awake,' he said softly. He had a cultured voice, clear and melodious. Rom swallowed. The man's composure scared him more than any display of aggression ever had. He opened his mouth to speak, then thought better of it. 'Very good,' the young man said, 'don't bore me with useless questions and protests. I have no patience for it.'

He drew a small knife from his belt. He started to cut the nails of his left hand. His movements were curt and precise. Rom stared at the sharp, controlled movements of the knife with horrified fascination.

'I'm called Feyir,' the man said. 'I intend to get some information from you. I advise you again not to lie. If you do, I'll turn you over to my men. They have crude, but effective methods to persuade people to be informative.'

Rom shuddered. He tried to shut down his mind against the images it was conjuring up for him. A feeling of despair rose from deep within his belly.

'Here we go,' the young man said, his voice light and pleasant, as if they were having a picnic on a summer's day. 'One: what is a *Tzanatzi* doing in the Forests of Gardeth?'

'I'm not *Tzanatzi*,' Rom said habitually. In a heartbeat, Feyir was at his side, grabbed his hair and pulled back his head with force.

Rom felt the cold steel of the knife at his throat.

I knew I should have cut that hair.

A new explosion of pain racked the left side of his head. He laboured to control his breathing.

'What did I tell you?' Feyir said, his face so close to Rom's he could feel his breath on his cheek. His voice was low.

'I'm half-*Tzanatzi*,' Rom said, surprising himself. 'I didn't lie to you.' Feyir laughed and let go of his hair. He took the knife off Rom's throat and sat back again, completely composed.

'Two: why is a half-*Tzanatzi* travelling through Gardeth Forest with the leader of the *Einache*?'

'I really don't know who you—' The knife flashed through the air. It flew straight at his face. He gasped and yanked his head sideways. He screamed as the knife seared straight through his right ear and struck the tree behind him with a thump. Something warm began to flow down his neck. There was a short pause in the clamouring of the pots and pans near the fire. Then the normal sounds of the camp resumed. Rom's ear throbbed with a dull, hot pain.

'I warned you,' Feyir said.

'I—I really don't know who you mean.' Rom was shaking. Blood trickled down his right arm.

'You were seen with the man they call Yldich,' Feyir said slowly. 'The beast-caller. The mage. The rebel leader.'

'Yldich, a mage and a rebel leader?' It was ludicrous. 'He's a farmer or something, a story-teller. He tells dreams, and stories about *rabbits*.'

Feyir leaned over to him, his amber eyes narrowed. 'Where did he go?'

Rom shook his head. 'I don't now. We parted company. His stories got on my nerves.'

Feyir smiled. 'Very convincing. I don't believe you.' He moved as if to leave. He turned and grabbed Rom by the front of his tunic. Rom held his breath. 'I'll have my riders break you in the morning,' Feyir said softly. 'They'll tear you apart if they have to.' Rom stared at him and swallowed. Feyir looked at him with a pensive expression. 'Pity,' he said, 'you're not unpleasant to look at. After tomorrow, I doubt if any girl will look at you a second time. If you'll live.' He threw Rom back against the tree.

A movement caught Rom's eye. He turned his head and saw the boy standing not three paces away. He was staring at Feyir. The boy's face was ashen. He had his arms around his small, frail body as if to steady himself. Feyir turned around and noticed him. He smiled. Rom suddenly felt sick.

'What's a child that age doing here? Where did he come from?' He hardly recognized the sound of his own voice. It was hoarse. Something dark began to well up inside him.

Feyir looked at him, his eyes narrowed like a satisfied cat's. 'If you want these *Einache* mongrels to be useful servants, you break them while they're young—' Rom lunged forward and thrust Feyir to the ground with his bound fists.

'You bastard,' he cried. A surge of black rage gave him strength. Feyir was taken by surprise and fell back under his weight. Rom grabbed Feyir's neck with his bound hands and hit his head against the ground. He'd ceased to think altogether. 'I'll kill you, you bastard....' His blood was ringing in his ears. Riders came running from all directions, but he didn't notice.

He was pulled back with force and hauled off Feyir's body by many hands. He fought like a cornered animal, instinct taking over, kicking and yelling. He heard a bone snap and a cry as he kicked someone's hand away. A heavy blow to his chest had him reeling. Another threw him back against the tree, where he lay sprawling. He was barely conscious. A rider kicked him in his ribs, another in his stomach. He doubled over and coughed up blood. Then he lay still, his eyes closed, panting. Someone leaned over him. He heard Feyir's cool, level voice as if from a distance.

'That was a foolish thing to do.'

He fell into darkness.

The sound of painful, laborious breathing woke him. He found it was his own. He slowly opened his eyes. His head throbbed. It was completely dark, save for the dull red glow of the embers of the fire in the middle of the camp. He heard no sounds, saw no silhouettes against the light of the fire. Apparently, the riders were so sure of themselves they didn't even keep watch at night. It struck him as strange. The silence seemed unnatural.

He tried to move, and groaned as he felt a sharp pain shoot through his chest. The leather strip that bound his wrists had been tied to something, a thick tree root perhaps. He couldn't move more than a few inches. He lay still and closed his eyes. What use was there in trying to do anything? Tomorrow he was a dead man. He tried not to think of what they might do to get him to tell them what he didn't know. He wished he knew *something*. To be killed over nothing seemed even more horrid. A wave of panic went through him and he nearly choked on it.

'Roëm,' a voice said near his ear. He would have jumped if he had been able to. It was the boy with the Northern accent. Eald. He stressed the vowel just as Yldich had done, but more markedly so.

'Are you awake?'

'Yes,' he whispered.

'Please, keep still.' He heard a sound above him. The boy pulled the knife out of the tree with some difficulty. Feyir had apparently forgotten it after the unexpected brawl. The boy kneeled in front of Rom and carefully cut through the leather binds.

Rom peered at him through the darkness. 'What if someone sees you?'

The boy smiled his lopsided smile. 'I put some herbs in the beer. Watcher drank most of it. The others had enough to keep them asleep. I hope.' He gave a final tug at the leather binds. They gave way and Rom sat up gingerly. He rubbed his wrists and winced at the pain in his chest. 'You must go now, while they are still asleep,' the boy said. 'Don't try and get your horses. Too dangerous. Just go.' He handed Rom the knife.

'They'll know you did this,' Rom said. 'You'd better come with me.' He saw the boy hesitate.

'They'd kill me if they caught me running away.' Eald's voice was a whisper. 'Or my family. That's what *he* said.'

Rom swallowed down a curse. 'You're not safe here either. What are you going to say when they see this?' He motioned at the cut binds, hanging from the tree root. 'The pixies did it?'

The boy grinned wryly. His eyes were filled with fear. A sound came from a few feet away, where most of the men lay sleeping. It sounded like a groan. Maybe one of them was tossing in his sleep.

Then a low voice rasped. 'Who's taking watch? Hey, Marteld, that you?'

Rom's heart leaped up, his throat constricted. 'Someone's waking up! Come on!' he hissed to Eald. 'Quickly now!' He gestured towards the trees. Behind them lay a low mound. Rom took the boy's hand and started to half help, half drag him up. His ear started to throb with pain again and his chest felt as if it was on fire. He set his teeth and hurried Eald along. 'Go, now!'

They went over the mound and half slid into a ditch. Rom nearly passed out from the pain. He blinked to clear away the specks of black in his vision. Eald dragged him up with difficulty. They scrambled through the trees, trying to make as less noise as possible.

Rom had no idea where they were, what direction to take. First a straight line away from the camp, he decided. There were no sounds of pursuit as yet. Maybe the rider had not noticed anything amiss, and had fallen asleep again.

They had run for quite a while, Rom clutching at his side and coughing, when they heard the sound of horses' hooves behind them. Eald moaned.

Rom looked around. Panic surged through his chest. There was a steep, narrow gully to the left. It was the only place where they could possibly hide.

Rom grabbed Eald's arm and pulled him into the gully. They half fell, half slid into it. It was fairly deep. There was still water at the bottom. It was cold and muddy. Rom noticed there was an area where the roots of a large tree had eaten away into the bank, creating an overhang covered with moss and old leaves, with a dark niche behind it. He crawled towards it. Eald followed. They crawled into the narrow dark place and kept still. The sound of their breathing sounded alarmingly loud in the stillness. Hopefully, Rom thought, the tree roots would hide them from anyone looking down from the side of the gully.

Hardly had they settled into the muddy hole when the riders arrived. They were bearing torches. There were four of them, including Feyir. They heard his smooth, confident voice from the lead.

'No use blundering about in the dark,' it said. 'Cal. Can you see any tracks?'

'Too hard in the dark with this bloody thick carpet of leaves,' another voice said.

'All right then,' Feyir's voice sounded. 'You two, go northwest a bit further; see if you can catch up with them. Cal, we'll move around, back to camp. If we don't find them now, we'll do so in the morning. They won't get far.' He turned his horse. Feyir and the rider called Cal went back. The two other riders went off ahead.

Rom was strangely reluctant to get moving again. His head was swimming. He closed his eyes for a moment.

'Rom? Rom!' Eald was shaking him hesitantly. He had drifted off into a state of semi-consciousness. 'I don't think we should stay here,' Eald whispered. They clambered out of the gully with difficulty and made their way through the Forest. Eald was nervously listening for hoof beats or voices in the distance. Rom was plodding along doggedly. He felt strangely disconnected from his body. A buzzing noise filled his head, making it impossible to think clearly. His chest burned. He coughed painfully.

They came upon a wide, dry riverbed with rocky banks overgrown with moss and followed it. They had to clamber over rocks and boulders. Apparently, the river had once run a wild course from the mountains in the North, through the forests, foaming over rocks, only to ease down when it reached shallower waters in the South. The river bed was now overgrown with small bushes, plants, and moss. Rom stumbled over a rock and fell down hard. His breath was coming in painful gasps. Lights were going off in his head, like exotic flowers of exploding pain. He closed his eyes.

'I'm sorry.' His breath was wheezing. 'I don't think I can go any further.'

Eald anxiously tugged at his arm. 'We can't stay here. They'll see us when it gets light.' He bit his lip. Rom laboured to sit up. The grey light of dawn was filling the sky. 'Maybe we can hide somewhere for the day,' Eald muttered.

He left Rom sitting against a boulder and went a few paces ahead. He studied the rocky sides of the river bed in the increasing light. There were places where gnarly trees had grown into the river bank, dislodging rocks and creating small crevices. Years of determined growing in rock and hard soil had widened them. Some were near the ground, others higher up. A few seemed big enough to hide in. Eald went back to where he'd left Rom. He found him lying against the boulder, breathing hard and coughing. There was blood in the corner of his mouth. Eald shook him softly.

'There's a hiding place a few paces away. Please, just a little further.' He helped Rom up with difficulty. They stumbled to the rocky side where a narrow crawl led to a dark opening. 'Here,' Eald said. Rom crawled forward, and moved slowly through the crack in the hardened soil, holding on to tree roots and branches. He slid down a short slope. He fell down with a gasp, landed in a small cave-like hole and lay still. It was dark and smelled of earth and dead leaves. Eald clambered in after him. 'They won't find us here,' he said hopefully to the darkness.

Eald found himself walking through the trees in the light of early morning. The sun had gone up, and the warm, golden light fell in beams on the forest floor. The forest already smelled of autumn. A blackbird was singing in a tree a little further up the trail. Its song was piercingly sweet. It filled him with gladness. Eald felt strangely light-hearted. He walked softly, delighting in the sounds and smells of the early morning.

After a while, he became aware of a deep, soft humming sound. He realized it had been with him all along, like an undercurrent in his mind. He felt curiously unafraid. The sound attracted him in a strange way. It seemed to softly draw him towards the source, as if friendly, ghostly fingers were tickling him, tugging at his will in an almost teasing way.

He came upon a small clearing. A large, heavily built man sat a few paces away from him in front of a small fire pit. He had ginger hair and a short beard. The man looked at him and ceased his humming. The piercing grey eyes seemed to laugh at Eald. Eald smiled, completely at ease, and moved closer. The man gestured at the ground before the fire. Eald sat down and looked at him. He became aware of a low, vibrating voice in his head.

Who are you?

His name flowed out of his eyes, across the fire to the man. *Eald.*

Eald, he sensed, *I'm Yldich. Can you help me? I'm looking for someone.* The strange thing was that Eald heard no words, but meanings. The wonderfully complex, soundless speech that flowed through his brain was composed of bits of knowledge, faint images, impressions, and feelings. He saw a dark young man that reminded him strongly of Rom. The picture differed subtly from his own image of him. Concern and a question of location went with it.

He nodded to the man across the fire and let the images and feelings pour out of his eyes to him. *He's with me. We're in trouble. Can you help us?*

Yldich was alarmed by the violent images the boy emitted. Urgency and fear accompanied them. He allowed them to pass through his awareness without holding on to them. If he did, they would possess him. He steadied his breathing to stay calm. If he broke his concentration, he might lose the boy and not be able to connect with him again.

Where? He conveyed.

Eald showed him.

Eald woke up with a sense of urgency. A slender beam of sunlight penetrated the entrance to the hole above. Motes of dust danced in the light. It had been a dream. Yet Eald felt compelled to act on it. He turned to Rom and gently shook him. 'Rom. Wake up. We've got to go.'

It was hard to get Rom to crawl up the slope to the entrance. It was even harder to get him out and down to the river bed. He was barely conscious. Somehow Eald managed, pulling and tugging. When they had gotten out, he looked around anxiously. Maybe he was being foolish trusting in a dream. The big man had said to get out and wait for him near the entrance of the hole. What if the riders got there first? What if the man existed only in his dream? The sun was already high and he felt awfully conspicuous. Anyone coming down the river bed or from the forest above would see them immediately.

Rom's horribly ragged breathing rasped in his ears. It scared him. He tried to shut it out of his awareness. Then he was afraid he would stop hearing it altogether. He hardly dared to look at him. The thought of running occurred to him for an instant. To run into the woods and leave the man to die alone was somehow even less appealing than to stay and wait. He sat down beside him and waited.

When Yldich found them, they were sitting on the ground, leaning against each other in the shadow of a large rock. The boy looked as if he were asleep. Rom looked as if he were dead. Thoroughly alarmed, Yldich dismounted as quickly as he could. He shook the boy gently, while he peered into Rom's face. It was deathly white. His breathing was shallow. Tiny bubbles of blood formed between his lips.

'Eald,' Yldich said. The boy woke up and stared at him anxiously. 'It's all right. I want you to do something.' Eald nodded. 'There's a large crystal in my saddle bag. Take it and go up the river bed for a mile or so. Put down the crystal in the middle. Turn it until it catches the sun and point it away from us. Say this word: '*Ílumae*'. Say it three times. Don't look directly into the light. Repeat it to me now.'

'Ill... *Ílumae*,' Eald said. '*Ílumae*.'

'Can you do that?'

Eald nodded.

'Go!' Yldich said.

Eald found the crystal quickly and ran off. He was relieved to be away and doing something, anything. He ran until a bend in the river bed obscured the others from view. Then he carefully set down the crystal. He took a few small rocks and set them against it on all sides to steady it. He started to turn it. It wasn't long before a ray of light found it and shone through it. He spoke as Yldich had instructed him.

'*Ílumae. Ílumae. Ílumae*.' He carefully pointed the crystal away from him.

The strangest thing happened: the ray of light flowed with the movement of the crystal as he was turning it. It seemed to become tangible somehow, like honey or fluid amber, caught by the crystal, changed into something malleable. It grew stronger and stronger, until it shone like a second sun. The air around it was affected too. It shimmered and changed, until it seemed as if he were looking through a glass curtain. Everything behind the curtain was distorted. From one side of the river bed to the other, a shimmering curtain of glassy air rippled and obscured everything behind it from view.

While he was giving directions to the boy, Yldich was already turning his attention to Rom. He sensed the young man was slipping away fast. He pulled open Rom's tunic and saw bruises covering a large portion of his body. The skin had broken in places; dried blood had caked his tunic to the skin. Yldich breathed in sharply when he saw the extent of the damage. He deftly searched the area with his fingers, closing his eyes, almost touching the skin but not quite. He frowned with concentration.

Rom was sinking into an immensely deep, black sea. The feeling of sinking was not unpleasant. What was cruelly painful was to try to keep his head above water and breathe. Breathing hurt, and with every painful exhalation, life seemed to flow out of him. The water pulled at him. He could almost hear it whisper.

Come away, let go, come with us....

The voice of the water was seductively sweet. He had been struggling to get away from it for a long time now. He was so tired. The voice of the water was getting clearer every time he expelled a breath.

Let go, with us there is no pain, no hurt, no grief.... He struggled for another painful breath.

Let go....

There was a small pinpoint of light somewhere above him in the dark above the sea. It was like a tiny sunbeam seen through deep water. He only saw it when he took in breath. He tried to focus on it, but it was hard. The sea was stronger. It wouldn't hurt to let go. The pain would cease. He would have peace.

But somehow the light kept him from letting himself sink into the soothing blackness completely. It was like a nagging voice that wouldn't leave him alone. He heard it murmur. It turned into a strange wordless song. It sang its way down to him and connected itself to him. He struggled for another breath. The energy of the song somehow gave him strength. It filled him with golden light.

Initially, it hurt even more. Then it got a little easier to breathe. His lungs were filling with light. It was warm and soothing. The song reminded him of sunlight, of the sounds and smells of spring. He breathed in a little deeper. It hurt less than before. He felt life return to him. The black sea receded. It murmured mournfully to itself behind him as it retreated, like a ghostly lover turned away. He was lying on a shore that was basking in light. The pain drained away into the sand.

He opened his eyelids a little. Sunlight was seeping through them. Someone peered into his eyes. He couldn't see clearly who it was. The sun was behind him. Rom opened his mouth as if to speak.

'Don't move yet, Rom,' he heard. 'Easy, now,' and he recognized Yldich's voice. He tried to move and found it hard. His arms were heavy as lead. His legs were somewhere down below, far away. He was hardly aware of them. His hands twitched.

Yldich took them into his own. 'You will never do as I say, will you?' Rom tried to grin. He imagined it probably looked hideous. The taste of his own blood was still heavy in his mouth, his teeth stained red. He coughed.

He heard quick footsteps coming closer. Eald was back, his eyes still full of the miraculous feat he had performed with the crystal.

'Eald, please get the water skin for me,' Yldich said. Eald blinked and looked at Rom, then back to Yldich with a question in his eyes. 'He'll live,' Yldich said. 'For now.'

After he had had a few sips of water, Rom closed his eyes again and drifted off into a sleep of exhaustion. Yldich checked his breathing. It sounded normal and healthy. While Eald looked at everything he did with wide eyes, he started to peel off the mud- and bloodstained tunic.

'Keep an eye on him, will you?' he said. Eald nodded. Yldich took one of his own spare tunics out of the saddle bag. When he carefully lifted Rom into a sitting position to get the clean tunic over his head, he heard Eald gasp. 'What is it?' The boy was staring at Rom's back. Yldich moved over so he could see. He swallowed. The young man's back was a map of scar tissue. Lines of old welts formed ridges of white flesh that crisscrossed like old mountain trails. Yldich felt a surge of nausea. Then a black thundercloud of anger welled up inside him. He released it with difficulty, closing his eyes for a moment, and let it soak into the dry earth of the river bed with an inaudible sigh.

'Sir, look here,' he heard the boy say. His face was tense and white.

'It's Yldich, son,' he said, his thoughts elsewhere for a moment, 'not sir. What is it?'

'Here,' Eald said, 'I've seen this before.' He pointed to Rom's left upper arm near the shoulder. A mark had been burned into the skin at one time, leaving the inverted sign of a stylized animal. It looked like a misshapen dog or boar. The mark was old, like the other scars. Yldich cursed under his breath. 'Feyir has a ring with the same picture on it,' the boy said.

'Feyir?' Yldich looked at him sharply. '*Lord* Feyir?'

Eald looked confused. 'He's a lord?'

'Is that who he's run into?' Yldich's face was tense. Eald nodded. Yldich shook his head. 'A wonder I found him alive at all.'

A while later, the sun began its journey down into the west. It would be a few hours yet before it went behind the trees. Yldich made a quick meal of powdered grains and herbs which he soaked in water. He tried to get some spoonfuls of the stuff into Rom's mouth, but he wouldn't wake up thoroughly enough to swallow properly. After a few attempts, Yldich gave him some more water, mixed with honey, and let him sleep.

Eald fetched the crystal. He kept all his senses alert in case the riders were nearby. Yldich had told him the crystal would be of no use for protection once the sunlight had faded away.

Yldich carefully lifted Rom onto the horse and let Eald sit behind him to steady him. They followed the dry river for a few more miles. Rom was deeply asleep, leaning back heavily against the boy.

They came upon a place where there had once been a shallow ford. The sunlight was fading away when they climbed the river bank, abandoning the relative shelter of the riverbed, and went back into the woods. Yldich started his habitual soft humming. This time, the humming was so low-key it was barely audible, yet it stretched over the ground over a large area. It washed against trees and bushes as it flowed through the forest, and created a tapestry of sound that stretched for miles. If any living being bigger than a mouse entered the area, he would know of it.

They made camp in an area where small trees had grouped together in a rough half-moon shape, creating a secluded area. Yldich dug a deeper fire pit than usual, to hide the light of the fire, and made some more broth. Eald had gone to sleep, sprawling by the fire like an exhausted dog, arms and legs in all directions. He twitched in his sleep. Yldich pulled a blanket over him. He took a bowl and went over to Rom, who lay on the other side of the fire, under the trees.

'Rom.' Rom was faintly aware of someone calling his name. He was reluctant to wake up. The voice kept calling him. 'Rom. Wake up. You should really eat something now.' He opened his eyes a little and peered in the darkness ahead. A large shape sat before him, painted in reds and yellows by the light of the fire.

'Yldich?'

'Come on, let's get you up.' He was grabbed under his arms and gently dragged up against the larger of the tree trunks. He had never felt so exhausted before. He sighed and noticed breathing didn't hurt any more.

'What happened?'

'Eat first,' Yldich said. 'Questions later.' Rom accepted the bowl, bringing it to his lips with difficulty. He took a few careful mouthfuls. His hands were shaking.

'I feel as if I've been run over by a herd of cattle,' he said finally.

'No wonder,' Yldich said. 'You nearly died.'

Rom looked at him over the rim of the bowl with wide eyes. 'What?'

'You were drowning in your own blood when I found you. A few heartbeats later and I wouldn't have been able to bring you back.'

Rom stared at him, white-faced. 'I remember.' A spasm of pain crossed his face. 'I remember dying.' He closed his eyes.

Yldich shook him softly. 'One more.' He helped him lift the bowl again. Rom obeyed, his eyes closed. He took another sip. 'Good.' Yldich put aside the empty bowl.

Rom leaned his head against the tree. He opened his eyes again. 'How—how did you bring me back?'

'Well, I am a *Yaever*.' Yldich sat back into a more comfortable position. 'I told you it means *true-dreamer*, or dream-walker, in my language. But it's a lot more than that. I've been taught to, how would you say it, touch the living web that is life, and work with it. Manipulate it. Sometimes it means healing people. Or animals, or fields, or trees. Sometimes it means other things, like helping them to die. It's hard to explain exactly,' he said with a grin. 'Your language is not equipped with the words to describe it well.'

'But I was nearly dead. I felt it. How did you bring me back? Can you heal anyone? Anything?'

'No. No I can't,' Yldich said, looking sober. 'Some hurts are beyond my help. Some beings don't want to be healed. Or can't be healed,' he said, searching for words. 'It's a matter of feeling your way, balancing, understanding, and focusing energy.'

'I thought I... heard you sing,' Rom said.

'You probably did. Sound is an important part of it. Touch, as well.' Yldich looked serious. 'Listen, Rom. I wouldn't have been able to heal you if it hadn't been the way things should be.' He frowned, trying to explain it properly. 'If it had disturbed the purpose of your being, of the lives you touch, of the reason why you're here, I would have had to let you go.' Rom was silent for a while. Yldich thought he had fallen asleep again. Then he spoke.

'How did you know where to find us?'

Yldich smiled. 'Eald told me.'

'Eald? But he was with me. How could he have...?'

'He found his way to me while he was asleep. I had a feeling you might get into trouble, so I was looking for you, casting a net of awareness, so to speak. Eald responded to it and came to me in his dream. He has a great talent for dream-walking. As do you.' Rom stared at him in bewilderment. 'Rest now,' Yldich said. He helped Rom back into his blanket between the roots of the tree. 'We'll talk more tomorrow.'

Rom was awakened by the sound of voices. He sat up slowly and carefully. It appeared to be early morning. A low mist drifted past over the grass. Watery sunlight illuminated the glade. Droplets of water had formed on the blanket. The voices were a little distance away. They were speaking in a language he didn't understand.

Laughter rang in his ears. It was the boy, Eald. He heard Yldich's deep, booming laughter follow it.

Rom drew the blanket around him and walked unsteadily towards the sound of their voices. He found them sitting opposite each other in the middle of the glade. They didn't notice his presence. It suddenly occurred to him how similar they looked: Yldich with his ginger-coloured hair and beard, his big nose, his merry grey eyes, his ironic grin, and Eald, with his slightly darker shade of lanky hair, almost copper, his skewed smile, his boyish features that might just grow into a countenance like Yldich's. His high voice had the same lilting accent Yldich's had. Rom stood still, and watched them, fascinated by the strange speech and exuberant laughter. He had never laughed like that, not even as a boy.

Yldich was aware of him. He smiled at Rom. 'Well, good morning to you,' he sang. Rom was reminded of the morning he had imposed his company on him at the inn. 'How are you now?' Rom felt subtly excluded by the intimate laughter and the language he couldn't share. He drew the blanket around his shoulders more tightly.

'I'm fine,' he said stiffly. Yldich sprang up lightly and came up to him. He put his hands on his shoulders and looked him closely in the eyes. Rom had to force himself not to look away from the clear, piercing glance. Eald happily hobbled along a few paces behind Yldich. He looked up at them expectantly. If the boy had a tail, Rom thought, it would be wagging.

'Let's have breakfast,' Yldich said.

'Rom!' Eald said while they were eating. 'Yldich's going to teach me *flestrérer*.' Rom blinked at him in bewilderment. Yldich saw the flustered look on his face and grinned.

'It's the humming,' he said to Rom. 'The kind that makes you aware of your surroundings.'

Eald nodded eagerly. 'I can help Yldich keep watch, so no riders will find us.'

Wonderful, Rom muttered to himself. *Now there's two of them.* He nodded at Eald, doing his best to look at the boy approvingly. Eald beamed at him. Yldich cleared up the bowls and mugs.

'Eald, why don't you go and practice *flestrérer*. And keep on the lookout for anything we might be able to eat. Like berries. I want to talk to Rom for a while.' Eald nodded and sprang away. Yldich helped Rom up and motioned toward the trees. 'Let's have a seat.' Rom tried to sit down on his own, using the tree for support, but his muscles trembled so much that Yldich had to help him down so he wouldn't topple over. 'Now then,' Yldich said when he had settled in the grass. 'Tell me what happened. The day before yesterday.'

Rom looked uncomfortable. He would rather keep the episode shut out of his mind. But Yldich was looking at him intently. And there was a question that was beginning to nag him, now he thought about the day he ran into Feyir and his riders. 'Well, I met someone called Feyir. A refined gentleman.'

Yldich nodded gravely. 'Eald mentioned his name. Do you have any idea who he is?' Rom shook his head. 'He and his riders were first seen in the Forest five or six years ago. Soon after, small villages and houses on the Southern fringe of the Forest were found burnt down or empty. The inhabitants were found slain, or were never seen again. We—I guessed that they had been taken as slaves. Or worse.'

Rom shuddered. 'He was going to have his men torture me. He was having a go at it himself.' He pulled away the hair on the right side of his face. Yldich stared at the mass of clotted blood that was his ear. 'He seemed to be under the impression I was travelling with the leader of the *Einache*.' Rom studied Yldich's face sharply. 'He wanted to know where he had gone. I tried to convince him I had never heard of such a person. He wouldn't believe me. So he did this.' He motioned at the bloodied ear.

Yldich closed his eyes. His tanned face was a shade paler than it had been. 'I am sorry.'

Rom stared at him. 'Who are you?' he said finally, his voice hoarse.

'Feyir has got a somewhat distorted notion of what it entails, but in a sense, I guess it's true. I am the *Hárrad* of the *Einache*.'

'What does that mean?' Rom's face was tense. He felt strangely betrayed.

'It means I am at the head of a—a group of people who want to change things for the better. But it's not what Feyir thinks.'

Rom shook his head and scowled. His eyes had turned black. 'Why didn't you tell me this? Before you let me go off into the forest by myself....'

Yldich fixed his gaze on him with a stern expression. 'It's not the kind of thing one goes and tells a man he has only known for three days. Besides, you hardly left me time to explain. You were too busy running away from yourself.' Rom swallowed. He leaned his head against the tree and closed his eyes. To his horror, tears pushed to the surface. He brushed them away with a gesture of annoyance. Yldich looked at him with an unfathomable expression.

'You haven't been too forthcoming with details of your personal history either,' he said softly.

'But that's hardly the knowledge that would get another man killed.' Rom sounded bitter.

Yldich laughed. 'You've got me there.' Rom didn't speak. He sat against the tree with his eyes closed. He felt drained, tired and empty. Yldich looked at him and shook his head. 'Rom,' he said in a gentle tone. Rom remained motionless, his eyes closed. Yldich took his hand. Rom's eyes flew open. He flinched and tried to pull back his hand. Yldich held on to it. 'If I had meant to harm you, would I have gone through all that trouble to find you and keep you alive?' Rom looked at him and swallowed with difficulty. 'Maybe it's time you learned to trust a little.'

Rom shuddered. Something strange happened. Something that had been coiled and knotted inside his chest ever since he could remember was loosening. It scared him. He felt he would drown if he let it uncoil. He would dissolve. Yldich saw the panic rise in his face. He carefully laid his hand back down in the grass. He took a deep breath.

'I'm sorry your trip to the North is turning out to be such a nuisance,' he said in a cheerful tone.

Rom pushed the hair out of his face. He smiled wryly. 'I guess I'd have been better off listening to your warning.'

Yldich grinned. 'Welcome to the North.'

'Why, thank you,' Rom said. 'I think I'll turn around and go home as soon as possible.'

'Unfortunately, it's far too late for that.' Before Rom could retort, Eald came back from his expedition, running through the glade with his shirt filled with orange-red berries. They had stained it thoroughly.

'Look what I've got,' he called. 'The bushes near the stream are full of them.' He dumped his load at Rom's feet.

'What are those?' Rom said, as he eyed the squished things. He'd never seen them before.

'Weyberries,' Yldich said. 'They only grow in the north of Gardeth Forest. Have some, Rom. And let me have a look at that ear.'

Yldich studied Rom's cut ear and carefully cleaned it with a damp cloth, while Eald looked on with the same fascination he would have for a dead animal or a curiously mottled bird's egg.

'You've been lucky,' he said. 'It looks like the heavy bleeding has cleaned the wound thoroughly enough. I don't think it will get badly infected. Just don't touch it, and it will heal by itself.' He put away the cloth. 'Now, there's one thing I'm still wondering about. How did you manage to get yourself in such a state that you almost bled to death?' Rom was silent. Eald answered for him. He sat up proudly, tossing back lanky wisps of hair.

'He fought all of the riders at once,' he said. 'Of course, there were too many of them for him.' Yldich raised his eyebrows and looked at Rom. Rom looked away, feeling uncomfortable.

'It really was the other way around,' he said to the grass. 'I attacked Feyir, and they pulled me off him and—'

'*You* attacked Feyir?'

'It was something he said.' Rom frowned darkly at the ground and was silent.

Yldich was about to ask another question. Then he thought better of it. Instead, he got up and went over to the saddlebags. He pulled out a sword. With it went a scabbard of deep indigo that was beautifully adorned with silver needlework. Hundreds of thin lines of silver formed curly patterns that intricately connected forms of birds, leaves, stars and symbols Rom had never seen before. Yldich pulled out the sword. It had the same forms and symbols on it, subtly engraved in the shiny steel. The sun glinted on its sharp edge. Yldich tapped it lightly with a fingernail. Immediately, the sword resounded with an eerily high, clear note.

Rom stared at the sword. He had never seen such a strange and beautiful weapon before. It looked more like a work of art than an effective weapon.

Yldich saw his glance and grinned. 'Don't underestimate it. It's well-balanced and extremely sharp.' He threw the sword into a tree with little effort. It ripped through the air like an arrow, and burrowed itself deeply into the trunk with a thump. Rom and Eald stared at it as it quivered, Eald with his mouth half open and his eyes shining.

'I had it made in Newbury for my daughter Maetis.' Yldich touched the hilt with a fond smile. 'She has an un-girlish fascination with weaponry.' He pulled the sword out of the tree and sheathed it. He held it out to Rom. 'I think you should have it for now.'

Rom made no move to touch it. 'I don't much care for weapons. Besides, I haven't any skill with a sword.'

Yldich lifted a brow. 'Would you rather fight Feyir with your bare hands again next time you run into him?'

'I intend not to run into him at all.' Rom frowned. 'I'm going home as soon as possible.'

Eald sprang up and tugged at his sleeve. 'But, Rom, you can't leave us now. You've got to stay with us.' He turned to Yldich. 'Please tell him to stay!'

Yldich gently pressed his arm and turned to Rom. 'Rom, you're in no state to travel by yourself. Even if you hadn't lost your horse and pony, you wouldn't be able to get through to the South on your own safely now. You had better stay with us for a while. The most important thing is that we stay out of the way of Feyir and his riders.' Rom sat down in the grass. He felt too weak to argue. He held his face in his hands and nodded. 'That's settled, then,' Yldich said cheerfully. 'Eald, let's go pack. Rom, you rest now. We'll be leaving shortly.'

They cleared the camp quickly and efficiently. Yldich showed Eald how to hide all signs anyone had been there. They raked the floor with branches and buried the fire pit.

The day before, Yldich had left Rom's tunic in a shallow pool for hours to soak the worst of the bloodstains. It was the only one he had now, and he needed it since Yldich's spare one was much too big for him. Yldich helped Rom mount the horse.

'His name is *Elda*. Just give him free reign. He'll follow my lead.' He walked alongside the horse.

'Where are we going?' Rom said, when they were moving for a while.

'We'll try and find Eald's parents, first,' Yldich said. Eald was a few paces ahead, humming softly. He was practicing *flestrérer*. 'This morning, he told me he was taken in a raid by Feyir's men a year ago.' Yldich spoke softly. 'His family lived in a small village on the outskirts of the Forest. They were surprised at night, and Eald doesn't know what happened to them. They might have been looking for him all this time. Or mourning him.' Rom looked at the boy.

'Yldich,' he said softly. 'What do you think happened to them?'

Yldich shook his head. 'There's always hope.'

When they had reached a wide, hilly glade in the forest, Yldich signalled them to stop.

'I need to get my bearings.' He went and sat down cross-legged in the middle of the glade. Rom and Eald looked at his movements in silence, wondering what the man was up to.

Yldich closed his eyes. The mellow autumn sun warmed his face. He let the sunlight fill his heart and breathed in slowly. As he breathed out, he let his awareness pour out over the forest floor. He let it spread around in all directions. The golden threads of Life were everywhere. To touch them, and know himself to be part of it, filled him with gladness.

He was aware of the small creatures working in the earth, turning leaves to soil, their busy, productive lives unnoticed by human beings. He let his awareness rise up beyond the forest floor. He felt the slender presence of young saplings, their fresh leaves rejoicing in the light of the sun, and he rejoiced with them. He sensed the slow heartbeats of the old, wizened trunks of their elders. Their leaves, high above, whispered to him and he listened respectfully. Further and further away he reached.

He passed Rom and Eald, who looked on in wonder. He felt Eald's presence, a blend of exuberance and amazement, vibrating at a high pitch, like any young life. There was only a little scarring there, at the surface. He felt Rom's, darker and more introverted, old hidden pain, and power beneath it.

He felt a strange connection with the young man that went further than the few days he had known him. It felt like a subtle thread he couldn't define, running along from somewhere far back in the past, right through his heart, to somewhere far ahead in the future. He had felt it before, in his true-dreams. His skin prickled.

He let them go and let his vision expand beyond their immediate surroundings. He rose up into the sky, sensing more animal life further ahead. There were geese in the air, flying in V-formation towards the south, all business and purpose. He became aware of a dark area in his field of awareness to the northeast. Feyir and his riders. He swooped over them, then turned and went through them. He felt the riders' energy. Theirs was a common mixture of brutal ignorance, callousness with fear underneath. They were mainly concerned with survival and competition. Then he came across a different form of energy altogether. Feyir. His vibrated at a much higher frequency, yet there was something about it that made it more unnerving. Something repulsive, like the hidden rotten core in a piece of fruit that looked otherwise attractive and healthy. There was brilliance to his energy that somehow sickened Yldich.

He pulled back quickly and breathed out, then returned to the glade where he'd left his body. He strengthened his connection with it. For a moment, he rested lightly above the earth, and let the interconnectedness of life sustain him. He touched the roots of the grass and trees and shared the nourishing energy of the earth.

He felt something dark pull at him. It came from deep down below, from far beneath the tree roots. Yldich frowned. A strange metallic taste was in his mouth. He tried to pull back, and to his rising horror, the darkness wouldn't let go. An acrid smell filled his nostrils. He struggled like an animal caught in tar. He started to choke.

Rom gingerly dismounted and stood beside the horse. He studied Yldich silently as he sat down and closed his eyes. He wondered what the man was doing. Yldich was breathing slowly. Rom slowed down his own breathing instinctively. He half closed his eyelids and let his awareness drift. Then he saw the other man frown. An expressing of pain crossed his face. He cringed. It was alarming.

'What's happening? What's he doing?' Eald said. His voice was high with uncertainty.

Driven by an impulse he didn't understand, Rom ran towards Yldich and dropped on his knees before him. He gripped the big man's arms and shook him forcefully. 'Yldich. Come back.' Yldich groaned, but his eyes did not open. All colour had drained from his face.

'Do something,' Eald cried out.

Rom hesitated. Then he closed his eyes. He concentrated fiercely. First, he saw nothing but the dark of the insides of his eyelids. He tried to locate Yldich by sight alone, but it was to no avail. Desperately, he tried to feel for him with his senses. He groped around wildly, finding nothing. He panted, his chest filling up with fear and despair. Suddenly, he was aware of a thin thread that wound through his heart. He followed it out. It stretched before him, into the dark. Without knowing what he was doing, he sent a call through the thread and felt a response. He hurried towards it. He became aware of another being, far below, partially trapped in a horrible living darkness. It struggled faintly. It felt like Yldich.

He plunged down towards the darkness, and felt its substance reach for him. It felt like something sentient, something conscious. Touching it made his skin crawl. It was cold. It leeched onto him greedily. He grabbed at the energy form that was Yldich, and cried out to him. He felt a faint response. It was as if someone grabbed hold of his hand. He pulled out of the darkness with all the force he could muster. It was almost unbearably heavy.

'*Ayàdi eymíraz,*' he cried, and he did not know the language. The darkness gave way a little. He gave one last desperate pull, moaning with pain and effort. All at once, there was no more resistance. He fell back heavily and found himself back in his body. He was lying on his back in the sunlit grass, shaking uncontrollably. He heard Eald cry out with relief and run towards them. He heard Yldich's voice. It was hoarse.

'I'm fine,' Yldich said. He sounded badly shaken. Rom clambered up and sat up in the grass. He looked across at Yldich. Yldich wiped his brow, his eyes closed. He composed himself, taking deep, ragged breaths. He suddenly opened his eyes and looked at Rom. 'How, by all the gods, did you....' he burst out abruptly. Rom shrank back from his glare. He drew a hand across his face. He was shocked at what he had done. He didn't even know how he'd done it. He didn't want to think about what it meant. It frightened him more than the sickening blackness he'd felt reaching for him.

'I—I don't know,' he said. 'I just—I don't know.' He bit his lip and stared at the ground. Eald looked at him with anxious wonder. Yldich stared at him fixedly with his deep grey eyes.

'It can be a dangerous thing,' he said slowly, his voice still hoarse, 'for a man not to know who he is.' Rom buried his face in his hands. Yldich sighed and got up slowly. He walked up to Rom and kneeled beside him. 'Whatever it is you're running from,' he said kindly to his bowed head, 'whatever you may be, you may have just saved my life with it.'

Eald dropped down beside them in the grass. His clear voice rang in their ears. 'I know what you did. You were dreamwalking. I felt you go. Only you were awake.' Rom lifted his head and stared at the boy.

'Eald may be right.' Yldich looked at Rom. 'What was down there is not of this plane. The only way to reach it may be *ayúrdimae*, the waking dream.' He didn't mention the strange words he had heard Rom cry out. Somehow the darkness had shrunk before them. He couldn't remember where he had heard them before, but it was a long time ago. It disturbed him greatly.

'Our safest course is north-west, I think,' Yldich said as they were preparing to move on. 'I sensed the riders on the other side of the river to the east.' He helped Rom mount the horse. 'We may be able to find Eald's village that way as well.'

Rom looked down at him, frowning. 'How do you know?'

'Well, right before I was... trapped in the darkness, I surveyed the area around us. By *ayúrdimae*, dreamwalking. But apparently it has become hazardous to do so.' Yldich's face was grim. 'It appears whatever is down there in the earth can entrap anyone who's dreamwalking.'

Eald looked at him with wide eyes. 'It can grab me while I'm asleep?'

'Well, I would advise you to be careful where you dream yourself to, lad,' Yldich said. 'Just as long as you don't stray too far, you should be fine.'

Rom shook his head in bafflement. 'You talk about this—this dreamwalking as if you're talking about cleaning the dishes.'

Yldich chuckled. 'With the *Einache*, we teach our children from a young age how to dream well. But they're not all as talented as Eald. Or you. These days, most of them don't get to the stage where they have true dreams at all.'

Eald smiled at Yldich. He seemed to grow a little with pride. Rom fidgeted uneasily with the reigns.

They moved through a green woodland area that was fed by several little streams. Blue-green dragonflies glided through the air above their heads. Eald and Rom filled the water skins while Yldich went hunting. He returned with two rabbits.

'How did you do that?' Eald said, his eyes big.

'I called them,' Yldich said. 'I'll teach you.'

In the afternoon they came upon an area where the trees stood back in thickets and a strip of grassland bordered a small river.

'Let's make camp here,' Yldich said. 'We could all do with a wash. Eald, you look like a pair of muddy boots left out to dry.'

Eald laughed. 'And Rom looks like a bag of dirty laundry.'

'If we went to the *Squealing Pig now*,' Rom said, studying his grimy fingernails, 'I doubt they'd let us in even there.'

Eald and Rom descended to the river bank. It was lined with small pebbles that stung their feet. They waded carefully into the river and stood there shivering. After they had washed their clothes in the stream, they wrung them and threw them on the grass. Then they plunged into the water, gasping with the cold. Rom habitually made sure his back was turned away from Eald while he washed. Eald noticed.

'You don't have to hide it,' he said. His tone was matter-of-factly. 'I've seen your scars.' Rom winced. 'How did you get them?'

Rom's eyes turned dark. 'It was a long time ago,' he said in a low tone. 'It doesn't matter now.' Eald opened his mouth to ask about the mark that was shaped like Feyir's ring. Before he could speak, Yldich's voice boomed through the air.

'Hurry up you two. Dinner's almost ready.'

They hurriedly dried themselves off with bundles of coarse grass and spread out their damp clothes over the bushes to dry. Then they went up the river bank, Eald in the lead. Rom followed more slowly, holding on to roots and tufts of grass.

They wrapped themselves in their blankets and sat down before the fire. They looked at it in amazement. Yldich did not only have two rabbits roasting above it, but he had also filled the small kettle with an assortment of wild potatoes, herbs and roots. It smelled delicious.

'Don't tell me,' Rom said. He looked at the potatoes. 'You called these as well?'

Yldich laughed. 'No, I had to dig these out myself.' He grinned. 'Eat, now.'

They went to sleep early, wrapped in their blankets around the fire. Rom heard Yldich and Eald softly murmur in their own language for a while. He was too tired to talk. He stared at the stars until he drifted away into sleep.

The next morning Rom retrieved their clothes from the bushes. Yldich had gone off on his own. Rom and Eald ate some leftover stew as they waited for him to return. Eald babbled about calling rabbits, ducks, deer, and wolves. A whole menagerie filled the campsite in his imagination. They heard Yldich's voice from the other side of the field.

'Good morning to you,' he called in a merry tone. 'Sword practice today.' He tossed two staves at their feet.

'Where did you get these?' Eald said.

'Went into the woods and cut them while you were still snoring,' Yldich said with a grin. He gestured at the staves and looked at Rom. 'Choose one.'

Rom stood up slowly and picked up a staff. He frowned and looked at it with distaste. 'I told you, I don't want anything to do with weapons.'

'Really?' Yldich moved forward so suddenly Rom had no time to blink. He took a swing at the staff with a precise, curt move. It flew out of Rom's hand and hurtled to the ground. In one fluid motion, Yldich turned his staff around and pushed at Rom's chest with just enough force to make him topple backwards. He hooked his foot behind Rom's right leg. Rom gasped and fell over like a felled tree. He lay on his back in the grass and before he could move, Yldich was on the ground beside him and lightly held his staff across his throat.

'Too bad,' Yldich said in a sober tone. 'You're dead.' It had taken less than five heartbeats. Rom swallowed and breathed out slowly. Yldich took the staff from his throat. He grabbed Rom's right hand and pulled him up.

'That was perfect!' Eald jumped up and down with excitement. His eyes were shining. 'Do it again!' Yldich grinned. Rom looked shaken. His face was pale, but his eyes were dark with some emotion Yldich could not fathom. He clenched his hands into fists.

'I won't do it. I've been able to survive for years without picking up a sword. I won't start now.' His voice was strained.

'Eald, you get some practice with this,' Yldich said, and lightly threw his stick at Eald's feet. 'I need to speak with Rom.' His grey eyes were stern. He took Rom by the arm and pulled him across the field until they were out of earshot of the boy. Rom tried to loosen his arm, but Yldich held it in a tight grip. At the other end of the field, he turned Rom around briskly and faced him, gripping his upper arms.

'Now you listen to me,' Yldich said forcefully. Rom stared back, his face tense. 'I don't know what happened to you, but you can't afford to run from it any more. I won't let you. What will you do if Feyir's riders catch up with us? What if they capture Eald? Torture him? Kill him? Or me? Will you just stand there and say that you don't want to fight? Will you let yourself be killed?' Rom swallowed and closed his eyes. Yldich felt him fade away. He shook him sternly. 'Rom. You must stop this, now. You can't do this any more.'

'Please. Leave me alone,' Rom whispered. He was shaking. Tears were running down his face. Yldich stared at him in perplexity. He shook his head.

'If you go on like this, you'll get yourself killed. You're running towards your death.'

Rom looked at him with non-seeing eyes. 'Better mine than another's.'

Yldich's eyes widened. 'What do you mean? What did you do?' He let go of Rom's arms. Rom sat down heavily against a tree. Yldich squatted in front of him. 'Tell me.' Rom closed his eyes. 'I've seen your scars,' Yldich said, his brows knit. 'I know something horrible must have happened to you. The kind of thing that changes a man.'

'Not a man,' Rom whispered.

'What?'

'I was not a man. A child. Eald's age.' Yldich gazed at him with wide eyes. Rom stared blankly at his hands. 'I was apprenticed to a man called Aldr,' he said finally. 'Lord Aldr. I was sent to his Keep to serve as a page. I must have been eight or nine years old....'

They heard Eald shouting challenges to imaginary foes in the distance. Apparently he was bravely attacking and killing stones, bushes and small trees with his staff. The merry sound contrasted sharply with Rom's wan face, Yldich thought. He felt his heart sink. He sat down before him and looked at him intently. Rom was speaking with his eyes closed. He held his face in his hands.

'Where I come from,' he said huskily, 'the family of a young boy that showed an aptitude for battle, or other skills, would be paid a small amount of silver for his apprenticeship at the Keep of one of the local Lords.' He took a deep breath and steadied himself.

'Maybe it was once a good system. Boys were taught their letters and their manners. They were introduced by their elders into their way of life and into their professions, of men-at-arms, guardsmen, falconers, and so on. First, you would learn the ways of the Keep by being a servant to the lords and ladies, by working in the kitchens and stables. Then, from the age of eight or nine, we were taught fighting skills.' He paused.

'Go on,' Yldich said.

'As I said, maybe it was once a good system. By the time my mother sent me away, it had become a life of servitude.' He swallowed. 'We—we were broken down and taken apart bit by bit. We were each assigned to a master, to teach us obedience, discipline, and unquestionable loyalty.' He emphasized the words with force. The list sounded as if it had been beaten into him many times over, Yldich thought grimly.

'That meant that you could only speak when questioned, to never ever look your master in the eye, to never ever question anything he did or said, to never have a thought of your own.' Rom's eyes were dark as pitch. 'We were to follow any order without question and without delay. I was assigned to Lord Aldr himself. I suppose he thought it an honour.' He grimaced. 'But

Lord Aldr was the worst of them all. He resented anything *Tzanatzi*. And they made me his personal servant and page. A half-breed.' He swallowed bitterly.

'From the age of eight until I was about twelve, he was the centre of my life. He ruled it from the early morning till late in the evening. At night he had me sleep at the foot of his bed, on a sheepskin rug on the floor. The slightest mistake, the smallest mishap, and his fist would be in my face, or his belt on my back. Maybe it wouldn't have been so bad if I had been better at pretending to be submissive.' He grimaced. 'But when he ordered me about, when he chastised me, my eyes betrayed me every time. He would look at me and *see*. I couldn't hide my thoughts. I wasn't really obedient. I didn't show him due reverence. So I was beaten even more often than the others.' He held himself as if he were cold.

'As I became older, it became worse. He seemed to be haunting me, tricking me into making mistakes, so he could punish me for it. He wouldn't leave me alone.' He hid his face in his hands like a child. 'I've often wondered why he hated me so much,' he whispered. Yldich swallowed down a curse.

'I know,' he said. 'He knew he could never get from you what he wanted.'

Rom looked up, his face wan. 'What was that?'

'Respect,' Yldich said, his voice stern. 'True respect. Furthermore, he probably sensed you were stronger than him.'

'Stronger?' Rom said. He sounded incredulous.

'Indeed,' Yldich said with a grimace. 'Why else would he need to beat you down so much? You were the more powerful, and he knew it.'

Rom stared at him, unbelieving. 'Do you really think so?' Yldich nodded. Rom frowned, trying to make sense of it.

'Go on,' Yldich said softly.

'One afternoon, my lord had me bring him a cup of heated wine during a gathering of nobles. I must have been twelve or thirteen. As I came up to him, carrying the heavy cup on a tray, he turned their attention to me. He said,

"Here's that half-breed mongrel. Can't do anything right." He moved as if to cuff me again. And I flung the tray at his feet. Warm red wine splattered on the stone floor and on his trousers. I did it on purpose. I couldn't help myself. I heard someone laugh. It was one of the nobles. Lord Aldr flushed red and beat me to the floor with one heavy blow of his fist.' Rom swallowed. He closed his eyes.

'The next day, one of the other boys was accused of stealing something that belonged to lord Aldr. A piece of jewellery or something.' He looked at his hands as if they belonged to someone else. 'We were all summoned to the practice court, a hall where the swordsmen used to practice. All the pages and many of their masters were there. Lord Aldr took it upon himself to punish the boy.' He blinked.

'The worst thing was, I knew the thing hadn't been stolen. It couldn't have been. I knew the whereabouts of every garment, every piece of jewellery my lord owned. The boy had no reason to take it and no chance to mislay it. He must have lost it himself.' He paused, and absently tugged at a tuft of grass. He pulled the blades to bits before he let them fall to the ground.

'Lord Aldr took the whip he used for this kind of routine. He had the boy forced down over a stool. Then he proceeded to beat him.' He swallowed. 'I knew the boy. A lanky boy with red hair and freckles. I liked him, insofar as it was possible to know him. We weren't encouraged to socialize. Any talk amongst pages was habitually discouraged. We were kept at our chores and exercises all day, so we didn't have much chance to talk. Still, I liked the red-haired boy. He had laughing eyes, and a wry grin, a little like Eald. And my lord was flogging him until the blood was dripping out of his mouth. His shirt was drenched with it.' Rom paused a moment, then continued, his face white and drawn.

'I thought he was going to kill him. And then something strange happened. Lord Aldr spoke to him, in between the lashings of the whip. I heard him say:

"This'll teach you, you despicable little bastard," and he looked at me across the hall. He looked straight at me. It was a look of hatred. So then I realized. He wasn't flogging the red-haired boy for stealing. He was punishing me. For defying him. He knew I liked the boy. He'd seen us talk. So thrashing this boy to death was just another way to subdue me.' He closed his eyes and clenched his hands into fists.

'What happened?' Yldich said, his voice strained.

'I went over to him,' Rom said. 'It was as if my legs were on strings, pulled by someone else. I walked up to him. And then I hit him in the face. In front of everyone.' He closed his eyes. Yldich stared at him. Rom breathed deeply, as if he had been under water. He opened his eyes, and gazed in the distance without seeing.

'Time stood still. I could hear the other boys gasp. I looked at Lord Aldr's face. It was wrenched with cold fury. I felt like sinking into the earth. I wish I could have.'

'What did he do?'

'He became deadly calm. He had the boy dragged away. I didn't dare look at him, to see if he was still alive. And then Aldr ordered his men to bring two swords. He said,

"If you really want to fight me, you filthy little bastard, you'd better do it right." He ordered me to choose a sword.' Rom shuddered. 'I'd had a little practice. Some years of basic training. And I was tall for my age. But to have to fight him, with a real sword....'

Yldich cursed. 'A boy is no match for a grown man.' His voice was low with disgust. 'It was never a fair fight.'

'For an instant, I thought that he only wanted to humiliate me, put me in my place,' Rom said. 'To be an example to the other boys. But when he came at me, his sword drawn, I could see in his eyes that he truly meant to kill me.' He stared at the ground. 'I couldn't move. I saw him advance, but it was as if I was frozen to the floor. Then he lifted up his sword and aimed it at my head. I blocked it by pure habit. We had practiced the same move over and over, outside on the field in weapons practice.' The ghost of a smile pulled his mouth awry. 'Lord Aldr wasn't an accomplished swordsman. He had strength, but not skill. Still, he could have had me down in two, three strokes.'

'What happened?'

'I blocked the first blow, and a second with effort. The sword was heavy. I could just manage to parry his moves. The third time he aimed a long thrust at my heart. I backed away to avoid it. I stumbled and fell to the floor. The sword fell out of my hands. He gripped me by the front of my shirt and lifted me up. He meant to cut my throat right then.' He swallowed. 'I closed my eyes. And then he spoke to me.

"By the way,' he said, 'your little friend is dead. I just had him put out of his misery." Rom's face was drawn, the skin taut. Yldich scowled. 'Something came over me,' Rom whispered. 'Something dark. From deep within. I felt pure rage, pure darkness. And it was as if the light of the sun was cut off. The hall was darkened. I heard people gasp in surprise.' Yldich stared at him.

'I looked up at Lord Aldr. I looked him straight in the eyes. Something went out of me. And he shrank back from me. I saw a look of horror in his face. He let go of my shirt. He backed away. Sunlight returned to the hall. The tension was broken. I saw him wipe the sweat from his brow.' He released a breath. 'When he was at a safe distance he stopped and looked at me. He took care not to look into my eyes.

"I'll not waste my time with you again," he said over my head, loudly so all those present could hear. He nodded at his men. "Twenty lashings," he said, and then he left.' Rom shuddered.

'They held me down over the same stool. And they flogged me like he had the red-haired boy.' His breath quickened. 'I wanted not to cry out. But by the fifth stroke, I couldn't stop myself.' He shook and put his arms tightly around his body. 'By the tenth stroke, I had fainted. So they waited until I

came round. And then they went on again.' Yldich clenched his teeth and
breathed out slowly.

'When they were finished, they dragged me from the room. I hardly
noticed. I only felt pain. Like fire, and ice. Red and white. My back was
screaming.' He stared in the distance.

'When I woke up, I was in a little cell. It was one of the old dungeons
that were no longer in use. I welcomed the silence. I was resigned to die. I
almost looked forward to it. But at night, one of the kitchen servants came to
me. I was barely conscious. She gave me water. She told me one of the pages
had told her what happened. Lord Aldr had given orders for them to stay away
from me. He wanted me to die slowly, alone in the cell. But she had heard
what had happened to the red-haired boy. She was related to him. So she took
a great risk and took care of me in secret.

At night, she came to me and dressed my wounds. She stole soup from
the kitchens and ripped up old sheets for bandages. After a day or two, when I
was delirious with fever, she had one of her cousins take me out of the castle
in secret. In a cart loaded with empty beer barrels.' He sighed and drew a
hand over his face.

'He brought me to a small inn. After a few days, when I was able to sit
up again, the innkeeper came to me. He told me Lord Aldr's men were
searching the country, looking for a dark-haired half-breed boy. Apparently,
when they had gone down to the dungeons to take away my dead body to be
buried, they discovered my disappearance. Lord Aldr was furious.

The innkeeper hid me in the wine cellar. After a few days, strange
rumours came to the inn. It appeared Lord Aldr had caught a mysterious
disease. He had a fever of sorts, they said, that made him hallucinate. He kept
to his rooms and trusted no servant to get him his food. He had his men
prepare it for him. He had them stand guard by his door day and night. He
saw things that weren't there, and ranted about *Tzanatzi* curses and black
magic. He suffered from a strange fever that wouldn't go away. And then one
night, after a series of painful convulsions, Lord Aldr died.' Yldich stared at
him. Rom continued, oblivious of his gaze.

'I went away one night, not long after. I didn't want to get the innkeeper
and his family into trouble. I took some food and a knife. I walked by night,
and slept by day in ditches. I managed to get to another town a little further
from the Keep where they didn't know me. I would do dishes, laundry, any
work they'd let me do for food. And sometimes I had to sleep under bushes
and steal it. Then I moved on further away from the Keep to another village.
And so I managed to survive. Once or twice I had a narrow escape. Aldr's
men just missed me on the road, or in a village. But they never caught me.'

He leaned his head back against the tree and closed his eyes. He exhaled slowly. He looked completely spent. After a while, he spoke again. 'The innkeeper also told me what happened to the red-haired boy.' His voice was husky. It had nearly gone. 'He told me Lord Aldr's men had dragged him away from the practice hall still alive. And then they'd cut his throat.' He winced. 'If only I hadn't smiled at him, passing him on the stairwell. If only I hadn't talked to him... if I hadn't provoked lord Aldr and defied him every chance I had, maybe he'd be still alive.' He leaned forward and hid his face in his hands. Yldich shook his head.

'It's not your fault, lad,' he said softly. 'He wasn't killed because of what you did or didn't do. He was killed because your lord Aldr was filled with fear and self-hatred.' He sighed. 'You were just a child. There was nothing you could have done.' Rom's breathing was shallow, his eyes closed behind his hands.

'I'm so tired,' he whispered. His voice sounded faint in his own ears, as if it came from far away. Yldich went over to him without a word. He sat down next to him and put an arm around his shoulders. Rom shuddered, but he didn't pull away. He turned towards Yldich as if involuntary, grasped his tunic with one hand, and hid his face against his shoulder. He cried without making a sound, shaking, and soaking Yldich's tunic with tears. Yldich sat with him against the tree for a long time, and held him silently, until he was still.

Rom disengaged and drew a sleeve across his face. Yldich handed him a piece of cloth without comment. Rom blew his nose, and stared in the distance, avoiding the other man's gaze. Yldich seemed not to notice his embarrassment. He sat back and looked at him for a moment with his clear grey eyes. He nodded and released a sigh.

'We should go and see what Eald is up to,' he said. 'I hope he hasn't taken his own foot off with his pretend sword.' Rom managed a bleak smile. 'Come on.' Yldich helped him up. 'After a tale like this, we need a second breakfast. I wish I'd taken a bottle of mead with me.'

They slowly walked back to camp. Eald came running towards them over the grass, the staff in his hand.

'Rom!' he called. 'You must come and look at my moves. I can take a man's head off like it's nothing.'

Rom smiled at him with an effort. 'Show me.'

It was far past noon. Yldich had left Rom under a tree with Eald after they had eaten. Rom already looked half asleep. Yldich had decided to give travelling a rest for the day. Rom needed some peace after his tale. And he himself could do with some time to think. He needed to clear his head of disturbing images.

Softly humming low-key he went into the woods. He let his song brush against the low trees and bushes, to increase his awareness of his surroundings. He didn't want to do any dreamwalking. Instead he used his senses to connect to the world around him. He felt his way around with his singing, like the small creatures of the woods use the tiny hairs across their bodies.

He increased the pitch of his song so it rose higher, until it became like a bird of prey's piercing cry, rising up into the air. He let his heart rise with it. He sighed and let the high north winds blow through his awareness, and clear his heart and mind. They brought to him the ghost of perfectly formed snowflakes from the far mountains. Focusing on their clear, crystalline perfection cleared his mind. He breathed out and let all uneasiness drain away into the ground.

Then he started to think. There were aspects of Rom's story that snagged in his mind like catch weeds. They bothered him. He turned them over and over in his mind.

When he returned to the camp site, Rom was fast asleep. Yldich heated some more stew and had Eald wake Rom to eat a few mouthfuls. He drifted away as soon as they left him alone. Yldich talked to Eald for a while until they fell asleep.

He was standing on a cliff at the edge of a great plane. Clouds of a grey that was almost black rose in the north, nearly blotting out the sky that was stained a deep indigo by the last light of the sun. Dark shapes moved on both sides of the vast plane beneath him. He heard the sounds of clashing swords. He felt a nameless horror approach. It coiled over the earth like smoke and smothered everything it met in its path.

Habit made him feel for the hilt of his sword. He found it at his left hip. Its familiar weight reassured him.

He woke to the sound of wood clacking on wood. The sun was already up. The sunlit field seemed strangely peaceful after the dark plane of his dream. Birds twittered in the trees at the edge. The distant rushing of the river was brought to his ears on a slight breeze.

Before he made a move, Yldich cast his awareness about him. He found nothing disturbing. The whole area was quiet and peaceful. He sensed Eald and Rom a few paces away, the only humans near. Yldich was surprised and a little unnerved. He'd never slept through the others waking before. They were practicing basic fighting moves near the fire. Eald worked hard to keep up with Rom's movements. Yldich heard Rom's clear voice ring across the field.

'Don't stand there holding that staff like a dead fish, Eald! Hold it up properly.'

Eald giggled. Yldich sat up. Rom noticed he was awake. He lowered his staff and met his gaze. There was something in his face Yldich hadn't seen there before. It was reflected in his eyes. It reminded Yldich of fireflies dancing in the dark.

'Good morning to you,' Rom called. He was smiling.

Three
Conflict

While Yldich made himself a belated breakfast, Eald and Rom went into the woods to gather firewood. Yldich once more impressed upon them the need to be cautious.

'I don't sense any other humans about. But we don't want to leave any trace for the riders. They might still be on our trail. So be careful.'

They moved gingerly through the underbrush, taking care to leave as little trace of their passing as possible. Eald was more adept at it than Rom. His lithe body moved through the thickets like a slender fish through water. Rom wondered how he managed to move about so noiselessly. Compared to Eald, he felt about as inconspicuous as a band of travelling jesters. Another dry twig snapped under his foot and he winced.

'Eald,' he whispered. Eald looked over his shoulder. He was obviously enjoying himself. 'Where did you learn to move like that?'

Eald grinned. 'You're really not from around here, are you?'

Rom shook his head. 'I grew up in village streets and castle halls.' Eald stood still and scratched his nose. His eyes went vague.

'It's like... you have to move with the Forest,' he said finally. 'Like swimming with the current.' His eyes lit up. 'Oh, and you... you have to *feel* around you before you move your arms or put down your feet.'

'How?'

Eald shook his head. 'Don't know. Just do it. Feel your way. It's like... like feeling the warmth of a kettle before you touch it.' Rom frowned, not understanding. 'My mother taught me when I was small, by letting me walk through the forest with my eyes closed,' Eald said.

Rom snorted. His mouth pulled in a wry smile. 'I think I'll try another way.'

They entered a small clearing. The leaves on some of the trees had already turned a soft yellow. It was like a hollow space in the wood, filled with golden light that danced on the delicate threads of spider webs. Eald moved to the middle of the space and sat down. Rom followed and settled down next to him in the grass.

'I'll try and send out a call for some game,' Eald said.

'Do you know how?' Rom felt a little uneasy. He knew Yldich did so habitually, but he had never actually seen him do it. He didn't understand it, so it unnerved him.

Eald nodded confidently. 'Yldich told me how. It's easy, really.' Rom looked aside at him, his brow lined with doubt. Eald settled down and closed his eyes. 'I'll try for something better than rabbits.' He took a deep breath and slowly released it. Rom looked at him with uneasy fascination. The boy's face looked serene in concentration.

A humming sound rose, soft and vibrating. It did not seem to issue from the boy's throat, but rather from the edges of the clearing. It was like sitting in a fuzzy bubble of golden sound. Rom's skin tingled. The humming increased, but rather than increasing in volume, it expanded, enlarging the bubble ever more, until it encompassed a large area around them. An expectant silence was growing inside it. Rom felt it fill his chest. A small tingle of anticipation grew into a feeling of excitement. Eald breathed out.

They heard a noise at the edge of the clearing. Something large was coming through the undergrowth. A sniffing, grunting sound reached their ears. Twigs were snapped underfoot by a dark shape that moved towards them from the other side of the clearing. Eald opened his eyes.

Rom jumped to his feet. 'What's that?' Eald stared open-mouthed in the distance. He looked directly into the small, angry eyes of a large black boar. It was moving straight for them. Rom looked down at Eald, frowning with uncertainty. 'Did you do this?' Eald stared mutely at the creature, his face pale. Rom scowled and grabbed Eald's arm. He pulled him up with force and started to run. They dived into the bushes and stumbled through the trees, back to the field where Yldich was clearing up the campsite. They rushed breathlessly across the field, closely followed by the boar.

The boar was confused by the strange song that had called it away from its root digging. It didn't know what to think of it, so it had decided it was angry. It had gone for the first thing that moved at the edge of its vision. Once it was running, its course was set.

When they reached the edge of the field near the river, Rom veered off to the right and threw himself over the side of a steep incline. He pulled Eald with him. They tumbled into some thorny bushes. The boar, still following its determined course, ran straight into the river and stood there, stopped short by the cold water that lapped its chest. It looked stupefied. Yldich came running towards them.

'What happened?' he shouted. Eald clambered up with difficulty while Rom disentangled from the scratching brambles, muttering curses when they tore his skin. Eald guiltily looked up at Yldich.

'I just wanted to call something big....'

Yldich raised his eyebrows at him. 'Well, you certainly got what you wanted.' He heard Rom laugh out loud. It was a sound he hadn't heard before.

'Eald, you fool....' He was wrestling the thorny branches, helpless with laughter. Eald looked at him sheepishly. Yldich grinned.

'Next time you send out a call,' he said, 'be sure to call something your own size.'

They cleared the site and gathered their things. Rom looked soberly at the broken branches of the bushes and the clods of earth the boar had thrown up in its passage.

'So much for not leaving any traces,' he muttered. Yldich heard him.

'Possibly the riders won't come this way at all. We've been careful so far.'

They moved on, walking in a north-west line, and kept the river on their left hand. The area was a mixture of grassland and woods. Eald took his turn to ride the horse. His eyes shone with delight. He looked small on the tall horse, trying hard to sit up straight and keep his legs around the horse's large body.

'Why don't you try and keep a circle of awareness around us by *flestrérer*, Eald,' Yldich said. 'But contain yourself. We don't want any more large game coming our way.' Eald's mouth pulled into a crooked smile. Rom snorted with amusement.

In the afternoon, they made camp in the area of grassland between the river and the woods. While Yldich and Rom took care of the horse and built a fire, Eald went into the woods. He came back a while later with a triumphant expression on his face, and with two rabbits, one in each hand.

'Well done, lad,' Yldich said, looking pleased.

'Don't tell him I got a swarm of stinging flies first,' Eald whispered to Rom when Yldich turned away to skin the rabbits.

When the rabbits were stewing with some herbs, Yldich got out the staves from the saddlebags and turned to Rom. 'Let's have some practice before dinner. Show me what moves you remember. And maybe I can teach you a few new ones.'

Rom felt uneasy as he faced Yldich with the staff. The older man was at least a hand span taller and more heavily built. An old, formless fear stirred deep within him and he frowned. His hands gripped the staff tightly.

'Not like that,' Yldich said. 'Tell me. What were you just thinking?'

Rom grimaced. 'I was thinking you could easily defeat me with that thing.'

Yldich nodded. 'Exactly. You were already projecting your thoughts outward. If that's what you're thinking in a fight, that's what you'll get.' He advanced; making a move at Rom. Rom blocked it, holding on to his staff with force. Suddenly Yldich's staff changed direction and moved around Rom's in a fluid motion. The move took him by surprise. The staff was thrown out of his hands and Yldich pointed his at his chest.

'One,' he said. Rom held his breath. 'Again.' Yldich made the same movement forward. Rom tried to block him the same way. Abruptly, Yldich froze. 'Now what are you feeling?'

'Nothing.' Rom avoided Yldich's eyes. Yldich looked at him, his grey eyes impassive.

'Just tell me the truth. There's no room for shame or avoidance in fighting. Avoidance will get you killed.'

'All right,' Rom said. 'I was feeling fear.'

'Good. Tell me what you're afraid of.' Rom frowned, his eyes dark with introspection.

'I suppose I'm afraid to die,' he said slowly.

'Good. Now you know what you're up against. It's not the man opposite you that you're fighting. It's your own fear. You have to get to know the thing you fear, befriend it, or it will defeat you.'

'Are you telling me I have to befriend death to be able to fight?' Rom looked incredulous.

'Exactly.' Yldich grinned. 'Once you've made your peace with death, fighting should be easy for you.'

'I should think death was something to be avoided in a fight at all times.'

Yldich laughed. Then his expression was sober again. 'Rom, this is important.' He looked at him intently. 'This is the thing about fighting. In a fight to the death, you meet the clean truth about yourself. And it will meet you without mercy. If you try to flee it, it will kill you. If you befriend it, you will survive. It's as simple as that.' Rom looked at him uncertainly, a line of thought between his brows. Yldich drew a slow breath.

I should have found you ten years ago, not the last moment before the storm.

'Again,' he said, and held up the staff.

After a while Eald came to watch them. He sat down cross-legged in the grass, a few paces away. His narrow face was unusually serious. Yldich had a way of moving that was fluid, unpredictable, and forceful. He had floored Rom at least a dozen times, or knocked the staff out of his hands with two, three easy strokes. Rom was panting. He wiped the sweat of his brow. Apprehension made way for irritation.

Yldich was calm as ever. He hit the staff out of Rom's hands for the thirteenth time. Rom's brows were knit. His dark eyes flashed.

'Thirteen.' Yldich's voice was dispassionate. He was not sweating at all. 'What are you feeling now?' Rom scowled. He felt a brooding sensation deep down in his belly. 'I'm guessing it's anger,' Yldich said. 'What are you going to do with it?'

Rom stared at him. 'Use it?'

'Do it,' Yldich said. Rom frowned. He turned his attention inward for a moment. He reached down towards the brooding sensation. It was like a small, dark, intensely hot fire. He tried to let it grow bigger. He thought of all the fights he'd been in since he was eight, older boys challenging him, calling him half-breed, or worse. He fed the fire with the memories. He thought of all the men in the taverns who had tried to corner the *Tzanatzi bastard* since he was thirteen years old.

The fire blazed up and he lunged forward, aiming short, fell sweeps at Yldich's staff. Yldich parried them with a look of mild surprise on his face. It turned into an expression of interest. Rom worked hard to pass his defensive strokes. Anger gave him speed and energy. He managed to drive Yldich back a few paces across the clearing. Eald hissed out a breath. His face was tense.

After about ten moves, Yldich nodded as if he had seen enough and changed his stance. He suddenly seemed to be made of air. Rom aimed a powerful thrust forward and Yldich moved with it, and around it. He ducked under the arm that held the staff. He turned, gripped Rom by the neck of his tunic and whirled him around. He threw him lightly with his back against a tree. Rom felt the air being forced out of his lungs and sank down with a gasp. The staff fell out of his hand. He closed his eyes and sat panting.

Yldich squatted in front of him. 'Is this how you got at Feyir?' Rom coughed and nodded. 'Let me tell you something about anger, lad.' Yldich sat down in the grass before him. 'It may give you force, it may help you forget your fear of death for a while. But ultimately, it will defeat you as surely as your fear will.'

Rom frowned. 'I did drive you back with it. And I did get at Feyir.'

'Yes you did. For a moment. And then you got yourself killed. If memory serves me right.' Yldich looked at him intently, his grey eyes stern.

Rom sighed. He closed his eyes and leaned his head back against the tree. 'Then what am I supposed to do?'

'Face your fear of death. Befriend it. And learn to channel your anger.'

'How?'

'I'll teach you.' Yldich grinned. 'If you'll let me.'

'All right,' Yldich said when they had finished eating. 'Let's talk about anger.' Eald went off for a walk along the stream. Rom and Yldich settled next to the fire. The sun was about to sink behind the horizon and set fire to the sky. A few wisps of cloud blazed in orange and gold.

'Now then,' Yldich said, 'when you got angry just now, what set it off?' Rom searched his mind, going back to the moment when he felt the first prickling of irritation. He hesitated. 'Tell me what you felt right before you got angry.' Yldich looked at him across the fire.

Rom felt his face grow hot. He didn't speak. Yldich pressed him, his face impassive. 'Was it shame? Because I managed to beat you thirteen times in a row?' Rom nodded, his eyes dark. He fidgeted with a piece of wood, turning it in his hands. 'So you chose to forget for that moment that I've been doing this for a very long time. And that you haven't held a weapon in your hands since you were about thirteen years old.'

Rom's mouth pulled into a wry smile. 'I suppose you're right.' He tossed the wood on the fire.

Yldich nodded. 'So you were being rather hard on yourself.'

'I guess that's true.'

'See how your judgment of yourself fuelled your anger?' Rom nodded, staring into the fire, his eyes dark with thought. 'So what were you trying to do with your anger?' Yldich went on. Rom felt hounded by his questions. He was silent. Yldich kept staring at him, and he yielded.

'I suppose I wanted to prove that I—that I wasn't—'

'That you weren't some weak young boy too scared to hold up a staff?' Rom sprang up, his eyes dark as night. He clenched his fists and stared at Yldich, his face white with anger. 'Easy, now,' Yldich said. 'I'm not saying you are. I'm trying to get you to see what you're fighting against.' He patted the ground with his hand. 'Sit down, Rom.'

Rom breathed out slowly. He unclenched his hands. He sat down. An old wellspring of grief tried to fill his eyes with tears. He pushed down the stream of tears, swallowing them before they could surface. He moved a hand across his face, as if to wipe away any sign of them. Yldich looked at him. His expression subtly changed. He was aware of the wellspring as if it was right before his eyes. He sighed and let the pain pass through him into the earth.

'Don't be so hard on yourself, Rom.' Rom blinked. 'You're still fighting your past.'

'I thought I was fighting my fear of death.' Rom's face was a door, closed and bolted.

Yldich grinned, unperturbed. 'No. Your fear of death keeps you from fighting altogether. But when you are pushed into it anyway, you're fighting your past.' He threw some twigs and pine cones on the fire. They crackled; the heat of the fire threw glowing sparks into the darkening sky. Rom listened to the sound. He felt numb, his mind empty.

'When you fight out of anger, to push away shame, you reject a part of yourself,' Yldich said. 'And you can never do that without it coming back to haunt you.' Rom looked up. 'Think of your Lord Aldr. He was filled with fear and hate. He tried to obliterate it by killing you. Think about what happened to him.' Rom saw again the sun-filled hall that was emptied of light, the gathering darkness, the look in Aldr's eyes when he had backed away in fear from Rom's eyes. He shuddered.

'If you acknowledge all that is in you, if you embrace it all, even the fear, the shame, the pain, then there's nothing to be afraid of. Not even death,' Yldich said softly. 'Then you're ready to fight.'

Rom was silent. He stared into the fire. He turned inward, trying to get an impression of what was there, what was haunting him, driving him on. He sensed the outline of a deep core of darkness and pain. It was outlined in grief, like the corona of the sun when the moon hid its face. He shrank back before it. His throat constricted. He choked on tears.

'I can't,' he said huskily. 'I can't.'

'You'll have to,' Yldich said softly, 'one of these days.'

Eald came running back to the fire when the sky had turned almost black and a myriad of stars wheeled slowly overhead. He was panting and wildly flailing his arms.

'Rom! Yldich!' he shouted. They turned towards the small figure that came running towards them, ready to jump in case of trouble. Rom reached for his knife. When Eald had come close enough to the fire so they could see his face, they relaxed. Rom put away the knife before Eald could see it. Eald's eyes shone with excitement. He dropped down on the ground. It took a while before he could speak coherently.

'Breathe first, lad,' Yldich said. Eald closed his eyes, and breathed deeply a couple of times. His eyes flew open again.

'I know where we are. I've seen the Standing Stones.' Rom shot Yldich a puzzled look.

'It's an old burial mound, from the time the *Einache* still lived all over this area,' Yldich said. He gazed at Eald, who still struggled to get his breath back. Eald began speaking impatiently. The words rolled out of his mouth like pebbles in a fast flowing stream.

'The Standing Stones. I've seen them before. My father took me to see them. It means we're not far from my home.'

The next day they followed the route Eald had taken along the river towards the Standing Stones. Eald rode the horse again. He was bubbling with excitement. He was brimming with memories and details of his life before his capture, stories of life in a small *Einache* settlement on the edge of the Forest. Rom listened to him attentively while Yldich walked ahead. He was humming. Eald was in no mood to be cautious, so he kept watch, creating a large circle of awareness around them by *flestrérer*.

'How far are these Standing Stones from your home, Eald?' Rom said.

'I don't know for sure. My dad took me there when I was small. But it can't be that far. It only took us a day or two to get there. My mum would never have let us go away longer than that.' He grinned. 'She wouldn't even let my dad go to the Midsummer Festival alone.'

'Why not?'

'She said something about with that much beer around, it was possible to have too much fun.'

They reached the Stones before noon that day. Rom stared at them. He had never seen anything like it before. A little distance from the river, five large conical stones, as high as three men standing on each other's shoulders, jutted upward from the grass. They looked ancient. Years beyond count had left their marks on them in passing. Patches of light green and orange coloured lichen grew on their northern sides. Centuries of rain and wind had all but erased the markings that had been carved above eye level. Rom walked up to them and tried to make them out. He squinted and held one hand above his eyes.

'I see a sun, a moon, something that looks like a wheel,' he murmured. 'A bird, a crow maybe? And some sort of symbol... a lot of curvy lines, weaving into each other. I've never seen it before.'

Yldich nodded. 'The Sun is for the active principle, the male. The Moon is for the receptive, the female, the mystery. The Wheel is the Wheel of Life. The Crow is for the invisible, the Underworld, and death.' Eald turned his head in surprise.

'How did you know that? Nobody from my village knows what they mean.'

'They are old, the Standing Stones,' Yldich said. 'Not even the *Einache* remember what they were for nowadays.' Rom joined them. 'What is the fifth, the symbol?'

Yldich smiled. 'It's the All-encompassing. Its name is seldom spoken.'

Yldich decided to change course, veering off to the northeast. It meant they had to leave the river. They washed and filled the water skins to capacity. They moved on, with Eald in front on the horse. He had calmed down a little and was humming again.

Rom looked aside at Yldich. He had been unusually silent. Though he did not always speak while they travelled, he seemed to be continually communicating one way or another: with his humming, his eyes, his hands, and his face. Since they had passed the Standing Stones, his attention seemed to be turned inward.

When the sun started its slow descent, Rom asked: 'Yldich, I've been wondering. Who are the *Einache*, exactly?' Yldich nodded thoughtfully.

'The name *Einache*, in your Southern language, means something like *They who are of the Earth*, or *They who guard the Earth*. The name is used for all the forest-dwelling clans of the North.'

'But—you told me you were the *Har*—the leader of the *Einache*,' Rom said. 'Does that mean you're their King or something?' Yldich laughed out loud. Eald stopped *flestrérer* to look at them in surprised amusement.

'No indeed,' Yldich said. 'The *Einache* are a group of different clans, families, called Houses, and every clan has its own Head. They are all self-ruled. No-one rules them or tells them what to do.' His eyes glinted as if the thought of anyone telling a Head of an *Einache* clan what to do was highly amusing.

'When Feyir called me the leader of the *Einache*,' he continued, 'by *Einache* he meant a certain group of us from different clans who gather for a specific purpose, not the people of the *Einache* as a whole.' Rom frowned as he tried to understand.

'I am the *Hárrad* of that group, but it doesn't mean I rule them or lead them as Feyir would understand it.' A look of disgust fleetingly crossed Yldich's face. 'It's more like, I give them advice. You know I'm a *Yaever*. I'm one of the few left. I receive messages in my dreams, and I pass on my knowledge to them, so they can make informed choices.' He grinned. 'And because I'm eldest and speak with a little authority, they sometimes listen to me.'

'But what's the purpose of this group? What do they do?'

Yldich released a slow breath. 'Rom, what do you know of the history of this realm?' Rom looked surprised. He shrugged.

'What everybody knows, I suppose…'

Yldich raised his brows. 'And what is that?'

'Well….'

'For instance, do you know why the sons and daughters of the *Einache* are not allowed to settle outside of Gardeth Forest? Why the *Einache* are required by King Farhardt to pay taxes, but cannot demand justice at his court like his own people in the South can? And do you know why the *Tzanatzi* people are looked down upon as a lower class of beings, while they were the first ones to conquer and subdue this land, driving out the *Einache* by the power of their magic and the edge of their swords?'

Rom stared at him open-mouthed. He'd never heard Yldich speak in such a tone of voice before.

'I didn't think so,' Yldich said. His grey eyes were unusually serious, the colour of wind-swept seas under a cloudy sky. Eald looked down at the two men with wide eyes, his shoulders hunched, his narrow face pale and tense. Neither of them noticed. Rom frowned. He spoke hesitantly.

'The only thing I was told as a child is that the Southerners, King Farhardt's people, conquered the *Tzanatzi* long ago. They lost their lands and were cast out of their homes. And now they live on the road and travel from village to village. They keep to themselves, but sometimes people seek them out for their debased sorcery.' Yldich nodded.

'And before they were killed on their doorsteps and thrown out of their temples, they ruled this whole country with iron determination for three hundred years.' His face was grim. 'With the exception of Gardeth Forest.'

A nameless tension seemed to be spun in the space between the two men like a tautly stretched thread. Yldich suddenly noticed Eald looking at them anxiously and drew a deep breath. He smiled at the boy.

'Don't take any notice of me, lad. This is all ancient history. I'm an old fool for letting myself get worked up over it.' He squeezed the boy's hand. Eald sighed and visibly relaxed. Rom was still digesting what he heard.

'I never knew the *Tzanatzi* conquered your people… I just thought they'd always been here, before the Southerners arrived.' Yldich shook his head.

'I'd better tell you the whole story. Listen up, lad,' he said to Eald, 'this concerns you too. You should know your history.'

'Before the *Tzanatzi* came, the *Einache* lived in all the corners of this land. They lived, as the remaining families in Gardeth still do, in small villages, with the main House, the home of the Head of the clan and his family, at the centre.' His eyes went vague as he stared in the distance.

'The Houses were not the homes of the ruling class, but more like the hearth of a home, the heart of the family. They were great wooden homes filled with music, laughter, and talk. There you could go for justice, advice, learning, and healing.' He smiled wistfully.

'The ancient tradition of the *Yaever* people flourished in the *Einache* Houses. My foremother, Yealda, was raised in such a home. She was a famous *Yaeve*. She lived in the House of the Bear, which lay in a village in the woody hills some miles to the south of here. Any inhabitant of the village could go to her seeking healing or council.

She taught the children of the village everything they needed to know to live a good life. She taught them reading and writing in the ancient script. She taught them how to see the wisdom of their dreams. She gave them knowledge of herbs and taught them how to commune with nature. And when she noticed a child having unusual gifts, such as a potential talent for dreaming or healing, or seeing portents and omens, she would train such a child as her apprentice. I am of that tradition.' He smiled at Eald.

'Had you lived in those days, someone like Yealda would eventually have noticed you and taken you under her protection, teaching you to be a *Yaever*.' Eald gazed at him, spellbound.

'About five hundred years ago,' Yldich said, 'the *Einache* who lived at the coast saw the ships coming. They were large, graceful ships, with many sails and unfurled pennants of a dark red like old blood. They had beautiful figureheads carved in the likeness of birds and beasts of prey. They carried a dark-haired people that was graceful to look upon, men and women alike, great in knowledge and magic, and deadly in their hunger for land and dominion.' Yldich paused for a moment. He had lapsed into his chanting tone of voice again, as he did when telling tales.

'No-one knew where they had come from,' Yldich continued. 'But once they had debarked, no-one stopped to marvel at it. The day the *Tzanatzi* came, the sky darkened to black and a dark, nameless fear took the inhabitants of the coastal villages in an icy hold. It crept into the hearts of their warriors and it emptied their houses. Women and children were found dead in its wake, with no visible wounds on their bodies. The men that managed to stand and do battle were easily overcome, disheartened by the deaths of their wives, their children, and by the creeping horror that took them in a stranglehold. By the second day, the *Tzanatzi* had taken over the coast and were moving north, spreading all over the land.' Eald's eyes were wide with horror.

'Was there nothing that could stop them?'

'My people had never encountered anything like this before,' Yldich said. 'The dark terror that crept into their villages, crawled under their doors and rolled into their fields was unknown to them. As they did not understand it, they did not know how to fight it.' Rom swallowed, and put his arms around his body as if he were cold. His eyes were impenetrable, dark as night in his pale face.

'As they moved up north, conquering village after village, taking the lands for themselves, they finally met with resistance halfway the Forest of Gardeth. You see, when it became clear that the *Tzanatzi* would not stop until they had overrun our whole world, a handful of our people gathered to find a way to stop them from moving further north. It was a forerunner of the group that is now known as the *Einache*, or by people like Feyir as *rebels*.' He smiled wryly. 'It consisted of the last of the Headmen, the last of the *Yaever*, and the warrior leaders. They gathered to find a way to learn about the threat the *Tzanatzi* were using against them, so they could stop them in their path.' Eald bit his lip.

'With the help of the *Yaever*, the *Einache* found there was one individual, one great mage who was the source of the darkness that crept into their lands, drove grown men mad with fright, turned warriors against each other, and stole the breath of their children.' Something darkened his bright eyes.

'Go on,' Eald pressed him.

'They decided to meet him head-on in battle.' Eald let out a sigh. 'You see,' Yldich continued, 'the *Einache* had sent out a call to every House that was still standing, every family that still had sons, grandfathers, even daughters who were able to stand on their feet and hold a sword. The *Yaever* worked day and night, and used their joined voices to arouse anyone still able to fight. When the army of the *Tzanatzi* emerged at the edge of the Plain of Gardeth, they were met with what looked like a fully equipped, professional army. The *Yaever* had used their best abilities to create an illusion that would dishearten the *Tzanatzi* army.' Eald listened with his mouth open. 'Spears would look twice their size, boys of sixteen years would look like grown men in full battle gear. Of course, the illusion wouldn't be maintained if they got too close. But the *Yaever* hoped it wouldn't come to that.'

'Why?' Rom said, drawn into the tale despite a strange aversion he had been feeling to it since Yldich had mentioned the creeping darkness.

'Well, they wanted to keep the army busy, while they found a way to the mage. If they could get at him, they still had a fighting chance.'

'And did they? How?' Eald's eyes glittered with apprehension.

'I'll tell you tomorrow,' Yldich said. 'We should look for a place to put up camp and do some hunting.'

'No, Yldich, go on, please! I want to hear how they defeated the evil mage.'

He smiled. 'Why don't you think of a way. I'll be looking forward to your theories at breakfast.'

'Yldich,' Rom said that evening, while they were sitting by the fire. Yldich was mending a torn harness strap. Eald had gone off between the trees, humming softly as he went.

'What is it?' Yldich looked at him, at the eyes that looked like dark polished glass. Rom's face was worn and pale. He had been silent all evening. 'Are you not well?' Rom lowered his eyes and studied his worn boots.

'It's—it's only... don't you hate them?' Yldich looked surprised.

'Who?'

'The... the *Tzanatzi*. Don't you hate them for what they did?' He avoided Yldich's eyes. Yldich breathed out slowly. He gathered his thoughts.

'No, I don't hate them,' he said finally. 'It's been a long time since I've done any hating.' Rom looked up. 'Besides, all that was a long time ago. Things have changed a lot since then. As you well know.' Rom sighed. He seemed to let go some of his tension. 'Don't worry about it, lad,' Yldich said in a kind tone. 'Whatever some far-removed ancestors did in a distant past, has no bearing on you.'

That night, when Eald and Yldich were immersed in a dreamless sleep, Rom lay awake and stared into the darkness above his head. After a while, he heard a strange music just below the surface of his awareness. He strained to hear it with his ears, but the harder he tried, the less distinct it became. He closed his eyes and tried to follow the eerie sounds to their origin.

They were like the thin, piercing wails of flutes, the touch of strings, and the slow, sensuous beat of drums. The more he reached into himself, the clearer the music became. It was like a strange, sensual lament. Little bells accompanied the dark, flowing melody of the flutes and accentuated the subtle rhythm of the drums. Every few beats, a deeper bass note reverberated, like the beat of a great heart. He felt his own heart join in its rhythm.

The music pulled him into a great open hall. It had no roof that he could see; overhead the sky was a deep blue that was almost indigo. He could see no sun, no moon, nor stars. A large trellis overhead supported living vines that were in full bloom. Their sweet, intoxicating scent made his head swim. Slender trees had been braided into living walls. Copper braziers with burning coals hung from thin chains and added light and scent.

He moved into the hall like in a dream, led by the music, and could hardly feel the floor under his feet. He felt strangely weightless. He noticed spirals of elegantly wrought iron, with burning candles and incense, on beautifully carved tables. Wooden lattices were carved into the likeness of interlacing vines, and numerous hummingbirds, their feathers so scrupulously copied from living example that they seemed almost real.

He felt someone's eyes on him. He turned around to face the middle of the hall. A woman was standing there. Her gaze pulled him irresistibly to her. Her body moved subtly, almost imperceptibly, attuned to the slow pulse of the music. Her long hair, dark as night, seemed to possess a life of its own, and swayed around her as she moved. Her pale face glowed like alabaster in the semi-darkness. Her eyes smiled at Rom, pulling him to her. They were dark in her pale face, like living black velvet.

She held out a hand to him and he responded to the inviting gesture, feeling as if his movements were inevitable, beyond his control. There were others there, in the background, men and women, dark-haired like her, dancing slowly, elegantly, gazing at them like cats, their eyes catching the glow of the candles.

The woman's gaze pulled him all the way across the hall. Their hands met in the middle, touching softly, until she pulled Rom into the slow, stately, sensual dance. He held his breath as he looked into her eyes. They were of a height; their eyes met like a pair of birds, like two fighters engaging. Hers were warm and inviting, yet he suspected something behind them that was hidden beyond the surface, like a thought, not spoken aloud.

Somehow he knew exactly how to move with the music. He matched her movements like a mirror image, as he let his hands travel along her arms, her waist, and their eyes locked into each other. Her smile deepened as she moved a hand across his back, and he held his breath, the touch of her hand sending a shiver through him that shook him to the core. He looked up.

It was then that he saw the mountain in the distance. A great cloud of ash loomed above it. The smell of smoke was in the air, and suddenly he tasted bitter ashes in his mouth. A ripple of panic moved through the crowd of people until they started to run, and he ran with them, pulled into the stream of fear as if he were without a will of his own.

Clouds of ash and soot obscured his vision, and he felt the people around him struggle for breath, their lungs bursting with heat, choking on the ashes. He heard them scream until they had no breath left to scream with, and they fell to the side while he was pulled along with the ones who were still able to run. The hot air seared his lungs and he felt his skin pull taut with the heat of a merciless wind that threw him to the ground. He saw the ships in the distance, as he fell screaming, fighting for air.

He woke up with a gasp, tears running down his face. He opened his eyes to the sky and saw it burning red and gold. It took a moment before he realized it was not the fire of the volcano, but only the glow of the sun rising above the forest. He sat up, panting, struggling to get his breath back.

Yldich and Eald sat in front of him, blinking like owls, looking at him concernedly with their grey eyes that looked dark in the dim light of the dawn.

'I saw them,' he said, when he could speak again. 'I saw them.' He coughed. 'They were running. They were burning alive.'

'Eald, please get the fire going and heat some water,' Yldich said. Eald nodded and ran off, his eyes big. Yldich turned to Rom. 'Tell me what you saw.' Rom brushed the sleep out of his eyes.

'It was like a dream... but if felt so real....'

'You were dreamwalking.'

'Maybe....' Rom stared at the ground in wonder.

'Where did you go?'

'It was a place, somewhere beautiful...' He remembered the melody that had pulled him away. 'There was music. There were people dancing. They were *Tzanatzi*. It was a great hall, with vines and flowers, and beautiful carvings....' he released a sigh. 'I always thought anything or anyone *Tzanatzi* was bound to be ugly, horrid, beyond contempt.' His eyes lit up with wonder. 'But everything I saw there was graceful and beautiful.'

Yldich nodded. 'Go on.'

'There was a woman there. She was beautiful. She drew me into a dance.' Rom's eyes unfocused. 'The way she looked at me, touched me... I've never seen a woman look at me like that.' He gazed in the distance as if he'd forgotten Yldich was even there. 'I felt different... as if there could possibly be something desirable about me....' his voice trailed away and he flushed when he saw Eald had come back and stood listening to his words with great amusement.

'I don't believe no woman ever looked at you like that,' Yldich said, his brows arched. 'You were probably too busy surviving to notice.' Eald snorted, a teasing grin on his face. Rom felt his face burn with embarrassment. He found a fir cone under his hand and threw it at Eald's head. The boy ducked just in time and giggled. Yldich shook his head and suppressed a smile. He gave Eald a gentle shove.

'Now then,' he said, his brows knotted together. 'Leave Rom alone. Wait till you're his age and let's see how you'd feel. Now go do something useful.' Eald chuckled and fetched their mugs.

'Tell me,' Yldich said, when Eald had returned with their mugs filled with hot herb tea. 'What happened that was so bad you had to wake us up like that, this early in the morning?' Rom took the mug between his hands, and warmed them with it. He stared into the steaming liquid.

'Something happened, something horrible. A mountain erupted into fire. People ran to get away, but the heat and the ashes got to them before they could reach the ships. They were killed as they ran, their lungs filled with fire....' Yldich stared in the distance.

'We never knew why the *Tzanatzi* appeared as suddenly on our coasts as they did,' he said softly. 'Maybe they were running from some disaster of their own.'

When they were moving again, clouds gathered in the northeast. They thickened and clotted together until they obscured the light of the sun altogether. A light drizzle started to fall. The trees still sheltered them from most of the rain. Eald was in the lead on the horse, looking out for landmarks.

Rom still pondered his dream, walking through the hazy, dim light that was all around them; it made him feel as if he was still surrounded by the eerie music. The essence of it ran through his veins, like a stream flowing into whirlpools with slowly opening water flowers. It made him feel strangely light-headed. His feet seemed to make less noise when he walked. It was as if the dream had sharpened his senses and made him more sensitive to his surroundings and the movements of his body. He experimentally reached out and slowly moved his fingers, and felt the tiny droplets of water in the air brush against them. He laid his hand on the horse's flank and it was as if he could feel hundreds of individual glossy hairs, instead of one indistinct patch of coat. He suddenly felt Yldich's gaze on him and started. He guiltily pulled back his hand.

'What's the matter, lad?' Yldich said.

'Nothing,' he whispered.

'Something seems different about you.' The deep grey eyes probed him gently.

'It's just—I seem to feel more than I did... I don't know how to explain....'

Yldich turned and looked at him curiously. He breathed out slowly, changing his focus. He reached out to the young man's energy until he could almost see it. Whereas before there had been something defensive and sharp, like a cloud of tiny needles, he was now aware of an opening, a shy, tentative flowing of energy.

Good. He's dropped some of his self-hatred at last.

'I think you've let go of something that cut you off from yourself and the world around you,' he said. Rom gave him a quizzical look. Yldich grinned and nodded at Eald. 'I'd been wondering when our *Einache* influence would start rubbing off on you. We'll have you singing for rabbits yet.' Rom snorted and shook his head.

When they stopped in a field to make a quick fire and have some soup to warm their stomachs, Eald moved towards the line of the trees, looking around for specific trees and boulders he might recognize from his past.

'Don't go off too far now, Eald,' Yldich called. Eald nodded and disappeared in the thickets without a sound.

'I've been thinking,' Rom said when they were waiting for the water to boil. 'If the *Tzanatzi* were fleeing some disaster when they came, why didn't they simply ask for help when they arrived? Why did they have to overpower the *Einache*?'

Yldich smiled grimly. 'Knowing the *Tzanatzi* as they were then, it wasn't in their nature to *ask*. They saw what they needed and they simply took it. Maybe,' he added, 'they had a strange idea about the people they met when they came here. I've been thinking about that. What would a sophisticated, cultivated people have thought of the *Einache* as they were then, the forest dwellers, the people who lived in simple huts of wood and clay, their children running naked through the fields with their dogs? Maybe they thought us savages.' He stared into the fire. 'It's easier to conquer a people you consider beneath you,' he said softly. 'It was the same when the Southerners came, two hundred years later. When the *Tzanatzi* were already diminishing, robbed as they were of their greatest source of power.'

'How did they lose it?'

'I'll tell you when I continue the story of the Battle of Gardeth, when the *Einache* defeated the great mage,' Yldich said. 'Eald will want to hear that.' He stood up and fetched their mugs. 'Now where has that boy gone off to?'

They waited a while for Eald to return, but by the time the water had gone cold again, there was still no sign of him. Rom started to feel restless. He paced around the area, fidgeting, a cold, queasy feeling in the pit of his stomach. He walked back to the fire.

'Something doesn't feel right.' His face was pale and tense. Yldich sprang up.

'I'll have a look around.' He walked to the middle of the field and closed his eyes. As he breathed out, he swept around the area with his awareness. He felt the hidden life of the trees, some of them already turning inward for winter. He sensed the activity of insects and small mammals in the vicinity. There was no sign of any other life nearby. He opened his eyes. 'I can't feel him anywhere.'

They searched the area in a large circle around the field. They found nothing. They returned to the fire finally. The drizzle had extinguished it hours ago.

'What's happened to him?' Rom said, his face drawn. He slumped before the remains of the fire. 'Could he have wandered off so far he got lost?' Yldich shook his head.

'I can't feel his presence anymore. He couldn't have gotten that far in such a short time.'

'What if he was attacked by something large, a boar, or a wolf or something?'

Yldich's face was grim. 'We would have found the traces.'

Rom started to shiver with cold. The persistent drizzle had drenched his clothes, soaking them through to the skin. His throat constricted. 'What are we going to do?'

Yldich went over to the saddlebags and took out a cloak. He threw it around Rom's shoulders. 'We'd better stay here, for tonight at least. I'll try and call him through *ayúrdimae*. If he's anywhere near, I'll find him.'

Rom went to the edge of the clearing for some dry wood. It took several futile attempts before he had a fire going in the soft, dreary rain. He shivered under the woollen cloak. Yldich seemed to be impervious to the wet and the cold. He had gathered some things from his saddlebags and sat before the fire, frowning at them.

Rom looked at him. 'What are those?'

'These are some of the oldest heirlooms of my House,' Yldich said, indicating the large crystals on the floor before him. 'They can focus and align energy of all kinds. If I can't find Eald through *ayúrdimae*, I may have to use these.' Rom looked at the small assortment of rocks, bones and bundles of soft leather that lay next to the crystals.

'And what are those for?' he said, pointing at the bundles.

'Those are powerful *Yaever* herbs. If they are burned while a trained *Yaever* uses the crystals to focus his attention, the smoke can help someone who's not trained in *ayúrdimae* to leave his body and walk the path of the unseen, into the other world.'

His anxiety about Eald forgotten for a moment, Rom asked: 'What is *ay—ayúrdimae*, dream-walking, exactly, Yldich?' Yldich released a breath. He dropped some of his tension, his voice taking on its usual story-telling tone.

'Did you ever notice that you have different kinds of dreams?' He sat back a little more comfortably. 'You may have noticed that some dreams are wistful or whimsical, some dreams are just a repetition of the day's events. They are called *lágea*. Everybody has *lágea*. Then, there are true-dreams, dreams in which you may see something hidden or far away, or find out something important about the world, or yourself. They are called *énthemae*. And then there's dream-walking. And that is called *ayúrdimae*.'

Rom wondered silently how many times he must have repeated the lesson to *Einache* children.

'You've seen me do it in the glade where the darkness rose. *Ayúrdimae*, dreamwalking, means that you can enter the other worlds while you are dreaming.' Yldich sorted the bundles. 'Mostly this is done while asleep, but some people, trained *Yaever* like me, can do it whether asleep or awake. Because the dreamworld touches on our world, when you're dreamwalking, you can go anywhere and do anything. But there are rules. Dreamwalking can be dangerous.'

'Why?' Rom said, fascinated despite a slight feeling of unease.

'Well, there are other beings, other forces in the other world,' Yldich said, choosing his words with care. 'A dreamwalker has to be cautious, because not all of them look friendly upon humans.'

'You said there were other worlds, beside the dreamworld,' Rom said, his brows lifted in curiosity.

'Yes, there are many other worlds beside this one, the visual plane,' Yldich said. 'There is the dreamworld, which you have visited twice now, through *ayúrdimae*. It in itself consists of many layers. You might meet your past there, or your future. You might meet your darkest fears and greatest desires.' He picked up a crystal and weighed it in his hand. 'One should be careful, entering the many planes of the dreamworld. A dreamwalker might lose himself in the other world, and not be able to return.' He pointed the crystal at Rom. 'That's why dreamwalking is only done after much careful preparation and instruction.' He put it down again and met Rom's eyes.

'And then there is the Underworld, a deep layer of darkened consciousness.' His grey eyes were serious. 'No-one should enter that world unprepared. The Underworld can be dangerous if you don't know what you're doing. It can draw you in, and you'd never be able to find your way back.'

Rom shivered. 'But what's it like?'

Yldich gazed at him from under his brows, his grey eyes overcast with some dark memory.

'I hope you'll never have to find out.'

Rom propped himself up on one elbow, bundled in his cloak, while Yldich prepared to send out a call for Eald. He sat down cross-legged in front of the fire and closed his eyes. Rom looked on in fascination.

An arrow whizzed past his ear. It buried itself in his left hand. He cried out with pain and surprise. Yldich's eyes flew open. He saw the arrow, the bleeding hand, and looked around sharply, following the trajectory of the arrow to find the source.

'You should take more care where you leave your servants,' a level voice sounded from the other side of the clearing. 'I've already found one other loitering about in the forest.' Two men were standing at the other side of the clearing, in the shelter of the trees. One of them held a bow, a fresh arrow notched to the string. The other Rom recognized immediately.

'I've taken him into my keeping, so do not worry,' Feyir said. Yldich stood up straight, his movements slow and careful. He kept his hands at his sides.

'I don't believe we've been introduced,' he said in a calm voice. Feyir smiled.

'Nevertheless, I've got a fairly certain notion of who you are. Even though,' he said, and indicated Rom with his amber eyes, 'your *Tzanatzi* half-breed had some trouble admitting it.' Rom flinched, his eyes flashing with anger. He stood up, holding his injured hand with stiff fingers. Yldich laid a hand on his shoulder like a warning.

'I'd appreciate it if you returned the boy to me.'

'Well now, that depends,' Feyir said. 'By rights, he still belongs to me. However, I'm prepared to discuss some terms under which I might let you take him off my hands. Tomorrow, at sunset. The Standing Stones. We might come to an arrangement.' He turned to leave. 'Oh, and just to be clear about things.' He smiled. 'If you decide not to come, I'll terminate his service to me. Permanently. I don't like loose ends.' The men disappeared between the trees without a sound.

Rom's face had gone ashen. He sat down heavily and stared at the trees where the men had stood, clutching the hand with the arrow still sticking through. Yldich kneeled beside him.

'Show me your hand.'

Rom held it out without thinking. Yldich took his wrist in a firm grip and drew out the arrow in one quick movement. Rom cried out with pain and fell back into the grass. Blood welled up from the wound. He set his teeth. Darkness began to obscure his vision at the edges. He laboured to stay conscious.

'Sorry about that,' he heard Yldich's voice above him. 'Better get it out quickly.' He felt Yldich grab his hand again and winced. Yldich held a water skin over the wound, rinsing it thoroughly with water. He took a piece of cloth and bound it tightly around Rom's hand.

'Keep pressure on it,' he said. He helped Rom up and had him sit up against a rock, then went off to the fire. He mixed some herbs in a bowl with boiling water until he had thick green paste. It emitted a sharp, tangy smell. He went back to the rock. Rom sat with his eyes closed, breathing heavily, his face white and tense.

'What are we going to do?' he said. Yldich took his hand and carefully peeled off the already blood-soaked bandage. 'What do they want? Why didn't they just attack us and be done with it?' Yldich covered the wound with green paste. Rom winced as its sharpness bit into it and hissed in a breath.

'I don't know. Seems to me this Feyir likes to play games according to his own rules, in his own time. And he seems to think I can be of use to him.'

'So why not take us now?'

'Maybe he doesn't want to risk a fight, without his riders here.' Yldich smiled grimly. 'I've been known to split some heads in my time. And don't underestimate yourself. You can do quite a lot of damage when you're properly motivated.'

The drizzly rain had finally relented. Yldich went off into the woods to gather more dry kindling. He tried to get a sense of Eald without *ayúrdimae*, using only the instincts that linked him to the world around him. He got an impression of the boy's light, buoyant energy. It was faint, as if he was unconscious or asleep, and far away, nearly smothered by the surrounding dark, heavy energy of the riders. But it was there, miles away to the west. Relieved to feel he was still alive, he returned to the camp site to find Rom pacing impatiently around the fire. He held onto his bound left hand compulsively. His eyes were glittering with fever.

'Where did you go?' His voice was harsh.

'Got some more wood and food,' Yldich said in a calm tone. 'I found Eald's trace as well. He's still alive.' Rom released a sharp breath.

'What do we do now? Do we just do as Feyir wants, go to his camp like a pair of sheep to the slaughter?'

Yldich dropped the wood and filled the kettle, moving slowly, his face impassive. 'What else do you propose?'

Rom shook his head and scowled. He kicked at a burning piece of wood, and sent it flying over the fire in a rain of sparks. Yldich stopped what he was doing and looked sharply at Rom. Rom glared at him. His face was rigid.

'How can you stay so calm?' His voice was edged with despair. 'How can you gather food while you know he's with them? We should go there immediately. Who knows what they've done to him, what they're going to do when we get there.' He clenched his fists. 'Feyir's ruthless. He'll do anything to get what he wants. Maybe he's torturing him right now, so he'll tell him everything he knows about you—' Yldich walked over to him and took him firmly by the shoulders.

'Rom. Stop it. You're driving yourself crazy.'

'How can you stand there so calmly and not *do* anything?' Rom struggled in Yldich's grip, and hit him in the chest as hard as he could, wincing as he hurt his injured hand. He fought with all the force of a feverish rage, until he was spent and went limp in Yldich's hold, sinking to the ground.

Tears ran down his face. Yldich shook his head at him. He let him go and sat down in front of him.

'I'll tell you.'

'The reason I'm not running off right now in anger or despair,' Yldich said in a calm voice, 'is that I know my place in the order of things. I know my purpose.'

Rom stared at him. 'What are you talking about? What's this got to do with anything?'

Yldich sighed. 'Listen, Rom. There's something I've been meaning to teach you. Something the children of my people are taught at a much earlier age. I'm sure Eald knows it.' He paused. Rom frowned with incomprehension.

'There's so little time.' Yldich stared pensively at the sky. 'The only way I can teach you now is by showing you directly. In order for me to do that, you'll have to trust me.'

'I—I trust you.'

Yldich shook his head and smiled briefly. 'For this, you'll have to let go of any mistrust and control completely. Can you do that?'

Rom swallowed. 'Do I have a choice?'

'Yes, you do. You can choose not to learn this. You can choose to remain as you are.' Rom was silent for a while. He stared in the distance. His eyes were unreadable. Yldich waited patiently.

'I'll do it,' Rom said finally. The feverish glitter had left his eyes. 'What do I have to do?'

Yldich went over to the fire and came back with two large crystals, a bundle of herbs and a lighted branch. He stuck it in the ground like a torch. 'Close your eyes.'

Rom closed his eyes. A tingle of fearful anticipation started deep down in his belly. He forced his breathing to slow down. It took some effort not to open his eyes to see what Yldich was doing.

'Hold this.' Something cold and heavy was put into his hand. He closed his fingers around it. It felt like one of the large crystals. 'Now hold it firmly in both hands. Whatever you do, don't let go of it.'

Rom nodded and swallowed. A smoky smell was filling his head. It was sweet and bitter at the same time. His thoughts started to wheel and swirl in his head. It was like being caught in a whirlpool that wanted to draw him out of the top of his skull. He clutched at the crystal. His breath started to come in ragged gasps. He swayed, a sense of panic rising from within his belly. He let go of the crystal with one hand, reaching out wildly, trying to find anything to hold onto, anything solid. He heard Yldich's level voice as if from far away.

'Hold onto the crystal, Rom.'

He withdrew his hand with an effort, and held the crystal in both hands again. Yldich started to hum softly. It sounded different from his usual tentative, questing chant. It was purposeful and powerful. Like a dark undercurrent in Rom's awareness it pulled at him, and began to turn and whirl. Rom could discern words in the strange Northern language. Their vibration filled his head and his body. Yldichs tone deepened; the song increased in power, quickening, pulling at his being like a surging vortex. He moved his awareness to the space between his eyes, and for a moment he balanced in the middle of the current like in the eye of a storm, where there was only silence. He held on to himself, the storm whirling about him. He felt he had a choice: to go with the words, or to stay. He wavered, trembling with indecision.

He let go.

The vibrating chant pulled him out of his body so fast he nearly lost consciousness. He felt as if he fell apart, no longer one entity, no longer a person. He wanted to scream, but there was no voice to scream with. He felt wave upon wave of fear pass through him. He thought he heard Yldich's voice.

'Let it go, Rom. Let it pass.'

He realized he held onto the fear as if it were the only thing that still defined him as a person, the last thing that kept him whole. He let it pass through him like a fast flowing river. He breathed out, and breathed in pure light. He was hovering in an undefined space of deep black, his body no longer a physical thing but a constellation of many little twinkling lights, like stars against the dark. They wheeled around his heart, invisible yet pulsating strongly, an inflowing and outpouring of a strong, unfocused, impersonal sense of love. He felt oddly unsurprised and very alive, though there was no body, no breath, no ebb and flow of blood. He was at peace in the great pulsating centre that was his heart. He heard Yldich's voice once more.

'Come back, Rom. Take a look around you.'

He drew his awareness back to the world of living things with reluctance; he felt he could have stayed there for ever. He became aware of the grass in the clearing, its myriad little roots, finer than human hair. There was no difference between him and the grass. They were part of the same living entity. He became the grass, feeling a peaceful sense of satisfaction at receiving the light of the sun. He turned, casting his awareness around him in one large wave, and was conscious of all life in a wide radius around him. It was all one. He was aware of the riders, of their unrest, their strife, and knew it as if it were his. He felt Feyir's presence, sickly brilliant and sharp, and recognized his hunger for power as if it were his own. They were part of the same, living whole. He felt Eald's presence, like a small sun, radiating joy and life. He held it for a moment, cherishing it, then was drawn back to the clearing.

He felt Yldich's presence near and melted into him, feeling a sense of shock at the depth and width of his being. A deep calm welled up from him, which, moving up into the air, changed into a strong brisk wind, clear and sharp, showering him with beautiful, tiny crystals of ice that were reflected in the grey twinkle of his eyes.

Rom pulled away in surprise, and fell back into his body with a jolt. The crystal rolled out of his hands.

It took a while before he could speak. Yldich handed him a mug of steaming herb tea. He started and nearly knocked it out of his hand when he couldn't tell which hand was Yldich's and which hand was his own. The invisible link that connected all life was still in his mind, confusing his orientation in space. He laughed at the absurdity of it. When he tried to take a sip of tea, he felt tears run into his mug and realized he was crying at the same time. He shook his head to try and clear it.

'Easy, now,' he heard Yldich's voice. 'Take your time.'

Night settled around them like a cloak of sable velvet, and stalked their fire like a soft-footed cat. They had a late makeshift meal. The forest was silent but for an occasional rustle of leaves and the cry of a prowling animal. The stars had come out one by one.

After he had eaten Rom sat back, and stared at them meditatively. He hadn't yet spoken a word. Where he had been, there had been no need for any. He felt strangely reluctant to break the silence. Yldich did so finally. He spoke softly, his voice just loud enough to be heard over the crackling of the fire and the rustling of the Forest.

'We call it *Eärwe*, the all-encompassing. It is knowing you are part of the Whole, of the living entity that is the world. It is the All.' He threw some pine cones on the fire and poked it up with a stick. 'It is a state of being all children of the *Einache* were made familiar with in the old days. It's how they knew who they were. It was the reason they were able to live without disturbing the Balance.' He paused, his eyes seeming to focus on something far away and long ago.

'It's also the reason why *Einache* fighters were not afraid to go into battle. They knew their true being. They knew death wouldn't change that.' Rom swallowed and tentatively cleared his throat. A thought occurred to him. He tried his voice.

'If all the *Einache* knew this,' he said huskily, 'how could the dark fear overpower them when the *Tzanatzi* came?' Yldich looked at him.

'If I knew that, we would probably not be sitting here trying to find a way to stop it from rising again.'

Rom started. 'Is that what this is all about?' Yldich nodded.

'Not all the people of my House agree with my conjectures,' he said, staring into the fire, 'but that is my belief.'

They slept for a few hours, keeping the fire burning low between them. They woke before dawn and had some leftover stew.

'Yldich,' Rom said, as he finished his stew, 'what are we going to do about Eald?' Yldich put away his bowl.

'It would have been no use to run over there straight away and attack the riders on their own turf. They would have overpowered us at once. I've been trying to figure out a way to get him back without us all getting killed.'

'How?'

'I have been surveying the area tonight by *ayúrdimae*. There are a few disused huts, a few miles away from their camp site, at the edge of the Forest. I got the impression he was there, with at least two riders keeping guard.'

Rom sprang up. 'We should go there as soon as possible—' Yldich checked him with a move of his hand.

'No, Rom. Feyir will have the area watched. If he finds out I don't plan to meet with his agreement, he will have him killed immediately.' Rom swallowed.

'So what do we do?'

'I will go to the Standing Stones and talk to Feyir. I'll keep him occupied. Meanwhile, you try and free Eald. After what happened yesterday,' he motioned at Rom's bound left hand, 'I don't think Feyir will be surprised my 'servant' doesn't accompany me to his meeting.'

'Won't he be suspicious?'

'It's a risk we'll have to take.'

'But what will you do once you're there? Feyir will have you right where he wants you, powerless....'

Yldich chuckled. 'I may have some tricks up my sleeve.'

'Like what?' Yldich looked at him inquisitively, then shook his head. 'You'll see.'

They rode back in a straight line towards the river. On horseback it only took a few hours to reach the Standing Stones. When it was past noon, they halted in the grassland between the river and the Forest. Yldich took out the slender sword in the indigo scabbard.

'You'd better take this, now. You might need it.' Rom stared at the sword. He hesitated. If he took the sword, something would be irrevocably changed. His old life would be lost. There would be no way back. He wavered. Yldich seemed to sense his uncertainty. He motioned for him to sit down. When they were seated in the grass opposite each other, Yldich drew the sword and placed it on the ground between them like a dividing line.

'To carry a sword is both a responsibility and a burden,' he said softly. 'In the old days, young *Einache* warriors did not earn the right to carry one until they had passed through several tests and rites of passage, a process that took years.' A distant look was in his grey eyes, as if he were remembering a faraway past. 'It was demanded they possess rigorous self-knowledge, integrity, and responsibility towards all life, before they were granted the right to carry one.' He looked at Rom, his gaze sharp and clear as ice. 'Before you pick up this sword, you might need to ask yourself what you're going to use it for.'

Rom took a deep breath. He looked at the sword that lay in the grass like a sharp threshold. He imagined what it would be like to use it in a fight. He pictured the kind of damage that could be done with it and shuddered.

'Although the Southern people consider the sword a weapon of attack and conquest,' he heard Yldich's voice from what seemed like a distance of years, of centuries, 'the *Einache* did not see it so. The *Einache* warrior knew that how he wielded it sealed his own fate. To wield a sword in anger, or lust, to gratify one's desire for power, would mean he was no longer a true warrior. It would mean his downfall and ultimately that of his people.' Yldich paused, and gazed at Rom as if he were measuring him.

'To ensure the aspiring *Einache* warrior used his sword wisely,' he said, 'it was asked of him that he consecrated it, dedicated it to a specific purpose.'

'How would he do that?' Rom whispered. He felt he knew the answer already.

'He would make sure the first blood drawn with the sword was his own,' Yldich said calmly. 'It was a token of sacrifice, of commitment. It would forge a link between fighter and sword that could only be broken in death. With his blood, he would dedicate it to a worthy purpose.'

Rom stared at the sword and held his breath. Images began to whirl through his head. He saw Lord Aldr coming at him, his face distorted with hatred and fear. It shifted into Feyir's, cold and aloof. He was surprised by a sudden image of his mother, her blue eyes dark with bitterness. He swallowed away a sudden wave of pain.

He blinked and saw Eald running through the Forest. The boy turned his head and smiled at him. The vision expanded until he could see a large area of grassland and trees. He saw small houses, irregularly shaped from reed and clay. Children of all ages were playing, running barefoot through the grass. A tall woman, her hair the colour of a sunset stood there and smiled, her hair whipped up by the wind, a baby on her arm and a toddler grasping at her leg, trying to balance itself on wobbly legs. He looked up and nodded as if he had reached a decision. Yldich took the sword and held it up.

'Give me your right arm.'

He held it out. He felt a strange feeling of inevitability pass through him. He kept his arm still with an effort. Yldich rolled up his sleeve and set the sharp point of the sword on the inside of his arm near the elbow. Rom took a deep breath.

'Tell me now,' Yldich said softly. 'To what purpose do you dedicate this sword?'

'Love,' he said, his voice like a breeze, barely audible in his own ears. He closed his eyes when he felt the cold point of the sword pierce his skin. He hissed out a slow breath as Yldich slid the sword all the way down his right arm. The cold steel burned, leaving a thin, fiery trail of pain. When he had reached his right wrist, Yldich quickly and deftly cut a small design in the palm of his hand near the wrist. Rom felt the sharp steel finally lifted from his hand and swallowed. He breathed heavily, as if he had been running up a steep hill. Yldich put the hilt of the sword into his bloodied hand and carefully closed his fingers on it. He went off and returned with a strip of cloth.

Rom was engrossed by a strange feeling in his arm. It felt as if something was flowing out of him with his blood, energy that purposefully seeking, connected itself to the sword in his hand, and trailed down the length of the blade, until it was infused with it. Something bright, like the spirit of silver glinting in the sun, sprang alive and pulsed back through the blade. It travelled upwards through the palm of his hand and his arm. It felt as if the sword came alive in his hand, as if it became part of him. The bright energy travelled upwards through his heart, and filled it with light.

'Rom. Let me bind your arm.' He felt strangely reluctant to let go of the sword. He slowly opened his fingers. Yldich laid the sword aside with care and bound his wrist and arm. Rom sighed.

'It spoke to me.'

Yldich stared at him, taken aback. 'What did it say?' Rom opened his eyes and stared at the sword.

'It said something about joy.'

They left Elda behind and walked the rest of the way, to a bend in the river where birch trees obscured the Standing Stones in the distance from view. The sun was already sinking in the west. The light turned the trees a soft golden yellow. Rom felt awkward walking around with the long sword that weighed down his belt.

'I will probably trip over it and fall flat on my face at the worst possible moment,' he muttered. Yldich chuckled.

They stopped when they had reached the shadow of the trees. Yldich pointed north, to a place where the trees at the fringe of the forest had thinned out a little.

'Now, enter the Forest that way,' he said. 'Go some miles to the north where you'll find a small clearing encircled by old oak trees. A few huts are still standing. I think that's where they keep Eald.' Rom felt an uneasy tension take root in his stomach. 'There will be at least two riders there, I think,' Yldich continued. He appeared not to notice his disquiet. 'You should be able to get past them and get Eald out. Meanwhile, I will go upstream to the Standing Stones and meet with Feyir.' Rom frowned at him.

'And then what?'

'We will meet here afterwards, after nightfall,' Yldich said, ignoring the worried look on his face. 'If all goes well, we should be able to continue our journey tonight.'

'But, Yldich,' Rom started, 'how will you—' The other man laid his hands on his shoulders and directly looked into his eyes, stopping him from speaking further.

'Make sure you get back in one piece,' he said. Rom blinked. '*Encalimae, fayïre éntme,*' Yldich said softly. He surprised Rom by embracing him briefly and tightly. He released him and turned away. He walked towards the birches without looking back. Rom stood and watched him go. He felt strangely moved. He blinked and took a deep breath. He turned and made for the Forest.

Rom entered the Forest moving gingerly. His heightened awareness of the world allowed him to move more quietly than he had been able to before. The light of the sun fell through the trees in long slanting beams, and threw patches of light before his feet, illuminating ferns and plants he had no names for.

He thought of the riders and touched the hilt of his sword with hesitant fingers. He wondered if he would be able to use it against another man if the need arose. He shuddered and let the thought go.

When Yldich reached the birch trees that sheltered him from view of the Standing Stones, he stopped and kneeled down in the tall grass. He opened a leather bundle. He took out a double-pointed crystal and a small packet of herbs, rolled up and held together by shiny threads as fine as human hair. He lighted it carefully. A thin trail of smoke, at once bitter and sweet, encircled him. He began to chant softly.

Rom reached the circle of oak trees as the sun was setting. The trees cast deep shadows into a small clearing that was overgrown with ferns and weeds. A few wooden huts were still standing. They looked as if they kept themselves upright with difficulty. Two huts looked sturdy enough to provide shelter to humans. Torches had been stuck into the ground before them.

Rom stood still at the edge of the clearing, taking care to keep out of the light of the torches. He listened intently. He saw a dim light appear at one of the windows. Someone had lit a lantern in the house nearest to the edge of the trees. Rom moved carefully in its direction. A branch snapped under his weight and he bit his lip, standing still immediately. He waited. Nothing happened. He walked on towards the house. He treaded even more lightly than before.

The sun was just about to sink below the edge of the trees when Yldich reached the Standing Stones. When he had reached the central Stone, he stood still and surveyed the area. There was no sign of a camp. He sat down and waited patiently.

Rom crept alongside the small house, going round the back. He heard a murmur of voices coming from within. It sounded like two men having a muffled discussion. One of the voices was suddenly raised.

'All right then, have it your way.' The sound of heavy boots on wood neared the front of the house. Rom crept to the side of the house and peered along the corner. The door creaked open and a tall blond man stepped out, muttering curses under his breath. He walked away to the other end of the clearing, and disappeared between the trees.

Rom held his breath and moved stealthily towards the door that hung crookedly in its hinges. He peered inside. A lantern hung from a wooden beam, and cast a dim yellow light into the single room. It had once been a kitchen and living quarters in one. Pots and pans still hung from the wall. An indistinct shape lay huddled in a corner.

A brown-haired rider in his early thirties sat on a bench at the other side of the room, turning a knife around in his hands. He looked like he'd recently been in a brawl. Blood had leaked from his nose and along the side of his mouth. A soft moan came from the huddled shape in the corner. The rider cursed. 'You try anything like that again, you little rat, and I'll slit your throat right now, orders or no orders.'

Rom swallowed. The shape moved and groaned, and turned his head towards the light. He recognized Eald's copper hair and pale face in the dim light of the lantern. His left eye was swollen shut and there was a cut in his lower lip. He tried to sit up, and peered defiantly at the rider with his one good eye.

Rom stepped into the room without thinking. The rider sprang up, quickly tossed the knife from his left hand to his right and lunged at him. Rom tried to move aside, out of the way of the knife. The rider grabbed him and they fell to the floor locked together, like dancers too drunk to stay on their feet. Rom twisted and fell on his side. The rider threw him on his back and went for his face with the knife. Rom gasped and grabbed his wrist in both hands, struggling to hold it off. He managed to free his right leg and jabbed his knee forcefully into the rider's ribs.

The rider doubled over and Rom managed to throw him off. He saw something gleam in the corner of his eye and grabbed it. It was heavy. As the rider came at him again, aiming a stab at his chest, he knocked him on the side of the head with it. The rider groaned, went limp, and fell over.

Rom's breath was heaving. He looked at the object in his hand. It was an old saucepan.

A row of lights advanced to the Stones. It formed a rough half-moon shape and gradually closed in from all sides. Yldich took a slow, deep breath and stood up. Six riders with burning torches stepped up to the central stone. Yldich held his hands a little away from his sides, the palms outward, to show them he was unarmed. The light of the torches gleamed on the blades of swords being drawn.

Rom dropped the saucepan and got up. He went over to Eald and helped him sit up.

'Are you all right? What did they do to you?'

'I tried to escape,' the boy said huskily. 'They dragged me back. I tried to fight them off. I gave one of them a bloody nose.' He grinned. The motion pulled awry his face that was already distorted with swelling. 'They weren't too happy about it.' Rom shook his head at him, appalled.

'They could have killed you.'

'Where's the other one gone?' Eald's face was suddenly anxious. Rom heard a sound near the door. He turned his head in alarm. The tall blond-haired rider stepped inside, and gazed at the scene with a look of surprise that turned into an angry scowl. He drew his sword.

'You half-breed bastard. I should have finished you off the first time.' Rom recognized his face. He was one of the riders who had nearly beaten him to death in Feyir's camp. He stared up at him as if frozen, his breath stuck in his throat. The rider lifted his sword and brought it down in a heavy two-handed stroke that would have split his skull. Eald screamed. The sound brought Rom out of his frozen trance.

He threw himself at the rider's legs, bringing him off-balance. The man fell down heavily, the sword clanging to the floor. Before he could get up, Rom cracked his fist across his face as hard as he could. The man groaned and got up again, furious with pain. Blood was trickling from his nose. Rom reached for his knife. Before he could get it out, the rider hit him on the side of his face. He fell back, dazed by the force of the blow. The rider threw him to the ground and hit his head on the floor. He grabbed Rom by his throat and started to choke him.

Rom felt his head start to throb. It was as if he was under water. Pressure was building in his ears. He desperately fought to get the rider off, but the man was too heavy. His hands closed ever tighter around Rom's neck. A sound like the roaring of the sea filled his ears. He clawed at the rider's fingers. Black specks filled his vision. A shudder went though him. His hands went limp. Bright stars exploded soundlessly in the blackness inside his head.

Suddenly the pressure was off his throat. The rider fell away from him with a dull thud. Rom turned over, frantically struggling for breath. He opened his eyes, wheezing and coughing. Eald dropped the saucepan and went over to him. He peered worriedly into his face. The rider lay face-down on the floor; a dark trail of blood trickling out of his hair and into his eyes.

'I'm glad you could make it.' Feyir's cool, cultivated voice reached him across the clearing. Yldich looked around sharply. The riders had escorted him to an area in the woods, not far from the Standing Stones. Tall trees surrounded a glade that was lined with burning torches. Lanterns were suspended from the lower branches of the trees. Feyir stood before the fire. One of the men who had brought him motioned Yldich to move towards him. He walked up to Feyir and stood still.

'So,' Feyir said. He inclined his head. His voice was calm. 'I see your *Tzanatzi* servant has declined.'

'He felt a little indisposed after your visit the other day,' Yldich said, matching Feyir's neutral, unconcerned tone of voice. 'I left him to take care of the horse.'

Feyir smiled slowly. 'Really. Well, it doesn't matter. I have something I would like to discuss with you. A proposition, if you like.'

'Let's hear it, then.'

Eald helped Rom sit up. Rom's breath was still ragged. He wiped his hair out of his face.

'We should get out of here,' he said finally, his voice hoarse.

'Where's Yldich?'

Rom hesitated. 'Feyir gave him an ultimatum,' he said slowly. 'He was to meet him at his camp. He wanted to discuss a proposition or something.'

Eald went pale. 'He went to Feyir's camp? He's there now?' Rom nodded. 'What's he going to do? How does he think he'll get out?'

'I don't know,' Rom said. He felt uneasy. 'He wouldn't tell me, exactly.'

'What did he say?'

'That he might have some tricks Feyir wouldn't expect.' Rom searched his memory. 'And he said something in *Einache* to me.'

'What was it?' Eald looked at him intently. Rom frowned as he tried to retrieve the words from memory.

'It was something like Encali—Encalimé....'

'*Encalimae*?'

'That's it. *Encalimae... fayïre éntme*.' Eald widened his eyes. 'What does it mean?'

'It's from the old tales... it's what the warriors used to say to their families when they went into battle. It's a farewell.' Rom stared at him. A sense of alarm, dull and heavy, was rising in his stomach. He swallowed a curse.

'He doesn't expect to get back.' He sprang up and nearly lost his balance when the blood drained from his head. He bowed his head and waited for his vision to clear. Eald fluttered anxiously around him like a moth around a candle. Rom straightened slowly and gripped the boy's arms.

'Eald. Go in the direction of the river and follow it downstream until you reach a bend in the river with tall birches. Wait for me there.'

'What are you going to do?'

Rom's face was pale and tense. 'I'm going to try and get him out.'

'You may have heard,' Feyir said softly, 'that the honour of my House has been severely compromised.' He turned a cup of red wine around in his hands. Yldich had declined the offer for a drink. 'About seven years ago, my father, Lord Aldr, was killed in a bizarre attempt on his life by one of his servants.' Yldich looked up with a sudden flare of interest. 'One of his own pages apparently slew him with *Tzanatzi* magic. My father died an unexplained and horrible death.'

Feyir took a sip of wine and stared into the cup. 'I was his only heir, and too young to accept the rule of the house. King Farhardt, who had already been questioning my father's loyalty to the Crown, decided to confiscate our lands and our House.' His cool, level voice was devoid of its usual amused disdain.

'Our lands were divided among the surrounding nobility. My mother had to leave the Keep with a few of her remaining possessions and servants. We were led away by an armed escort of Farhardt's soldiers. I was fifteen years old at the time.' He looked at Yldich, his handsome face hard.

'We were forced to live in a simple house in one of the neighbouring villages, like ordinary peasants. Our honour, the privileges that were ours by right of birth, were taken from us. My mother never recovered from the humiliation. She died a few years later, in bitter disappointment.' His eyes had turned to burnt umber.

'I intend to restore the dignity of our family and get back the rule of our lands. In order to do that, I will have to gather support from everyone Farhardt has ever wronged.' He studied Yldich's face, his eyes sharp with speculation. 'I have come to understand that you, as leader of the *Einache*, have considerable influence on the remaining clan leaders of the North.'

Rom ran through the Forest, back to the river. He muttered sharp curses under his breath and forced down the cold sense of dread that wanted to stop him in his tracks.

He saw lights in the distance, to the east of the Standing Stones. He stopped running and advanced more slowly, taking care not to step on dead branches that would snap under his feet to betray him. He stole along warily until he could see the lanterns hanging from the trees. He heard a voice above him and stopped dead.

'We weren't expecting *you* again... but you're welcome to join us.' He whirled around, feeling as if he'd stepped into a nightmare. Three riders dropped silently from the lower branches of the trees behind him. His hand moved for the hilt of his sword.

'I think you may have the wrong idea about the kind of influence I can exert,' Yldich said slowly.

'Aren't you the *Hárrad* of the *Einache*? The one they turn to for council? And do you not possess the kind of wizardry that gives you power over the elements?' Yldich smiled carefully and shook his head. A fleeting look of sadness passed over his face.

'I am, but it's not what you think. I don't exercise control over anyone or anything. I balance and I heal. That is all.'

Feyir frowned, his eyes narrowed with displeasure. 'Do you not want to restore your people to power? Do you not want to right the wrongs that were

done to them? If what I hear is true, Farhardt and his nobles are treating them
like serfs.' Yldich sighed. His grey eyes were stern.

'I do want justice for my people,' he said slowly, his voice low. 'I'm
sorry for what happened to your family. And I don't agree with the King's
reign in many ways. But I don't think overthrowing Farhardt's regime is the
way to restore the balance. It will destroy more than it will build up. It may
cause a civil war that will drench this whole country in blood.'

Feyir's eyes had turned hard, his mouth set. He was about to speak, when
a disturbance at the edge of camp captured their attention. There seemed to be
a small struggle going on. Feyir tossed his cup of wine in the grass with an
impatient movement of contempt. He strode towards the men that were
coming towards them.

'What is going on? Can't I have a conversation in peace?' One of the
men stepped forward. He was a rider in his forties, his hair shot through with
grey.

'I'm sorry for the disturbance, my lord,' he said. 'We found an
unexpected visitor lurking around camp. He's been a bit of a nuisance.' The
other two riders moved ahead, dragging another man in between them. He
seemed barely conscious. His head was hanging forward, dark hair obscuring
his face. Yldich clenched his hands at his sides.

'Well,' Feyir said, his voice smooth with contentment, 'good to see you
after all.' He went over to Rom and pulled his head up by his hair. Rom
started and opened his eyes. Blood ran over his face from a cut above his eye
where the blow of a rider's fist had torn the skin. He blinked at Feyir.
'Where's the boy?' Feyir said calmly, addressing the grey-haired rider. He
fidgeted.

'Gone, my lord. This here fellow helped him escape. The two guards
have been injured badly.' Rom stirred, and tried to stand back up on his feet.
The riders that held him increased the strength in their grip. He winced with
pain and groaned. A sword cut on his upper arm had stained the sleeve of his
tunic with blood. The grey-haired rider coughed. 'There's something else I
should tell you, my lord.'

'What is it?'

'When we apprehended this *Tzanatzi* intruder, I noticed something that
might interest you.' He went over to Rom and pulled at the blood-stained
tunic. 'Here,' he said, pointing at Rom's left shoulder. Yldich heard Feyir take
in a slow, hissing breath. He stared in Rom's face.

'Where did you get this mark?'

Rom coughed. 'What are you talking about?'

Feyir hit him sharply across the face with the back of his hand. 'Don't
play games. Tell me where you got the mark of the Boar.'

Rom reeled from the blow. 'The—the mark of the signet ring? Why do you want to know?'

'Because,' Feyir said slowly, 'that mark was used only by my father, Lord Aldr, before he was killed by a cursed *Tzanatzi* half-breed.'

'That was... he was your father?' Rom stared at him, his face pale, as recognition struck. The noble's son who only came home in winter, the one with the haughty smile a lowly page only saw from afar. Lord Aldr's son.

Feyir stared back. Cold realization stilled his features. He stood still a moment, as if deliberating. Finally he took a step back and drew a long, slender dagger. He grabbed Rom's hair and pulled his head backward with force, lifting up his face. He held up the dagger and moved it towards his eyes. Rom gasped and struggled frantically. The riders kept him still with an effort. The grey-haired rider looked uncomfortable and averted his eyes.

Yldich took a step forward in alarm. He was immediately seized by two riders who held him in a tight grip.

'Do you know,' Feyir said slowly, 'what the Southern nobles used to do with *Tzanatzi* sorcerers in the days of old?' Rom stared at him, his dark eyes wide with terror. 'They would blind them.' Rom felt the touch of the sharp, cold point of the dagger touch the skin under his left eye. His breath came in shallow gasps.

'Please,' he whispered. He closed his eyes.

'Lord Feyir.' Yldich's voice rang across the glade. 'Tell me what it is you want. I will do what I can. Just stop damaging my servant.' Feyir turned to him, his brows raised.

'You seem improperly attached to your servants.' He smiled coldly. 'What do I want, besides giving this *Tzanatzi* filth the treatment he deserves? I'll tell you.' He let go of Rom's hair and took a step towards Yldich. Rom shuddered and sagged in the rider's grip.

'I want you to go and convince your rebels to work with us. I want you to use your power over the minds of men and the elements to help me and overthrow Farhardt's reign.' To his surprise, Yldich began to laugh softly. Rom lifted his head a little and looked at the two men. Feyir stood facing Yldich, dangling the dagger idly by its point. Yldich shook his head. He laughed soundlessly.

'How do you think,' he said softly, 'understanding the nature of the earth and the minds of men could possibly aid you in a conquest of violence?'

'I understand you can do a lot more than that, *wizard*.'

Yldich smiled faintly and shook his head. 'All that a *Yaever* does is dependant on his understanding of the Whole. The Balance. I could not help you hurt a fly if it went against the way the World wants to unfold.'

'I see,' Feyir said. His voice was cold. 'You have no intention of working with me. Maybe,' he added, you will only work against me...' He turned the dagger around between his fingers. Rom stared at Feyir's hands. He took a deep breath. '...which makes you a liability.' Feyir moved back his arm, preparing to thrust the dagger at Yldich.

Rom threw himself forward with all his weight and tore himself free of the rider's hands. He stumbled into Feyir and threw him off balance. The dagger fell out of his hand. Rom drew the sword that was still at his side. The riders had not bothered to take it from him. He had been struck down before he had been able to draw it. Feyir turned calmly and looked at him with amused contempt. He held back the riders with a gesture of his hand.

'Do you *really*,' he said slowly, 'want to challenge me?'

Rom clenched his hands around the hilt of the sword, labouring to keep it steady. 'Let him go.'

Feyir narrowed his eyes. 'I've no intention to let either one of you go. Especially you. However, I might let you earn your death in a fight. I would recommend it to the other treatment I had in mind for you.' Rom swallowed. Feyir had a rider bring him his sword. He looked at Rom speculatively. 'Let's have some fun before you go.' He drew his sword and advanced.

Feyir moved confidently, as if he were in a practice court. He handled his sword with contemptuous ease. He struck suddenly, like a snake, aiming short, smooth stabs at Rom. Rom parried desperately. It took all his strength to keep up with the silver flashing of Feyir's sword. It swished dangerously close to his face. The cut on his arm throbbed dully. He breathed hard and swallowed down his fear. Feyir stalked him like a predator, moving in circles, forcing him to move with him.

'You fight like a girl.' Feyir smiled disdainfully. 'How disappointing. But then, what can one expect from a *Tzanatzi* bastard.'

Rom flinched at the words. Feyir aimed a sudden deadly stab at his chest. Rom fell back and lost his balance. He desperately warded off a second blow coming down at him. The swords screeched at the impact. Blue sparks flew through the darkened sky. He clambered up and stood back, panting.

'Be careful, Rom,' Yldich said in a calm voice. 'He doesn't fight fair. Expect some vile tricks.' Feyir laughed.

'Come on now,' he said. 'I'm getting bored. You should really make this more interesting. Or I'll finish what I started right now.' He moved to strike at Yldich. Rom sprang at him and warded off the thrust. The swords clashed with a clang, slid down and caught at the hilt. They were momentarily locked together. Rom moved as if to dislodge the sword. Instead, he thrust his knee up as far as he could. It slammed into Feyir's stomach. The air was knocked out of him and Feyir pulled back hastily, couching with pain.

'You low-life bastard,' he spat, his amusement gone.

'You were lucky. I was aiming for your groin,' Rom muttered. He heard Yldich's voice in his head and nearly dropped his sword in surprise.

Rom. Keep him busy. When I tell you to, close your eyes.

A low humming sound began to fill the empty corners of his awareness. It seeped into his head and began to surround the clearing. The humming was getting louder. It throbbed and vibrated. A strange tension was in the air. Feyir didn't seem to notice. His handsome face was a mask of controlled viciousness.

'I'm tired of this exercise now,' he said. 'Let's finish it off.' He launched a series of powerful sweeps that drove Rom back all the way across the clearing. A strong wind was rising. It whipped their hair into their faces. The leaves of the trees rustled as if in the throes of an autumn storm. The branches started to sway. Rom stumbled backwards, away from Feyir, and stumbled over a bump in the grass. He gasped. Feyir hit the sword out of his hand with ease. He stood over Rom and leaned the tip of his sword in the hollow of his throat.

'Any gods you'd like to pray to?'

Now. Close your eyes.

Rom turned his face away from Feyir and closed his eyes. A brilliant flash illuminated the clearing, followed by a powerful crackling sound that ripped through the air and ended in a thundering boom that shook the earth. Rom could see the blood vessels in his closed eyelids. His ears popped. He put his hands over his ears, crying out in pain. A strong burst of air made the trees sway.

Feyir stepped back with a shout of surprise or pain. He dropped his sword and held his hands over his ears. The air smelled of ozone and singed hair. Several riders lay dead.

Go. Now.

Rom sprang up and collided with Feyir. The impact had Feyir stumble backwards. Rom saw a glint of silver in the grass and grabbed it. It was his sword. He scrambled towards Yldich. One of the riders still held him, the other had gone.

Before Rom had reached him, a dagger ripped through the air and buried itself in Yldich's chest. He still stood for a moment, his grey eyes locked into Rom's dark ones. Rom stood as if frozen and stared at him in sheer unbelief. A dark stain spread around the dagger that, by coincidence or perfect aim, had buried itself in Yldich's heart. As he fell, a wordless cry wrenched through Rom's body. Darkness rose from the earth and enveloped him.

Eald had reached the half-circle of birches. He bit his lip with impatience. Suddenly a flash of light illuminated the sky. A loud crackling noise had him cover his ears. A low boom shook the earth under his feet. Stunned, he looked in the direction of the Forest beyond the Stones. The trees were burning.

Darkness pushed away the grief that threatened to overwhelm him. It filled him with a deep, dark, impersonal sense of power. All feeling was swept away by a black wave, which left only a dark sense of purpose. The wish to destroy. The world around him was completely silent. A word rose to his mouth and chilled the air.

'*Calamêntiré.*'

The voice rang in his ears as if it was someone else's. He didn't even recognize the language. Darkness swirled around him like a living entity. Rom turned around slowly and focused his gaze on Feyir. Feyir looked into his eyes. The satisfaction in his face wavered.

Rom took a deliberate stride in Feyir's direction. He raised his sword. It gleamed a fiery red in the light of the burning trees. The dark rage that had risen from the earth and surged through his veins was growing. It reached his eyes. They went completely black. Feyir went pale. His eyes searched the ground in haste. He grabbed the sword that lay next to a dead rider and raised it.

Rom swept his sword down in a gleaming arc of red. The two weapons clashed with a scream of metal. Rom aimed another heavy thrust at Feyir that he could only escape by stumbling backwards. Rom fought like a cat. He struck quick, merciless blows that drove Feyir back until he stood before a large tree. The last thrust was too quick. The sharp steel of the sword almost pinned him to the tree. He cried out. The sword fell from his hand as he sank back against it. Instinct made him clutch at his side. Blood welled up through his fingers. Rom stood over him, his sword stained red.

Feyir looked up at him, his face tense with pain. Cold hatred filled his eyes. 'Finish it, you bastard.' Rom raised the sword. Feyir closed his eyes.

The blood that stained Rom's sword filled in the strange *Einache* designs that curled along the blade. An eerie high note resounded through the steel and made it sing. The sound travelled up along the edge of the blade and ran into Rom's hands. It flowed into his arms. He wavered. Threads of light ran through his body. The cold that had driven him on dropped away and a sweet pain pierced his heart. He lowered the sword, trembling, breathing as if he had been under water too long. Feeling returned to him. The darkness left his eyes. He looked at Feyir, who gazed up at him through his pain with icy spite.

'I knew you couldn't do it. You low-life coward.'

Rom breathed out a last remnant of cold. He sheathed the sword and went over to Feyir. He hit him across the face with his fist and knocked him out.

Eald gazed at the burning trees in the distance. He stirred, and made as if to move towards the Forest. He heard a rustling noise behind him and froze.

Rom left Feyir lying unconscious by the tree. He went over to Yldich's body that lay on his back in the grass. He sank down onto the ground beside him and took his hand. It was already growing cold. He let grief wash over him like the sea, like rain.

Rom heard a sound behind him. He slowly turned his head. A rider had come up behind him and watched him sit beside the body. Rom stared at him through his tears. He didn't move.

'You'd better get out of here.' It was the grey-haired rider. On the other side of the clearing, survivors of the blast were busy putting out the fires that raged among the trees and threatened the tents. Rom blinked at the man in confusion. The rider shook his head. 'I've a son at home about your age.' He motioned towards Feyir, lying limp at the tree. 'The way his lordship's going about his business doesn't entirely agree with me.' His mouth pulled in a wry expression of distaste. 'Now, get away,' he said in a gruff voice. 'Before either he wakes up or I change my mind.'

Rom got up slowly. He looked down at Yldich's form lying on the forest floor. It seemed indistinct, hazy, as if it were changing into grey smoke before his eyes. He tore away his gaze with difficulty. He turned and started to run in the direction of the river. Behind him, smouldering branches fell down into the grass.

Four
Loss

The world around him seemed unreal, insubstantial, as he crossed the distance between the Forest and the Stones. The birches at the river loomed up before him.

He tried to think of a way in which to tell Eald of Yldich's death. He quickly shut down his mind against the feelings and images that arose and focused his attention on running, the sensation of earth beneath his feet. He had almost reached the river and stopped for breath. He felt reluctant to move on, to do anything. If it had been possible to put down roots and stay there forever, he would have done so.

Eald came towards him at a run. 'Rom. Are you all right?' A large, dark form stirred behind the boy and advanced towards them. Rom felt a surge of panic. He unsheathed his sword and drew Eald to him with a forceful pull at his clothes. He threw the boy aside quickly, out of the way of the dark shape.

'Rom. It's all right.' He blinked. The voice was Yldich's. The sword fell from his hand. His legs gave way as if they had turned into water. Yldich caught him before he could fall to the ground. He held him upright by his arms.

'I saw you die,' Rom whispered. 'I held your hand. It was cold. You were cold.' He stared at Yldich as if he were a ghost. Something stirred and swam into focus beside him. It was Eald. He, at least, looked remarkably lifelike and normal. Not ghost-like at all. His face was smeared with dirt. He threw Rom an indignant look out of the eye that wasn't swollen shut.

'What did you do that for? It's only Yldich.'

Yldich carefully lowered Rom to the ground. Eald frowned at the men in confusion. Rom stared at Yldich. His face was ashen. He touched Yldich's arm to make sure he was real.

'How—how is this possible?'

'I'll explain it to you. But we mustn't stay here. Feyir may think I'm dead, but he could send his riders after you.'

Rom laughed. He sounded more than a bit hysterical. 'I don't think he'll do anything anytime soon. I just about killed him.' Yldich widened his eyes in bafflement. Rom felt a coldness rise in his bones. He couldn't stop shaking. His teeth were chattering. The world became a blur. He closed his eyes and heard Yldich's voice as if it were coming from far away.

'Rom, stay with me now. Eald, please, help me support him. We need to get away from here.'

Somehow they managed to get back to the copse where Yldich had left the horse. They half dragged, half carried Rom between them. Safely out of sight of the Stones and the Forest, Yldich made a small campfire in a hollow in the ground. Rom sat hunched beside it, shaking with cold and shock. Yldich heated some water and put in some dried herbs. He sat down beside Rom, put the cup in his hands, and helped him lift it to his mouth. Rom wrinkled his nose at the pungent taste of the herbs. Some colour came back to his face. The warmth flowed out from his stomach and into his arms and legs. The trembling subsided. It left a heavy and dull feeling behind. Yldich fetched a blanket and drew it around him as he sank down in the grass.

'Sleep now, Rom. We'll talk in the morning.'

Shortly after sunrise, Yldich went to fetch some dead wood for the morning fire. He stooped to fetch some twigs off the ground and winced. He stood upright and breathed carefully for a moment, releasing the pain in his chest. He went back to the others. Eald and Rom were still sleeping next to the fire pit. He sat down and started to build a new pile of twigs and small branches. He moved with care. Every slight movement of his arms pulled at the bruised muscles of his chest, and roused a dull pain that made it harder to breathe.

He got a fire going and prepared breakfast. He looked at the others while he worked. Rom was murmuring softly, moving in his sleep. Dark bruises on the side of his face contrasted sharply with his pale skin. Eald's face looked little better, though the swelling of his left eye seemed less pronounced than the day before. A pitiable lot, the three of them, Yldich thought with a wry smile, as he looked at the blood that stained his own tunic.

He was struck by a thought. Things could have been very different, had they been less fortunate. He breathed in deeply with a sense of gratitude, and took in the light of the sun, the crispiness of the morning air. He breathed out slowly, and felt a deep inner calm return. Once more he was aware of the subtle emanations of life around him. He strengthened his connection with it. The pain slowly subsided.

Rom was dreaming of the black *Tzanatzi* cat. They circled each other, walking soft-footed through the grass. The shiny black coat of the creature rippled with the movements of powerful muscles underneath. It panted slowly. Their tread was like a dance, a game.

Rom was on his guard, though the fear that had filled him when he had first met the creature had left him. A great wariness had taken its place. He carefully approached the cat. He looked into the dark feline face. The green eyes stared into his with a knowing, dispassionate look, a hidden power in their depths. Words rose into his awareness. He let them flow out.

'Taôre, eccêloz, Taôre....' He reached out his hand.

'Careful, Rom!' Yldich's voice rang in his ears.

Rom started awake. He was almost reaching into the fire with his fingers. He jerked back his hand. He rolled away from the fire, sat up carefully and glanced at Yldich. He brushed the hair out of his face and blinked away sleep.

'Well now, good morning to you.' Yldich handed him a bowl. Rom accepted it without comment. He looked at Yldich. The morning sun was low, the bright light making him squint. His face was still crumpled with sleep, his dark hair in wild disarray. He looked very young.

'You must be real,' he said, with the unabashed directness of one just awake. 'I can see you by daylight.'

Yldich's mouth pulled into a half-smile. 'I owe you an explanation, I think.' Rom nodded silently. He took a sip while he looked at Yldich over the rim of the bowl. 'Well,' Yldich said. He felt strangely scrutinized by Rom's unwavering gaze. 'I had been deliberating, whether or not to tell you what I was going to do. The only way to get into Feyir's camp and get out of it alive, I thought, was by *ayúrdimae*, that is, a heightened level of *ayúrdimae*.' He reached for his own bowl.

'Before I left for the Standing Stones, I used an *Einache* song that is rarely used, and for good reason. It is extremely dangerous. Even the eldest *Yaever* would hesitate to use it.' He took a sip. 'The chant, along with certain herbs, makes you leave your physical body so completely, and transfers such a substantial part of your essence into the dream body that it seems real in the waking world. It's harder to pull off in broad daylight,' he said with a smile, 'but at night, no-one would notice that you're not really there.' He paused, taking another sip.

'What makes it so dangerous is that concentrating so much of your being into the dream body makes it more physically dense, hence making it more vulnerable to physical hurts. If you are wounded, or killed, in such a heightened state of *ayúrdimae*, your physical body might actually *believe* it is hurt or killed, thereby making it true.' He stared thoughtfully into the fire. 'It is a precarious balance to hold,' he said, 'believing you're somewhere else, and yet not believing it too strongly.'

Rom sat up. 'Like when the daemo cat scratched me.'

'Yes,' Yldich said. 'That's how I knew you must have a great talent for dreamwalking.'

'Go on.'

'There's not much left to tell. When Feyir threw the knife at me, I drew back from the dream body as quickly as I could. He took me by surprise, so I had some trouble getting away.' He grimaced. He pulled aside his tunic and revealed dark bruises on his chest. 'A substantial part of me was left behind. When I came to at the place near the river, I had to recover it, slowly and deliberately. It took some time. It wasn't... easy.' He stared in the flames, his eyes momentarily darkened by pain.

Rom stared at him. 'It hurt.'

'Yes.'

Rom hissed out a slow breath. 'You took a great risk.'

Yldich was silent for a moment. 'Yes.'

Rom shook his head slowly, his face tense. 'Why,' he said in a low voice, 'didn't you tell me what you were going to do?' Yldich frowned.

'I was afraid you might not... understand, and besides, I didn't think it was necessary. By the time you and Eald had returned, I would be back at the river, I thought.' His mouth pulled in a wry smile. 'I didn't count on you running back, straight into the fire.' Rom stared at him. He spoke carefully, as if he were holding onto something dangerous that could be unleashed at any moment.

'*Encalimae fayïre éntme.*' Yldich raised his brows in surprise. Rom's *Einache* accent was flawless. 'I asked Eald what it meant. I thought you were going to have to fight your way out of there alone. I didn't know you were pulling off an even more dangerous *Yaever* spell. You didn't tell me.' Yldich stared at him. 'You knew, didn't you,' Rom said slowly. 'You knew Feyir would never let you go.' Yldich was silent for a while. He contemplated his bowl. He looked up.

'It seemed unlikely he would.'

'You should have told me what you were going to do.' Rom's voice was thick with suppressed anger. A glimpse of uncertainty crossed Yldich's face. 'I was mourning you,' Rom said heavily. 'I thought you were dead. You should have told me. You should have trusted me.' Yldich moved his gaze to the fire, taken aback. His grey eyes were shadowed with thought, his attention turned inward for a while. Then he looked up at Rom.

'You're right. I've done nothing but ask for your complete trust. You have the right to demand the same from me.' Rom blinked. The anger that had been fuelled by pain flowed away. The shaking subsided. Yldich stared at the fire, deep in thought. 'It's been a while since I taught young *Einache*,' he said. 'You're the first to remind me trust goes both ways.' He fixed his clear grey eyes on Rom. 'It was a courageous thing to do, going back to Feyir's camp, and fighting him like you did.' Rom lowered his eyes and stared in his bowl. He suddenly felt shy.

Eald stirred and sat up, still half asleep. 'What's the matter?' He blinked against the bright morning sun. 'What's going on?' Rom turned his head to look at him, thankful for the distraction. Eald's hair, stiffened by days of dirt and dust, was all sticking out to one side. His face was smeared with dirt.

'Breakfast,' Yldich said lightly. He lifted an eyebrow at his appearance and handed him a bowl. 'And then, I think, a bath.'

Rom got up and felt his muscles protest. He groaned and moved gingerly. Yldich shook his head at him.

'That's what you get for not practicing.'

While Eald and Rom scampered off to the river, Yldich washed the bowls and prepared some more green paste to treat their wounds with.

'You first,' Eald said. They were standing on a large, flat stone that lay halfway in the river. They were putting off the plunge. The water was icy.

'No, you first,' Rom said, shivering.

'What happened, anyway?' Eald asked Rom, to put off the inevitable. His eyes grew wide when Rom explained. 'He was in two places at once?' he said in awe. An idea seemed to strike him. His eyes glittered. Rom was alarmed.

'Now don't you get any ideas, Eald. It's much too dangerous to try for yourself.'

'Why?' Eald said, unperturbed.

'Because,' Rom said slowly, 'you're much too young. And you wouldn't know what you'd be doing.'

'Like when you went after Yldich when he was trapped by the black thing?'

Rom looked flustered. 'That was different.'

'Why?'

'Because I'm old enough to do *this*.' Rom scooped him up and unceremoniously dropped him in the water. Eald surfaced splattering and coughing. He glowered at Rom.

'I'll get you for this....' Rom grinned at him. Then he gritted his teeth and slowly lowered himself into the water.

They returned to the fire shivering with cold, stamping their feet to keep warm. When they were warm enough to sit still, Yldich treated their wounds.

'Now,' he said when he was finished, 'tell me how you managed to free Eald.' Yldich listened attentively while Rom told him the story. Eald interrupted him at intervals. Finally, Yldich shook his head in disbelief.

'Let's see if I understand this right,' he said. 'I give you a perfect *Einache* sword, and you start attacking riders with kitchen utensils?' Rom looked down at his hands and bit his lip. Eald smirked. Yldich started to chuckle. His face pulled into a wide grin. Rom looked up. A tentative smile pulled at the corners of his mouth. 'Wait 'till I tell this tale at home,' Yldich said. 'They won't let you forget it, ever.' Lights of amusement danced in his eyes. Rom's smile wavered. He looked at him uncertainly. Yldich noticed. 'You'll come with me, of course.'

'But, Yldich,' Rom said. 'I can't... won't they mind you bringing along a stray *Tzanatzi*?' Yldich snorted.

'They should be used to me taking home eccentric visitors by now. It's become a family tradition. My daughter Maetis takes after me that way.' He smiled. 'She's taken home frogs and squirrels from the age of five. She even lured in a wild fox once. You can imagine the look on her mother's face when she saw it under the dinner table that night.' He chuckled.

'Oh, and another thing.' He focused his sharp grey eyes on Rom. 'I don't think they will let five hundred-year-old history get in the way of entertaining guests.' A tension seemed to leave Rom's face. He released a sigh and nodded. 'Good,' Yldich said. He nodded contentedly. 'That's settled, then.'

They decided to stay that day in the shelter of the willow trees. Eald went into the woods to catch some dinner. When Rom turned to go and gather firewood, Yldich stopped him.

'Rom.' He froze, and felt strangely reluctant to turn back. 'I still need to hear what happened to Lord Feyir. Is there any chance he might seek us out?' Rom turned around.

'I don't think so... I wounded him rather badly.' His voice was strained.

'Tell me what happened.'

'Well, after you—after I saw him kill you, I was filled with a—a dark rage. I went cold. Everything dropped away but the wish to destroy him. I... I didn't know myself.' He stared in the distance. 'I felt no fear, only a dark anger.' He couldn't bring himself to mention the strange word he had heard himself utter.

'What happened?'

'I attacked him. I wounded him in the side. He lay helpless against a tree. I was about to slay him right then and there.'

'What stopped you?'

'It was the sword.' Rom looked down at his hands in wonder. 'It sang to me.'

Yldich's eyes widened. 'The sword sang to you?'

Rom nodded. 'The song went right through me. I couldn't hear any words, but I felt it somehow. I felt what it was saying to me.'

'What was it?'

Rom hesitated, clenching his hands. 'It was as if it said that if I killed out of rage, for revenge, I would never know true happiness...it said that love and pain and happiness were one.' He grimaced. 'I guess I was trying to erase the pain I felt by killing him.' Yldich nodded slowly. 'So I left him there. I started to grieve. Not knowing you weren't actually completely dead.'

Yldich laid his hands on his shoulders. 'I'm sorry.' Rom swallowed. Yldich drew back his hands. 'I'm glad you didn't kill him. It would have changed you. You would have lost something, and it would have been irrevocable.'

Rom blinked at him. 'What would I have lost?'

Yldich smiled faintly. 'Your innocence.' Rom gave him a quizzical look. Yldich smiled. 'What I mean is, the innocence that comes from not having spilled another's blood unnecessarily. Listen, Rom. The memory of every man you slay stays with you for the rest of your life. So you'd better have a good reason to kill them.' Yldich turned and put away the cooking gear.

'Now,' Yldich said, 'there's something you're not telling me.' He straightened and fixed Rom with his piercing gaze. Rom lowered his eyes. 'I don't know if it's important,' Yldich continued in a light tone, 'you must judge for yourself.'

'I don't know what it was... it scared me.' Yldich waited patiently. Rom sighed. 'A word... a word I heard myself say, when the black rage took over.'

'What was it?'

'I'm afraid to say it again. I don't know what might happen.' Yldich frowned.

'Words of power only work when there is sufficient energy and purpose behind them, Rom.' Rom took a deep breath to steady himself. He looked up.

'*Calamêntiré.*'

His voice was unusually dispassionate. The air parted before it. The sun wavered. It was as if a sudden cloud cut off the light. A chill shivered through the two men. They stood as if frozen. The birds stopped singing. The world seemed to hold its breath. Rom's eyes grew wide.

'What—what is it?' Yldich had turned slightly pale. 'Do you know what it means?' Yldich shook his head. He resisted the urge to start whispering as well.

'No.' His face was grim. 'I don't. But I remember where I've heard it before.'

Yldich paced up and down in the grass, raking his hair absently with his fingers until it resembled an abandoned bird's nest. Rom had never seen him act like it before. It unnerved him. He walked up to him, and brought him to an abrupt halt.

'Yldich. Please. Tell me what you know.' Yldich stopped fidgeting. 'You just said you've heard that word before. Tell me. Where was it?'

'I need to think about this. I need to be sure about this before I can tell you anything.' Rom shook his head.

'You can't leave me in the dark. I need to know.'

Yldich stared into the clear blue sky as if it could clear his thoughts. Finally, he nodded. 'I'll tell you what I know. But I'm going to wait until Eald is back. This concerns him, too.'

Eald returned with a load of berries, roots and even some apples. He tossed the fruit on a small heap and they sat down to eat.

'Listen closely now, Eald,' Yldich said. 'I'm going to finish the story of the *Einache* and the *Tzanatzi* mage.' Eald beamed him. His face and shirt were stained with berry juice. Rom looked up sharply and stared at Yldich with his dark eyes.

'So it was,' Yldich said in his story-telling tone, 'that the last *Yaever* had gathered five hundred years ago to rouse their people to action and fight the *Tzanatzi* army on the Field of Gardeth. They devised a plan to lure the mighty *Tzanatzi* sorcerer so they might defeat him.'

'What were they going to do?' Eald said.

'Listen, and I will tell you.' There was an amused glint in Yldich's eyes. He was enjoying himself despite an underlying seriousness that put an edge to the story like a sharp knife.

'They had decided to send one of their warriors out alone to challenge him. He was to distract the mage with a fight. Meanwhile, the *Yaever* would use an incantation, a powerful *Yaever* song that would separate the mage from his body forever. It would condemn him to walk the earth unseen and unheard, to inhabit the dark places, to dwindle and finally, to die.'

Eald listened with his mouth open. Rom looked uncomfortable.

'One of the young men who were training to be a *Yaever* came forward. He had lost almost everyone he loved when the *Tzanatzi* had advanced to the

North. He was filled with a righteous anger. He felt he had nothing to lose.' Something changed in Yldich's eyes. Only Rom noticed.

'At first, the *Yaever* wouldn't let him go. They thought he was too young. But as the novice insisted, they relented.'

'He must have been very brave,' Eald said.

'He was very stubborn,' Yldich said. Rom was silent.

'In those days, novice *Yaever* were not only taught the magic of dreams, herbs, and song. They were fully trained as warriors as well. This novice *Yaever*, carrying no other weapon but his sword, went to the edge of the plain. He stood at dusk on top of the cliff as the *Tzanatzi* army advanced on his people, and waited.' Eald held his breath.

'Meanwhile the *Yaever* had sent a messenger to lure the mage to the cliff. He brought a challenge to a fight to the death. The mage, sure of himself and his power, accepted. As the two armies advanced, he came to the cliff at the south edge of the plain, alone.' He stared into the distance.

'He was dark-haired with dark eyes, fair as all his people, and almost as tall as the young *Yaever*. He looked him straight in the eyes and smiled silently as he drew his sword. The fight was terrible.' His eyes unfocused.

'It lasted for hours. The mage and the novice *Yaever* nearly matched each other in their skill with the sword. The mage surpassed the *Yaever* in experience and agility. He moved like a hunting cat, graceful and deadly. The novice surpassed the mage in strength. His anger fuelled him as he fought. Over and over they charged at one another. Their swords flashed red in the light of the torches. Meanwhile, the group of *Yaever* came together and began to sing.' His eyes darkened.

'The song was called the *Eyurimae*. It had already begun. There was a tentative thrill of sound at the edge of the warriors' awareness. The young *Yaever* was at the end of his strength. He wavered. The loss of blood had weakened him. He could hardly keep to his feet. He desperately drew together his last strength, to fight back the mage one last time....' Eald had trouble sitting still.

'What happened? What happened?'

'As the *Eyurimae* became stronger and stronger, the thickening of sound around him finally alarmed the mage. He looked into the novice's eyes and saw that he had been deceived. They became black as night. He uttered a string of words to break the circle of sound. It did not relent. He knew his power was equalled. He knew he would not get out. Hatred filled his eyes. He looked at the novice who desperately held on to his sword as he waited for the final confrontation.' Eald bit his lip, his eyes wide.

'The mage said a word,' Yldich said. 'It was as if time stood still. Everything was frozen. The *Einache* novice gasped for breath. The mage walked up to him and drowned him in darkness and cold. The novice's sword fell out of his powerless hands. He started to choke, clawing at the air in desperation.' He closed his eyes. 'The mage spoke again.' Rom had one hand at his throat, his face pale.

'*Calamêntiré.*' Yldich's voice was low and cold. Eald froze. A sudden chill made him shudder.

Rom stared at Yldich in horror. A surge of panic ran through his body and made him jump to his feet. He stumbled back, away from the others. Yldich opened his eyes and looked at him, surprised. Rom stared at them wildly, as if they had suddenly changed into the inhabitants of his nightmares before his eyes. Yldich went over to him and grabbed him by his arms.

'Easy, now. Take a deep breath.' Rom's breathing was quick and shallow; he was shaking with some undefined emotion. Eald stared at him in puzzlement.

'What's the matter, Rom? It's just a story.'

Yldich had Eald go fetch some water. When he got back, Rom sat in the grass with his eyes closed, his face hidden in his hands. Eald sat down before him.

'Rom? Here's some water.' Rom opened his eyes. He looked at the boy's narrow face, the red hair tossed to all sides by the wind, the bruises that made him look very human. He held on to the normalcy, the familiarity of it, while he accepted the bowl and drank some water.

'How,' he said hoarsely, 'how can it be I knew this—this spell?'

Eald looked up at Yldich in confusion. Yldich reverted to his own language. Rom listened to their rapid *Einache* while Yldich filled in the gaps in the story for the boy. Strangely, it appeared as if the words flowing to and fro were at the edge of his understanding. It was as if he could almost feel the words, see them as they pulsed through the air. If he listened only a little while longer, he would understand what they were saying. Still, every new sentence was as foreign to him as the last. He shook his head, feeling as if the world as he knew it rapidly slipped away from him, taking his identity with it. He looked up at Yldich.

'What does it all mean?'

Yldich shook his head. 'The only thing I can tell you,' he said carefully, 'is that you're somehow connected to this ancient history.' He paused, musing. 'It does make a strange kind of sense. Seven years ago, the darkness that was called forth by the *Tzanatzi* mage and nearly vanquished my people started to manifest itself again. About the same time, I dreamed you and started to search for you.' He carefully neglected to mention the darkness that had risen in Lord Aldr's hall and driven him mad. 'I knew in my heart I had to find you, because we need you to stop it from rising again somehow.' Rom was silent.

But what if I am the focal point of this power? He shuddered.

'How does the story end?' Eald said. Yldich sat back.

'As the circle of sound tightened about him,' he said, 'the mage looked the young *Yaever* straight in the eyes and used his last strength to curse him. The novice was smothered in darkness.' Eald shivered. 'As the novice lost consciousness, the *Yaever* song was completed. The mage cried out as he was torn out of himself. His body was left for dead, his spirit lost for ever, doomed to wander the dark places under the earth.

The *Einache* novice was caught in darkness, bereft of his courage, his connection to all life. He was nearly lost. But just as the novice was about to cross the threshold between life and death, the head of the *Yaever* sent out a song for him. It reached him just in time. The song reminded him of all that was familiar, of all that he loved. It returned him to his life and his body.' Eald sighed.

'The loss of the mage and the darkness that had empowered them discouraged the *Tzanatzi* army. They called for a truce. It was agreed that they would cease their advance. They had already conquered over two-thirds of the country. They agreed to leave the north of Gardeth Forest and treat it as an *Einache* enclave, never to set foot in that area again. And so it was that the *Tzanatzi* never conquered Gardeth Forest, and the *Einache* heritage and way of life was preserved.'

They used the rest of the day to rest and gather supplies. Eald washed out his shirt and went off to catch some game. He wore Yldich's spare shirt. It reached to his knees.

'Now don't you tear my last shirt, Eald,' Yldich called as he was about to disappear into the bushes. 'Or I'll have your hide.' Eald grinned.

That night, when Eald was already sleeping, Rom and Yldich sat around the fire and waiting for sleep to find its way to them. Rom stared silently into the fire as he fed it twigs and acorns. His expression was grave. Yldich looked at him. He stretched out his awareness to get an impression of the young man's energy. It felt as if he carried a great weight, frowning as he contemplated it. Finally, Yldich spoke.

'What's the matter, lad?' His voice woke Rom from his reverie. He had almost forgotten the other man was there. He looked up.

'Yldich, do you believe in evil?' Yldich looked at him, taken aback. He thought for a moment, weighing his words.

'No,' he said finally, 'I don't. I don't believe there is such a thing as pure evil.' He released a sigh. 'I've been taught that darkness is only the absence of light. And without the grace of darkness, we wouldn't know light.'

'But what about people like the *Tzanatzi* mage? Like Feyir?' Rom's eyes were dark with thought. 'Aren't they evil?' Yldich slowly shook his head.

'When I was your age, I used to think in opposites like that – good and evil, light and dark. I used to think that if only we could rid the world of people like Feyir, everything would be all right. Divine order would be restored.' He smiled. 'I had no idea they were actually part of the same Divine order.'

'But shouldn't people like that be fought, be stopped at all costs?'

'You have given the answer to that yourself already,' Yldich said, his expression sober. 'When you had the chance to finish off your enemy. Think about what stopped you.'

Rom studied his hands. 'Maybe if I had slain him when he was already down, defenceless, I would have become just like him....' Yldich nodded thoughtfully.

'Feyir is like a spiteful child, trying to get his way at any cost, striking at everything that reminds him of what he hates most about himself.' He took a burning twig that had fallen in the grass and tossed it back on the fire. 'He's fighting what he perceives as weakness. If you engage in his fight, you could be at it for ever.'

'Then what should I do?'

Yldich smiled. 'Explore your own darkness. Instead of fighting it in others. Which isn't to say,' he added with a grin, 'you shouldn't defend yourself when necessary.' Rom frowned with uncertainty. He sighed and pushed his hair out of his face. 'Why don't you get some sleep, Rom.' Yldich fetched a blanket and draped it around Rom's shoulders. '*Nâstreher ehéminae palári êstre.*' Rom looked up, puzzled.

'What does that mean?'

Yldich smiled. 'Night is never as dark as the setting sun would have you believe.' It's an old *Einache* expression. Sleep well, now.'

The next day they resumed their journey to Eald's village. They abandoned the river once more and went in a straight line through the Forest towards the northeast. Yldich and Rom walked beside the horse.

'I want to find Eald's parents as soon as possible,' Yldich said. 'The weather will be turning. I can feel it. We'll need warmer clothes, and fresh supplies. If we can't find Eald's village and get help there, we'll have to push on to Woodbury.'

That night they kept the fire burning low between them as they slept.

Rom was walking along a deserted field. He saw a small cottage on the edge of a village. He recognized it with a sense of wonder. It was the cottage he and his mother had lived in until he was eight years old. He was surprised to see it still standing. The whitewashed door creaked as he carefully shoved it open. He went inside the house, blinking in the gloom that was dark after walking in bright sunlight.

A figure stood before the familiar old hearth. It turned slowly as he approached. He felt his heart pound in his chest.

'Mother?' He recognized her face, her tawny hair. Unlike he remembered, she had to turn her face up to look at him. She gazed in his direction, a vague smile on her face.

'Rom?'

He walked up to her. He felt strangely tall, the sword on his belt an unwieldy thing in the small house. As her dark blue eyes focused on his tall form, his dark hair, a frown creased her brow. She drew back. Her expression changed.

'It's me, mother.' He moved as if to touch her arm. She shuddered and made a sign to ward off evil. He froze and stared at her, shaken.

'You. *Tzanatzi*. You're cursed. Get away from me.'

He turned around and fled.

He woke up with a gasp. It was still dark. He lifted his head and noticed Yldich beside the fire, his face distorted by dancing shadows. He was putting brushwood on it to keep it burning. Yldich turned his head and looked at him.

'Bad dream?' Rom blinked and nodded. 'Try to get some more sleep, now. We have a long way to go tomorrow.'

They got up early the next morning. Dawn presented them with a grey, overcast sky. There was almost no wind. As they continued their way through the forest, Rom felt as if they were moving about in an enclosed space. The Forest looked so uniform in the murk that they might as well be travelling in circles.

Yldich looked around sharply as he walked, humming occasionally to get an impression of life around them. Eald sat on the horse, keeping an eye open for recognizable landmarks.

Around noon, the grey clouds thinned out and opened up to a sky that was already stained with the sun bleeding out towards sunset. The ground had started to slope slightly upwards, until they came to an area where the Forest was less dense. Eald stirred and sat up straight in the saddle. Yldich noticed.

'What's the matter, lad?' Eald shook his head.

'I'm not sure....' They came upon a low wall of broken stones covered with ivy. Eald stiffened. 'I recognize this....' A path meandered through the forest and trailed along an old well made of roughly hewn stones. Eald's face lit up. He turned to Yldich. 'This is the well of my village. I'm nearly home!'

Yldich studied the well closely. Tall grass grew between the flagstones. The path that trailed alongside the well was overgrown with weeds. He frowned and looked at Rom. Rom felt a sense of unease creep upwards along his spine. He met Yldich's eyes. An unspoken thought crossed between them. He nodded almost imperceptibly.

Eald slid off the horse and hurried along the path. Yldich went over to Elda and took the horse's head in his hands. He murmured softly. Then he let it go. The horse slowed its pace, and fell behind as it followed them at its leisure. Yldich rushed over to Eald and overtook him.

'Eald,' he said carefully, 'why don't you let me go up front. Just in case.' Rom went and walked beside Eald.

As they neared a glade in the forest that bathed in the last light of the sun, Rom took Eald's hand. Eald hardly noticed. The boy took in the village that was his home and wondered what it was that made it unfamiliar. He stared at it until he realized it was the silence. There were no dogs barking, no women singing or chattering, no sounds of children playing. The place was eerily silent. He frowned, uncomprehending.

Yldich had reached the edge of the village. Rom looked down at Eald. The boy's face was tense.

'Maybe they left for help after the raid,' he said softly. 'Maybe they all went away to another village.' Eald stared at the dusty earth of the empty centre of the village. He nodded blankly.

Yldich had reached the first house. He held up a hand. 'Keep back, now. Just in case predators have made their den inside. I'll have a look first.' He stooped to pass through the low doorway.

They waited a while. Eald was getting restless. 'I'm going. I know this place better than he does.' He slipped out of Rom's hold and broke into a run towards the houses. As he saw the boy's bobbing figure move away, Rom felt a strong sense of alarm, like a low buzzing sound, filling his head. At the same time, Yldich reappeared from a house. His face was grim. He saw Eald approach and shouted in alarm.

'Rom! Keep him back. Stop him, now.' His voice was uncommonly harsh. As a horrible realization of the truth shuddered through him, Rom threw himself into a run. He grabbed hold of the boy. Eald struggled in his grip.

'Let me go!' He looked at Yldich's face, and as he saw the expression that was there, he started to cry. He struggled violently, kicking and flailing his arms. Rom closed his eyes and held onto him, feeling as if he was the eye of a storm. A piercing wail of desperate grief tore through the boy's small body. As it broke free, it shattered the silence of the Forest like breaking glass. Rom felt the sound pass through his bones, grating against his core until he felt tears run over his face. As another desperate wail was loosed, Eald sank down in his grip onto the ground. Rom kneeled down on the ground and held on to him. Waves of grief passed through the boy as he lay in Rom's arms, shaking and sobbing uncontrollably.

Yldich sat down beside them. His face was pale. He closed his eyes and started to murmur softly. The sound merged with the sound of the boy's violent sobbing and carried it away, a low dirge without beginning or end. Rom felt the pain that constricted his heart melt away with the song and let his own sadness flow with it.

After a time, Eald's wild sobbing had softened into a low weeping. Rom moved a hand across his eyes and looked up at Yldich.

'Give him to me,' Yldich said softly. He carried him back to the place where the horse still waited patiently. Rom looked back over his shoulder. The sun had gone down. The moon was rising, and lit the village with its own eldritch light. Dark shadows filled the windows and doorways of the empty houses. He shuddered and turned away.

They walked by the light of the moon until they reached a clearing with low trees and shrubs. While Rom started to gather twigs and fir cones to build a fire, Yldich carried Eald over to a sheltered space under some low trees and swaddled him in blankets.

When Rom had gotten a fire started, Yldich returned. He sat down heavily beside the fire. Rom looked at him. Yldich looked tired, the lines in his face etched more deeply, making him look older than usual.

'I finally got him to go to sleep.' He sighed deeply and brushed his hands over his face. Rom handed him a mug with steaming tea.

'Yldich... are you sure they're all dead?' Yldich nodded grimly over his mug.

'I saw the remains of at least ten adults and two children.' Rom shook his head as if it could loosen the images in his mind. Yldich took a sip. 'Scavengers have been at the bodies and scattered the bones. But I saw the kind of damage you only sustain in a fight. Sword cuts on the bones of the arms, superficial cuts on ribs... they put up a struggle before they died.'

Rom swallowed. He imagined the forest dwellers, armed with knives and simple tools, fighting Feyir's well-armed riders. He felt a slow, heavy anger start to build up inside. His eyes darkened. 'It's not fair.'

'No,' Yldich said. 'It's not.'

That night in his sleep, Rom walked a winding path through the forest that took him to the top of a steep hill. It looked out over a small settlement. Small houses shaped of reed and clay were scattered over the sunlit field below like mushrooms or like pebbles, dropped on the ground by a careless giant.

A tall, slender girl in a long dress, the colour of young leaves, was standing in the field. She had her back towards him. Suddenly he was in the grass behind her, without knowing how he got there. She turned around and met his eyes. She was almost of the same height. Spiralling curls of burnished copper had escaped her braids and were lifted up by the breeze, catching the light of the sun.

He gazed into her eyes. They were of a clear grey, bright against her dark eyelashes. Her eyes reminded him a little of Yldich's. Her eyebrows were a darker shade of copper, with a slant to them that made her face look both wilful and beautiful. Her skin was fair and her nose was dotted with little freckles. Her mouth had a curve to it that might be drawn into either a smile or a mocking grimace. She parted her lips as if to speak. He waited, breathless. He heard her soft, melodious voice in his head.

Please tell him to come home.

Yldich awoke with a heavy feeling of sadness that pressed on his chest and weighed him down. He breathed deeply, trying to release it. It felt as if it were clinging to him, refusing to let go. He opened his eyes and sighed. He knew what he would have to do.

He went over to Elda and greeted the horse by running his hand lightly over its long face. The horse whinnied softly in reply. Yldich rummaged through the saddlebags and took out some crystals wrapped in leather and some bundles with herbs. He went over to Eald and kneeled by his side. The boy was deeply asleep, wrapped in his blankets. Only the top of his head was visible; his hair stuck out in rusty wisps. Yldich murmured a few soft words in *Einache* and left the boy sleep. He walked over to Rom, who lay beside the burnt-out fire. He was also deeply asleep. He moved a little as if he was dreaming.

Yldich moved for the trees, humming softly. The horse followed him without a sound. When they had reached the edge of the clearing, Yldich mounted and disappeared between the trees.

The village lay empty and quiet in the light of the morning sun. Yldich carefully felt around with his senses. The air was heavy with a lifeless silence that made it harder to breathe. He sat down on the hardened earth in the middle of the village and unwrapped a stick of herbs. He lighted it and breathed on it to make it glow. A thin trail of smoke spiralled into the air, and released a sharp smell that cleared the air in its wake. Yldich closed his eyes and began to sing. The sound spread out from him, rippling the air like water.

The shadows in the empty doorways and windows thickened. They began to move. Elda whinnied and shied away, his eyes rolling with fear. Yldich kept singing until he was surrounded by a circle of darkened air that rippled and swayed, reaching out for him. He opened his eyes. *'Ohênstre Eldiri, verésimer Eärwe,'* he murmured. He stared at the dark shapes that came towards him.

Rom woke up shivering with a persistent chill. The weather had finally started to turn. He wrapped himself in his blanket and shambled over to the remains of the fire. He was surprised Yldich had let it go out. Both he and the horse were nowhere to be seen. He saw Eald lying under the small trees, an indistinguishable shape wrapped in blankets, thankfully still asleep.

He got a small fire going and warmed his hands above it. He heated some water and made some tea. He had just decided to go look for Yldich, when he saw him return with the horse. He made some more tea and handed Yldich a mug without comment. The man looked more worn and tired than he'd ever seen him. Rom let him take a few sips before he started to speak.

'Where did you go?'

'There was something that needed to be done,' Yldich said softly, motioning in the direction of the empty village. Rom waited for him to continue. Yldich closed his eyes and released a sigh. He opened his eyes and met Rom's. 'When something like this happens,' he said in a low voice, 'sometimes the dead remain behind, restless, unable to pass on and resume their journey.' Rom shivered.

'You may have felt it, yesterday in the village, a heaviness in the air, a chill that has nothing to do with the wind or the weather.' Rom thought of the eerie silence of the moonlit village and nodded mutely. 'The dead still needed to be released.'

'Why didn't they... pass on?'

'When people are killed suddenly, or when they cannot accept that they have died, they can linger on, believing they're still alive, or holding onto the world of the living on purpose, in anger or in spite. The people of Eald's village had been surprised at night. One moment, they were asleep, the next, they were fighting for their lives. They weren't truly aware of their condition. So I... helped them understand.'

'Was it... difficult?'

Yldich studied his hands. 'Some of them were still in agony, re-living the moment of their deaths over and over. I had to help them release the pain. For a *Yaever* to do that, he or she may feel some of it, too.' He grimaced. 'It's all right, now. I'm just tired.'

Rom took the empty mug out of his hands and put it away. He stood up. 'You'd better get some rest. I'll see if I can find us something to eat.' Yldich looked up. Some private thought pulled his face into a weary smile. He nodded and drew the blanket Rom had left by the fire around him. 'But I'm not going to sing for rabbits,' Rom added in an impulse. He turned around briskly and left. Yldich snorted. A tiny sparkle of amusement returned to his eyes. He lay down huddled in the blanket and fell asleep almost immediately.

Rom entered the forest moving diligently. He carefully avoided the village, despite the knowledge that there was nothing there that could harm him now. Instead, he went around the campsite in a large circle, and looked around for shrubs or trees that might carry nuts or berries. He stumbled over a tree stump that was partially hidden by trailing ivy. He cursed, and nearly fell face down into something that looked like a small field. He noticed it might once have been a vegetable patch. Weeds and saplings had started to infringe on its borders, slowly taking back territory for the Forest, but the signs of human cultivation were unmistakable.

He began to dig into the earth with his fingers and discovered something that reminded him of a carrot or a small turnip. He continued digging with enthusiasm, pulling out as many as he could find. When he went back to the campsite, his arms filled with grubby roots, he felt as if he'd unearthed a hidden treasure.

Eald had finally woken up. Rom neared the camp and saw Eald and Yldich in front of the fire, talking softly in their own language. Eald was crying. Rom dropped the roots next to the cooking gear and brushed the earth off his sleeves. He felt slightly awkward, not knowing what to do with himself. He sat down next to the heap of roots and began to clean them and cut them up while the sound of the murmuring voices brushed his awareness. Again, he felt he could almost make out the words. After a while, Yldich came over to him.

'How is he?' Rom said.

'As well as can be expected.' Yldich sighed softly. Then he noticed the heap of vegetables. He pulled up an eyebrow in surprise. 'Where did you get those?'

Rom's mouth pulled into a crooked smile. 'You're not the only one who can conjure up a supper out of nothing.' He tossed the last of the cleaned roots on the heap with a jaunty movement.

While Yldich cooked the roots together with some dried herbs and mushrooms, Rom sat back with his arms around his knees.

'Yldich,' he said softly. 'What about Eald? What's going to happen to him? He's got nowhere left to go.' Yldich nodded.

'I've talked with him about it. He's agreed to come home with me. I'll raise him as my foster son. He's already decided he wants to be a *Yaever* when he grows up.' He smiled. Rom swallowed. An odd, tiny sensation of jealousy went through his heart like a sharp needle. It embarrassed him. He pushed it away quickly and looked down at his hands. Yldich gazed at him with his piercing grey eyes. 'You, on the other hand, may not have any aspirations to become a *Yaever*.' He grinned. 'But you may want to stay with us, anyway.'

Rom looked up sharply. His eyes reminded Yldich of dark, fragile glass. They were lit by a shy, careful smile. Yldich felt a sudden tingle of foreknowledge.

Moreover, we will need you, when the storm comes. His skin prickled.

They ate in silence, each of them occupied with their own thoughts. Afterwards Yldich brought Eald back to bed. His face was still pale, his eyes puffy with crying. He went without protest.

Rom sat staring at the fire, deep in thought, when Yldich returned. Yldich sat thinking for a while. He turned his gaze on Rom's face. 'You never told me about your parents.' Rom stiffened. 'After you escaped from Lord Aldr's Keep.' Yldich raised his brows in wonder. 'Why didn't you return home?'

'I'd rather not talk about it,' Rom said in a low voice. Yldich looked at him attentively.

'Why not?' he said simply.

Rom was suddenly reminded of Eald and his childish way of hounding him with questions. His mouth almost pulled into a smile. 'It's—it's not a nice tale.'

Yldich nodded. 'This seems to be the time for sad tales.' He motioned in Eald's direction. Rom stared in the fire in silence, his brows knit. Yldich looked at his face intently. Finally, Rom relented. As usual, he thought, only a blunt refusal would make Yldich leave the matter be.

'When my mother was a young girl,' he said in a soft voice, 'she was engaged to be married to a wealthy merchant's son. They had met at a Harvest Fest. People said she was beautiful, with her tawny hair that danced around her as she moved, and dark blue eyes. She lived in a small village in the South, near the coast. Her family had a sheep farm, and they were not so well off. So it was considered a fortuitous match.' He stared into the fire.

'One evening, she was walking home late from bringing in the sheep. The sun had almost gone down, and she walked past the dark woods that bordered the fields as she took the path that led back to the village.' He clenched his hands.

'My mother told me she had never been afraid in the dark before. But as she walked along the path, she felt a strange coldness rise up from the ground and chill her to the bone. Darkness rolled over the path towards her. She was shaken, confused. She blinked her eyes, swaying with dizziness. When she opened them again, a man stood before her.' He breathed out slowly. Yldich stared at him, his face expressionless.

'She—she told me he was different from the men she knew. He had dark hair and dark eyes, a pale skin that was luminous in the faint light of the moon.' He frowned. 'The *Tzanatzi* were not often seen in that part of the South at that time. Sometimes they passed through the villages by night. But she had seen enough of them to know what they looked like.' He paused, and stared at his hands.

'She told me the man spoke to her in a strange language. He almost seemed to chant the words as he came towards her. She—she was swayed by his voice. He touched her face. She told me it was like a dream. It didn't seem real. He... overpowered her. She felt unable to resist, swept away by his song, his dark eyes that seemed to gaze into her being.' He bit his lip. 'When she got home, she told her family that she had been raped by a stranger.'

Yldich stared at him, his face grim.

'Her father and brothers searched the whole area for the dark-haired man. They found no-one. Eventually, they started to think that maybe she had made the whole thing up. But a few months later, it became obvious to everyone that *something*, at least, had happened to her.' He paused to pick up a small twig. He sat turning it around and around in his hands. He threw it into the flames.

'The merchant's son broke off the engagement as soon as he heard she was pregnant. She was a shame to her family. For months, she didn't go into the village, afraid of what people might say. And then she gave birth to a son.

With hair like charcoal and eyes almost as dark, just like the man she said had raped her. A *Tzanatzi*.' He stared into the fire, his eyes like obsidian.

'By that time, her family had begun to suspect her story was a lie. They thought she had secretly been with a travelling *Tzanatzi*. Which was even worse than being raped by one. So they disowned her and drove her out.' Yldich shook his head in silence.

'An elderly lady that lived at the edge of the village took pity on my mother and took us in. She was considered a little strange herself so she lived alone. We lived with her in her little cottage. After she died, we stayed there.' He pushed his hair out of his face and sighed softly.

'When I was small, my mother did her best to love me. I think she really did. But as I got older, it became harder. I grew up faster than other children. I was a serious child. After five, six years had passed, I was no longer a chubby infant. I think I reminded her more and more of the man who had ruined her life.' He swallowed. 'And there was more. There were the dreams.'

Yldich sat up. 'What dreams?'

'From an early age on, I had nightmares. I used to wake up screaming, waking the whole house. It was always the same. I would wake up in terror, and tell my mother I was lost, lost in blackness, that I couldn't find my way home.' He shuddered and drew up his knees, and put his arms around them. He looked like a frightened boy, unable to chase away the shadows that hid under his bed and crept up the covers.

Yldich frowned. A strange chill passed through him. Something seemed to catch in his mind, trying to get his attention. As he tried to touch it, it was gone. Rom didn't seem to notice. His gaze was turned inward.

'The nightmares unnerved my mother. She was, as all her people are, afraid of sorcery, of anything magical, especially anything *Tzanatzi*. And then I started to... dream true, as you would say.'

Yldich looked at him sharply. 'Tell me.'

'I would... know things, little things, which I wasn't supposed to know. I knew it beforehand when a storm came and hit the village, and ruined the crops. I knew where my mother had lost her necklace, the one with the little pendant she loved. I knew it... when the old lady was going to die.' He swallowed. 'At first, I would tell my mother everything I dreamed. But as I saw the look of fear in her eyes grow to loathing as more of my dreams came true, I didn't speak of them again.'

'You must have been very lonely,' Yldich said softly. Rom started. He blinked. Something, some hard shell that covered his eyes, was threatening to break. He looked away quickly.

'The children of the village had no trouble spotting me as different,' he said. 'They targeted me. I tried to avoid them, but sometimes they would hunt me down and corner me. So I would have to fight them.' He frowned. 'Finally, my mother had enough. I was nothing but trouble. I always got into fights. So when I was eight, she sent me away to lord Aldr's Keep.' He swallowed. 'She stood in the doorway as Aldr's men came to collect me. I looked into her eyes. I saw the relief in her face. She was glad to be finally free of me.' He paused and drew a hand over his face.

'The first time I ran away from lord Aldr's Keep was after a month. I ran home and begged my mother not to send me back. She wouldn't listen to me. She walked me back to the gates, and had the guards take me in again.' He closed his eyes. 'That's when I got the mark, the mark of the Boar. Lord Aldr had me brought to his personal quarters. He had a signet ring he always wore. He had it heated in the fire by one of his servants. He—he had his men hold me down, and he burned it into my skin, saying it would never let me forget that I was his.'

His breath shuddered out of him. His face was pale and drawn. Yldich was about to speak, when Rom stood up abruptly. He left Yldich sitting by the fire and stumbled a few steps across the field, grabbing a slender tree for support. He sank down next to it, his head bowed, choking, struggling for breath. Yldich went over to him and gently laid a hand on his back.

'It's all right, lad,' he said softly. 'Stop fighting it.' Rom started to shake with violent sobbing. He held onto the tree like a drowning man. Yldich let out a sigh and sat down next to him. He laid his arm around Rom's shoulders, murmuring softly in *Einache*.

'*Entewé, di eldimae, sa roë....*' The words mingled with the painful sobs, like a song, and softened them, until they became a steady flow of silent tears.

Rom became aware of an elusive sensation of light and warmth that enveloped him. Slowly, the shaking subsided. A long sigh shuddered through him, leaving him strangely empty. He stirred, trying to get up.

'Come on,' Yldich said. He gently helped him up and led him back to the fire. The sun was already going down. A blackbird was singing its evening song. Yldich pulled a blanket around Rom's shoulders. He made some tea and brought him a mug. Rom sat with his eyes closed, clutching the blanket around him. He accepted the mug and closed his hands around it to warm them. Yldich sat watching him silently. After a while, Rom started to speak again.

'Ever since I can remember,' he whispered, 'I've been afraid there was something wrong with me. Something... evil.'

Yldich shook his head slowly. 'If you had been born into an *Einache* family, you wouldn't have been made to fear your heritage. You would have learnt how to deal with your dreams.'

Rom opened his eyes. 'It's—it's not just that.' He stared into the mug. 'The story of how my mother got pregnant had gone round the village. Sometimes, when I walked past a house, a field, people would make the sign against evil.' He shuddered. 'Once an old woman spat before my feet. She— she called me demon child.' His eyes were dark with an indeterminate fear. Yldich shook his head, frowning, his grey eyes the colour of storm clouds. 'You were right, you know.' Rom looked up. 'That night in the Forest. All my life I've been running from myself. I think I've always been afraid that if I stopped running, I would bump into myself and be horrified by what I'd see.'

Yldich was silent for a moment, his brow lined with thought. He started to speak slowly. 'These people from your village,' he said, his voice stern. 'They created their own demons for fear of what was different. Of what they didn't understand. They saw a little *Tzanatzi* boy and made a demon out of him.' He grinned. 'They wouldn't know a *real* demon if it hit them on the head with a stick.'

Rom was appalled. 'Are you saying there is such a thing as real demons?'

'I told you about the different levels of consciousness in the dream state. They are inhabited by all sorts of beings. Some of them you might call demons.' Yldich smiled. 'You are nothing like them, I assure you.' Rom gazed at him. He began to feel strangely relieved. Something seemed to loosen inside him. 'Sometimes the dream state bleeds into reality, and demons and other beings may be encountered in our world.' Yldich gazed thoughtfully in the fire. 'Sometimes it's the other way round and people get lost in the dream state, when they are in a different state of consciousness.' He met Rom's eyes. 'However, experience has taught me that *human* beings can be much more dangerous than any demon.' He smiled.

Tension flowed away from Rom's face. He sat for a while and watched the fire, leaning his chin in his cupped hands, his thoughts adrift. 'Yldich... what do you think really happened to my mother?'

Yldich frowned. 'I wonder.'

That night, while the three of them lay curled up in their blankets around the low-burning fire, Yldich felt himself move away from the camp site and into the Forest. He trailed along the trees, not knowing where he was going, following a faint call that pulled him along. He travelled in a blur of colours and sensations, until he found himself on the edge of Gardeth Battle Plain.

A bitter fight was taking place. Two armies clashed against each other in a flurry of movement, a clamour of metal, and cries of men, filling the midnight air.

In the midst of the chaos of screaming horses, fighting men, spears, swords and whistling arrows, a small figure was trying to find its way. Yldich gazed at it, trying to make it out. He felt his heart pound in his chest when he realized it was a small, dark-haired boy. A low sinking feeling of dismay filled his stomach as he saw the child stumble across the battlefield. Only a few paces away, a lithe *Tzanatzi* archer was hewn down by a heavy battleaxe, blood spraying over his clothes. A little further to the left, an *Einache* warrior was thrown off his horse. He fell down in a tangle of bodies, his legs caught under the horse's heavy body, shouting for aid until he was killed by a *Tzanatzi* spear thrust through his chest. Arrows whistled through the air, right over the head of the little boy.

Yldich threw himself into a forward movement, and somehow managed to scramble off the cliffs and onto the battlefield. He ran as hard as he could. Arrows whizzed past his head. He only just managed to dodge a spear that was aimed at another man behind him.

When he had finally reached the place where he had last seen the little boy, he looked around in bewilderment. There was no-one there, only a rising darkness, that curled itself around him, and filled him with cold. His body went numb. His throat constricted. He uttered a last desperate cry before cold darkness closed his mouth.

He was thrown back into consciousness, gasping, like a swimmer thrown back onto the beach, his eyes half open and gritty with sleep. He saw the sky that was blushing light orange in the light of the rising sun.

Yldich sat up slowly and looked around. The fire had gone out hours ago. A damp chill was rising from the forest floor and seeped through his blanket. He looked at the other side of the fire pit. Eald and Rom had moved towards each other for warmth in their sleep. They lay huddled against each other in a confused mass of blankets and cloaks like a pair of bear cubs in a den.

Yldich got up carefully so as not to wake them, and gathered some dry twigs and kindle wood for a fire. He reviewed the images of his dream in his mind, trying to trace their origin. The sense of unease that had been with him since waking remained.

He became aware of a need for help, for the mirror of another's mind. His heart filled with a longing for home, for the familiarity of the great wooden House, for the sound of his daughter's voice, for the sharp, aged wisdom of Yealda, his teacher. He breathed in deeply, feeling the depth of his longing, and breathing out, sent out a call through his heart, like a thin thread, that rolled out and winded through the trees, reaching towards the North.

When he got back to the camp site, Rom was just waking up. He blinked at the light of the early morning sun.

'Good morning to you,' Yldich called. His voice was airy and didn't convey any of his uneasiness.

'Morning.' Rom sounded sleepy. He pushed his hair out of his eyes and disentangled from the blankets. He began to help Yldich build a fire. He picked up the small tinder box to light some dry grass and twigs. He had trouble filling it and producing a spark. His hands were numb and shook with cold. Yldich watched him for a while and took it out of his hands.

'You go get some bigger branches, lad,' Yldich said. 'Moving will get you warmed up.' Rom grumbled, grabbed his cloak and disappeared between the trees. He was shivering.

Eald's head popped out of the blankets. He yawned and rubbed his face. He stuck his nose into the air and sniffed it like a fox. His lip curled up in distaste. 'It's cold.'

Yldich pulled his blankets away and rolled them up. 'The sooner you get ready and moving, the sooner you'll get warm.'

When they were moving again, Yldich insisted Eald go up front on the horse and *flestrérer*. He looked at him, surprised.

'But Yldich, I can walk now, really. Let Rom ride for a while.'

Yldich shook his head. 'He should walk and keep moving.' They looked at Rom, who walked a few paces behind them. He was shivering despite the cloak and some spare woollen leggings Yldich had dug out of his saddlebags. He had to roll up the hem at the top and put his belt over it to keep them from falling down as they were several sizes too big.

Eald frowned. 'Why does the cold bother him so much? It's not that bad.'

'It's a difference in temperament, I think. The *Einache* are used to this climate. I've noticed before *Tzanatzi* do not stand the cold as we do.' Yldich frowned. 'We're not that far from Woodbury. I want to try and get there today, tomorrow at the latest. We can buy some winter clothes there, and some supplies. Hunting will become more difficult as the cold increases.'

They followed a decline in the forest floor that turned itself into a narrow path embanked by walls of earth covered in ferns, moss and birches. It widened into a road. As they moved along the road, yellow leaves were falling from the trees like premature golden snow. Some trees were already baring their skeletal arms against the cloudless sky.

As the sun rose, the sharp chill of the air softened. A little colour came back to Rom's face. Some time before noon, they stopped for a rest.

'Let's get off the road,' Yldich said. Rom looked at him sharply. 'I don't expect any trouble,' Yldich said. 'But I don't want to take unnecessary chances either.'

After a short rest they returned to the road. As it widened, the trees thinned, the Forest making way for grassy fields and hills.

'Well,' Yldich said. He looked pleased. 'We've come further than I thought. This is the road to Woodbury.'

Five

Woodbury

A large enclosure of wood and stone came into view in the distance. Yldich turned to Rom.

'Maybe I should warn you, lad,' he said. 'Woodbury is an old *Einache* settlement. It does have some contact with the outside world. They have trading contacts with the South and speak the Southern language. But some of the people there haven't seen a *Tza*—an outsider for years. Don't take it personally if they look at you a little strangely.'

They approached the walls and passed through the gates. They were wide enough to let two horse carts pass through at a time. No-one seemed to man them, but as they passed, Rom looked up and noticed a heavy wooden structure, like a trap door, that was held up by thick ropes and ended in iron spikes. He guessed it could be lowered quickly in case of trouble.

As they neared the village, more and more *Einache* passed them on the dirt road. The men were dressed in simple woollen garb, tunics and trousers in beige or dusty terracotta, embroidered with stylized nature motifs. They wore big leather belts and boots. Rom saw no-one overtly armed, though some men had knives in their belts.

Women were wearing long, flowing skirts and dresses of thin wool and other fabrics in more adventurous hues: bright yellow and the green of young leaves, and sometimes a rare purple, contrasting with their hair, which ranged from light mahogany to copper or ginger-blonde. They wore it loose, in long braids, or done up in buns with copper pins.

Some men nodded politely, even respectfully at Yldich. Rom wondered how many people knew who he was. As they passed Yldich and Eald on the horse and set eyes on Rom, some men stiffened and stared. He noticed a few women avert their eyes. One or two older men stared at him with an indeterminate look of hostility in their faces. Rom swallowed and tried not to show his unease.

When they had passed several houses made of wood, plastered with clay, their roofs thatched with dark reed, Yldich stopped in front of a large, two-storey building that had a painted sign over the door. Rom tried to read it, but it was in *Einache*. It had a picture of a beer barrel on it. He guessed it was a tavern or an inn.

A serving boy came out of the building as they approached. Yldich nodded to him and tossed him a coin. The boy took over the reigns of the horse and led Elda to the stable. Rom looked back at him.

'Aren't you afraid someone will go through your saddlebags?' he said under his breath.

'This is not the South,' Yldich said with a look of amusement. 'Besides, around these parts, people still have some respect for a *Yaever*.' He grinned. 'One never knows what ill luck it will produce if you dare touch his belongings.' Rom and Eald followed Yldich into the inn. On the left side of the room, a big, red-haired man with a ruddy face leaned over a wooden counter. He wore a leather apron over his clothes.

'*Ya'haeve*,' he greeted them in *Einache*.

'*Ya'haeve*, to you,' Yldich responded, reverting to the Southern language. The innkeeper had a loud husky voice, which rose easily over the noise of a crowded common room, and a thick, lilting *Einache* accent. Rom had to listen intently to understand him. Yldich started speaking about the possibility of restocking supplies, the state of the roads beyond Woodbury, and the local gossip.

When Rom and Eald lost interest in the conversation and started to look around, the man leant over his counter towards Yldich.

'Now, it's none of my business, I'm sure,' he said in what for him probably served as a soft voice. He eyed Rom carefully. 'But are you sure you and the boy are quite safe travelling around with an...,' he whispered under his breath, 'an *ohênstriër Tzanatzi?*' Rom stiffened. He turned and shot the man a dark look. He opened his mouth as if to speak, then closed it again. He clenched his hands at his sides.

Yldich laid a hand on his shoulder. 'If it weren't for him, neither of us would be standing here alive today.' The innkeeper held up his hands in an apologetic gesture.

'I meant no offence, gentlemen, I'm sure....' Rom noticed him look furtively at the *Einache* sword at his side. He wondered what the man was thinking. Maybe he took him for a hardened swordfighter with a foul temper, he thought with a wry grin.

They moved into the common room and sat down at a table in a corner, out of earshot of the innkeeper. After he served them beer and a sweet drink for Eald he left to busy himself in the kitchen with their orders. Some locals and a traveller or two were at the other tables, and threw curious glances at the newcomers over their mugs.

'Yldich,' Rom said in a clear voice, 'What does *ohênstriër* mean?' Yldich coughed, nearly choking on his beer.

'Trust me,' he said in a low voice, 'you don't want to know.' He took another draught. 'Also, I would advice you not to say that word out loud in these parts... it might get you into trouble.'

After a while the innkeeper came back with their plates.

'Real food,' Eald said with a happy grin, as a large plate laden with steaming food was put before his nose.

When they had eaten their fill, Rom sighed. 'It would be nice to sleep in a real bed, as well....'

Yldich nodded in sympathy. 'So it would,' he said. 'Still, I'm afraid we'd best not linger here. We should move on. I don't want us to attract too much attention. Besides, I've a feeling we need to get home as soon as we can.' Rom frowned as a memory stirred in his mind. 'What is it?' Yldich said.

'Something I dreamed. Something... something about going home.' Rom frowned as he tried to recall it exactly. He stared in the distance. 'I saw a girl... a tall girl, with red hair. She had grey eyes like yours.' Yldich sat up and looked at Rom with a piercing glance. Rom didn't notice, focusing on the vivid dream imagery that filled his mind. 'She was standing in a field, with little houses that looked like they had been shaped out of reed and clay. She turned around and spoke to me. She said—she said, "Please tell him to come home." ' He looked at Yldich.

'Maetis.' Yldich's face was serious. 'Did she say anything else?' Rom shook his head. 'I wonder why she came to you and not to me. Or how she knew to go to you at all. When was this?'

'I think it was the night we were at—at Eald's village,' Rom said. Eald lowered his eyes and stared at the circles that had been worn into the table top. Yldich squeezed his shoulder without speaking. He sat thinking for a while.

'I'd better go into the village and restock our supplies. You two have a look around; see if you can find a shop that stocks winter gear. If we leave in an hour or so, that leaves us enough daylight to travel.' Yldich signalled the innkeeper and paid for their meal. Rom fidgeted. He was suddenly painfully aware of the loss of his own luggage. It had included a small amount of coins to pay for lodgings along the way. Yldich saw his expression and shook his head.

'Don't worry about it, lad,' he said.

Once outside, Yldich took the road to the right. The innkeeper had mentioned some shops that sold dried goods, herbs, and the like further down the road.

'Now don't get yourselves into trouble,' he said over his shoulder. 'We'll meet at the inn in about an hour.'

They took the main road to the left, where the innkeeper had said they might find the workshops of weavers and leatherworkers. Yldich had given them an assortment of Southern and *Einache* coins that would buy them clothes if they could find any. As they walked along the houses and shops, and looked around, they heard music in the distance. Someone was playing a flute. Sweet, meandering notes filled the air. The notes reminded them of the wind in the trees and the call of forest birds. Eald listened as if in a trance. His eyes went vague. He pulled at Rom's sleeve.

'Rom. Let's have a look.'

Rom shook his head. He had just noticed the stand of a leatherworker's workshop. 'You go, and don't take too long.' Eald sprang away. Rom looked over the leatherworker's goods. There were some fur-trimmed coats that might actually fit him. After a while, he began to feel as if someone was watching him. He turned around and saw a little girl stare up at him with an inquisitive gaze. She looked as if she was about eight years old, and had a mass of copper blonde curls that spilled over her shoulders.

'*Ya'haeve*,' he said, remembering the way the innkeeper had greeted them earlier. The girl smiled. She pointed at his head.

'Why is your hair so dark?'

He thought for a bit. 'Well, one day, I stayed up too late in a tavern and when I went home, a piece of the night sky fell on my head and painted it black.' The girl shook her head at him.

'No it didn't,' she said. 'You just made that up.' He made a face and she giggled. He smiled at her. She was about to ask another question, when he heard a shrill voice.

'Ylóna!' A woman ran across the street in a flurry of skirts. She pulled the girl away by her arm and snapped over her shoulder at Rom. 'You leave her alone.' She dragged the girl away and left Rom staring at them as if frozen.

A heavy hand fell on his shoulder and forced him to turn around. A familiar feeling of apprehension made him tense his muscles. He clenched his fists, ready to fight off whatever was before him. He looked straight into the sharp green eyes of a young man. He was about Rom's age, and like most

Einache, he was taller and heavier of build. His hair was the shade of hay. He fixed Rom with a stare, his brows knit.

'Are you troubling these people?'

Rom scowled. The young *Einache*'s hand weighed on his shoulder like an accusation. He pushed it off with a sharp, angry movement of his arm. The *Einache* grabbed him by the front of his tunic and forced him backwards into a small alley. He pushed Rom with his back against a wall.

'I asked you a question.' An old feeling of helplessness and rage flared up and Rom growled.

'Leave me alone.' He threw himself forward and moved to push the man out of his way. The *Einache* moved swiftly. He grabbed Rom's left hand while he lashed out with his right fist. Rom gasped and fell back against the wall. The young man squatted before him and peered calmly into his face.

'Have you had enough?' Rom gingerly touched his mouth and winced. 'Now,' the other said. 'What's a *Tzanatzi* doing in Woodbury causing trouble?' Rom felt another flare of anger. He moved to get up. The *Einache* grabbed his tunic in a firm hold and held him back against the wall. Rom's arm moved up by instinct. The *Einache* saw the scar on Rom's arm and froze. A look of wonder crossed his face.

'*Faraër*,' he whispered. He let go of Rom's tunic. He sat back and stared at him. 'Who are you?' He spoke in a hushed voice.

Rom glared back. 'Where I come from, people introduce themselves, before they hit other people and ask for their names.'

The *Einache* laughed. 'I'm Eldairc.' His eyes glinted with amusement. He waited, then lifted an eyebrow. 'Well?' Rom looked at him with distrust. 'Where I come from,' the *Einache* said, 'people introduce themselves after they've been introduced to their assailant.' He grinned. Rom felt his mouth twitch in response.

'I'm Rom. I wasn't causing any trouble.' He shook his head in defiance.

'So why did that woman run away from you as if—'

Rom scowled. 'When you look like me, it's the kind of reaction you can expect.'

Eldairc leaned his chin in his hand and looked at him pensively. 'I see.'

Rom got the strange impression that, in fact, he did. He fidgeted under the calm green stare. He was suddenly reminded of Yldich and his relentless gaze. He swallowed, feeling painfully visible.

'Will you let me go now or will you keep me sitting here all day answering questions?' he said, to get away from the eyes.

'Just one,' Eldairc said. He grabbed Rom's right hand. Rom flinched. Eldairc turned his hand palm up and pointed at the *Einache* symbol. It curled along the palm of his hand and trailed upwards along his wrist.

Rom frowned. 'What of it?'

Eldairc stared at him in amazement. 'Do you even know what it is?' Rom opened and closed his mouth, not knowing what to say. 'Who gave it to you?'

Rom hesitated. He doubted whether it was safe to mention Yldich's name to any *Einache* he met. 'A—a *Yaever* did.'

Eldairc widened his eyes. 'What *Yaever*? This mark hasn't been used for at least four, five hundred years.' Rom stared at him, taken aback. 'It's the mark of *Farae*,' Eldairc said. 'It was used long ago, in the old days, before the Great Battle. Young *Einache* warriors and *Yaever* received it when they were considered ready to wear arms and do battle.' Rom felt a strange chill run over his back. He shuddered. Eldairc's eyes moved to the slender *Einache* sword at Rom's side. 'Is this yours?' There was a look of fascination in his eyes as he studied the curling spirals and signs that trailed along the scabbard. Rom nodded. Eldairc shook his head in amazement. 'Have you any idea how old this design is?'

Fragments of Yldich's stories, things Yldich had said rose in Rom's memory. They surfaced in his awareness and were left like pieces of driftwood after a flood. He sorted through them in his mind. A disturbing question rose in his throat. He closed his hand over his mouth as if he wanted to keep it from leaping out. He turned to Eldairc and asked another.

'How do you know all this?'

Eldairc apparently pulled his gaze away from the sword with difficulty. 'I've a fondness for the old tales.' He smiled, and shook his head again in wonder. 'I never thought I would see a *Tzanatzi* walk into my town covered in the stuff of *Einache* legends like a warrior from the old days.' His green eyes glinted.

'Half-*Tzanatzi*,' Rom said absently. He felt dazed.

'Come on,' Eldairc said. 'I'll buy you a drink to make up for that blow to your face. And then you should tell me all about this.' He lifted Rom by his arm and pulled him along before he could protest.

They came out of the alley and almost walked into Eald who was looking for Rom.

'Rom! There you are.' Eald looked up into Rom's face and noticed the cut on his mouth. His gaze moved to the tall *Einache* beside Rom and he scowled, his narrow face tense. 'Did he do this to you?'

'It's all right, Eald,' Rom said.

Eldairc looked at the small boy in bewilderment. 'You two are travelling together?' Eald looked up, frowning with uncertainty. 'I'm Eldairc,' the tall *Einache* said to the boy. 'I was just about to get your friend here a beer to make up for a slight, uh, misunderstanding.' He grinned. 'Come with us.'

He made a broad gesture with his left arm as if to include Eald in the company, while he moved Rom along with his right. They felt strangely disinclined to protest. As they arrived at a small house that had the wooden sign of a tavern over the door, he ushered them in.

'Tell me Rom,' Eldairc said, after they had found a table in the corner and sat down. 'Why are a young *Einache* boy and a *Tzanatzi* travelling through these parts?' His green eyes glittered with curiosity.

A large mug of beer was planted in front of Rom by a busy serving girl. She put a similar mug at Eldairc's elbow and handed Eald a cup of milk. Eald wrinkled his nose at it. He eyed Rom's mug with interest. Eldairc took a deep draught of beer. He leaned his face in his hands and studied them at his ease.

Rom hesitated. 'I'm not sure how much is safe to tell you. We had some... trouble on the way.' Eldairc frowned slightly.

'What sort of trouble?'

'We were attacked by Lord Feyir's riders,' Eald said abruptly. 'They nearly killed us.' Rom started.

'Eald! Don't say that name out loud,' and looked around the common room as if he expected riders at the other tables drinking beer. 'You don't know who's listening.'

Eldairc stared at him. 'I heard a rumour about a group of riders harrowing small Forest villages. They were supposed to be led by a Southern noble. I didn't think it was true....' Rom shook his head. A dark sense of foreboding rose from within. He looked down at the table top, his eyes black.

'We shouldn't be telling you this. It might be dangerous for you to even know our names. If he ever comes this way...' He thought of the little girl, of the unarmed *Einache* in the market street and shuddered at the thought of the riders descending on Woodbury in the dark of night like a pack of hungry wolves.

'So why is this Southern lord after you?' Eldairc said. Rom swallowed.

'It's a long story. He—has a personal grievance.'

'*And* he's after Yldich,' Eald said. Rom lifted his head and looked at him with something akin to despair.

'Eald!'

Eldairc shifted in his seat. 'Yldich?'

'The *Yaever* I told you about,' Rom said, exasperated. He cursed himself for bringing Eald along. The boy was too young to understand the danger of misplaced trust.

'He's called Yldich?' Eldairc said. Rom looked at him questioningly. 'It's probably just a coincidence... there's an ancient legend about a *Yaever* called Yldich. Supposedly he led the *Einache* in the great Battle of Gardeth.

There's a tale about him being the *Hárrad* of the *Einache*, a mysterious rebel faction that will free our people from the rule of the Southern kings.' He grinned. 'I'm one of the few people here who go in for that kind of thing, old legends and the like.' Rom had turned pale and pressed his fingers against his mouth as if he were stifling a cry.

'All this time,' he muttered. 'All this time it was under my nose and I didn't see it.'

'Rom? Are you all right?'

Rom apparently tore himself away from some disturbing inner vision and turned to him. 'Eldairc. Is there any way you can warn the people of this town, make them understand the danger they might be in?'

'You mean the riders?'

Rom nodded. 'Are there any people in Woodbury bearing arms?'

Eldairc cocked his head. 'Farhardt has forbidden the *Einache* to bear arms. But I'll be able to find some people who have kept old swords hidden in their cellars.' He grinned mischievously. 'And I know some boys who've been practicing archery in secret.'

'You need to warn as many people as you can. The town must be guarded.' Rom thought for a moment. 'It would be just like them to try and raid it at night.' Eldairc stared at him.

'You're serious, aren't you?'

Rom nodded grimly. 'Yes.'

Rom and Eald met Yldich in front of the inn a little while later. Yldich met them with a pensive expression on his face.

'I've heard some strange rumours around town.' He looked at Rom, his head a little to the side. 'When I was at the herbalist's shop, a customer was telling him about a fight between two young men, one dark-haired and one red. Apparently, the dark-haired one was a ferocious foreign warrior.

When I was at the weaver's, a young boy was telling his uncle about a mysterious *Tzanatzi* who was having a meeting with two *Einache* in a tavern. They seemed to be discussing some grave and secret business.

Not long after, I heard family members of the weaver and the leather worker are digging up swords from their cellars that belonged to their great-great grandfathers. Boys are busy the edge of the Forest cutting branches for arrows. The town elder has been asking for volunteers to man the gates of Woodbury. There seems to be a mysterious danger threatening the village.' He looked at Rom levelly. 'Do you know anything about that?'

Rom pulled his fingers through his hair. He looked up at Yldich with an expression of slight desperation. 'I had no idea word spreads so fast around here.'

Yldich shook his head at him. 'Maybe you'd better tell me what you've been up to.'

'I heard that the inhabitants of this village are ignorant of the danger of Feyir's riders. They are unarmed; they hold no watch at night. They even think the rumours about the raids on Forest villages are stories to frighten the children with. If the riders come upon them, they'll be defenceless.' He paused, frowning. 'If word gets out that a *Yaever*, a *Tzanatzi* and an *Einache* boy travelled through Woodbury, they're in danger.'

'How did you convince them to arm themselves?' Yldich cocked a brow in curiosity.

'I met an *Einache* who was willing to listen to me.'

'Is he the same one who gave you that cut lip?'

Eald grinned. Rom smiled wryly. 'We had a slight... misunderstanding at first.'

'Rom and Eldairc were fighting,' Eald said cheerfully. 'But then they made up.'

Yldich's mouth pulled into a smile. Then his expression sobered. 'Rom. Do you realize that if Farhardt finds out these people are arming themselves, he'll think they're planning an insurrection?' His voice became low. 'Did you give any thought to what will happen then?'

'I'm afraid the danger of Feyir's men raiding the town is much more immediate than Farhardt finding out what the *Einache* in an obscure little town in the high North are doing.' Rom met Yldich's eyes and lowered his voice. 'I've a bad feeling about it. I don't know why.'

Yldich's gaze went vague until he seemed to be staring in the distance, beyond Rom and Eald who stood before him, beyond the village street, into the hills and trees that bordered the Forest. Finally he turned his eyes on them again. 'Maybe you're right.' He sighed. 'I wanted to leave town quickly and quietly, not giving rumour a chance to spread. But apparently,' he said with a grimace, 'rumour spreads around you like fire in a haystack.'

They decided to spend the night in Woodbury and took lodgings at the inn. The red-haired innkeeper with the loud voice, whose name, Rom learned, was Meldritch, had the stable boy take their luggage upstairs to a reasonably large room with two single beds. Two windows looked out into the main street. A door in the left-hand corner of the room led into a small side room with a little window that looked out into the yard. The innkeeper had a makeshift bed made in it for Eald with thick pillows, sheepskins and blankets. In a corner of the main room, near the door, were a sturdy table and two heavy chairs with sheepskins on them. A large oak clothes chest was in the other corner.

'The washroom is down the corridor to your right,' the stable boy said as he left. 'Tell Eldi, the kitchen girl, if you want water heated for a bath.' Rom's eyes lighted up at the prospect of the first warm bath in weeks.

'Me first!' Eald exclaimed, before he could open his mouth to speak.

Yldich shook his head. 'We must go back to the weaver's shop and buy some winter gear before we do anything else. We leave early tomorrow morning. I hope we reach my home before winter sets in. It's the worst time of year to be travelling through the Forest, and I truly hope we can avoid it.'

Eald wandered out into the corridor to explore the rest of the inn. Yldich unpacked his things. He carefully laid out the bags, the bundles of herbs, and the crystals on a piece of cloth. Rom watched him work.

'Have you ever travelled through Gardeth in winter, Yldich?'

'I have, and I don't recommend it.' Yldich's voice was solemn. 'Remember what I told you about the Forest being ancient battle ground. In some places, the dead still rest uneasily. Their voices are heard more clearly on the wind in the still of winter, when the trees are silent and snow covers the earth like a shroud.'

Rom felt a cold shiver run along his back. The question he did not know how to ask rose in his awareness. It felt like a strange, hidden space in his heart that subtly ached. It would not form into words. He decided to let it go for the time being. He would have plenty of time to ask unnerving questions on their long journey north.

They went back to the weaver's workshop where Rom watched helplessly as Yldich pulled woollen tunics, trousers and sheepskin coats from the shelves and stacked them in Rom's arms.

'Try them on; see if any of them fit you.' He proceeded to send Eald for three pairs of fur-lined boots at the leather worker's place. Rom selected some tunics that didn't look too oversized and tried one on. It was of heavy cloth in a dark shade of green with a leather strap at the neck. Yldich eyed him critically. 'That one doesn't look too bad.' He selected another one of similar fit, of a dusty red, as well as some shirts and trousers and added them to the slowly growing heap of clothes at Rom's feet. Next, he searched for some clothing for Eald and himself. He pulled a new tunic over Eald's head. 'At least now you don't look like a scarecrow.' Eald grinned shyly.

Yldich also found some heavy woollen cloaks. They were lined with fur and had large hoods that could be pulled over their heads to keep out the wind. 'We will need these if winter sets in while we're on the road.'

'But, Yldich, you can't—' Rom protested weakly as Yldich paid the weaver.

'Nonsense,' Yldich said in a cheerful tone. 'I'm the one who insisted you come to the North. The least I can do is see to it you don't freeze on the way.'

When they got back at the inn, Meldritch the innkeeper motioned them to come and speak to him.

'A while ago, a young man who called himself Eldairc was here to speak to someone called, ah, Roëm,' he said in his lilting *Einache* accent. He studied Rom cautiously. 'I'm guessing that would be you?'

'Did he leave a message?' Rom was curious.

'Only to say that it was all taken care of.' Meldritch eyed Rom with a hint of wonderment. 'He seemed to be amused about something.'

Yldich lifted an eyebrow. 'Resourceful young man,' he said. 'Pity I don't have time to meet him.'

'We'd better have dinner upstairs, instead of going down to the common room,' Yldich said when they entered their room. 'I think we've attracted enough attention for one day.'

After they had eaten, Yldich began to refill his leather bundles with dried herbs. He was humming softly as he worked. Eald had just started to argue about who should have the first bath, when Rom heard soft music coming from downstairs. He waved vaguely in Eald's direction.

'You go,' he said. Eald ran off without another word. Rom went out into the corridor and sat down on the top of the stairs that led down into the common room. Someone downstairs was playing a harp. The piece was soft and strangely melancholic. Sometimes the notes were tentative, as if the harpist doubted in which direction to go, then they meandered strongly and purposefully, tumbling over each other like water running over stones.

Rom listened breathlessly. The music seemed to flow right through his heart, filling it with longing. He couldn't get himself to leave. He had never heard harping like it in Lord Aldr's Keep, although he had heard musicians play there on occasion. Nothing he had ever heard compared to the playing of the *Einache* harpist downstairs.

After a while, curiosity tempted him to descend a few steps, to see if he could get a glimpse of the musician. He was about to take another step down, when the kitchen girl came up the stairs. She almost bumped into him.

'Excuse me, sir,' she said. 'Just getting the water ready for you.' Her small mouth was pulled into a secretive smile, her eyes downcast. A multitude of skirts brushed against him as she passed in a whiff of soap. Startled, he stepped back, to get out of her way.

He walked back to their rooms to find Eald wringing the water out of his lank hair with a towel. His cheeks were pink. He looked thoroughly soaked.

'You're next,' he said with a happy grin.

Rom went into the washroom, where he found a large wooden tub filled with hot water. He left his worn clothes in a heap on the floor. His new ones lay ready on a low bench. He stepped gingerly into the tub and lay back in the steaming water, slowly relaxing every muscle in his body. He closed his eyes with a contented sigh. He was drowsing, nearly dropping off to sleep, when there was a noise behind him. The door flew open. He jumped, splashing water over the floor as he moved around to face his assailant.

'Sorry to disturb you.' The kitchen maid whirled past and dropped some towels on the bench beside the tub. 'Forgot to give you these.' She giggled and disappeared.

'Girls.' Eald snorted disdainfully when Rom returned, washed, dried and slightly shocked. 'She probably fancies you.' Rom stared at him in perplexity. Yldich chuckled and shook his head.

'Better lock the door, next time you're having a bath.'

They went to bed early that night. Rom was drifting in a deep, dreamless sleep. He was shaken roughly and started. Still half asleep, he backed away instinctively. Someone shook him again.

'Rom. Wake up. The village is burning.' He opened his eyes and looked into Yldich's face. It was grim and set.

'What?' He was completely disoriented. Yldich was already fully clothed. He moved away from Rom's bed and motioned towards the window. A faint red glow illuminated the room. Rom jumped out of bed and grabbed his clothes. He pulled them on quickly, watching the sky with a low, dull sense of dread.

'What's happening?' Eald stumbled into the room, his face swollen with sleep. His eyes widened as he saw the red glow from the window.

'You stay here now, Eald,' Yldich said. He girded on his sword. It was longer and heavier than the slender sword he had given to Rom. The scabbard looked worn and old. 'Stay and bolt the door. We'll be back as soon as we can.' They left him staring after them in dismay.

As Yldich and Rom ran towards the fire, they met people running away from it in a panic, or towards it with buckets and blankets. The thatched roof of a big building not far from the inn was alight. The blaze was spread towards the other roofs by the wind. The house itself was a roaring wall of fire. They heard an alarming tearing sound. The roof was caving in. Rom held his hands at his mouth.

'If they didn't get out in time....' He heard a faint cry far behind them. It came from the gates. He turned around quickly; just fast enough to see the dark silhouette of a watcher, pierced with arrows, tumble from the wall. His throat constricted. 'It's a diversion.' His voice was stifled. 'They're coming from the other side.'

They ran in the direction of the gates and heard the sound of horns, and an indistinct cry that was being picked up by everyone who heard it. It echoed through the streets, passed from one house to another, arousing the whole village. As they paused for a breath they heard it again.

'*Na'Héach*,' a young boy cried as he ran past them towards the gates with a bow and an armload of arrows. Yldich started in surprise. Rom looked at him.

'What does it mean?'

'It—it's an ancient war cry.'

Rom smiled despite an underlying sense of dread. 'Eldairc's doing. He told me he loves the ancient tales.'

When they reached the gates, the fight had already broken out. The attackers used hooks and ropes to climb the walls. The watchers were easily overpowered in man-to-man fights. Others tumbled down the walls, their bodies pierced with arrows.

Rom watched in horror as the riders spilled over the walls and entered the village. They were soon met by villagers armed with rusty swords, kitchen knives, and even pots and pans.

'I doubt they'd counted on such fierce resistance,' Yldich said with a grim smile. He drew his sword. His eyes were like grey ice.

Rom winced as he saw the first villagers slain. Their weapons were hit out of their awkward hands before they could use them. Something stirred deep inside him, a slow, hot anger that made his blood run faster. His breath quickened. He laid a hand on the hilt of the *Einache* sword. A tingling sensation ran through it. It vibrated at a high, almost imperceptible pitch. He took a deep breath and drew it. The motion wakened the blade. It sang softly as it was drawn. Yldich turned and looked Rom in the eyes.

'*Encalimae*,' he said. 'Be careful.' Then he was gone.

Rom watched as if frozen as Yldich engaged the riders. It was like watching a trickling mountain stream change into a roaring river, a summer breeze erupting into a gale. He moved as if he were made out of water, surprising the riders with his swiftness. Before any of them could move, he had disabled three of them with quick, powerful sweeps and thrusts.

A cry to his left caught Rom's attention. Some villagers had gathered to fight off the riders, who were initially taken aback by the fierce counterattack with sticks, mallets and bread knives.

One rider was down. He bled heavily from a blow to the head. But as the fight progressed, the riders gained the upper hand. Two *Einache* men lay dead. Another was cut down before Rom's eyes. Two young *Einache* were still standing. They faced the riders with rusty swords. Their faces were grim and desperate.

Rom's heart sank as he saw one of them was a girl. He threw himself into a run, just as the *Einache* man was hit. He fell back with a smothered cry. The rider was about to kill him with a downward thrust when Rom had reached him. He had to move his sword in an awkward angle to turn the rider's sword. The rider turned his head in surprise. Recognition flared up in his eyes. A look of loathing mixed with wonder crossed his face.

'You.' He cursed and spat on the ground. 'You'll regret this.'

He attacked swiftly and launched vicious strokes at Rom's chest. Rom parried them by pure instinct. He laboured desperately to keep the rider back. Then he heard an angry cry of pain. The other rider had disarmed the girl. She was down on one knee, wincing as she grasped her right arm. Her eyes were on the rusty sword that lay just a few steps away. The rider lifted his sword to cut her down with one heavy stroke.

Rom saw the rider's sword reach its zenith before it would fall. Time stilled around him. A calm sense of purpose filled his heart. He stopped breathing. He stopped thinking. He changed the grip on his sword and set his teeth as he aimed a powerful double-handed blow at the rider. The man fell back heavily, blood spurting from a deep gash. Before he had touched the ground Rom was away, and threw himself between the rider and the girl. He blocked the falling sword and aimed another at the rider. The *Einache* sword slashed through muscle and bone with frightening ease. The rider fell back with a short cry and lay still.

Rom kneeled on the ground, panting, staring at the blood that stained his sword. He shuddered and got up. He saw the girl sit next to the fallen man. He went over to them.

'Are you all right?' he said. The girl lifted her face. She looked at him warily. He winced as he saw the familiar coldness of distrust in her eyes. An old sense of not-belonging, a barren loneliness froze him where he stood. 'You had better go to the inn.' His voice was hoarse. 'There's a *Yaever* staying there called Yldich. He'll treat your wounds.' He turned to walk away.

'Wait,' the girl said. Her voice was melodious and clear. It barely had a trace of an *Einache* accent. He turned around slowly. 'What's your name?'

'I'm Rom.'

'Thank you, Rom.'

He blinked at her, then nodded stiffly. The sound of fighting near the gates drew his attention. 'I've got to go.' He turned and made for the gates. A strange sensation nagged him, like a string attached to his heart, which stretched painfully as he ran away. He pushed the feeling away as he ran.

As he reached the walls, he noticed something had changed. As more villagers were roused by the war cry echoing through the village, the riders began having trouble getting over the walls. While some villagers climbed the walls themselves and fought off those that came up, formations of boys and some girls assailed the riders that got through with bows and arrows. They were surprisingly effective, Rom noticed as he saw another rider fall from the wall with a raw cry, pierced with arrows.

A young boy ran across the street carrying an armload of ammunition. Rom was appalled when he recognized the familiar features and copper hair.

'Eald!' he cried. The boy stopped short and slowly turned to face him. 'What are you doing here? It's far too dangerous outside. Didn't we tell you to stay indoors?'

Eald bit his lip. He lifted his face, and stared up at Rom in defiance. 'The other boys are fighting, too. Besides, you might need my help.'

Rom shook his head in desperation as he saw the boy was serious. 'Have you seen Yldich?' Eald shook his head. 'When you do, stay close to him. I'm going to the gates. And in the name of all the gods, be careful. Stay away from the walls.' Eald nodded. 'And from any riders,' Rom added. Eald nodded again, seemingly meekly. His eyes glittered. 'And *be careful*!' Rom shouted over his shoulder as he began to run towards the gates.

'You said that,' Eald said softly to Rom's back. He stared at him as he disappeared. A look of worry creased his brow.

Why he felt such a persistent need to check on the gates, Rom didn't understand, as the danger seemed to come solely from above, from the top of the walls. He neared the heavy doors that were bolted with a thick slab of oak. The trap door with the iron spikes hadn't been lowered. Obviously someone hadn't thought Eldairc's warning too pressing or serious enough to bother. Rom cursed under his breath, and looked around for the ropes or chains that held the thing in place.

When the tide of riders getting over the wall slowed into a trickle, and the immediate danger seemed over, Yldich sheathed his sword and looked around for Rom. When he didn't see him anywhere near, he deliberated, frowning. Finally, he made a decision. He turned and ran back to the centre of the village, to the house next to the herbalist's shop. The day before, he had learned the village midwife lived there.

Rom stood a few paces before the gates. An acute cold was rising from the ground. At first he thought nothing of it. It was probably just the chill of early morning, though there was no sign of dawn. Then, as the chill persisted and crept up along his body, he frowned. His hands were stiff with cold. His breath came in puffs of cloud. A feeling of unease grew into a sense of alarm. He looked around for the source of his anxiety.

It was then that he noticed dark tendrils of something that looked like mist, seeping through the crack in the wood where the doors met. He walked towards the doors to get a closer look and heard a faint whispering. It seemed to come from behind the doors. The hair in his neck clambered up. He stepped towards the doors as in a dark dream, as if pulled against his will. As he came closer, the whispering became more distinct. It sounded like many voices speaking at once. He did not know the language. It was not *Einache*. The voices filled his head.

These are not the voices of living men.

He recoiled and watched in horror as the door latch began to shudder. It seemed to be moving out of its own accord. He opened his mouth to cry out. No sound would come. He felt faint, indistinct, as if something was drawing him out of his body. Panic went through him in a wave. Paralyzed with fear, there was only one thing he could think of to do. He moved his hand towards the *Einache* sword and closed his stiffened fingers on the hilt.

He drew it with effort. For a moment, it stayed dull, lifeless, and he felt his despair rise, as he was being drained of the last of his energy, his sense of self. Darkness closed in and clouded his vision.

'*Na'Héach*,' he whispered. His voice was barely audible; his mouth was dry. He had started to sway like a tree in a storm. He was about to lose consciousness. The blade slowly began to vibrate. '*Na'Héach*.' His voice gained in strength.

The sword sprang alive and emitted a high, silver tone. It cleared his mind, breaking the voices' stranglehold. He drew back into his body and stumbled backwards, away from the doors. He turned around and began to run.

'To the gates!' he cried as loud as he could. 'To the gates! They're coming through the gates!' Behind him, a heavy blow made the wood crack. Another dislodged the heavy latch.

Yldich roused as many villagers as he could. He sent some elderly women for cloth to tear into strips for bandages. He sent children to the village well to fetch water. A young girl went running to the inn to get his *Yaever* supplies. The others followed him to the midwife's house.

The midwife was a sturdy middle-aged woman called Meryel. She had wayward ginger curls that escaped a thick braid that reached to her waist. They framed a broad, friendly face. Her tranquil grey eyes hid a will as patient and unyielding as an ancient oak.

At a glance at the small gathering in front of her house, she opened her door wide and went to get her tools.

Rom noticed several villagers respond to his call. Men and women of different ages, armed with various tools and weapons came running towards him. They stopped short as they saw the young man who came at them brandishing a sword was a *Tzanatzi*. One of the men, a large, bulky *Einache* who was a woodworker in daily life, took a step forward. He pointed a heavy spear at Rom.

'And who might you be?'

Rom stopped short, the spear point a finger's length away from his chest. 'Listen to me.' His voice was hoarse. 'We've got to lower the trap door. They're breaking through the gates—'

'Isn't that the strange *Tzanatzi* who's been seen in town?' a woman said. 'My niece told me about him... said he'd been starting a brawl....'

'Rom!' Rom was relieved to recognize Eldairc's friendly face among the growing crowd of suspicious ones. Eldairc pushed his way through and laid a hand on the woodworker's arm. 'It's all right, Yeald,' he said. 'He's with us.' The man slowly lowered the spear, his face shadowed with doubt.

'They're breaking through the gates,' Rom cried, his voice edged with frustration. 'Eldairc, someone's got to lower the trap door—'

A spear hurtled through the air. A man to Rom's left fell without a sound. Rom whirled around in dismay. The riders were on them.

Rom caught a glimpse of burning torches, and of a dark, rolling mist. A heavy sword came down towards his head. He blocked it with effort and fought to keep the rider at a distance, waiting for an opportunity to disarm him. The other villagers fought back fiercely with their makeshift weapons.

The woodworker called Yeald used his heavy spear with surprising agility. He used it to ward off blows, and then turned it to strike down several riders at once.

While he held off the first rider, Rom noticed the group of young archers only a few feet away. He caught a glimpse of Eald and cried out to him.

'Eald. The trap door at the gates. Release it!'

Eald nodded wordlessly and cried out a stream of rapid *Einache* to the other children. Two other boys, their bows slung across their backs, joined him in a quick run to the walls, and climbed the steps that were placed at regular intervals. When they had reached the top, they started to hack at the heavy ropes that held the thing in place with their knives.

Keeping an eye both on Eald and on the fight at hand nearly turned out to be fatal. A sharp pain slid across Rom's left arm. He recoiled and tumbled backwards over the body of a villager. A rider leaned over him and lifted his sword to thrust it through his throat.

Before Rom could move, the woodworker loomed behind the rider and struck a blow behind his ear with his spear. The woodworker nodded at Rom and went over to the other *Einache* who were struggling to drive the riders back to the gates. Rom scrambled up, panting, and joined them.

Despite the loss of several *Einache*, the remaining group was growing as more and more villagers came running towards the sounds of the disorganized fight. The crowd was about to become large and wrathful enough to drive the riders back to the splintered gates.

Rom froze. He stared at the gates. Something was pulling at him. The shadows behind the gates were thicker than normal. They seemed to be moving. His breath caught in his throat as he became aware of the lone figure of a woman. She stood in the dark before the gates. Her raven hair spilled over her long cloak and dress, and floated upon the air like a black mist. She reminded him strangely of the *Tzanatzi* woman of his dream. He wondered if she was real. Even though she stood completely still, he got the impression she was looking, no, *feeling* her way around. He shuddered.

Her head went up. She looked with alarming precision straight at the spot where Eald and the other boys were cutting through the thick ropes with their knives. They were engrossed in their task, their backs to the fight below them. The woman uttered a few words. A few riders turned and faced the wall. They aimed their spears at the boys.

Rom felt a red wave of desperate fury. He ceased to think. He threw himself into a run. He flung himself at the riders and knocked a few of them to the ground. He incapacitated one by sheer luck as the man fell onto another rider's knife. Chaos ensued.

'Help him!' Eldairc's cry didn't seem to reach the other *Einache*. Rom disentangled with an effort from the confusion of arms, legs and weapons. He clambered up and faced the riders. A sinking feeling of despair turned his limbs to water. He had managed to get himself cornered.

The wall was behind him. Three riders stood before him. They slowly advanced. Eldairc and the other villagers were too far away and too busy fighting off the riders that had assailed them immediately. They couldn't help him.

Yldich looked up from his work and stared in the distance. It was as if he saw something dark, something alarming, beyond the range of normal vision. It filled him with a vague sense of dread. His scalp prickled. He stood up abruptly. He handed his instruments to a woman who helped him tend to the wounded.
'Tell Meryel I've gone to the gates.'

Rom stared at the riders. He clenched his hands around the hilt of his sword. Fear crept up to him and slid cold fingers over his skin. He shuddered. He remembered what Yldich had said about the fear of death. He faintly tried to let it go. Instead of growing less, the fear only embraced him the more thoroughly, and quenched the fire in his heart that had given him a semblance of courage. He gritted his teeth and decided to try and do as much damage as he could before it was all over.

Yldich left the main street and was in sight of the walls, when he became aware of the disorderly battle that progressed before it. He drew his sword. As he saw the splintered gates and the dark mist that floated over the ground, he felt a chill creep along his spine. Tendrils of mist tentatively reached for his ankles.

A heavy two-handed sword flashed in the light of the torches. Rom sprang back. He blocked it with an effort. The *Einache* sword screeched in protest as it slid across the rider's blade. A second stroke sent him reeling backwards into the wall.

Yldich heard a familiar high, thin wail of metal over the din of the fight. He started to run.

Rom aimed a desperate thrust at the rider. There was not enough room to strike sideways. The rider countered it with a powerful stroke that sent Rom's sword flying. It sang softly as it fell to the ground. The rider struck swiftly. A sharp, white light seared through Rom's chest and blinded him with pain. His own cry echoed in his head.
The rider calmly sheathed his sword as he saw Rom was defenceless. Rom stared at him, clutching at the wound. The sword had cut into his chest just under the collar bone. Blood seeped through his fingers and trickled down

his left arm. He looked left and right for a way of escape. Both ways were blocked by the other riders.

'Well,' the rider said as he drew a knife. 'Looks like you've made a nuisance of yourself for the last time.' Before Rom could move, the man grabbed his tunic and pushed him against the wall. Rom stared into his eyes. The rider set the knife at his throat. He was about to slash it with a strong, efficient movement when he froze. The knife dropped to the ground. Rom blinked. There was an arrow, sticking through the rider's throat.

He stared at it in vague amazement as the rider sagged at his feet. He wanted to move. Instead, he sank down against the wall. He stared at the stars in the dark night sky, and heard the swish of arrows in the air above, the cries of the other riders as they fell. He wondered why he didn't get up. His eyelids were heavy. His mouth was dry as dust.

A shadow passed before him. He blinked and looked into the face of the dark-haired woman. She stood over him and gazed into his face. Her dark eyes were unreadable, her fair, pale face still as a moonlit lake. Then she was gone.

The trap door fell down with a rattling sound. Its heavy iron points buried themselves in the earth. As chance would have it, it killed the last rider, who stood directly beneath it.

Yldich had no trouble finding Rom among the fallen riders. He made straight for the place where he had last heard the shrill cry of the *Einache* sword. Rom lay still against the wall, his clothes soaked with blood. His eyes were open. Yldich dropped down before him and took his hand. It was cold. He felt for his pulse. 'Rom. Can you hear me?'

Rom blinked slowly. Eldairc dropped on the ground beside Yldich. He was panting, wiping sweat and blood off his brow.

'He threw himself straight at them.' He stared at Rom's ashen face. 'Never seen anything like it. Don't think he even knows how to use that sword properly.'

Yldich lifted a brow at his rambling. 'You must be Eldairc.' The young man nodded. 'I'm Yldich. We must get him to the inn as swiftly as possible. If you carry him, I'll keep pressure on the wound.' Eldairc stared at Rom's blood-soaked tunic and swallowed. He nodded. A rasping sound came from Rom's mouth. They looked up.

'*Tzanatzi* sorcery... outside the gates....' Rom closed his eyes.

Eldairc stared at him. 'He must be delirious....'

'I doubt it.' Yldich's face was grim. He tore a strip of cloth from his shirt for a makeshift bandage. He padded the wound with a piece of bandage he still had in his pocket and rolled the cloth tightly around Rom's shoulder.

Eald dropped from the steps. 'We shot the riders. Is he all right?' He stared at the blood in horror.

'Eald, run to the inn and boil some water,' Yldich said. 'And get all the blankets you can find.'

When they had reached the inn, Eldairc carried Rom upstairs. Yldich took Eald aside.

'Eald, can you find the herbalist's house?' The boy nodded. 'Next to it is the house of Meryel, the midwife. Tell her I'm here if she needs me. And get my *Yaever* bags.' Eald was still pale, his narrow face taut and serious. Yldich laid a hand on his shoulder. 'And don't touch my *Yaever* things, if you know what's good for you.' A flicker of mirth lit his eyes. Eald's mouth pulled into a skewed grin. A little colour returned to his face. He nodded and took off.

Yldich went into the kitchen and came out with an armload of supplies. He heard Eldairc call out.

'Yldich! Come quickly. Something's wrong....'

He ran up the stairs as quickly as he could. Eldairc had laid Rom on a bed and covered him with blankets. He was alarmingly pale. His lips were blue. He was convulsing, his breathing fast and shallow. He stared vaguely in their direction, his eyes wide and anxious. Eldairc wondered if he recognized them at all.

Yldich dropped his things on the floor. He took Rom's hand and laid a hand on his brow. It was damp with cold sweat.

'Rom. It's all right.' He addressed Eldairc without taking his eyes off Rom's face. 'Eldairc, get those pillows and put them under his legs. And make a pot of tea with those herbs. Lots of honey.' Eldairc moved swiftly. He heard Yldich murmur behind him.

'Don't leave us now, lad.' Yldich began to hum softly under his breath, slow, meandering notes that cleared the atmosphere like waves of light. Eldairc noticed the humming had a calming effect. He turned back to the bed with the bowl. Colour was coming back to Rom's face. His breathing had steadied. Yldich accepted the bowl and was about to bring it to Rom's mouth, when he managed to speak.

'The dead,' Rom whispered. Eldairc raised his brows. 'The dead... at the gates...'

Eldairc stared at Yldich. 'What's he talking about?'

Yldich shook his head in puzzlement. He swallowed away a sense of unease. He turned to Rom. 'I'll make sure the walls are guarded at all times. I'll use my own *Yaever* tricks.' He smiled. Rom seemed to be reassured. He drank some of the heavily laced tea. Yldich helped him lay back.

'Eald... is he all right?' Rom said.

'He's fine,' Yldich said. 'In fact I think he shot your assailant.' Rom managed a faint smile.

'He said I might need him....' he sighed and closed his eyes again. 'Sorry about the mess....' Yldich shook his head.

'Don't worry. Get some sleep now, Rom.' Rom nodded faintly. He dropped off immediately.

He woke feeling feverish and hungry. He tried to sit up, and winced. Eldairc was in the chair next to his bed. A large, leather bound book was in his lap. He looked up and smiled.

'*Ya'hey*',' he said. 'Good to see you awake.'

Rom looked at him. He felt strangely light-headed and disoriented. '*Ya'hey*'.' He looked around. Sunlight entered the room at a sharp angle. 'Where... where's Yldich?'

'Off to sleep, finally,' Eldairc said. 'He's been up for two nights now. Wouldn't leave until he was sure you were alive and staying that way. Meryel, that's the midwife, she threatened to put some sleeping draught in his tea when he wasn't looking.' He grinned. 'But he agreed to go and get some sleep if I promised to stay here while he was gone.' He pulled a pillow up behind Rom's back so he could sit up.

'Two nights....' Rom sat back. He carefully touched his left arm. It was bound from elbow to shoulder. More bandages covered his chest.

'You know, if it comes to stubbornness and wanting to get their way, I wouldn't know who to put my money on, the *Yaever* or the midwife,' Eldairc said. 'They're both as bad as each other.'

Rom swallowed. 'Eldairc... do you think you could get me something to eat?'

Eldairc sprang up. 'Of course! Here I am, talking your ear off while you're just returned from the dead. Well, not literally,' he added as he saw the look on Rom's face. 'I'll be right back.'

He returned a few moments later with a bowl of soup. It had a muddy brown colour and unidentifiable greens floating in it. It smelled strongly of herbs. Rom wrinkled his nose at it.

'I know.' Eldairc smiled in sympathy. 'But Meryel says it's good for you. You lost a lot of blood you know.'

He tried to force down the unappealing meal by himself but in the end Eldairc had to help him for his hands trembled too much to hold the bowl steady. After he had finished, he sank back into the cushions and closed his eyes. Eldairc was telling him of the battle; his voice droned on pleasantly in the background, like the sound of bees in summer. Rom let his awareness float with it until he drifted away in a fuzzy haze.

He stood at the edge of a large elevated plateau and looked north over a vast plain below. The wind was in the West and blew strands of midnight hair across his eyes. He brushed them away and felt for the hilt of the long, double-handed sword. The silver dragon's head shaped itself under his fingertips. He heard the sounds of clashing swords, the swish-and-thump of many arrows. He looked down.

A battle was taking place. In the east, he saw many *Einache* warriors, tall, red and golden haired men with long swords and battle axes. They were outnumbered by the dark army that threatened from the west.

Two *Einache* warriors desperately fought to keep back the black tide of swordfighters that threatened to overwhelm them, their swords flashing silver in the light of the moon. He recognized their faces and started to run.

Somehow he got down the plateau and onto the battlefield. As he reached the place where he had seen Yldich and Eldairc fight, he drew the dragon-headed sword. They turned and looked at him. There was no sign of recognition in their faces. To his astonishment and utter horror, Yldich lifted his sword and aimed it at his head.

He woke gasping for air. He was fighting off the sheepskins in a feverish sweat. Someone tried to keep him down. He opened his eyes and looked straight into the face of a tall woman with a broad face and ginger curls. He stopped struggling and stared at her.

'Easy, now.' She had a kind, steady voice. It was calm and unrelenting as the sea.

The room was dimly illuminated by the light of a few candles. The woman took some of the heavy blankets away and returned with a bowl of tea that smelled strongly of sage. She helped him sit up and held the bowl up for him so he could drink.

After he had finished, she sat for a while, staring at his face. He began to feel uneasy under her gaze. He shifted nervously. She seemed to suddenly realize she was staring.

'I'm sorry,' she said. 'I'm Meryel. I've been looking after you with Yldich these last couple of days.'

'Why—why were you looking at me like that?'

She sighed. 'Well, it's been about five hundred years since the *Tzanatzi* were seen around these parts.' She had a stronger *Einache* accent than Yldich or Eldairc. 'For some of us, the sight comes as a bit of a shock.' He felt a strange pain under his heart.

'Why?' he whispered.

'Well,' she said, 'I guess in the ages past, the image of your people has grown into something... legendary, something demonic.' He felt an old sadness well up and swallowed. Fever made him speak more openly than he was wont to do.

'When they look at me like that, it's as if the weight of all those dead is on me.' Meryel shook her head. She took his hand and pressed it carefully.

'Don't take it on yourself,' she said softly. 'It was ages ago. It's not your fault.' It was like hearing an echo of Yldich's words. Meryel smiled. 'After the day before yesterday, you should expect the people of this village look at you a little differently. Eald and Eldairc have seen to that. And the harpist.'

He looked up in surprise. 'What do you mean?'

She shook her head. 'You'll see.'

After Rom had finished the bowl of sage tea, Meryel changed the dressing on his chest. She made a rumbling sound in the back of her throat, and frowned at the wound as if it offended her personally. The edges were closing, but the skin around it was an angry red.

'Infection,' she said curtly. She crushed some dried herbs into a bowl of hot water. The sharp, clear smell reminded Rom of the green paste Yldich had made. As she cleaned the wound, Rom winced and set his teeth. Meryel only nodded as if his pain confirmed her opinion. After she had padded and bound his chest, she pulled a fresh tunic over his head and let him sink back into the pillows like a rag doll, shaky and exhausted. He did not hear her leave.

He woke with the bright light of the early morning sun seeping through his eyelashes. Something moved at the end of the bed. He blinked in an effort to focus.

'Rom.' Yldich perched on the edge of his bed like a large owl. He peered into his face.

'*Ya'hey.*' Rom's voice was hoarse with thirst. A smile lit up Yldich's eyes.

'*Ya'hey.*' He poured some water in a cup. Rom sat up carefully. Fever made him feel peculiarly weightless. Yldich helped him hold the cup so he could drink. He pulled up some pillows behind Rom's back. Rom sat back and wiped the hair out of his eyes.

'What happened?' he said huskily.

Yldich raised a brow. 'Before or after you threw yourself at the riders?'

Rom fidgeted with his cup. 'They were about to... kill Eald and the other boys... I stopped thinking.' Yldich nodded.

'You let yourself be led by your anger again. It nearly got you killed.' Rom stared at the sheepskins. Yldich pressed his hand. 'They would have been slaughtered if it hadn't been for your ill-advised action.' He grinned. 'And that wasn't the only thing you did, if the stories I hear around town are true.' The familiar lights of amusement were dancing in his eyes.

'What do you mean?'

'Well, there are tales going around about a handsome and ferocious dark warrior who mysteriously appeared out of nothing, rescued *Einache* by reducing riders to shreds, bowed courteously and vanished like a figure out of an old ballad.' He chuckled. Rom stared at him.

'Handsome?'

'Also, there is a tale going round about a lone *Tzanatzi* warrior who sided with the *Einache*, and held off the riders before the gates with a legendary singing sword. I suspect Eldairc is responsible for that one.' Yldich shook his head and grinned. 'That young man has an overactive imagination.' His expression sobered. 'Which reminds me.' He looked at Rom. 'What was it you saw at the gates?' Rom swallowed.

'A dark mist,' he said in a low voice. 'I heard strange voices. Before the gates. I don't think they were... the voices of living men. I heard them in my head. They... pulled me out of myself.'

Yldich's eyes narrowed to a piercing stare. 'What happened?'

'I remembered the ancient battle cry Eldairc taught the villagers. It woke the sword. The sword... sang me back.'

Yldich rubbed his face and held his chin in his hand, deep in thought. It was as if for a moment he'd forgotten Rom was there. Rom studied him. The faint lines on his brow seemed deeper than usual. The morning sun caught some silver in his short beard Rom had not noticed before.

'I saw the mist,' Yldich said. 'Something not of this plane was seeping through the gates. I felt it before I saw it—'

'There was a strange dark-haired woman,' Rom said. Yldich looked up. 'She appeared before the gates... as if she was connected to the mist. She seemed to be... feeling her way around. It was unnerving....'

'A *Tzanatzi* woman?' Yldich looked baffled. 'Well. For centuries, no Tzanatzi has dared set foot across the border. And now, we have *two*.'

Rom shook his head. 'There was something eerie about her, as if she wasn't... real. Though she seemed in league with the riders.'

'Are you sure?'

'It's all become a bit of a blur....' Rom closed his eyes. Talking had drained him. Yldich touched his shoulder.

'You'd better get some rest. I have to get back to Meryel's house to check on the other wounded.' Rom opened his eyes.

'How many are there?'

'Two dozen, not counting the dead and the ones I've already lost.' Yldich raised himself from the bed. His face was grim. 'We buried about twenty riders.'

After Yldich had left, Meryel had a kitchen boy bring up some soup. Apparently, Rom thought as he stirred the broth and tried to identify the lumps that floated on its surface, she now trusted him with a meal that had a little more substance to it.

He ate some of the soup and slept for a few hours. He woke up with a faint sense of boredom. Restlessness had settled in his bones. He looked around for something to distract him, and found the big, leather-bound book Eldairc had left lying on the chair. He took it back to the bed and settled in the cushions and sheepskins, huddled in a blanket.

The book smelled pleasantly of age and sun-faded parchment, the creased, ancient leather was soft under his fingers. He leafed through it slowly. The *Einache* writing danced before his eyes, short, sturdy letters made with strokes and slashes that made him wonder if they had once been based on the scratching of stone onto stone.

He found sketches of trees, flowers and plants, their delicate leaves and blossoms lovingly drawn and coloured with what must once have been bright reds, greens and blues. Another section seemed to deal with kinds of animals. Then he came across pictures of different kinds of habitation. His heartbeat quickened as he recognized the simple, round clay-and-reed houses from his dream. He wondered if any *Einache* still lived in such houses. He planned to ask Yldich about it later.

He turned the page. A whole chapter was dedicated to ships. He frowned, deep in thought. The *Einache* had never had anything to do with ships, as far as he knew. They kept to their forests and fields. He turned another page and saw some drawings of weaponry. His breath stuck in his throat as his gaze fell on a detailed drawing of a dragon-headed sword. The blood drained from his face.

When Yldich returned to their rooms, he found Rom at the head of the bed in a heap of scattered cushions, his face ashen, his dark eyes fixed on a large leather book in his lap.

'Rom. What's wrong?'

Rom looked up. He had a faraway look in his eyes. He pointed at the pages that lay open before him. 'What does it say?' he said, pointing at the *Einache* words he could not read.

'It's... a description of a *Tzanatzi* weapon,' Yldich said carefully.

'What kind?' Rom whispered. He had closed his eyes. He didn't need to look at the page. The image of the dragon-headed sword was burned into his mind. Yldich hesitated.

'It... was once wielded by the *Tzanatzi* mage, the one who was slain to end the Battle of Gardeth,' he said slowly. Tears were running over Rom's face. He seemed oblivious to them. A pained expression was in his face.

'Why would I dream of such a sword belonging to me?' he whispered. Yldich stared at him.

'Tell me of your dream.' His voice was strangely flat. Rom took a deep breath. He dug his fingers into the sheepskin, grasping at the fleece.

'It was a nightmare. I was standing at the edge of a large plain. A battle was going on. I was wearing a sword, *that* one.' He motioned at the page. 'I saw you and Eldairc nearly overrun and I ran across the battle-field to help you. You didn't recognize me.' A mirthless laugh escaped his mouth. 'You were about to kill me when I woke up.' He let go of the fleece and wiped a hand across his face. He looked at the wet streaks on it in surprise.

Yldich sat down on the bed. He stared in the distance, not-seeing.

'What does it mean?' Rom whispered. 'Why would I dream a thing like that?' Yldich met his eyes.

'I'm not sure,' he said softly. 'I told you once before, somehow you are connected to this ancient history.'

Rom's eyes darkened. 'Somehow I've got the feeling you know more than you are telling me.'

Yldich released an inaudible sigh. 'If I do, it is because I am not sure about these things myself.' Rom stared at him. Yldich startled him by taking his hands. 'Please trust me in this,' he said gently. 'I'm telling you all I safely can.' Rom swallowed and cast down his eyes. Yldich got up and went to the door. 'I'll get you something else to eat,' he said, lifting a brow at the remains of the lumpy soup.

Rom looked up. The question he had not known how to ask suddenly formed into words.

'Yldich,' he said. There was something in his voice that made Yldich stop. He turned around slowly. 'If I ask you a question, will you give me a straightforward answer?' Yldich nodded warily. 'How often do legendary *Yaever* walk out of five hundred year old tales to go south, searching for lone *Tzanatzi*?' Yldich drew a deep breath.

'A far as I know,' he said in a soft voice, 'this is the first time.' Rom began to shake. He closed his eyes. A buzzing sound was in his ears. He vaguely felt around for something to hold onto. A cup was pushed into his hand.

'Drink this.' He nearly choked on the fiery liquid. 'Easy, now.' He opened his eyes and coughed. His vision had cleared.

'How,' Rom said, 'how old are you, exactly?' To his dismay, Yldich chuckled.

'After about two centuries, you stop counting the years.' Something glittered in Yldich's eyes like the sun sparkling in clear, sea-grey water. Rom stared at him. He felt faint. 'Better have another,' Yldich said. The cup was pushed into his hands again. Rom managed to swallow a second gulp without choking.

'I'm getting better at this.' He sounded surprised.

Yldich grinned. 'You get used to it.'

Rom sat looking at him for a while in silence. 'What—what are you?' He suddenly wondered if he really wanted to know.

'I told you,' Yldich said. He sat down on the sheepskins at his ease. 'I'm a *Yaever*.'

'Do all *Yaever* grow to be as old as you?'

'They used to.' Yldich's eyes were clouded for a moment by a vague sadness. 'Times have changed. I'm one of the last of the ancient *Yaever*.'

Rom was taken by a strange thought. 'Are you—are you human?'

Yldich looked at him. 'Are you?'

'What do you mean?' Rom whispered. A strange anxiety tugged at his mind.

'Well,' Yldich said, 'it all depends on your definition.' Rom stared in the distance. The image of whirling snowflakes and glittering ice-crystals suddenly appeared in his mind's eye.

'The Northern wind,' he said softly. Yldich started. 'You're connected to it in some way.'

Yldich looked at him, perplexed. 'How did you know?'

'I felt it—when you helped me travel in the dream-state,' Rom said. 'To know *Eärwe*. I... became you for a moment.' Yldich stared at him. Rom's thoughts suddenly took a different course. He looked up. 'Does Eald know?' Yldich shook his head. His expression had sobered.

'Besides my family and the people of my House, you are one of the few who know this. I would ask you to keep it to yourself for the time being.' Rom nodded slowly. 'And whatever you do, do not breathe a word of this to Eldairc.' Yldich snorted with wry amusement. 'Or you might as well have it cried around town.'

Rom held his face in his hands. 'I wonder how much he's already guessed,' he said through his fingers.

Yldich went downstairs and returned balancing some bowls on a tray. A whirl of red and dusty green ducked under his arm and landed on the bed, scattering the pillows.

'Rom!' A clumsy embrace had Rom reeling. He steadied himself, leaning on his left arm without thinking. Pain made him hiss in a sharp breath through his teeth. Yldich made a grumbling sound.

'Careful now, Eald.'

The boy drew back and studied Rom's face. 'You look better.' A tentative smile dispersed the worry in his face. 'I'm glad. You looked horrible last time. I thought you were going to die.' He paused to take in air. 'Yldich wouldn't let me see you earlier. Said it would be too tiring for you.' He shot an accusatory look at Yldich's back. Yldich, well aware of the glance, only lifted an eyebrow. He turned and handed Rom a bowl filled with stew.

Rom gazed at Eald. Somehow, it seemed as if the boy had grown taller in the last few days. The crisp, savoury smell of autumn clung to his clothes. His face was flushed with colour; his copper hair was swept into a tangled mass by the wind. His grey eyes glittered.

'You look well,' Rom said. 'What have you been doing with yourself?'

'Me and the other boys have been taking turns patrolling the walls. Yldich's taught me some new *Yaever* tricks to chase off spooks.' Eald grinned. Rom's eyes widened with slight dismay. Yldich took a seat on the edge of the bed.

'After what you said happened to you at the gates, I didn't want to take any chances.'

Rom tried to send Yldich a worried glance without Eald noticing. 'Are you sure they're safe?'

'As safe as they can be, in these times.'

That evening, restlessness had Rom itch to get out and do something, any other thing than to lay in bed. Yldich had just returned to their rooms when Rom voiced his feelings.

'You'd better get a wash and a shave before you do anything else,' Yldich said. 'Let me know if you need any help.'

To get to the washroom, wash and change his clothes took more of Rom's strength than he had anticipated. He had to sit down frequently for fear of toppling over. His muscles trembled alarmingly. It was disconcerting that a few days in bed could leave him so weak.

He was sitting cross-legged on the wooden bench and shaving as Yldich walked in to check on his bandages. Yldich looked at him with slight surprise. Rom refrained from looking in the mirror, a sheet of polished metal that hung on the other wall. He habitually felt his way while he shaved. The sharp knife moved with the ease of familiarity.

'Tell me, Rom. Don't you ever use a mirror?' Yldich said.

'I don't need to. I know what I look like.'

'Do you, now.' Yldich lifted an eyebrow. 'How?'

Rom shrugged before he continued scraping the sharp knife across his cheek. 'The look in people's eyes tells me all I need to know.' There was a faint bitter tone to his voice. He put down the razor and dried his face with a washcloth.

'What people, exactly?'

'Everyone.' Rom shook his head in impatience. 'My mother, the people from my village, the people at Aldr's Keep... the *Einache* in Woodbury....'

Yldich held his head to one side. 'Maybe their eyes weren't the most trustworthy mirrors. Maybe you should look for yourself.'

Rom's eyes turned black. He put down the cloth. 'I know what you're trying to do.' Sudden tears of anger or fear, he could not tell which, tried to push to the surface of his eyes. He blinked angrily. 'I won't do it. I won't look. You can't make me.' He was surprised by his own vehemence.

'If you don't look, you'll never know for sure,' Yldich said softly. 'I won't make you do anything you don't want to do. But Rom, shouldn't you at least see the truth for yourself?' Rom had started shaking. The mirror was only a step away. 'Come on, now,' Yldich said. He took Rom by the shoulders and coaxed him gently towards the shiny surface of the mirror.

Rom stood trembling before the mirror. He drew a deep breath and looked up. He saw a second Yldich in the mirror, the familiar broad shoulders, the ginger hair and short beard, the bright grey eyes. Beside him stood a young man he didn't recognize. He saw a pale face sketched in graceful, slender lines, dark, slightly curved brows shading eyes like a warm midnight sky, which stared back into his own. As he put his hands to his mouth in shock, the young man did the same, putting strong, slender fingers to a well-formed mouth the colour of a pale winter sunrise. His breath stuck in his throat.

'I thought as much,' Yldich said.

'That's—that's not me,' Rom whispered through his fingers.

'What did you expect to see?'

'Someone... someone dark and repugnant, someone detestable.' Tears were running down his face.

Yldich released a slow sigh. A fleeting sadness crossed his face. 'Relying on other people's vision isn't always the wisest thing to do.'

Rom sat staring at his hands in a daze as Yldich changed his bandages.

Yldich sent him back to their rooms so he could clear up the washroom. 'We'll go have a drink downstairs in a moment. I'll be right with you.' Rom walked slowly, trailing the fingers of his right hand along the wall for balance.

When Yldich got back to their room, he found Rom slumped in a chair, deeply asleep. When he didn't respond to his name, Yldich carried him over to the bed and pulled some blankets over him. He stood gazing down at him for a while. Images from a past long gone filled his eyes, blotting out the present. They were darkened by an old sadness. He gently pushed aside the hair that had fallen over Rom's brow.

'*Nâstréhi ea,*' he said softly. He sighed and turned away.

That night, Rom walked a path through a thick layer of virgin snow. The boughs of the trees were heavy with it; the sun glinted on the snow crystals and made them glitter like tiny gems. The Forest was eerily quiet but for the crunching of his boots on the snowy path.

He reached the doors of a great wooden house. They were large doors, high and wide, wide enough to let several men on horseback pass through. They were made of sturdy oak and fortified with iron. One of the doors was open. The warm light of candles and hearths streamed out onto the snow. He became acutely aware of the cold. It had seeped through his clothes, chilled his skin, and settled in his bones. He shivered.

A tall, slender girl stood in the doorway, framed by the amber light. Her hair was a blaze of colour, red and gold, as if it were kin to the open fire in the hearths behind her.

When he reached her, he noticed they were of equal height, her sea-grey eyes level with his dark ones. He stood still. A vague sense of expectancy made his heart beat faster. They stood so close to each other he could feel her breath on his face. She reached out a hand and lightly touched his cheek. He shuddered. Her eyebrows pulled into a puzzled frown. She whispered.

Who are you?

He woke up with the light of the sun blazing into the room. Judging by the angle of the light, it was late afternoon. He stirred.

'Finally! I thought you were going to sleep the day away.'

He turned his head to see Eldairc grinning at him from the side of the bed. '*Ya'hey,*' he said, and yawned.

Eldairc chuckled. '*Ya'hey* to you too. Now get out of bed before you go into hibernation.' The tall *Einache* directed a steam of talk at him before he had managed to sit up. 'Yldich told me to go and get you to get up and to eat some normal food,' he began while Rom crawled out from under the heap of blankets and sheepskins. 'He's busy helping Meryel right now or he would chase you out of bed himself. I've had the kitchen girl heat some water for the washing room. Can you manage by yourself? I'll be here while you get ready. Don't take too long, now....'

Eldairc's voice followed Rom through the hall as he made for the washing room. He looked around carefully before he entered, mindful of the incident with the kitchen girl.

He paused a moment to look at the stranger in the mirror. He blinked at the dark young man, still taken aback. It would take time to get used to his face.

The sun was setting when Rom and Eldairc went down into the common room. Rom walked carefully, using the backs of chairs to steady himself. Eldairc had fastened a sling around his neck to rest his arm in. He ushered him into the room and helped him into a big chair by the hearth. The fire had already been lit. Eldairc got Rom a bottle of mead and a cup.

'Prefer beer, myself,' he said. 'Be right back.'

Rom took a sip of mead and leaned back in his chair, half closing his eyes. He felt someone's gaze on him. He opened his eyes and stared into the face of Yeald, the woodworker. He had been about to go home, when he had noticed Rom sitting by the fire.

'Well, how are you now?' He took a seat opposite Rom.

'All right, I suppose.' Rom shifted gingerly in his seat. His thoughts went back to the night of the battle, when the big man had pointed a spear at his chest. It seemed ages ago. 'I have you to thank for that....' The man made a movement with his right hand as if to say it was nothing.

'Fighting didn't entirely agree with you.' He motioned at Rom's bandaged arm in the sling. He took a sip of mead and looked at him.

'Well, I'm not a warrior.' Rom stared at his hands.

'I could see that.' The woodworker gazed at Rom, his calm, grey-eyed gaze curious. 'What are you, then?'

Rom hesitated. He tried to grasp at the shreds of his old identity. They eluded him. He pulled at his hair in vague despair. A flare of inspiration hit him.

'I'm a lost *Tzanatzi*, travelling north to fulfil a secret purpose foretold in a *Yaever* dream,' he said, enlivened by his own words. His dark eyes glinted. He smiled mysteriously. The woodworker shook his head at him.

'Don't get carried away, lad. You've been listening to Eldairc's stories, I wager. Also, I suspect you have had quite enough of this stuff.' He finished his mead in one gulp and got up, groaning a little with effort. Before he left the room, he placed a big, calloused hand on Rom's right shoulder. 'Take care, now.'

Tentative harping caught Rom's attention. He turned his head and peered across the common room. In the far corner of the room, beside the other hearth, someone was tuning a great harp. Rom left his seat by the fire and went over to the other side of the room. He sat down quietly, so as not to disturb the harpist. He saw with surprise that it was a girl. Her auburn hair fell over her face, partly obscuring it from view. He saw a softy curved cheek, a small nose, dark eyelashes shading eyes the colour of which he couldn't discern.

She played a slow, sweet piece. The notes she plucked from the strings reminded him of dewdrops falling from branches, catching the light of the sun. He closed his eyes and let the music run through him. The song quickened; the notes were like liquid sunlight, running through his veins, making his heart swell. He let himself be taken away, sometimes drifting, then hurried along by dazzling glissandos. After a while the music slowed down again, trickling away. He sighed regretfully and opened his eyes. He started. The harpist was staring straight at him. It was the girl he had saved from the riders. Her eyes were a dark amber that was almost brown.

'*Ya'hey,*' he said.

'I know you,' she said in a clear voice. 'You're the mysterious stranger I've been singing about.' Her mouth curved mischievously, making her face look boyish.

A thought occurred to Rom. 'Did you start those rumours about a fierce *Tzanatzi* warrior?'

She plucked a dramatic chord. 'I may have been embellishing somewhat, for artistic effect.' She winced as she stretched her muscles. Rom noticed her right arm had been bandaged up to the wrist. 'If you hadn't shown up when you did, I wouldn't be here to embellish at all,' she said.

He shifted, looking at his feet.

'I'm Alyra,' she said.

'I'm Rom.'

She smiled. 'I know.'

'What was that song you were playing?'

She shifted her gaze to the harp. 'It's very old. I don't know what it's called. I learned it when I was little.'

'Would you play it again? I could listen to you play all evening. I would even forget to eat,' he said.

She smiled. Her face, while pleasant and fairly unremarkable, would spring into wild beauty now and then, when she smiled. '*Beware the song of the Náeriae,*' she said, her eyes alight, '*for it will lure men even from their deathbed.*' Rom stared at her. 'It's an *Einache* saying,' she said, as she saw the bewildered look on his face. She chuckled, and looked boyish again. 'A *Náeria* is a female harpist.'

Rom studied her face. He had never met a girl like her before. Her shifting features and manner perplexed him. She was nothing like the girls he had met in the South. He had no idea how to talk to her. But then, he had had no idea how to talk to Southern girls either. They had never seemed to want anything to do with him. He decided to just say anything that came into his head. He wondered if it was the mead deciding for him. He had had nothing to eat since he had come out of bed that day.

She played for him a while, some country dances, a funny song about a little troll that skipped and skidded, and made him laugh. Then a slow, sensual song which stirred something deep within him. He sighed as she finished. A big hand landed on his shoulder and he jumped.

'There you are.' As Eldairc saw the faraway look on Rom's face, a glint of amusement sparked in his eyes. 'I'm sorry I took so long. I sort of got sidetracked on my way to the kitchen.' He grinned. 'Anyway, I've ordered some food. You look like you could use it,' he added, as he noted Rom's pale face and the feverish glitter in his eyes. He turned to the harpist, and bowed almost imperceptibly. '*Ya'haeve, Náeria* Alyra.'

She smiled at him. '*Ya'haeve,* Eldairc.'

'I'm glad your injury hasn't impaired your mastery of the harp. That was beautiful.' Rom heard a note of respect in Eldairc's voice he hadn't heard in it before. It was devoid of irony. He wondered about it absently.

Alyra smiled. 'I had a gracious audience.'

'I'll take him off your hands to have some supper.' Eldairc started to pull Rom out of his chair.

'Good night, Rom. I'm looking forward to see you again.' The fire struck sparks off the golden inlay of Alyra's harp and her auburn hair. Rom nodded at her, dumbfounded. He let Eldairc drag him along to the other side of the room.

Not long after they had taken a seat at one of the tables, the serving boy put two plates before them. Rom hadn't known he was that hungry until the smell of roast meat wafted up from his plate. It was wonderful to eat real food instead of the nasty broths Meryel had been feeding him.

'Listen, Rom, I feel that I should warn you.' Eldairc looked at him from the other side of the table.

'Warn me? About what?'

'What do you know about *Einache* culture? In particular, what do you know about *Náeriae*?'

'About Né—the *Náeriae*, next to nothing, I suppose.' Rom wondered where the young *Einache* was heading.

'*Náeriae* are not like other *Einache* women,' Eldairc said. 'They are... *aguéri*, divinely inspired, and therefore... sacrosanct, I guess you would call it in your language. They travel from village to village, sometimes staying for days, sometimes for years, as it suits them. They don't take husbands, they remain free all their lives.' His eyes sparkled mischievously. 'Which isn't to say they don't take lovers.' Rom felt the blood rush to his face.

'So why are you telling me this?'

'Well,' Eldairc said carefully, 'as someone who has had his heart broken by a *Náeria* before, I'm merely warning you. They can be extremely fickle. They love with great abandon, but it seldom lasts.' Rom shifted uneasily in his seat.

'I don't know what you're telling me this for....'

'Of course you don't.' Eldairc grinned. He turned the conversation to other matters. 'Did you see the gold inlay on that harp? No-one knows how to do such intricate work anymore. It's a lost art.'

'How do you know?'

'Well, I work for Teldric, the village smith. Amongst other things. I never could stick to one job.' He smiled with wry self-knowledge. 'Teldric is easy on me because he knows I won't be any good otherwise.'

'What other things do you do?'

'Oh, I copy gold and silver work, like on Alyra's harp, I make jewellery, I study old texts, I work as a carpenter, I hunt... and for the last couple of days, I've been trying my hand at sword-fighting.' Rom raised his brows. 'I don't want to be taken by surprise like that ever again.' Eldairc's usual cheery face was grim. 'I've even been thinking of remaking that antique sword of yours.'

A cough that was a little too loud to be discrete halted their conversation. The innkeeper, Meldritch, had suddenly appeared at their table. 'Well now, gentlemen, I trust everything is to your satisfaction?'

Rom looked up at his face. The man looked straight at him. He obviously expected him to answer. Something in his ruddy face was different. He couldn't quite define it. 'Yes, thank you,' he said.

'If there's anything else you need now, please don't hesitate to call for me.'

'Thank you,' Rom said, somewhat flustered. The man nodded at them politely and left. Rom turned a look of wonder at Eldairc. The young man chuckled.

'He's had to revise his opinion of *Tzanatzi* warriors somewhat.' His green eyes glinted. 'You didn't know, but one of the boys you saved is his sister's son.'

The next few days, Yldich woke Rom early each morning and sent him on a series of small errands. Some of which had him walk all the way across the village to see how a patient of his was doing, or across a field to get a certain herb for his *Yaever* work. It took some time before Rom realized the tasks were really meant to get him out and about. He smiled wryly when he found out that *Eletheria Kaména,* a supposedly rare and special specimen that grew only in the shade of a particular ancient oak at the other side of the village was really a common cooking herb that could be found in the cupboard of any *Einache* kitchen.

Eldairc was shaking with suppressed laughter when he enlightened him. Rom resisted the urge to go and throw the thing at Yldich's head when he realized he had grown strong enough to do so in the first place.

Yldich only chuckled when he confronted him. 'I had to give you something to do to get your strength back. Eldairc wanted to practice sword fighting, but you weren't strong enough yet for that.'

'Well, at any rate you've expanded your knowledge of *Einache* vegetables.' Eldairc snorted with amusement. Rom grumbled, trying to hold on to the remains of his dignity.

In the evenings Rom, Eald and Yldich usually had dinner together. Sometimes Eldairc joined them, and told them of the latest goings on in the village, the progress he made on making his first sword. Sometimes, Rom could hear Alyra play in the background. Her harping pulled at him, drawing him subtly, the notes like tiny fingers tickling his skin, filling his heart with wonder and a vague longing.

One evening he wondered if this was what Yldich's rabbits felt as they were pulled in irresistibly by his song. He grinned sheepishly.

'What's the matter, lad?' Yldich said.

He shook his head. 'Nothing.'

Though there had been no sign of hostile activity in the vicinity of Woodbury since 'The Battle', as it was now officially called, the villagers remained wary and did not go beyond shouting distance of the gates. The repairs were well on their way. Several tall, sturdy oaks had been felled on the border of the Forest and dragged to the clear space before the old gates. Woodworkers, carpenters and volunteers had been busy sawing the trunks into thick planks and fitting them together. The village smith was working on the iron fortifications.

It was a clear, sunny autumn day when Rom stood watching the new gate being put into place. He had got up that morning aware of a new sense of well-being. He realized it was because he could move without pain. The weakness of the first days of his recovery had left him. He turned his face to the sun and closed his eyes, basking in the mellow light.

As the great iron bars were put into place, he felt Yldich's presence beside him.

'We'll have to get ready to leave soon,' Yldich said. 'We mustn't linger here.'

Rom turned his head to look at him. Though Yldich looked completely at ease, there was something in his eyes that hinted at some inner disquiet.

'What are you worried about, Yldich?'

'Winter.'

That day Eldairc insisted Rom practice sword fighting with him. With the help of Teldric, the smith, he had made an *Einache* sword that was nearly identical to Rom's. Rom trailed a finger over the symbols that curled along the blade and looked at the sword with amazement.

'It's not perfect, but it will do.' Eldairc shook his hair out of his face and eyed the work of his hands with a proud smile.

'Better practice outside the gates,' Yldich said. 'It won't do to attract unnecessary attention. And use staves, not swords. We don't want any accidents.'

The weather was still fair and after practicing in the autumn sun for a while, they were sweating. To his satisfaction, Rom discovered that, although the young *Einache* surpassed him in strength, he could use his slightness of build and his swiftness to his advantage. He concentrated on letting Eldairc try and disarm him with powerful sweeps, waiting for the opportunity to surprise him with a sudden move. He almost managed to do so for the third time when Eldairc outmanoeuvred him and struck the staff out of his hand with a powerful blow. His staff flew all the way across the field and disappeared in the bushes.

Rom ran to fetch it. He had just found his staff and was about to turn back when he noticed something that made his blood run cold. A dead raven was pinned to a tree with a silver dagger. There were strange symbols, cut in the bark beneath it. They were stained dark with the raven's blood. For a reason he could not fathom, the sight made him feel sick. He walked back slowly, his face taut and pale.

Eldairc narrowed his eyes. 'What's wrong?'

'I'm not sure... I think I found the remnants of... *Tzanatzi* sorcery, over there.'

Eldairc raised a brow. He went to have a look. He came back with a puzzled expression on his face. 'Do you know what it is? Do you know what those signs mean?'

Rom shook his head. 'No, I don't. I don't know how to read *Tzanatzi*.' He shuddered. 'But I think it's got something to do with the strange woman I saw at the gates.'

'Why?'

'I can feel it,' he said in a hushed voice.

When they mentioned it to Yldich back at the inn, his face was grave. 'How long do you suppose the bird had been there?'

Eldairc held his head to one side. 'Judging by decay and the weather... I'd say seven days, more or less.'

Yldich nodded. 'That would mean it had been done the night of the Battle. It makes sense. Probably it was used in a ritual to call the spirits of the Dead.'

Rom stared at him, aghast. 'Do you really think that was what I felt at the gates?' Yldich nodded slowly. 'I thought it was a just fever-dream....'

Yldich shook his head. His face was serious. 'I doubt it.'

A little later that evening, Rom found himself alone in one of the big chairs by the hearth. It was made of wood and woven reed, wide enough to accommodate the burliest *Einache* frame and stuffed with big cushions in which he almost disappeared. Eald was wandering about the inn and Yldich was away for some *Yaever* work. Eldairc had already left them after dinner.

He stared in the fire, thinking of their departure that came closer day by day. He knew Yldich was already taking in supplies for their journey. He felt oddly reluctant to go. As he sat there wondering about it, soft, melancholic music trickled into his awareness. He listened without looking up, and let his feelings flow with the music; it shaped them until they seemed inseparably intertwined. When it had finished, he released a slow breath. He heard Alyra's warm voice close by his ear.

'You seem sad.'

He opened his eyes. He realized that he did, indeed, feel sad. He looked at her. She had pulled over a chair and sat gazing at him, her chin resting on her hand. The light of the fire turned her hair to warm dark gold. Unlike most *Einache* women, who wore long skirts, she was dressed in a long-sleeved tunic and soft fitted leather trousers. The clothes didn't make her look masculine at all, he realized, as he noticed the way they accentuated her shape. He suddenly saw her eyes, a tiny sparkle of amusement in them as she watched him gaze at her. He blushed and cast down his eyes.

'Eldairc told me you will be leaving soon,' she said in a soft voice. He nodded. Something made him decide to just speak his mind. He wondered briefly if her presence always had that effect on people.

'Somehow it makes me feel sad. I don't know why.' He swallowed. 'Maybe it's because I've started to feel almost... welcome here. At home, almost.' He stared at his hands. 'I've never experienced that before.'

She stared at him. 'Why is that?'

'Where I come from, in the South, *Tzanatzi* are despised by most people.' He wondered vaguely at the absence of bitterness in his voice. 'Being half-*Tzanatzi*, like me, is nearly as bad.'

She raised her brows. 'How sad to be judged for your ancestry. It never made a difference to my family.'

'What?'

'Being part *Tzanatzi*. It never bothered the people around me.'

'You—you're part *Tzanatzi*?' Alyra nodded. Rom suddenly realized she was indeed darker than most *Einache* he had seen. Her amber eyes were almost brown. She was also less tall than most women he had seen in Woodbury and more lightly built.

'Ages ago, during the siege and battle of Gardeth, some *Tzanatzi* blood found its way into the family line,' she said. 'Every once in a while, dark-eyed children are born to us. I'm the only one in my family who shows the signs. My brothers are all tall, ginger-haired, and green-eyed. Not to mention loud,' she said with a grin. 'My father thought the *Tzanatzi* blood in me had made me *Náeria*. He said my music had a haunting quality.'

'It does,' Rom whispered. 'It's beautiful.' Alyra gazed at him. She leaned forward ever so slightly. Slender fingers touched his hand. His breath stuck in his throat. He blinked at her. Time seemed to stand still.

The noise of new guests arriving at the inn broke the spell. Alyra withdrew her hand. Rom sat back, wondering faintly what had happened.

'I'm expected to perform a few songs this evening.' She smiled, a thought hidden behind her smile. 'There's a birch grove not far from the gates. One could build a fire there that would be sheltered from sight and from the wind. A fire would be convenient if someone was to meet you there. After the moon has risen, for instance.' She rose. He stood up, flustered. The new arrivals began to crowd the common room.

Alyra nodded at Rom politely, almost formally. '*Ya'haeve*, Rom.'

'*Ya'haeve*,' he whispered. She went back to her seat by the harp in the corner. She moved her fingers over the strings. A soft, mellow sound followed Rom as he left the room in a slight daze.

It was a clear night. The moon was nearly full, its light softened by a thin veil of cloud. Rom had found the small grove of birches with ease. He had made a small fire and sat feeding it small twigs. He had taken some blankets from their rooms at the inn and drawn one around his shoulders, though the night wasn't really all that cold. He shivered with apprehension. He wondered why he was there at all. He must have misunderstood Alyra's words, dazed by her presence, the touch of her hand, something he didn't quite understand.

He heard the dry snap of a twig broken underfoot and cursed himself under his breath. The birch grove was well out of sight of the village walls. If anyone with bad intentions was about, he would be an easy target. He felt for his sword and cursed again. Of course it was in their rooms up at the inn. He hadn't worn it since the battle. While he fumbled for his knife, he nearly ceased to breathe, becoming all ears, and eyes, and sense of smell.

'Don't jump,' a voice said in his ear. He jumped and whirled around. 'I hope I didn't startle you.' It was the *Náeria*. Her mouth curled in a mischievous smile. She wore a heavy cloak, which moved aside a bit as she sat down. Rom noticed a dagger on her belt. She saw him look. 'I don't want to find myself in a situation where I'm wishing in vain I brought one,' she said as she touched the dagger.

'Like the night of the Battle.' Rom thought of Eldairc's sudden interest in sword-fighting. He sat down beside her.

'Like that.' She turned to him and smiled. He gazed at her. Dark shadows played around in her hair. The light of the fire lit her face and danced in her eyes. It made her look mysterious and achingly beautiful. He swallowed.

'Alyra, why are we here?'

'Why are we?' She leaned over to him and pressed a light kiss on his mouth. She turned back to the fire and threw on a handful of dead leaves. They rose up in the air as they caught fire, sparks flying as they spiralled down like beautiful dying birds.

Rom was still trying to get his breath back. He'd forgotten how to breathe as soon as Alyra's lips touched his. He gazed at her, shaking.

'It's simple, really,' she said softly. 'I'm here, you're here. We have a whole night. All the time of the world.' She looked at him. 'It's up to you.'

She held out a hand. He didn't think. He felt his hand reach out to her of its own accord. She drew him to her and kissed him, a wild, fiery kiss this time. Rom felt a flare of desire leap up from somewhere deep within his body and quicken his breath. He brought his hands up to her face and held it carefully as he kissed her.

She drew him down towards her on the ground. She caressed him, kissing his face, his neck, while she pulled at his clothes. He paused for breath as she attacked the lace of his shirt. They laughed as it defied her and got tangled into knots. Finally, Alyra just pulled the shirt over his head. He touched her in wonder, breathless, and moved his hands along the curve of her hips, her breasts. Her hands moved down his body. As she loosened his belt and began to undo his trousers he froze.

'Alyra, I—I've never done this before.'

She stared at him a moment. 'Don't worry,' she said gently. 'You'll be fine.'

She made him laugh once more as she wriggled out of her tight trousers like a snake out of its skin. She kissed him and guided him with her hands. He merged with her breathlessly, gazing into her eyes, a hand linked in hers. He felt as if something broke free in him; it filled his heart with a wild, elated joy. Waves of desire travelled through his body. She became a wave beneath him, writhing and holding on to him fiercely as he moved ever faster, her body beneath him pale and beautiful as a young, naked moon.

Their pace quickened. Rom felt a hidden well of liquid fire start to rise. It passed through his body; it filled him from his feet to his fingertips. As the waves reached his head, blinding him with their light, he fell apart in a fiery eruption. He cried out, bewildered, and found himself whole again in her arms, panting and shaking.

They lay embracing each other on Alyra's cloak, a blanket pulled over them, their legs entwined. Alyra's head lay cradled in the hollow between Rom's shoulder and neck. He kissed the top of her head.

'I could just lie here for all eternity and be content,' he said softly.

She chuckled. 'Eventually, you would become hungry.'

'Loving you would sustain me.' She smiled against his chest. She didn't speak. 'I may be leaving tomorrow, or the day after that.' He smoothed her hair, trailing his fingers along her neck, the soft skin of her shoulder. He felt a stab of regret. 'I wish I could stay.' She leaned on an elbow so she could look into his eyes. She pushed the hair out of his face and kissed him.

'Let's not speak of that now.' She moved until she was on top of him and captured him with her hands, her mouth.

They didn't talk again for a long time.

'Rom.'

He stirred.

'The sun is almost rising. We've got to go soon.'

He had fallen asleep in her arms, his head against her chest. Alyra had remained awake, trailing her fingers through his dark hair, staring into the embers of the dying fire.

He lifted his face and smiled up at her. His eyes were soft with sleep. '*Ya'hey.*' He lifted a hand to touch her cheek with his fingers.

She smiled at him. 'You were talking in your sleep.'

'Was I? I don't remember....'

'I think you were dreaming about someone called Maetis,' she said. Rom started. 'Who is she?' Alyra said.

'Someone I've only met in my dreams....'

'Well, you know what they say about that,' she said. Rom shook his head. 'It's said that if you meet someone in your dreams before you do in real life,' Alyra said, 'your fates are entwined.'

They slowly walked back to the village, their hands linked. As they were nearly in sight of the village walls, Alyra stopped and turned to him. She looked into his eyes.

'I'm glad our paths crossed.' Her eyes were warm. She smiled, and kissed him on the mouth. He stared at her, lost for words. She let go of his hands.

As they walked on towards the gates, she took care to keep a discreet distance between them. Rom felt a faint sense of loneliness settle under his heart as she did so. When they had reached the gates, she spoke to him softly.

'You go on ahead now, Rom. Take care. And don't look back.'

Dazed, he did as she bade him. But after he had walked a few paces, he could not resist turning around. Alyra had gone.

By the time he reached the inn, he was trying to balance happy elation with a sense of sadness. The resulting confusion had him move like a sleepwalker. Yldich sprang up as he entered the common room. He had been sitting at one of the tables, talking with Eldairc.

'You had us worried.' He took one look at Rom's face and pulled up a chair for him. 'Eldairc, will you get him some breakfast?' It was still early morning. Rom sat down and held his face in his hands. 'What happened?' Rom was silent. 'If Eldairc hadn't told me someone had seen you with the *Náeria*,' Yldich said, 'I would have organized a search party.' He smiled, but there was an undertone of seriousness in his voice.

Rom swallowed. 'I'm sorry. I didn't think. It—it just happened.'

'What just happened?'

'She—Alyra and I, we—' He faltered.

Yldich widened his eyes. 'Do you mean....' Rom nodded. 'Well, now.'

'I never dreamed it would be like that,' Rom whispered. 'That... wonderful. And then—she let me go. She left me.'

Yldich stared at him. 'Do you mean to say you had never—?'

Rom looked up and met his gaze, his eyes dark.

'Oh. I see,' Yldich said. Well, now.' A thought occurred to Rom.

If I didn't feel so lost and confused, I'd rather enjoy seeing him truly taken aback for once.

Eldairc returned with a full plate and a bowl of steaming soup. 'What happened, Rom?'

'We'd better leave him in peace for a bit,' Yldich said. 'He can talk about it later, if he wants to.' Rom stared into the bowl of soup as if the answer to his confusion lay at the bottom. Yldich shook his head. 'I had planned for us to leave today. The weather is in our favour, and I've made all the necessary preparations.' He stood up and gripped Rom's shoulder. 'You eat now, Rom. There's still time for a bath. If we leave in an hour or so, we have plenty of time to travel before nightfall.'

Rom was reluctant to wash away the night. He could still feel the *Náeria's* touch on his skin. When he had finished, he came downstairs and was met with a small crowd. Yldich seemed to be in the middle of it.

'There you are,' Yldich said. 'There are some people who would like to see us off.' He motioned at Meldritch, the innkeeper. 'Our host has graciously given us a horse, and a pony for Eald.' Rom stared at the man. Meldritch's ruddy face reddened even more.

'It's a gift from my family,' he said. 'We can never repay you for what you did for us, *Yaever*, and you, Mr. Roëm.'

'Thank you—thank you for everything,' Rom said, flustered, and shook the hand that was thrust in his direction.

Eald came forward, dragging along two boys who carried large leather bundles. 'Look what Elyr and Dághrad have made for us!' The boys each handed a bundle to Yldich and Rom.

'They're bows, and arrows,' the one said with a shy smile.

'We made them ourselves,' the other boy said. He looked up expectantly. Rom and Yldich thanked them profusely. The boys stepped back with wide grins. Someone passed along the mead. Even the boys had some. Meryel, the midwife joined the company. She handed Yldich a small packet of herbs, rolled in oiled leather and bound with strands of her own hair.

'I know you'll make good use of these,' she said. She turned to Rom and took his hands.

'Thank you,' he said, 'for everything you did for me.' She smiled at him.

'Take care of yourself, now.'

Eldairc joined the group. He had his new sword slung over his back, and wore new boots and a cloak that looked as if they were made for heavy weather. Rom shot him a surprised look.

'That's right, I'm coming,' Eldairc said. 'Someone's got to keep an eye on you lot.' Rom hadn't realized how much the dangers of the road, travelling with only two armed adults, had weighed on his mind. To his own surprise, he found himself embracing the tall *Einache* with a sense of gratitude. He quickly drew back.

Eald grinned. 'I'll finally have the opportunity to get some sword-fighting practice. And I'd like to see Yldich's House. Apparently, it's legendary.'

Yldich had already packed Rom's clothes. Meldritch's horse was a slender chestnut mare.

'I'll leave it to you to find out what her name is,' Yldich said.

They rode towards the gates at an easy pace, Eald bringing up the rear on the pony. When they had reached them, Eldairc joined them on a grey horse. His saddlebags were big and jam-packed. Rom wondered what he kept in them.

As they left the village, Rom looked over his shoulder. Some children had climbed the walls and waved. He waved back and turned around in the saddle. The one he had wanted to see most had not come to say goodbye.

Six
The North

They rode along the empty fields in the pale light of the early autumn sun. Rom was silent, staring at the way ahead. He and Yldich were riding in front. They heard the occasional laugh or remark from Eldairc and Eald, who rode a few paces behind them. Yldich hummed softly. Every now and then he glanced aside. Rom's expression did not change.

Finally, Yldich spoke. 'You're very quiet.'

Rom did not answer. He fidgeted with his reins. After a while, he spoke. 'She—she did not even ask me to stay.' His voice was husky. Yldich nodded in silence. 'I would have found a way to be with her.' Rom gestured fervently. 'She could have joined us. Or I could have returned to her, later —'

'It doesn't work that way, Rom.' There was a touch of sadness to Yldich's voice. 'She is *Náeria*. They don't tie themselves to one person. It's not their way. They are *aguéri*, they belong to their art.'

Rom hung his head. He bit his lip. 'Eldairc warned me this would happen. I didn't heed him.' He moved a sleeve across his eyes.

Yldich sighed and shook his head. 'Listen, Rom. *Náeriae* are like... spring flowers, like butterflies. They will fill your heart with joy, for a little while. But you can't hold on to them. It's just the way they are.'

Rom envisioned the Náeria's slender hands touching the strings, caressing his skin. He saw her face glowing in the light of the fire. He could almost hear her voice. A dull, sweet pain was under his heart, like a small bruise. He released a breath. 'You must think I've been very foolish...'

'No.' Yldich smiled. 'Just very young.' He gazed in the distance for a while. 'At your age, I'd probably have gotten myself in the same predicament.' He chuckled.

Rom looked at him. A smile began to light his face. The pain under his heart lessened a bit. A thought occurred to him and he laughed.

Yldich turned his head to look at him. 'What?'

'I was just thinking... when we arrived at Woodbury, you warned me that being *Tzanatzi*, I might get a cold reception. I never expected my virtue to be at stake.'

A few miles further down the road, Rom started to hum softly, in tune with Yldich's *flestrérer*. He found that somehow, it eased the pain that was under his heart. His humming shaped itself into the ancient song Alyra had played at their first meeting. The refrain had stuck in his mind; the *Einache* words came back to him in bits and pieces. Unaware of what he was doing, and of Yldich's surprised gaze, he began to sing, trying the unfamiliar words on his tongue. Two voices, one high and clear, the other low and pleasantly husky, joined in with the refrain.

Rom stopped in surprise. He turned around in the saddle. 'Do you know this song?' Eald and Eldairc lifted their brows at him.

'Every *Einache* knows this song,' the boy said. He shook his head at such ignorance.

Eldairc grinned broadly. 'It's the oldest *Einache* love song there is.'

They rode at an easy pace, keeping the woods to their left and the flowing hills to their right. In between the hills were small fields, patches of human cultivation. Some were dotted with bee-hives. After an hour or two, the road forked: one branch went southeast and travelled in a wide circle back to Woodbury and its fields. The other went north. Yldich took the north branch without comment.

Gradually, the road became a path, trailing in an increasingly vague way through the woodland hills, until it disappeared completely. Yldich steered them on through the trees without hesitation, as if there was a path only his eyes could see. Rom shifted in his saddle.

It's as if the Forest has eaten the path.

'Yldich?' he said.

Yldich stopped humming and turned his head. 'What is it, lad?'

'What happened to the path?'

Yldich turned his attention inward for a moment. 'Well,' he said finally, 'the paths have a tendency to shift in the Forest. They disappear and reappear for reasons that aren't always clear.' He stared in the distance, his grey eyes filled with thought. 'Most paths north fade after a while. It has been that way for hundreds of years.' There was something in his face, something sad, that had Rom wonder. 'This one started to fade when the darkness manifested itself in the Forest about seven, eight years ago.'

Rom felt a tightening in his stomach. 'How did it start?'

Yldich turned around in the saddle and looked at Eald, who was having an animated conversation with Eldairc about the catching of rabbits. He turned to Rom.

'I'll tell you about it later,' he said softly.

They made good progress, stopping only at noon for a meal of bread, cheese and apples. The Forest was not yet as dense as it would become further north. There were still large open spaces in between the trees, covered with grass, ferns, and moss.

Late at midday, they stopped and made camp in a large glade. There was a little stream nearby where they could refill the water skins.

While Yldich taught Eald how to build a campfire that wouldn't collapse on itself and go out with a sputter, Eldairc challenged Rom to some fighting practice. Rom grudgingly assented.

When they had been at it for some time, he found he had actually started to enjoy himself. Eldairc had a way of making light of things, making him laugh by pulling silly faces when Rom beat him, and shouting with triumph when he won. His cheerful mood was infectious. Gradually Rom started to relax, and get into the spirit of things.

He was aware of the weight of the staff in his hands and how it moved through the air. He learnt to use speed as a means to get through the taller *Einache's* defence. He forgot the dull, heavy feeling of dread that always assailed him when he had to fight with a weapon, be it a real sword or a staff.

Then he became aware of Yldich's gaze. The man was standing a few paces away and studied the fighters with visible interest. Eldairc stepped back.

'I think I've had enough for now.' He wiped the sweat off his brow. 'I'm getting hungry.' Yldich approached them.

'I'll have a go with your staff, Eldairc, if you don't mind.' Eldairc tossed the staff through the air, lightly so Yldich could catch it. He turned to Rom.

Rom swallowed away a slight feeling of unease. He had always thought that it was his fear of fighting that made him feel the heavy sense of dread, or the fact that Yldich was both taller and heavier than he was. But it was different when he fought Eldairc, and he was even taller than Yldich, although less heavily built. He wondered about it as he looked into the bright grey eyes that seemed to see everything.

Yldich moved suddenly. He surprised Rom and drove him back across the grass. Rom caught his breath and concentrated. All his attention was focused on countering Yldich's movements, going with the fight like water, as if it were a dance. He fell in with the rhythm of it, to and fro, strike and parry, until he felt his awareness widen, like the rippling of water when you throw in a pebble, ever wider, until it encompassed them both. He was no longer battling an opponent. He and his opponent were one, like a dancer and his shadow.

He forgot his fear. He forgot everything around him except the movements of the dance. He became the centre of a silent whirlpool, completely still while everything else around him was turning, a flurry of colour and movement. It was as if time was about to stand still.

He felt for the right moment, took a deep breath and moved forward, cutting through time, in between two moments, between the particles of air. He struck swiftly and forcefully, like a cat, knocked the staff out of Yldich's hand and hit him between the ribs. He saw a look of utter surprise on Yldich's face before he fell back into the grass with a short gasp of pain.

Rom's staff fell out of his hands. He held them against his mouth, staring at Yldich in dismay. Eldairc turned away from the fire in alarm. Rom dropped down in the grass beside Yldich and peered at his face.

'I'm sorry,' he muttered. 'I'm sorry.' He helped him sit up. Yldich stared at him in amazement. He coughed and winced.

'How,' he said breathlessly, 'did you do that?'

Eldairc came running. 'What happened?'

A broad smile formed on Yldich's face. He began to chuckle. He ended up coughing. Rom's face was drawn with concern.

'I'm sorry,' he said for the third time.

'Don't be,' Yldich said. His eyes glinted. 'I'm glad.' His mouth pulled into a broad smile. 'I don't for the life of me understand how you did that, but believe me, lad, I'm glad.'

Eldairc stood staring at Rom. '*You* floored Yldich?'

Yldich grinned widely. 'I've always thought that, once he calmed down a bit, there must be a fighter hiding in there somewhere.'

They had settled around the campfire. Eldairc had made some soup to accompany the bread and cold meat and warm their stomachs. They had just begun to eat when a noise at the edge of the forest caught their attention. Something was stumbling through the underbrush. The sound of breaking branches and shouting quickly drew nearer.

Yldich rose and pulled Eald behind him. Rom and Eldairc sprang up and got out their swords. Then they saw the men who were coming towards them.

They looked like ordinary *Einache*, except for the blood and soot on their clothes. There were two of them, men in their forties or fifties. Before they had reached the fire, they began to shout in husky voices.

'A raid... we were attacked in the night...'

'The village is burning—' The man in front, a large *Einache* with a nasty head wound that had been bandaged with a dirty piece of cloth set eyes on

Rom and froze. 'You—you travel with an *Ohênstriër Tzanatzi*?' Rom swallowed and stared at them in silence.

'He's with us,' Yldich said in a calm voice. 'Now. You'd better sit down and tell us what happened. Eldairc, can you get them some soup?' Eldairc put away his sword and fetched some mugs. Eald stared at the bloodstained men with wide eyes. Yldich had them sit down by the fire. They sat looking at the company in slight amazement. Eldairc handed them steaming bowls of soup. The man with the head wound was blinking heavily.

'Now, tell me,' Yldich said when they had had some mouthfuls.

'I'm Oldghar,' the man with the head wound said. He wiped his mouth with his sleeve. 'That's Ulrich,' he said, and indicated the other man with his chin. 'We're from Elbury, that's a two, three days' walk to the northeast. If it's still standing,' he added. 'Two days ago we were attacked in the night. Houses had been set alight and while most of the men were busy putting out the fires, a band of raiders entered the village from the other side. They slaughtered anyone who put up resistance.' He swallowed heavily, his eyes dark with images of horror. 'We're probably the only ones who managed to get away.'

'It's them,' Rom said. The man turned his head and shot him a wary look.

'Who?'

'Lord Feyir's men,' Rom said.

'If it was, they weren't alone,' the man called Ulrich said. 'There was something dark, a black horror that crept in behind them, into the village.' Rom and Yldich stared at him.

'It's true,' Oldghar said, misinterpreting the look on their faces. 'There was some kind of... weird magic involved. I saw it as well. What's more, I felt it, too. It—it nearly froze me solid with fear.' To hear a tall and heavily built *Einache* admit to such a fact made it seem all the more credible.

Yldich stood up. 'I'll have a look at your injuries. And then you'd better go on to Woodbury. It's only a day's walk to the south.'

Oldghar stared at him. 'Then where are you going?'

'We're bound for the North,' Yldich said calmly. The two men gaped at him as if he had announced they were on their way to visit the Underworld.

'The North? Are you mad?' Ulrich said.

'Well, no. Not as far as I know.' Yldich smiled.

'You can't go to the North,' Oldghar said. That's were all the trouble is. What happened at our village is only the beginning. On our way here we were assailed by—by—' the man fell silent and would say no more.

Yldich stood looking at him, a puzzled frown on his face.

'The forest isn't safe,' the man called Ulrich said. 'Some parts are haunted by something—something *unnatural....*' He shook his head in fear, lost for words.

'What are they talking about, Yldich?' Eald said. His face was pale and anxious. Yldich's expression had changed subtly.

'The way north has always been a perilous one to take for those who don't know what they speak of,' he said. There was a ring to his voice that made Rom and Eldairc look up. His expression was stern. 'I have travelled it many times. I know the dangers, and I know the way through.'

The men fell silent, but their faces spoke their thoughts aloud for them.

'Eldairc, please boil some water so I can treat their injuries,' Yldich said in a level voice. 'Let's get these gentlemen on their way to Woodbury.'

After Yldich had treated their wounds, the men made ready to leave. Yldich gave them instructions to find the southbound road.

'You should at least let us take the boy with us,' Oldghar said. 'It's not safe for a child to travel north. He'd be safer in Woodbury.' Eald looked up at Yldich, his small face troubled. He stepped a little closer to him, away from the men.

Yldich laid a big hand on his head. 'He is safe enough with us. Have a safe journey, now.'

The man shrugged and turned away. Yldich stood and watched the two of them take off. Rom noticed he didn't turn away until they were completely out of sight. He stood beside Yldich and sighed.

'There was something about them,' he said. 'I don't know what it was. Something unpleasant I've only felt with Southern men. I'd never have thought I would... sense it with *Einache.*'

Yldich smiled grimly. 'Why do you think they were the only ones to get out of Elbury alive?' Rom turned to stare at him. His face was strained. 'You do not think they were the ones who defended the women and children, do you?'

Rom swallowed. He felt slightly sick. 'Then why did you help them?'

'It's a *Yaever's* way to bring healing without judgment.' Yldich sighed softly. 'But to tell you the truth, I'm glad they've gone.'

The thought of staying the night where the men would know to find them made Yldich uneasy. He decided to go a little further along the stream to find a place to put up camp. They found a more secluded spot, further away from the stream, sheltered by low, evergreen trees and small, gnarly oaks and birches. Eldairc and Eald set about building a fire.

'What about the riders?' Rom said.

'We should keep watch from now on, take it in turns,' Yldich said. 'And I'd better teach you how to expand your awareness.'

Eald and Eldairc lay a few paces away from the fire, rolled into shapeless bundles of thick wool and fur. Rom and Yldich took the first watch. Rom had put on his fur-lined coat and drawn a heavy cloak around his shoulders. Yldich did not seem to mind the chill of early night. He sat facing Rom from across the fire, a light woollen cloak drawn around him.

'All right. It's about time I taught you how to use your senses in a focused manner, to get an impression of the world around you. We can't go about *flestrérer* all the time. But we need to be wary, and this is another way to be vigilant.' Rom looked at him in silence. 'Now. Pay attention. Use your senses, all of them. What do you feel?'

'Well... I feel the ground underneath me....' Rom took a deep breath. 'I can feel the air against my skin.' He closed his eyes. 'I feel my heart beating. I can feel the blood going through my veins.'

'Good. Now expand your awareness. Let it go beyond your bodily sensations.'

Rom frowned. 'I don't really know how....'

'Just try and sense if there are any other creatures about. Get an impression of life around you.'

Rom breathed out and waited. Nothing happened. A feeling of doubt crept up from deep within his belly. He shook his head. 'I can't do this.'

'Try again.'

He waited and took care to breathe slowly. He concentrated hard. Nothing changed. A feeling of inadequacy rose and changed into a prickly sense of irritation. He rose abruptly. 'I can't do this. I'm not like you and Eald. I'm no good at this.'

Yldich gazed at him. His grey eyes were impassive. 'You're right. You'll never learn if you give up this easily.' Rom stared at him. He sat down again and determinately closed his eyes. He set his teeth. Yldich shook his head. 'You're trying too hard, Rom. Don't *try* to make it happen. Just *let* it happen to you.'

Rom opened his eyes and drew up his brows. 'How am I supposed to do something without actually doing it?'

Yldich chuckled. 'It's a matter of being receptive enough to make a connection with the area, then actively reaching out towards other life. Imagine this whole clearing being part of you. Feel it in your body. Connect with it. *Be* it. Then reach out.'

Rom closed his eyes again. He envisaged the clearing in his mind's eye: the dark grass, the shadows of the trees that stood in a rough circle around them, the crackling fire to his right, the huddled shapes of Eldairc and Eald in their blankets. He listened to the crackling of the fire, and let it fill his head until there was no room left for thought. A calm settled down on him that was like the rustling of the leaves on the evergreen trees, the wind whispering along the bare branches of the oaks. There was a searching, a nervous running of little legs, a hungry sniffing, whiskers trembling, *watch out, humans, be careful*, a furry presence running through the grass, a little... little...

'Mouse!' Rom jumped up. 'A mouse! I felt a mouse! I felt it!'

Eldairc rolled over with a grunt and pulled his heavy blanket closer about him. 'Wonderful. You felt a mouse. Now be quiet, will you? I just felt a nice girl.'

When it was Rom and Yldich's turn to sleep, Rom drifted away to the sound of the crackling fire. When he opened his eyes again, the light of another fire threw dancing shadows into a great hall.

He did not recognize the hall and yet somehow it was familiar to him, as if he had been there before. The walls were made of heavy oak. It had aged to a dark brown that was almost black in the gloom. They were covered with tapestries. It was too dark to see what was depicted on them. High above his head, spears and old shields had been put up. They had a practical look to them, as if they were more than merely decorative in function. The fire was lit in a large hearth of grey stone.

A figure lay curled up in a large chair in front of it the hearth, wrapped in a large leaf-green shawl. It was the girl. Maetis. She looked as if she had fallen asleep reading. A leather bound book had fluttered to the ground and lay open on the stone floor, spine up. The fire glowed in the girl's copper hair that fell in long, loose curls over her shoulders, and poured pools of light in it like molten gold.

Rom stood before the fire, and gazed breathlessly at the girl. Something prompted him to move towards her, like a thread that wound through his heart and pulled him towards her. He took a step forward, and another. He kneeled in front of the chair so their faces were level. He slowly reached out a hand towards her face. He brushed her right cheek with his fingertips. The girl stirred. She opened her eyes and looked straight into his face.

'You.' Her voice was a whisper. The thought occurred to him that he should probably draw back his hand. For some reason he couldn't fathom, he didn't. 'The way is becoming ever more dangerous,' she said softly. 'You mustn't linger. Tell him.' He nodded. She sighed, and reached out a hand to touch his mouth with her fingertips. 'Why don't you ever speak?'

He stared at her. He tried his voice. It was husky. 'I didn't think I could.'

To his surprise, the girl's face drew into a broad grin. Bright lights danced in her eyes.

'You simply never tried!'

He smiled sheepishly.

Someone was shaking him by the arm. He tried to ignore it, but they wouldn't go away. He grumbled. He didn't want to wake up and leave the hall.

'Rom, wake up.' He recognized Yldich's voice. He reluctantly opened his eyes. It was still quite dark. 'We have to go soon.'

They had a quick and cold breakfast as the morning sky was blushing in pale peach and gold. When they were moving again, the morning sun threw long shadows across their path.

Eald and Eldairc took the lead. Eald softy practiced *flestrérer*; Eldairc yawned and muttered half-hearted complaints about the early hour under his breath. Rom and Yldich followed a few paces behind.

After a while Yldich turned to Rom. 'Why don't you try and put into practice what you've learned yesterday. Try and sense what life there is in the forest around us.' When he saw Rom hesitate, he added: 'Remember how you used the fire yesterday. How did it help you?'

Rom thought for a while. 'It took me away from myself, I guess,' he said finally. 'I just stopped thinking I couldn't do it, and then suddenly I could.'

'Exactly.' Yldich chuckled. 'Often it is more a question of dropping the rules you have set up for yourself and the world, then of actually having to do anything special. Now, see if you can do it again. Find a way to drop the restrictions you have put upon yourself.'

Rom was silent for a while. He found he could tune into the rhythmic movement of the horse's hooves, concentrate on its sound on the forest floor and the movement of the horse's back. It was such a comfortable rhythm that he nearly fell asleep again. He drifted with the monotonous, lulling rhythm; receiving faint impressions of the area around him, until something brought a vague memory of his early morning dream back to him, like a squirrel that moved in the corner of his eye. He started.

'Yldich.'

'What is it?'

'I dreamt her again. Maetis. This morning.'

Yldich stared at him. Rom didn't notice. He was gazing at his hands as he concentrated on retrieving the dream. 'It was a great hall, of wood and stone. There was a large hearth. She was sitting by the fire....'

'Did she say anything to you?'

Rom concentrated, frowning with effort. 'She said—she said to tell you we shouldn't linger, that the road was getting ever more dangerous. Yldich, what danger was she speaking about?'

Yldich released a breath. He stared at the path ahead. It was nearly invisible; the only thing that made it a path was that the trees and bushes grew slightly less close to each other.

'I had a feeling it might be so,' he said softly. He turned his head and met Rom's eyes. 'There are some things I need to tell you about the Forest. All of you.'

They sat down to a small fire and a simple meal at midday. Yldich was uncommonly thoughtful and silent. When they had finished, he took a stick of rolled-up leaves from a *Yaever* bundle and lit it at the tip. Smoke curled up into the sky and started to fill the area around them. The smell entered their heads. It had a slight, strangely calming effect.

'This smoke,' he said, 'is called *Párscha*. It has been used by the *Einache* for thousands of years when discussing matters of grave importance. It clears the mind and calms the emotions. Particularly useful when handling feuds between hot-headed *Einache* clan leaders.' Eldairc chuckled, his green eyes glinting. Apparently he had some idea of the kind of heated discussion Yldich was referring to.

A broad beam of sunlight fell through the opening of a large tent. It fell across a wooden table that nearly disappeared under the folds of a large, ancient map. A slender young man sat on a low stool in the middle of the tent and poured over the map. The light fell in his hair and turned it a warm shade of gold. His face was pale. Shadows pooled under his cheekbones.

A man came to the opening of the tent. 'The messenger from the South has arrived, my lord. Shall I....?'

'See him in.' The young man folded up the map, moving slowly and gingerly, while he silently cursed the weakness that was still on him. If that idiot rider had gotten to him sooner, maybe he wouldn't have lost so much blood. Well, he had seen to the man. Ten lashings with the horsewhip had taught him the value of a swift response. He smiled a small smile of satisfaction. The man returned.

'The King's Messenger, my lord,' he announced.

Feyir stood up.

'The northern part of Gardeth Forest,' Yldich said, 'is not the same as the Southern part.' He paused and threw some twigs on the fire. They burned up quickly; they glowed for a little while, like the red-hot ghosts of branches, until they fell into ashes.

'Where the change begins, is not always clear to see. Some years the boundary lies further north, some years it shifts, like the paths of the Forest, and moves further south. When the boundary travels south, it sometimes comes across small forest villages. They are usually abandoned by their inhabitants.'

Rom and Eldairc stared at him. Eald sat with his face cupped in his hands, listening intently.

'When this change came into being, when the North and South started to drift apart, no-one knows for certain. But I think it was during the Last Battle of Gardeth, five hundred years ago, that something started to change.' Rom shifted uneasily. Eldairc frowned, staring at Yldich.

'You may have heard something of the Last Battle on Gardeth Battle Plain,' Yldich said to Eldairc, 'when the last of the *Einache* stood up against the *Tzanatzi* army, and the *Tzanatzi* sorcerer that was the main source of their power was slain.'

Eldairc nodded. A look of wonder crossed his face. 'As a matter of fact, I've been able to find some references to it in the old books. And Eald told me the story as you told it.' He looked at Yldich's face intently. 'There are also the legends.'

Yldich smiled faintly. 'I wonder how much truth there is to them.' He threw some more twigs on the fire. 'Whatever the case may be, time in the North seems to pass in a different way, not slower, or faster, but *different*, making it easier for the old ways to be preserved, and for dreamwalkers to walk their dreams.'

Rom remembered the little round houses of reed and clay in the sunlit grass of his dream. The vividness of the image surprised him.

'Somehow,' he heard Yldich go on, 'the veil between this world and the other worlds is thinner in the North than it is in other places. A traveller that passes the boundary might suddenly find himself in a place and time not his own. Or rather, a reality not his own might intrude upon his reality. Briefly, he might hear the dying cries of falling warriors, and hear arrows whistle though the air.' Eald shivered under his woollen cloak and looked at Yldich with wide eyes.

'Some travellers have even had actual encounters with the other reality,' Yldich said, 'but most of them, I fear, did not return to tell the tale.' He checked himself, suddenly aware of Eald's narrow, anxious face at the other side of the fire. He released an inaudible sigh.

'Tonight Rom dreamwalked his way to my daughter, Maetis. She warned him that the way north has become more dangerous than before.' Eldairc turned his head to look at Rom in slight amazement.

'Why she came to him, rather than to me, is a mystery to me,' Yldich said softly, as if following some private thread of thought, 'though my daughter has always had a tendency to do things her way.' He chuckled. Then his grey eyes were sober again. 'We will need to take care as we travel further north, and stay close together. We can't afford to be separated.' His expression softened as he looked at Eald.

'Now, it probably won't be as bad as all that. I have travelled this way and back many times, and, as a *Yaever*, I know how to deal with these things. But, as they say, better carry one sheepskin too many than to freeze for want of one. So, if you feel anything strange, be on your guard, stay close, and report it to me.' He looked at Eald. 'That means no more going off on your own, lad.'

Yldich took the first watch that night. As Eald and Eldairc where making ready to go to sleep, Rom came and sat beside him by the fire.

'Yldich,' he said. 'I was wondering. How will we know when we've crossed the boundary?'

Yldich turned his head and looked at him a moment with his clear grey eyes. 'Trust me. You'll know.'

The next day was a clear and sunny one. The air was cold and crisp, and there was almost no wind. At midday, they came to an area where the forest floor rose and the trees thinned out; eventually, they found themselves climbing a small, green hill overlooking the Forest ahead. They stopped about half-way up, where there was an area with rocks and small trees. While the others busied themselves with the campfire, Rom felt an urge to climb the top of the hill to get an impression of the landscape around them.

'Be right back,' he said over his shoulder. It took him only a few minutes to get to the top of the hill. It was nice to have an unlimited view of the landscape. He looked out over the Forest. Beneath him, he could discern the glimmer of a river running northeast. It was probably the same river they had followed two days ago. He closed his eyes for a while, enjoying the warmth of the sun on his face. The air smelled of sunlight on grass. It reminded him briefly of summer. He breathed in deeply and filled his heart with wellbeing.

There were sounds in the distance. He opened his eyes in surprise. Voices like tinkling little bells rose up through the air. It sounded like children, playing in the distance. They seemed to be coming up the hill. He looked around, but there was no-one to be seen.

'*Ya'elemni aerwascht'e?*' A high, clear voice rose behind him. He turned around in surprise and saw a little *Einache* girl. She had come up behind him, followed by five or six other children.

The girl wore a simple dress of emerald green wool that came to her knees. Her arms and legs were bare. Red-golden curls framed her face. She looked up at him curiously with her clear grey eyes. The other children, little ginger-haired girls and boys of various ages between three and eight, gathered around them, gazing at his dark hair and unfamiliar face from a safe distance.

'I'm—I'm sorry,' he said to the girl. 'I don't speak *Einache*.' He tried hard to remember the smidgen of *Einache* he'd learned in Woodbury. 'Uh... *Ya'haeve.*'

The girl giggled, and burst out in a stream of *Einache* to the other children. They laughed and came a little closer.

'*Na durga est'e Faraër?*' a little boy asked, pointing at the sword in the sky-blue scabbard that hung at his side. One of the strange words caught in his mind. The memory of the alley in Woodbury came into his head, of Eldairc telling him of the mark of *Faraër*. He kneeled down and showed them his hand.

'*Faraër,*' he said. An excited chatter rose about him. The little girl took his hand to examine it closer.

'Rom?'

He blinked his eyes. Something whirled around him. He shook his head in confusion. Someone was shaking him. He opened his eyes. The bright sunlight had gone, the shadows of the trees told him an hour or more had passed by.

'What?' he said. 'Where are the children?' Eldairc eyed him in amazement.

'What children? There's nobody here but us.'

'What?' Rom shook his head, trying to clear it. 'They were here just a moment ago.'

Eldairc stared at him, dumbfounded. A shiver crept along his back. 'Let's get back.'

'He just stood there, staring,' Eldairc said. 'It was unnerving.' They sat around the fire. Yldich had made them some herb tea.

Rom sat staring in his mug. He shook his head. 'They—they seemed so real. They spoke to me. They even touched me.'

'Well,' Yldich said. 'I think I can safely say we have crossed the northern boundary.'

Eldairc looked aside at him. 'What would have happened to him if I hadn't woken him up? What if he'd been on his own?'

Yldich nodded, his expression grim. 'That,' he said, 'is exactly the reason we shouldn't get separated.'

They rode on through the Forest until it was nearly dusk and Eald's stomach was telling him it was time for dinner.

'Can we stop now, Yldich,' he called from the rear. Yldich and Rom were riding up front. 'I'm getting hungry.'

Yldich turned and was about to speak, when a chill wind rose. Rom noticed his breath was pluming white. He turned his head to mention it to Yldich when his horse shied away from something that wasn't there. It whinnied anxiously. Before he could grab a tighter hold of the reigns, it bolted.

Rom found himself on the forest floor without knowing how he'd got there. His head spun and he groaned. He heard a sharp curse. Eldairc had been thrown off as well. The grey and the chestnut mare had disappeared between the trees. Eald tried desperately to keep his pony from running off. It whirled around nervously. Yldich dismounted and kept a firm hold on Elda's reigns. Elda fidgeted, whinnying and snorting, his eyes rolling in fear.

'Eldairc, help him!' Yldich took hold of Elda's head and tried to calm him down. Eldairc managed to get hold of the pony's reigns. Eald dismounted gingerly. Rom was about to get up, when he noticed something strange.

Little crystals of ice formed on the grass at an amazing speed. It was like seeing autumn change into midwinter within seconds. His eyes grew wide as he saw a muddy puddle freeze over in an instant. It changed into crackling ice before his eyes. He wanted to cry out to Yldich, but his voice stuck in his throat. The cold crept up his body and he was gripped in a stranglehold by a strange, formless fear that took his breath away. He swallowed and coughed.

'Yldich,' he croaked. It was like being in a bad dream where he was unable to cry out. He tried again. 'Yldich... Eldairc... look!' He finally had their attention. Their heads turned and he saw their eyes widen in dismay.

'Rom, don't look back. Just come to me, now.' Yldich's voice was strangely level. He held out a hand. Rom scrambled to his feet, looked back over his shoulder and froze. A ghostly army formed itself out of ice, snow, and mist. It approached like a nightmare come to life. All around them, night fell at the same, unnatural pace as winter had set in.

The warrior leader had obviously been a big-boned *Einache* when he was still alive. In death he was still impressively tall and powerful. The cold mist swirled around him. The bones of his haggard face showed through his ghostly flesh, which had a sickly sheen in the light of the moon.

He stepped forward and looked at the company. His gaze went past Eald, who looked as if he thought he was dreaming, past Eldairc, who had let go of the pony's reigns and stood staring, his face pale. He nodded almost imperceptibly at Yldich. Then he laid eyes on Rom. He stiffened. Rom saw him move a fleshless hand to his side, where the gleam of a great sword hung suspended in the air. He heard a voice like the northern wind howling around ancient cairns.

'You. *Tzanatzi*. Prepare for your death.'

Rom's eyes widened in horror as he watched the haggard form move purposefully towards him, the host of dead men close behind. The moon glinted on their helmets.

'Stop,' Yldich said. He let go of Elda's reigns and stepped forward. The ghostly leader turned his head to look at him from the dark caverns that were his eyes.

'We have no quarrel with you, *Yaever*. Our business is with the enemy.' He pointed a bony finger at Rom. 'We'll have his head, and then we'll be on our way.' He stepped towards Rom, who shrank back in horror.

Yldich stepped in the dead man's path. 'He's not the enemy. He's under my protection. You will not touch him.'

'He is the enemy, and one way or another we will have him, *Yaever*.'

'Well, you'll have to get past me.' A clear ring of metal rang through the trees and echoed against the ice crystals. Yldich's great sword glinted in the dark like a sharp barrier.

The ghost that had addressed Yldich gathered strength. Its presence became more palpable. Flesh clothed the bare bones of his skull. A thin, long stretch of metal that was a ghostly echo of Yldich's great sword hissed as it was drawn from thin air. He advanced towards Yldich.

Eldairc stepped in and moved to Yldich's side. He drew his sword. Rom saw a massacre in his mind's eye of *Einache* slaying *Einache*. He moved before he could think.

'Stop it!' Before Yldich could prevent him, Rom stepped in between the men, the dead and the living. He faced the ghostly *Einache* warrior. 'Stop it. All of you. You're *Einache*. You can't go fighting each other.' He was shaking with fear, trying desperately to keep control over his voice, and his body, which wanted to fold in on itself and disappear.

If the ghost still had had eyebrows, he would have lifted one. 'What?' His voice was like stones being grinded together.

'Isn't it bad enough that you were killed in your thousands five hundred years ago without you turning on each other now?' Rom looked up at the *Einache* warrior, who even in death was a couple of hand spans taller. The dead man stared at him, speechless for a moment. Then he began to shake.

Rom stared at him, trembling with cold and fear. A strange sound came forth from the dead man's mouth. It grated along Rom's ears and frayed his nerves. It took a few moments before he realized the man was laughing.

'In all my years, alive or dead, I never dreamed I would one day be lectured by a *Tzanatzi* brat.' The warrior leader took a step forward and gripped Rom's tunic with an icy hand. Rom felt his boots scrape across the frozen ground before he was lifted up, his feet dangling in the air. 'How do you propose to stop me?'

Rom stared up at him, white-faced. The silver glint of the ghostly sword was less than an inch away from his neck. His breath stuck in his throat. 'I—I can't. I'm relying on your sense of what's just.' The entire host of ghostly men laughed, a low, grisly sound that echoed between the frozen trees. The sound chilled Rom to the bone. He closed his eyes and waited for the cold touch of the sword.

'Just for amusing me,' the dead man said, 'I'll let you live. This time.' He dropped Rom abruptly. Rom felt the blood drain from his head and passed out, falling to the ground before Yldich or Eldairc could catch him. The ghostly army disappeared between the trees. The icy sound of their laughter followed in their wake.

Rom came to suddenly, gasping for air and moving his arms in a panic, like a man who can't swim and has been dropped in deep water. He was gripped by his arms.

'It's all right, lad. Easy, now.' Yldich helped him sit up. He shook his head at him, speechless for once. 'Well,' he said after a while. 'Well, now.'

'Have they gone?' Rom's voice was shaky.

'Oh yes, they've gone.' Yldich chuckled. 'But if we ever get home, I doubt if they'll believe me when I tell them you stopped an *Einache* army by making them laugh.'

The temperature rose steadily and the frost melted away. Elda came trotting back. He whinnied softly.

'You two better stay here and build a fire,' Yldich said to Rom and Eald. They sat next to each other on the ground, huddled in their cloaks, their faces pale, like two children who had just been awakened from a bad dream. 'We'll go and try to get the horses back. Don't you go off on your own, now.' They shook their heads vehemently.

Yldich and Eldairc followed the trail the horses had left in the soft forest floor. Soon, they found them standing next to each other in a small clearing. Eldairc's grey nuzzled up to him, whinnying softly, sounding as if he was glad to see him.

They rode back and joined the others around the fire. Yldich made some soup with dried mushrooms, herbs and dried meat. Eldairc was unusually silent. After they had finished eating, he spoke.

'These *Einache* ghosts,' he said. 'They obviously haven't realized the war has finished. Why do you suppose that is?' Yldich nodded.

'Though they are able to manifest and even contact the living from time to time,' he said softly, 'they live in a world of their own. To them, the *Tzanatzi* are still the enemy, and they are still riding out to war. Although sometimes, the truth might get through to them briefly. Like it did just now.' He chuckled.

Eald shuddered. 'What if they come back?'

Yldich shook his head. 'I don't think they will.'

'Why not?' Eald still looked anxious. The thought made his blood run cold.

'Well, for some reason we came to this place when the veil between realities was unusually thin,' Yldich said. 'Conditions seem to have returned to normal, now. I think we'll be safe for the time being.'

'There's something I don't understand,' Eldairc said. 'We were all able to see these ghosts, but when Rom encountered the children, I saw no-one.'

'When Rom met the children,' Yldich said softly, 'he was slightly out of touch with this reality, so to speak. He had attuned to another world, another time, without even knowing it.' Rom stared at him. 'When the *Einache* host came, they had moved beyond the confines of their reality. They had crossed the boundary themselves.'

'How is that possible?' Rom said.

'The power of their anger might do it,' Yldich said. Don't forget the *Einache* warriors, who fought and died here did so in defence of their families, their world, their entire way of living. They had a good reason to feel passionate about what they were doing.'

Rom looked down at his feet. A weight settled on his shoulders like a heavy cloak. Yldich looked at him.

'For you to get through to them, and let them drop their hatred, however briefly, is quite unheard of. It's something few people have managed to do.' He smiled briefly at Rom. A part of the heaviness seemed to fall away from him and he sighed.

'Well, I didn't like them one bit,' Eald said with feeling. 'They nearly went and cut Rom's head off. They can take their hatred somewhere else, next time.'

The following morning, Rom woke up with the nagging feeling he had forgotten something, something important. He sat up and pushed the hair out of his face. He looked around. Everyone was still asleep, including Eldairc, who was supposed to take the last watch before sunrise. He sat propped up against a tree, his long legs stretched in front of him, his mouth half open. He was snoring softly.

Rom felt an urgent need to find a tree to relieve himself in private. He walked until he was just out of sight of camp. To his surprise, he heard the rushing of water over stones. He went a little further to investigate, and found that they had either followed the course of the river, or had run into another little stream that ran through the Forest. The banks were rocky and steep; the water below looked cold and clear, as it hurried over the rocks.

Maybe there had been snow up in the mountains in the high north, he mused, as he fastened his trousers. He found a spot where access to the river seemed easiest and climbed down. He washed his face and hands in the stream, wincing at the sharp coldness of the water. He found a flattened rock and sat staring in the running water a while. He wondered about the nagging feeling that had woken him up. Its source was elusive. It wouldn't reveal itself on close inspection, like a star will disappear when you look at it directly, so he let it hover, and drift before his mind's eye.

He felt he nearly had it when he heard a sound behind him. He felt for the nature of the source in the brief moment before he got up and turned around, fumbling for his knife at the same time. He got a brief impression of something peaceful, and ancient, like the stars of the early morning sky reflected on the surface of a calm mountain lake. There was an ancient sadness, hidden somewhere deep within, that almost brought tears to his eyes. He turned around and met Yldich's gaze. The man had come up behind him without making a sound and stood looking down at him with his hands in his sides.

'Good morning to you,' Yldich called. He made his way down to the stream. Rom put away the knife. He became aware of a familiar feeling of apprehension, a strange tension, as he looked into the clear grey eyes. Suddenly, the thing that had been nagging him fell into place.

'He knew you.' He looked intently at Yldich, his face tense. 'The dead *Einache* warrior leader. He called you *Yaever*. He knew who you were.'

Yldich chose another rock for a seat and sighed. He nodded silently. Rom sank down on his rock, his hands at his mouth. Yldich stared into the water just as Rom had done a moment ago. He picked a pebble from the ground and rolled it over in his hands. Finally he looked up.

'I thought you would work it out sooner or later.'

'But—if he knew who you are,' Rom said, 'that means you were here when the Battle took place.' Yldich nodded slowly. Rom swallowed. He felt an inexplicable reluctance to pursue the subject further. But he knew it would keep nagging at his mind until he unravelled its tangles all the way. A thought hit him. 'When the two armies met on Gardeth Battle Plain, five hundred years ago,' he said, 'where were you then?'

'I think you're starting to have a fairly good idea,' Yldich said softly.

'Did you—are you the *Yaever* who fought the *Tzanatzi* mage?'

A fleeting sadness crossed Yldich's face. 'I was.'

Rom stared at him. He was shaking. 'You—you might have told me. Why didn't you tell me?'

'Remember the first time I told you too much, too soon,' Yldich said with a wry smile. 'You ran off and nearly got yourself killed.'

'I think I've calmed down since then,' Rom said in a low voice.

Yldich chuckled. 'So you have. All right, then. Ask me what you want to know.'

Rom studied his face. 'You—you told us that the young Yaever had lost everything, and everyone he loved, when he came forward to fight the *Tzanatzi* mage.' Yldich nodded. His grey eyes darkened an instant. 'So how can you not hate them?'

'I told you,' Yldich said softly. 'I stopped hating a long time ago.'

Rom's expression was pained. 'Why?'

Yldich sighed. 'After I fought the mage, and Yealda, the *Hárrad* at that time, pulled me back from death, I was ill for a long time. It was when I was finally able to walk again, that the dreams started.' He moved his gaze to the water. A hint of pain fleeted across his face.

'At first, the dreams were only of darkness. I felt a strange, disembodied feeling of despair, of being lost in the dark. But steadily, night by night, the dreams became worse. I wandered the darkness alone, disoriented, and afraid. In the end, I woke up every night in a cold sweat, crying out in blind panic, not knowing where I was.' His fingers tightened around the pebble. Rom stared at him. A cold sense of recognition made his heart sink.

'It took me some time to realize I was dreaming the *Tzanatzi* mage,' Yldich said. 'You see, when the last of the *Yaever* had banished him from his body, they hadn't actually killed him. Instead, the song separated him from his body, banishing him to a lifeless state of total deprivation in the Underworld.' He tossed the pebble in the stream. 'And there, after years of torment in the dark, he finally must have found a way to manifest again.' Rom shivered as he thought of the rising cold, dark mist.

'I was so young. I was so sure of myself and my actions, my righteous anger.' Yldich paused, staring at his hands. 'That is, until I could hear him scream night after night, in my nightmares.' He looked at Rom and released a slow breath.

'When I fought the mage at Gardeth Battle Field, he was lured to me thinking it was a fair fight, when in fact, it was a trap. It was a strategy that was born out of despair, a last resort to end the battle and save what was left of our people. But it went against everything I'd been taught as a warrior and a *Yaever*.'

'But, Yldich—he was responsible for the deaths of hundreds, thousands of people. He misused his power in a horrible way. He slew your kin. He nearly killed you.'

'If you had that kind of power,' Yldich said softly, 'what would you do with it?'

Rom stared at him. 'I—I would try to do good with it, I suppose.'

'And how would you do it? Where would you begin?' Rom knit his brows and hesitated. 'When I was about your age, and still in training to be a *Yaever*, learning to work with the elements,' Yldich said, 'I once created a clear sunny season for a poor village that had had several years of bad crops—only to find out later that my good intentions with rain and cloud had caused major floods lower down the country.' He chuckled. 'What I'm saying is,' he continued, his face sober again, 'that to hold that much power and wield it responsibly, is a great challenge and a great burden. It's a lesson that few learn without stumbling and falling. So who are we to judge another?' Rom shook his head, feeling dazed.

'I've always thought it the strangest thing of all,' Yldich continued in a soft voice, 'that this mage, who was my greatest enemy, taught me more about compassion than any of my gentler teachers ever did.' Rom stared at him in silence. He blinked back tears.

'Come on,' Yldich said, and rose from his rock. 'We shouldn't discuss this kind of thing before breakfast. Let's have something to eat.'

They clambered back up the river bank and walked back slowly to the camp site. Eldairc had just woken up. He looked at the two men as they walked over to the burnt-out fire. He frowned. There was something about them, something that always seemed to hover in the air between them, a strange tension, a thing he'd never been able to figure out exactly. He wondered about it as he got up and began building a fire.

'*Ya'hey*,' he called out cheerfully as always as they approached.

'*Ya'hey*,' Yldich replied. Rom sat down in silence. He seemed far away.

'You know, Yldich,' Eldairc said as they sat around a crackling fire, warming their hands around their mugs, 'there's something I've been wondering about.' Eald was still blinking sleep out of his eyes. He yawned and scratched his head. 'You told me you're a *Yaever* of one of the ancient Houses of the North. Beyond the boundary you told us about yesterday.'

Yldich nodded. 'Now why would a *Yaever* travel all the way to the South to find someone like Rom, and take him with him all the way back north again, seeing as how people in the North feel about *Tzanatzi*?'

Yldich grinned. 'I can see how that would seem strange to you.' Eldairc looked at him curiously over the rim of his mug. 'About ten years ago,' Yldich said, 'trouble in the Forest was starting to get worse. Now,' he added, 'I'm not just speaking about the sort of trouble we ran into yesterday.' Eald shuddered. 'That kind of thing has been going on in the Forest for hundreds of years and although it seems to be getting worse and can get a bit hazardous at times,' Yldich said with a faint smile, 'we of the North have been able to deal with that. The trouble I'm speaking of is the kind we don't know and don't understand.' He looked at his hands.

'An ancient menace, a dark and deadly power has been awakened in the earth, and threatens to destroy us. I've been dreaming it for the past seven years. It has been rising, manifesting ever more strongly. And somehow, Rom is connected to it.' Rom started. To hear it put so bluntly was disconcerting.

'How—how could he be?' Eldairc asked, as he looked at Rom.

'I don't know.' Yldich shook his head. 'What I do know is that I've been dreaming him for the past seven years, knowing that somehow, he is connected to it, and is our only hope if we want to survive it. We need him. That is why I went searching for him.' Eldairc stared at him for a while, his green eyes narrow.

'You're—you're no ordinary *Yaever*, are you?' Yldich nodded.

'I have been around for…a very long time,' he said softly. He sighed. 'I suppose I'd better tell you everything now we're talking about it. You'll find out sooner or later anyway.' He paused and stared into the fire a moment. 'I have seen the *Tzanatzi* come to our shores, and I have seen the last Battle on Gardeth Battle Plain. I saw it because I was there.'

Eald sat up, his eyes wide. 'You were?'

Yldich nodded. 'Remember how I told you the story of the young *Yaever*, who fought the *Tzanatzi* mage,' he said. 'That young *Yaever* was me.'

Eald stared at him. His eyes began to sparkle. 'So…you're a kind of hero?'

Yldich laughed out loud, his grey eyes glinting. 'Hardly. I was young and angry, and stubborn, and I thought I knew it all. Like many a young man that age.' He grinned.

'But the battle of Gardeth was ages ago,' Eldairc said. 'Four, five hundred years… how can it be that you were there?'

Yldich sighed. 'For you to understand that, there's something I need to tell you about some ancient *Einache* beliefs. In particular, about the *Sha'neagh d'Ea*.' He motioned in Eald and Rom's direction. 'You two have seen it, at the Standing Stones,' he said. 'The *Sha'neagh d'Ea*. The Wheel of Life.' He finished his soup and sat back.

'In the old days, long before the *Tzanatzi* came,' he continued, 'the *Einache* believed that Life was like a great Wheel, that we are born, and die, and are reborn, according to the lessons that the soul chooses as it develops and grows. Beyond that individual Wheel of Life, each living creature was also thought to be part of the Greater Wheel of life, which is *Eärwe*, the all-encompassing.'

He paused for a moment and stared in the distance, his grey eyes focused on something beyond their range of vision. 'Now, most of the time, people do not remember being part of their individual Wheel, living as if they are here only for their one brief time on the earth. But long ago, the *Yaever* people started to remember. They started to remember who they had been, and where they were going, and why. After hundreds of years had passed, some *Yaever* chose to commit themselves to a certain community, or a specific place, for many turns of their individual Wheels. I am one of those *Yaever*, my teacher, Yealda, is another.' An expression of sadness and wonder briefly crossed his face.

'Now it is not always clear, even to a *Yaever*, what choices the soul makes, and why. But whatever the reason may be, I remember being at Gardeth Battle Plain, and I remember fighting the mage, and living out my life as a *Yaever*, and returning to that same life, time after time. I have served the House of the Deer for a very long time.' He fell silent. The others were staring at him, digesting what they'd heard.

Finally, Eldairc spoke. 'So…if we go from one life to another, and travel round the wheel of life, dying and being reborn…then what are we, really? What were you before you decided to become a *Yaever* all those hundreds of years ago?'

Rom stared at Yldich, snowflakes whirling before his mind's eye in a clear, brisk wind. 'What,' he said, 'is the *Einache* name for the north wind?'

Yldich met his eyes. 'Yldich,' he said softly.

Eldairc sat staring at Yldich, his green eyes wide.

Eald shivered and looked up at the sky. 'Is that—is that what I think it is?' he muttered.

Yldich looked up. 'I'm afraid so.' He sprang up and started to gather his things.

'What—what is it?' Rom said.

'Snow,' Yldich said. His face was grim. 'We'd better get moving. And pray to all the gods you can think of it doesn't get to us before we've found some shelter.'

'Already?' Eldairc muttered while he put out the fire. 'It hasn't even started freezing yet.'

Rom gazed at the grey clouds that loomed over the trees in the distance. 'Are you sure it's going to snow? They look like ordinary rain clouds to me....'

'Trust me,' Yldich said. 'I know snow clouds when I see them.'

Eldairc hastily buried the blackened remains of the morning fire while Rom stuffed the cooking gear in his saddlebags. Yldich pulled out the heavy woollen cloaks they had bought in Woodbury and handed them out. They were of a darker shade of green, like the leaves of the evergreen trees, with large hoods trimmed with dark fur.

They mounted their horses. Yldich went in front, in a course that would take them right through the heart of the Forest, where the trees were tall and dark, interspersed with low hills and open spaces dotted with ancient burial mounds.

As they made their way through the trees, the first snow began to fall. Eald turned up his face to catch the first snowflake on his tongue. As yet, there was no wind, and the snow fell soft and silent as eiderdown. They came upon a low hill that had already been covered in purest white. The branches of the trees were crested with a thin layer of snow that made them look like frosted works of art. The Forest was eerily silent.

'It's beautiful,' Eald said.

'Beautiful... and deadly,' Yldich said.

As they rode on, the temperature dropped, and they got out their gloves. Rom was shivering.

'Yldich,' he said. 'Is this normal for this time of year?'

Yldich stared at the way ahead. He frowned with concern. 'It is early for snow,' he said. 'Very early.'

After an hour or two, the snow fell so fast, and the carpet of snow became so thick it was hard to see where the earth stopped and the snow filled sky began. A chill wind had risen and blew the snowflakes into their faces. The world had become one whirling, greyish white flurry of snow.

'Yldich, where are we going?' Eldairc shouted from the rear. His clothes were covered in white. His wind-whipped face was red with cold. His eyes were watering. Yldich turned around in the saddle.

'There should be a shelter further up north,' he cried.

After toiling for another hour, they came upon a low hill where some rocks and boulders provided some rudimentary shelter. 'Stop here,' Yldich called. 'We need a rest.'

They had the horses stand at the bottom of the hill, near the rocks, so they were largely out of the wind, and Yldich made Rom and Eald sit right next to them while he and Eldairc gathered some firewood. After a while the wind dropped, although the snow still fell down steadily.

When they got back, they found Eald shaking Rom to no avail.

'I can't wake him up,' he said miserably.

'This won't do,' Yldich said, his brows knit with worry. He lifted Rom from the snow-covered ground. 'This won't do at all.'

Rom was walking though the Forest, wondering why his boots made no noise. It was eerily silent. The snow had stopped falling, although the ground was still partially covered with a white blanket.

After a while he heard noises in the distance. The smell of wood fires was in the air. He heard voices, the sounds of horses, and crackling fires. He was nearly on top of a low mound, at the edge of a large clearing in the Forest. He carefully crept closer, keeping close to the ground. He was about to peer over the top of the mound when he heard a voice close behind him.

'*Caleërte, alcánte. Aléir?*'

Two men stood behind him and looked down at him. His breath caught in his throat. They were unmistakably *Tzanatzi*.

'What's the matter with him? Why won't he wake up?' Eldairc frowned in puzzlement. Yldich was shaking Rom, but he got no response from him at all.

'Keep him upright for me, will you.' Eldairc held Rom up by his arms while Yldich peered in his face, and touched it with the tips of his fingers. Rom's eyes were moving behind the closed eyelids; his breathing was slow. His face was almost as pale as the snow.

'He is in a deep state of *ayúrdimae*,' Yldich said. 'This is no good, no good at all. If we were in a safe place, I would simply let him sleep it off. But out here in the snow, his temperature will drop to a dangerously low level. In fact, I think it's the cold that set this in motion in the first place. *Tzanatzi* do not tolerate the cold as we do.' He shook his head. 'Besides, there's no telling what might happen where he is, without protection of any kind. It's dangerous to have so much of your essence walk into the dream world, especially involuntarily.'

'What are we going to do? We've tried everything to wake him,' Eald said in a shrill voice. He shivered, stamping his feet to keep warm.

'Well, the body has its own instincts for survival,' Yldich said with a wry smile. '*He* may not listen to me, but if I can make his body believe it is in danger, it might rouse him.'

The two *Tzanatzi* could have been elder brothers to the young stranger he had seen in the mirror. They were dark-haired like him, and had the same almond shaped eyes, of a deep brown that was almost black. They were pale-skinned and slender. The man on the left was dressed in a chain mail hauberk over a tunic of dark red. The other wore a leather jerkin and a cloak of olive green. They were fully armed; both wore dangerous looking swords on their backs, and long knives on their belts. The one in green had a long bow slung over his shoulder.

'*Aléir? Taz Aléir?*'

He stared at them with wide eyes. He had never seen *Tzanatzi* up close before. They gazed at him, then exchanged a puzzled look.

'*Enteroz,*' the one with the hauberk said finally, with a tone of decisiveness in his voice. There was something in his bearing that made Rom suspect he surpassed the other in rank, or seniority, or both. He hauled Rom up by his arm. They were both slightly taller than he was, he noticed as he stood before them. The one in red pushed him in the direction of the campsite. It was a gentle enough push, though Rom doubted the man would tolerate any resistance on his part. The archer in green went in front.

They reached the top of the low mound. Rom looked in astonishment at the large clearing. It was swarming with people. Thirty or forty tents had been pitched and he saw at least ten large fires burning. The area was teeming with activity. Many men were dressed more or less like the two *Tzanatzi* he was with. Some of them were busy tending to the fires or the many horses. He heard the clang of a smithy nearby.

He started in surprise when two children crossed their path. They were chasing each other and laughing. He looked at them in astonishment, until the *Tzanatzi* in the hauberk gave him another push to move him along. Then he remembered. It was not just an army that had set up camp in the hills of the North. The *Tzanatzi* ships had left bearing all that was left of a whole people, men, women and children alike, before they landed on *Einache* shores.

They passed a fire to their right where a slender youth practiced sword fighting moves. He wore dark trousers and a leather jerkin over a long-sleeved tunic. When the youth turned to look at them as they passed by, a dark braid swung to his waist, and Rom realized the youth was a girl. He remembered the battle field of his dreams, the chaos and the violence of two armies clashing into each other, and was shaken at the thought of a young woman in the midst of it all, wielding a slender sword against the broad swords and battle axes of the *Einache*.

They neared a large tent that was set apart slightly from the others, and the *Tzanatzi* stopped. The archer opened the tent flap and motioned to Rom to enter. Inside, there were small copper braziers hung from the beams. They spread light and a subtle scent. The floor was covered with carpets in dark red and purple. There was a low wooden table with cushions on the floor around it. In a corner of the tent, there was another table.

The archer gestured again. '*Oyente sá,*' he said, and communicated with a motion of his hand that Rom should wait there. He nodded. The two men left.

He looked around in curiosity. There was something about the interior of the tent that was vaguely familiar. He noticed elegantly wrought candleholders in spiralling curls of silver, and realized with a sense of shock that he'd seen them before, in his dream. He went over to the tall table in the far corner of the tent. There was a silver dagger on a dark purple cloth, a map, and a scroll. He shuddered when he saw the dagger. It reminded him of the remnants of *Tzanatzi* magic he had found at the edge of the woods. His scalp prickled. He backed away from the table.

Then he noticed a sword that hung from a pole in the other corner of the tent. He stiffened. It was a long sword with a dragon-headed hilt. A sense of dread rose in his belly and changed into something akin to panic as it reached his chest.

If this is a dream, I would really like to wake up now.

He hastened to the opening of the tent. He was about to make for the forest when the *Tzanatzi* swordsman saw him. He uttered a sharp cry.

'*Oyente sá, ílderae me. Taoroz!*' Two other *Tzanatzi* swordsmen came over to Rom and grabbed his arms before he could run off.

'You don't understand,' Rom said, his voice tense with urgency. 'I cannot be here. I need to leave, now.' They frowned and stared at him with their dark eyes. They only tightened the grip on his arms.

A movement at the edge of the clearing caught his eye. The swordsmen turned their heads, but did not relax their grip. Someone was approaching; a tall man clad in a hue of indigo that was so dark it was almost black. A hush fell over the clearing. The clanging of metal on metal in the distance stopped; all around, people stopped speaking, stopped moving.

The sense of dread Rom had felt in the tent was getting stronger. His heart was beating wildly. He knew the man coming towards them must be the man who wielded the dragon-headed sword, the source of the creeping horror he had felt in the earth and before the gates of Woodbury, the dark mage who would be fighting Yldich on Gardeth Battle Plain. The thought of meeting him face to face filled him with terror.

'Let me go!' he cried. He struggled violently. A sharp, hot pain seared through his chest and he cried out, striking out with his fist, kicking and struggling to get free. He heard a short cry as his fist made contact with someone's face. Someone slapped him and he reeled. He blinked dizzily to get rid of the black spots that started to hover before his eyes.

'Easy, lad. Come back, now.'

He gasped and opened his eyes. Darkness swirled around him like water. The world tilted at a nauseating angle. He doubled over, fell on his knees in the snow and was violently sick while someone held him so he wouldn't topple over.

'Well,' Yldich said. 'I think he's back now.'

After he had had a drink of water, the world fell into place again. It still jarred at the edges, as if it were trying to fit around him, or he into it. He moved a hand across his face and groaned. He still felt sick. Someone made him sit down and he blinked, trying hard to focus.

'Yldich?' he said hoarsely.

'Easy now, until you've come back all the way.'

He peered through his half-opened eyelids. 'What happened to your face?' A dark bruise on Yldich's cheekbone was already beginning to swell up.

Yldich grinned. 'I didn't move fast enough to get out of the way of your fist. I must be getting old.'

'I—I don't remember hitting you... I was fighting to get away. They wouldn't let me.'

'Who?' Eldairc said.

'The *Tzanatzi*.' Eldairc and Yldich exchanged an astonished look. 'There were so many of them,' Rom whispered. 'I was taken to their camp. There were women there, even children....' He looked at Yldich. 'Did you know that there were women fighting at Gardeth Battle Plain?' Yldich slowly shook his head. Rom tried to move and winced. A dull pain throbbed through his chest. He put a hand on his chest. 'What—what happened?'

Yldich smiled wryly. 'I had to hurt you a bit to wake you up. Don't worry, it won't last long.' He motioned at his bruised cheek and grinned. 'This will take longer to fade away.' He extended a hand. 'Now, up you get. We can't stay here. We must find some shelter, or we'll all have changed to ice sculptures in the morning.'

The sky was still overcast, but the heavy snowfall had stopped, and the clouds were thinning out. They revealed a watery sun that was already low in the sky. Yldich insisted Rom should walk for a while to fully come to his senses. He had to support him as he stumbled through the snow.

'Can't we rest for a while, Yldich?' Rom asked through chattering teeth.

'And have you go off dreamwalking again? I don't think so.' Yldich had his right arm firmly around Rom's waist to prevent him from falling, and moved him along at a brisk pace. 'Besides, you need to keep moving to stay warm.'

They plodded through the snow while Eldairc went a little ahead on his grey mare to find any kind of natural shelter for the night.

'What—what do you suppose happened just now, Yldich? How could I be that far away?' Rom muttered in wonder. 'It felt as if I was really *there*. That's never happened before.'

'You were in a deep state of *ayúrdimae*. You had gone into a different reality. A lot of your being had gone into it in fact, leaving you unresponsive.'

'But—I thought you said that could only be done by trained *Yaever*.'

Yldich frowned. 'I did. And it's true. I've never known anyone go into *ayúrdimae* like that without any preparation or formal training. You must have a talent for it that's even greater than I thought. But it's an erratic one, and all the more dangerous for that. Also, I suspect the cold makes you more susceptible to other realms of consciousness. Your body tends to shut down in the cold. You should really be careful, Rom. If you get lost in another reality, there's nothing I can do to help you.'

Rom shivered.

'How can I prevent it from happening again?' 'You can begin by staying awake,' Yldich said with a smile. 'And I'll think up some exercises that might help you stay grounded in this reality.'

After a while the wind picked up again, a moderate but chilling wind that picked through their clothes with icy fingers and chilled them to the bone. More snow had begun to fall. Yldich was beginning to have trouble to keep Rom awake. He was plodding along, stumbling and blinking his eyes against the wind. He looked as if he could hardly keep to his feet. He shivered uncontrollably.

Yldich shook his head and thought for a while. He turned to Eald. 'Eald, do you know any walking rhymes?'

The boy looked at him, surprised, and nodded. 'Of course.'

'Will you teach one to Rom? An easy one, one he can remember.'

Eald searched his memory. Then he recited in a rhythmic, chanting tone:

'*Éldamae,*
Yéldimae,
Tárarer,
Erst!

Méldower dure mó kálander est.'

Yldich repeated the unfamiliar words to Rom, and had him repeat them. After two, three times, he got it right.

'What does it mean?' he muttered.

'My dad taught it to me,' Eald said. 'It's a song for walking, to keep you going when you're tired. It used to be a nursery rhyme, I think. It goes something like this:

First
Fastest
Quickest
Gets best!

Who's late for dinner must make do with the rest.'

'It's based on an old warrior marching song,' Yldich said softly. 'But no-one remembers that now.'

They sang to the rhythm of their footsteps for an hour or so. Then Yldich had them stop and got out a bottle of spirits. He gave them a mouthful each. Eald made a face at its sharp taste and coughed. It warmed up their stomachs, for a little while.

The temperature dropped sharply as the sun descended behind the clouds. By sunset, Rom had nearly lost consciousness and Yldich had to drag him along.

'Stay awake, lad,' he muttered. 'Don't fall asleep on me now.'

By evening, Eldairc found a place where an overhanging rock and a few trees with low branches provided some shelter from the snow and the wind. Yldich lowered Rom to the ground. He curled up into a ball, shivering convulsively. Eldairc came over to them. Rom was muttering something under his breath.

Eldairc kneeled on the ground before him, trying to make out the words. 'What's he saying?'

Yldich held his ear close to Rom's face, then sat back. He shook his head and chuckled softly. '*Éldamae, Yéldimae....* '

Yldich had Eald sit next to Rom to keep him warm and shake him every once in a while to keep him awake. While Yldich dug a large pit in the snow for a fire, Eldairc went off and came back with some big branches. He stuck them in the ground and tied them together at one end. He took some large sheets of leather from his saddlebags. They were made of oiled hides sown together. He pulled them over the branches, fastening them with leather cords, effectively forming a makeshift tent. He left a small opening at the top to let out the smoke from the fire. Yldich lifted his brows in surprise.

'Well,' he said. 'I did say you were a resourceful young man, and that's the truth of it.'

When the fire was crackling and they all sat huddled together, the temperature in the shelter rose steadily. Yldich made some stew with dried meat and mushrooms. The warmth from the fire slowly brought Rom back to his senses. After a while he was able to sit without support and have some soup.

When they had finished eating, Eldairc sighed and stretched his long legs towards the opening of the tent. He gazed at Yldich. 'How much further 'till we reach your House, Yldich?'

'Well, that depends,' Yldich said.

Eldairc looked at him sharply. 'What do you mean?'

'The distance to the House of the Deer shifts and changes over time. Sometimes it's closer, sometimes it's further away from the border.'

'How can that be?' Eldairc looked astounded. 'A house can't move, can it?'

'It's not the House that moves,' Yldich said. 'It's the way.' He sighed and sat back.

'The *Einache* way of life has not changed much over the last thousand years in the high North. Because of the boundary, trading has been limited and the clans of the North haven't had much contact with Southerners. Unlike the *Einache* in Woodbury, for example. Woodbury has had trading contacts with the South for hundreds of years. It has changed their way of life. Life in the high North is different.'

'How?' Eldairc said.

'You'll see soon enough, I hope,' Yldich said. 'If the weather doesn't keep us plodding through the Forest indefinitely.' He chuckled. 'There's an old story about an *Einache* clan leader who was lured into the Forest by an elfin spirit in the likeness of a hauntingly beautiful woman. He kept trying to catch her, but she always kept just out of his reach. She kept him going in circles, and eventually he and his men were so tired they couldn't walk anymore, and they turned to stone. They became the Standing Stones.'

Eldairc raised a brow. 'Let's hope it doesn't come to that.'

Eald shook his head. 'Why would they follow some strange woman through the Forest until they turned to stone? That's just silly.'

When they made ready to go to sleep, Yldich turned to Rom. He had taken something out of his *Yaever* bag. Rom took it and studied it in the light of the fire. It was a double-pointed crystal, kin to the large ones he had seen Yldich use in his *Yaever* work. It was about the length of his index finger and twice as thick.

'It will help you stay focused on the reality of this earthly plane,' Yldich said. 'Keep it with you at all times, and if you get into trouble, keep it in your hand, and concentrate on the here and now.'

Rom stared at him. 'But, Yldich,' he said hesitantly. 'You told me these were the oldest heirlooms of your House.'

'All the more reason to put them to good use,' Yldich said. 'Now, don't forget. Keep it in your hand as you go to sleep, and if you get into trouble, focus on it.' Rom nodded. He felt somewhat lost for words.

'Thank you,' he muttered.

'And don't you lose it.' Yldich grinned. 'Or you'll be in trouble.'

Rom felt a faint reluctance to go to sleep that night. The prospect of suddenly finding himself somewhere else kept him awake. Each time he felt himself drop off he woke with a start, clutching the crystal in his hand. Finally he had enough and sat up. He moved closer to the fire at the entrance of the shelter and sat there with his blankets drawn around him, staring into the flames.

He heard a sound and turned his head. Yldich had joined him.

'I don't believe it,' Rom muttered. 'All day I've tried so hard not to fall asleep, and now that I should sleep, I can't.'

Yldich nodded. 'When I had nightmares about the *Tzanatzi* mage,' he said softly, 'it became so bad that eventually, I tried everything not to fall asleep. But it was useless. You can't stop it, Rom.'

Rom sighed. 'I saw him, you know. Well, I nearly did,' he said under his breath.

'Who?'

'The mage.' Rom shuddered. 'He came over to me, in the *Tzanatzi* camp. They wouldn't let me go. You pulled me out just in time, or I would have come face to face with him.'

'Well, now...' Yldich muttered. His grey eyes were dark with images of the past. Rom didn't notice.

'It was so strange, being there, seeing them,' he said. 'They—they looked just like normal people, going about the business of daily life. Not demonic at all. Dark-haired and slender, and strangely pale, but human, just like you or Eldairc. Only...they looked just like me.' He sighed and shook his hair out of his eyes. 'If *he* hadn't come, I wouldn't have minded being there just little longer. It was almost—almost nice to see people like me for once...'

He felt oddly guilty as he spoke the words.

Yldich looked aside at him. 'I wouldn't be surprised if that's the reason you ended up at their camp in the first place,' he said. 'It's your *Tzanatzi* blood. I think you're drawn to them, like I would be drawn to anything *Einache* if I had been separated from my people, living in isolation all my life.'

'But—I didn't choose to go there. I don't want to be like them.'

Yldich smiled. 'But that's what you are, and you'd better get used to it,' he said kindly. 'Besides, I think there's a reason why you are what you are. It's no coincidence things turned out as they have. Why else would I have dreamt you and not another all those years ago?' He shook his head. 'There's a reason why things are as they are, even if I cannot see it yet,' he muttered.

Rom woke up. He carefully opened one eye, and then another. He let out a sigh of relief. The first thing that met his eyes was the brown leather roof he had been staring at until he fell asleep. He heard Yldich and Eldairc snoring softly. The familiar sound was like music to his ears. When he turned his head, he saw light streaming in through the opening of the shelter.

He crawled out of his blankets and peered outside. The early morning sun glittered on the snow. The sky was a clear blue. He crept out through the opening and turned his face to the sun. He closed his eyes and let it fill him with light and warmth. Soon he felt his blood running again, and his spirits rising.

'*Ya'hey!*' he called out cheerfully to the others as they crawled out of the shelter one by one, squinting in the light of the sun.

'And a good morning to you too,' Eldairc grumbled. He pushed his shaggy hair out of his eyes. He looked as if a few more hours of sleep would have been more to his liking. Eald was yawning.

While Eldairc prepared breakfast, Yldich went and took care of the horses. He came back with a small piece of leather from his saddlebags, and busied himself with it until soup was ready. Then he motioned at Rom.

'Here, lad,' he said, and tossed something through the air. Rom turned it over in his hands. It was a small pouch on a leather cord. 'Something to carry your crystal in,' Yldich said. Rom put the crystal in the pouch and hid it in his shirt. The weight of the crystal felt oddly reassuring against his heart.

When they had eaten, they rode trough the hills and trees at a steady pace for a few hours. The snow was melting in places, dripping off the branches of the trees. Sunlight caught the falling drops, and turned them to liquid gold before they fell.

Rom was riding at the back, next to Eldairc. He felt exceptionally good-humoured and light of heart. He hummed under his breath, searching for *Einache* words and phrases in his head to accompany the tunes he remembered from Woodbury. He was having a go at the skipping troll-song when he heard Eldairc laugh out loud. Eald snorted. He turned around in the saddle to grin at Rom in amusement.

'What?' Rom said.

Yldich chuckled. 'Well, you'll want to work a little on your *Einache*, lad. You seem to have changed the words to that song somewhat. I wouldn't recommend you repeat that in decent company.'

Eldairc grinned. 'I'll teach you get it right.'

After they had stopped for some food and rest, they resumed their journey through the Forest. The weather was still fair; there was no wind and the light of the sun made them all feel more cheerful than they had felt for some time.

Eald taught Rom the words to many Einache songs; Eldairc joined in the refrains with his deep, husky voice, which contrasted pleasantly with Rom's clear tenor. Every now and then, Yldich stopped *flestrérer* to join in. His grey eyes glinted with amusement, though he kept a sharp eye on their surroundings.

After they had sung all twenty-two parts of *the ballad of the bard of Eyskillin*, about an *Einache* bard who sits drinking at a tavern late at night and comes up with increasingly bizarre excuses why he should not go home to his wife, it was near the end of midday. The ground sloped slightly upwards, and the trees were thinning out, until they reached what looked like an old path that went steeply up the hill. Rom felt a strange sense of expectation in his stomach. It changed into exhilaration as he saw the path.

'Let see what's at the top,' he cried, and spurred on his horse before any of the others could react.

'Rom, wait!' Yldich cried, but he was already out of sight. He turned around to Eald and Eldairc. 'You two wait here,' he said in a stern tone. 'And stay together.' He spurred Elda on and followed Rom up the hillside. Eldairc and Eald exchanged a puzzled look.

The path winded and curved along itself, along rows of prickly bushes and stunted trees that obscured the view as it took Yldich to the top of the hill. There was a broad ledge, a cliff that overlooked a large plateau to the north.

Yldich dismounted and held his breath. The dark figure of a man stood motionless at the edge of the cliff. A slight wind had risen; it lifted strands of hair, the colour of deepest night. The hand of the figure rested on the hilt of his sword. Yldich felt his skin prickle at the familiarity of the image.

'Rom?' he said softly.

The figure turned around. Rom's face was pale and taut, his eyes like obsidian. They seemed to look straight through Yldich's.

'It's here,' he said in a voice that was strangely level. Yldich hardly recognized it as his. 'The place of my dreams.' He turned around, and began to walk across the ledge. His eyes feverishly searched the ground. Suddenly he stopped and dropped to his knees. He frantically started digging in the earth with his fingers. Yldich came over to him and laid a hand on his shoulder.

'Rom. Please, stop it.'

'It's here, isn't it. He's here. You buried him here, didn't you. You buried him right where he fell.' Rom stopped digging to turn his head and look at Yldich. His dark eyes fixed on Yldich's face, but he didn't seem to truly see him. 'He doesn't even have a stone to mark his grave.' A dark anger seemed to possess him, a silent anger that was growing. When it reached his eyes, his arms, it would be unleashed.

Yldich swallowed. A chill shivered through him. 'Yes, he's here. Here, we fought, and here he was buried.' Rom stared at him. The dark anger was growing. It reached his heart, his throat. He rose and drew the *Einache* sword with a soft metallic hiss. Yldich's eyes widened, but he did not move.

'Rom,' he said softly.

'You killed him.' Rom's voice was low. He lifted the sword. Yldich took a step forward. He reached out, over the sharp blade, and gently touched his face.

'It's all right,' he said. 'It's over.'

Rom shuddered at his touch. Something, a spell, seemed to be broken. He blinked and stared into Yldich's eyes. The darkness left him. 'Yldich?' He was trembling. He looked at the sword in his hand. 'What—what was I doing? Why did I feel so—so angry?' Yldich shook his head and took hold of his arms. 'I've no reason to be angry with you,' Rom said. 'You've been nothing but good to me....' Tears rose to his eyes.

'I don't think it was you,' Yldich said.

Rom looked up. 'It was him,' he whispered. 'The mage. I felt it. It was him.' Yldich nodded, his face slightly pale. 'We need to get away from this place,' Rom said. 'Now.'

They hastened back down the path, and met Eldairc and Eald at the bottom of the hill. Rom avoided their eyes. Eald and Eldairc sat staring at him.

'Let's go find a place to camp for the night,' Yldich said. 'We'd best not stay here, at the edge of Gardeth Battle Plain. Too many dark memories.' Eald looked up sharply at the name.

'I didn't know we were there already,' Eldairc muttered.

They rode on for a couple of miles, and chose a dry spot under the evergreen trees where Eldairc could use the rocks and branches of the trees to build a shelter. Eald and Rom went through the undergrowth to search for kindling and dry branches. Rom was silent. Eald looked aside at him every once in a while, but said nothing.

When they all sat around the fire, and nurtured mugs of soup between their hands, Eldairc broke the silence.

'Now, I would really like to know what all the fuss was about. What was going on this afternoon? Why did you two look as if you'd seen a ghost?' Rom shuddered and stared at his hands.

Yldich stared into the fire. 'Maybe because in a way, we had.' Eldairc's eyes widened in surprise. Yldich addressed Rom. 'Maybe you should tell them in your own words what happened.'

Rom winced. 'I'd rather not speak of it.'

Yldich's expression was grim. 'Keeping it to yourself won't make it go away. I thought you'd know that by now.'

Rom swallowed and cast down his eyes. 'All right then.' He took a deep breath. 'Ever since I can remember, I've been having strange dreams. Nightmares.' He sighed. 'I'd dream of being lost in the dark, and wake up in a panic. Yesterday, Yldich told me he had been having the same dreams. After he fought the *Tzanatzi* mage on Gardeth Battle Plain. After the mage had been separated from his body, banished to a living death in the Underworld.' He clenched his hands into fists and stared in the fire.

'When—when I fought Lord Feyir, when I thought Yldich was killed, a dark rage came over me, and I spoke a word I didn't know. A—a *Tzanatzi* spell. Yldich recognized it. It was the same one the dark mage used when they fought.' He closed his eyes.

'When we were in Woodbury, I had fever dreams of a great plane and two armies clashing into each other. I stood on a cliff overlooking the plane, wielding a dragon-headed sword. It was his. The mage's.' He swallowed, picked up a twig and thoughtlessly started to break it in little pieces.

'When we reached the path to the cliff overlooking Gardeth Battle Plain this afternoon, I didn't know where we were. I just knew something called me up there. When I reached the top of the cliff—' he paused, clenching his hands. 'A darkness came over me. I felt a great pain, and a great rage.' He closed his eyes. 'I knew he was there. I felt his bones calling to me. I felt a dark rage over his death.' He swallowed. 'I drew my sword against Yldich.'

He hung his head. Eldairc hissed in a sharp breath. Eald stared open-mouthed at Rom. They both turned their heads to look at Yldich.

'It wasn't you,' Yldich said softly. He sighed. 'Somehow, there is a connection between you and this—this moment in history.'

Eldairc gazed at him with his chin in his hands. 'What do you suppose the connection could be?' A thought hit him. 'Could it be—could it be Rom is related to this man?' Rom lifted his head. 'Would that explain these strange events?' Eldairc turned to Yldich. 'What was the mage's name, anyway? Do you know?'

Yldich met his eyes. 'His name has not been spoken in five hundred years,' he said quietly. 'You see, the *Einache* have from the earliest times believed that in someone's true name lies power, and that to speak someone's name is to summon something of his essence.' He smiled. 'I have come to understand the *Tzanatzi* hold the same belief.'

'I'd still like to know,' Eldairc said.

Yldich glanced aside at Rom. 'I believe you have the right to know. But I will only speak his name once.' They sat up. 'His name... his name is Riórdirým.'

A hush fell over the company. Rom stared at Yldich's face. A thought drifted past and chilled him to the bone.

He didn't use the past tense.

That night in his sleep, Rom felt the same irresistible call he had felt during the day, drawing him to Gardeth Battle Plain. He passed through the Forest as if he had no will of his own, while a sense of alarm was growing in his belly. An irresistible force pulled him to the top of the cliff that overlooked the plain. When he reached the edge, alarm grew into a sickening sense of fear.

The place was dark. There was no moon to light the way, yet he could see perfectly in the gloom as if he had gotten the eyes of a nocturnal creature. A tall, black figure stood at the edge of the cliff. His back was turned to Rom. Rom's skin prickled. He longed to turn around and flee, but fear had drained him of strength and he felt unable to do anything. His hand went to the crystal around his neck, but the small, hard thing seemed lifeless, devoid of power or meaning, unable to break the spell.

The man started to turn around. Rom wanted to close his eyes. He couldn't. He had to watch. Dark hair swirled around the man's head. His face was haggard and pale. Rom's breath stuck in his throat. The face was his own.

He woke with a gasp. Waves of horrified nausea rolled through him. He quickly crawled out the entrance of the shelter. Outside, he stumbled a few paces, fell on his knees and was sick in the snow. After the last wave of nausea had passed, he grabbed a handful of fresh snow and rubbed his face.

He rose slowly and looked back. He gazed at the shelter were the others lay sleeping. Loneliness settled on him, a horrid sense of not-belonging, as if the ground was sliding away beneath his feet.

'I shouldn't be here,' he whispered. 'I'm cursed. I shouldn't burden you with this.' He swallowed back tears and stumbled back a few paces. Then he turned around and walked away.

He walked through the snow for hours. The cold numbed his senses. It seemed to him that, as long as he could keep walking, he wouldn't have to think. The numbness was almost pleasant. It took away the sharp edge of the pain in his heart, until the clamouring had stopped and there was nothing left but a dull throb. He had no idea where he was going, only that he was going as far away from the others as he could.

He stumbled a few times, a foot caught behind a hidden tree root or rock, and fell face down in the snow. The white stuff clung to his hair and nestled in the folds of his cloak. It melted in places and soaked his clothes. It became harder to keep moving. It was like swimming against a high white tide of snow that was intent on throwing him back onto a cold shore. He set his teeth and doggedly kept going.

There was a sound of muffled hoof beats in the distance. He looked up. Had the others already noticed his disappearance? He looked around, but there were only the bare trunks of the oaks and evergreen trees. There were no bushes. There was no place to hide. The hoof beats were getting closer. Strangely, they did not come from behind him, but from before him. He stopped walking, puzzled, and waited. He had stopped thinking entirely. A vague buzzing sound filled his head.

Six or seven horses came towards him through the Forest. A clear voice called out. One of the riders had seen him. They stopped right in front of him and dismounted all at once, in an orderly, practiced fashion. Quite different from Feyir's riders. They were tall and heavily armed; they were clad in wool, leather, and fur. Some wore their hair long, in thick, tawny-golden or copper braids.

'*Ya, Tzanatzi. Ya'elemni aerwascht'e?*' The tallest rider, a young man with barley-coloured hair, stepped up to Rom and stared at him from under a blond frown. His voice was harsh.

'Leave me alone. I'm cursed,' Rom said hoarsely. He tried to move around the man, but a big hand against his chest stopped him.

'You answer my question,' the young man said in a thick *Einache* accent.

Rom reached out to move the hand. The ring of five swords being drawn stopped him. He felt the cold steel of a sword point in his neck. One of the *Einache* riders had come up right beside him. Despair rose to his throat and he turned to the rider. He grabbed him by the front of his clothes, heedless of the sharp steel next to his face.

'When will you people leave me alone?' he cried. The *Einache* warrior stared at him a moment in surprise. His sword wavered. Then he deftly turned it around and hit Rom on the side of the head with the pommel. He went down as if he had been struck by lightening.

Two tall *Einache* stood looking down at him. They stared into his face.

'*Alyúrimae erdántwe Tzanatzi*,' the first rider said in a stern voice.

'*Ya'kalánte*,' the other remarked, shaking his head.

Two other riders sheathed their swords and grabbed Rom under his arms. They hoisted him up and laid him across a horse. The entire company mounted and rode back the way they had come.

Yldich woke up with a sense that something was wrong. He swept his awareness around him quickly, but he felt no danger in the immediate vicinity. Then he was aware of something missing. He opened his eyes and noticed it was morning. Rom was gone.

'Eldairc,' he said.

'Mm... what?'

'Have you seen Rom leave?'

The young *Einache* sat up slowly and looked at the empty bedding next to him. He shook his head. 'Probably went out for some private business.' He scratched his head and yawned. Eald stirred and turned over in his bedding, still half asleep.

Yldich grabbed his cloak and crawled out of the shelter. There was no sign of Rom, apart from a trail of footsteps in the snow. A light snowfall in the early hours of the morning had already started to fill them in. He studied the footsteps, and followed them until he came to a place where the snow had been soiled and disturbed more thoroughly. Eldairc came out of the shelter and watched him. Yldich followed the footsteps until they reached the edge of the trees. Then he stopped and turned to Eldairc.

'He crawled out of the shelter and was sick,' he said. 'Then he just went off. The trail goes in a straight line, away from camp. He didn't even go back for his horse or sword.' Eldairc stared at the tracks.

'What—what's gone into him?' he muttered. 'On foot through the snow, with no supplies. He won't last a day.' He shook his head and looked at Yldich. 'Whatever would he do that for? Leave us just like that?'

'I'm not sure, but I have my suspicions,' Yldich said. His face was grim.

They went back to the shelter, where Eald was just crawling out.

'Where's Rom?' His voice was shrill.

'You two stay here and make a fire,' Yldich said. He grabbed his sword and a blanket. He saddled Elda hastily, rolled up the blanket and fastened it to the saddle. 'Get some water boiling. I'll try and catch up with him.' He turned the horse and shot away.

About an hour's riding took him to a place where the trail in the snow stopped abruptly. Yldich frowned at the confused muddle of tracks. There were markings of horse's hooves and large boots, next to Rom's smaller ones.

'A fine riddle,' he muttered, and bit his lip. He dismounted and carefully walked around the jumbled markings.

Six horses coming, and six horses going. And his footsteps end here. They must have taken him with them.

He studied the tracks intently, hoping to find a clue to the identity of the riders. When they taught him nothing, he straightened in the middle of the path. He closed his eyes and started murmuring softly. He breathed out and opened his eyes. A tiny glimmer to the right caught his eye. His hand shot down like a hawk for its prey. It was a single long, golden hair.

'*Einache.*' He rose and mounted his horse, and rode back as swiftly as he could.

Yldich dismounted. 'He's been taken by riders.' Eald gasped and turned pale. Yldich laid a hand on his shoulder. 'No, not those riders...I think they were *Einache.*'

'Where?' Eldairc asked while he started to unfasten the strings that held the shelter together. He motioned for Eald to start packing their things.

'He met at least six riders, about an hour on horseback from here. There were signs of a struggle, but I found no blood. So I gather he's still alive, though I doubt he's gone willingly.' He shook his head, his mouth pursed.

'Who could they be?' Eldairc said.

'Well, I found this.' He opened his hand. The long golden hair drifted away on the wind. 'There's only one people I know of whose warriors wear their hair long. The *Einache*. My people.'

'But then... he's all right, isn't he? If he is with them?' Eald said.

'I'm not too sure about that.' Yldich frowned. 'They don't know him. All They'll see is an *Ohênstre Tzanatzi* wandering their woods, and if I assess the state Rom is in correctly, he'll be in no mood to be cooperative.' He buried the fire pit and got up. 'We'd better go quickly. They have a lead of at least six hours.'

Rom woke up and groaned. His head was throbbing. He carefully opened his eyes. It seemed to be early morning. He was lying on his back under a large fir tree. He tried to sit up, and had to lean on an elbow, his head low. It was spinning.

'*Ya'elérwe, Tzanatzi,*' a deep, clear voice sounded. Rom looked up. A tall *Einache* warrior towered over him. 'Get up,' he said in the Southern language. When Rom just stared at him, the man took one step towards him, grabbed him under his arms and roughly set him on his feet. Rom gasped. His head felt as if it were being hammered on an anvil. 'Now, walk.'

In the end, the *Einache* had to half drag him across the clearing by his arm. Two warriors were tending to the horses; the other three sat at the edge of the trees around a fire. The first warrior gave Rom a push. He stumbled up to the fire.

The light-haired *Einache* who had addressed him the day before gazed at him. He was maybe two or three years older than Rom, and his eyes were grey and piercing, like Yldich's. But they showed none of the cheerful amusement Yldich's' usually did.

'I am Aeldic. Tell me your name. And then tell me what you're doing in these woods.' Rom clenched his fists and kept silent. It took all of his strength to keep standing up. Aeldic frowned at him. 'Answer my question.'

'You have no right to hold me here.' Rom's voice was hoarse. 'Let me go.'

'We are the *Einache*. These are our woods. We have every right to hold you here. Now tell me what you're doing here, *Tzanatzi.*'

Rom stared at him. Even if he'd wanted to, he wouldn't have known how to begin explaining his presence. And there was the dark nightmare, looming over his thoughts, chasing him on. He closed off his mind against it. He set his teeth and was silent.

'*Aléyante éya.*' Aeldic motioned at the other *Einache*. They grabbed Rom's arms. He began to struggle instinctively, but they simply dragged him along through the snow. 'Take him to the lockup,' Aeldic called after them. 'A few hours in cold storage might make him more reasonable.'

There was a small building, a few feet away from the fire. It was made of sturdy oak. The windows were closed off with thick shutters that had slits in them to let in some light. The warriors unceremoniously dragged Rom inside. They closed the door, bolted it from the outside and walked away.

Rom sat up dizzily. He was in a single room, which was bare save for a wooden bucket that had some water in it, and an empty one. A layer of hay was strewn across the floor. The room was dimly lit by the light of day that seeped through the slits in the shutters. He huddled in a corner and pulled his cloak around him. He could see his breath plume in the air before him. He started to shiver.

Yldich had decided to leave Rom's horse and the pony behind so they could travel faster. Eald sat behind Eldairc on the grey mare.

'If he met the *Einache*, your people,' Eldairc said as they hastened along the snowy path, 'that must mean we're not far from your House…'

'The path has taken us further than I thought, and faster, if that's so,' Yldich said. 'But we still have hours to go. If we don't catch up with them while daylight lasts…' He frowned and stared at the way ahead.

Rom paced around the room to keep warm. His breath came in white puffs of cloud. He was thirsty; a few hours ago he had gone over to the bucket to drink some water, only to discover it had frozen over solid. There was still some liquid at the bottom. He had reached for his knife to break the hard surface, but the *Einache* had taken it from him when he was unconscious.

He stopped pacing and explored the door with his fingers. There was no way to open it from the inside. It closed without leaving so much as a crack. It was the same with the shutters. The slits let in some daylight, but were useless as a way of escape. His hands were getting stiff and numb with cold. He was shivering uncontrollably. He paced up and down the room some more, his hands under his armpits to try and keep them warm. He was getting tired. His head was buzzing, making it impossible to think clearly.

Daylight had nearly seeped away. He was too tired to walk around any more. His muscles had seized up. He slowly got down on stiff knees and gathered the straw that was on the floor. He heaped it up in a corner of the room. He crawled into the heap of straw, moving with difficulty, and drew his cloak around him.

He closed his eyes. The buzzing that filled his head extended to the rest of his body. It was a strange sensation. At first it was painful, and he fought it, holding himself to keep it from taking over. After a while, the pain subsided. It left a strange numbness behind.

If I fall asleep now, I won't see the sun rise again.

Panic rose to his throat. Then it subsided, like an iceberg disappearing under the water. He let his awareness drift, and random images rose from the icy sea, to hover before his mind's eye a moment before they disappeared.

One image stood out. He was in the Forest. He looked down at the little *Einache* girl with the copper curls. She smiled at him. Her smile woke a faint sense of wanting to live. Something made him reach for the crystal that lay across his heart. Fumbling with stiff, cold fingers he pulled it out of his tunic and held it in his hand. Holding it sharpened his focus.

The little girl peered into his face. Her clear voice reached him over the sea. '*Ya'erwé?*'

He frowned. How could it be that he heard her voice? He laboured to see her face more clearly. There was a large hall, with blazing fires and many candles. They were mirrored in the clear grey eyes of a girl. Long, copper curls framed her face. Maetis. She frowned with concentration. Her lips moved, but her voice was lost in a cold mist. He tried to reach out and touch her face, but he couldn't summon enough strength to bring up his arm. He gathered all his remaining strength to reach her.

'Help me,' he whispered. The icy sea closed above his head.

Maetis released her breath with a sharp hiss. Her face was taut with tension. She clenched her hands into fists and resisted the urge to hit them on the table. She mustn't lose her concentration. She closed her eyes again and relaxed her hands. She reached out through the hall, through the falling darkness outside, through the trees and the snow.

Yldich. Dáydach. Hear me now.

Yldich looked up sharply. The sun was setting and they had just dismounted to eat and get some rest.

'Maetis,' he murmured. He closed his eyes and tried to get a clear impression of her surroundings. She conveyed a sense of urgency and desperation. 'I'm here,' he said out loud. He got a faint impression of rushing folds of cloth. Then she was gone. He sighed.

'Yldich?' Eald stood before him. 'Everything all right?'

'We have to go,' he said. 'Something's wrong. I can feel it. Maetis has felt it too. She's coming this way.'

Eldairc stared at him. 'How will she know where to find you?'

Yldich smiled. 'She'll find me. She has an uncanny ability for it.'

They had just finished their soup when they heard hoof beats in the distance. A large grey horse approached them over the snowy path at great speed. They caught a glimpse of flowing folds of cloth, of whirling colours and a confused mass of long red tresses. Then a tall girl dismounted and threw herself in Yldich's arms. Eldairc stared at the horse. It wore neither saddle nor bridle. It stared back at him, reared its head and snorted as if in defiance.

The girl disengaged from Yldich. '*Dáydach.* Something's wrong with your companion. The dark one. I've seen the *Ulúme.*' Yldich's eyes widened. His face was tense. Maetis let go of Yldich's arms. Eldairc stood staring at her. She turned to him. 'What—have you never seen a woman in her nightwear before?'

He looked at her clothes. She wore a long nightgown woven of thin creamy wool. Layers of some green undergarment swirled at the hem. She wore a heavy fur-trimmed cloak over it all. Incongruously large and heavy dirt-crusted boots were at her feet. 'I have,' he said. A mischievous grin pulled at his mouth. 'But never riding bareback.' His green eyes glinted. 'What's the *Ulúme*, anyway?'

Her grey eyes met his. 'It is the fore-image of a person's death.'

His smile faded. 'If I get my hands on him,' he muttered, 'I'll tell him a thing or two. Running off in the snow like a fool—'

'After I've had my say,' Yldich said. 'But we have to find him first.' He turned to Maetis. 'Could you get an impression of where he was?'

'It was somewhere inside, I think, somewhere dark.' She frowned with effort. 'There were slits for windows. There was straw on the floor.'

Yldich tried to remember why the description was familiar. 'The walls... were they made of stone?'

Maetis shook her head. 'No... I think they were made of wood. I saw some wooden buckets—'

'The lockup. The lockup in Aeldic's camp.' He shook his head in dismay. 'It's only a few feet away from the House.' He whistled in a high tone and Elda came trotting over. He mounted quickly.

'What—what about the fire? And the rest?' Eldairc said.

'Leave it,' Yldich cried. 'We have no time to lose. Get Eald and follow us. Go.' He shot away. Maetis had already disappeared on the grey horse.

Maetis was the first to arrive at Aeldic's camp. The warriors jumped to their feet and stared at her as if she were a wraith. They were not prepared for the sight of the tall girl in her nightwear, her wild hair flaming around her.

'Where's Aeldic?' she cried. They murmured amongst each other, their eyes wide. One of them ran off to get him. When Yldich arrived only moments later, the warriors stared at him in even greater consternation. Yldich searched the camp with his sharp eyes. When he saw the cabin, he threw himself into a run. He lifted the heavy bolt on the door, suddenly apprehensive of what he might find inside. He held his breath and entered the dark cell. Aeldic arrived and followed him in carrying a torch.

A dark, motionless figure lay huddled in the straw. Yldich hastened towards it. He lifted it from the cold floor and peered into Rom's face. It was ashen. His lips were bluish-grey. His eyelids fluttered. He moaned faintly.

Yldich released a sigh of relief. He turned his head to glare at Aeldic from under his heavy brows. 'After dragging him all the way across Gardeth and dragging him back from death at least two times, you'd have him die right on my doorstep of exposure.' Aeldic swallowed and opened his mouth as if to protest. 'Get someone to the House and have them heat as much water as they can,' Yldich said before he could speak. 'And get me some blankets. Now.' Aeldic blinked, then nodded. He turned and ran out the door.

Yldich carried Rom through the doorway. Maetis and Eldairc came running, Eald a few paces behind.

'Is he still alive?' Eldairc called.

'Only just,' Yldich said. The gruffness of his voice was in sharp contrast with the care with which he lowered Rom to the ground. Eald stood a few paces away, his face pale. Maetis took his hand. Aeldic and another warrior came running laden with blankets. Eldairc helped Yldich swaddle Rom in the blankets. 'Now help me get him on a horse,' Yldich said. 'I've got to get him to the house as quickly as I can.'

An old *Einache* woman stood straight as a pine in front of a broad hallway paved with flagstones. Behind it was a great hall. The fire from many hearths spilled through the windows and fell in her hair. Unbound, it streamed over her back like a river of white silk, threaded with silver. She greeted Yldich with a faint smile.

'Yealda,' he said. He lowered Rom off the horse. Eldairc and Yealda carefully took him from his arms and carried him away.

Aeldic came in next, followed by Maetis. She had taken Eald with her on the grey horse. He had buried his fingers in its manes, terrified he would fall off. He had never ridden a horse without a saddle before. Maetis gently pried his fingers loose and helped him dismount.

'That wasn't too bad now, was it,' she said softly.

Aeldic turned to Yldich. 'I—I didn't mean to kill him.' His face looked pale in the light of the torches. 'He refused to state his business. He defied my authority. I didn't think a little time in lockup would do him harm…'

Yldich sighed and laid his hand on his shoulder. 'You couldn't have known. *Tzanatzi* don't withstand the cold like we do. Now, why don't you go inside and get everyone something to eat. I have work to do.' He gave the tall young man a gentle push towards the doors and went in the direction Yealda had gone.

Yldich found they had put Rom in one of the bedrooms with a window facing west. It was a large chamber with a hearth, some heavy wooden furniture and a low bed covered in sheepskins opposite the door.

To his surprise, he noticed Yealda had left, and had sent a young apprentice to help him in her stead. The apprentice, a young girl with flushed

cheeks and copper braids to her waist, had already started to order Eldairc
about. He carried warm moist towels to the bed for her, which she took and
draped over Rom's upper body. When they cooled off even the slightest, she
took them away and replaced them with fresh ones. The room was stifling
with the heat of the fire and the steaming cloths.

Yldich kneeled beside the bed and peered in Rom's face. He laid a hand
on his brow. It was still cold. His face looked waxy and pale. He was
murmuring vaguely. Yldich couldn't make out the words. He took his right
hand and started to sing softly in *Einache*.

After a while, he closed his eyes, using his inner senses to get an
impression of Rom's energy. It felt weak and confused, as if he was lost in a
cold mist. Yldich tried to get through the mist. He felt a darker energy, hidden
within it. He reached out and connected with it. His eyes opened wide and he
recoiled, nearly stepping away from the bed. There was a deep pain,
loneliness, and a longing for death that drove tears to his eyes. He gasped and
let it pass with difficulty. He was shaking. The apprentice turned her head to
look at him.

'Are you all right, *Yaever*?'

He swallowed and nodded at her. He looked back at the bed. Rom's
hands were twitching, the eyes behind his closed eyelids moving as if he was
dreaming. He muttered something under his breath. Yldich bowed over him to
hear.

'Don't bury me,' Rom said. 'Still alive. I'm... still alive. Please hear me.
Oyéntere calatíroz, êlcme. Ílde me. Ílde....' Yldich felt the blood drain from
his face.

The girl stiffened and stared at him. 'What—what's he saying? What's
that language?'

Eldairc looked at him open-mouthed. 'I thought Rom didn't speak
Tzanatzi?'

'He didn't,' Yldich said.

It was like fighting his way back through heavy layers of ice-cold mist.
For hours he seemed to struggle, like a swimmer lost in deep water, fighting
to get back to the surface. Once or twice he simply wanted to drop away and
give up, but then a murmuring sound came to him, and carried him further. It
held a promise of warmth, of sunlight, and laughter. It wakened a faint will to
live in his heart, and at the same time a deep sadness. He knew that if the
sadness won, he would be lost. It weighed on his heart and darkened the light.
It was suffocating. He coughed, struggling for breath, and groped around with
his hands for something to hold onto. Someone took them.

'Easy, lad. Keep breathing, now.'

He opened his eyes a little. 'Yldich?' Yldich's familiar grey eyes came into focus. There was something he had not seen there before, a faint sense of pain or sadness.

'Take your time, now.' Yldich took a bowl and filled it with water. 'Élora, please help me.' A young girl with red braids to her waist came over to the bed. She lifted Rom's head so he could drink. After a few sips, he sank back into the pillows and closed his eyes.

Yldich put away the bowl and sat looking at him. Rom's face was pale, almost translucent. There were dark circles under his eyes. Yldich sat with him for a while, silently sending threads of energy through his hands, like golden strands of light, strengthening the young man's connection to life. After a while, Rom seemed a little stronger. He opened his eyes again.

'I had—a horrible nightmare,' he whispered. 'I was... buried alive. I cried out, but no-one would hear me.' He closed his eyes. 'I was in the dark, under the earth, and I couldn't get away....' Something splashed on his hand and he peered up at Yldich's face in surprise. 'Yldich, are you—are you crying? I've never seen you cry before... you're scaring me.' His eyes widened in apprehension. 'Is—is everyone all right? Is something wrong with Eald?' Yldich shook his head.

'Everyone's fine,' he said quickly, and pressed his hand. 'Don't you mind me.' He drew his sleeve across his face. 'We're all fine, now.'

'Yldich... where are we?'

'We're in the House of the Deer, in the heart of the high North.' A smile lit Yldich's eyes. 'We made it.'

Seven
The House of the Deer

'Eldairc.'

'Hmm.'

'Are you awake?'

'Huh—huh.' The tall *Einache* grumbled and turned around on his sheepskins.

'I am. I'm hungry.' Eald tugged at his blankets. An unkempt mass of straw-coloured hair surfaced.

'Well, why don't you go and get something to eat, then?' The shaggy head disappeared again. There was another tug at the blankets.

'I don't want to go on my own in this strange place. It's big. What if I get lost?'

Eldairc sighed. He sat up and pushed the hair from his face. 'All right then. Just let me put on some clothes.'

The door opened to a corridor with many heavy doors. Eldairc hesitated to knock on the doors at random. He decided to follow his nose instead. A few paces down the hall it was alerted by the smell of freshly baked bread. They followed it until they came into a large, sunlit kitchen.

There was a chubby woman with cheeks that were rosy from the heat of the ovens. Ginger curls had escaped her low bun and clung to her brow and neck.

She turned around and gazed at them. 'Well, look at you!' They stood still in the doorway and stared at her. 'Come in, sit yourselves down,' she said, and started fussing over them immediately. 'Poor thing,' she added, as she pushed Eald towards a chair and patted him on the head. 'You must be famished after riding all day and all night, if what I've heard is true.' Eald did his best to look his most hungry. He didn't have to work hard at it.

She had them sit at a large table. Before they could open their mouths, bowls of soup and plates laden with bread, cheese, butter and cold mutton had been put before them. As they were wolfing it all down, she stood before them, work-reddened hands on her ample hips.

'You boys look near famished. What's that *Yaever* been feeding you, crickets and mice?'

Eald grinned, his mouth full of bread. 'Rabbits,' he mumbled. 'But mostly, it's been mushroom soup these days.'

'Or soup with mushrooms,' Eldairc said. His eyes glinted with amusement.

The cook stood shaking her head. 'Well, it's a near disgrace. No wonder the other one looks no more than skin over bone. Took a peep at him this morning, when I was getting the *Yaever* his breakfast. Never seen a *Tzanatzi* before in my life. I would have thought he'd look more, well, fierce, or something. Scary-like. But he seemed like no more than a boy to me. And a skinny one at that.' She turned to the stove to check on a roast, and turned back to serve them more soup, talking as if to herself. 'I wonder if he'd grow a little more, if I could get some decent meals into him....'

Eldairc chuckled. 'I don't think he'll get any bigger than this. He's all grown up. Apparently, it's just the way they're built.'

Eald snorted. Then his expression sobered. 'I hope he's all right now. He looked awful.' He turned to the cook. 'Can you tell us which room he's in?'

The light of the morning sun streamed through the open windows, and poured over the oaken chests, tables and chairs like honey. It glinted in the silver that sprang up here and there in Yldich's hair. He was seated at a large table and leaned his head in his hands. His eyes were closed.

'You look tired, my son.' Yealda had entered the room without him noticing. She stood at his left hand and gazed at him. The golden light was kind, but could not disguise the thin lines in his face. There seemed to be more than she remembered. He opened his eyes and turned his head to smile at her. The smile, she noticed, also did not hide the hint of worry that was in his eyes. She took a seat at the table and took his hand. 'You seem troubled.'

Yldich sighed softly. He stared at the tabletop. 'I know you never really agreed with my journeys south.'

Yealda sat back. 'I never could see how a stranger from the South could solve what is essentially an *Einache* problem.'

Yldich smiled faintly. 'Neither could I. But since my dreams were telling me so, I kept searching anyway.' He grinned at her. 'You were the one who taught me to have faith in my dreams in the first place.'

She lifted a brow. 'I also taught you to distinguish between *lágea* and *énthemae*, wistful dreams and true-dreams.'

Yldich laughed softly. 'Well, it appears they were *énthemae* after all. I found him.'

Yealda sat very still, as if she were holding something in check. 'You found *a* man. A *Tzanatzi*.'

'Yes.' He sighed. 'And he's the one. The one from my dreams. I know it. I knew it the first time I laid eyes on him. What's more, since yesterday night, I think I finally understand why. Why him.' The troubled look in his eyes deepened. 'I'll have to tell him sooner or later. And he's not going to find it easy to hear.' He closed his eyes and drew a hand across his brow. 'It took a lot to even persuade him to come. It's taken even more to gain his trust.' He grinned. 'A bit like taming a wild fox.' His expression sobered again. 'I fear I might lose him after all when I tell him.'

She stared at with her lavender eyes. 'You had better tell me everything.'

The warm, mellow light was nice. It filled the room and made everything seem cheerful and warm. Rom peered through his half-closed eyelids and enjoyed the sense of warmth and light. It was a relief to be able to let himself drift for a while, and forget the heavy darkness that pursued him through his dreams, always on his heels, breathing down his neck like a predator.

He brought a hand up to his chest. His own clothes had disappeared; someone had put a white nightshirt on him while he was asleep. It was *Einache*-size, which meant it was at least two sizes too big. The crystal in the leather pouch was still there, on the cord around his neck. Holding it made the dark recede even further.

He tried to sit up. By the time he had managed to get a pillow up behind his back, he was shaking. He let himself sink back into it with his eyes closed. He fell asleep again.

The sound of the door woke him up. Yldich was in the room. He filled a mug with water from a large earthenware pitcher. He perched on the edge of the bed. 'Can you manage?'

Rom nodded and took the mug in both hands. They trembled while he drank. Yldich gazed at him, his grey eyes unreadable and very clear in the bright light of the room.

'Here,' Yldich said, and took the mug from him. 'Before you spill it all over the bed.' He sat for a while peering at him. Rom grew self-conscious under his gaze and fidgeted with the sheepskin.

'Do you want to talk about it?' Yldich said finally. Rom cast down his eyes. 'About what made you run off into the snow without telling anyone. Which got you a slightly rough introduction to Aeldic and his warriors.'

Rom lifted his head. 'I found the *Einache* dead easier to reason with.' His voice was husky.

Yldich grinned. 'Aeldic is young. Two, three years older than you. He still has something to prove. I'm guessing he needed little provocation, and you gave it to him.'

Rom frowned at the sheepskins. 'I just wanted to be left alone... they wouldn't let me go.'

Yldich sighed. He shook his head. 'You stubborn, obstinate fool. Have you any idea how much worry you put us all through?'

Rom swallowed and stared at him. He blinked back tears. 'I—I didn't realize. I'm not... used to people worrying about me. Besides, it just seemed... you'd be better off without me.'

It was Yldich's turn to stare. 'What on earth do you mean?' Rom looked at his hands. His face was pale. 'What happened?' Yldich said.

'It was a dream,' Rom whispered. He closed his eyes.

'Tell me.'

Rom sat with his eyes closed. For a while, Yldich thought he wasn't going to. Then he spoke. 'I was drawn to the cliff at Gardeth Battle Plain. I couldn't stop myself. There was a dark man standing at the edge. It was *him*. He turned around. I was afraid, but I couldn't turn away. And then I saw his face.' He shuddered. 'It was the one you showed me in the mirror in Woodbury. My face.'

Yldich closed his eyes. He composed himself, taking a deep breath. 'And so you ran off into the snow, thinking—what?'

'I wasn't thinking. I just wanted to make it all stop.'

'Well, you almost succeeded.'

Rom stared at him, his eyes dark with pain. 'I might be dangerous, don't you see. What happened at the cliff was—I nearly attacked you. I don't know what came over me. I don't want it to happen again.'

Yldich took hold of his hands. 'But you didn't. You came back.'

Rom swallowed. 'There's something dark, something that's pursued me all my life. It's finally catching up with me. When it does, I don't know what will happen....'

'All the more reason not to run off on your own when it does.' Yldich gently pressed his hand. 'Now, promise me you won't do anything like that again. Promise you'll come to me, first.'

Rom looked up. He nodded.

That night, Yldich walked past Rom's chamber and saw a soft amber light fall through the doorway. Surprised, he peered into the semidarkness. A fire was lit in the hearth.

Yealda sat in the chair across the low bed where Rom lay sleeping. The light of the fire glinted in her silver hair. A sword lay over her knees. She gripped the hilt with tight fingers, her eyes non-seeing. Her face was still.

'Yealda,' he whispered. She stirred. 'How long have you been sitting there?' Yldich went over to her and noticed the sword in her lap. He stiffened. 'Yealda,' he said, a tone of concern in his voice.

'I wanted to know what it was like to sit here with a sword in my hand and not kill him.'

Yldich sighed. He kneeled before her chair. He gently took the sword from her hands and laid it aside. Yealda breathed out and shuddered, blinking as if she was aroused from a deep sleep. She suddenly looked very old.

'He's so very like him,' she said, looking over Yldich's shoulder at Rom, at his dark hair spilling over the sheepskins like ink. Yldich took her hands into his own and kissed them.

'Alike, and yet not,' he said softly.

Rom was awakened by a faint growling sound and discovered it was his own stomach, demanding his attention. He blinked in the bright light of the morning sun. Apparently, someone had lit a fire in the hearth earlier that morning, but now that he was awake, he was alone in the room. He looked around for anything to eat, but there was only the pitcher of water on the table.

He slid out of the sheepskins and looked around for his clothes, but they had been taken away. There was only the oversized nightshirt he had been wearing in bed. Underneath it he had been dressed in woollen leggings and thick socks. He decided it would have to do.

The door led to a long, circular corridor with many doors. They were all closed, and had a somewhat forbidden look to them. He did not dare knock on one, let alone open one. The length of the corridor made him wonder just how big the house really was. He kept walking slowly and carefully, until he smelled herbs and spices, and freshly baked bread. His stomach rumbled enthusiastically. Two doors opened into a large kitchen with windows facing east. The early morning sun bathed it in bright golden light. He stood blinking in the doorway.

'My, there he is now, your *Tzanatzi* companion,' he heard a husky female voice in a thick *Einache* accent exclaim. Before his eyes had adjusted to the light, Eald had risen from his chair and thrown himself at Rom. The boy drew back and Rom did his best to regain his balance, only to be nearly thrown off-balance once more by an even bigger embrace by Eldairc. As the tall *Einache* drew back to look at him, Rom grabbed the back of a chair for support.

'Sit yourself down, lad, quickly,' the woman said as she turned to one of the stoves to fill a large bowl with soup. 'You look like you're starving. Here.' She put the bowl in front of him and patted him on the back. 'Eat, now.' She went to a stove and returned with a large plate laden with bread rolls. She sat down across the table and stared at him with curious eyes.

The soup was thick, filled with all sorts of vegetables and meat. He ate until it was all finished and sighed with contentment. He looked up, and met three pairs of eyes, two grey pairs and one green. They gazed patiently at him from the other end of the table. He blushed, with the hot soup and with embarrassment.

'I—I'm sorry,' he said to the woman. 'I didn't even introduce myself, I was that hungry. You must wonder where I've left my manners.'

'Not at all,' she said. Her smile dimpled her round, rose-colored cheeks. She got up and took his bowl to refill it. 'Now, I'm Saráyah, but everyone calls me Yárah. That means cook in *Einache*.'

'I'm Rom.'

'So these two tell me,' she said, motioning at Eldairc and Eald.

Eldairc was grinning. 'Yárah has let us make her kitchen our new haunt,' he said.

'She thinks Yldich has been feeding us crickets,' Eald said, his mouth pulled awry in a wide grin.

'And spiders, and frogs, and things with a hundred legs each,' Yárah said, and tickled him. Eald giggled and nearly fell off his chair trying to get away from her. 'Well, I hope you're feeling a bit better, lad,' she said to Rom. 'If you need anything, just ask.' She rose and busied herself at one of the counters at the other end of the kitchen, chopping up vegetables and grinding spices in a mortar. She hummed softly to herself as she worked.

Eldairc's eyes were luminously green in the bright morning light, like a curious cat's. He leaned his elbows on the table and put his hands under his chin. He studied Rom's face. Rom seemed even more pale than usual, the dark eyes large in his lean face. There were faint dark circles under his eyes.

'We wanted to go and see you yesterday, but Yldich caught us and sent us back,' Eald said. 'Said you weren't strong enough yet to see visitors.'

'He chased us off like a couple of chickens,' Eldairc added. 'Now, tell us what happened. Why did you run off like that?'

Rom stared at his hands. 'I'm—I'm not sure I can explain it.'

An elderly man with white streaks in his hair entered the kitchen behind Rom. He set a bowl of soup on a tray with some bread rolls and turned to leave. When he noticed the dark young man at the table, he started, staring at him with wide eyes, and nearly dropped his tray. Soup sloshed in the bowls, spilling over onto the bread. He hastily kept his tray level and left without a word.

'Apparently, not everyone is aware of the *Tzanatzi* guest,' Eldairc said with a grin. 'Though I'm pretty certain word will spread anytime soon.'

Rom winced. 'I'd best not start walking about on my own. He looked as if he'd seen a wraith.'

'Speaking of which,' Eldairc said, not losing track of his subject. 'What did *you* see that made you run off like that in the snow?' Rom swallowed. It was like talking to a younger version of Yldich. Once the young *Einache* caught scent of something, he pursued it like a hunting dog a rabbit.

'It—it was a nightmare.'

'Did it have anything to do with what happened the day before, at the Battle Plain?' Eldairc said. Rom nodded.

'Nightmares, you say?' Yárah cut in. She had moved to the stove next to them to check on some spiced bread. A sweet smell wafted from the oven before the door closed with a metallic clang. 'You should talk to the *Yaever*. He knows everything about dreams. My cousin suffered nightmares once. Talked to him once, they never bothered her again.'

Rom looked at her round and pleasant face. She radiated an energy that was cheerful and wonderfully mundane. In her kitchen, he could almost believe that the darkness that pursued him was only the stuff of nightmares; like dark clouds, easily diffused by the light of the sun.

He smiled at her. 'I will.'

When they were done eating, Eldairc insisted on helping Rom back to his chamber.

'I can manage, I'm fine,' Rom muttered.

'You don't look it,' Eldairc said calmly, and proceeded to support him through the corridor. 'Besides, what would Yldich say if he found you passed out in some corner of this labyrinth? Eald and me would be in for a right scolding.'

When they had reached Rom's chamber, they found the door open. Yldich had just arrived to find it empty.

'Well, there you are,' he said. The frown that had creased his brow faded away. 'I was just about to go look for you. I'm not sure how people would react to a strange *Tzanatzi* wandering the hallways of the House.'

Eldairc grinned. 'We just witnessed the effect in the kitchen. It was quite amusing.'

'Maybe,' Yldich said with a wry grin. 'Still, I wouldn't want there to be any… accidents because we haven't yet announced Rom's presence officially.' He started to help him back into the bed. Rom was inclined to protest, but when he felt his muscles tremble with effort, he let him. He sank back into the pillows with a sigh and closed his eyes.

'We'd better leave you alone for a bit,' he heard Yldich's voice. It sounded as if it came from miles away. 'Get some more rest, Rom.' He wanted to nod, but it felt like too much trouble. He slid away into nothingness.

Eldairc followed Yldich out of the room. Two doors down the corridor, Yldich opened the door to a large room with windows to the west. He sat down at a large table. It was littered with papers, maps, scrolls and old books. The loose papers were secured with crystals and pieces of rock.

Eldairc eyed the papers with interest and took a chair opposite Yldich. He stared at him with his clear green eyes. 'Something's worrying you.' Yldich looked up sharply. 'He doesn't look well,' Eldairc continued, unperturbed. 'He looks as if… something's hunting him. It's not just the after-effect of nearly freezing to death, is it?' Yldich slowly shook his head. 'And you're not going to tell me what it is?'

Yldich sighed and looked him in the eyes. 'It's not that simple.' He raked his fingers through his hair. 'The reason why he is here, the thing that's hunting him…it's only part of the story. I don't even know all the parts yet.'

Eldairc stared at him. 'Does it have anything to do with the dark mage you've been telling us about? Riór—' Yldich stopped him with an abrupt gesture of his hand.

'Don't speak his name out loud,' he said in a level voice. His eyes were stern. 'Especially not here,' he motioned towards the windows, 'in sight of Gardeth Battle Plain.'

Eldairc rose and went to the windows. They were made of many little panes of thick glass, set in lead. He gazed out over the snow-covered fields. In the distance, he could just discern the top of the cliffs that overlooked the Plain. He drew up his brows. 'You have a study with a view of Gardeth Battle Field?'

Yldich joined him at the window. 'I never thought anything of it, but now you put it like that… well.' He sighed and turned to Eldairc. 'Listen, Eldairc. I know you only want to help. But Rom has a tendency to run and get himself into serious trouble when confronted with too many painful truths at a time. So please, trust me. I think it's best if he finds out the truth in his own time.'

Eldairc turned back to the windows and stared at the cliffs in the distance. 'But what if it finds him first?' he muttered.

The light had changed. It must be near midday. Rom was aware of it before he opened his eyes. Something else was different in the room, too. There was an energy that was vibrant and lively. It felt as if spring had wandered into the room in the heart of winter. He opened his eyes and stared straight into Maetis' grey ones.

'*Ya'hey,*' she said, and smiled.

'*Ya—Ya'hey.*' He sat up hastily. The sudden movement had his head reel.

'Careful.' She came over to the bed and placed some pillows behind his back. She gathered her skirts and sat down on the edge of his bed.

He stared at her, wondering what to say. When he had met her in his true-dreams, he had felt drawn to her like a vine to the light of the sun. He had simply followed the thread that ran through his heart and led him straight to her. There had been no need for clumsy words. Now, he felt thoroughly intimidated by her vibrant presence and singular beauty.

She drew up one eyebrow, reminding him of Yldich. She tucked a loose red curl behind her ear. 'You were never one for words, were you?'

'It's just that it's... different, meeting you in waking life,' he said.

She gazed at him. 'It does feel strange, meeting you for the first time, while you've appeared in my dreams for weeks....' She handed him a mug of water. 'You gave me quite a scare, that last time. I thought you were lost.'

Rom wondered if there was anything that could truly scare her.

She stared at his face, his dark eyes, with a pensive expression. 'My father has travelled for years, looking for the dark young man from his true-dreams. Most people were beginning to think he was just a myth.' Her mouth curved into a smile. 'They didn't expect *Dáydach* to actually bring him back with him, in the end. And now here you are.' She eyed him curiously. 'Tell me, Rom. How did he find you? How did he persuade you to come all the way up here?' Rom hesitated. He stared at his hands.

'I—I didn't want to come at all, at first,' he said. 'It sort of just...happened. I suppose I finally agreed to come when I realized I had nowhere left to run.'

Her eyes widened. 'What do you mean? What are you running from?'

He lifted his face. 'I've come to think that the thing I've been running from is the same thing that had Yldich go and search for me all those years ago.'

'What... what about your family? Do they know you're here?' He shook his head. 'Why not?'

'It's a long story,' he said huskily. 'My mother...sold me to a Southern lord when I was small, and I was almost killed serving at his Keep. I ran away, and I've survived on my own ever since.'

'Well... I can see there is more to you than can be told during a harvest song.'

'It must have been so much different, growing up in this house.' There was a wistful look in his eyes. 'Yldich told us about you, how you used to bring home a fox when you were small, and other things....'

She chuckled. 'He told you about that?'

'Tell me what it was like,' he said almost hungrily.

She leaned her elbows on the side of the bed. 'Well, my mother always said that I was running wild, that I would grow up to be a wolf, or worse, a boy, if she let *Dáydach* have his way.' She grinned. 'I suppose he spoiled me no end. He let me come and go into the woods as I pleased, only coming home when I was hungry. *Dáydach* taught me how to ride a horse, shoot a bow, and sing all the songs he knew, the ballads, the love songs, the healing songs....'

His dark eyes lit up. 'It must have been wonderful.'

She smiled. 'We went into the woods and hills, and he taught me how to call the birds, and how to move so that I could walk straight into a herd of deer.' She grinned. 'Of course, sometimes it went wrong. Once, I spooked a big stag. Yldich had to rescue me, and we both ended up face down in a muddy pond. We had to walk all the way home covered in mud, with the prospect of facing my mother's scorn if she caught us before we could sneak in the back way. Which of course, she did.'

Rom chuckled, thinking of Eald's confrontation with the black boar. He found himself telling Maetis the tale with verve, and continued with the story of how he had met Eldairc, when the tall *Einache* hit him on the face by way of introduction, and how the entire town of Woodbury had armed itself with pots and pans behind Yldich's back while he had tried to remain inconspicuous.

Yldich heard the sound of their laughter walking through the corridor. He entered the room, his brows lifted in surprise. 'I hope Maetis isn't bothering you with her fanciful tales.' He laid his hands on her shoulders.

Maetis smiled up at him. 'Rom has been telling me of your journey north.' Yldich looked at Rom. The sickly pallor had lifted from his face. He smiled; lights were dancing in his dark eyes. He seemed a different person when he smiled.

'Well, mind you don't wear him out with talk,' he said to Maetis. 'Tomorrow is the big day.'

'What day?' Rom said.

'The heads of the Northern clans are coming to the House. I'm going to officially introduce you.'

That evening, Yldich, Eldairc and Eald joined Rom in his chamber for dinner. Rom was glad to notice he could sit at the table for an hour or two without his hands shaking or his legs feeling like they were giving way. Eldairc and Eald were bubbling with excitement about the gathering of the clan leaders and their people.

'It's going to be wonderful,' Eald said, after he had just stuffed his mouth full of bread.

Yldich lifted a brow and nudged him lightly. 'Chew first, then speak.'

Eald swallowed the lump of bread quickly, almost managing to look meek. He smiled his skewed smile and continued. 'There's going to be music, and singing, and dancing...' His eyes were glinting with excitement.

'And I've heard there will be a hunt, the day after,' Eldairc added.

'Which no doubt will be a great success after the heavy drinking the night before,' Yldich said. Eldairc snorted with amusement.

Rom stared at them, his mind filled with images of a great hall filled with tall, rowdy *Einache* warriors. 'I'm—I'm not supposed to attend, am I? After you've introduced me to the clan leaders. I'd only be in the way... I know nothing of *Einache* customs. I wouldn't want to be a nuisance....'

'Nonsense,' Eldairc said. His green eyes glittered. 'You're going to come, and you're going to dance as well, even if I have to pull you onto the dance floor myself.' Rom stared at him in slight shock.

Yldich grinned widely. 'Or maybe you'd rather dance with the girls. Maetis would appreciate you joining in.'

'She would?' Rom said as if to himself. He gazed in the distance. His eyes went vague.

Yldich and Eldairc stared at him, then looked at each other with their brows lifted. Eldairc's mouth pulled into a grin and he opened his mouth to speak, but something in Yldich's eyes made him close it again.

'I'm sure she would,' Yldich said to Rom. 'Though you might want to take an effort to make yourself a little more presentable.' He looked at Rom's appearance with a critical eye.

Rom brought a hand to his face and felt the days' worth of stubble on his chin. He'd long ago noticed a difference in beard growth between *Einache* and *Tzanatzi*. The stubble was by no means as heavy as Eldairc's would have been. However, a bath and a shave were long overdue.

Yldich thought for a moment. 'Maybe I can get you something a little more festive to wear than that travel-worn tunic.'

That night, despite his worries about the clan gathering, Rom slept deep and long. He woke up feeling better than he had in days.

Someone had left some towels and a bar of soap on the chair next to his bed. There was also a tidy pile of clothes. There was a pair of long fitted trousers made of supple leather; a white shirt and a sleeveless tunic in dark red with elaborate embroidery like the kind he had seen the men in Woodbury wear. They had probably been made for an *Einache* adolescent, he thought as he held them up to get an impression of their size. There was a knock on the door and Eald rushed in, his face sticky with some kind of icing sugar.

'There's a washroom behind the kitchen,' he said. 'Yldich said to tell you breakfast is ready after you've had your bath. He wants to see you when you're ready. In his study. That's two doors down, on the left.' He was about to rush off again.

'Hold on, what are you up to?'

Eald grinned. 'They're baking lots and lots of these cakes with icing on top. The ones that come out of the oven lopsided or fall off the trays are fair game. But you have to be fast. The other boys know it too.'

Rom managed to make his way to the washroom without frightening strange *Einache* on the way. The washroom was a large chamber with a flagstone floor. In the front section were two wash basins made of stone, two large wooden cabinets and some benches. In the back to the right there was a section that was partitioned off by large wooden screens. He suspected it was a sort of steam room. There was a large stove and a pile of logs, and a few buckets with copper ladles. There was a large bath to the right. Steam was rising from the water; apparently, Eald had warned someone in the kitchen that he was up. Rom pulled off his clothes and lowered himself into the water before it could cool off.

After he finished soaking, scrubbing and shaving while still in the bath, out of habit, he got out and tried on the clothes. They fit almost perfectly. He put the crystal on the leather cord back around his neck and hid it in his tunic.

There was a mirror on the wall above the washbasin. It had been fashioned from a kind of metal that looked like silver, and had been polished until it was clear as glass. Rom approached it with a slight sense of apprehension. He was still not used to his own face; in the wild, there had been no mirrors. He had only seen it three times: twice in the mirror in Woodbury, and once in his nightmare.

He held his breath and looked up. The young man that stared back at him from the mirror looked lean and pale. He could see the slender bones of the face beneath the skin. He touched his hair. It was really in bad need of a trimming. He experimentally stuck the front locks behind his ears.

He was reaching for his knife when he was surprised by a clear mental image of the *Tzanatzi* he'd seen in *ayúrdimae*. Unlike the Southern men he had been used to all his life, they had not cropped their hair short, but had worn it shoulder-length or even longer. Some he had seen wearing it tied back into tails with leather strips, others had the parts that fell back into their eyes tied behind their ears.

Something, some inner decision, made him put back the knife with a sense of finality. He took a deep breath and nodded at the young man in the mirror. 'Better get used to it,' he said under his breath. A smile lit up his dark eyes.

He went to the kitchen, which was buzzing like a bee-hive with activity. Yárah and a group of young *Einache* boys and girls went to and fro taking trays of hot pies out of the ovens, kneading dough for new ones, and turning roasts on spits. Children ran about, trying to keep out of the way and avoid a scolding while keeping an eye out for fortunate mishaps involving cookies.

Rom's arrival made a hush fall over the kitchen. Children suddenly went uncommonly quiet and still, and stared at him with wide eyes. Two older girls started to whisper behind their hands and giggle nervously.

'Now, you girls get busy and finish that dough,' Yárah said. She put some bread, a jar of honey and a slab of butter on a big plate and handed it to Rom. 'Here, lad. See if you can find a place to eat in peace.' Activity in the kitchen resumed; children went back to their hunt for scraps, though they looked back at the strange young man every once in a while to see what he was up to.

Rom looked around for a space to sit down but everywhere he looked there were pairs of eyes, blue, green, and grey, staring at him with great curiosity. He fidgeted with his plate. He heard a familiar voice call out over the general din.

'Rom, over here.' Eldairc beckoned him from his perch on a bench in the corner of the kitchen. Rom hastily sat down beside the tall *Einache*, trying to become invisible while he ate. 'It's a right hornet's nest, isn't it?' Eldairc popped a piece of bread into his mouth. 'And it's going to get worse after the guests arrive.' He looked as if he thoroughly enjoyed himself. He winked at one of the young girls, who stared at them from under her long eyelashes. She blushed and quickly turned back to her work. Eldairc grinned.

'Some young warriors have invited me to join them in practice this afternoon,' he said. 'Why don't you come too. See if you can show off that move you used on Yldich.'

Rom was about to decline, when something in Eldairc's expression stopped him. 'I might, if Yldich doesn't keep me too long with his introduction to the clan heads.' He thought for a moment. 'Eldairc, have you any idea what I should expect?'

Eldairc shook his head. 'Anything, when Yldich is concerned.'

After breakfast Rom took leave of Eldairc and went to Yldich's study. He knocked three times, but when there was no answer, he decided to wait for Yldich inside. He looked around curiously.

Yldich's study was a large chamber with windows to the west and south and a large hearth to the east. The north wall was almost entirely hidden from view by bookcases; their shelves were laden with old books and scrolls, boxes, ink pots, bundles of quills, and jars containing all sorts of strange objects, including nuts and seeds, the skeletons of small mammals, and glittering crystals. In the south corner of the room there was a large oak table littered with papers, some with writing, others with watercolours of plants and trees. There were six chairs around the table, and a couple of big wicker chairs with thick cushions before the hearth. The cushions looked as if they had once been a deep red colour. Time had faded them to a soft dusty pink.

In the southwest corner of the room there were two heavy chests with iron locks. Rom wondered what Yldich kept in them. He walked over to the windows, and gazed out over the snow-covered fields and hills. Far away in the distance he could see the tops of the cliffs he had been standing on only a few days before. He recognized them immediately. Below them must be Gardeth Battle Field. He stared at the cliffs, the miniature trees and shrubs, and envisioned the Plain below.

He could see the gathering armies in his mind's eye: the slender *Tzanatzi* archers in green, the swordsmen and women, in hauberks of steel, and tunics in dark red like old blood, their dark hair bound back from their brow, their dark eyes proud as they rode their horses through the Forest. He could see the gathered *Einache*, waiting for their arrival at the edge of the bowl-like Plain with grim and desperate faces. Veterans and inexperienced youths gripped their swords and axes with white-knuckled hands, their breath pluming white against the evening sky.

A dark horror crept over the Plain. It slowly made its way towards the gathered *Einache*. Rom could almost feel it. A soft humming sound was rising in his ears. The *Yaever* were singing their song to ensnare the master of the black terror. His breath was coming fast and shallow when his gaze was pulled towards the cliff.

Two men faced each other and drew their swords. He could almost hear the screech of metal as they threw themselves at each other, again and again, like the armies below as they charged and the swordsmen in the front lines engaged in battle. Arrows whistled and when they hit their targets hoarse cries

tore the air. Over it all the dark sense of dread was rising. It squeezed the life
and breath out of the *Einache* warriors and drained them of courage. Rom's
breath came in shallow gasps; his hands, laid flat on the window panes were
trembling.

'Easy, lad.'

He felt a hand on his shoulder and flinched. He whirled around. Yldich
had come in behind him without making a sound.

Rom stared at him with wide eyes. 'It's—it's as if it never stopped....'
Yldich looked at him with a puzzled expression on his face. 'The battle,' Rom
said. 'I can feel it. It's—it's as if there's a rent in the fabric of time, a tear, and
all the pain, all the anguish were sucked into it, and it's still there, all of it,
only it's gone twisted, and evil, and dark—'

'Hold on, now.' Yldich went over to one of the chests. He got out a flask
and filled a cup. 'Here. Drink this.'

Rom accepted the cup and took a gulp. He swallowed and coughed. A
fiery sensation travelled down to his stomach and eased the pain. The
trembling subsided. He managed a wry smile. 'I'm starting to understand why
the veterans in the towns of the South keep themselves drunk as often as they
can afford it. It takes the edge off.'

'Off what?'

'The memories,' Rom said huskily. He gazed at the cliffs. They seemed
to pull at him. He tore away his gaze with an effort and turned to look at
Yldich. 'It never stopped. It's all still there.'

Yldich nodded slowly. 'I know. I can't feel it as clearly as you, but I
think I've always known it.'

Rom was aware of an old, heavy sense of grief that rose to his throat and
nearly closed it up with unshed tears. 'How can you stand it?' His voice
sounded strangled. 'How could you live here all these years, almost on top of
it, and not go mad?'

Yldich smiled. 'It's a little different for me.' He motioned for Rom to
come and sit at the table.

'I told you how I was ill for a long time after the Battle. Several times, I
was near death. I went further and further in the experience of *Eärwe*, the all-
encompassing, each time before I was pulled back by the *Yaever*. It...made
me reconsider my life, question the convictions that I had, that had been the
rock-solid foundation of my life.' He stared in the distance. 'I began to see
beyond the opposites of good and evil. I released my hatred and my fear. I
began to realize the only solution lies in unity. I devoted my life to it, healing
and teaching.'

Rom stared at him. 'Still, you came back to this life, this place, again and
again, for five hundred years. Why?'

Yldich motioned to the window and the cliffs in the distance. 'Because, as you say, it never stopped. The rift, as you call it, is still there. Something has yet to be resolved before I am released from this life. That is my belief.' He sighed. 'I have been balancing, healing, and teaching for five hundred years, yet the darkness hasn't lifted, and the rift is still there, all the anguish and pain turned to darkness, poisoning the earth, threatening my people and our way of life. It has separated the northern part of Gardeth Forest from the southern part. It has enabled the dead to linger. It has instilled a deep mistrust of anything not-*Einache* in the majority of my people. And it has made the Forest into a place of horror for some. It has worsened in the last seven years.' He looked at Rom. 'And then I began to dream you.'

Rom blinked and stared at him. 'Tell me.'

'It began with an image that came back in my dreams, again and again... I saw the Plain of Gardeth Battle field. It was eerily silent. The earth was black and barren; the sky a deep, dark red. I saw a young man in the middle of the plain. He stood there with his eyes closed. His sword glinted silver as he held it up to the sky. Light seemed to infuse it, and stream through his hands like lightening. He plunged the sword into the earth, and the light streamed through his hands, through the blade of the sword. The hard, blackened surface of the earth started to crack. Tiny green shoots appeared through the cracks, and lifted their little heads. They were budding and growing, leaves unfurling, until the young man was standing in a field of lush green grass, plants and trees, buds opening in an explosion of flowers of yellow, and pink, and gold...'

Rom released a breath. Tears had risen to his eyes. 'What—what did he look like?'

'Almost exactly like the stray young half-*Tzanatzi* I met in the common room of the *Squealing Pig*.' A smile deepened the wrinkles at the corners of Yldich's eyes.

Rom sat back and blinked away tears. He felt strangely moved by the image, by its beauty that contrasted sharply with the heavy sense of guilt, and the dark horror that haunted him in his dreams. He swallowed. 'But... I wouldn't know how to begin healing this—this great wound. What could I possibly do?'

Yldich cupped his chin in his hands and sat looking at him with his eyes half-closed. 'If there's something I've learned in all my long years, it's that intention is everything. When you are clear about what it is you want to accomplish, the how will come to you as you go along. So, when you think of that image, what does your heart tell you?'

Rom sat staring in the distance. He concentrated on his heart; unbidden the images came to him of *Tzanatzi* and *Einache* falling to the earth, and the snow covered them all like a shroud. He felt his heart go out to them. 'I would have peace. I want the pain to end. I want the rift to heal.'

'Well. If that is your intention, the how will come to you as you go along. Just have a little faith.'

Rom stared at him. 'Faith in what?'

'In *Sanáyah*, the Unfolding of the World.' Yldich smiled. 'Or, if that's too *Einache* a concept for you: have some faith in your own heart.'

Rom stared at the table top. He looked up. 'And you had enough faith in a dream to go and convince a complete stranger to travel north with you.' He thought back to their first meeting, and saw himself as Yldich must have seen him: a dark, withdrawn young man, his eyes hard with caution and deep-seated mistrust. 'It—it must have been no easy task.'

Yldich shook his head and smiled. 'The hard part was not to convince you. The hard part was getting you here alive.'

Sunlight peeped through the south window of Yldich's study and threw a warm beam of light across the table.

'The clan heads will be coming soon.' Yldich got up. 'You'd better get ready.'

'What do you expect me to do?'

'As little as possible.' Yldich grinned. 'And you'd better let me do the talking. Some of these clan leaders are rather set in their ways. Their opinions are a little…old-fashioned. Any idea not traditionally *Einache* might ruffle their feathers. But don't let them intimidate you. Just go along with the spirit of the thing, and you'll be fine.' Rom frowned. He couldn't think of an event he'd rather miss than the gathering of the clan heads.

'I'll have to start getting everything ready now. Why don't you join us in an hour. Oh, and better get your sword,' Yldich said airily, as he walked towards the door. 'The old warriors like that sort of thing. Now, it's one door down the hallway, the large chamber on the left with the double doors. Can't miss it. See you later.'

Rom went back to his room and sat staring at the dying fire for a long time. He stood up and girded on the *Einache* sword. He stood before the hearth, gazing at the blackened remains of the fire. Instinctively, his hand went to the crystal that lay against his heart.

'*Na' Héach*,' he whispered. He took a deep breath and left the room.

When he stood before the doors, he hesitated a moment. The sound of voices was coming from within. Apparently, the clan leaders had arrived and the council was already underway. He was about to knock, when one of the voices was raised. It was deep and booming.

'We've always held you in great respect, Yldich, but to bring in a stranger, because of a dream....'

'And not just any stranger, if the rumours are true,' another voice said. It was slightly rougher than the first one. 'An *ohênstriër Tzanat*—'

Rom set his teeth and pushed open the doors. He looked around. The chamber was large, and sparsely furnished. The walls were decorated with old spears and shields. A tapestry in green and gold added some colour to the north wall. There was a window to the west. The sun had not yet risen high enough to light the room sufficiently, so thick candles had been lit in the heavy chandelier, a great wheel that hung suspended from the ceiling. There was a table in the middle of the chamber that seated six impressively tall *Einache* men in their travelling gear.

They were clad in leather, fur, and wool in the green and earthy hues of the forest and hill clans. They wore broad leather belts, and Rom could see the hilts of belt knives and swords sticking out. Apparently, none of the *Einache* of the high North cared much about the King's ban. They turned around to stare at Rom with their clear grey and green eyes.

Rom released a breath and looked around for Yldich. He was seated at the head of the table, directly opposite the door. Yldich held out an arm in his direction.

'There he is now,' he said calmly. 'Rom, please come in. Let me introduce you to the clan leaders of the North. They are Eldich, Morven, Ullwich, Aërven, Wérdyris, and Olwen.' The men sat staring at Rom in silence.

'*Ya'haeve*,' Rom said. He looked around the circle of unfamiliar faces, and tried not to betray his nervousness.

'*This* is the man you have told us about? The one who is supposed to help us defeat the dark terror?' Ullwich, a younger *Einache* clan leader with hair and a short beard the colour of light beer, lifted a brow.

The clan leader called Morven, a big-boned warrior in his late forties with eyes the colour of steel, knit his bristling brows. 'Man?' he said in a gruff voice, and looked at Rom with his sharp grey eyes, taking in his slender build, his narrow face. 'Looks more like a boy to me.'

'Or a girl,' Wérdyris, a sandy-haired giant, said with a wry grin. Deep, booming laughter rose around the table. Rom felt his face burn. His eyes turned black with anger. His hand instinctively searched for the hilt of his sword. Yldich shot him a warning glance and stood up. He placed his hands on the table and looked the gathered leaders in the eye one by one.

'If you question my wisdom in this,' he said, 'maybe you would like to challenge my authority as a *Yaever* and *Hárrad* of the *Einache* as well.' The laughter died down.

'No-one wants to question your authority here, Yldich,' Morven said. His expression was grave. 'But you have to see our side. We have to deal with the reality of this black danger. It has been getting worse these last few months. Livestock has been disappearing. Crops are withering on the fields. People living at the edge of the Forest have been found dead, with no visible wounds on their bodies. Now how is this young stranger going to be of any use to us?' Rom thought the man had a point. He had no idea, himself.

'How Rom will be able to help us will become clear with time. However, I have enough experience as a *Yaever* to know the truth of my dreams. I know I have brought the right man at the right time.' Yldich looked around the table, his grey eyes stern. The conviction in his voice, that was almost palpable, silenced the clan leaders, at least for the moment. 'Now, please take a seat, and introduce yourself, Rom.' Yldich motioned at the empty chair at the other end of the table.

Rom sat down and looked around the table. Six pairs of eyes peered back. He noticed glances that were curious, others that seemed vaguely apprehensive. Morven gazed at him with a pensive expression. One or two clan leaders stared at him with eyes that were cold with hostility.

'Well, speak to us then, lad,' Morven said. 'Tell us the name of your House. Tell us about your ancestry, your forefathers and foremothers.' He leaned back into his chair and looked at him expectantly.

Rom swallowed. He hesitated. He glanced at Yldich at the head of the table, who gave an almost imperceptible nod. 'I—I don't know much about my ancestry,' he said. 'My mother was a Southern woman called Astara. Her mother was Maira. The name of my—my father no-one knows.'

Morven lifted his brows and stared at him with something of surprised pity in his eyes. Obviously, in his world, where family and lineage was identity, was everything, it was unthinkable not to know one's ancestry. Another clan leader spoke.

'You must have some idea who your father was.' Olwen, a thick-set *Einache* with ginger hair and an impressive braided beard, had a deep, booming voice that carried easily across the large table.

Rom looked at him. 'Only that he must have been *Tzanatzi*.' Ullwich and Eldich, a clan leader in his late fifties with a shock of grey hair, muttered amongst themselves, a cold look in their eyes. Rom shifted uneasily in his seat.

'I was sent to the court of a Southern noble, Lord Aldr, when I was eight,' he said. 'His hatred of *Tzanatzi* nearly had me killed. I had to flee for my life when I was about thirteen. I travelled from village to village to escape his men. I've been on my own ever since.' There was a surprised murmur across the table. Rom was vaguely surprised to see some of the icy stares thaw somewhat. Apparently, the *Einache* clan leaders shared a dislike for the Southern nobility that almost surpassed the deep-seated collective dislike they felt for anything *Tzanatzi*.

'Well,' Olwen said after a while, and pulled at his beard. 'As we can't judge your character from your lineage, you'll have to prove yourself some other way.' There was a murmur of approval across the table.

Yldich scowled. He stood up abruptly and planted his hands on the table. He leaned forward to look them in the eye. 'Now you listen to me.' They all turned to him. 'I have travelled with this young man for many days, and I trust him completely. I would gladly put my life in his hands, and my daughter's, and the responsibility of my house and everything in it.' Rom stared at Yldich. He seemed to mean every word.

'I appreciate your sentiment, Yldich,' Morven said, 'but you have to understand our reservations. He is a *Tzanatzi*, one who knows nothing of our customs, who has no ties to this land. What would a stranger care for the fate of our people and our way of life?' There was a murmur of assent across the room. Ullwich fixed Rom with a cold stare.

'Who can trust a *Tzanatzi*?' he said loudly. 'And a bastard at that.' Yldich's eyes had turned the dark grey of storm clouds. He was about to speak.

Rom swallowed. A sensation akin to indignation, like a bright light, was rising from somewhere deep within. He stared at Ullwich with non-seeing eyes, and saw instead a vision of green sunlit fields, and small round houses of reed and clay. He could almost hear the ringing laughter of children running barefoot through the grass. He stood up abruptly, moved back his chair and stepped away from the table. He took a deep breath and gripped the hilt of the *Einache* sword. A tingling sensation went through his hands, his arms, and into his heart. Words came to him and he opened his mouth before he knew what he was going to say.

'*Eyespragae Faraër, entewé ya élorae.*' His clear voice carried through the large chamber. He drew the sword. It sang as it was drawn, its high, piercing voice reverberated through the steel and flowed with the words. Driven by an impulse he did not understand, he walked over to the table, turned the sword and drove it into the wood with as much force as he could muster.

The sharp blade went in for almost a third of its length before it stopped. It quivered for some time before it was still. Rom stepped back and stared at the clan leaders with his dark eyes. They sat gazing at him, speechless.

The clan leader called Morven stood up and stared at the sword. Then he looked at Rom. He seemed to be deliberating. He moved around the table and stepped up to him. Rom had to look up to look him in the face. He was shaking, wondering what on earth he had just done. Morven took his wrist and stared at the mark of *Faraër*. He gazed into Rom's face as if he were measuring him. Rom held his breath.

'Very well, then,' Morven said. He gripped Rom by the arms and kissed him firmly on both cheeks. '*Ya élorae Faraër,*' he said in a solemn voice. He released Rom and stepped back. 'Let's give the boy a chance. Can't see the harm in that.'

There was a hesitant murmur of agreement from the other clan leaders. One by one they stood up and nodded at Rom.

'*Ya élorae Faraër,*' they murmured under their breath.

Yldich was the last to join them. Lights danced in his clear grey eyes. 'Now that's settled, you had all better get some rest after your journey. Tonight there will be a feast in the Great Hall in your honour. Your chambers have all been made ready. *Ya'herwe sá eldérwera.* Enjoy the hospitality of my House in peace.'

Rom felt slightly numb as he watched the clan leaders leave.

Yldich came and stood beside him. 'I think that went rather well.'

'They didn't seem overly impressed.

Yldich chuckled. 'It takes more than thrusting a sword through the table to impress these old war-horses. But you did well. Better than I expected. They didn't even demand you prove yourself in a man-to-man swordfight with one of their warriors. It's an old custom, but I wouldn't put it past them.'

Rom turned to him in dismay. 'You might have warned me.'

Yldich grinned. 'I don't think I could have convinced you to come if I had.' He went over to the table and poured them both a cup of mead. 'Now tell me, where did you learn the words to the Pledge of *Faraër*? Did Eldairc teach you?'

'The—the what?'

'You spoke them, just now,' Yldich said.

'I don't know what I said. The words just came to me and I spoke them.' Yldich stared at him. Rom was starting to feel slightly anxious. 'Why, what did I say?'

'You took the pledge of *Faraër*, swearing to dedicate your sword and your life to the *Einache* people.'

Rom's eyes grew wide. 'I did?'

Yldich chuckled and shook his head. 'Now you had better think of a way to get that sword out again.'

Eldairc shook his head at the sword that was stuck in the table. He had tried several times to pull it out, but his efforts had only resulted in a painfully pulled muscle. He moved his arm gingerly and winced. Yldich had already sent for the smith and a woodworker.

Eldairc turned to Rom. 'I never would have thought you had it in you.'

Yldich grinned. 'It's an ancient custom. You may not have heard of it. When a warrior who wears the Mark swears the oath of *Farae*, he is supposed to perform some sort of impossible feat to prove his integrity and intention. Passion can lead to improbable results—'

'It was more than passion,' Rom interjected. 'It felt as if I was... led somehow.' He bit his lip. 'Those words... I don't know where they came from...'

'Words shape energy and direct it,' Yldich said. 'Words of power can momentarily lift the limitations you have placed upon yourself and the world.'

Eldairc lifted a brow. 'They certainly changed the way Rom handled his sword. Yldich, if this was the kind of thing that would sway the clan heads to your way of thinking, why didn't you teach them to Rom instead of just waiting to see what would happen?'

Yldich smiled. 'It's not just the words, it's the intention behind them. You have to be, how shall I put it, *inspired* for them to work. Do you really think Rom could have pulled off a feat like this just because I told him he could?'

Eldairc looked at Rom, who stood staring at his hands with a look of uncertainty. He grinned. 'I see what you mean.' Rom looked up.

'Yldich... did you mean what you said, just then? Do you really have that much faith in me?'

Yldich smiled at him. 'When I look at you with my eyes, I see a stubborn, obstinate youth with a temper. When I look at you with my heart, I see a man with compassion, love, and courage—' Rom swallowed. He turned away abruptly and went over to the window. He closed his eyes and leaned his brow against the cool glass, pushing back the tears that closed up his throat. 'Even if you can't see it yet,' Yldich said softly.

While Eldairc joined the young warriors in their practice rounds, Yldich sent Rom back to his chamber to get some rest. He went without protest. He was relieved he didn't need to face any more curious or hostile glances for the rest of the day. He let himself drop into the sheepskins and realized the day's confrontation had worn him out. He fell into a dreamless sleep. He woke up a few hours later at the opening of the door.

'*Ya'hey*,' Eldairc said. He stood looking down at Rom, his hands on his hips. 'Better get up now, or you'll miss all the fun. What's more, you'll miss dinner.' Rom sat up and pushed his hair out of his face.

Eldairc had changed and was wearing dark green trousers and a tunic the colour of bright young leaves with elaborate embroidery, with a slightly darker green sleeveless tunic on top. His hair, which was usually an unkempt mass of shaggy snarls and curls, had been brushed until it shone like gold leaf. Rom lifted a brow at his elegant appearance.

Eldairc grinned. 'Élora, the healer apprentice, said she would dance with me if I promised to brush my hair.' His green eyes glittered. 'You wouldn't think it to look at her, she is such a slight thing, but the girl has quite a temperament.' There was a jug of water and a bowl on the table. Rom washed his face and hands. 'That's you ready,' Eldairc said. 'Let's go.'

The Great Hall lived up to its name. It boasted three great hearths with blazing fires. Tables and chairs, which in winter were usually grouped around the hearths, had been placed in large concentric semicircles in the middle of the Hall. They faced the podium, a raised platform that had been set up for the musicians and for dancing. People serving food used the paths that had been kept clear between the tables.

A few musicians were still busy tuning their instruments. Rom noticed small stringed instruments like lutes, flutes and a great harp.

Chandeliers with burning candles, like the one he had seen in the council chamber but even bigger, had been suspended from the ceiling. Oil lamps on the walls provided additional lighting.

Rom noticed that the clan leaders and their people, easily identifiable by the shade of their clothes, tended to band together. He saw Ullwich and his people, mostly warriors dressed in the ochre and brown colours of the hill clans, at the tables to the left. Morven and his people were sitting nearest the dance floor on the right, talking spiritedly amongst each other. They wore the green and yellow hues of the forest clans. The other clans he found less easy to identify in the throng. Yldich's people were sitting or standing about in small groups in between the larger groups of visiting clan heads.

Rom looked around and wondered what it was about the Hall that made it different from the familiar Hall at Lord Aldr's Keep. He realized it was the arrangement of tables. In the keep of a Southern noble, his immediate family and distinguished guests would have taken their seats on a raised dais in one section of the hall. The other people would have been awarded seats according to rank or status, with the ones highest in rank closest to the dais. Their tables would have been arranged in the form of a rough square instead of concentric circles. Servants, children and other inhabitants of low status would not have been allowed in the great hall during a feast at all, except for the kitchen staff.

As a page, he had often sneaked in to watch the musicians play. Pages who did not have to attend their masters during a feast were not allowed in the hall. The ones that got caught paid for their transgression with a severe beating. Rom had been caught more than once, yet the music and the sounds of laughter lured him to the hall every time.

The hall got more and more crowded. The hubbub reminded Rom of a busy market-place on Harvest Fest day. Eldairc pulled him over to a table in the right hand corner where Yldich and Eald had taken place.

'We saved you a seat,' Eald called out.

'I thought we might have dinner together,' Yldich said. He had changed into a slightly more colourful version of his usual simple attire: a sky-blue tunic embroidered with spiralling abstract motifs in silver-grey, a broad leather belt and indigo trousers. Eald was dressed in an apple-green tunic and dark green trousers much like Eldairc's.

As Rom sat down, he became aware of several people at the other tables staring at him with wide eyes. Some people even turned their heads to get a better look. Some looks were just curious, or abashed, but he noticed some *Einache* staring at him with clear hostility in their eyes. He stiffened.

Yldich passed him a basket with bread. 'Don't let it get to you, lad. Give them some time to get used to you.'

'Maybe you'll get a chance to sing the skipping troll song tonight,' Eldairc said with a grin. 'That should warm them towards you.'

Rom snorted. 'I don't think there's enough beer in this hall to get me to sing the *eylérwe conache*.'

Eald giggled. 'You said it again.' Rom gave him a puzzled look.

'It's the language,' Eldairc said. 'When you reverse the order of words in *Einache*, the result can be rather…unexpected. For instance, *conache eylérwe*, skipping troll means a hopping troll. *Eylérwe conache*, troll-skipping means bedding one.' Eald smirked.

'I think I'm catching on,' Rom said with a wry grin. 'I think I'll better refrain from speaking *Einache* altogether. Just to avoid any misunderstandings.'

Yldich chuckled. 'You'd better.' He passed around a bowl of vegetable preserves. A serving girl passed their table and filled their mugs with beer from a small casket. Rom tasted it. It was slightly sour and went surprisingly well with the bread and salty onion preserves.

The Hall had gradually filled up with people. Rom saw some standing about with plates in their hands. The harpist had started to play a soft, mellow tune.

'Well, it is customary for me as Head of the House to speak a few words,' Yldich said. He rose and went to the low platform, where he motioned for the harpist to stop playing. The buzz of voices in the Hall died down.

Yldich took his time calling each clan leader by name and welcoming him and the people of his House. A cheer went up at each name and mugs were raised with gusto. Much of Yldichs speech consisted of traditional and elaborate greetings and well-wishes in *Einache*, and therefore went right over Rom's head.

Eldairc and Eald joined in with each cheer; Eldairc took a large draught of his beer every time he had raised his mug. As he looked around, Rom saw most men do the same and he wondered how long it would take before they were thoroughly intoxicated.

It shall depend on how long Yldich takes with his speeches.

He grinned as he thought of the man's long-windedness.

'Good to see you enjoy yourself, lad.' A booming voice sounded from a table to his right. Morven, the clan leader of the forest clan of the Red Fox, raised his mug to him and took a large draught. Rom smiled and copied his gesture.

Maybe this evening isn't going to be so bad after all.

Suddenly he heard Yldich call out his name. He coughed and nearly spilled his beer. To his horror, he saw Yldich motion for him to come over on the platform. Faces turned to him expectantly. He wiped his mouth with his sleeve and stared back.

Eldairc nudged him with an elbow. 'Go on then. They won't expect you to sing. I hope.' He grinned and gave him a push towards the platform.

Rom passed many an *Einache* looking at him with undisguised curiosity. As he stood beside Yldich he held his breath, unnerved by the sight of a whole Hall full of *Einache*, staring at him with their clear eyes. Yldich put a hand on his shoulder. He abandoned his own language for the Southern speech so Rom could understand as well.

'Many of you may know of my reputation for oddity, whether it be deserved or no,' he began. There were a couple of grins from members of the household in front. They obviously had first-hand knowledge of Yldich's self-proclaimed peculiar behaviour. 'Some of you might think that the announcement I'm about to make falls into the same category,' and Rom noticed some of the people sit up with expectation. 'I think most of you are aware of the trouble that we are having, the Disturbance that started many years ago and is growing in the high North. These last years I have travelled far and wide, on the trail of a *Yaever* dream, a true-dream that showed me there is a way to restore the Balance.'

The Hall had grown eerily quiet. Most *Einache* seemed to have some understanding of the Disturbance Yldich was referring to. Rom noticed some whispering to their neighbours, making animated gestures. 'In this true-dream, I saw a dark young man who would restore the Balance and free us of this evil. I have searched for him for seven years, and this autumn, I have found him.'

There was a murmur across the Hall. Yldich laid a hand on Rom's shoulder. 'This is Rom, the one I have seen in my *Yaever*-dream, the one who will help us heal the Disturbance. I have travelled with him for many weeks, and together we have survived many dangers. I have come to regard him as *hwérwoden*, as family. I ask of you that you do the same, and treat him as such, whether in my House or without. *Kalantíri fayïre hwérwoden*. Behold my beloved family.'

A hum of agitated whispers went through the Hall. Rom blinked his eyes. He had expected anything but this. Yldich made a gesture with his right hand, silencing the Hall.

'There is another I would like to present to you,' he went on. He gestured towards Eald, who sat on the edge of his seat, his eyes shining. He was on the platform in two heartbeats. 'This is Eald, of the village of *Wýntheir*. His people were lost in a raid by Southern riders. He has travelled with us this long journey and has shown all the signs of an aspiring *Yaever*. I have decided to adopt him as my foster-son as well, and to teach him the way of the *Yaever*. *Kalantíri fayïre hwérwoden*.' There was another murmur in response. This time, most *Einache*, having recovered from their initial shock, gave the correct traditional response.

'*Kalantíri hwérwoden érda*.'

As they sat down at their table, kegs of beer and cider were passed around the Hall. Youths carried trays with an assortment of earthenware pots and bowls of steaming food and put them on the tables so the guests could serve themselves.

'Well,' Eldairc said to Rom as he stood up and began to ladle out the stew, 'I suppose this is as close to becoming a true *Einache* as you're going to get. But don't expect it to speed up beard growth. It is a purely metaphysical thing, I'm afraid.' Yldich chuckled. Rom was still recovering from the shock.

'Did you know he was going to do this?' he said to Eldairc.

'With Yldich, you can expect anything,' he replied.

Eald sat smiling broadly at Rom. 'Now no-one can give you a hard time about not being one of us ever again.'

'Don't be too certain about that,' Yldich said in a sober tone. 'Prejudice is like blight weed. Once it gets into your vegetable patch, it is hard to get rid of.' He took a large bowl with fruit preserves and served them from it. 'Now, let's enjoy our food and have some fun. But don't overdo it,' he said with an eye on Eald's plate, which started to resemble a mountain landscape in miniature. 'You can't dance on a full stomach.'

Rom was surprised at the different kinds of preserves being passed around the tables. There were bowls of sweet apple preserves tasting like cider and cinnamon, carrot slices in golden syrup, *weyberries* in a spicy yellow sauce that tasted well with meat. There were also onions in vinegar and dried tomatoes in oil that smelled like cloves. He commented about it to Yldich.

'In the North, fresh fruits and vegetables are hard to come by in winter,' he responded. '*Einache* cooks have perfected the craft of preserving until it became a form of art. They have all sorts of secret recipes they guard as closely as a mountain troll its hoard.'

Rom looked up from his plate. 'Just to be certain…there's no such thing as mountain trolls, is there?'

Yldich grinned at him. 'You might be surprised.'

Rom shook his head, perturbed. 'Well, at this point, I'm ready to believe just about anything. I won't even be surprised if pixies do dance in the market square the night before Harvest Fest and there really is a gateway to the Underworld guarded by dragons.'

Yldich felt a tingle of foresight. 'Perhaps that's just as well,' he muttered in his beard.

When most people had finished their meals, a band of youths went through the Hall and took away the empty plates and bowls. The harpist started to play, and gradually more and more musicians joined him on the platform. He began to play a more vigorous piece. Two girls with deerskin drums accompanied the plucking of the strings in a rhythm that was steadily increasing. A man with a lute took over the cheerful tune from the harpist and quickened the pace even more, until the melodies were tumbling over each other like children playing in the snow. Eldairc had trouble sitting still; he drummed his fingers on the table and tapped his feet on the floor.

Some of the younger guests and members of the household got up on the platform and started to dance. It was a vigorous dance, Rom noted, with a lot of grasping of hands, turning, and swirling of skirts. The lively tune was contagious, and he noticed many people at the tables stamping their boots or clapping their hands to the beat of the music to encourage the dancers.

A slender girl with copper hair in a thick, waist-length braid threaded through with silver stepped up to their table. She wore a flowing azure dress.

She greeted Yldich in the traditional way, putting her right hand on her heart and bowing slightly. '*Ya'haeve, Yaever* Yldich.'

Yldich smiled at her. '*Ya'haeve*, apprentice Élora.'

The girl nodded at Eald and Rom, then turned to Eldairc. 'I believe you promised me a dance, master Eldairc,' she said.

'I believe I did,' he said with a broad smile, and got up quickly. His green eyes glittered. He accompanied her to the dance floor, one arm around her waist.

Rom sat watching them dance. A growing smile lit his face. Eldairc and Élora moved around the dance floor as if they had it all to themselves. The tall *Einache* moved confidently; he danced with a kind of flair that pulled all eyes in the Hall to them. The slender girl, who had to tilt her head back to look him in the face, easily kept up with his energetic movements. She whirled and grabbed his hands, laughing as he lifted her from the floor as if she weighed nothing more than a child. As he put her back down again, Rom could see her round cheeks blushing and her eyes shining with delight.

Eald used the table top as a drum, like many of the other guests, and after a while, Rom found he couldn't resist joining in. They had been at it for a while, Yldich grinning broadly, when the musicians changed pace and started to play a slow, almost solemn piece. A girl played a haunting melody on a reed flute. Eldairc returned to his place at the table with a broad smile on his face. He was panting and wiping the sweat off his brow with his sleeve. A young boy carrying a beer casket refilled his mug and he emptied it in one draught.

Rom listened to the yearning melody of the flute. It wakened something in him, something he couldn't quite define. The dancers left the floor and others took their place. They danced at a slow pace, in pairs, in a way that was much more stylized than the loosely choreographed dances of a moment ago. Though there was nothing formal or stiff about it. The dance flowed effortlessly around the melancholic tune of the harp and reed. One of the drummers began thrumming a slow, sensuous rhythm with her fingers.

Yldich sat staring at the dancers with a faint wistful smile. He became aware of Rom's glance and turned to him. 'This is an old *Einache* dance,' he said softly. 'It has been danced for thousands of years. It dates back to a time long before the Battle. No-one knows its exact origins, but I think its roots lie in the ancient ceremonial dances that celebrated the movement of the Sun and the Moon, the seasons, and the *Sha'neagh d' Ea,* the Wheel of Life.' He stared at the dancers. 'In settlements that have had more contact with the South, like Woodbury, they don't know this dance anymore. Here in the high North, we still do, although the real meaning of the dance is all but forgotten.'

Rom felt a light touch on his shoulder. Maetis had come up beside his chair. She wore an emerald-green dress that flowed around her ankles. Her long copper curls had been partly put up in spiralling shapes held together by brass pins. Most of it curled over her shoulders and down her back in a fiery cascade. Her eyes were very bright. She held out her hand. He stared at her, taken aback.

'I can't,' he said breathlessly, shaking his head. 'I can't dance. I don't know the paces. Better ask Eldairc.'

'But it's *you* I'm asking,' she said, her mouth curved in a smile. 'Come on, Rom.' Teasing lights were in her eyes.

She took his hand and he dared not refuse her. He let her pull him to the dance floor while he threw a worried glance over his shoulder. Eald and Yldich sat looking at him with wide grins. Other *Einache* they passed stared at them with unfathomable expressions on their faces.

'Now, don't worry,' Maetis said as she took his hands. 'It's easy. Just do whatever I do.' He held his breath and let her pull him into the dance, while he kept an eye on the other dancers to see what he was supposed to be doing. They circled each other, and held up their arms like the branches of trees, leaning into each other and out again, their hands touching lightly. They whirled around each other, their arms locking. The dance ended with a curtsey that was almost formal and reminded him of the mating dance of birds. Then the whole sequence was repeated with variations.

He copied Maetis' movements, frowning with concentration, until he found there was a pattern to the dance that repeated itself, and he eased into it, letting the music guide him. The subtle drumming and the undulating notes of the flute had a soothing effect and after a while he forgot to worry about the paces or about stepping on Maetis' toes. He even began to enjoy himself.

He looked into Maetis' face; her bright grey eyes were sparkling with merriment, and something else, something that was almost like a challenge. Unlike most other pairs they were of a height and able to meet each other's eyes without having to tilt their heads. Each time they completed a circle and turned back to each other, touching hands and looking into each other's eyes, Rom felt a strange sensation stir deep inside, a warm blend of happiness, excitement and nervousness. He felt it travel upwards, and run through his heart and his hands. Like in his true-dreams, he felt a pull as if from an invisible thread, that ran through his heart and connected him with Maetis.

As the music quickened, and the dance pulled him along ever faster, the other dancers and the crowd seemed to drop away. There was only the music, and the girl that smiled at him, then nearer, then farther away, eyes and hands beckoning, sometimes so close he could feel the warmth of her body. He ceased to feel the wooden boards under his feet, and the ceiling with the heavy chandeliers fell away, until it seemed to him they danced under the open sky, the blinding light of the sun shining in their eyes. There were tiny daisies in the grass under their feet, and in the girl's hair, like many white stars.

He could see circling forms everywhere: in Maetis' whirling skirts, the hearts of the flowers, the movement of the earth, the dome of blue over their heads. It seemed to him they were the centre of a great turning spiral, like the many-armed myriad of stars at night, an ancient, ever widening circle, whirling out into infinity.

As the music stopped, he heard Maetis release a sigh, and looked into her face. She stared at him, transfixed, and he wondered what she saw. His hand went up to her face of its own accord and he touched her cheek with his fingertips. Suddenly he realized where they were and he withdrew it quickly.

The harpist began to play a tune that was as different from the one they had just danced to as the morning from the evening. An *Einache* youth stepped up and touched Maetis' shoulder. She turned to him, and looked back over her shoulder once before she let him pull her into another dance. Rom walked back to the table in a daze. He noticed two or three *Einache* staring at him with something akin to icy disapproval. It was a slap in the face after the experience of the dance. He sat down and sighed.

'What is it, lad?' Yldich said.

'Nothing,' Rom said. 'Well…just the way some people looked at me.'

Yldich took a draught of beer and studied him with a pensive expression. 'Well, it will need some getting used to, a half-*Tzanatzi* dancing an ancient fertility dance with the daughter of the *Hárrad* of the *Einache*.'

'But—I thought you said it was a dance to celebrate the movements of the sun, and the moon, and seasons and such?'

'Same thing,' Yldich said with a grin. 'At least, that is how it was to the ancients, who first danced it in spring, to perpetuate the movement of life.' He took another draught of beer and looked at Rom with interest. 'It's been a long time since I saw it being danced as it's supposed to. Usually they just go through the movements without touching the essence.'

'It was as if it danced me, and not the other way around,' Rom said softly, thinking out loud. 'As if I was taken up in a movement of life that is greater and older than I am....'

Yldich drew up a brow. 'Well, I know my daughter has a certain effect on young men…' Eldairc laughed softly. Rom's face flushed. He frowned.

'It was the dance,' he said. 'There's something entrancing about it.'

'I'm sure there is,' Yldich said in a mild tone.

Much to Rom's surprise, one of the young girls he had seen working in the kitchen that morning came to their table, blushing, and asked him to dance. The harpist was playing a cheerful, simple tune, and Rom found it not too difficult to follow the girl's movements. She was about fifteen or sixteen, and had large, dark blue eyes with long lashes, from under which she looked at him with a mixture of fascination and awe. Feeling a little more confident, he whirled around with verve, only to find he was thoroughly lost. The girl laughed and helped him back into the dance. Before it had finished, Élora relieved the girl and pulled him into another. Then Eldairc came over and led her away with a cheerful grin. He danced with her tune after tune, and didn't let anyone else near her.

Rom stood to the side of the platform, watching the people turn, and bow, and laugh. Somehow, it felt as if he were part of it, although he was only watching. He felt strangely happy. He smiled as he saw Eldairc spin Élora around. Suddenly he was aware of another's presence beside him. It was Maetis. Her fingers stroked along the inside of his hand. The touch made him hold his breath.

'There will be a hunt tomorrow,' she said softly. He felt the warmth of her touch travel through his fingers, through his arm, and his heart made a little jump. 'It will be nice to be out, riding our horses into the hills. Will you come?' He hesitated. 'Please say you will,' she said, as she felt him waver.

'If you want me to be there, I will.'

She lifted her other hand to his face, and pushed the dark hair aside with a smile. 'Good,' she said with conviction. She kissed him lightly on his mouth. Rom felt his heart beat in his throat. He brought his hands to her face and kissed her back. They stood still for a moment, their faces touching. He could feel her breath on him, like in his true-dream. It felt as if they were the centre of the world. Time stood still. He dared hardly breathe, for fear he would break the fragile spell of the moment.

'I have to go,' she said softly, and drew back. She traced her fingers along his cheek with a look of regret. 'I promised Aeldic and Érdogan another dance.' He let her go. His hands suddenly felt strangely empty. 'I'll see you tomorrow.' She smiled and walked away. He stood blinking for a while in wonderment, and waited for his heart to resume its normal pace.

He felt someone's eyes on him and turned, vaguely expecting Yldich or Eldairc. Two young *Einache* warriors came up to him. He didn't know them, but by the colours of their garb he guessed they were in either Ullwich's or Eldich's party.

'*Ya'hey*,' the warrior in front said with a cheerful smile, but his eyes were cold. He took Rom's arm in a friendly gesture, and effectively pulled him through one of the side doors, while the other stood guard in the doorway.

The first *Einache* pushed Rom against the wall, lightly, but with an underlying sense of threat, that showed in his eyes, and the set of his jaw. Rom stared at him. Instinct made him clench his hands into fists.

'You,' the young man said, his voice heavy with contempt. '*K'álestre*. Descendant of demons. Why did you come? You're not wanted here.' He was standing so close Rom could smell the beer on his breath, but he did not seem drunk, or else, it was the kind of drunkenness that caused an unnatural calm. There was a look of dark loathing in his eyes. Rom felt a deep, sickening feeling in his stomach he could not put a name to, though he knew it well.

'You leave her alone, monster,' the young man spat. 'Get away, if you know what's good for you. You'll regret it if you don't.' There was a sound at the other end of the corridor and he stepped back. The warriors were gone in the blink of an eye. They left Rom staring at the doorway.

He slowly walked back into the Hall. The young warriors had disappeared in the crowd. He looked at the dance-floor. The music was as merry as before, but now he was no longer part of it, and it grated along a horrible sense of separateness. He turned and left the Hall. He walked through the great doors and stood staring at the snow with burning eyes.

The mellow light of the candles, the music and laughter spilled through the doors. He stood with his back to it, blinking in the cold, wondering why he had come at all. It didn't matter where he went; he took his face with him, and the bitter sense of separation, the loneliness to the bone. There was no escaping it. He cursed himself for believing it would ever be different. It would have been better if he had never come.

'Come out for some air?' He heard a familiar voice behind him. Eldairc was wiping his brow with his sleeve. He looked at Rom's face. It was pale and taut. 'What is it?' Rom shook his head. Eldairc went and stood before him. He peered in his face with his bright green eyes. 'What's happened?'

Rom swallowed. He felt an uneasy sense of shame, a reluctance to speak, as if by telling Eldairc he would make the words that had been said to him true. 'Nothing.'

'Really.' Eldairc lifted a brow. 'I suppose it's nothing that made you look as if you've been stabbed in the stomach?' Rom looked up. 'And you thought that by turning your back on it, it would go away?'

Rom frowned darkly. 'It was probably better if I went away, like he said.'

Eldairc stared at him in surprise. 'Who?'

Rom looked away. 'Just some men,' he said, and stared at the shadows in the snow.

Eldairc raised his brows. 'Tell me.'

'It was just the usual. He pushed me into a corridor, called me—called me a name. Said I'm not wanted here. He's probably right. Why should I be here, and cause trouble, when I don't even belong here?'

'What did he call you?'

Rom was silent for a while. He could hardly bring himself to utter the words. 'He—he called me monster. Demon. Something *Einache. K'álestre.*'

Eldairc sighed and pulled his fingers through his hair. It had already regained its usual dishevelled appearance. 'And I suppose it's because you're such a monster that Yldich goes to so much trouble for you, and that Eald fights the other boys if they say anything bad about you?' He shook his head at Rom. 'Right now, Maetis is wondering what happened to you and turning down every man who wants to dance with her.'

Rom looked up. 'She is?' Some colour came back to his face.

Eldairc grinned. 'I thought I saw something going on between you.' He laid his arm around Rom's shoulders, and shook him playfully. Rom nearly lost his footing. 'Now stop sulking outside and come with me. I know what the trouble is.'

'What?' Rom said, slightly dazed by the rough treatment.

'Not enough beer,' Eldairc said with a sober expression, and ushered him back into the house. 'But we'll soon have that fixed.'

Eight
The Hunt

Rom crept out from under the covers. He peered through his hair, squinting against the bright morning light. The door opened without so much as a knock to prepare him.

Eald stormed into the room, a whirl of colour and sound. 'Come on, get up, quickly! Or you'll miss the hunt.' Rom groaned in protest, holding his head in his hands. Eald stood before the bed, his hands in his side. 'Real *Einache* beer too much for you?' He grinned. 'Eldairc thought it might be.'

'It wasn't the quality, it was the quantity.' Rom wiped the hair out of his face. 'I lost count.'

Eald chuckled. 'But you were still sober enough to sing the skipping troll-song.'

Rom looked appalled. 'Please, tell me I didn't sing.'

'Don't worry, Eldairc only made you sing it once, then Yldich shut you up. But you should have seen the faces of the guests.'

'What—what else did I do?'

'O, nothing to worry about.' Eald smirked and made for the door. 'Now hurry, or you'll get no breakfast. I'll see you outside!'

Rom found a pile of clean clothes outside the door and took them to the bathroom. He was relieved to find it all to himself. He plunged his head in a ewer with cold water, and shaved at one of the stone sinks. As he stood before the mirror he realized he was on his guard, listening for any sounds outside the door.

He dressed quickly and walked into the kitchen, where Yárah shoved a plate with bread, butter and honey under his nose.

'Better eat fast, lad, or they'll be gone without you,' and Rom wondered if that would be such a bad thing. But then he thought of Maetis. He ate hastily and washed away the bread with a herbal brew Yárah had put beside his plate. He shuddered at the taste.

She laughed. 'That bad, is it? It chases the demons away, though.' He stared at her. 'The hangover,' she said. 'Now, away with you!'

He went outside, and found a host of *Einache* up and about in the snow before the great doors. Their horses reared and snorted, even more eager to be away than their riders. It didn't take him long to find Yldich and Eldairc, and Eald on his pony. They had brought Rom's horse saddled and ready.

'Good morning to you,' Yldich called cheerfully. His breath formed clouds in the crisp morning air. The sun had only been up for an hour or so.

'How's your head?' Eldairc said with a grin. Rom mounted the chestnut mare and grumbled. Eald chuckled.

'Get ready, now. They are impatient to start.' Yldich motioned at the head of the group. One of the clan leaders had brought his hounds. They were sniffing and yelping, tugging at the leash. A hunter blew a great horn, and the hounds were away. The hunters followed at breakneck speed. Yldich and the others followed at a considerably more leisure pace.

As they rode through the snow-covered hills, Rom sat wondering. 'Shouldn't we pursue them?' The distance between them and the head of the hunting party was steadily increasing. He was starting to feel a lot better. Apparently, Yárah's potion really did chase the demons away.

'Not really.' Yldich leaned back in the saddle at his ease, his face turned to the sun. 'The hunt is just an excuse for them to be out and about and make a lot of noise. I'll be surprised if they catch anything at all. Let them run. Enjoy the sunshine.'

'But—couldn't you use your *Yaever* senses to find game?'

'I could, but that would defeat the purpose of this day. It requires patience and silence, and it would be much too effective.' Yldich's mouth curved in a smile. 'They wouldn't enjoy themselves half as much as they are now, galloping through the hills and showing off.'

Eldairc laughed. 'I think I'll go and join them,' he said. 'I feel like showing off a little myself. Let's go, Rom,' and he spurred on his horse. Rom's horse followed before he had a chance to think.

Soon, he found he was enjoying the fast pace, the cold wind that whipped the blood to his cheeks. It was the first time he was out since their arrival at the House, and he revelled in his renewed sense of health. He was aware of the horse's powerful muscles beneath him and the creatures' desire for speed, and felt more alive than he had for days.

The group in front had split up. One party had disappeared into the woods to the west; the others deliberated whether or not to follow them. Apparently, one group of hounds had started to follow the trail of a stag through the trees, while the others had found the scent of snow hares in the hills. Their tracks were easily discernable in the fresh snow.

Maetis was among those who were about to steer their horses through the hills and fields. The party consisted mainly of young *Einache* warriors and stable boys. They turned when they heard Eldairc and Rom approach.

'*Ya'hey*,' Eldairc cried. Two or three youths grinned at him. He had met them before in weapons practice. Maetis was dressed much the same way as the young men, in leather trousers, boots lined with fleece, and a green woollen tunic that almost reached to her knees. She wore a long cloak trimmed with dark brown fur. Her long hair blazed like fiery gold in the morning sun.

Rom stared at her, fidgeting with his reigns. She turned her horse, and smiled when she saw him.

'I'm glad you decided to come.' Her bright eyes were shining. 'Let's go race the hares,' she cried, and spurred on her horse. The cry was taken up by the others. They shot away over the fields, trying to outrun each other through the snow.

Rom spurred on the chestnut mare. She seemed eager to run some more. Despite Yldich's teachings he still had not taken the time to find out her name. Although, he thought with a wry smile, it probably was something like "runs until her rider drops off with weariness". Once she was running, she seemed inexhaustible.

While Eldairc and the other warriors took the lead at great speed, laughing and shouting friendly insults at each other, Maetis lagged behind a little, until she was riding next to Rom.

'*Racing* the hares is just what it will amount to.' She chuckled. Her fair skin was flushed with the wind. 'And the hares will win. They're much too clever to get caught. But that's what it's all about, isn't it? Galloping through the snow.' She seemed to share Yldich's attitude towards the hunt.

'Have you ever hunted them another way?' Their pace slowed gradually, until the others were tiny dark figures against the snow in the distance.

'Of course. If you want to catch snow hares, you have to outsmart them, which isn't easy. They're quick as water over rocks. They like to bewilder you with their tricks.'

'So how do you catch them?'

'By not underestimating them, as these lads are doing.' She grinned. 'You have to have eyes in the back of your head, and sing them into a semblance of safety, until they get cocky. Then you pounce them.'

He laughed out loud. He couldn't help it, she sounded so self-assured, much like the cocky hares she was describing. She turned her face to him and drew up a brow.

'Are you laughing at me?' Her expression was serious, but there was a sparkle of amusement in her eyes, and her lips seemed ready to curve into a smile.

'I wouldn't dare.' His mouth twitched.

'If you're so sure of yourself, why don't you try and catch *me*.' Maetis spurred on her horse. She shot away like an arrow. The hooves of her horse hardly seemed to touch the pristine snow. Rom spurred on his mare. They shot over the white fields, laughing with the joy of pure speed, while the wind whipped the hair in their faces.

They ran until they reached a line of trees. They marked the fringe of a patch of woodland that sheltered a frozen lake. Maetis sprang off her horse and looked back at Rom, motioning for him to be quiet. They left the horses behind and approached the lake with caution. Rom wondered why she was suddenly moving so carefully. Her boots made almost no sound. He followed slightly less noiselessly. He gasped with surprise when Maetis pulled him to the ground and pointed to a spot at the edge of the lake.

They lay in a hollow in the ground behind a small mound of earth, and he peered breathlessly over the top in the direction she indicated. A hind and a fawn stood at the water's edge. They drank cautiously. The hind lifted her head to sniff the air every once in a while, her tail wiggling nervously. Her dark, soft eyes were watchful.

Rom felt a strange sense of exhilaration. The blood still coursed wildly through his veins because of the ride, and the tension of the moment. There was also his proximity to Maetis. She lay so close to him he could feel her body press against his.

A sound, or the ghost of a sound alerted the hind. One moment she stood as if frozen. The next, like autumn leaves that quivered and were taken by the wind, she and her fawn were gone. Maetis sighed and turned around.

'Weren't they beautiful?' she said. 'I keep a part of the lake open in winter, so the animals can drink here. You don't see many fawns that young in winter. The hind must have birthed out of season.' She sat up. 'Now if you keep very still, sometimes you can even see lynx here.'

She got a bundle out of her saddlebag. She spread a blanket on the ground, sat down cross-legged next to Rom and opened the bundle. It contained some thickly sliced bread and slices of meat. She handed a piece to Rom. 'If we sit here long enough, perhaps he'll smell it and come pay us a visit.'

'Who?'

'You'll see.' She grinned, reminding him of Yldich, and tore off a piece of bread. She saved a few pieces of meat, which she laid on the ground before her.

'This is my secret place,' she said. 'It has been since I was a child. No-one else comes here but me. Or maybe *Dáydach*.' She smiled, a wistful expression flitting across her face. 'Most young *Einache* don't have the patience to lie still in the dirt and wait for lynx to come by.' A couple of wild swans flew overhead. They were flying so low that Rom could hear the swoosh of their wings. He heard the cooing of woodpigeons in the trees and the rushing of reeds along the water's edge. The sun spilled through the trees and warmed his face. The light filled him with a sense of peaceful well-being. The lake was like a hidden jewel, set in a hollow of the landscape.

'It's beautiful,' he said softly.

'I had a feeling you might like it.' She smiled and touched his hand. 'I suppose you haven't had much peace in your life,' she said softly. 'To appreciate it like you do.'

He swallowed and gazed at her face. She leaned in and kissed him lightly on his mouth. He sighed as she drew back. She took his hand and trailed a finger along the scar on his wrist.

'*Farae*,' she said softly. 'You know, I have this strange memory, I don't know if it was a dream. I must have been five or six years old. We lived further to the south then, in the heart of the Forest. I used to sneak into the woods with the other children. One day, we went up a hill and met this man, this dark-haired stranger. He was very dark, and strangely handsome.' Rom felt a shiver run along his spine.

'Did—did he say anything to you?' he said breathlessly.

'He showed us his hand. He bore the mark of *Faraër*. Of course, we couldn't tell anyone, because we'd been in the woods when we weren't supposed to. Later, we agreed we must have made it up. Because it was impossible. First, because he was *Tzanatzi*. Second, because he had the Mark. But I never forgot.'

Rom stared at her. 'You wore an emerald green sleeveless dress, and you had shoulder-length copper curls.'

She widened her eyes. 'How did you know?'

'Because I was there,' he said. 'It was a couple of days ago, when we crossed the north boundary. I was in a kind of haze, when these children came up to me. If Eldairc hadn't woken me up, I'd still be standing there.'

'Well, now.' She shook her head in amazement. 'Maybe that explains why I felt drawn to you, even before I met you, in my dreams.'

'Like I was to you.' He brought his hands to her face. He moved forward and kissed her. Maetis stiffened, and Rom let her go, wondering if he'd been too forward.

'Don't move,' Maetis said. There was a sniffing sound. An animal approached on stiff legs. Maetis smiled. 'Come on, Whiskers.' Rom sat still in apprehension. He recalled Maetis' reputation for taking in strays and silently hoped Whiskers wasn't a wolf. Then he saw the creature. It was a fox, its shabby coat, which was probably red in summer almost white, with brown patches near its belly. It stared cautiously at Rom with its eyes of dark amber.

'It's all right,' Maetis said. 'He won't hurt you.' She made little inarticulate noises and held out her hand. The fox peered at her, its body low to the ground and its muscles taut, ready to spring away. Quickly and carefully, it snapped a piece of meat from her fingers and pulled away to eat. 'I took care of him when he was wounded,' she said. 'He was an older fox kit when I found him, so he never grew accustomed to humans. I let him go after his leg healed up, but he still comes to visit me sometimes. He knows the sound of my voice.' She looked at the fox. 'When you want to earn the trust of a wild creature, you have to be honest,' she said. 'Animals don't care for pretence, they see right through you.'

He suddenly felt an overwhelming urge to kiss her. She felt it, like a physical sense of warmth radiating from his body. A little fire of excitement sprang up in response, deep in her belly. She turned to him and he pulled her towards him. He held her body against his, his fingers entangled in her hair, and sought her mouth with his. They fell over on the blanket, touching each other blindly, feverishly exploring the exciting uniqueness of each other, like fire and water, earth and sky touching.

After a while Maetis disengaged, suddenly aware of the sun's progression along the sky. She pulled away gently. 'Rom,' she said, and put her fingers against his mouth. 'The others will start to wonder where we are.' She sat up and smoothed back the curls that had escaped their pins.

Rom sat up and stared straight into the face of the fox. It sat on his haunches and looked at them with mild interest. It panted softly with its mouth open, grinning like a dog. He had finished the meat, and their bread, even the crumbs that had fallen on the blanket. He turned and trotted off into the trees at his leisure. Maetis chuckled.

'I wonder what he thought of that.' She deftly coiled up some copper curls and secured them with a pin on top of her head.

Rom sat gazing at her. 'Maetis, I don't know much about *Einache* traditions. I don't know how to—to go about courting you…'

Maetis chuckled softly. He bit his lip. She felt him stiffen. She took his hand and kissed it. 'I don't care much for traditions, unless I see a point to them.'

He snorted. 'I gathered as much.'

She grinned at him. 'But I do see the wisdom in not stepping on too many toes at a time. Especially with all these battle-hardened old warriors here, now. Maybe we should tread lightly for a while. Warriors can be frightful gossips.' Rom smiled wearily as he remembered how rumour had spread through Woodbury in the time it took to boil an egg.

'I wouldn't be surprised if word was going round already.' He thought of the young *Einache* warrior who had threatened him. 'Maetis, are you sure you—you want this? I wouldn't want you to get into trouble.'

She pushed back the hair from his brow with a light touch of her fingers. 'Would you keep back because of a little trouble?' He gazed into her eyes. He shook his head. 'Neither would I,' she said.

They returned to the path the others had taken. Soon they met them coming back from the chase empty-handed.

'Those hares are cunning little *skélgae*,' Eldairc cursed in *Einache*. His hair was standing out to all sides, and he was sweating. He grinned much like the fox had done. 'I guess you two didn't fare any better?' He gazed at Rom with a look in his sharp green eyes that made Rom suspect he knew exactly what they had been up to.

He shook his head. 'Nothing.'

'Told you those hares are smarter than they look,' Maetis said. Rom noticed a few young warriors staring at him. He wondered what they were thinking. Maetis turned her horse. 'I'm going to speak with my father. Maybe he knows where we might find some game.' She smiled at Rom. One of the youths who had a severe cold and had enough joined her, wheezing and sniffing.

'I'm going into the woods to see if they've caught that stag yet,' Eldairc said. 'Rom, are you coming?' Rom was about to answer when one of the hounds seemed to have picked up a new scent. It ran in the direction of the hills to the east, baying loudly, the others following suit.

'They've found a new track,' one of the youths cried. He was a redheaded youth of about fourteen from Yldich's House called Réydin. 'Come on,' he said to Rom with a challenging grin that bared white, irregular teeth. 'Show us what kind of hunter you really are.' Rom looked at Eldairc, who shrugged and nodded slightly. He spurred on his horse and joined the boy.

Two other riders caught up with them, galloping through the fields and hills with the hounds. It was only when he turned around briefly, that Rom recognized the two warriors. They were the same ones who had threatened him the evening before. He felt a vague, cold sense of alarm. It seemed unthinkable they would attack him in broad daylight, with the boy as a witness, yet he felt his muscles stiffen.

Réydin seemed impervious of any threat. He rode a sleek grey horse that ran like quicksilver, and was completely absorbed by the pursuit. Suddenly a hound in front stopped running and dove into the bushes. Réydin dismounted and ran towards it. As Rom got of his horse, he felt a tingle of alarm along his back and turned around. The other warriors were standing directly behind him. He stared at them, wondering what to do. Before anyone had moved, Réydin came running back.

'That silly dog has got himself stuck in a rabbit hole,' he cried. 'Come help me dig him out—' he noticed the others standing completely still and stopped short. 'What's going on?'

The *Einache* who was facing Rom held out a hand without taking his eyes of Rom's face. 'It's none of your business, Réydin. Go join the others. We have something to take care of here.' The boy stared at him in doubt. The other warrior turned and took a step towards him.

'He said, go away,' he said in a gruff voice. 'This is none of your business. Go get some help for the hound,' and the boy stepped back. He turned and mounted his horse. Soon he was only a small black figure against the white snow of the fields.

Rom stared at the warrior in front of him. He had sandy hair and dark grey eyes. His face looked harsh and grey, though he was only the same age as Rom. A familiar feeling of anger and helplessness rose inside. He was surprised by an unbidden memory, sharp and clear, of when he was about eight years old.

To his surprise, a girl from the village had smiled at him and talked to him. One of the boys had seen it and sought him out, a band of village children behind him for support. They had hunted him down until he was standing with his back to a wall, and a fight had ensued that left both parties with a great number of cuts and bruises. To Rom's mother it had been the last straw. After the other boy's parents had complained to her about Rom's behaviour, threatening to rouse the village against them, she had sent him away to the Keep.

It was a strange thing, Rom thought vaguely, to be a man and still feel exactly like that eight-year-old, standing with his back against the wall. He clenched his hands into fists and waited for the *Einache* to make a move. He didn't have to wait long. The warrior in front grabbed a hold of Rom's tunic.

'I told you to stay away,' he said in a harsh voice.

'Maybe you should mind your own business,' Rom said with a scowl, and regretted it immediately. The *Einache* tightened the grip on his tunic, his face distorted with anger.

'It *is* my business when a low-life *K'álestre* lays his filthy hands on our girls.' His voice was a low growl. He pushed Rom away. 'She must have been disgusted. Did you have to force her?'

A dark, hot fire of rage rose in Rom's belly. His eyes turned black. He lashed out before he knew what he was doing. The warrior backed away, but he wasn't fast enough to dodge the blow completely. He wiped his mouth with the back of his hand and saw blood.

'*Tzanatzi* bastard.' He struck at Rom and hit him full force on his cheekbone. Rom fell back with the force of the blow. The *Einache* lost his balance and toppled forward. He landed right on top of him. Rom struck his head on a rock that was hidden under the snow.

A shock went through him. The world trembled at the edges. There was a low throbbing in his ears. Nausea came over him like a sickening wave and he closed his eyes.

When he opened them again, he was walking through the snow, wondering where he was. He was completely disoriented. He could see no distinguishable landmarks. There was only the snow. He wondered vaguely how he got there.

He heard a soft sound. It sounded like muffled sobbing. He stood still, wondering if he'd come across a wounded animal, hidden in a hollow in the ground. Then he became aware of two pairs of eyes. They were watching him intently. He heard a sharp intake of breath and stared at the eyes. They were dark, like his own, and human. *Tzanatzi* eyes. Children's eyes.

Eldairc had dismounted and studied the tracks of the first party that had gone through the forest, when he heard the sound of horse's hooves behind him. A slender grey horse stopped right before him and a young boy dropped panting from the saddle.

'El—El—,' the boy said.

'Eldairc,' he offered helpfully. Réydin stood with his hands on his knees, waiting until he got his breath back.

'It's your *Tzanatzi* friend,' he said finally. 'I think there's trouble. You'd better get help.'

Rom's eyes grew wide as he stared at the faces that turned up to him. Two children stared back. They had pulled their cloaks over their heads to keep out the cold. Because they were made of undyed wool, they almost disappeared against the background. He had nearly stumbled over them before he saw them. His mind was racing. A shock went through him as he realized he was dreamwalking. He must have ended up near Gardeth Battle Field at the time of the Battle.

One of the children drew back the slip of her cloak. She was a girl of about twelve.

'*Aléir?*' she said. The boy stared at Rom, his eyes wide with fear. His lips were blue with the cold. '*Taz Aléir?*'

Something about the words sounded familiar. He realized he'd probably heard them in the *Tzanatzi* camp. He kneeled on the ground before them, taking care not to make any sudden movements. 'I'm sorry... I don't speak your language.'

'*Altheíra calavéno,*' the girl said, her voice high with urgency. '*Laôtha. Élderoz me?*'

'I don't understand...'

'*Íte,*' she said urgently, '*élderoz, Einache calavéno, íte!*'

'It's all right, I'm not going to hurt you—' He saw the fear grow in her eyes and realized she wasn't looking at him, but at something behind him. He turned his head.

Two *Einache* warriors had come up behind him. They stared at Rom and the children with their bright eyes. Their swords were drawn. The boy whimpered softly. Rom looked at the *Einache* warriors. They seemed subtly different than the ones he had seen. Their swords were more crudely made, their clothes too, made of coarse felt, untreated leather, and fleece. Their hair hung in long, matted braids.

The warriors moved forward in unison. The one in front tightened the grip on his sword. Rom saw the girl close her eyes and realized with a sense of horror she was waiting for death. The blood drained from his face. He didn't even have a knife on him. He turned to the warriors.

'Stop,' he said huskily. They approached steadily. 'Listen to me. They're children. You can't do this.' He held up his right hand. Maybe they would recognize the Mark of *Farae*. '*Hwérwoden,*' he said, desperately searching his mind for the few *Einache* words he knew. '*Farae. Hwérwoden....*'

The warriors appeared to hesitate. They looked at each other and argued in rough *Einache*. Rom looked at the warrior in front. He tried to reach him with his eyes by lack of language. There was a hint of doubt in the grey ones that stared back. The man seemed to be deliberating.

'*Elderána k'álestre Tzanatzi,*' the other warrior said, with an impatient gesture of his hand. His face was distorted with disgust. The sound of a horn tore the air. There was a hoarse cry and the sound of clashing swords in the distance. Something hardened in the first man's eyes. He tightened the grip on his sword. The boy hid in the girl's arms, who sat frozen, her eyes on the sword. Rom held his arms around them.

'Please,' he breathed. The sword was raised. He bowed his head and screwed his eyes shut. The girl's scream rang in his ears until it was cut short by the sword.

Maetis found Yldich and Yealda in a quiet spot at the foot of a small hill. She sat back against a tree. She closed her eyes against the midday sun and sighed.

'Had enough of the chase?' Yldich said.

She smiled. 'I wanted to sit with you for a while.' Yldich looked at her face. Something was different about her. Usually, she would be running with the lads right now, trying to outdo them. But today, she radiated a warm contentedness, a sense of hidden excitement.

They had enjoyed the sunshine for a while when Eald arrived on his pony. He almost dropped in the snow in his haste to dismount.

'It's Rom.' He was panting. 'He's having one of his spells. Eldairc sent me. You should come quickly.'

'Spells?' Yealda said in a sharp tone.

Yldich rose hastily. 'He has a tendency to go dreamwalking at the oddest and most inopportune moments.'

'He goes into *ayúrdimae*? Then he must have *Yaever* potential. You should have told me.' She walked him to his horse, her brows knit. Maetis handed him his cloak, a look of worry darkening her face.

'I'm not sure *Yaever* potential is what is causing it.' Yldich mounted his horse. 'I'm afraid it's something else entirely. Something much more dangerous. Show me the way, Eald.' He reached down to hoist the boy up. He set Eald before him in the saddle. They took off and left Yealda and Maetis staring after them.

When they reached the place Eald indicated, Réydin came running to meet them. The older boy helped Eald off the horse as Yldich dismounted hastily.

'They're over there.' Réydin pointed them to a spot between some rocks. A few young *Einache* warriors crowded together, having a heated discussion under their breaths. One of them was gesturing wildly at another.

A couple of paces away Eldairc sat in the snow, a motionless body wrapped in a cloak in his arms. He looked up when Yldich approached. 'He won't wake up.'

Yldich kneeled beside them and studied Rom's face. It was ashen. His eyes were moving rapidly behind his closed eyelids. Yldich noticed a bruise on his cheek. Rom's lips were moving as if he were speaking, but there was no sound. Yldich touched his face with the tips of his fingers and closed his eyes, murmuring softly, and tried to get a sense of where he was. The only impression he got was one of fear and great urgency. He had no time to lose. He quickly rubbed the knuckles of his hand forcefully over Rom's breastbone. Rom cried out in pain, wildly flailing his arms.

Yldich grabbed them. 'It's all right now, lad,' he murmured. 'Come back.' Rom shuddered and opened his eyes. He stared right into Yldich's.

'They killed them,' he whispered. 'They decapitated them.' Yldich and Eldairc stared at him. 'I tried to intervene, but they wouldn't listen. They were going to kill us all....' he brought a hand to his neck and winced. He stared at his fingers. They were covered in blood.

'It's not a deep cut.' Yldich dabbed at Rom's neck with a piece of cloth. 'You were fortunate this time.' He sat back and put the bloodied cloth away. 'I told you going into *ayúrdimae* was dangerous.'

'It's not like I choose to go dreamwalking.' There was a defiant tone to Rom's voice.

'What set if off, this time?' Yldich peered in his face. Rom looked at the warriors who continued their debate in hushed voices. He shifted his gaze to his hands.

'I must have stumbled and fallen on a rock.'

'Really.' Yldich eyed the darkening bruise on his cheek with a doubtful expression. 'Amazing how you managed to find a fist-shaped rock in all this snow.'

Eldairc snorted in amusement. 'I'll go and take Eald back. I'll see you two later.'

Yldich helped Rom up. 'Do you think you can ride?'

'I'll manage,' Rom said, a little uncertain. The world still trembled at the edges.

'All right then. Let's go home. We'll speak about this later.'

An hour later, Rom sat with a blanket around his shoulders before the hearth in Yldich's study. His teeth were chattering.

'D—do you feel like this after every time you go into *ayúrdimae*?' Yldich gazed at him from the other chair. He shook his head. 'Then—then why do I feel like throwing up every time?'

Yldich smiled. 'Because your body's not used to it. A *Yaever* pupil has years of training to prepare himself gradually. You just throw yourself in head first, and the gods know where you're off to.' He shook his head. 'What set you off this time?' Rom stared into the flames in silence. Yldich sighed. 'Why don't you tell me who gave you that bruise on your face?'

Rom lowered his eyes. 'I don't want to cause any more trouble.'

Yldich drew up a brow. 'Looks more like someone was causing trouble for *you*.'

Rom looked up. 'I hit him first. But he provoked me.'

Yldich's eyes narrowed. 'I hope it wasn't one of my household.'

Rom shook his head. 'I think they were with Ullwich's party.'

'They? There was more than one? You'd better tell me the whole story.' As the story progressed, Yldich's eyes turned to slate. The usual twinkle of amusement was gone. 'Now,' he said sternly. 'Why didn't you tell me this yesterday, after those two cornered you?' Rom stared in the fire.

'I guess I thought there'd be trouble.' He sighed wearily. 'I suppose I'm still afraid of being sent away for it.'

Yldich stared at him. 'What do you mean?'

'Like when I was small,' Rom said, and looked at the floor. 'When I kept getting into fights, and was sent away to Aldr's Keep.'

'I see.' Yldich stared at his face, suddenly aware of the lost little boy, looking through the eyes of the nineteen-year old man. It made him look small and forlorn. 'Listen, Rom. When I declared you *hwérwoden*, family, that was more than just a gesture. It means you have the same rights as anyone of my family. Now, if a member of my family was threatened by a guest in my own House, you don't think I would send them away, would you? I would speak to the offending party.'

Rom looked up. Something seemed to change in his face. 'But what if they take offence, and leave, and start a clan conflict, or something?'

Yldich grinned. 'I would find a way to keep the peace. But even in the unlikely event Ullwich takes offence, it'd be his own warriors who would be an embarrassment to him, starting all this in the House of the *Hárrad*, and he'd know it.'

There was a knock on the door. A young girl entered carrying a tray with a kettle and two mugs. 'Here's that brew you wanted, *Yaever*.' She put the tray on the hearthstones. She looked at Rom as Yldich began to pour. 'I heard you were taken ill.' She fidgeted with the fabric of her skirt and looked at him from under her long lashes. He realized she was the girl that had danced with him the night before. She smiled a shy smile. 'I hope you feel better soon.'

'Thank you.' He smiled at her. She blushed and hurried out of the room.

'Now,' Yldich continued, when they sat nurturing mugs of steaming tea between their hands, 'why do you suppose Héyoden targeted you?'

Rom stared at him. 'I thought it was obvious. Anyway, he said so himself...' Yldich lifted up a brow. 'Because—because of what I am...'

Yldich smiled a little sadly and shook his head. 'No. That's only the weapon he uses to get at you. That's not what it's about at all.' He met his eyes. 'It's because of the way Maetis looks at you.'

Rom widened his eyes. 'How...how can you know?'

Yldich smiled. 'I've known him since he was small. Héyoden has been in love with Maetis ever since I can remember.' He looked sharply at Rom. 'So what exactly is going on between you two?'

Rom stared in the distance, envisioning the time they had shared that morning at the lake. The memory filled him with gladness. Everything else dropped away into insignificance. His face was lit up by a joyous smile.

Yldich lifted a brow. 'Well, now.'

While Yldich poured a second round *Eldairc* strode into the room. He draped his sodden cloak over one of the chairs to dry.

'Would you like to hear the latest gossip?' He placed a cushion on the hearthstones for a seat. He shook the hair out of his eyes and grinned at them. 'They say there's been a skirmish involving Ullwich's young warriors. Two of them got into a fight, probably over a girl, posing a threat to the dignity of the Wolf clan. Their friends made them return home before news of the brawl could reach Ullwich's ears. They didn't even take time to pack.'

'Where did you hear all this?' Yldich's eyes were bright with curiosity.

'In the kitchen, which is the best source of information in this house. Also, it seems the dark and mysterious guest, who from what I've heard is a surprisingly good dancer, has been taken ill while hunting. The cook has made a batch of honey cakes to speed up his recovery. Eald will bring them in shortly. If he hasn't eaten them on the way.'

Yldich drew up a brow. 'To what extent have these events been inspired by a young man named Eldairc?'

Eldairc chuckled. 'I thought I'd speed up the process by dropping a hint here and there.' He turned to Rom. 'Actually, Héyoden and Udyn were all too happy to leave without having to face the wrath of Yldich or Ullwich. This way, everybody gets to keep their dignity. Most of it, anyway.' Eald came in carrying a large tray.

'Honey cakes,' he said with a skewed grin. There were crumbs on his clothes. 'Compliments of Yárah. She hopes you'll get well soon.'

The pale, wintry sunlight fell in long beams through the slit windows and onto the stone tiles. It lit up the hair of the men who sat facing each other.

'Now, tell me of the purpose of your visit.' The speaker was a man in his forties, broadly built and well-muscled, with hair the colour of ripe wheat. 'It seems you have travelled a long way to come and speak to me.' He took a sip of warm red wine.

'I have, my King,' the younger man said. His amber eyes narrowed. King Farhardt was not a tall man, but there was something about him which made him seem taller than he was. He radiated a kind of direct, simple authority. It irked Feyir, who felt a deep dislike for the man and everything he stood for. He inclined his head and forced his lips into a smile. 'And I thank you for your graceful reception.'

He studied the man seated in a heavy chair covered in furs. King Farhardt wore his clothes like a necessity; a heavy woollen cloak trimmed with dark fur, woollen trousers of a heavy quality that didn't quite match the colour of his cloak tucked in simple brown leather boots, a large leather belt. The overall impression was one of a man who did not care overly much for appearances but had other things on his mind when he dressed in the morning.

Feyir, in contrast, was dressed in a dark blue velvet tunic and cloak that lent him a kind of effortless elegance. He had washed and shaved meticulously for the occasion.

'As Your Majesty may have heard, after the death of my mother, the former lady Erwine, I have been living a simple life in the woods up north.' He took a sip of wine and took in the details of his surroundings: the rich tapestries, the heavy furniture, and the rows of candles in their candlesticks of heavy silver. 'After the ill luck which has befallen my family, I have been content to live in the woods with my fellow hunters. However, this autumn, there has been a sequence of events that have been, how shall I put it, *disturbing*. Events which I thought would be of great interest to you, as they might threaten the peace of this land.'

Farhardt gazed at Feyir's face with a pensive expression. There was something about the young man's manner that repelled him ever so slightly, though he was hardly aware of why this should be. He only felt a slight aversion. His interest, however, was raised. 'Tell me.'

After they had finished the last of the cakes, Yldich brushed the crumbs off his lap and looked at Rom.

'Now, maybe you'd like to tell us where you dreamwalked off to this morning.' Rom looked up. In his seat before the cosy fire, he had forgotten for a moment. His eyes darkened.

'I think—I was somewhere around here, at the time of the Battle,' he said slowly. 'I nearly stumbled over two children who had hidden in a hollow in the snow. *Tzanatzi* children.'

Eldairc's eyes widened. '*Tzanatzi* children? Here?'

'Go on,' Yldich said in a level voice.

'I tried to talk to them, but I speak *Tzanatzi* even less than I speak *Einache*. But it was obvious they were terrified. Two *Einache* warriors came up to us—' he looked at Eald, and wondered if this was the kind of thing he should be discussing in the boy's presence. Yldich noticed.

'I think there aren't many things that can still shock Eald,' he said softly.

'They were about to decapitate them.' Rom's face was strained. 'I tried to talk to them. I couldn't believe *Einache* warriors would slay children, just because of—of what they were.' He drew his hands over his face and stared at the floor, his eyes black. 'You drew me back just in time.'

Eldairc looked at Yldich, an expression of perplexed doubt in his face. 'Did you know this?'

Yldich nodded slowly. There was something in his eyes Eldairc hadn't seen there before. A sense of regret, an old, lingering sadness. 'During the war, *Einache* warriors would have perceived any *Tzanatzi* as the enemy. In the old songs, and in the stories that we still tell our children, the emphasis is always on the raiding of our lands, the invisible threat that nearly was the downfall of our people. This is a part of the story that is seldom spoken about.'

'Perhaps it should be,' Rom said. There was an unusual ring to his voice. He straightened. 'Perhaps someone should tell these stories for once.'

Yldich looked at him. A faint smile was on his lips. 'Perhaps that someone should be you.'

'These are indeed disturbing tidings.' King Farhardt gazed in the distance. His sharp blue eyes were narrow under the straight line of his brows. He frowned and absently rubbed his fingers over his short beard. 'To think that a renegade *Tzanatzi* would inspire the Northern clans to take up arms against the Crown.' A shadow of doubt flitted across his face. 'One would think they have enough trouble as it is, with their harsh winters and sober means of existence.'

'Their discontent has been brewing for a long time.' Feyir took care to keep his voice level. 'Perhaps it needed only a spark to set it off.' He took a sip of wine. 'But the signs were unmistakable. The barbaric Northern clans have even attacked their own kind, at the border of their territory. Elbury, a village that had trading contacts with the South, has been looted and burnt to the ground. I saw it with my own eyes. No-one was left alive.'

Farhardt shook his head. 'This cannot be tolerated,' he said slowly. 'I will speak with my advisors tonight.' He turned a sharp look at Feyir. 'I'm curious. How do you suppose a *Tzanatzi* would incite the Northern clans to rebel? One would think they'd chop off his head before he had a chance to speak.'

Feyir smiled. 'Maybe they are united by their hatred against Southern rule. It surprised me as well, to see the *Hárrad* of the *Einache* lead an attack on my men with a renegade *Tzanatzi*. But it's true. I barely escaped death in the onslaught.' His hand went to his side, his eyes momentarily narrowed by the memory of pain. 'Perhaps,' he added as an afterthought, 'the *Einache* have a use for his kind's debased magic, as they lack the means to build a fully equipped army.'

'Perhaps,' Farhardt said. An expression of disgust fleeted across his face. He had an abhorrence of anything magical or mystical. He was a man who liked things to be clear-cut and visible in the light of day.

After Eldairc and Eald left the study, Rom sat staring in the fire for a long time. Yldich had left to take care of some *Yaever* business. There was a soft knock on the door. Rom looked up. It was Eald. He took the other chair in front of the fire and drew up his legs. He put his arms around his knees, gazing at the floor.

'Do you think it hurt?' Eald said. Rom stared at him. 'Those children.' Eald swallowed. 'Do you think it hurt, when they were killed?'

Rom hesitated. For some reason, he felt he dare not lie to the boy, not even to reassure him. 'I don't know,' he said carefully. 'I think… it was over quickly. They were scared more than anything else.'

Eald looked up. His narrow face was drawn. 'When you told us I started to remember something. The night they came and took me away. Until now, I remembered only lots of screaming, and people running about, and then nothing.' He tensed his fists. 'Now, suddenly, I see the face of my mother as they come. And my dad, shouting at us to go inside. And Eyléra, my niece, cut down as she runs.' He started to shake. 'I struggled to get away, and someone knocked me on the head, and they took me away.'

Rom kneeled beside his chair. He laid an arm around his shoulders. 'It was a horrible thing to happen to you.'

Eald wiped his eyes with his sleeve. 'What if they ever come here?'

Rom shook his head. 'I don't think Feyir and his riders would dare go this far north. It's unfamiliar territory, and besides, they would risk facing all the *Einache* clans at once. I don't think you need worry about it.' He realized he was trying to convince himself as much as the boy.

When Yldich returned, Rom was alone in the room. He seemed not to have moved at all. He sat staring into the fire, his brow lined with thought. He looked up and gazed at Yldich with his dark eyes.

'I want to know everything,' he said. 'Everything there is to know about the war. About the *Tzan*—about my people. About dreamwalking. And I want you to teach me how to use that sword properly.' Yldich went over to the bookshelves without a word. He took a stack of heavy leather bound books and dropped them in Rom's lap.

'There you go.' There was something in his grey eyes, a grim sort of gladness. 'You might want to get some help with those. Eldairc's, or Maetis'.' Rom opened a volume and stared at the yellowed parchment. The writing was all in scratchy *Einache*. He looked up. 'I will speak with Yealda about your impromptu wanderings,' Yldich said. 'If I can't keep you from wandering off, maybe there's a way for me to reach you when things go wrong.'

The sun was sinking in the West. The mellow afternoon light streamed through the little panes of glass and set Maetis' hair ablaze. She sat next to Rom, one of the books open across her lap.

Eldairc sat on his usual perch by the hearth, frowning at another. 'I wish someone had taken the effort to translate these into everyday *Einache*.' He sounded disgruntled. 'In some parts the style is so archaic as to be totally incomprehensible.'

Rom leafed through a collection of sketches. 'I had no idea there were so many records.'

'Most of these are by my father,' Maetis said. 'Or to be more precise, by one of the *Hárrad* before him.'

Rom looked up. 'Did it never strike you as strange, the idea that he was here then?'

She smiled. 'I never knew any different,' she said. 'I think it's a comforting thought, that he was here always, and always will be.' Rom felt a vague, fleeting sense of sadness.

But will he?

'What are you looking for, anyway?' Eldairc scratched his head.

'Anything that will shed light on who the *Tzanatzi* were,' Rom said. 'Especially anything to do with dreamwalking or magic.'

Eldairc raised his brows. 'I thought you didn't want anything to do with any of that?'

Rom's face was set. 'If I'm going to master this thing, instead of it mastering me, I'd better learn everything I can. And there's another thing.' Maetis looked up and gazed at his face. 'It feels as if there's a side to the story that needs to be told, will there ever be any real peace....'

After another hour or two, Eldairc yawned broadly. He closed his mouth with an audible clap. 'I'm sorry.' He grinned. 'I need something to eat. Are you coming?'

'Just a little longer,' Maetis said absently. She waved at him without looking up from her page. 'We'll join you later.' She motioned for Rom to come over. He went and sat next to her by the hearth. 'It says here,' Maetis said, a finger marking scratchy runes on a faded page, 'that the *Tzanatzi* had a magic that transcended the confines of space and time. A magic that enabled them to walk through walls, and enter their enemy's stronghold to get an impression of their strengths and weaknesses.'

Rom was reminded of the strange dark-haired woman he had seen in Woodbury. 'Go on,' he said breathlessly.

'It says here some of them mastered a form of *ayúrdimae* that was more developed than that of the oldest *Yaever*. They could leave their bodies at will, and walk wherever they wanted. Many of them mastered this skill to some degree, but none so well as the Unnamed One. He could go wherever he wished. For this, he was most feared and respected.'

'The mage,' Rom said. His voice was strained. 'Does it say anything about how they did it?'

Maetis frowned as she read the ancient lettering with effort. 'There's a word here I don't quite understand,' she muttered. '*Ayurië*... it seems to have something to do with emotion....'

Rom sat back. 'The first time I had what Yldich called a true-dream, it was after trying to discover my *érstwae* all day. The second time—' blood rose to his face when he thought of the dream in which he was pulled into the sensual dance. The following eruption rose in his mind's eye. 'Yldich had told us of the War. I was shocked. Perhaps I was trying to understand what had driven the *Tzanatzi* to conquer....' he drew his hands over his face.

'Why don't you get some rest, Rom,' Maetis said softly. 'These books will still be here tomorrow.' She closed the one on her lap and put it away. She leaned over to him and took his head between her hands. She pressed a soft kiss between his eyebrows, and one on his mouth. He released a soft breath as she drew back and smiled at him. It was strange, he mused, how her touch made him feel at peace, yet had his heart beat wildly at the same time.

'Maybe,' she said, 'we can find a place to be alone together one of these days, if the weather holds up.'

'I'd like that,' he said softly.

That night, Rom had a simple meal in the kitchen with Eldairc and Eald. Eald was unusually quiet. Afterwards, Rom went back to Yldich's study, telling himself he wanted to take another look at the old drawings. He felt a vague reluctance to go to bed. As he sat before the hearth, staring in the flames, he let his thoughts drift. His eyelids were getting heavy. He was sinking, drifting away. Someone touched his shoulder and he started.

'Rom. Wake up.' He straightened and opened his eyes. Some parchments had slid off his lap onto the floor. Yldich stooped to pick them up. Yealda stood in the doorway and gazed levelly at him. She wore a long, blue-grey robe. Her silver hair flowed loosely over her shoulders and back. Her eyes, he noted, were of a curious blue, a blue that was almost lavender. There was something about the way she looked at him, an aloofness that made him uncomfortable.

'Yldich tells me you are experiencing difficulty with *ayúrdimae*,' she said in a low voice. She took a chair and placed it opposite him. She sat down and gazed at him. 'It is time you and I speak.'

Yldich put the books and parchments back on the shelves. 'Yealda and I have been concocting a special brew for you, a blend of herbs that will help strengthen your connection to your body. It will ground you and keep you in the plane of everyday reality.'

'I'm sure it'll taste horrible,' Rom said with a wry expression.

Yldich chuckled. 'I daresay it will.' He turned back to the row of books.

'I will need to know more about your experiences with *ayúrdimae* if I am to advise you,' Yealda said in a sober voice. 'Tell me.'

Rom told her as much as he could remember. He told her of the black cat and the time he went after Yldich, who had been entrapped by the black horror. He told her of the dreams that had led him to Gardeth Battle Field, the *Tzanatzi* camp and the children in the snow. Yealda nodded.

'It's as I thought,' she said. 'When a trained *Yaever* goes into *ayúrdimae*, he or she does so with a clear purpose in mind. *Yaever* attain a high level of concentration and disengage from the body with the use of herbs. When you go into *ayúrdimae*, it's a different thing altogether. It is haphazard, spontaneous, and driven by subconscious emotion rather than purpose.'

'Isn't emotion just another form of purpose?' Rom said. Yealda's cool, detached attitude aroused a sense of defiance in him.

Yldich chuckled. 'Rom has a point. Emotion is a form of energy in and of itself. When used to guide him in the right direction, it is as powerful, maybe even more powerful, than mental clarity and concentration.' He looked at Yealda. 'He has pulled off feats of dreamwalking that would take novice *Yaever* years of training.'

'Maybe,' Yealda said a little stiffly. 'However, it seems to me emotion as a driving force is substantially more difficult to guide or control.'

'*Ayurië.*' Yldich traced a finger along the worn spine of a leather volume. His eyes went vague. 'Heart, or spirit. That is the name the *Yaever* of old used to describe processes inspired by emotion.'

Rom looked at him. '*Ayurië*, that's the word Maetis was trying to translate. In one of your books, there's a description of how *Tzanatzi* used it to attain a heightened state of *ayúrdimae*. It said the Nameless One was most adept of them all, that he could go wherever he wished....' He felt Yealda's eyes on him and fell silent.

'We do not speak of him in this house.' Her voice was cold.

Rom's eyes darkened. 'If you want to understand why, after five hundred years, his shadow still haunts these lands, maybe you should.' Something in his voice made Yldich turn from the row of books he was studying. Rom and Yealda sat facing each other, their eyes like swords in the hands of warriors about to engage in battle. He raised his brows.

'It's late,' he said in a calm voice. 'We're all tired. Maybe we should continue this discussion tomorrow, in the clear light of day.'

Rom swallowed. 'I suppose you're right.' He lowered his eyes.

Yealda nodded and stood up, gathering the folds of her robe. 'We will speak about this later.' Her voice was level once more. '*Nâstréhi ea*, Yldich. Rom.' She turned and left without making a sound.

Rom sighed as the door closed behind her. He drew his hands over his face. 'I'm sorry,' he said. Yldich took a seat opposite him and looked at him with a curious expression. 'She makes me feel uneasy.' Rom looked up. 'Why do you think she dislikes me so much?'

Yldich stared at him. 'She doesn't dislike you. She hardly knows you.'

'Still, every time she looks at me, I feel cold inside,' Rom muttered.

Yldich sighed. 'Listen, Rom. There's something about Yealda you should know if you want to understand her. She has her own reasons to feel strongly about the War. About the Unnamed One. Yealda's daughter led a small band of *Einache* rebels. The Unnamed One had her executed before Yealda's eyes.'

'But—why should she look at *me* like that?'

'Because,' Yldich said carefully, 'you seem to resemble him quite a lot.' Rom stared at him. 'How much so?'

Yldich released a breath. 'Uncannily so,' he said softly.

Yldich walked Rom back to his room, and left him on the edge of the bed. Rom stared numbly at the floor.

Yldich returned with a steaming mug of herbal brew.

'Now drink this,' he said, and gently pushed a cup into Rom's hands. Rom obeyed. He felt dazed, his mind a jumble of thoughts he didn't dare pursue. The tea tasted like a mixture of ginger root, sage, and something bitter he couldn't quite place. When he was finished he looked up. Something in his face made Yldich lay a hand on his shoulder. 'Don't worry,' he said softly. 'Get some sleep, Rom.' He turned at the door. '*Nâstréhi ea.*'

Nine
Ríórdirým

It was a cloudless, sunny morning. The light of the sun bounced off the sea and was thrown back as sparks of yellow fire. Gulls cried overhead. Two children ran across the deck, laughing and yelling. When they saw him standing at the bow they hushed, and whirled past with their eyes cast down demurely. A few moments later, he heard them yell at each other again from the other side of the ship. He smiled indulgently. The wind rose, and blew long strands of raven hair across his eyes.

He turned around, and the wind whipped his hair out of his face. He stood there for a moment, his hands at the rail. He took in the sea-salt air, listened to the sound of the gulls, the wind in the sails, and the rushing sound of the water that was parted by the keel of the ship. Ahead, he could see a narrow strip of rocky coastline. One of the boys had spotted it early that morning, the first land they had seen in over three months. It had sent a ripple of excitement across the ship. For the boatman and his crew, and for him, it had mainly meant relief. Their supplies of food and fresh water were dangerously low.

'Ríórdirým.'

He heard a young male voice to his left and turned his head. It was one of the apprentices, Lakíthra. The dark-haired young man bowed slightly in the old gesture of reverence, his right hand on his stomach. He still managed to look dignified, despite the downy hair on his chin, the streaks of dirt on his cheeks and his somewhat dishevelled clothes. They had all stopped bathing weeks ago.

'The scouts have surveyed the area,' Lakíthra said. 'Some of them had trouble concentrating. They are getting anxious. Restless. But it appears the lands are inhabited.'

He nodded as if he knew it already. 'Have they been able to get an impression of the inhabitants?'

The young man grimaced. 'Yúriel woke up screaming, and said they looked like ghosts, with their pale hair and bright, fell eyes. Nonsense, of course. They must be human. Yúriel really is too young for this kind of exertion. But they all agreed they were savages. They live in crude dwellings of reed and clay, in loosely knit groups, and fight each other with primitive swords and battle axes. There are no cities, no other signs of civilization.'

'Aren't there any ports? Any seaside towns?'

'None, my lord. Only little huts, clinging to the rocks along the coastline.'

He shook his head and frowned. It was worse than he had thought. No place to dock, no sign of civilization anywhere. Only a fierce, savage people, who would no doubt prepare them a savage reception. He looked in the distance, at the waters behind them, where he could just discern the masts and pennants of the other ships that had survived the storms of a week ago. They carried all that was left of his people. Five, maybe six thousand, he thought bitterly, and swallowed away a heavy sense of loss. Fear hooked its icy talons in his bowels. He could not afford to take any chances. His jaw tightened.

He turned to Lakíthra. 'Get everything ready in my quarters. I will summon the *Tahiéra*.'

The young man went pale. His dark eyes widened. 'Yes, my lord.' He bowed and took three steps backwards before he turned and strode away.

Rom woke wondering what was strange about the room. He realized it was the absence of movement, the way his bed was perfectly level and still. After more than three months at sea, he'd gotten used to the rolling and thumping of the waves.

He shook his head abruptly, and pushed the hair from his eyes. The ship. It had been a dream. He had never been at sea in his life. Then he recalled what the young man in the dream had called him and he went pale.

There was a knock on the door to Yldich's study. He lifted his head and groaned. He had fallen asleep at the table, his cheek cushioned on a thick pile of parchments. He pulled his fingers through his tangled curls.

'Come in.' His voice was hoarse.

Rom came in, still in his nightclothes. He stopped abruptly as he took in Yldich's dishevelled state. 'You must look worse than I do. Didn't you get any sleep at all?'

Yldich drew a hand over his face and yawned. 'I think I fell asleep pouring over these papers.'

Rom shook his head. 'Wait here. I'll get us something to eat. And then we must talk.'

He returned from the kitchen with a large tray laden with bread, butter, fruit preserves, cold mutton and a pot of steaming tea. 'Yárah patted me on the back and insisted I should eat more.' He set the plate on Yldich's table and snorted. 'She thinks I'm a fourteen-year old boy who needs to be fattened out.'

Yldich chuckled. He washed two bread rolls away with tea and sighed contentedly. Then he looked at Rom. 'Now, tell me. What was so important you had to burst into my room at this hour?'

'A dream.' Rom frowned. 'At least, I think it was.' He told Yldich what he still remembered. Yldich listened intently, his clear grey eyes impassive, his chin on his hands.

'It was different from dreamwalking,' Rom said. 'It wasn't as if I was truly *there*. It didn't feel as if I could change the course of events. But I saw through his eyes, thought his thoughts, and felt what he felt...' Yldich gazed at him in silence. 'It wasn't at all as I would have expected.' Rom looked at his hands as he spoke his thoughts aloud, as if Yldich wasn't there. 'I didn't feel like a monster, a dark sorcerer intent on ruin and destruction. They were running from something. They were afraid and desperate, and I felt the full weight of responsibility for the survival of my people....'

He turned his gaze at Yldich. 'Five, six thousand people. That was all that was left of them.' He shook his head. 'He thought they would have to fight for their lives as soon as they'd landed. So he made a decision. To summon something—something deadly, something terrible....'

'Fear makes people take to roads they would normally avoid.' Yldich's eyes were dark.

'The *Tahiéra*,' Rom whispered, as if he were afraid the thing might come up behind him and jump him. 'Have you ever heard of it?'

Yldich shook his head. 'No, I haven't. But I've witnessed its effect. What's more, I have felt it. So have you. In the woods, when I was trapped by darkness. And at the gates of Woodbury.' He drew his hands over his face, as if he wanted to clear away the memory of the dark horror that had crept over his skin. He gathered the parchments together and slammed his hand on the pile with a thump. 'I will search the old writings.' He smiled at Rom. 'Maybe your nightly escapades will help us find it, and ultimately, destroy it.'

'But why is it still here? Why didn't it perish along with the mage?'

'Maybe you'll find the answer to that question.'

'I'll ask Maetis to help me translating the old writings.' Rom stood up. 'There must be a reference to it somewhere.'

Yldich looked at Rom's crumpled nightshirt. 'You might want to change first.'

On his way back from the washroom, Rom ran into Eldairc.

'Good morning to you,' Eldairc said. He stood still and yawned at his leisure. 'You're up and busy early.' He brushed the shaggy hair out of his face.

'*Ya'hey*,' Rom said. 'If you run into Maetis, would you ask her to meet me in Yldich's study? I want to go through more of the old writings.'

Eldairc's mouth twitched. He nearly managed to suppress a grin. 'You two are spending an awful lot of time together.'

Rom fidgeted. 'I need her help translating the ancient script... I can't very well start reading *Einache* all of a sudden.'

'Now there's a thought. Why don't you? Start learning *Einache*, I mean. I'll help you.'

An hour later, the three of them were seated at the large table in Yldich's study. It was laden with books, scrolls, sketches, empty cups, and plates with crumbs. Eldairc balanced his chair on two legs, a heavy book in his lap, and a quill behind one ear. He was humming softly. Rom frowned over a large sheet of parchment. He laboriously copied a list of *Einache* runes Eldairc had written down for him. His quill made scratching noises on the parchment. Maetis leafed through a stack of papers.

There was a knock on the door and Eald ran in. 'What's all this about? What are you doing?' His eyes were lit with curiosity.

'We're trying to find references to the dark menace,' Eldairc said. 'Rom has had one of his true-dreams. Apparently, it has a name and everything. Maybe we'll be able to find out more about it.'

Eald walked over to the table and picked up one of the folders with sketches. 'Maybe I'll find a picture of the monster.'

'It's not a monster,' Rom said absently, his attention focused on his runes. 'It has no real life, nor a purpose of its own, apart from the one it has been imbued with. It induces fear, and fear is what it feeds on—'

There was a hushed silence. He felt their eyes on him. He looked up and saw the amazement in Maetis' clear grey eyes.

'How did you know that?' she said in a small voice.

He swallowed. 'I—I don't know....'

'Well,' Eldairc said, 'I guess this means there won't be any pictures for you to find, Eald. Maybe you'd like to run some errands instead? I could do with some more tea. And maybe something to go with it.' Eald nodded and ran out of the room, a hopeful expression on his face. He had seen Yárah take out a fresh batch of honey cakes not an hour ago. Eldairc resumed his reading and good-humoured humming while Rom stared at his parchment. His face was still and expressionless.

Maetis gazed at him a while. The air in the study smelled of old leather and parchment, of dust and the past, gone and forgotten. She felt a sudden need to be outside, to move and enjoy the present. She put down her papers and stood up.

'I feel like going out for some air.' She put back the curls that had escaped from their pins and looked at Rom. 'Will you come with me?'

He looked up, his dark eyes impenetrable. He seemed far away. 'I'd like to,' he said finally.

'You two go and enjoy yourselves, and don't mind leaving me with all these musty books.' Eldairc snorted and waved them out the door. 'But don't complain to me when Eald and I have finished all the cookies.'

'I'll just get my things,' Maetis said as they stood in the corridor. 'I'll see you outside.'

Rom sat on his bed and put on his fur-lined boots, when his gaze fell on the *Einache* sword that stood against the wall. In an impulse, he decided to take it with him.

He pushed open the great doors and found Maetis waiting. She rode a grey mare and sat smiling down at him. The sun lit up her hair, turning it a fiery bronze.

'Come on, get your horse, quickly.' Her eyes were bright. 'Before the weather turns on us.'

It was a calm and beautiful day, sunny and cloudless. They rode their horses into the hills at a fast pace and enjoyed the wind in their faces. They tied their horses to the birches at the bottom of a wooded hill that was crowned with large slabs of stone. The stones were worn smooth with centuries of wind and rain, and warmed up by the sun. They looked like the ancient foundations of some circular building. Slender birches had taken root in between the stones.

Maetis spread a blanket over a large slab of stone. Rom sat down beside her as she opened a bundle that smelled of cinnamon. She took out the crumbled remains of freshly baked honey cakes. She handed Rom a piece and grinned.

'Eald is not the only one who knows his way to the kitchen.' She popped a large piece into her mouth, sat back and closed her eyes against the light of the sun. She sighed contentedly. Rom finished his cake and looked at her. He couldn't help but smile. She looked like a cat that was sunbathing after a satisfying kitchen raid.

A long, curly lock of golden red hair was lifted up by a breeze and curled itself around his hand. It was sticky with honey. Maetis opened her eyes. She laughed and freed him. The touch of her fingers sent a peculiar thrill through his arm and made his heart beat a little faster.

'Here,' Maetis said, 'your hand is all sticky.' She lifted it to her mouth. She kissed his hand, and licked off the honey with a delicate movement of her tongue. Rom felt it send a shiver over his skin. When she lifted her face to smile at him, he cupped her cheek with his hand and leaned over to her.

'Here,' he said, 'your lips are all sticky.' He kissed her softly and tasted the honey on her lips. When she opened her mouth to kiss him back, something warm and breathtaking began to rise from deep within. The sensation of her tongue, flickering delicately into his mouth, sent a wonderful thrill through his body.

They sat holding each other a while. Rom could feel Maetis' heart beat against his chest.

'I've wanted to do that for a long time,' she said.

Rom stroked back her hair. 'So did I.' She turned around and nestled under his arm. 'What is this place, do you know?' Rom said, to distract himself. He had trouble thinking of anything but the feeling of her slender body leaning against his.

'I don't know, exactly. I think it's an ancient place of worship.'

He frowned. 'An *Einache* one?'

'I should think so.' He looked around, at the circle of trees, the ancient stones. Something seemed to tug at his mind, something vague that he could not shake off.

'Maetis,' he said, and wondered why he was on the subject now, of all times, 'have you ever encountered the dark menace, as Eldairc calls it?'

'No, I haven't,' she said softly, 'but I met someone who has. A beekeeper who lived at the edge of the Forest.'

'What happened to him?'

'Nobody knows. He ranted for four days and nights, and then he died.' Rom shivered. 'It's getting colder,' Maetis murmured. She pulled her cloak about her.

Rom felt something tighten in his stomach. 'Maybe we should head back. The weather seems to be changing.'

Maetis sat up and looked around. A chill wind had risen and whirled her hair around her. She frowned. 'Strange,' she said. They heard the horses whinny at the bottom of the hill.

Rom rose and fastened his cloak. 'Something doesn't feel right.' His face was tense. They descended in haste, while the air grew steadily colder around them. 'Do you think the hunters would have followed us?' Rom said.

'The clan warriors? No, they all left for their homes yesterday afternoon.'

Rom stared at the footsteps in the snow. There were several, and they were all larger than their own. 'Then whose are these?'

Maetis hissed in a breath. Rom looked up and followed her gaze. Across the field at the bottom of the hill, three dark shapes stood in the snow. Their cloaks floated on the wind. A dark mist curled at their feet. One of the figures, a tall man, turned around slowly. Darkness swirled around him. The light of the sun was cut off. Despite the sudden gloom Rom could see the hair move around his head, like tendrils of blackest smoke.

He acted before he could think. He drew the Einache sword. It cried out as if in protest, a high-pitched wail. He turned to Maetis. 'Take your horse.' The dark man stiffened. He took a step forward. 'Take it and go.' Rom pushed her in the direction of the horses. 'Run!' Maetis hesitated. She stared at the dark shape as if she doubted her eyes.

'*Enteroz.*' A voice was raised and chilled the air. '*Íte, elcánte Einache. Elcánte Yeave...Oyente sá!*' Maetis stood as if frozen. Rom went cold inside. He grasped the sword in his numb hands. Three other dark shapes closed in.

'Run,' he whispered. His mouth was dry. The dark-haired man came closer. His blood turned to ice. Rom stood frozen, unbelieving, staring for a moment at dark eyes in a pale face almost exactly like his own. Time stood still.

There was a soft murmur, a low humming at the edges of his awareness. Pressure built up inside his head. There was a blinding flash of light. It was followed by a boom that shook the earth and threw him to the ground. Someone grabbed his arm and pushed him in the direction of the horses.

'Go!' he heard Maetis' cry and scrambled until he was on his feet again. They ran without looking back, darkness at their heels. The horses snorted and tossed their heads in fear, their bits slippery with froth. They mounted and shot away over the snowy fields. As soon as they were out of sight of the hill, the darkness lifted. It was gone as suddenly as it had descended.

When they were about halfway home, Rom slowed his pace. He turned to look at Maetis. 'How—how did you do that?'

She grinned at him, although her face was still pale. 'Something I learned from *Dáydach*. Calling down the thunder.' There was another flash of lightening in the distance. Rom felt a drop of rain on his hand.

'An unfortunate side-effect,' Maetis said with a wry smile, as the first ice-cold raindrops started to fall on their heads. She pulled a fold of her cloak over her head.

By the time they were back at the house, the sun was setting and they were soaked through. The cold wind had plastered Rom's wet clothes to his skin. He shivered as he handed the reigns of his horse to one of the stable lads with stiff hands. Maetis pulled him into the house.

'You'll catch your death if you're not careful,' she said frowning, as she saw his lips were turning blue. 'Come with me.' She pulled him into a corridor, and led him to a large room at the south side of the house. As soon as they were inside, she started to peel off his wet clothes.

'Maetis....' he said in faint protest as she unlaced his tunic with quick fingers.

'I won't hear of it,' she said in a decisive tone, and proceeded to pull the cold and wet thing over his head. She made him sit on the side of the bed so she could pull off his rain soaked boots. Then she unfastened his trousers. She pulled the stiff, water-soaked leather off him with difficulty. Rom was shaking uncontrollably, too cold to be embarrassed anymore. Maetis pulled the heavy blankets and sheepskins over him.

'If—if you wanted me in your bed, you could have just asked,' Rom said through chattering teeth. She chuckled, kneeling beside the hearth to light the fire. She rose and wrung the water from her hair.

'I'll be right back.' When she returned with a large kettle and two mugs, Rom seemed only half-conscious. She called his name, but he only murmured vaguely in response. His eyes remained closed.

'Well, this is no good,' she muttered. She took off her own clothes. They were waterlogged and heavy, her undergarments cold and damp. She left them lying on the flagstones before the hearth and slid between the blankets. She put her arms about him. His skin was cool to the touch.

She couldn't resist exploring his shoulders and back with her hands while she held him. The muscles underneath his skin were spare but well-developed; his skin was smooth, except for the scar tissue that ran in ridges over his back. She held her breath as they formed under her fingers.

He stirred and opened his eyes. 'I... I think I dropped off for a bit.'

'Yes, you did.' She pushed back the hair from his brow. He sighed and gazed into her eyes. He brought a hand up to her face and touched her cheek with the tips of his fingers. He trailed his fingers down along the soft skin of her neck. She closed her eyes and released a slow breath. She was silent for a while. Then she opened them again.

'What do you think it was? The darkness we met at the ruins. I've never seen anything like it.'

Rom's eyes widened. 'Didn't you see the dark man? He was coming straight for us. He spoke to you.'

She shook her head, and stared at him with her bright eyes. 'I saw only a dark mist, and I felt something... something that made me feel cold right through. I only knew that we had to get away as fast as possible. As if something dangerous was just at our heels. A trap that would snap shut any time. I've never felt anything like it.'

'It was him,' he whispered. 'The mage. I saw him clearly.'

'Why would you see him, while I saw only a dark mist?'

'I don't know.' He held her closer to his chest, his fingers caught in her hair.

'Lucky for us I didn't grow up with a *Yaever* father without picking up some of his tricks.' She caressed him, almost without thinking, her fingers trailing from his neck to the lower part of his back. He was suddenly very aware of her naked body lying close to his. Something warm leapt up in his loins. His breath quickened and he gingerly pulled back.

'Maetis, you—you're making it very difficult for me to think straight.' Maetis chuckled. Something in the sound of her voice made him suspect she knew exactly what awkward position her caress had put him into.

'In the old days,' she said, 'before they lived in houses like this, the *Einache* shared their beds naked in winter all the time. It's the most effective way to keep warm.'

'They must have been a prolific people,' he muttered. She laughed and snuggled up to him once more. He felt Maetis' fingers draw a trail of tingling sensations along his chest and stomach. A thrill of desire went through him and made his breath quicken. Something made him gently take the audacious hand before it moved further down.

'Maetis... are you sure you want this?'

She tilted her head back a little so she could look at him. Lights danced in her eyes. 'Now, would I be here if I didn't?'

'But—you don't know what I am. *I* don't know what I am.'

'What do you mean?'

'I'm pursued by a dark power. I have memories not my own. Last night Yldich told me I'm walking around with the face of the Unnamed One. I don't know what it means... maybe I'm dangerous.' She looked at his face a while in silence. A thought like a searing pain went through his head.

If she rejects me now, she will tear me apart.

He stared at her with his dark eyes like fragile glass. She put a hand on his heart and gazed into his face.

'I can feel you,' she said softly. 'I know who you are.' A wellspring of desire sprang up from deep inside and he drew her to him. He kissed her deeply and a thrill of joy sang through his body as she received him.

It was different from the first time. The first time was a stroke of lightening, a torrent that took its course and left him senseless, with no choice but to obey. He had neither the chance nor presence of mind to truly heed the woman he had shared himself with.

This time, he was very aware of Maetis, of the touch of her hands as they ran along his body and let the blaze of his desire rise higher, of the shine of the hearth in her moist curls that lay spread over the sheepskins like hammered gold. He traced his fingers over the freckles that dotted her face and stared into her sea-grey eyes; he held on a moment before he would lose himself in their depths. Something small leapt up in his belly in fearful excitement at her clear gaze. She smiled at him, a joyous, welcoming smile, and he let go.

Wonderfully soft, she opened for him like a flower and one moment, it struck him how perfectly they fit together; her pleasure his pleasure as they moved in unison, rising and falling like the waves of the sea.

For a while, he managed to take it slow, but Maetis uttered little cries in his ear that spurred him on to go faster, faster. She arched her back, and brought up her hips to meet him; she cried out a word he didn't know, and he couldn't keep back any longer. For one long blinding, dazzling moment they were one. Then he fell back to earth, panting.

He lay on his back, her head on his chest, stroking her hair, slowly and softly. She almost frightened him, she was so much alive, so uncompromisingly herself. It was what drew him to her at the same time. She was like fire, like the wind, unpredictable and powerful. But lying against his heart right now, she was all warm, soft curves of naked skin, soft curls that smelled like summer, warm breath that rose and fell.

He pondered how fragile a naked human body was, how vulnerable. He felt a sudden fierce urge to protect her. He tightened his arms around her. She murmured softly and held him closer in response, a vague smile on her lips. They fell asleep together, a content tangle of naked limbs under the sheepskin covers.

They had pitched their tents in a rough, wooded area a little inland, out of sight of the ships. Thin columns of smoke, the only remains of the huts along the coastline, were rising in the distance. It was early morning, the first morning in this strange, inhospitable land. A chill seeped through his clothes and he shivered. He girded on his sword.

'Riórdirým.'

He turned and looked at the low bench that served as a bed. Ciórdynn raised herself on one elbow. She swept her long, black hair out of her face.

Her eyes were still puffy with sleep. He went over to the bed and kneeled beside it. He laid a hand on her hair and kissed her lightly.

'I hope you slept better than I did.' He turned back to his preparations. Ciórdynn drew up her legs under the blanket and folded her hands over her knees. She looked at him. There was a hard edge to his face that had not been there before. He seemed to avoid her eyes.

'Where to today?' she said.

'The scouts have found out where the highest concentration of resistance will be. If we attack swiftly, the barbarian tribes will have no chance to unite.'

She got up and began to dress. She brushed her hair and quickly worked it into a thick braid that reached to her waist. She pulled a leather jerkin over her head and reached for the slender sword that hung from the tent pole.

He looked up. 'You're not coming with us.'

'I am, though.'

He gripped her arms. 'I will not have you come with us. It's too dangerous.'

'Do you think I want to be left behind when you risk your life for us?' Her pale, oval face was set.

He brought a hand to her cheek. 'You're the only one I've got left. I will not lose you now.'

'Riórdirým—'

'No.' He took her face in his hands and kissed her. 'It's time. I'll see you when we return.'

Darkness rolled before them and trailed behind them as they led their horses through a narrow pass a few miles north of camp. Lakíthra and the others shivered when the dark mist touched their ankles and crept up their legs. Both sides of the pass consisted of rocky boulders, with small, gnarly trees holding on to the earth in between the rocks. At the end of the pass, they heard a harsh resounding cry.

'*Na'Héach.*'

Their horses reared as they hastily tried to turn them. It was too late. A band of straw-haired, leather-clad men descended on them from all sides of the pass. Within moments, they were in the middle of a heavy fight.

When he had managed to free himself from his attackers, Riórdirým sheathed his sword and put his hands to his temples. He tried to shut out the sounds of the fight around him and concentrated fiercely.

'*Calamêntiré,*' he murmured. The coldness increased, and the mist thickened as it began to rise. '*Calamêntiré, ti eyíldi, Tahiéra, óyirtaz....*' An eerie silence descended, enveloping him and everyone around him. Tall warriors with bright eyes clawed at their throats with their fingers. Others were hewn down by *Tzanatzi* swords, helpless in their terror, their eyes wide.

As the *Tzanatzi* warriors finished off the last savages with their slender swords, he stood and stretched out his awareness around him, trying to feel any more resistance in the immediate vicinity. There seemed to be none. He approached Lakíthra, who stood wiping blood and sweat off his brow with an expression of vague disgust. The young man had never been in a real sword fight before, and he stared at his blood-stained hands, which were trembling. He straightened hastily as Riórdirým walked up to him.

'Only a small pocket of resistance,' Riórdirým said. Lakíthra nodded. 'We should press on. No doubt there are a few small settlements nearby, like the ones we found yesterday. They must have been warned somehow, and sent their warriors ahead to surprise us.'

They left the pass and rode north, crossing foothills and green, empty fields. After a while Riórdirým frowned. His eyes went dark. A strange sensation had come over him, like a dark cloud looming over his head. His throat closed up and he swallowed, trying to understand what was causing his discomfort. He cast about his senses and was suddenly thrown by a raw, painful feeling in his heart. It was as if a part of him had been forcefully cut off and left him with the frayed edges of a lost connection. He swayed in the saddle, bending over in pain.

'Back,' he uttered through clenched teeth. 'Something's not right. Back to camp, now.'

They smelled the smoke before they saw the burning tents in the distance. They dismounted quickly and were immediately beset by *Einache*. While the others engaged in battle Riórdirým frantically searched the area calling Ciórdynn's name. He found her lying on the ground at the entrance of one the larger tents. Her sword was still in her hand. He dropped to his knees beside her body and cradled it in his arms.

'Ciórdynn,' he whispered. He carefully brushed some soot from her cheek. There was a large gash across her abdomen, where the blood had stained her jerkin and the tunic underneath a dark red. She did not move. Her face was white and unnaturally still. A raw cry of pain and loneliness tore through his body, and he closed his eyes as he was engulfed by darkness.

He sat with her for hours, while the women and children returned from their hiding places in the woods and trickled back into camp. As time passed more and more people came and stood in a circle around him. They stared at him in silence with their dark eyes, witnessing him as he sat there with her body in his arms. It was as if he sat in a bubble of anguish and dark, tightly held-back fury. None dared approach him.

In the early hours of the morning, when most people had silently drifted off to their tents and Lakíthra was the only one left watching over him, Riórdirým passed out. The body fell from his arms as he hit the rocky ground. When he opened his eyes, he was lying in his tent, covered with blankets, alone.

Rom woke with a gasp. He was completely disoriented. It was still dark and for a moment, he was unsure of where he was, of who he was. He rolled on his side and became aware of someone lying beside him. Maetis. He heard the reassuring sound of her breath.

He carefully pushed aside the curls that had fallen across her face. She murmured softly and moved towards him in her sleep. He put his arms around her and held her close to his heart. He held her as if she were his last connection to the world of joy, of love, and laughter.

He left her before dawn. He dressed without making a sound and stood staring down at her for a while. He kissed her temple.

'*Aye sûa*, Maetis,' he whispered, and no longer knew what language he was speaking in.

At first light Yldich woke up with a strange, heavy feeling in his heart. He went to the kitchen, the oppressiveness hanging over him like a cloud. He wondered if it was the change in weather. Since the sudden rains the day before, the sky had remained clouded, and the atmosphere was dull and still.

'*Ya'hey*,' Yárah said. She handed him a mug of tea. 'Will you be having your breakfast now, *Yaever*, or shall I have it brought to your study?' He took a sip and looked at her over the rim of his mug.

'I think I'll be back for breakfast later,' he said. 'I've a feeling there's something I have to do, first.'

He opened the door to the study and noticed a familiar figure in front of the windows, looking out over the fields in the distance. As the figure turned, Yldich felt a tingle of foresight.

'I dreamt him again,' Rom said in a low voice. His dark eyes burned in his pale face. Yldich took a chair and sat down.

'Tell me,' he said softly. When Rom finished the story, Yldich nodded. His grey eyes were sad. 'I think I understand now. Why someone as adept and powerful as *Riór*—the Unnamed One would fall for such a feeble trick as a challenge to a duel. He must have felt it was a ruse. I always thought it was arrogance that made him come nonetheless.'

'If it wasn't arrogance, then what was it?'

'He was longing for death,' Yldich said in a low voice. 'Maybe he wasn't aware of it. But that's what it must have been. Think about it. He lost his home, most of his people, and the woman he loved.'

Rom's face was strained. 'But he was still responsible for the remainder of his people.'

Yldich smiled, but his grey eyes kept their grim expression. 'When they arrived in the high North he had done everything for them he could. He had conquered a whole country for them and nearly wiped out the original inhabitants. What more was there to do? What more was there to live for?'

'So he came to the top of the cliffs, and was killed,' Rom said. His voice was husky.

'Not exactly,' Yldich said. 'He was torn from his body, and his body was lost.' Rom held his arms across his stomach as if he were in pain. 'Yet somehow his presence, or rather the presence of the *Tahiéra*, has become palpable again. Since the entity, as you said, has no will of its own, it must mean that the mage has found a way to manifest, if not in the world of tangible things, then at least in the world of spirit. For him to rise, and send the *Tahiéra* to trouble us, he must have had some kind of focus, an anchor in the world of living beings.' He gazed in the distance. 'Someone alike in temperament, and energy, even in body.'

Rom stared at him. 'What—what are you saying?' He went cold.

Yldich went on speaking as if he hadn't heard him. 'It would have to be someone with some kind of resonance to his energy.' He leaned his chin in his hand. 'Someone related, however far removed. Or, even better: his own next turn on the *Sha'neagh d'Ea*, the Wheel of Life. His own, newly born self.'

Rom's breath caught in his throat. 'What?'

'You,' Yldich said, turning his clear gaze on him.

'No,' Rom whispered.

'Yes,' Yldich said calmly. 'Think about it. It makes sense. The unusual gifts you had as a boy. The nightmares of being lost in darkness. It was what he felt as he was torn from his body. I know it well, because I dreamt it time and time again, after we fought on the cliff at Gardeth Battle Plain.' Rom stared at him, his face ashen, a horrible, sinking feeling in his stomach. He wanted to scream, to run from the room, do anything to stop Yldich speaking.

'When darkness rose in Lord Aldr's hall,' Yldich said in a dispassionate voice, 'it was the *Tahiéra*, coming to your call, even though you didn't know it. It was the first time your spirit reached out for it, because you were helpless and in dire need. Its calling upon started a chain of events you were not aware of. Far away to the North, darkness rose in our fields and woods, and I started to dream you. Later, on our journey through the Forest, when you thought Feyir had slain me, you even summoned it without being aware of what you were doing.'

'No,' Rom said, but it was like trying to push away the tide coming in. He was shaking.

'And your proficiency in dreamwalking.' Yldich smiled mirthlessly, shaking his head. 'I've had five hundred years to practice, yet you unwittingly pull off feats the oldest, most famous *Yaever* would feel intimidated by.'

'No... no,' Rom whispered, but all the time he could feel something inside saying *yes, yes*. It was as if a thin cloth that had veiled his memory was forcefully torn away and he couldn't help but know. Images whirled before his mind's eye. They came into focus one by one. He saw people running before they were swallowed by a hungry river of fire, and the figureheads of slender ships. Swords flashed in the light of the torches. Black hatred filled his veins and gave his sword arm strength as he fought a tall ginger-haired *Einache* youth with Yldich's eyes. His legs turned to water. He grabbed the edge of the table to keep himself upright.

Yldich came over to him and took hold of his arms. 'Careful, now.' He pushed him into a chair.

'How—how long have you known?'

A faint smile crossed Yldich's face. 'I've had my suspicions since you pulled me out of the darkness in the woods. But when we brought you into this house and I heard you raving in *Tzanatzi*, saying you were buried alive, I was sure.'

Rom's face was ashen. 'So... shouldn't you kill me now, or something?'

Yldich laughed softly. 'Kill you? And start all over again? Silly lad. I haven't brought you all the way up here to kill you. I've brought you here to heal you. So you can lift the curse that threatens us all.' Rom sat staring as if in a daze. Yldich sighed and pressed Rom's shoulder. He stood up. 'I'll get us something to eat. Breakfast was ages ago. We could both do with something.'

Rom nodded absently. Yldich walked towards the door. He was about to leave the study when he heard a low, strangled cry behind him. He looked back. Rom had sunk to the ground and sat with his head in his hands, shaking as waves of grief tore through him. He started sobbing violently. Yldich shook his head and went back.

'I was wondering when it would sink in,' he murmured. He kneeled beside him. He laid a hand on his back and held him as his body was racked by hoarse sobs.

After a while Rom seemed to have no more strength for tears. He sat back, trembling, staring at something behind Yldich.

'I can see them,' he said. His voice was raw. '*Calênte áyoroz.* I can see their faces....'

'Whose faces?'

'*Elérimaz io, éldere....*'

Yldich shook him gently. 'I don't understand you, Rom. Speak your own language.'

Rom grabbed Yldich's tunic, grasping it as if it could keep him from sliding into an abyss. 'Yldich,' he whispered, his eyes wide with fear. 'I don't know who I am anymore....'

'Easy, now.' Yldich carefully disengaged and went over to one of the chests. He returned with a cup. 'Here, drink this.' The liquid was bitter, but Rom didn't even wince. Soft, fuzzy-edged darkness enveloped him, promising forgetfulness and sleep. Thankfully, he embraced it.

Eldairc was in the kitchen, having breakfast with Élora. They were talking with their heads close together. Eldairc said something under his breath that had Élora toss back her hair and laugh. Her eyes glinted. Yldich came in and stood before their table. He looked unusually serious. His grey eyes were dark. A hush fell upon the room.

'I need your help,' he said.

'I don't believe it.' Eldairc stared at Yldich, his hands at his mouth. He sat at the table in Yldich's study. Yldich stood with his back to the hearth, his hands planted in his sides.

'Believe it.'

'Are you sure?'

'As sure as I can be, after travelling with him for the better part of two months. Yes. I'm sure.'

Eldairc shook his head. 'Somehow I'm having trouble picturing Rom as a battle-hardened sorcerer, the scourge of our people.'

Yldich grinned, though his eyes remained sober. 'So would I, if I hadn't witnessed the dark take him over. Still, it's not him, it's his former self. They're not the same.'

'So... where's he now? How did he take it?'

'That's where you come in. I need someone to help watch over him. We can't afford to leave him alone.'

Eldairc stared at him. 'What happened?'

Yldich sighed and dragged his fingers through his ginger curls. 'There's a reason why people don't remember all the Turns of their Wheel of Life.

Yaever only do so after years of preparation. It takes a special kind of awareness to juggle the conflicting personalities and points of view... it's dangerous territory for the untrained to be pushed into.'

'Why?'

'When you're not ready, it might break your mind.' Yldich's face was grim.

Eldairc looked at him with wide eyes. 'What did you do?'

'I drugged him. His dreaming mind has a better chance of incorporating the knowledge without him going mad.'

Eldairc plucked at his lower lip. He looked up. 'How will you know whether he's all right?'

'I'll know when he wakes up.'

They stood outside the door to Rom's chamber. Eldairc hesitated, his hand at the handle. 'Do you hear that?' Yldich looked at him. There was a faint whispering, like the sound of many voices speaking at once. He didn't know the language.

'Open it,' he said, his eyes like slate.

They entered and halted abruptly. Eldairc gasped. The room was so cold he could see his breath plume in the air. A black cloud, a column of darkest smoke hovered over the bed where Rom lay sleeping. It loomed over him, reaching for him with tendrils of mist, like impossibly long fingers. At their entrance it turned and wavered. Something inside it stilled. They saw a fair, pale face emerge from living midnight hair. A woman gazed at them with dark, almond shaped eyes. Then she was gone.

Eldairc stood frozen in the doorway. 'What, by all the gods, was that?'

Yldich took a deep breath. 'His past, catching up with him.'

Yldich moved over to the bed and sat on its edge. He bowed over Rom, touching his face gently with the tips of his fingers. Eldairc stood watching him and wondered not for the first time how the heavily built man could move so gracefully. He reminded him more of a mother with a sick child than of a warrior and leader of men. A soothing energy emanated from his hands and eyes. He addressed Eldairc without taking his eyes off Rom. 'In the large chest near the door in my study there's a leather bundle. Get it for me, will you?'

Eldairc swallowed. 'What if that—that thing comes back?' He furtively eyed the sword that stood against the wall.

'That won't do you much good against *Tzanatzi* ghosts,' Yldich said with a faint grin. 'Don't worry. My song will clear a space where they will not be able to enter. At least for now.' He turned back to Rom and started to hum softly. The song sent out ever widening ripples of sound, just above the threshold of hearing. Warmth returned to the room, and the atmosphere began to lighten.

Rom fell into the sky. It was a curious sensation. There was a force that carried him upwards, ever higher, past the dome of azure that covered the earth, and into the night. When he passed the moon, he faintly wondered if he would see the face of *Janta*, the wizened old woman who lived in the moon, whom his Southern mother had told him about as a child. But he saw no-one, only the faint glow of the moon as he passed, floating upwards.

Stars were overhead, myriads of stars, whirling out into infinity. There was no-one else there, yet he did not feel alone. He felt strangely comforted, cradled by the invisible force that carried him upwards, bathed in the light of a countless stars. Feeling completely safe and at ease, he curled up and fell into a deep and dreamless sleep.

After what seemed like a long time, although he wouldn't have known how to measure time in that place, he became aware of something pulling at him. Someone was trying to get his attention. He attempted to ignore it. He was so perfectly at peace. He wanted to stay there forever. But something kept tugging at him, trying to wake him up.

Reluctantly he turned his attention outward. Something swirled around him and suddenly he was in the world again, or rather, the world was before and below him. He could see the waves of the sea crashing at the rocky coast. He could see endless forests, winding rivers, lakes and snowy fields, stretching out beneath him. It was like flying over the surface of the earth at great speed.

The presence that had woken him up became denser, and he became aware of someone at his left side, someone pointing out something to him. He looked down, screwing up his eyes to see clearly. It seemed as if tiny fissures were running in the bedrock beneath the earth's surface, beneath the grass and the snow. They looked like the hairline cracks across the ice when it is broken.

As he looked at them, the fissures seemed to deepen and run further and further across the earth, like lightning running through the sky. He stared at it in alarm. Where the cracks in the bedrock widened, darkness seeped into the soil above, curling up into the air like smoke. He could see dark shapes form themselves out of the smoke. Fear went before them, and fear went behind them. The earth rumbled and shook like a wounded animal in the throes of death.

Fear rode through the streets of Érskitha, the capital in the South where King Farhardt reigned. People did not dare go out after nightfall. A child had gone out and was lost, unable to find his way back. His mother wailed behind a closed door, while her family kept her from going out the door. An icy wind howled through the streets. In the early hours of the morning they would find the child, dead, an expression of frozen horror on his face.

In the fields further east and north, arrows were flying and the cries of warriors slashing away at each other tore the silence. Farmers and their families fled their homes in terror. Those that were not caught in the invisible battles raging outside were frozen on the way by the cold, or the black terror creeping up to them.

In the forests to the north, the *Einache* dead arose and sounded their battle cries. Little *Einache* settlements were abandoned by their terrified inhabitants. Some refugees were caught in ghost fights when the *Einache* dead attacked *Tzanatzi* sentries and set fire to their invisible tents. Villagers who were sensitive to the other realms found themselves face-to-face with *Tzanatzi* swordfighters, but they had no time to cry out. They would be found with their throats slashed.

Rom saw the settlement of Woodbury empty of its inhabitants while the streets filled with a dark, rolling fear and the houses filled with the whispers of the dead. His gaze was led steadily northward by the presence at his side. Rom could see it got worse the further north he looked. The forests of the high North were filled with the battle-cries of the *Einache* and *Tzanatzi* dead, while darkness enveloped them all and froze the breath of anyone who dared near them.

The House of the Deer was a small island of light in a black sea of despair. Soon, it too would be engulfed. Rom imagined Yldich's people, as the darkness finally broke through the heavy doors and streamed into the great Hall. He saw the young *Einache* warriors, pulling their swords in vain against the incorporeal terror. He saw Eald and Maetis, powerless against the dark power of the *Tahiéra* as it engulfed them. Acrid smoke entered their mouths and nostrils, stole their breath and stopped their hearts.

'No,' he cried, although he had no voice to scream with. The images swirled, and suddenly all was quiet again.

'There is still time,' he heard the presence's voice in his head. There was something familiar about it. He searched his mind in wonder.

'Lakíthra?'

A dark-haired young man shaped himself out of nothingness. He smiled slowly at Rom. '*Caleërte*, Riórdirým.'

Rom stared wide-eyed at the dark young man. 'I'm not *him*,' he whispered. The young man held his head a little to one side, like an inquisitive raven. An expression akin to amusement was in his dark eyes.

'That's were you are mistaken. You are both him and you. The sooner you acknowledge this, the sooner you can help lift the curse and stop the storm from destroying us all.' He motioned at the earth below, where all was now quiet.

'What—what is it?'

'The result of the forces set in motion five hundred years ago.'

'The *Tahiéra*?' Rom said in a hushed voice, afraid to arouse the living darkness.

Lakíthra shook his head. 'It's not that simple. Ask her who is eldest, the white-haired one.'

Rom stared at him. 'Yealda? The eldest *Yaeve*?'

'Ask her why the dead are lingering.' Lakíthra's pleasant face was stern. 'If you find out, maybe you can prevent all this from happening.'

'How? How can I stop it?'

'I cannot tell you,' Lakíthra said in a soft voice. 'You'll have to find out for yourself. I am, however, permitted to give you *this*.' He held out his hands. A warm glow shone through his fingers, as if he had taken the heart from a fire.

'Permitted? By whom?' Rom eyed him a little suspiciously. 'What is it?'

'Something you lost a long time ago,' Lakíthra said. He smiled. 'Hold out your hands.'

Rom hesitantly held out his hands before him. Something warm filled them and he closed his fingers on it. A warm orange glow filled his hands, filling them until he felt he could hold no more, and travelled through his arms, his heart, and deep down into his belly.

He gasped in surprise, and fell on his knees as he was overwhelmed by images, sounds and sensations. A beautiful dark-haired woman held him up into the sky, laughing, and he felt perfectly happy and safe, able to do anything, be anything. He noticed his own hands, the tiny fingers of an infant no more than a few months old, grasping at her hair.

He was a boy of five summers and sat on sun-warmed rocks, gazing out over the blue sea, the sun glittering on the water. He saw creatures that looked like big fish but laughed like joyous children. They jumped from the water, and dived down with a splash as if it was their only business to enjoy themselves. He left his body on the rocks and swam with them, one with their powerful, perfectly synchronized movements.

He was a young lad in a place where dark-haired people were dancing a slow, graceful dance. The roof was made of living vines giving off an intoxicating scent. He could see the stars through their bows and leaves. A girl with eyes the colour of night gazed at him from the other side of the field, and he felt the powerful pull of desire in his heart and his loins. As they lay together he could feel their energy mingling, expanding in a deliriously powerful soundless explosion of pleasure. It seemed to him they were earth and sky meeting, sea and shore, fire and air, re-creating the world. He held out his glowing hands and could see the light dancing at his fingertips.

'What—what is it?' he whispered. He looked up.

Lakíthra looked down at him. 'The source of your power.' Rom stared at him in astonishment. 'Wield it carefully,' Lakíthra said, the shadow of a smile around his mouth, 'this time.' He helped Rom up and embraced him. He met his eyes. '*Aymíraz*, brother.' Then he was gone.

The light of the setting sun painted the room in peach and gold. Rom carefully opened his eyes. There was a sharp smell in the room, which reminded him of tree resin and forest fires. His eyelids felt heavy, his body unfamiliar, like an old garment he had left lying about somewhere and not worn for ages. His mouth was dry. He coughed and tried to move from under the heavy sheepskins.

Yldich came over to the bed. He sat down and stared intently into his face. Rom tried using his voice.

'Yldich,' he croaked.

The older man's face was shadowed with wariness. When he saw Rom's eyes were clear, with no sign of madness, the wariness dissipated. He released an inaudible sigh of relief. 'How are you feeling?' He helped him sit up.

'Like a piece of old driftwood,' Rom said huskily. He coughed in an attempt to get his voice back. He shot Yldich an accusatory glance. 'What was that stuff you gave me?'

'Something strong enough to knock down a horse, especially on an empty stomach.' Yldich grinned. He handed Rom a mug filled with water.

'Yldich—what's that smell?'

'Ah. That. Well, we had an unexpected visitor. I'll tell you about that later.'

'I think I had one as well.' Rom frowned, trying to clear his head. 'One of my kinsmen. Or who used to be my kinsman—no, well, *his*, really.' He shook his head in confusion. 'Anyway, he showed me something—something important....'

'Can it wait?'

Rom's brows lifted in surprise. 'I think I'll be able to remember... I don't think I could forget if I wanted to. Why?'

'Because there's someone here who wants to see you.' Yldich pressed his shoulder and went to the door. 'I'll be right back.' He left and Maetis stepped into the room. Her face was pale and strained, as if she had been crying. A horrible certainty made Rom's heart sink.

She's turning away from me. I can hardly blame her.

Maetis sat at the edge of his bed, her hands in her lap. She looked at him.

'Maetis,' he said. His voice was hoarse. 'Did—did Yldich tell you?'

She nodded. 'It was... a bit of a shock,' she said softly.

Cold loneliness settled down on him. He closed his eyes, steadying himself inwardly. 'It's all right,' he whispered. 'I understand....'

Maetis looked up. She took his hands. 'No, that's not what I'm saying at all... I am not turning away from you.'

'You're not?' His eyes lit up.

She smiled at him. 'Would I keep back because of a little trouble?'

'Not you.' He released a breath and relaxed a little. 'But Maetis, this is more than a little trouble.'

'I know.' Her mouth pulled in a crooked smile. 'I wonder what my mother would have said if she had known I'm courting the man who was once the scourge of our people—' She saw the pained expression in his face and fell silent. She bent over him and kissed his brow. 'It was a long time ago,' she said softly. 'Things have changed. So have you.'

He brought his hands to her face and kissed her with great care, as if she would melt away like snowflakes under his hands. Maetis slipped her arms around him. He held her as tightly as he dared, as if he needed the touch of her embrace imprinted upon his skin for ever.

One day, I may need the memory dearly.

A shiver went through him. He pushed the thought away quickly and buried his face in her hair. He filled his senses with her touch, her scent, and the sweet sound of her voice.

They had their evening meal, which in Rom's case was a very late breakfast, in Yldich's study. The sun had set and Eldairc had lit the candles in the large chandelier that was suspended above the table. Eald sat opposite Rom and Maetis and nibbled on a piece of bread. He stared at Rom with a pensive look on his narrow face. Yldich had taken the boy aside and explained matters to him. He looked at Rom with his brows knit, as if he were trying to reconcile two different images of him. Rom fidgeted with his food. He could almost feel the boy's clear gaze on him.

'So... can you make the table disappear, or pull a flower from my ear?' Eald said. Yldich chuckled in his beard.

Rom felt his mouth pull into a smile. 'I don't think he was that kind of sorcerer.'

'Then what kind was he?'

'Well... I don't really know....'

'When we were in the woods, Yldich told us he was a dark sorcerer, that he did bad things... like call a dark mist that killed people,' Eald said in his clear voice. Rom winced.

'He wasn't like that to begin with, Eald,' Yldich said, and ladled some more stew on his plate. 'No-one ever is.'

'He thought he should strike first, to avoid his people being hurt,' Rom said huskily. 'They were desperate, you know. There were only a few of them left, and they felt they had nowhere left to go. They didn't know the *Einache*, so they feared them.'

'So he used his magic to slay them,' Eald said.

'And when the *Tzanatzi* advanced to the North, the *Einache* did exactly the same,' Yldich said. His gaze was turned inward a moment. 'They struck back out of fear and slew any *Tzanatzi* they met. And when they were threatened to be overcome, the last *Yaever* used their magic to kill, just as the mage had done.'

'But they were only defending themselves, weren't they?' Eald took another spoonful of stew.

'The *Tzanatzi* would have told you the same,' Yldich said.

Eald munched his stew, a thoughtful expression on his face. 'But...the *Einache* were here first. And the *Yaever* only cursed the mage to protect themselves.'

Yldich gazed in the boy's direction, but he seemed to be staring at something far away. 'That's how it's always been told.' Something in his voice made Rom turn his head to stare at him.

Eldairc cleaned his bowl with a piece of bread and popped it in his mouth. He sighed and sat back. 'Still, I wonder where we would be now if the *Einache* had tried to reason with them, instead of drawing their swords on the spot.'

'So do I,' Yldich said softly.

After dinner they sat by the hearth and drank their tea in silence. Eldairc sat on his usual perch by the hearth. Rom and Maetis shared one of the large chairs.

'Now, maybe you want to tell us about your visitor,' Yldich said to Rom.

'Visitor?' Eldairc's green eyes lit up.

'It... it was someone I once knew,' Rom said. He felt slightly uneasy as he felt their eyes upon him. 'A kinsman of mine, or rather, of *him*. Lakíthra.

He was my—his apprentice, I guess you would call it.' He released a breath, and saw the earth torn apart by the dark force, and the people driven from their homes by the rising Dead.

'He told me a storm is coming. Something is about to break free, and when it does a darkness will rise. The dead will roam the earth, and no-one will be safe once they pick up their fights again. No village will be left standing.'

Eldairc stared at him with his green eyes. Eald shivered. Maetis took Rom's hand and held it, as much for her own comfort as for his.

Yldich nodded, his brow furrowed with thought. 'I've known it was coming for a long time.' His gaze was far away a moment. 'Tell me what you saw.'

'It came from below. The earth could hold it back no longer. Darkness rolled into the fields, and the streets of towns and cities, while the dead fought each other heedless of the living.' Rom shivered. 'I asked Lakíthra whether it was the *Tahiéra*. And how it could be stopped. But he said: "Ask her who is eldest, the white-haired one. Ask her why the dead are lingering." I think he meant Yealda.' Yldich stared at him in bewilderment.

Maetis sat up. 'What would Yealda know of this? Surely it's the darkness that has been rising in our woods, the one that was once called forth by the enemy?' Rom stiffened at her words. Maetis felt it and cursed herself in silence.

Yldich gazed at the two of them. They looked so different, yet somehow they seemed to match each other perfectly in some way: his daughter, lively and bright, like copper flashing in the sun, free like a bird in flight, and Rom, his eyes like the surface of a deep, dark lake, fire and power hidden in their depths. For a fleeting moment they seemed painfully divided by the past. It lasted only an instant. Maetis took Rom's hand and kissed it. Rom looked up and smiled. The tension dissolved.

Yldich released a breath. 'We'll go and speak to Yealda in the morning. Maybe she can shed some light on this vision of yours.'

Eldairc and Eald were about to return to their own chamber as Maetis stood up and turned to Rom.

'*Nâstréhi ea,*' she said in a soft voice. He held her lightly and kissed her. He forgot everything but her touch, and her mouth on his. He heard a chuckle behind him. He felt his face burn and quickly let her go. He turned around and saw Eald grinning widely. Maetis smiled.

'Away with you, now,' she said to the boy. Eldairc grabbed his arm and pulled him out the door with an equally wide grin. His *Nâstréhi ea* trailed behind him through the corridor.

'Rom.' The remainder of a smile was still on Yldich's face, though his eyes were serious. 'Just a moment. I've got something for you.' He rummaged in a chest and tossed something at Rom. He had to move quickly to catch it. It was a small bundle of herbs, rolled up and bound together with thread, as thin as human hair. It had a pungent smell, like wood resin, with a hint of something bitter underneath. He wrinkled his nose at it.

'What's it for?' He frowned with distaste.

Yldich grinned. 'You light it and clear the room with the smoke. The smell may not appeal to you, but it helps to keep uninvited guests away. This morning, while you were still unconscious, Eldairc and I encountered a... presence in your room. A fair, dark woman with dark eyes.'

Rom's eyes went wide. 'The woman from Woodbury... who do you suppose she is?'

'Well, as I see it, there are two possibilities. Either she is like you, a *Tzanatzi* with an uncanny talent for dreamwalking....'

'Or?'

'Or she is from the realm of the Dead.'

Rom shivered. His hand went to the crystal that was on the leather cord on his neck. 'Yldich... what do you think she wants?'

'Maybe that's not the question you should be asking.' Yldich cocked his head. 'Maybe the question should be: who does she think you are?'

Rom turned the bundle of herbs around and around between his fingers. He closed the door of his chamber behind him and toyed with the idea of barring it. Then the futility of it, barring the door against a ghost, made him snort at himself.

He went over to the hearth. Someone had lit the fire earlier in the evening, and it was still burning low. He lit the tip of the bundle carefully until it glowed, and breathed in the bitter smoke that filled the room. It cleared his head, though it did not lift his feeling of unease. He left the bundle glowing on the hearthstones and lay down on the bed, still fully clothed. He held the crystal in his hand, while he closed his eyes and tried his best to fall asleep.

His thoughts went back to Woodbury, to the eerie darkness that seeped through the gates, the whispering voices that tried to tear him from his body. Now they had even penetrated the House of the *Hárrad*. He shuddered and sat up. It was no use. He grabbed a blanket and drew it around his shoulders. In an impulse, he took his sword with him.

The corridor was dark. The lamps were turned down low for the night. He could just discern the doors and walls. He took the left passage and passed a few doors, trying to find Eldairc's and Eald's room. In the dark, all doors looked the same to him. He thought of knocking on a few doors at random. The idea of barging into some unsuspecting *Einache's* bedroom or worse, Yealda's, made him grin with wry amusement.

He stood still for a moment and wondered what to do. The silence and dark, the absence of human sounds, made him feel lonely and forlorn.

'Prrew?' A sound at his feet made him look down. Two luminous green eyes stared back. A black cat curved itself around his legs and looked up expectantly. He bent down to stroke it. It started purring instantaneously, the sound loud in the empty corridor.

'*Ya hey*', cat,' Rom said. 'Looking for a place to sleep, too?' The cat made a little '*prr—aw*' sound as if in agreement, and proceeded to walk through the corridor, its paws soundless on the stone floor, its tail in the air like a flag. Not knowing what else to do, Rom followed it. The cat stopped every once in a while to look back at him, as if to make sure he still followed.

Finally they reached the Great Hall, where the fires were still burning low. No-one was about. The cat walked straight across the Hall and leapt on a bench in an alcove. Rom sat on the bench, sank back in the cushions and drew his blanket around him. The cat leapt in his lap, turning a few times to find the most comfortable position. Rom laid the sword beside him, began stroking the cat and felt strangely at home.

'You'll wake me if anything bad comes, won't you?' he said. The cat gazed at him a moment with its green, dispassionate eyes. Rom leaned back and drew up his legs. Slowly but surely, he drifted off into sleep.

The fires had gone out. The early morning chill had crept up to him in his sleep and crawled over his skin. He began to shiver. Something started to glow in response. A tiny orange flame that flickered deep in his belly. He felt it grow, like a tiny sun that grew bigger and bigger. A pleasant glow spread through his belly and suffused his arms and legs, filling them with warmth until it reached the tips of his fingers. Warm and comfortable once more, he released a contented sigh and stretched a little, at the edge of sleeping and waking.

'*Fírte! Éya a'elmni fírte!*' A high, clear voice rang in his ear. He started and opened his eyes. Three *Einache* children stood staring down at him.

'What?' He shook the hair out of his eyes. A little boy with sun bleached hair pointed down at Rom's hands. A soft light washed over his skin and made it look as he were on fire. Bewildered, he held out his hands. They were glowing. Soft flickering flames danced at the tips of his fingers. He gasped and instinctively brushed his hands over the blanket to quench the flames. It was useless; they were coming from under his skin.

As he stared at his hands, the flames dissolved, leaving only a faint warm glow, so faint he might have been able to tell himself he had imagined the whole thing. His three witnesses, however, vouched to the contrary:

'You were on fire! I saw it!'

'Me, too!' They turned and ran away, chattering like squirrels, no doubt on their way to spread the word. Rom pulled his fingers through his hair and groaned.

'Well, it sounds like your heritage is truly catching up with you.' The shadow of a grin flitted across Yldich's face. He poured Rom some tea. Rom sat on the hearthstones in Yldich's chambers, shaking his head in bewilderment. Yldich looked at him with interest, his head at a curious angle. 'Do you think you could do it again?'

'I've no idea. I don't even know what I did, let alone how.'

Yldich sat down in the chair before him and narrowed his eyes. 'Apparently, you have hidden your gifts so deep they only surface when you are either asleep, or in great need of them.'

'But when I was freezing to death in Aeldic's lockup, I couldn't do this.' Rom shook his head. 'This is not like dreamwalking. This is something I've never done before.' He stared at his hands. Somehow, the glowing sensation in his belly had been familiar. He closed his eyes and searched his memory. 'I dreamt it,' he said. 'When I met Lakíthra, my former apprentice. He gave me something, something he said I'd lost a long time ago. It felt exactly like this, but it was much more....'

'Tell me.'

Rom closed his eyes, his fingers at his temples, and grasped at the remnants of his dream. He frowned. The experiences of *ayúrdimae* had a tendency to fade in daylight. It was like trying to catch fish with his bare hands. When he had a careful hold on the dream, he recounted the experience to Yldich without opening his eyes. Finally, he looked up.

Yldich sat staring in the hearth. 'Apparently, the Unnamed One mastered much more than the forces of darkness,' he said. 'He had some kind of affinity with the elements as well. With fire, at least.'

'It didn't feel like ordinary fire,' Rom said. 'It felt like... like something from deep within me, something to do with passion, and life, and joy....'

Yldich looked at him. Something was different about the young man, he mused. He couldn't quite put his finger on it. 'You seem no worse for adding Riórdirým's talents to your own,' he said in a kind tone.

Rom shivered at the open use of the name. 'Should you say his name out loud?'

'But it's *your* name, isn't it, really? Rom. Riórdirým....' Rom winced. Yldich seemed not to notice. 'And in your real name lies power. I think your kinsman, Lae—Laekita....'

'Lakíthra.'

'Yes. Lakíthra. I think he was right. The sooner you acknowledge who you really are, and make peace with yourself, the sooner you'll be able to wield the power you once possessed. So you can stop the forces that threaten to destroy us.'

'I'm afraid of it.' Rom's face was drawn. 'I don't know what it is... I don't know what I'll become once I... let it take over.' Yldich smiled.

'You wielded it led by fear and hatred once already,' he said in a kind tone. 'I don't think you'll make the same mistake again.' Rom looked up. Something changed in his face. The haunted look in his eyes faded a little. 'Why don't you go and have some breakfast, and clean yourself up a bit,' Yldich said. 'Then we'll have a talk with Yealda.'

'Yldich tells me you had an important dream about the coming storm,' Yealda said in her level voice. They were in her drawing room, a sparsely furnished chamber with windows facing north. Yealda occupied a large chair that appeared to have been carved from one solid log of honey-coloured wood. Interlacing branches with stylized leaves ran along the armrests and back. Rom wondered what kind of the tree had supplied the wood. It must have been immense.

Yealda sat straight, her face composed, her hands in her lap. She wore the same kind of blue-grey robes Rom had seen her in before. He took a deep breath to steady himself. Being in Yealda's company made him uneasy every time.

'You may wonder about this chair,' Yealda said with a motion of her hand. 'It is very old. It was carved from the Tree that was most sacred to our people, the eldest tree. We performed our ceremonies under this tree for the turning of the Wheel of Life, the changing of the seasons, the births and deaths. It was cut down by the *Tzanatzi* right before the Great Battle. We saved it right before they could burn it.' Rom stared at her. He didn't know what to say. 'Now, please tell me about your dream.'

Rom cleared his throat. 'I saw the... darkness rise and roam the earth.' He shivered. 'Fear held cities and villages in its grip from the South to the utmost North. I saw the dead do battle in the fields and village streets, *Einache* and *Tzanatzi* alike—they simply cut down the living if they were in their way. Darkness besieged the House of the Deer and burst through the doors.' He looked at Yealda's face, but her lavender eyes betrayed no feeling at all. He continued.

'There was one I knew a long time ago, during the War, one of my kin. I asked him if this was the *Tahiéra*, the horror that was summoned by the Unnamed One. But he told me I should come to you—to ask why the dead are lingering.' She stared at him in silence.

Yldich looked at the old, proud woman, a pensive expression in his eyes. 'I always understood that the song you sang and ended the War was the end of the Unnamed One, and of the darkness that assailed us,' he said. 'But since that time, it seems as if in some subtle way, we've been stuck in time. As if everything around us is moving, and we're still, like fish trapped in ice ... even the dead seem ignorant of the fact that time has moved on and the War is over.' Yldich looked at Yealda, but she remained silent. 'I also wonder how the rising dark could linger, even increase in strength, and poison our lands, while the Unnamed One was banished.'

Rom stared at Yealda's face. Somehow, he knew. 'You did more than banish him,' he whispered. 'You cursed him.'

Yealda turned to him. 'Yes, I cursed him.' Her voice was cold. 'I cursed him and his people, for every Turn of the Wheel, that they would not have peace until he is released by the sword that he once wielded against us. I chained him under the earth and then I cursed him.'

Yldich stared at her. His face had turned pale. 'You cursed a whole people to get at one man—why?' He sounded shaken.

Yealda motioned at Rom. 'Ask *him*. Ask him who is the mirror image of the one who robbed my life of happiness.'

Rom felt coldness rise from within. A heaviness settled on his shoulders. Unbidden images came into his head. His voice was husky as he started to speak. 'It—it was when we were moving camp towards the high North, on a cold autumn day...'

The sky was clear and blue, but the air was edged with the first chill of winter. Ríórdirým, Lakíthra and several archers rode in front, to survey the territory. Lakíthra fidgeted with his reigns. He seemed uneasy. Lately, he was the only one who had contact with him, who still talked to him. The others seemed to avoid his company. They still bowed respectfully, one hand on their stomach, as he passed. But no children laughed when he was near, no women talked to him, and the men avoided his eyes.

From time to time the thought came to him that he should do something about it. That it was important. But somehow, he couldn't get himself to care. Since that fateful first day on land, when Ciórdynn was lost, he didn't seem to be able to feel deeply about anything. There was a hollow where his heart used to be, and beneath it, a dark, tightly contained anger. He had wielded it like a sword, striking at every village, every *Einache* who dared cross their path. He fought back relentlessly if they dared resist them. His strategy had proven successful. They had taken nearly all the country, on their trek to the high North, where resistance was fiercest.

Some whispers had come to his ears as they pushed on relentlessly: why did they not stop, as they had more than enough land to settle comfortably? Why pursue this course of destruction? If anyone dared ask questions along these lines to his face, his answer was always the same: they could not afford to let the barbarian clans intact. If they left so much as one small village, the inhabitants would one day regroup and revenge themselves. They would never have peace.

Usually, when Riórdirým rode in front with Lakíthra, all his senses were alert. Though his emotions were dulled, his other senses were sharper than ever. But today, as they rode through the forests that seemed to go on forever, his thoughts had a life of their own. They pulled him this way and that, until he seemed to be drifting above an endless sea of treetops and boughs, their leaves whispering, whispering, dulling his senses, telling him it was safe, why not relax, why not let himself drift, it was easy, so easy, let go, sleep...

As they neared an open space in the woods surrounded by shrubs and young oak trees, he jolted awake from his strange reverie. He was alarmed and cursed inwardly. It was not like him to let himself go like that. He shook his head, sat up straight in the saddle and sensed about him.

There was something, beneath the lulling voices, beneath the soft cloud of sleepiness, an indeterminable tension. He held up his left hand to Lakíthra, as a signal for him to slow his pace. As they advanced more cautiously, he stretched out his senses to include the area around him. He felt something in the air, a tension like a tautly stretched thread. They were being watched. He felt a surge of alarm and turned in the saddle.

'Back!' he cried to the archers and swordsmen behind them, who protected the heart of the company, the women and children. 'It's an ambush.'

The words had hardly left his mouth when the earth under his horse's hooves shook and came up, shedding turf and clods of earth. The horse reared in surprise, his eyes rolling in fear. Riórdirým fell backwards and caught a glimpse of a wooden trapdoor studded with spear points. They had not advanced far enough, or they would have been impaled.

He heard the *Einache* battle cry come from all sides, and the deadly swish of arrows. He struggled frantically to get up. His foot was caught in the stirrup. A cry to his left told him they had gotten at Lakíthra, and a surge of black anger rushed through him.

'*Atáre*,' he cried, and the leather straps of his stirrups, along with every other strap, rope or belt within five yards snapped. He scrambled up, his heart filled with anger, his eyes dark as pitch. The company was beset by invisible archers. He saw Lakíthra on his back in the dirt with an arrow in his chest, pale as a dead man. To Riórdirým's relief, he coughed, and struggled to get up. He looked back.

The invisible archers used lighted arrows on the carts and wagons. One of them was already on fire. He felt a kind of detached horror as he heard high-pitched cries coming from inside. *Tzanatzi* warriors rushed towards the wagons to put out the fires and rescue whoever they could. They were beset by arrows.

Riórdirým felt a sense of hopeless panic in his stomach make way for a surge of dark, cold anger. It was growing. It filled him up until he felt twice his size. Darkness flowed through his veins like ink.

'*Calamêntiré,*' he said, and the sun was cut off. He was filled with a cold, impersonal sense of power. It was like being under water. Sounds were muffled, and movements were slowed down. The fires died down abruptly, smothered like snuffed candles. '*Calamêntiré, ti eyíldi, ti Tahiéra, óyirtaz me...*'

The stream of arrows trickled and stopped. He heard muffled cries, coming from the trees. As he released a breath, and let go of the darkness, sunlight returned to the glade. He moved quickly and addressed the warriors that were still on their feet.

'There. Between those trees.' He indicated them with a wave of his hand. It didn't take them long to find their assailants. The warriors returned within a few heartbeats, dragging along five struggling *Einache*. They were still coughing and wheezing.

He stared at the captives. From up close, he could see they were young, four youths and a girl. Their bleached hair was in disarray, covered in dirt and bits of tree bark. They were clothed in light greens and browns, which from a distance made them nearly invisible against the background of the trees and shrubs. They stared at him with their oddly coloured, disconcertingly bright eyes, grey and green. The girl was obviously the leader. She addressed him in a proud manner. Her eyes were cold and hard.

'*Ohênstriër Tzanatzi.*' She spat before his feet. His hand moved to the hilt of his sword. A cry sounded behind them.

'*Ni'érsi.*' It was a woman's voice. He turned his head. A tall woman stood on a low hill behind them. Her long hair floated about her on a breeze. It was so fair it was nearly white. She stared at Riórdirým. He saw the way her robes moved in the wind, her hair drifting around her, and suddenly he knew. She was the source of the sleepy voices, the song that had lulled him into a semblance of safety. She had nearly cost him his life, and the lives of his kinsmen. Something hardened in his stomach.

He turned to the man who held the girl. 'Decapitate her. And hang the others from the trees, as a warning.'

The young warrior hesitated. 'But—it's a girl, my lord... and the others, they're what, sixteen, seventeen years old?'

'Did they stop to ask how old Ciórdynn was when they killed her?' Riórdirým's voice was cold. 'You seem to forget that this is a war. If we let them go today, they'll be the ones who kill our women and children tomorrow.' The man stared at him in dismay. He didn't move. Riórdirým's eyes turned to pitch. 'If you cannot do your duty, I'll do it for you.'

He drew his sword. The young man stepped back involuntarily. Riórdirým swept the blade in a powerful arc. He heard a high-pitched scream behind him as the girl fell under his hand.

Rom held his hands over his eyes in abhorrence, then realized the futility of the gesture. The images were inside his head, not without. He shuddered under Yealda's clear, unwavering gaze.

'I remember,' he whispered. He held his head in his hands. 'I killed her. I killed your daughter.' Yealda looked down at him, her face impassive.

'Maybe now you understand why your very presence in this house is a curse to me. Each time I see you walk, hear you laugh, it is like a knife to my heart.'

Rom felt the heavy weight of guilt constrict his heart and throat. Thoughts of despair went through his head. They sounded like voices. They filled his mind. His heart seemed to have trouble beating.

That's right, a voice seemed to say. *Why go on beating?* A cold hand gripped his heart and started to squeeze it, slowly and deliberately. He began to shake. His lungs constricted.

Yes, why struggle to take in air. It's all futile. You're the last of a cursed race. They're all gone. You're all alone. What is there left to live for?

He coughed, his breath wheezing. Yldich turned his head in alarm. Rom sank to the floor, choking.

Why don't you stop, the voice told his heart, his lungs. *Stop struggling. Stop the pain.*

He fell over on his side and instinctively brought his hands to his throat to fight off the incorporeal foe. Yldich kneeled beside him and looked sharply up at Yealda. Her eyes were closed, her face was pale, almost translucent, the muscles taut with exertion.

'Yealda,' he said in a harsh voice. 'Stop this, now.' His voice was like a slap in her face that brought her out of her trance. She shook her head and blinked. Rom wheezed and coughed as he attempted to get up. 'Deep breaths.

Easy, now,' Yldich said as he helped him sit up. When Rom got his breath back, the shaking subsided a little. He looked up at Yealda.

'I'm—I'm so sorry,' he whispered, his voice hoarse. She stared at him in silence as Yldich helped him up. He walked Rom to the door. He turned and looked at Yealda.

'Your unwillingness to forgive,' he said, his grey eyes hard, 'may well prove to be the death of us all.'

'She took my heart in her hands and just willed it to stop,' Rom muttered. He sat before the hearth in Yldich's study. His hands were shaking. His heart was beating erratically, skipping a beat one moment, going too fast the next. Yldich kneeled beside him. Rom looked at him. 'Can you do that?'

'I suppose,' Yldich said carefully.

'Have you ever done anything like it?'

Yldich shook his head. His eyes were sad. 'No. I've never used my *Yaever* skills in anger.'

Rom sighed. 'I'm glad.' He closed his eyes.

'Let me help you, Rom.' Yldich laid a hand on his back, at the height of his heart. He held the other open before his chest. It felt as if a warm force enclosed his heart. Rom shuddered. After the experience of a moment ago, he wasn't keen on laying his heart in a *Yaever's* hands, not even Yldich's. But as the warmth suffused his heart, slowly and gently, it began beating more regularly. He sighed and felt muscles relax that he didn't even know he had tensed. He sat back in his chair as Yldich poured them some leftover tea.

'Now I understand why the *Tzanatzi* dwindled so fast after the Battle,' Yldich said. 'The curse was already upon them.' He took a sip of tea. 'It followed them wherever they went, and reduced them to a shadow of what they were. And when Farhardt's people came, it was the final straw. I've always wondered why the *Tzanatzi* would inspire such loathing and fear in Farhardt's people. Now I understand. It was more than the uneasy feelings the conqueror has for the people he has subdued. It was the curse.' He gazed in the fire.

'Yealda has always been my teacher. She saved my life, and everything I know of healing, I owe to her. But I didn't realize the depth of her hatred.' He shook his head. 'To think she would use her gift for healing to kill....'

'I do understand,' Rom said. He looked up. 'It was the same when Ciórdynn was killed... it's as if everything stops, as if you're dead inside, but you have to go on, and it's all grey, and meaningless... there's a burning pain where your heart used to be, and you begin to hate the ones that hurt you....'

Yldich nodded. 'Remember what your hatred brought forth.' His face was grim, his eyes like slate. 'Would you perpetuate the cycle of loss and revenge, until all this land is covered in darkness? Would you have Yealda slay you for her daughter, and me revenge myself on her for you? And so on, and so forth? Where would it stop?' He slowly shook his head. 'There must be a way to end this. To stop the storm. Somehow the curse is linked to it.'

Rom set down his cup. His face paled.

'What?' Yldich said.

'She said that—there will be no peace until he is slain by his own sword. And as Lakíthra told me, and you keep telling me, I am him, aren't I?'

'Now, don't you even think of it. There must be another way,' Yldich said. Rom swallowed and looked up. Yldich pressed his shoulder. 'Go and have some rest, Rom. Let it go. I'll think of something.'

The rest of the day passed in a kind of haze. Rom met Eldairc in the kitchen in search of something to eat, and the tall *Einache* suggested they practice sword fighting on the hill just outside the walls. Rom went with him, but his heart wasn't in it. Time and time again, Eldairc managed to disarm him with a few strokes.

'You're making it too easy for me,' Eldairc said. He knocked the staff out of Rom's hand for the fourth time. 'You should make more of an effort. Where are your thoughts today?'

'I guess I'm just tired.' Rom attempted a grin. 'Don't worry. I'll beat you some other time.'

Eldairc smirked. 'Not if your present achievements are anything to go by.'

In the evening they had dinner at one of the tables in the great Hall. Afterwards, Maetis took Rom's hand and led him to one of the hearths. A harpist practiced at the other end of the Hall; soft chords and melodies drifted through the air and rose above the low murmur of conversation.

They sat in one of the big chairs, Maetis leaning back against Rom, her fiery head against his shoulder. He held his arms around her, his face half hidden in her hair. The notes the harpist plucked off the strings were bright and cheerful like the sun on a clear blue sea, and as he felt her slender body rest against his within the circle of his arms, Rom felt a deep undertow of sadness, just under the threshold of awareness. The current was too vast, too great to be held back by one man. As it reached his eyes, he blinked and pushed back tears. Maetis didn't notice. She sat with her eyes closed, and caressed his arms, while she softly hummed to the harpist's tune.

In the grey light of early morning Rom woke with a gasp. His hand clutched at the crystal. He sat up and pushed the hair from his face. Frightful images slowly retreated from his vision. He breathed out and tried to release the bleak sense of horror that still clung to him. It had seemed so real: the living darkness that crept over his skin and numbed the fingers that reached for his sword, the creeping horror that penetrated the House and suffocated every living creature in its path.

He got up and donned his clothes. He girded on his sword. It felt as if a force from without directed his actions. He moved like a sleepwalker, afraid to stop and think, afraid the shred of courage he possessed would dissipate like smoke in the wind.

He encountered no-one as he walked through the silent corridors. Finally, he found the door to Yealda's chambers. He knocked softly. The door opened almost immediately, as if she had been expecting him. Yealda let him in without speaking.

She stood before him in the middle of the room and met his eyes. As they were of a height, she could face him without having to tilt her head.

Rom's face was pale, the skin under his eyes dark with lack of sleep. He pulled the *Einache* sword. The blade hummed softly as it passed through the metal sheath. Yealda didn't flinch. Rom handed Yealda the sword and kneeled down before her.

'Please do what you need to do.' His voice was strained.

She stared at him with her lavender eyes. She blinked. 'What are you saying?'

'You told us there would be no peace until I was gone. Do what must be done, so the curse will be lifted.' She stared at him and slowly lifted the sword in both hands. She held it against the side of his neck. He felt the edge, cold against his skin. He closed his eyes and waited, clenching his fists at his sides, trying not to shake.

'You would give up your life,' she spoke softly, unbelieving.

'Yldich doesn't know I'm here. He wouldn't agree,' Rom said in a hoarse voice. 'But I've seen what will happen if this curse isn't lifted. I've seen the dead rise, and darkness kill everything in its path. I've seen the downfall of your people. I saw Maetis die. It must be stopped.' He bowed his head and waited for the sword to fall.

Yealda stared at the dark head of the young man who kneeled before her. Something softened in her gaze. The hilt of the sword felt warm in her grip. It quivered softly. It melted away the cold, the rigidity that had kept her upright for a long time. She started to tremble. The sword fell out of her hand with a clang.

Rom looked up. 'Yealda—are you all right?' He stood up and grabbed her arms. He helped her into her chair. She sat with her eyes closed, her face pale. She looked frail and tired. Rom poured her some water.

She took a few sips and opened her eyes. 'When you were brought to this House, I did not understand why I avoided you. I guess it was because I wanted to hold onto my hatred.' She sighed and drew a hand across her face. 'It may have been the crutch that has kept me upright all these years.' He gazed at her wordlessly. Yealda shook her head. 'I've seen the way Maetis looks at you,' she said softly. 'I thought it was just a youthful folly. A fascination with what is different. Now I'm beginning to think there is more to it than that.' She closed her eyes. 'It was a brave thing to come here. Still, taking your life would have been useless. The curse can't be lifted that way.'

'Why?'

She looked up. 'Because of *him*. The Unnamed One. It is he I cursed. And he is still here.' Rom stared at her. 'I sung the spell that tore him from his body and imprisoned him in the Underworld. He is still there, after all this time. He has never passed on. There will be no peace until he is released.' The image of a dark, trailing mist curling along a winding path stole into Rom's mind. He shivered. Yealda sat back with her eyes closed. 'I need to rest now,' she whispered, 'Rom.'

It felt as if by using his name, the last remnant of cold between them dropped away. He took her hand and pressed it without speaking. He went and softly closed the door behind him.

Yealda sat staring in the distance with unseeing eyes for a long time. Finally, she stood up with difficulty and opened a clothes chest. She took out a little box. She kneeled carefully, opened it, and took out a single braid of shiny golden hair.

'Cáyla.' She began to cry, slowly and painfully.

Rom went to Yldich's study. It didn't surprise him to find the man up already, leafing through old manuscripts with the remains of his breakfast littering the table. Yldich took one look at his face and had him sit down before the hearth. He took some bread that had been left over from his breakfast and put it before him, and poured him a fresh mug of tea.

'Tell me,' he said.

Rom rubbed his face, and wiped the hair out of his eyes, as if he had just woken up. He stared into the fire in wonder. 'I had a nightmare,' he said softly. 'I saw what will happen if the curse isn't lifted. I felt the dark horror, and I saw you fall. I saw Maetis die.' Yldich's face was strained. Rom stared at his hands. 'So I went over to Yealda's chambers, and I gave her my sword.'

Yldich's eyes went wide. 'What?'

'I knew you wouldn't agree... so I went immediately after I woke up.' He looked at Yldich, his eyes heavy with anticipation. Yldich stared at him in disbelief.

'You reckless fool....' He sat shaking his head, lost for words. He rose abruptly and paced around the room, dragging his fingers through his curls until they stood up in all directions. 'You'll never do as I say, will you?'

'I'm sorry. I just felt it needed to be done....'

'So—what happened?'

'I think the sword spoke to her.' An expression of wonder crossed Rom's face. 'She had it in her hands and held it against my neck. It felt as if it... came alive somehow. Something changed in her, and she dropped it....'

Yldich released a breath. 'If you had taken any other weapon with you, I doubt you'd be sitting here right now.'

'I think it's over now... the enmity between us. She looked very old, and tired, when I left her.'

Yldich sat down again. 'I'll go and speak to her,' he said softly. 'She might need me.' He turned to Rom. 'You had better go and do something to take your mind off things. Go for a walk, practice with Eldairc, or something.'

'But—shouldn't I help you find a way to stop the darkness?'

Yldich stood up. 'It has been brewing for five hundred years. It can wait another day.' He gently pushed Rom towards the door. 'You're young. You shouldn't be cooped up inside with a load of musty books.' He shoved him out of the door. 'Now go and enjoy yourself, Rom. I'll do the studying for today.'

Without consciously choosing a direction, Rom's feet took him to Maetis' chambers. He found her in the windowsill, the sun in her hair, a piece of parchment on her lap. She was sketching in languid, careful lines. He stood behind her and looked over her shoulder to see what she was drawing. He was surprised to see his own face, looking up from the parchment.

'That's—that's me.'

She looked up and smiled, and he felt a weight lift that he hadn't even known he carried. He took a seat before her and took her face in his hands as if it were something fragile and precious. He kissed her carefully.

'Your eyes are like a summer night sky,' she said in a dreamlike voice. 'I could disappear in them.' He stared at her. 'What, has no-one ever said something like that to you before?' He shook his head. 'Well, then it was long overdue.' She smiled, and stood up. She took his hand.

The afternoon sun turned the sheepskins on Maetis' bed into a haze of gold. It entered the room in broad beams and lit up little motes of dust that whirled and danced in the air. Rom's tunic lay near the door, where Maetis had discarded it after she had pulled it over his head in haste. Her hair had escaped its pins, and cascaded down her body like a cloak of fiery silk. Her clothes lay in a muddled heap halfway across the room, along with Rom's boots.

Rom touched her in renewed wonder and kissed one breast as he curiously studied the effect it had on her. Her breath quickened and she stirred, releasing a soft sigh.

'You're so beautiful,' he said. 'Everything about you is beautiful. This part,' he moved his mouth around one breast, 'and this one....' He kissed the other with equal concentration and attention. She smiled and trailed her fingers along his body as he moved up to seek her mouth with his.

'So are you,' she said when he released her. 'I love your eyes, and your mouth, and your tender hands, and your *rúan*....' her hand travelled down toward his crotch, the bold touch making him blush. She chuckled. 'You have such an odd attitude towards your body.' Lights of amusement flickered in her eyes.

'I do not,' he said somewhat stiffly, and shifted awkwardly. 'Where I come from, we just don't talk about certain—parts of it.' She laughed, and his mouth started to twitch. 'I'm serious. In the South, people don't talk about bodily things.'

He lay down beside her, leaning on one elbow, while his right hand softly explored every inch of her skin.

'Where I grew up, children are kept in the dark about it.' His fingertips drew circles on the soft curve of her belly. 'Girls especially. They're supposed to stay innocent until their wedding night, which is only whispered about behind closed doors. They call it the "night of trepidation"....'

She snorted. 'How awful. A good thing you ended up here.' She trailed her fingers softly along his neck, his shoulder. 'We call lovemaking *lachéia*, an old *Einache* word that derives from *lachéire*, to share. It's woman's territory. I've heard that children in the South don't know where babies come from, that they think they're left at the doorstep at night by pixies. We don't entertain such strange notions.' She chuckled, and paused to kiss his neck, her fingers entwined with his.

'Now most *Einache* girls,' she continued, 'have some knowledge of herbs and moon cycles. They can be reasonably sure they're not blessed with a child if they don't want it to be. We're free to take lovers as we choose when we're young, although we're supposed to choose and marry when we've become of age. If a girl gets with child before she has announced her husband to be, it is assumed her lover is the father, and he's expected to take responsibility and acknowledge the child as his.'

Rom's knowledge of procreation was basic, but thorough enough to see the flaw in this manner of reasoning. 'But Maetis... how can anyone be sure who the father is?'

Maetis smiled. 'In these matters, the *Einache* have wisely chosen to give the woman the last word. Her word is considered truth. Because all *Einache* boys know this, they will think twice before *lachéie* with a girl—'

'Because if she got with child and he backed out—'

'He would face the wrath of her father, brothers, uncles, and cousins, who would make his life miserable until he took responsibility.'

Rom was amused by a sudden image of himself being chased through the Northern fields by Yldich and the *Einache* clan leaders. He chuckled and kissed her hand. 'We had better be careful, then.'

Maetis smiled. His right hand, following the curve of her inner thigh, awakened something warm deep within her, a yearning for, and opening to his touch. She sighed and pulled him towards her. She gently pushed aside the hair that had fallen across his brow and traced his face with her fingers.

'Why don't we,' she whispered, 'share *lachéia* once more. With care,' and she drew him within the circle of her arms. Exhilaration went through his heart like a bird taking flight. The little flame of orange fire deep within him leapt up and ran through his veins like a joyous river, hastening to meet her.

Ten
The Storm

It was a fine, clear winter morning. The sun glittered on the snow-covered hills. Rom enjoyed the warmth of the light on his face and breathed in the fresh morning air. He had not touched a book in days. Yldich had resolutely turned him away every morning, and ordered him to go and do something appropriate for a young man his age.

At first, he felt guilty leaving Yldich to his fate and his dusty archives. Eldairc had no such qualms. He took Rom along to every activity he was engrossed in, be it metal working, sword fighting, charming Yárah into feeding them more than their fair share of pastries, or going to see Élora and the other girls who were busy at their tasks. Eldairc would make the girls laugh with his dry remarks until the supervising *Yaever* chased them off, telling them to take themselves elsewhere, if they knew what was good for them.

It occurred to Rom once, as they ran laughing through the hallway to escape the *Yaever's* scorn, that for the first time in his life, he truly behaved his age. It was a strange thought. He dropped it like a pebble as he ran.

He had finished his practice rounds with Eldairc when he sat under an old oak tree on the hill for a rest. After a while he heard voices on the other side of the hill. He walked until he could discern their faces and saw Maetis sitting in a circle of entranced young *Einache* children. She was telling them stories. He sat down to listen.

'A long, long time ago, so long you could count the ages on your fingers, and your father's fingers, and your father's father's fingers and so on, and so forth, and still not have counted them all,' she began, and the children listened open-mouthed, 'the first Beings were created. They were the Animals. They weren't so different from us Humans, then. And they all looked more or less the same. Bear didn't have his thick furry hide, nor knew how to fish for his dinner. Cat didn't have her dainty nose and slashing tail. Wolf didn't have his teeth nor his howl.'

One of the children asked the inevitable question: 'How did they get them, Maetis? How did Cat get her tail, and Wolf his howl?'

'Listen, and I will tell you,' she said, and smiled. 'I will tell you the tale of Pyki, the Magpie. As you know, Pyki's incessant chatter irritated the gods so much they struck him with lightning, turning him black and white, and inadvertently gave him the ability to see both in the real world and the Other world. But he only used the knowledge for his own ends, and so made more trouble for himself.' Maetis sat back more comfortably and began her tale.

'One day, Pyki was flying over a stream when a ray of the Sun struck the silver scales of fish swimming in the stream. The beam of light caught his eye. He went down to investigate, and perched on a large branch at the bank of the stream. He saw Eldi, the water-rat, and said:

"Tell me, brother, what are those precious objects in the river?"

Eldi laughed at him and said: "Why, you silly bird, those are just slippery fish," and went about his business, his nose twitching, his whiskers guiding him along. Now Pyki was eternally hungry. His interest was raised.

He thought: "Those fish might make me a hearty meal," and he tried to get one. But however he tried, he could catch none. He fell in the water trying to catch them with his feet. He tried swooping them up with his beak in flight, but the fish were too slippery, and down he went again. He even tried to bang them on the head with a stick, but he was neither strong nor agile enough for the task. Soon Pyki was tired, and had a cold besides, from all those involuntary baths.

He could have gone home then, and have his usual insects for dinner. But his mind was set on the fish. So shiny, so lovely and fat. He went back to his perch on the branch, blew his nose, and started to think.

When he was done thinking, he looked about the banks of the river and soon found what he sought. There were water-sprites bathing in a shallow pool between the reeds, a bit further downstream.

Water-sprites are shy creatures you know, and because they are of the Other Realm, humans don't usually see them. They look just like very small Humans, but for that they seem made of flowing water and frothy air. To your eyes or mine they would look like the blurry images at the edge of vision, and you would probably not notice them at all.

These water-sprites were female, and Pyki took care to approach them respectfully. "I beg your pardon, O Ladies of Alluvial Loveliness," he said out loud, to warn them of his presence. There were little shrill cries at his approach, for the bathing nymphs were of course naked. Some of the cries sounded more excited than anxious, but Pyki covered his eyes with his left wing anyway, as he walked with care through the reeds, using his sweetest voice: "Please do not worry for your modesty on my account, O Wonderful Maidens of the Riveting Rivulets…"

Despite their cries, he was pulled into a large gathering of twittering water sprites enthusiastically. They splashed about in a small pool fringed with reeds and grasses. They made a place for him to sit while they crowded about him, fluttering excitedly. One cheeky sprite dared to pinch his feathered shoulder, giggled and blushed as she whispered to another.

"My ladies," Pyki said, "it pains me to see such luminous creatures as yourselves without the adornments your beauty deserves." The water-sprites were properly flattered, and interested too. "By the length of my tail and the brightness of my eye," Pyki said, "I have found a place where the brightest of gems and the rarest of silver necklaces are to be found for the taking. Though they are of the finest jewelleries the earth can bring forth, they would be but poor companions to your beauty…."

"Really?" the water-sprites said. They're not the brightest of creatures you know, on this Plane or the Other.

"Truly, it is so," Pyki said.

"Where would one find these precious ornamentations?" one of the sprites asked, her eyes bright with greediness.

"Alas," Pyki said, "'t is in a place where I cannot go, or I would have laboured to lay these fine specimens of earthly beauty at your feet long ago.'

"Take us to this place!" they exclaimed unanimously.

Pyki took them to the spot where he had glimpsed his fish.

"Behold!" he cried. The sprites were looking about them in confusion, until he said: "There! Look in the water!" The Sun's rays glittered on the shiny scales once more. The sprites wasted no time diving in; they hardly looked but aimed for the brightest reflections and threw whatever was there in a heap on the river bank.

After some time, Pyki was standing in an ever growing heap of delicious fresh river fish. When the sprites returned to behold the fruits of their labour, they stood looking at a heap of dead fish in bafflement.

"Where are the jewels?" they said. "Where are the gorgeous riches?" Then they spotted Pyki in the distance, running off with as much fish as his wings could carry. They knew then they had been deceived.

Water-sprites can cook up a storm when they are irritated, and this they were in the extreme, dripping mud and slimy fish scales still. The eldest and most eloquent of them cast a spell on Pyki, saying:

"May you ever be allured by shiny trinkets, gathering them whenever you can, even forsaking the gathering of food, until you have laid the promised riches at our feet!"

And so, children, the Magpie cannot resist the most worthless of shiny objects, and must fill his nest with them if he can. But I don't think he will ever be relieved of the spell, because if there is ever a way he can get out of doing an honest day's work, he will.'

Maetis rose and the children ran off to play, as noisily as they had been silent before. Rom was smiling. Maetis' style of storytelling reminded him of Yldich. He wondered briefly how many *Einache* children had heard these tales, and since how long ago.

At least for as long as Yldich has been here.

He felt his skin prickle as he wondered once more at the ancient agelessness of the man.

'How long have you been here?' Maetis' voice was like an echo of his thoughts. She had come up to him and gazed at his face, smiling.

He kissed her lightly. 'Long enough to enjoy your story.' She kissed him back and rested her arms on his shoulders, clasping her fingers behind his neck. 'Maetis, why didn't you tell the story in *Einache*?' he said. 'Why did you use the Southern language?'

'Ever since the Southern Kings established their power, and some *Einache* started trading with the Southerners instead of fighting them, Yldich has insisted on teaching the children both languages. It's a matter of survival, I guess. Also, Yldich used to say that if you want to understand your enemy, the least you can do is speak his language.' She grinned. 'So I alternately tell the tales in *Einache* and Southern.'

She released him and adjusted a hair pin that threatened to slide down and take a coil of copper with it. 'I'm teaching the older youths sword fighting next. Why don't you come with me. Maybe you can show them a thing or two.'

'I doubt it,' he said, and joined her anyway.

The practice field was not far from the hill. Three *Einache* youths stood staring at Rom as he and Maetis approached them. He guessed the boys were between thirteen and fifteen years old. They held wooden staves in their hands much like the ones Yldich had cut to practice with. The fourth's face split into a bright, toothy smile when he recognized Rom. It was Réydin, the youth who had ridden with him in the hunt.

'*Ya Hey'*,' he said, and made an odd gesture. He laid the closed fist of his right hand on his heart, opening it like a flower in Rom's direction. Maetis chuckled softly.

'What does it mean?' Rom whispered aside to her.

'It's how *Einache* warriors greet each other,' she whispered back. Rom repeated the gesture as best as he could.

Réydin grinned. 'Have you come to teach us *Tzanatzi* fighting skills?' His sandy brows were arched in hopeful anticipation.

Rom grimaced and shook his head. 'I'll just let Maetis do what she knows best.' He sat on a patch of dry ground, his elbows on his knees, and watched her instruct the youths. Something changed about her as she fought. Her vibrant energy was stilled, her face serene, as she whirled and turned, using her staff to block and attack. She looked like an aerial spirit, calm and detached, as she dealt potentially deadly blows, slowed down and softened for the boys' safety.

I wouldn't want to have to fight her in earnest.

Partly proud, partly ill at ease, Rom watched her in fascination as she deployed her skills.

After a while he noticed a small figure running towards them. He squinted, trying to see who it was. It took a while before he recognized Eald. The boy was running as if all the dragons of the Underworld were at his heels. When he reached them he dropped panting at their feet.

'An—an army, a Southern army,' he uttered. Rom stiffened.

'Easy, lad.' Maetis took a hold of Eald's arm. 'Take a deep breath.'

'Where?' Rom said simultaneously. His voice was strained.

'It's still—many miles away. But they're coming—in our direction.'

Rom shook his head. 'If it's still that far off, how do you know it's coming?'

Eald rubbed his nose. 'Through my scrying crystal,' he said. 'Me and Odún were practicing. And then I saw it coming.'

Rom's mouth fell open in incredulity. 'You can see armies coming from miles away?'

Eald sat up and righted his back. 'There's even more I can do.' He shook his lanky hair out of his eyes. 'Yldich's teaching me. He has me practicing *Yaever* tricks.' Rom swallowed. He felt slightly guilty as he stared at the boy's narrow upturned face. Between running around with Eldairc and being with Maetis, he had all but forgotten about him lately. 'It's all right,' Eald said, as if he had read his mind. Which he probably had, Rom thought wryly. The boy really did have *Yaever* potential.

Maetis rose. 'We must warn my father.'

'Well, this can't be good.' Yldich scratched his head. 'I doubt Farhardt has sent an army to join us for Midwinter Fest.' They sat around the large table in the study. Eldairc had brought in something to drink. Eald, who had just told his tale again for Yldich's and Eldairc's benefit, gulped it down thirstily.

Yldich turned to Rom. 'You know something of these people's ways. Can you think of a good reason a Southern noble would venture this far north?' Rom shook his head.

Only a bad one.

'None,' he said.

Maetis frowned. 'What should we do?' She estimated the number of fully trained *Einache* warriors at her disposal. The result wasn't reassuring.

'I'll summon the clan heads immediately.' Yldich set down his cup with a decisive clunk. 'They can be here tomorrow evening if they make haste or the morning after that if they tarry. I'll make sure they make haste.' His grey eyes reminded Rom of grey shards of ice.

'How will you get word out to them so fast?'

A brief smile crossed Yldich's face. He nodded in Eald's direction. 'My *Yaever* students will help me with that.'

At midday, Rom watched Maetis work with *Einache* of various ages and backgrounds. She tried to assess which ones would make good use of sword or bow. Eldairc had gone with the woodworkers and the smith to see about the fortifications of the palisades and gates. The steady beating of hammers on wood would be in the air all day.

The palisades were about as high as four tall men standing on each other's shoulders. They were constructed with the tall, straight trunks of pines, and had a walkway along the inside for the archers. There was a watchtower that provided a good view of the surrounding area. The House was built on higher ground, while the area around the palisades sloped downward, which provided an additional defensive advantage.

The palisades had fallen in disrepair since the last time they had seen battle. It had been sparked off three hundred and fifty years ago by a disagreement between the clan of the Boar and the clan of the Deer about the right interpretation of the Song of the Charging Bull.

Maetis selected a handful of young men and women to train with. The rest she sent to the other field to practice with bows, or back home, to help with repairs, as they were useless with any weapon.

Maetis had just disarmed a tall youth with two strokes of her staff. He stared at her with a somewhat shocked expression on his face. She turned to Rom with a grin. 'Rom, will you help me show these lads how it's done?' He stood up with a faint sense of reluctance. The lad tossed his staff through the air so Rom could catch it. He faced Maetis. Her grey eyes glittered like sunlight in clear water.

'Don't make it too easy for me,' she said, and he grimaced.

'I'll try.'

She suddenly lashed out and he stepped back in surprise. There was a loud clack of wood on wood and her staff slid off his with a hiss. She immediately changed position and attacked from a different angle.

Something clicked into place within him. He straightened, and was no longer Rom, hesitatingly fighting Maetis. He became the dance. Something within still registered the look of surprise in Maetis' eyes as he started to wheel and turn, attack and parry, feeling for a chance to break through her defence. He felt a tiny window, a crack in time, coming at her next turn. He felt for it, and thrust through it. Maetis uttered a small cry of surprise as she stumbled backwards and fell in the snow, her hand at her stomach. The youths stood staring in wonder and hesitant admiration.

Rom looked down at Maetis, his eyes black, his face pale and strained, as she coughed and laughed in wonder.

'Well, you took me by surprise there.' She tossed back a loose curl that had fallen over her face. Rom's expression did not change. He turned and walked away without a word. Maetis stared at his back. She handed her staff to one of the youths.

'Why don't you practice the opening move I just showed you,' she said. 'I'll be right back.'

'Rom.' He didn't turn. He kept staring in the distance, leaning against the trunk of an oak tree as if it could lend him some of its ageless sturdiness. Maetis walked around and faced him. She lifted a hand, slowly and carefully, and touched his face with her fingertips. The touch was so slight he could have imagined it was just the breeze, caressing his face.

'What's wrong?' Her voice was soft.

He released a breath. 'Maetis, have you ever killed a man?' She stared at him, then shook her head. 'I have. The last time was not so long ago. And it wasn't something I was particularly proud of. In fact it was horrible.'

She laid her hands on his lower arms. 'Tell me.'

'In Woodbury... I killed two riders who threatened the *Náeria*.' He swallowed and gazed at his hands as if they were someone else's. 'I slid through a crack in time, and I—I killed them with two blows. There was so much blood... I felt their life seep through my hands.' He shuddered.

She stared at him. 'You saved a *Náeria's* life?'

He looked up. 'Well, yes....'

'So... what was her gift?'

'What?' He looked at her, not understanding.

'Her gift. The Gift of the *Náeria*. It is said that whoever saves the life of a *Náeria* will be granted a Gift, a Gift only she can bestow. Some say she will give you your heart's desire, even if you yourself don't know what that desire is.'

Rom's mind filled with images of the last night at Woodbury, the autumn leaves rising in the fire, the *Náeria's* naked skin under his hands, flushed with the glow of the dying embers. He felt his face turn a particularly bright shade of crimson under Maetis' clear gaze.

'I—I didn't know. She just—kissed me and we...' he faltered.

'I see.' Maetis cocked her head and eyed him with a pensive expression. 'Well.' He held his breath, weary of her reaction. An expression of wonder crossed her face that shifted into one of amusement. 'Don't worry, Rom. Whatever you did before you walked into my dreams and my life, does not belong to me.' She kissed him lightly and he felt a weight fall from his heart.

He put his arms around her and pressed his face in her hair. 'I don't care if I never touch a sword again.'

'Somehow,' Maetis said, 'I don't think we will get out of this so easily.'

That night, as they lay entangled in Maetis' bed, Rom lay thinking for a long while. The knowledge of Southern rule approaching in the form of an army had his thoughts wander in directions he hadn't considered before.

'Maetis?'

'Hmm?' Her voice was a sleepy murmur against his chest.

'You do realize I have nothing to offer you?'

She opened her eyes and rolled on her side. She leaned on one elbow so she could look him in the face. 'What do you mean?'

'Well, where I come from, it's customary for a man to offer the woman he courts his farm, his livelihood, and all his possessions. I have none, I don't even have a horse to my name. I lost everything on the way. It wasn't much to begin with,' he added, his mouth pulled in a wry smile.

'I see.' Maetis thought for a while. 'Well, with the *Einache* a prospective husband's worth was measured by the number of heads he had taken in battle. Or, for lack of border disputes between clans, the number of wild boar he had killed in the hunt.' He stared at her. He looked slightly pale. Maetis laughed. 'Don't look so anxious, Rom. That was hundreds of years ago.' Her grey eyes glinted. 'I won't need you to prove your manhood that way before I'll have you as my husband.'

His breath stuck in his throat. 'So... you will?'

She smiled and answered him simply, without words.

There was a coldness in the air, a wordless murmur. Fear tinged the air like frost. There was a weight on his chest that made breathing an effort. He felt as if he was pulled back from a dreamless slumber, like a fish on a line being dragged from the water. He struggled feebly, twisting to escape the hook. Something snapped within him and his eyes flew open.

Rom stared at the ceiling above his head, but what he saw was not the whitewashed ceiling of Maetis' bedroom. He stared straight into the black eyes of a woman. He wanted to cry out, but one gesture of her hand made the words die in his throat. She touched his breast, and his heart grew cold. He began to feel faint. His right hand trembled as it tried to move, but the woman's dark eyes held his in a paralyzing spell.

Maetis cried out softly in her sleep, and turned over to him. Rom's left hand broke through the spell of motionlessness and moved to his neck, where the crystal lay. Touching it cleared his will.

'*Na'Héach.*' His voice was hoarse. The woman's eyes widened. She wavered. '*Na'Héach,*' he said, and felt for the sword that stood next to the bed. As his fingers brushed the hilt, the woman drew back. Her dark hair trailed behind her as if through water.

'*Eloreaz é na Tzanatzi?*' she said. He stared at her as she dissolved in the air.

'It must have been the same woman,' Yldich said. They had breakfast in his study. Eald came in last.

The boy rubbed his face and yawned widely. 'Maybe she's come to spy on us.'

Yldich shook his head. 'That would entail conscious reasoning on the part of a ghost.'

'I don't think she was a ghost.' Rom was still shaken by the night's experience. 'When I broke her spell, she spoke to me. She seemed surprised.'

'What did she say?' Yldich's eyes were bright with interest.

'I don't know.' Rom shook his head. 'It was in *Tzanatzi.*'

'Well.' Yldich sat back, and gulped down his tea. 'I wonder what—' He didn't get to finish his sentence. A distant rumbling swelled and rolled through the earth, as if a gigantic earth worm turned in its lair and started burrowing towards the House. The floor shook. Centuries-old wooden beams creaked and moaned; ancient stones grinded against each other. Rom felt his hair try to stand on end. A sound like living rock being torn apart shrieked through his head and he cried out, his hands over his ears.

Eldairc, who sat balancing his chair on two legs, crashed to the floor and wheeled around his arms in an attempt to get up, his face white as chalk. Maetis held on to the heavy table and looked up at Yldich, who had risen and stood staring, as he wildly felt around with his senses for the source of the disturbance. There was a crash somewhere within the House, followed by a scream. Plaster fell from the walls like dry rain. The heavy chandelier swung to and fro on its creaking chains. Then the rumble died down. The House settled grudgingly, like a great creature that had been painfully prodded, had protested, and settled down again. Rom shook his hair out of his eyes with a sense of deep unease.

But is it settling down on the edge of a precipice?

'What—what was that?' Eald squeaked from his hiding place under the table.

Rom clenched his hands into fists. 'It has begun.' His voice was hoarse.

'Well,' Yldich said. He sounded as if he kept his voice steady with an effort. 'When trouble finally finds us, it does so on all planes at once.'

The winter sky above the tiny Southern seaside village called Elder's Rock was sunny and clear. The flaxen-haired little boy placed the bucket on the pier with a sigh of relief. Filled to the brim with bait, it was cumbersome and heavy. He turned his face to the sun. Gulls flew overhead and studied the bucket with their greedy yellow eyes. He turned back to keep an eye on the sea and the sky above it. That was when he saw the ships in the distance. His blue eyes widened.

The ships were completely different from the small, brightly painted fishing boats his father and his uncles owned. They were unlike any ships he had ever seen. They were dark, and graceful, with tall masts and pennants of dark red like old blood. Despite their slender beauty there was something eerie about the ships. Dark, insubstantial shapes moved on their decks.

As they came closer the boy could see their sails were horribly torn. In places they were ripped to shreds. Though there was no wind, the dark ships were cutting a swift path through the water, straight towards the coast. Fear snaked through the boy's belly. His skin tingled and the little hairs on his arms stood on end.

As he stood watching, the ship in front had come close enough to discern the figures that stood on its decks, looking out over the small stretch of sea that still separated them from the coast. Dark hair swirled around pale, hollow

faces. The boy went cold. He gasped for breath and turned around. He started
to run.

A few miles further to the north, Ferwen took a seat on one of the ancient
stones that dotted the hill where he grazed his sheep. Though it was still early,
he had decided to take a rest and open the bundle his wife had prepared him
for lunch.

Ferwen wasn't the most athletic man in his little village, and he knew it.
Still, he couldn't resist the smell of freshly baked spiced bread, cheese, and
honey that rose from the bundle. He had decided his ample girth was really to
blame on his wife's cooking. Everyone knew she made the best cheese pies,
the best honey cakes and the most scrumptious apple pies in the village.

As he took a bite of bread and started to munch contentedly, a cold wind
rose. A chill shivered over his neck. As he put back the bread, wondering
about the sudden change in weather, the light of the sun was cut off. A
shadow fell over the rock on which he had taken his seat.

Ferwen slowly turned his head. It was as if it was attached to a string,
pulled by someone else, and he couldn't help but comply. As his gaze took in
the dark shapes looming behind him, he was vaguely aware of a high-pitched
screaming. Darkness swirled around the sword of the tall shape before him,
and he realized it was his own voice, screaming in his ears. The sword drew a
fell silvery arc. There was a dull thud. Something heavy crashed to the
ground. A few startled birds rose in the air, chattering. Then there was only
silence.

Later that afternoon the first clan leaders and their people arrived at the
House of the Deer. The first to come through the doors while the sun was still
above the horizon was Olwen, the red-haired clan leader with the booming
voice.

'Yldich!' the big man roared through the Hall, but despite the outrage his
voice was tinged with fear. He raised it a notch to drown it out. His face was
pale and there were red splotches on his cheeks. 'What in the name of all the
creatures of hell is going on. On the way here we were assaulted by—by—'

'By the likes of *him*,' one of his younger warriors blurted out, motioning
at Rom. Rom stared at them, shaken.

'They moved like the wind. They appeared out of nowhere, and took six
of my people.' Olwen's voice was hoarse.

'Come in,' Yldich said calmly. 'Sit yourselves down. And then tell me
what happened.'

Olwen and his men sat glaring at Yldich over their beer mugs while the
rest of their folk busied themselves with the horses, their luggage, and the

children, who sat looking around with wide eyes in pale faces. They let themselves be put to bed without protest.

'Tell us what happened,' Yldich said. 'From the beginning.'

'We were riding through the woods near the old temple ruins,' one of Olwen's warriors, a sturdy man with sandy hair in braids and a short beard said. 'There was a cold wind, and the earth rumbled. And suddenly, there they were. They came riding out of nowhere.'

'*Tzanatzi.*' Olwen spat out the word as if it were an obscenity.

'Did you engage them in a fight?' Yldich arched his brows in curiosity.

Olwen frowned at him. 'Now you're asking, that was the strange thing... they came out of nowhere, and there were some swords flashing, and before we knew what had happened, they'd disappeared again. They left six of my men slaughtered like cattle. They didn't even have the chance to draw their swords....'

Rom looked at Yldich. '*Tzanatzi* wraiths. Like the ones that attacked Maetis and me at the foot of the hill.'

'Wraiths or not, their swords were real enough,' the warrior muttered.

Later that night, Ullwich and Morven arrived with their people. Yldich took one look at their strained faces and hollow eyes and had them sit down in the Hall, where a long row of tables had already been prepared for them with food and drink.

'Get your breath back first,' he said. 'Then we'll listen to your tales.'

And tales they told him, while his household, including Rom, and Eald, and Maetis, sat listening, until the moon was high and the fires were dying down.

Morven's party had been halted by a small army of *Einache* ghosts, who demanded to know where they were going. When Morven, who'd managed to stay calm, told them what their business was, and it became apparent they were not riding out to war against the *Tzanatzi*, the ghost leader demanded they hand over their weapons. When Morven adamantly refused, a fight ensued that left five of his men dead. He sat shaking his head, his eyes full of horror, as he told the tale. He looked about ten years older than the last time Rom had seen him.

'They looked like corpses who'd made some half-hearted attempt at looking like mortal men,' Morven said in a hoarse voice. 'They chilled my blood and unmanned my warriors. There was no reasoning with them.' Eald thought of the *Einache* dead they had encountered in the woods and shuddered.

Next, Ullwich told his tale. When he was riding through the fields a strange chill rose from the ground and rooted his people to the earth, while a dark cloud blotted out the sun. Horses bolted and threw off their riders. Chaos ensued. When Ullwich came to his senses and sent out some warriors to get back the horses, the bodies of their riders were discovered. They looked as if they had been frozen to the ground writhing in pain, their faces distorted with terror. They had choked to death.

'The *Tahiéra*,' Rom whispered. He felt slightly sick. Yldich looked at him, a worried frown between his eyebrows. He stood up and held out his hands as if to include all the gathered clan leaders and warriors.

'You have withstood much hardship to get here,' he said in a sober voice. 'To help us face a hardship that has yet to show its face. A Southern army is coming in our direction. We don't yet know why. But this is the time when we *Einache* have to pull together and face whatever it is the gods are laying in our path, to set aside our differences and stand together. Tonight, at least, you can sleep knowing you are safe. Tomorrow we will speak of the road that lies ahead. Your rooms have been prepared for you. My daughter will show you the way. *Nâstréhi ea.*'

'*Nâstréhi ea*,' they muttered, their faces drawn and tired. They left the table and went to their beds.

They did not get the good night's sleep they craved. All through the night, people arrived from all over the area, clan leaders and their people, families from little woodland villages, farmers who lived at the edge of the Forest. They all had their own tales of horror to tell. By the time they had been heard and given a place to sleep, it was hours past midnight.

Eldairc sat nodding in his chair. Rom was yawning and blinking. Maetis had gone to busy herself with putting up the guests hours ago. Yldich shook Eldairc gently by his shoulder. The tall *Einache* gasped and sat up. He rubbed his eyes.

'You two had better go and get some sleep,' Yldich said. 'It's going to be a busy day tomorrow.'

That night it began to snow. The House and surrounding countryside were covered in a soft blanket that muffled all sounds and made the world seem unearthly peaceful. When Rom got up and looked out the window of Maetis' bedroom, he stared at the graceful lines of numerous tents, at banners and pennants flying in the wind, of horses and men sketched in black against a world of purest white. The Southern Army had arrived.

In the early afternoon the King's Messenger came to the House. The young *Einache* warriors who kept watch at the palisades heard the sound of a trumpet, and peered over the edge to investigate. There was a young lad on a pony. He had hair like pale honey and wore a rich velvet cloak embroidered with eagles.

'I am the King's messenger,' he cried. They stared at him. He looked slightly nervous. The pony fidgeted and the messenger reined it in with an impatient tug at the reins. 'Well, will you let me in to deliver my message?' he said testily.

The warriors looked at one another and shrugged. The messenger was alone, and seemed harmless enough. They climbed down and shoved back the heavy bolts that held back the doors. They opened the gate.

The messenger looked at Yldich and the clan leaders who stood with their arms crossed in front of the great doors of the House. He stared at their heavy beards, their strange embroidered tunics, their leather leggings and big fur-lined boots, their bright eyes glaring at him from under bristling brows. He hesitated, unsure of what decorum decreed when faced with barbarians instead of the finely dressed noblemen he was accustomed to. He decided to stick to his usual routine and kneeled in the snow, his face impassive, his back straight, and reached out a hand. It held a large parchment scroll.

'Behold, a message from your King,' he said. Yldich lifted a brow at the word *your*, but held his tongue. He stepped forward.

'*Ya'haeve.* I am Yldich, *Hárrad* of the *Einache.*' He reached out a hand to accept the scroll. 'Be sure this will be read with the utmost attention.' The Messenger nodded and rose.

'I will deliver your words to the King. Please take care to respond promptly. He will expect an answer by daybreak tomorrow.' He turned around and walked back to the gate. He did not afford the young *Einache* warriors who brought him his pony a glance, but mounted and left without as much as a turn of the head.

'Well,' Yldich said to Rom when he had entered the Hall. 'At least they adhere to some sort of protocol, instead of just barging in and sacking the House. It shows to me this King still has some scruples left.'

'And he will take over and subjugate the *Einache* just as scrupulously and with the same amount of protocol,' Rom muttered. He stared at the scroll in Yldich's hands with eyes that were already full of dejection.

'Let's go and read it first, before we despair, shall we,' Yldich said. While the clan leaders sat down in the middle of the Hall, he beckoned Rom over to a table near a hearth.

'Will you please read it to me?' Rom gave him a sidelong look, his brows raised in surprise. 'After all my years of travelling back and forth, the

Southern script is still somewhat of a mystery to me,' Yldich said with a grin. Rom took the scroll and unrolled it on the table.

'There's a long statement saying this is a message from King Farhardt the Third, sole sovereign of the territories of the *Eldr*, the *Harmad*, and so on, and so forth....' His eyes quickly roamed the parchment to get the gist of the message. 'He addresses you as leader of the *Einache* and vassal of the King, subordinate to his rule, and trusts you will receive this message in good health and act according to the status he has accorded you.'

Yldich snorted and shook his head. 'Go on,' he said. His grey eyes glittered.

Rom's eyes grew wider as he read on. 'It says that word has come to the King that the *Einache* of the high North have overstepped their bounds in annexing territories belonging to the Crown, and sacking Northern villages in the process. For this, they will have to pay a penalty. As well as paying this penalty, that will be set by the King and will not be negotiable, the leader of the *Einache*, as well as all the vassals under his leadership, will hand over the rule of their Houses. They will be replaced by the sons of Southern nobles, chosen by the King, who will take up leadership of their Houses and lands, and rule henceforth, to ensure the King's rule is duly administrated.' Yldich's grey eyes flashed.

Rom put down the scroll, a sickening feeling in his stomach. 'Yldich... they mean to take over.'

'Go on,' Yldich said in a stern tone.

'It says here, that if the *Einache* do not relinquish authority to the King willingly, Southern rule will be enforced.' He looked up at Yldich. Yldich frowned at the parchment in Rom's hands. His eyes had taken the colour of thunderclouds. 'There's more,' Rom said. 'Here, at the end. It says the *Einache* must also hand over the *Tzanatzi* renegade they have been harbouring. If this criminal is not delivered into the King's justice,' he said in a low voice, 'the *Einache* leaders and their families will be sold as slaves.' He let go of the scroll and sat down heavily. He hid his face in his hands.

'I'll get my cloak,' he whispered, and stood up.

Yldich halted him with a hand against his chest. 'Where do you think you're going?'

'To the King's encampment. If I go immediately, maybe he'll be lenient....'

'Rom, what does the King's justice entail for *Tzanatzi*, or a half-*Tzanatzi* like yourself, do you think?' Yldich held his head to one side.

Rom frowned. 'I've heard stories... it seems *Tzanatzi* prisoners usually do not survive captivity long enough to be brought to justice. But when they do, the ruling is almost always the same. Afterwards, it is said their bodies are sometimes thrown to the hounds,' he swallowed away a sense of nausea, 'to give them an edge.' He closed his eyes. 'I heard a story once about a pack of hounds that was so used to this that when they caught the scent of a *Tzanatzi* girl they chased her into the woods like a deer. They tore her to pieces like prey. Their owners apparently thought it good sport.' He clenched his hands, his face white as the snow outside.

'I thought as much.'

'I have to go. You heard what the message said. If I don't, they'll attack and take you away as slaves....'

Yldich smiled wryly and shook his head. 'Rom, do you really think the *Einache* are going to comply with the King's demands and give up authority?'

Rom stared at him. 'But—they will overrun you....'

'The *Einache* of the utmost North have never been subjugated. Even the *Tzanatzi* haven't been able to subdue us. We've been free for thousands of years. Do you honestly think the clan leaders will let these Southern nobles order them around?'

'But, Yldich—'

'I would be highly surprised if they would.'

'But—then what do we do?'

Yldich's eyes glittered. 'We fight.'

That afternoon, the Great Hall filled up with people. Word had gone round that there would be a meeting of the clan leaders, and that following the meeting an important announcement would be made.

Rom had to push his way through a mass of people to get to the large chamber with the double doors where the meeting took place. Yldich had him take a seat on his right. Then he stood up and looked around the table.

'We have been given a message by king Farhardt, whose army has arrived outside our walls this morning,' he said simply. 'He has sent us a message in which he demands our complete submission. He also demands I hand over the "*Tzanatzi* renegade" he deems I am harbouring.' He sat down.

Rom swallowed. Ullwich stirred uneasily. He opened his mouth, as if he was about to comment. Then he closed it again, fidgeting with his mug.

'These are the King's demands,' Yldich went on. As he listed them one by one, Rom noticed the clan leaders sat unnaturally still. They listened to Yldich with great interest which showed in the intensity of their clear gaze and the set of their jaw. As Yldich progressed, a grim silence descended on the chamber.

'I do not know where the Southern king would get the idea that the *Einache* are responsible for the sacking of villages on the fringes of the Forest. The matter doesn't seem open for discussion. It appears to me that the

King is eager to establish his influence in the North anyway. His demands are clear. Therefore, I think these are our choices.' He stuck his hand in the air and ticked them off on his fingers.

'One, we surrender to the King and comply with his demands. It would mean the youngest sons of Southern nobles setting up court in our Houses, and enforcing their rule upon us. It would mean the loss of our independence, and quite possibly the loss of our way of life.' He looked around the chamber, noting the grim faces of the clan leaders.

'Two, we gather all the *Einache* who are willing to stand and do battle, and resist the King as long as we can. As we are seriously outnumbered, our chances of keeping them off are slim. It may be the last battle we ever fight in freedom.' He sat down finally and looked around the table.

There was a brief silence, which was broken by Morven, the clan leader of the Red Fox clan. He stood up and looked at Rom. 'You know something of life in the South—what do you deem would happen to our people if Southern lords sat in our places?'

Rom felt their eyes turn to him and hesitated a moment. Then he stood up. 'I can't tell you for certain,' he said. 'But I can tell you what life in the South is like.' He took a deep breath.

'The Southerners are a—a practical people, I guess you could call it,' he began. 'They are deeply suspicious of anything out of their scope of experience. So anything mystical or mysterious is seen as witchcraft, and that has ever been punishable by torture, incarceration, or even death.'

Ullwich drew up a brow. 'Explain what you mean by witchcraft.'

Rom grimaced. 'For some of them, the calling of beasts and birds would amount to witchcraft. Or the sharing of *énthemae*, not to speak of *ayúrdimae*.' Ullwich's other brow was raised as the *Einache* words rolled from Rom's mouth without so much as a hint of a Southern accent. Yldich coughed in his fist to hide his amusement.

'Southerners do not allow their women to teach, or roam around the country to sing, like *Náeriae*, or practice sword fighting. They're married off young, to husbands who are often not of their choosing, and are not expected to have minds of their own.' Rom swallowed as he thought of Maetis, and pictured what it would be like for her to live under such conditions. A sense of indignation started to fill his belly. As it rose, it added strength to his words.

'You would not be allowed to bear arms and organize yourselves as you would.' His voice gained in volume as he pictured it for them. 'The Southern nobles would need to gain some sort of income off this land. They would not be interested in the slow, simple life of bee-keeping, sheep-shearing or hunting. They would have you burn down parts of the Forest and till the land,

and sell off the harvest to the capital for profit, leaving you to toil and scrape out a meagre existence under their watchful eye.'

He could see it clearly, the proud warriors, bowed down by back-breaking labour, by the loss of their pride, their sense of self. 'You would no longer be free,' he ended in a soft voice. He sat down and stared at the gathered clan leaders. They were eerily silent. They sat looking at him with their bright, fell eyes.

Wérdyris spoke. 'They would turn us into farmers, into serfs,' he said with visible disgust. His nostrils quivered with indignation.

'They would turn our women into kitchen wenches and breeding hens,' Morven said with a vague look of abhorrence.

'While if anyone should have the right to bully them around, it should be us,' Ullwich said, and got a punch in the ribs from his neighbour. Everyone started to talk at once. After a while, they fell silent one by one. Their eyes sought Yldich's, and Yealda's. The *Yaever* sat watching them expectantly. The tumult died down.

'You have heard Rom's speech,' Yldich said gravely. 'I fear his picture of events will be very near the mark. The choice before us is not an easy one. Which will you have, the certainty of death in battle, or the certainty of life without dignity under Southern rule? Will you submit or will you do battle?'

Morven rose. His grey eyes were shining with a feverish passion. '*Eyléa kanáchon.*' His deep voice resounded through the chamber. 'I will do battle.'

'*Eyléarana kanáchon,*' the other clan leaders responded. Their eyes glittered and their cheeks burned as they took up the cry one by one. Their voices resounded through the chamber and made the beams thrum. 'We will do battle.' One of the warriors began humming a march-like tune, and one by one they joined in, even cynical Ullwich. The song sounded both heartening and frightening to Rom's ears. He stared at them in astonishment. They actually seemed elated at the prospect of fighting to death.

Finally Yldich rose and the singing died down. 'I will let the King know of our decision in the morning,' he said. 'I will also plant the ceremonial spear. I would like you to be present. Afterwards, we will devise our strategy.'

As the clan leaders left the room, Rom turned to Yldich. 'I don't understand.' He shook his head. 'They almost seem glad to go to war.'

Yldich looked at him. 'Rom, you know the ancient *Einache* war cry, don't you?'

'Yes. *Na Héach.*'

Yldich nodded. 'But do you know what it means?' Rom shook his head. '*Na Héach,*' Yldich said pensively. 'It's difficult to translate, because the Southern language doesn't have an equivalent for it. But roughly translated it would be something like *joyful death.*' He saw Rom's expression and grinned.

'It may sound gruesome to you. But consider this. For hundreds, thousands of years, the *Einache* have known that they are more than just their physical bodies, that they are part of *Eärwe*, the Whole, and their individual Wheel of Life. To know this, to truly know it and feel it in your bones, means it's an easy choice between slavery and fighting to preserve your freedom, even until death. A death which is not considered the end, as the Southerners perceive it. But a death that is a new beginning.'

'But, Yldich—it will be the end of your people. They're horribly outnumbered....'

A sadness seemed to well up in Yldich's eyes. 'This is not the first time we're faced with impossible odds,' he said softly. Rom cast down his eyes. He looked up as he felt Yldich's big hand land on his back with a reassuring thump. He just managed to keep his balance. 'And just like five hundred years ago, we may yet find a way to save what is left of us.' There was a ring to Yldich's voice that made Rom look up sharply.

'I haven't forgotten my dreams,' Yldich said in a soft voice. There was something in his eyes that made them seem lit up from within. 'We may yet find a way to save ourselves.'

'I don't see how,' Rom muttered abjectly, shaking his head.

In the evening Yldich had Rom come to his study and write a reply to the King. After the formal heading, which Rom found easy to make up as he was used to the formal language of the Southern nobility, the main letter was direct and brief. Yldich composed it pacing up and down before the hearth, while Rom sat scratching a quill over the parchment by the light of a candle.

'The destruction of *Einache* settlements is a matter that distresses us greatly,' Yldich began. 'We must inform you that we have no part in this matter and therefore cannot comply with Your Majesty's demands. The *Einache* of the high North have not fought amongst each other for two hundred years, and when they did, they met in open battle. The destruction of these villages is a shameful act, for which we hope the perpetrators to be found and brought to justice. The *Einache* would be glad to assist Your Majesty to this end in any way they can.'

Rom stopped scribbling and asked: 'Shouldn't we tell him about Feyir and his riders?'

Yldich slowly shook his head. 'We don't know who will be reading this letter. Who says it will be delivered straight to the King? Besides, I don't think it would help our case if we start pointing the finger at others. If we can persuade Farhardt to come speak to us, we might get him to listen to our side of the story. Which reminds me.' He started pacing again and said:

'As *Hárrad* of the *Einache*, I had the dubious honour to be present at the recent battle of Woodbury. If Your Majesty is willing, he would be most welcome to come and listen to our account of it.'

He grinned. 'Maybe if we can get his curiosity piqued, we can get him to come and listen to us, instead of attack straight away.'

Rom finished writing and looked up from the parchment. 'What about his demand to deliver the *Tzanatzi* renegade?'

'Ah, yes.' Yldich raked his fingers through his hair and started to pace once more, making Rom wonder if he was able to think if standing still: 'The *Tzanatzi* renegade that is referred to in your message is a matter of concern to us, as we harbour no criminals here. The only member of this household that has descended from the *Tzanatzi* people is my foster son, and as he is under my constant supervision he cannot possibly be guilty of any crime.'

Rom snorted with wry amusement and shook his head as he wrote it down. He had never thought he would be moved by being referred to as a wayward adolescent.

Early in the morning the King's Messenger rode through the gates of the *Einache* enclosure. His face was taut with apprehension. The large double doors of the House swung open. An *Einache* delegation came out and stood in a semi-circle in the snow. He recognized the men he had delivered his message to the other day. The big, ginger-haired man with the grey eyes and the name he couldn't pronounce stepped forward. He carried an enormous spear. It looked as if it had been fashioned from the entire length of a young tree.

The young lad hesitated as the spear was lifted in his direction. Fear stirred in his bowels. Would the barbarians dare to attack the King's Messenger? He had always felt entirely safe in his function, aware of the traditional sacredness of the position. Now, for the first time he doubted if he would get away with his life. He swallowed, his hands on his pony's reigns stiff and cold.

The big man planted the spear in the frozen earth with one powerful motion of his arms and the Messenger breathed a sigh of relief. A murmur of grim satisfaction went through the gathered clan leaders and warriors.

'*Kalantíri kenéchie chamera*,' Yldich cried in a loud voice. He stepped back. 'Behold the Spear of Separation.' He motioned for the Messenger to come forward. The gathered *Einache* witnessed him in silence as he waded through the snow, shivering with cold. Their faces were expressionless; their bright eyes glittered under their heavy brows. 'Please tell the King that we wish no strife with him,' Yldich said in a stern voice, 'but neither will we allow our peace to be disturbed. This ancient spear signifies the boundary that we will not have crossed. I trust this message will explain matters to him more clearly.' He held out the scroll. 'Go in good health.' The young lad nodded, glad to be dismissed, and turned away.

The Messenger rode back to the King's encampment at his ease. Relieved his task was over and he had come back from the barbarian's stronghold unscathed, he started to sing under his breath. While he hummed a cheery tune he had recently heard in a tavern in Érskitha, his thoughts turned to spiced wine and fresh bread. He subconsciously spurred his pony on to go faster.

Meera wiped her wet hands on a cloth and pushed her lanky hair out of her eyes. She was a mousy girl of ten, whose hands were already aged from wringing out the laundry and scrubbing pans. She stood at the entrance to the large tent that served as a kitchen, leaned against a tent pole and yawned. She looked out over the fields to distract her mind from the tedious duties that awaited her next.

A man on a pony crested the low, snow-covered hill and came into view. She recognized the King's Messenger. She gazed at him wistfully, at his fine clothes, his lovely hair that spilled over his collar like fine silk. Only adolescent boys wore their hair long. From the age of sixteen it was usually cropped short.

A silver bird shot through the air. It flew straight at the Messenger. Suddenly he lay splaying in the snow. Meera stared at the scene with wide eyes. She heard a level voice.

'Finish him off for me, will you.' A rough voice answered.

'Yes, milord.' Meera stared in frozen fascination as a man clad in brown kneeled by the figure that lay in the snow and drew a knife. As he pulled back the boy's head by his hair and the knife flashed, she averted her eyes. She swallowed down a wave of nausea.

'Now bring me the scroll,' she heard the first voice say. Meera trembled so hard she wondered if she could refrain from falling over. But somehow she managed to keep to her feet. Shaking, she peeped through a rend in the tent's fabric at the man who had given the order. She gasped when she laid eyes on Lord Feyir's handsome face.

King Farhardt stood looking out over the snowy fields, a fur-lined cloak over his shoulders and a cup of warm spice wine in his hands. He shivered with the morning cold nonetheless. He heard a voice behind his shoulder.

'The Messenger is late.' Feyir walked up to him. Farhardt shook his head.

'I would have expected him back by now.' A frown deepened between his brows. A young page came running towards them and nearly threw himself at their feet. He was panting.

'The Messenger is missing, my lord. His pony has been found wandering alone at the edge of camp. There's no sign of him anywhere.'

'These barbarian clans,' Feyir said in an indignant tone of voice. 'They hold no respect for our traditions. Not even for the inviolability of a King's Messenger.' Farhardt cursed under his breath. Arda was family, the son of one of his distant cousins. He had personally seen to it that the boy had gotten the position, and he had liked him.

'Have all the nobles assemble in my tent in one hour,' he said to the page. 'And bring us some more warm wine.' The boy took off. Farhardt turned to Feyir. 'One would think that these Northerners would be wiser than to provoke us this way. They seem almost intent on their own destruction.'

'A rowdy lot,' Feyir said, as the King turned and started to walk back to his tent. He smiled.

The afternoon sun entered Yldich's study in long, slanting beams that turned the polished floors a warm golden brown. Yldich sat at the table with his eyes closed, deep in thought. There was a creaking sound and a rustle of soft fabric. A slender hand took his and pulled him out of his reverie.

'What are you worrying about, *Dáydach*?' He looked up and found Maetis' clear eyes gazing at him. He sighed and squeezed her hand.

'Maetis, do you remember when your mother and I used to argue about you?'

She nodded. A faint smile curved her lips. 'She was angry with you for raising me like a boy instead of a proper *Einache* woman.'

He nodded soberly. 'Your mother said I was being selfish, to raise you like the son I had always wanted. I disagreed with her vehemently. Now I'm starting to wonder if perhaps she was right.'

'But, *Dáydach*—'

'Maetis, Farhardt's army is upon us. Our chances of holding them off are slim. Even if we're not slain or led into slavery, they would force their Southern ways on us. I worry about what would happen to you. You have always been free. It would be like—like—'

'Like a wild thing locked in a cage,' she said in a low voice. She frowned at the table top. Then she looked up.

'Do you remember Sventi? The wolf cub I raised. I was seven. Do you remember what you said when I had to release him?' She smiled. 'I worried about all the things that could happen to him in the wild. You said that I had raised him the best way I could—and that now it was up to him.' She kissed his hand. 'You can't protect me from the world forever, *Dáydach*... you have to let me go sometime.'

He sighed, trying to dislodge the stone on his heart. 'I'd never have thought it would be so hard.' She went over to him and embraced him briefly. She smiled at him.

'I'll be fine.' She left the room, and closed the door softly behind her. Her eyes darkened an instant as she touched the hilt of the dagger hidden under the layers of skirts.

No more messages came from the Southern camp that day. Late in the afternoon, as the setting sun turned the sky an ominous red, one of the watchers gasped and dropped off his perch on the palisades. He burst through the doors. The Great Hall was filled with people having bread and stew.

'They're coming!' A hush fell over the Hall. Warriors jumped up and ran to fetch their gear. 'The army's on the move!'

'Well, what are they playing at?' Ullwich's voice was a grumble. A handful of *Einache*, including Yldich and Rom had gathered on top of the palisades. They looked out over the fields, were the snow was ploughed by the boots of many soldiers. Yldich shook his head.

'I think they're preparing a siege,' he said. 'Rom, what do you know of the way these people wage war?'

Rom bit his lip. 'I'm not sure.' The sight of hundreds of Southern soldiers, of archers, swordfighters and smiths, made him feel extremely uneasy.

'In the old days, we would have picked a field for the confrontation, appointed a time, held a ritual, and got on with it,' Wérdyris said. He stamped his boots impatiently. His feet were getting cold.

'I think Southerners have different ideas about strategy,' Yldich said.

Rom nodded. 'They don't like open confrontations. They would rather starve us into submission, or surprise us, so they can subdue us with a minimum of effort. They don't delight in battle, really. They just want to take over.'

Wérdyris snorted. 'Strange people.'

As they stood watching the Southerners pitch their tents and light their fires, Rom found he could discern different parties in the assembled army. Some wore the colours of the King, some of the different noble Houses. He recognized some standards from the time he was a page at Aldr's court.

There was one part of the field where a group of men seemed not to wear any specific colours at all. They looked like a disorganized bunch. Rom squinted to try and see more clearly in the fading light. His breath stuck in his throat. 'Yldich.'

'What is it?'

'Look, look over there,' Rom whispered, and held his breath. He heard Yldich inhale sharply.

'Riders. Well. At least now we know who's responsible for this sudden turn of events.'

Rom gazed over the field where Feyir's men were busy at their tasks. A chill ran over his skin as he noticed a dark, slender figure at the edge of camp looking back at him. It was too far away to discern her face, but the dark, trailing hair was unmistakable.

'*Tzanatzi*,' Rom hissed, as if he were an *Einache* warrior.

'What?' Yldich and Wérdyris uttered at the same time.

'It's the *Tzanatzi* woman, over there, at Feyir's camp. I knew it. I knew it when I saw her in Woodbury. She's with them.'

All that evening things remained disconcertingly quiet. Yldich had sentinels posted on the palisades. In the Great Hall, all talk was of war, of battles fought in the past, and, inevitably, of the Ancient War with the *Tzanatzi* that had culminated in the Battle of Gardeth.

As the evening dragged on, Rom felt the need to go out for a breath of air. The threat of war weighed down the atmosphere like smoke and clouded his head.

He walked out into the snow and breathed the brisk evening air. He reached the place where the ceremonial spear had been thrust into the earth and became aware of another's presence. His heartbeat quickened as he saw the slender figure of the *Tzanatzi* woman come towards him. It was as if she had melted through the palisades. Rom thought of the eerie voices at the gates of Woodbury and shivered.

'Well,' she said, and smiled. Her voice was smooth like velvet. Her dark hair floated about her. Her pale, oval face was shapely like a night blooming flower. He wondered again if she was real.

'Seems like you are on the wrong side of the fence, *Tzanatzi*.' His eyes widened.

'There are no sides here,' he said under his breath.

'Really?' She touched the ceremonial spear between them. 'I distinctly sense a boundary here.' She held her head to one side. 'Why are you siding with those red-headed barbarians? You know how they think of us. They hate our kind. They call us demons. They don't consider us human.'

'After what our people did to them, can you blame them?' He swallowed away something painful. 'Times have changed. They've been good to me.' He gazed at her. She looked young, now he could see her up close, maybe even younger than he was, and definitely human. He wondered how she had gotten involved with Feyir. He gestured towards the Southerner's camp behind her. 'They fear you more than the *Einache* ever hated you. After they're done with you, they'll discard you.'

Her lips curved in a haughty smile. 'I won't give them the chance.'

He shook his head in perplexity. 'Why do you let yourself be used by these Southern nobles? You can't trust them. You know how they feel about *Tzanatzi*.'

'There's a certain reward to be won helping lord Feyir get back his inheritance.' Her voice was cool. 'I've lived in squalor all my life, eighteen years on the road, being spat at by peasants.' A look of pain crossed her face and made her eyes seem even darker. He was suddenly aware of the little girl behind the proud young woman. Her dark eyes were scarred with humiliation and pain. A deep sadness was beneath them. He swallowed.

'What's your name?'

Her laugh was sharp. 'Why do you want to know? Do you believe it will give you power over me?'

'I just want to know who you are. I'll give you mine. It's Rom.'

She shook her head at him. 'You shouldn't go about telling people your real name, Rom. Especially not people like me.' She held her head to one side, and gazed at him as if she measured him. Something had softened in her face. 'I am Iryna.'

'Won't you come with me, Iryna? You don't have to work for Feyir and his men. You would be welcome here.'

She stared at him for a moment. Her eyes were almost wistful. Then they hardened. They glittered like black opals. 'And do what, exactly? Roll about in the hay with some sheepherder, make some *Einache* barbarian a dutiful wife? No thank you.'

'You're not safe with Feyir's men,' he said softly.

'I'll take care of myself.' Her eyes changed. A dark power filled her presence and made her seem taller than she was. Her pale face glowed. Rom's eyes widened. He involuntarily took a step back. She started to turn away.

He tried to reach her one more time. 'Iryna.'

She turned and reached out a hand. She touched his face with her fingertips. A faint look of regret softened her eyes. Then she was gone. Rom brought up a hand to his face. Where she had touched him, his skin was cold.

It was near dark. There was a single candle burning on the table. The only other source of light was a copper brazier filled with glowing coals. The slender man's face was still as he stared into the glowing embers. Not an eyelash moved. The tent flap was shoved aside and a figure entered. He stopped abruptly as the dark head turned to face him.

Lakíthra gazed at Riórdirým's face. The mage looked as if had been sitting in the gathering dark alone for hours, staring into the flames, as the young man suspected he did more and more often, these days. His face, that Lakíthra had once thought beautiful as those of the deities that were carved on their temple walls, looked strained and hollowed out, and there were lines on his brow and beside his mouth that had not been there before. Lakíthra swallowed and came forward, one hand on his stomach in the familiar gesture of reverence.

'I've heard there's been a messenger from the *Einache*,' he said breathlessly. 'I heard he's brought you a challenge—'

'You have heard correctly,' Riórdirým said, an eyebrow raised at the abrupt interruption of his thoughts. 'At sundown tomorrow, I will meet with their champion on the cliffs. The Battle may be decided there before it has even begun.'

'Don't go.' Lakíthra took a step forward and laid a hand on the mage's arm before he knew what he was doing. 'Don't do it, Riórdirým. It's a trap. I know it is. You're in danger. I can feel it—,' he froze and drew back as the dark eyes flashed in icy disapproval. 'My lord,' he added in a belated attempt to restore decorum. Riórdirým stared at the young apprentice who stood before him with a pained expression on his face. His eyes made him feel uncomfortable. He stepped back and commenced pacing around the tent.

'They told me they will have their greatest champion come to the challenge,' he said in a low voice. 'You may not have thought this through. If I can defeat this man, this symbol of *Einache* strength and resistance, maybe we can avoid this battle altogether.' He stopped pacing to touch the dragon-headed sword, which hung suspended from a tent pole. 'It will break their resolve to fight us, to waylay us at every turn. If he is defeated, surely they will give up their resistance. We may finally have peace.'

Lakíthra stood softly shaking his head. 'I don't trust them, my lord... I fear for your safety. Please, at least allow me to come with you....'

Riórdirým turned to look at Lakíthra's face. The expression in the young man's eyes stirred something within he didn't want to be reminded of. He stiffened and closed his heart against him. 'I hardly think your presence will be either needed or useful when there's fighting involved. You'd better stay behind the lines and take care of the wounded.' He turned away quickly as he saw tears rise in the young apprentice's eyes. 'Now go and leave me to my preparations.'

Lakíthra bowed. He moved stiffly, as if he was wounded. 'Yes, my lord Riórdirým.' He turned and left the tent.

Maetis surfaced from a deeper layer of consciousness and stirred. Her hand reached over to the other side of the bed and found it empty. She opened her eyes and sat up. Rom sat staring into the fire with a blanket around his shoulders. She moved over to him and laid a hand on his shoulder.

'What is it, Rom? Can't you sleep?'

'I turned him away.' His voice was strained. He kept his eyes on the fire. 'The only person who still cared for me. He tried to protect me. And I dismissed him....'

She kneeled beside his chair and took his hand. 'Who?'

'Lakíthra. My apprentice.'

'The same apprentice who came to you in *ayúrdimae* to warn you about the coming storm?' He nodded. 'Well. It would seem to me he has forgiven you a long time ago.'

He looked up at her. 'Do you think so?'

Maetis smiled at him. She pressed his hand and rose. 'Come back to bed, Rom. It's too cold to be sitting by the hearth on your own.'

The next morning Rom awoke to the pounding of steel on wood. After a quick wash and shave he joined Maetis and the others in the Great Hall.

'What's going on?' he said.

'They've been at it since dawn.' Yldich greeted him with a grim expression on his face.

'They're cutting down our trees,' Yealda added, her eyes flashing with anger. 'The Southern *Ulérstwe*. Some of those trees are over a thousand years old.'

Rom widened his eyes. 'Why?'

'We're not sure,' Yldich said. 'They're too far away to see what they're doing. But they might be building some sort of contraption to scale the walls.' He turned to Eald, who stood beside him munching a bread roll. 'Why don't you take Odún to the enclosure. You can use your crystal to try and get an impression of what they're up to. And Eald,' he added as the boy was about to take off, scattering crumbs in all directions, 'this is not a game. Be very careful.' Eald attempted a demure expression.

'Yes, Yldich,' he muttered. At a nod from Yldich, he was off. Yldich raked his fingers through his curls and sighed.

'I've posted the older apprentices at the palisades to keep an eye on them day and night. Now the only thing we can do is wait.'

As Rom soon discovered, by waiting, Yldich did not mean sitting around and doing nothing. He quickly began to assign tasks. Young girls filled earthenware pots with oil that could be heated or set alight to defend the palisades; children were cutting arrows and young lads were making spears, and Maetis kept the young warriors busy with practice rounds and drills. Elderly *Einache* cut cloth for bandages. Even the little children were busy gathering sharp stones and rubble that could be hurled from the top of the palisades to repel invaders.

Rom noticed some tasks were more trivial than others, and concluded Yldich kept people busy not only because the tasks needed to be done, but also to keep morale up. He and Yealda seemed to be everywhere at once. They were encouraging people, giving instructions, and generally keeping an eye on things.

He wandered around the House and wondered what to do with himself. Everywhere he went, people were busy at their tasks, and there seemed nothing in particular he could assist with. Eldairc was busy working with the smiths. They were sharpening old swords, and melting iron and bronze implements for spear points. At the field behind the House, Maetis was training *Einache* youths. Some of the refugees had shown promise with sword or bow, and she taught them basic fighting skills.

Rom stood watching her for a while. Whereas before, he had enjoyed seeing her work, if somewhat hesitantly, the proximity of the Southern army turned his thoughts in a more sinister course. As he watched her move, he thought of her smiling eyes as she lay with him at night, her golden-red curls a soft mantle for their naked bodies. He imagined those curves, that creamy skin and those slender limbs, crushed in battle, torn apart by sword or knife, or in the pitiless hands of Southern soldiers. He felt a hollow pain in his stomach and was suddenly reminded of Ciórdynn. His eyes turned black and he held his arms across his stomach as if he were ill. He turned away so Maetis would not see. That was when Odún came running up to him.

'Roëm,' he cried in his thick *Einache* accent. 'Roëm. It's Eald. I need your help.'

'What's wrong?' Rom said. He took hasty strides across the field. They had nearly reached the other side of the House. The boy had to run to keep up with him. He was panting.

'Don't know. We were—we were at the watchtower, scrying with our crystals—to see what the Southerners are doing. And he suddenly went limp.'

Rom shook his head. His face was grim.

Too dangerous. This is what you get when you let children play with Yaever powers.

Eald lay on his back on the wooden boards of the watchtower, a simple wooden structure on top of the palisades. Rom got him down the steps with difficulty. He carefully laid him on the ground. The boy's narrow face was pale, his eyes moving erratically behind the closed eyelids. His lips were moving, but no sound came from his mouth.

Rom swallowed a curse and turned to Odún. 'Go and get Yldich. I'll try to get him back.'

'What's wrong with him?'

Rom frowned. 'He's gone dreamwalking. And I think he went too far. Now go and get Yldich.' As Odún turned and ran, his eyes big, Rom touched Eald's face with his fingertips. He closed his eyes and tried to connect with the boy. Somehow it felt as if he was far away, too far to reach without following him. Rom took a deep breath and plunged in after him.

It was dark, too dark to see where he was, too dark to discern anything. Rom concentrated on Eald, on the memory of his lively and bright energy. He felt a thin thread, a connection of some sort, unroll from his heart into the distance. It was the only thing that could serve as a guide. He followed it out.

Yldich was talking with Maetis on the practice field, when Odún found them.

'Yldich,' he cried. 'You must come and help us. Eald's in trouble and Rom has gone after him.'

At the bottom of the watchtower they found Eald lying on his back, his face pale as snow. Rom sat on the ground beside him, holding the boy's hands, his eyes closed. He was as pale as Eald. He was frowning, his eyes moving behind the closed lids. Maetis ran towards him.

'Don't,' Yldich cried. 'Don't touch him. You don't know where he is.'

Maetis turned her head to stare at him as she kneeled beside Rom in the snow. 'Why—what could happen?'

Yldich shook his head. 'There's no telling where he is or what he's doing. If nothing else, you could disturb him trying to find Eald.'

Maetis stared at him. 'And in the worst case?'

Yldich did not answer. He took a small bundle of herbs rolled into a stick and reached for his tinderbox. He murmured softly. As the smoke from the lighted bundle began to swirl around him, he closed his eyes and started to hum, a soft, wordless song that drew a circle of sound around them. It somehow eased Maetis' anxiety.

Yldich addressed her without taking his attention off his work. 'Get the double pointed crystals from my study. The large ones. I'll need them.'

She turned and ran.

The darkness was deeper than the ordinary dark of night. The dark of night was just absence of light. If anything, it was quiet and peaceful. This was a different type of darkness altogether. It was thick and somehow seemed alive, riddled with some kind of presence that made it feel... *sticky*, for want of a better word. Rom shuddered. There was no way to avoid its touch. If he wanted to follow the thread that rolled from his heart, he had to move through it.

After a while, the dark became even denser, and he became aware of the presence of another. He knew it was her before he saw her clearly.

'Iryna.'

She lifted her head and smiled at him. '*Caleërte*... Rom.' She stressed the vowel just long enough for him to wonder what she was insinuating. Her midnight hair swirled around her like a living thing, and she held something in her slender hands that was bright and alive, a golden orb of precious light. She tossed the orb in the air and caught it, with a kind of playful nonchalance that made his stomach turn.

'Give him to me.'

'This?' She threw the orb into the air again, and smiled as she caught it.

'Please....'

'Oh, come now... you don't think pleading with me will do the trick, do you? Besides, there's something I want to ask *you* in return.'

'What do you want?'

She smiled at him. 'Your cooperation.'

He stared at her. 'What could I possibly do for you?'

She smiled again, shaking her head. 'Are you really that ignorant of who you are, of what you are?' He did not answer, but her words made him feel cold inside. 'Well, there are those that are not.' He felt a movement behind him and turned his head. Dark shapes loomed up behind him. He caught a glimpse of pale, haggard faces, and dark, hollow eyes. He heard their voices whisper, like dead leaves on the wind.

Caleërte, Riórdirým.

Maetis returned carrying two large crystals. Yldich took one and let her hold the other.

'They've gone a long way down,' he said. 'I may need your help to get them back.' Maetis' fingers closed on the hard, cold surface of the crystal. 'Hold it and reach inside your heart. Summon any love you have for him. You'll need it if you want him back.' Maetis swallowed and concentrated on her heart as Yldich began to sing under his breath.

'You could help me reach my objective,' Iryna said. 'Once, we were respected and feared across this whole continent. You could side with me and lend me your power. Your precious savages wouldn't even have to know.'

'To help Lord Feyir get back his inheritance—'

'To help me get back *mine*. Feyir is only a means to an end.'

His eyes widened. 'You're using him as much as he's using you.'

'Only he's not aware of it.' She smiled. 'Now, I'm not only doing this for myself. I would have the *Tzanatzi* reinstated in their proper place. To right the years of wrongdoing against us. Will you help me?'

He shook his head. 'There must be another way to get back your self-respect,' he said. 'There must be another way to get justice for our people.'

Her eyes narrowed. 'And you think you will get it by hanging around with the savages, listening to their sob stories, and staring moon-eyed at the daughter of their leader?' She shook her head. 'Although,' she said with a taunting light in her eyes, 'you have done more than just *looking*, if my observations are correct.'

His eyes flashed with sudden anger. 'Eald was right. You have been spying on us.' He felt a sense of indignation rise, and give him strength. He drew himself up. 'If the Unnamed One *had* been here, he would have had you whipped for such a breach of dreamwalking protocol.'

She smiled, her head to one side. 'But he's not, is he? There's only a helpless little boy, the shadow of his former self.' She tightened her hands around the orb of light that was Eald. 'Little boys shouldn't play at adult games. Especially little *Einache* ones.' A flash of hatred made her dark eyes glitter with a merciless light. She tightened her grip on the golden orb. It squirmed as if in pain.

Rom winced. 'Stop it!'

'Then side with me and give me your power.'

He had a sudden impression of the power she was referring to. It was like looking down a deep chasm and feeling an enormous reservoir of fiery energy, like lava, hidden in the deep, waiting to be called forth. He recoiled in astonishment. If he truly had had so much power, to hand it to her would be the end of the *Einache*, the end of the Southerners, of the world as he knew it. In her hands, it would destroy them all. He shook his head.

'No,' he breathed.

'Then I will make you. *Áya ecúrima moréaz.*' The shadows moved, and he felt their touch, the horrid sense of their dead fingers on his skin. They leeched onto him and sapped him of strength. He struggled and fought desperately to loosen their hold.

A beam of light shone from above, and another. The thick, clinging darkness seemed to lighten. He heard a soft singing that lightened his heart and loosened the hold of the dead *Tzanatzi* on him.

She'll never hold power over me.

An ageless joy filled his heart. He lunged forward and snatched the golden orb of energy from her hands. He concentrated fiercely on the world of sunlight, of joy, and laughter. He held the energy that was Eald tightly to his chest and closed his eyes. He hurtled himself in the direction of the light.

He surfaced coughing and wheezing. His arms were trembling with effort.

Maetis cried out with relief and grabbed a hold of him. 'You're back.'

'Eald.' Rom's voice was hoarse. 'Where is he?' His eyes widened in dismay as he saw the boy's face, deathly white as he lay motionless in Yldich's arms. Then he coughed and stirred.

'What?' Eald said. 'What happened?' Rom embraced him forcefully. The boy tried to break free from his grip. 'Rom,' Eald's voice was muffled, 'will you let me go now? You're smothering me.'

Eald sat curled up in a chair before the hearth in Yldich's study. He took a last sip of hot soup, and put down the bowl with a sigh. He looked up. Yldich and Rom sat gazing at him, one pair of stern grey eyes and one pair black. He swallowed. It was like being confronted with not one angry father, but two. He knew he was in for a scolding.

'Well,' Yldich said. 'Would you like to explain to us now how you got yourself in such a predicament?'

Eald nodded. 'Me and Odún went to see what the Southerners were up to with our scrying crystals. We climbed the watchtower... and then we sat and concentrated. But I could see much further than Odún....' He couldn't prevent a proud tone from entering his voice. 'It was so easy. So I thought, why not go one step further and go there myself?' Rom sat shaking his head in silence. Yldich's eyes had become the colour of steel.

'Go on.' His voice betrayed nothing.

'I sort of made a turning motion, and suddenly, I was out, and in the dark. I was trying to find my way. That's when this woman came up to me.' He shuddered, his face suddenly strained. 'She was dark, like Rom. She reminded me a little of him. She smiled at me, so I went to her. But something wasn't right about her smile. I felt it. Like... like too many honey cakes make you feel sick.' Rom bit his lip to hide a smile. Yldich's face was impassive.

'Go on.'

'She touched me, and suddenly I was dizzy, and—and taken out of myself,' Eald said. 'It was awful. There was pain, but I can't rightly remember... and then suddenly I was lying on my back in the snow, and I was back again.'

Yldich released a breath and shook his head at the boy. 'Do you realize that because of your folly we not only nearly lost you, but both of you? Do you realize Rom had to risk his life to get you back?'

Eald dropped his head and stared at his hands. 'I'm—I'm sorry.'

Yldich shook his head. 'You're too young to go dreamwalking on your own. In ordinary circumstances, you might get away with taking such foolish risks. But we're at war now.' He looked sharply at Eald. 'You don't have to take risks to show off your skills to the other boys. Believe me when I tell you, you have great *Yaever* potential. But if you go about like this, it will get you killed. Will you be tempted to take such risks again?'

Eald shook his head. 'No, Yldich.'

'Good. Now, off to bed with you.' He rose and ushered the boy towards the door. Eald felt inclined to protest, since the sun had only just set. But one look at Yldich's face told him he had better comply, this time.

'*Nâstréhi ea*, Rom,' he said demurely.

'*Nâstréhi ea*,' Rom said. He smiled.

'I met her before,' Rom said when Yldich had brought Eald to bed. He had taken some precautions to see to it the boy would not be troubled by ghostly *Tzanatzi* again, that night. His clothes smelled of pine resin and burnt herbs.

'Tell me.'

'Yesterday evening, I went for a walk outside. And there she was. She had gone through the palisades as if they were air.'

Yldich raised his brows. 'What did you do?'

'I spoke to her. She reminds me of myself, somehow.' Rom sighed. 'She's young, she's hurt and angry, she's been an outcast all her life...'

Yldich nodded slowly. 'Yet I don't see you siding with the likes of Feyir, and endanger the lives of foolish *Yaever* pupils to get what you want.'

Rom nodded. 'I tried to reach her. I told her she would be welcome here. But she wouldn't have any of it. She seems proud, and very bitter....'

'What did she want from you?'

'She wanted me to side with her. She knows. She knows who I am. Maybe she's been spying on us all this time, since Woodbury. She wanted me to work with her, to give her my power....'

Yldich drew up his brows. 'Well, now...'

'When I refused, she threatened to kill Eald. She had even called the spirits of the *Tzanatzi* dead to force me to comply.' Rom shuddered at the memory of their touch.

Yldich's eyes turned dark. 'If she is prepared to go that far, it seems to me she has made her choice a long time ago.' His voice was stern.

'What choice?'

'To walk the dark road.'

Rom stared at him. 'What do you mean by the dark road, Yldich?'

'Well,' Yldich said, a brief flicker of mirth in his eyes, 'you of all people should know.' He sat back in his chair. 'Ever since people became aware of the fact that there is more to this life than what they can see and touch, that there are other planes, and powers, beyond the visible plane, there've been those who abused those powers.' His voice steadily gained a chanting tone as he went on.

Rom settled more comfortably in his cushions. *He's going into story-telling mode again.*

'You might wonder what defines abuse of power,' Yldich said. 'Well, the *Einache* saw it this way.' He turned his bowl around in his hands. 'I've taught you the concepts of *Eärwe*, the Whole, and of *Sanáyah*, the Unfolding of the World. *Sanáyah* has always taught the *Einache* about Balance. You see, the World and everything in it, plants, rocks, trees, people, is perfectly balanced. Nothing is ever wasted. No-one is ever lost. No effort is ever in vain, as all is energy, and energy cannot be destroyed. It can only be transformed.'

He poured them some more mead and went on. 'The energy that I'm talking about, the main energy that governs the World, is the energy of Creation, of Love.' He took a sip of mead while Rom stared at him, transfixed. 'Remember the spiral dance you danced with Maetis. Remember the fire your apprentice returned to you. It is the energy of passion, and creation.' Rom envisaged the orange fire that leapt through his body and spilled through his fingers, filling him with joy.

'Now to use the energy, the power of the *Sanáyah*, for purposes that go against the Way the World wants to Unfold, is to create disharmony, or Imbalance. It is to invite Destruction.'

Rom blinked. 'So when exactly is power destructive?'

Yldich smiled grimly. 'Power is power. The energy remains the same. It's the purpose and the way in which it is wielded that determines whether it's in accordance with the Law of Love, or whether it will yield Destruction.' He shifted his gaze to the fire. 'To use your power out of fear, greed, or lust, to bend another to your will, to force other beings to act against their nature, is to act against the Law of Love. And it will bring forth Destruction, not just for those involved, but especially for the one who has misused his power.

The greater the power misused, the greater the destructive force that will come back to him, and bring hardship, a hardship that will ultimately cause him to return to Unity, to *Sanáyah*. You see, to live in destruction, cut off from the force of Love, is to be cut off from the Whole, from *Eärwe*, from one's true Self. In the end, it's that which is most unbearable of all.'

Rom felt his eyes burn with an old, wordless grief. Images rose and shifted into each other, and he saw the wrecking of the *Tzanatzi* ships,

Ciórdynn's lifeless body, the rising darkness that came to his call. He saw his mother's hostile eyes, the cold walls of Lord Aldr's dungeon, and images of his long journey north. A deep sadness welled up in him.

Yldich sat gazing at him. 'No-one is ever lost. The Law of Love governs everyone.' His tone was gentle. 'Eventually, all will return to it. It is inevitable.' Rom sighed.

'For some, the way back is longer than for others.'

'Rom. Wake up.' Maetis tugged at his arm. He opened his eyes and blinked at her in confusion. It was still dark. The low fire in the hearth created weird shadows in Maetis' face. 'The alarm has sounded. We're under attack.'

He leapt out of bed and hastily threw on his clothes. He was hurriedly fastening his belt, weighed down by the *Einache* sword, when he turned and looked at Maetis. Her hair looked dark in the gloom. Her quick fingers had caught her wayward curls in a long, loose braid. She was fastening the laces of a leather jerkin. He felt a cold, numbing sense of *déjà vu* as he saw her gird on her sword. He took her by the arms.

'Maetis,' he whispered.

'We must go.' Her clear grey eyes found his. He brushed a loose red curl from her brow. She lifted her face and kissed him on his mouth.

'*Ti'héldae*, Rom,' she whispered.

'*Aye sûa*, Maetis.' He touched her cheek with his fingertips. He let her go.

The House was in an uproar. The corridor was filled with *Einache* running one way or the other. They carried swords, spears, arrows, or were running to the kitchens for kettles of hot water and oil.

Rom ran through the great doors and was greeted by the sight of countless Southern soldiers about to climb over the walls. They had used ladders and ropes with hooks on them to scale the palisades. They had also brought a siege tower.

They must have worked day and night to build it in such a short time.

Rom stared at the thing. It outmatched the walls in height, and it was large enough to house at least fifteen archers and soldiers. It had a small drawbridge that was about to be lowered onto the palisades.

How could they build it so fast? Why haven't Yldich's pupils detected it?

A chill crawled over his skin as the answer leapt in his head out of nowhere.

Iryna. She's somehow managed to conceal it from the Yaever's dreaming eyes.

He stared numbly at the *Einache* warriors who ran to meet the advancing soldiers, their faces grim. He shuddered at the familiarity of the scene. The fighting commenced as the first soldiers leapt over the top of the palisades. A thought like a panicked bird flew through his head.

This is the end. We're all going to die.

It was then he saw the first *Einache* fall. Érdogan, a young *Einache* warrior of Aeldic's company Rom had seen dancing with Maetis on the night of the clan gathering. He had been one of the first to climb the palisades to fight back the stream of Southern soldiers. Totally engrossed in fighting two soldiers who had just set foot on the boards, he did not notice a third, who had slipped past the other *Einache* warriors. Before Rom could shout a warning, a knife flashed and the young man fell backwards. He plummeted to the ground and lay still in the snow. Stunned, Rom stared at the place where he had fallen.

Another cry turned his head. Maetis had joined a group of young warriors at the other side of the House, where a small band of Southerners tried to get over the wall unseen. The *Einache* warriors were threatened to be overcome.

Rom watched in horror as Maetis desperately warded of blows with her sword in one hand, while with the other she held a wounded lad, so he would not slide off the edge. Dimly he saw Yldich running towards them, his sword drawn. He would never make it in time. In an awful, endless second, Rom envisioned Maetis' death. A cold hand clawed at his heart and cut off his breath.

Unbidden, the image of the abyss came to Rom's mind, of the hidden source of power he had sensed in its depths. He could feel it, a liquid fire, whirling and moving, deep within his belly. A strange calm descended on him. All was lost. What did it matter what it made of him now? He closed his eyes and reached into the deep.

Now.

The fire leapt up; joyful, incredulous, it rushed through his veins and filled him until he thought he would burst. He gasped with surprise at its beauty. Light shone through his hands and fingers.

'*Ayáa elcailië,*' he cried. A dark bubble of sound left his mouth. It rippled and grew wider, as if a stone had been thrown into a dark lake. There was an eerie silence within that was charged with intensity. Particles of air danced in it. The light caught them and set them on fire. One after the other, they sparked and started to wheel and turn. He saw *Einache* warriors turn their heads to look at him with wide eyes. Fiery sparks leapt from his eyes and outstretched hands. They came together and formed a fast-growing spiral of burning air. Holding it filled him with a strange, raw joy. It grew until he could hold it no more. He breathed out and let it go.

Fire seared through the air and hurled itself at the palisades, leaving a stream of flames that raged along the top and set the siege tower alight. Southern soldiers drew back cursing. They fell off their ladders frantically trying to put out the fire on their clothes. The orderly Southern ranks quickly turned to chaos. Rom heard the cries of the men that hurtled down the palisades to the frozen ground below.

Most *Einache* stood staring open-mouthed at the fire from a safe distance. Some hadn't drawn back in time and were rolling in the snow to quench the flames in their furs.

Rom sank to the ground, dazed and totally spent. His eyes were burning. Darkness hemmed him in.

What have I done?

Morven caught him and heaved him up. The clan leader moved a muscled arm around his waist and walked him back to the House as flames continued to leap and dance on the palisades. Glowing sparks descended in the snow, where they were silently quenched.

Yldich stood looking at the fire. 'Well now,' he said softly, and sheathed his sword. 'That should keep them busy for a while.'

The King gazed at the walls, where the orange flames were still raging. They repelled his soldiers with their heat, although strangely, they didn't seem to want to consume the wood they were dancing on. The same could not be said for the siege tower. The flames crackled merrily as it burned like a gigantic torch.

Farhardt stood shaking his head in bafflement. 'What could it be?'

One of his nobles grumbled. 'Some weird *Einache* magic, no doubt, my lord.'

Rom sat before the hearth in Yldich's study, his head in his hands. He looked up as Yldich came in. Yldich smelled faintly of singed hair and scorched clothes. He absently patted a patch on his elbow that was still smoking.

'What am I?' Rom said hoarsely. His eyes were blood-shot. 'What am I that I can do such a thing?'

Yldich went over to him and kneeled beside his chair. 'Once, you were an incomparably powerful sorcerer,' he said softly. A sudden flare of rage went through Rom. His eyes flashed with dark fire. He grabbed a bowl and flung it in the hearth with all the strength he could muster. It crashed onto the stones and shattered into a thousand tiny pieces.

'I don't want to be this man,' he cried. He was shaking. 'I don't want to be this man who's respected only because of his power, who pushes away anyone who loves him, and is hated and feared by everyone else.'

Yldich sat shaking his head at him. 'Rom,' he said gently. He moved over to him and held him as if he were still a child. Rom stiffened and tried to push him away, but as Yldich simply held onto him, he relaxed in his grip.

'I don't want this power. I never asked for it. You don't know what it'll make of me.' Tears were running down his face. Yldich held him at arm's length, gazing into his eyes with a stern expression.

'I'm sure the caterpillar is scared before he pushes through his casing and becomes the butterfly. I'm sure the sparrow is scared as it jumps the nest to test its wings and fly. But there's no other way. You can't stay a frightened boy forever, Rom—you'll have to grow up sometime.'

'But what if I grow into *him*....'

'You won't. Not again.'

'How can you know?' Rom whispered.

'Otherwise, you wouldn't be crying right now.' A sudden smile lit Yldichs eyes. 'Besides, you can't abuse your power. I won't let you. Neither will Maetis.' Something softened in Rom's face. He met Yldich's eyes.

'Promise you'll stop me if I ever start being like him.'

But you are him.

'I promise,' Yldich said.

It was near dusk. Riórdirým had been staring in the fire for hours, thinking of Ciórdynn, of the others that had been lost. His heart felt empty, his eyes dry as dust. A weariness of someone far beyond his years was in his bones. He rose and took the dragon-headed sword. '*Aye camêna*,' he said softly to the gathering dark. 'I am ready.'

The sky turned a deep indigo as he climbed the hill and stepped onto the ledge of the cliff. A slight wind lifted strands of black hair and swirled them around his face. Someone was already waiting for him. It was a tall man. His hair was a fiery red in the light of the torches. Riórdirým felt his breath stick in his throat as he laid eyes on the face of the *Einache* champion that stood there waiting for him.

He's so young.

The *Einache* warrior looked no more than seventeen winters old. Soft downy hair covered the jaw of a face that still had to fill out into adulthood. Riórdirým felt a sense of relief, secure in his skill with the sword.

I'll have him down in two blows. He won't even know what happened to him.

He smiled as he advanced upon the young *Einache* and drew his sword. He nodded to indicate he was ready. The *Einache's* grey eyes flashed as he responded by drawing his double-handed sword. He seemed to brace himself.

'*Na Héach*,' he breathed. He attacked.

Riórdirým found out quickly that he would only underestimate the young *Einache* to his own detriment. What the young warrior lacked in skill and finesse, he made up for in passion and strength. His clear eyes flashed as he charged, and Riórdirým had to move swiftly to avoid being cloven in two by the great sword. His dark eyes widened in surprise and he changed his stance, concentrating fiercely and calling forth all his skill.

The fight took hours. The tall *Einache* and the lithe *Tzanatzi's* skills and weaknesses compensated each other so completely that when the stars came out, Riórdirým was assailed by the strangest notion. They complemented each other so perfectly they might as well be standing still. The sensation was so overpoweringly real that for an instant, he froze.

The *Einache* saw his chance and took it. There was a quick flash of the great sword and Riórdirým gasped for breath. He stepped back as blood began to flow from a fiery cut on his chest. The pain pulled him out of his strange trance. Riórdirým set his teeth and focused on the kill.

It was long after midnight. Riórdirým felt his strength drain with every gash, every drop of blood.

It will never end. We'll be fighting until we're both dead with exhaustion.

The young *Einache* seemed as tired and desperate as he was. His breath came in gasps, and his sword hand was white-knuckled with effort. He wiped the ginger hair, which was damp with sweat and blood, out of his face with his sleeve. He seemed at the end of his strength.

That was when Riórdirým became aware of the humming. It rose from the edges of his awareness, and drew a circle around him, like a bubble of sound. It was tightening. There were words in it he didn't understand. He suddenly knew he had been hearing it for quite some time. Somehow, he had not been aware of it until now. His eyes widened and he frowned, trying to assess the nature of the humming.

Riórdirým looked at the young *Einache's* face and met his eyes. His heart sank. The lad knew. He knew what was going on. He could see it in his eyes, like a tiny flickering of guilty knowledge. He stepped back and raised his left hand.

'*Atáre*,' he said in a low voice. There was a slight ripple in the bubble of sound. Nothing more. He felt his own breath quicken. He knew then that he was afraid. He tried again. '*Atáre, amelerië*.' Nothing. The circle of sound kept tightening; it enclosed him, pressing on his chest until he felt his lungs constrict. He started to fight for breath.

The young *Einache* stood staring at him with a vague look of dismay. A sudden surge of hatred went through Riórdirým's heart. It was a trap. The *Einache* had known all along. It was not a fair fight. They would finish him off, like they had killed Ciórdynn, with one contemptuous slash of cold steel. It would be the end of his people. Hatred and despair filled his being and lent him a strange, cold kind of strength. He drew himself up one last time. He fixed his eyes on the young *Einache*.

'*Calamêntiré.*' Darkness flowed out with the words. It flowed through the circle of sound. Darkness filled his eyes as he approached the *Einache* warrior for the last time. '*Calamêntiré.*' He saw the Einache's eyes filling with terror. The lad was swaying, blindly holding on to his sword as if for balance. He was choking. As the *Einache* dropped his sword and fell on his knees, gasping for breath, the circle of sound was completed.

Riórdirým felt a tearing sensation, as if he was being ripped asunder. A searing pain screamed through his body as he was forcibly torn away from it. He cried out with pain and terror. He groped around wildly for something to hold onto.

The last thing he saw were the grey eyes of the young lad, who stared at him with a kind of horrified pity. In his despair, Riórdirým reached out and felt a thread unroll from his heart, and latch unto him.

Darkness took him.

Rom woke up screaming, wildly fighting the blankets and skins while someone grasped his arms. He opened his eyes and stared right into Maetis' grey ones.

'It's all right,' she said. 'Rom, it's all right. It's me—' As he set eyes on her face, the bright eyes, the fiery hair, he recoiled, and tore away from her.

'*Einache,*' he spat, '*ayàdi eymíraz.*' Then he saw the hurt in her eyes. He shook his head, trying to clear it.

'Maetis,' he whispered, 'what—what was I saying? Forgive me. I didn't recognize you....' Maetis had let go of his arms and sat looking at him with wide eyes from the other side of the bed. She hadn't understood the words he had uttered, but the hostility in his eyes had been unmistakable.

Awareness of where he was, of who he was came back to him. His feeling for her returned, and with it came regret. He took her hands in his. 'I'm so sorry. I had a nightmare. I wasn't myself....' He drew her into his arms and to his relief, she didn't push him away. After a moment's hesitation, she tightened her arms around him. As they sat holding each other in silence, he closed his eyes, wondering if the war would ever truly be over.

Before the sun had risen, he went to Yldich's study and looked out over the dark fields. The remains of the siege tower were still smoking, the ashes carried away on the wind. The Southerners had retreated.

'I dreamt it,' he said as Yldich came in the room. His voice was strained. 'The night of the Battle.' Yldich nodded, as if he had been expecting the moment for a long time.

'Tell me,' he said softly.

'Do you know,' Rom said huskily, 'why the mage accepted the challenge to a fight to the death? He thought that if he defeated the *Einache* champion, it would decide the war. His people would finally be safe.' He grimaced, shaking his head. 'When you told Eald and me the story, you told us how the mage advanced on you, smiling in his arrogance. But it wasn't arrogance. He was smiling out of relief when he saw you were only an adolescent. He thought he would be able to end it quickly. Only he hadn't counted on your anger and your strength.'

'Go on,' Yldich said. His gaze was turned inward, as if he was seeing dark imagery of his own.

'I understand now. How you were able to find me, without knowing who I was or where. When I was ripped out of my body by the *Yaever* song,' a spasm of pain crossed his features, 'when I was torn away, yours was the face I looked upon last. And what I saw in your eyes was not hatred, but pity. And I reached out to you, and somehow, I connected myself to you. That is why,' he said with a sudden flicker of realization in his eyes, 'you nearly died with me. You were pulled into the darkness with me. But you the *Yaever* called back.' He sat shaking his head heavily.

'So that is why you dreamt me. You dreamt me being torn from my body and chained alive in the Underworld. And when my next Turn came on the Wheel of Life, you started dreaming me again. I guess without knowing it, I was still calling out for help. It only took you five hundred years to find me.'

He swallowed, his face drawn, his heart heavy with tears. Yldich came over to him without a word, and embraced him. Rom felt a grief too ancient to be put into words. His tears soaked Yldich's tunic. He saw in his mind's eye the battle field of his dreams, but this time, the Southerners were the ones that outnumbered the *Einache*. 'We nearly killed each other the last time,' he uttered hoarsely. 'Now we will be slain together.'

Yldich held him at arm's length and resolutely shook his head. 'I refuse to believe it's all been for nothing,' he said. 'I haven't forgotten my dreams.' He smiled. 'Don't bury us yet.'

Maetis sat in the windowsill of her room. She was staring in the distance, her face serene like a cat's, quietly contemplating its existence. She turned her head as Rom entered the room and smiled. There were faint circles under her eyes. It had been a long night.

'I talked to Kylára in the kitchen,' she said. 'The young girl you danced with at the clan fest. She saw you, last night. She saw what you did. I myself,' she added with a weary smile, 'was a little busy, so I only caught a glimpse of it. But she saw the whole thing. She described it to me.'

He took a deep breath to steady himself. 'What—what did she say?'

'She said that your face glowed like the moon, that your eyes were shining like twin stars, and that as you opened your hands, flowers of fire leapt through the air. She'd never seen anything so beautiful in her life. She gets a little carried away,' she added with a mischievous grin, 'when she's talking about you.'

'Beautiful?' he muttered.

Maetis chuckled. 'I think she has a little crush on you. Still, it must have been a wonderful sight. I wish I could have seen it.'

He stared at her face. 'Maetis, don't you fear what I am? Don't you fear what I'm capable of?' She took his hands.

'I could never fear you,' she said softly. 'I don't think you could bring forth anything that isn't beautiful.' An old sadness lodged in his throat. He tried to swallow it down.

'I'm carrying the face of an enemy. I come here with the remains of a broken life. I lay the shards at your feet, and you give me back a vision of beauty, and of love....'

She smiled and traced his face with the tips of her fingers. 'I only mirror what I see.' He released a breath and felt the tired heaviness of the night settle on his shoulders. Maetis took his hand. 'Why don't we lie down and rest a while.' She led him to the bed and lay down beside him. He sighed and closed his eyes. He let himself drift, pleasantly aware of her body, safe and warm beside him, her hand in his.

After a while, he felt the other lightly travel down his body. It felt as if he came alive under her fingers, as if she drew trails of light across his skin. A pleasurable shiver went through him. A spark of desire jumped up somewhere deep below, like one of those strange, laughing fish he had seen in his true-dream, leaping from the azure waters. His breath quickened as she moved down and released the clasp of his belt.

'Maetis—' he began, and stirred, feeling slightly embarrassed under such undivided attention. He moved to sit up. She pushed him back in the sheepskins with her hand.

'Shush,' she replied softly. 'Don't speak.'

His breath caught in his throat as she untied his trousers and he felt the warm touch of her mouth on him. A small, hard ball of tension melted away

and became warm, and fluid, and expanding. A soft moan escaped his mouth
as the warm, orange glow started to rise.

*It's the same. It's as Yldich said. It's the same energy. There's nothing
evil or dark about it.*

The fire was singing through his veins. A longing for Maetis, a physical
ache for her body made him take her hands, and pull her up towards him. He
cupped her face in his hands.

'*Aye sûa,*' he said. A bright light was in her eyes.

'Show me,' she whispered.

He gathered her up and she whirled around lithely like a water sprite. He
swept away the copper curls that spilled over her shoulders and back and
kissed the nape of her slender neck. She sighed as their bodies merged. He
clung to her, his face in her hair, his arms around hers.

Maetis gasped as waves of desire rose from deep within, and carried her
away in a surge of orange fire. A sound like the cry of a wild creature rose to
her throat, wanting to be loosed. She turned her head to look in Rom's face,
and her eyes widened a moment in surprise.

Rom felt Maetis' surge of desire as if it were his own. Hers was a joyous
energy, fearless and bright. It mingled with his darker fire as it rose. When the
fire reached his heart, and filled his head, he could hold it back no longer. He
trembled as he let it pass through. His awareness soared with it like a bird of
prey. Breathless, he circled up and found Maetis' presence rising with him.
They ascended together, two birds on a joyous wind, in a spiral flight into the
sun. Their breaths mingled as it reached its zenith, and the wind lay down, and
gently carried them back to earth. She turned and gazed at him. She touched
his face.

'You were glowing,' she whispered. 'I saw it. Your eyes were alight.'

The water of the bath was nice. He could let the tired heaviness of his
muscles sink away in it. When Rom finished soaking, he went over to the
washbasin to shave. He stared into the face of the young man in the mirror.
His eyes widened. Was it his imagination, or was there something glowing
under his skin? He moved closer to have a better look. He reached out a hand
to touch the face, forgetting for a moment that it was his own. The burnished
silver of the mirror was cold under his fingers. Then a ripple went over the
surface and he felt the warmth of living skin. He gasped and blinked, and
stared open-mouthed at the smooth surface. Then the sensation was gone, and
he stared in his own eyes, dark in his pale face.

He stepped back, shaking his head. It must have been his imagination.
The sensation was probably caused by lack of sleep. And food, he thought as
he heard a low rumbling in his belly. He turned and went to the kitchen.

He walked through the corridor, his thoughts circling back to Maetis and their being together. The memory was like a warm, sensual blanket enveloping his body. He smiled as he crossed the threshold.

Yárah noticed him and walked over to him, her hands open in a welcoming gesture. 'There you are, now! Come in, sit down. You must be starving after all that exertion.'

He stared at her, the blood rising in his face. Did everyone in the House know what Maetis and he were up to? Then he realized she must be referring to his performance of the night before. Apparently, it was on everyone's minds, and tongues, he thought uneasily as he looked around the kitchen. Bright, inquisitive eyes looked back at him. Then his gaze found Maetis. She sat grinning at him as if she knew exactly what he had been thinking.

'Come sit with me, Rom.' She patted at a spot beside her on the bench. As he sat down Yárah put a plate of bread and cheese before him.

'Nothing fancy this morning, I'm afraid,' Yárah said. 'Yldich has us ration the food.' He looked outside as he started on the bread. The sun blinked on the snow-covered fields and filled the kitchen with a cheery light, and if it were not for the banners of the tents in the distance, and the soot and the ashes from the burnt-out siege tower, it would have seemed just an ordinary sunny morning in the kitchen of the house of the Deer.

'*Elearána héwerda méldowae firte?*' A clear, high voice cut through his thoughts. He turned his head and looked straight in the bright grey eyes of a small boy. The child stood looking up at him expectantly.

'What—what's he saying?' he said to Maetis.

She laughed softly. 'He's asking when you're going to play with fire again.'

Yldich stood gazing out over the fields of Gardeth. A longing to be out, to reconnect with the earth, and speak with the Northern winds filled his chest. He sighed. The presence of the Southern army weighed on his mind; suddenly, the House felt as if it confined him. The air in the study felt stuffy and close.

All these years on the road have made me a wanderer. If I hadn't found Rom when I did, I might have turned into a Tzanatzi myself.

He chuckled at the thought. His amusement lifted the mood of listlessness that was on him.

He took some leather bundles from a chest. He laid out their contents on the table. Seven shining double-terminated crystals caught the light of the sun. He arranged them in a circle, each crystal pointing both to the centre and outward. He was humming softly while he worked. When he laid the last crystal in the circle, a barely audible, high-pitched sound started to fill the room. The crystals were resonating with his song.

Yldich stepped back and closed his eyes. He murmured softly under his breath, his hands out before him, palms up, while the atmosphere in the room changed completely. It became clear and sharp, as if he was standing on a high mountain top. He sighed, then breathed in the pure, clear air. He opened his eyes. They had changed; whereas before, the grey had dulled a little, like the steel of a knife that has not been used for a while, now they were clear and piercing as a hawk's. He straightened and righted his shoulders. Then he left the room in search of Yealda.

Yealda had seated herself in the chair carved from the ancient tree. Her eyes were closed. She let her thoughts and awareness drift while she relaxed her muscles, allowing her to sink deeper and deeper into herself.

She had noticed long ago that the tree could help her dreamwalking. She would imagine herself merging with the tree, becoming one with it. She could let herself travel through its roots or branches and take her out of herself. There was a place at the edge of the Forest, a quiet spot, with lush green ferns and grass, where it had stood undisturbed for centuries. There, she had a good view of the fields where the Southern army had pitched its tents.

She let herself float gently in the direction of the tents, hovering over the field. People walked to and fro and carried weapons, logs of wood, and sacks filled with supplies. Smoke rose from numerous fires, and from the top of the largest tent, that housed the kitchens.

It's like a small village, Yealda thought in amazement as she saw some children hurry from the large tent and return with sacks of snow for water.

She turned, trying to sense a driving force behind this people's presence, a sense of direction or purpose. She felt pulled in two directions at once.

In the one direction she discerned a large tent with tassels, and banners with the embroidered eagle device. The King's tent. She drifted a little nearer and became aware of the people inside. They radiated impatience, the desire for action.

The nobles. They are eager for battle. It will not be long now.

She rose and turned in the other direction that was pulling at her senses. There was a small camp at the edge of the field. She saw a motley crew of men clad in brown and green. They sat around or busied themselves with their tasks. In the middle of the camp a large tent was pitched. It looked surprisingly new. She reached out for it, and drew back instantly as if she had burned herself.

There were two entities there, different and yet equal in their intensity. Their energy had a scathing quality, like acid. Yealda gasped as she felt two dark eyes upon her.

Old woman, a vicious, amused voice sounded in her head. *Are you spying on us?*

Yealda felt a sinister coldness rise from the ground. It tried to pull her out of herself. *Na'Héach*, she thought intensely. She realized with a sense of shock that freeing herself was hard, like fighting her way through quicksand or tar. She turned and hastily returned to the room.

She felt the smooth grain of ancient wood under her hands and sighed with relief. For a moment, she felt the presence of someone dear. A presence that was warm and loving, it enveloped her like a soft cloak. She did not open her eyes for fear she would break the spell. She smiled as she became aware of the smell of summer grass, and flowers.

Cáyla.

Something had changed in her. Before, when she thought of Cáyla, she would only see that fateful moment, and feel the horror and helpless rage at her bloody death. Now, she could see her daughter's face, the sun shining in her flaxen hair, her broad smile and shining blue eyes. Yealda sighed and let the warmth wash away the unease of darkness.

There was a soft knock on the door. Yldich entered the room. Yealda opened her eyes.

'It won't be long now. We must speak. And then we must gather the clan heads.'

'I have surveyed the Southern King's encampment,' Yealda said. Rom and Maetis had joined her and Yldich in her chambers. 'I noticed two things of interest. One, that the Southern nobles seem eager to press on. They will make their next move soon.'

'And the other?' Yldich said.

'There was another force there, another source of purpose.' Yealda's eyes darkened. 'Apparently, this Southern King is not the only driving force behind this expedition to the North.'

'Lord Feyir,' Rom said in a low voice.

'If it is one of the lords, then he isn't working alone,' Yealda said. 'There was a dark presence there. A woman. She was aware of me instantly. She has power. She nearly overpowered me by some force of darkness.'

'Iryna.' Rom's eyes had turned black as pitch.

'Who is she?' Yealda leaned over a little, her eyes bright with interest.

'I don't know, exactly,' Rom said. 'I first saw her during the attack on Woodbury, where she seemed in league with Feyir and his riders. It seems she has been watching us ever since. She even appeared in the House, twice.'

Yealda drew up her brows. 'Really.'

Yldich nodded. 'At first I thought she might be a *Tzanatzi* spirit. One of the restless dead. But since then, Rom has had a chance to speak with her.'

'She's had a bitter life,' Rom said. 'She thinks Feyir will reward her if she helps him get back his inheritance.' He sat shaking his head thinking of the slender girl, outwardly so much like kin that she could have been his sister, alone in the riders' camp. 'She knows who I am. She tried to make me do her will. She has crossed some kind of boundary, and will stop at nothing to get what she wants. I tried to reach her, to get her to side with us, but she wouldn't hear of it.'

'Pity,' Yealda said pensively, 'she would have made a great ally—'

'Contrary to the *Tzanatzi* you do have on your side, who has no clue how to use his skills,' Rom finished, shaking his head. He stared at his hands.

'You'll find a way,' Yldich said softly. 'You already made a difference last night. Think of the lives that have been saved because you held back the Southerners.' Rom looked up.

But for how long?

The low afternoon sun lit up the council room, throwing long shadows across the table where the clan heads were seated.

Yealda rose. 'The Southern army is getting ready to make their next move. We must be ready for them. Also, another force is pitted against us. A *Tzanatzi* woman. She is a great sorcerer, who can dreamwalk like the most seasoned *Yaever*. We have to assume we are being spied upon,' she finished in a grim tone, 'all the time.'

Morven drew up a brow. 'A *Tzanatzi* enemy?' Yealda nodded. 'Well,' Morven said, looking somewhat perturbed. 'Just when I was getting used to a *Tzanatzi* being one of us, one pops up who opposes us like the enemy of old.'

'Just to make things less confusing,' Wérdyris said. 'In the old days,' he added with a grin, 'at least we knew who the enemy was. Even if he did not dare show his face for five hundred years.' The other clan heads chuckled in their beards. Yldich cleared his throat. Silence followed.

'We have to be careful of our speech, even our thoughts. We have to guard them all the time,' he said. 'This woman appears to have the ability to walk anywhere. So be on your guard, and mind whom you speak to about our plans. Now,' he went on, 'I have found seven *Yaever* pupils that are talented enough to help me in the counter-attack. Most are young and they're still in training. But they're the only ones who can help me counter this woman's sorcery. They may also be able to help us fight off the next attack.'

Morven turned to Rom. 'Can't you just make some more of your, uh… fire magic? Like you did this night?'

'It doesn't work that way.' Rom sat staring at his hands as if they did not belong to him. 'I've never done anything like this before. I'm not schooled in—in *Tzanatzi* magic. It's as foreign to me as it is to you. I don't even know if I can do it again.'

'Well, what good is a *Tzanatzi* sorcerer if he can't do *Tzanatzi* magic?' Ullwich's upper lip curved in a sneer.

Morven ignored him. He nodded pensively. 'Seven young *Yaever* pupils and one *Tzanatzi* novice. Seems like you will have to rely on our swords if you want to win this one, Yldich. But I don't like the idea of sitting here wondering when they'll come to get us, like so many rabbits waiting for the cooking pot.'

'Maybe we won't have to,' Rom said suddenly. 'I know the way these people think. They have no inkling of your way of life.' He sat up. 'You could make it appear as if you're carousing into the night to celebrate last night's victory. They will think the warriors are off guard.' His face lit up as he envisaged the scene. 'You could have the musicians play their loudest drinking songs, and have all the lights on in the Great Hal. Those that can't fight can sing and make the kind of noises the Southerners would expect of a barbarian Northern binge.'

Morven drew up his brows. 'Would they think us that dull-witted? To have a drinking bout while they are still here?'

Rom smiled grimly. 'They have no idea what kind of people you are. If you wanted to, you could make them believe anything you liked about the *Einache*.'

Yldich sat up. Lights of amusement danced in his eyes. 'We will turn their own prejudice against them, and gain the element of surprise.' He grinned. The idea appealed to his sense of justice.

'And what then?' said Wérdyris. 'When they take the bait?'

'We will be ready for them,' Yldich said with relish. '*Yaever* and warriors alike. We'll give them a welcome they've never experienced before.'

The rising moon was nearly full, its face the colour of fresh butter. Stars twinkled in the frosty night sky. An owl hooted in the distance. Flimsy clouds flitted across the moon. The silence was getting on Rom's nerves.

'Where are they?' he breathed.

'They'll come,' Yldich said. 'Don't you doubt it. I've never known Yealda to be wrong before.'

Rom sighed noiselessly. Waiting was irksome; it stretched his nerves until they seemed taut as the fiddler's strings. He could hear the man playing in the background, a cheerful tune, meant as an accompaniment to the festivities of warriors who were already more than a little intoxicated.

There was also the rowdy singing one would expect on such an occasion. It sounded thoroughly convincing, especially to someone who did not know that the singers were the elderly and the infirm, acquitting themselves of their task with full abandon. The cheerful glow of the candles spilled out unto the snow. Rom touched the hilt of his sword and wondered whether he would have to use it tonight.

There was sudden hiss of sound. Rom gasped as three arrows struck home and he saw the watcher tumble from the watchtower. It was a youth he had seen practicing with Maetis. A low murmur went through the ranks of the warriors who stood waiting, hidden in the shadows.

Yldich cursed under his breath. 'I had warned him to keep out of sight…'

Rom felt a hot surge of wrath rise from his belly. 'Bastards,' he muttered. He clenched his hands into fists. All at once, the fire deep within was seething like an angry ocean. Rom made a motion to go to the gates. Yldich turned to look at him. He stopped him with one hand on his chest.

'You had better control your anger,' he said in a low tone.

Rom's eyes flashed. 'They killed him. The boy was only fourteen years old. Southern bastards…' The fire rose to his chest, and hands, wanting to be released. His vision was blurring, his ears throbbing with a low, buzzing sound. Tiny flickers of fire leaked from under his fingernails.

Yldich took his arms in an iron-like grip and eyed him with a stern expression on his face. 'Do you want to let your anger and desire for revenge unleash destruction, or do you want to help me prevent bloodshed and save my people?' Rom stared at him. The fire died down. 'Good.' Yldich gave him a final firm shake, and released him. 'Now come with me.' He led the way to the ceremonial spear that was stuck in the earth. Rom trudged along through the snow, his hands in his cloak, his brow furrowed.

'I thought you said the *Einache* were ready to fight to the death,' he said.

Yldich made a rumbling sound in the back of his throat. 'They are,' he said, 'and it may yet come to that. But I will try and prevent it for as long as I can.' He stared in the direction of the Southern camp. 'I'm not only thinking of us,' he said softly. 'I'm thinking of the generations behind us. The Southerners are not going to leave this realm. We'll have to find a way to live with them.'

Rom pulled up a brow. 'Are the clan leaders aware of your line of thinking?'

Yldich grinned. 'They want the same thing I do. To live in peace according to their own ways. But I see further than they do. They may think that if we can defeat Farhardt this time, we will be left alone. But the South is a large territory. There will be other Farhardts. We must find a more permanent solution.'

'And if we can't?'

Yldich's face was grim. 'Then we find our end here.' He took a large double terminated crystal from a leather pouch on his belt. The smaller seven he had divided among the *Yaever* pupils. Eald was one of them.

Rom heard a low, thrumming sound and looked around. The seven *Yaever* pupils, five young boys and two girls, were sitting in a circle in the snow, hidden in the shadows. Their eyes were closed, their faces serene. Clouds were gathering over the House. They moved fast, despite the fact there was no wind. The pressure in the air was changing. Rom could feel it in his ears. They were buzzing. He looked at the *Yaever* pupils. The low humming sound came from their throats.

They're calling the clouds.

Rom stared at them in awe. He stood back as Yldich closed his eyes and started to sing under his breath. He held the crystal in both hands. The song seemed to circle, spiralling upwards, drawing the clouds to one point. They were growing as they wheeled above his head. There was a flash of lightning, and another. The earth rumbled. At the third flash, Rom became aware of the presence of the Southern soldiers. They had climbed the walls without making a sound and were about to come down to attack the House, just like Yldich had intended. The first soldier set foot on the palisades.

'*Na Héach*,' Rom cried. An arrow whizzed past his ear and he hastily stepped back. Yldich had finished his song. He stretched out his hands and a sudden flash of icy rain was hurled from the sky, right at the spot where the Southerners were setting foot on the boards. They stepped back in surprise, shielding their eyes from the vicious rain that stung them with darts of ice.

Rom watched Yldich form snow clouds and pull them towards the walls, where they burst out in disproportionately large hailstones that clattered merrily on the helmets of the Southern soldiers. They thumped rhythmically on the boards, where they froze to the surface to create a slippery slide. He began to feel an inexplicable sense of joy. His hands tingled as he watched Yldich work and after a while, he couldn't help but open them and let the joy run through his arms and fingers.

'*Ayáa a elcaëz*,' he cried, and unleashed a burst of fire that turned Yldich's rain to hot steam. The Southern soldiers held up their hands to shield their faces. The freezing cold turned the water to sleet and they slid cursing down ladders and planks that had suddenly turned to polished glass.

How wonderfully amazing, he thought entranced, *to feel such delight in something that scared me so much before*. It was only comparable to the sensation he had felt when Lakíthra gave him back his power, or the elation when he shared himself with Maetis, giving her his body and his heart. He let out another flare of fire that danced on the palisades. He heard himself laugh out loud for sheer joy.

'That's enough now, lad,' Yldich said.

Fireflies in the dark, he thought, as he saw the dark eyes shining with rare exhilaration. 'We only want to defend ourselves.' Yldich made him step back. 'I don't want to give Farhardt any reason to keep this war going longer than it should.'

While the soldiers who had climbed the palisades were driven back, the *Einache* warriors crept through the side doors to attack the Southerners in the flank. Because they had not been used in years, they were almost completely hidden by mossy growths and ferns.

'*Na'Héach*,' the warriors cried in one loud voice as they leapt out, nearly scaring the first Southerners who laid eyes on them out of their wits. They did look frightfully like *Einache* ghosts, with their hair flaming in the light of the torches, their bright eyes and fell swords. Lightening flashed as they attacked, and blue fire leapt from the tips of their swords. It was the last straw.

'Retreat,' a Southern captain cried, his nerves already frayed by the freak hailstorms that drove the horses crazy and the deadly ice, that sent his men crashing to the ground before his eyes. He had counted ten fallen already, and the attack had not even truly begun. The call was taken up by the others.

'Retreat,' the cry went around. 'Retreat. Back to camp, now.' The earth rumbled one more time as they hastily started to wade through the snow that had turned to mush, and was already freezing over.

Iryna stood looking out over the dark fields in the direction of the *Einache* defences that proved so unexpectedly difficult to breach. She was standing just out of reach of the icy pellets of hail. A slow, dark anger welled up in her and she clenched her hands into fists.

'*Câladirce*,' she muttered. The dark night air seemed to swirl around her, lifting dark tendrils of hair around her face. Feyir looked aside at her and a shudder ran over his skin. He felt a dislike for the young woman that bordered on hatred, although why this should be so, he wouldn't be able to say. He didn't care enough to want to find out.

When all this is over, he promised himself, *I will be rid of her*.

One by one, the clan heads and their warriors returned to the Great Hall. The musicians were still playing, and at one point one of the clan heads decided they might as well have a modest feast to celebrate the Southerners' retreat. Kegs of apple cider were brought in and after a while, most clan heads were grinning inanely at their tables, hoisting large mugs full of cider at every elaborate toast.

Morven had pulled Rom over to his table. More and more warriors were returning from the fight. Some of them clapped Rom on the back with gusto and made him spill his cider.

'*Ya'érsi,*' one said with a grin. 'You may not have much skill with the sword, but you've shown yourself to be one of us.'

Ullwich was sitting at the other end of the long table with his party. 'One might wonder if we aren't digging our own graves, nurturing a *Tzanatzi* in our midst,' he grumbled. Rom flinched. Then something shifted within him. He drew himself up.

'You may have forgotten,' he said in a clear voice, 'that I have pledged the Oath of *Faraër*. But I haven't.'

'And what would a *Tzanatzi's* word be worth, I wonder,' Ullwich mumbled, just loud enough for Rom to hear.

'One might wonder at the trustworthiness of a man who habitually doubts the word of another,' Morven remarked in a dry tone. There was nothing wrong with his hearing. He looked Ullwich calmly in the eye, until the latter seemed to shrink a little. He muttered something under his breath and turned to engage in conversation with the man next to him. 'Don't you mind him, lad,' Morven said to Rom. 'He's always been like this. Habitually ill-tempered.'

After sharing one celebratory drink with the clan heads, Yldich left the hubbub of the Great Hall and stood at one of the windows. He stared out over the snow, in the direction of the Southerners' camp.

Maetis found him there. She took his right arm and nestled up to him as she had done so often when she was a child. He sighed and pulled her against him without taking his eyes off the fields.

'We won't hold them off indefinitely.'

After a few more rounds of cider, Morven's warriors managed to talk Rom into joining in their song. He got many of the words wrong, much to their hilarity. Eldairc sat looking at them with a grin on his face. Rom looked different, he thought. For as long as he'd known the *Tzanatzi* there had been a kind of defensiveness to him, an invisible wall of reservation. It seemed to have thawed a bit, to the point where he sat grinning shyly when the warriors cheerfully mocked his halting *Einache*, or laughed when they nudged him to get him to join in with some rowdy refrain. His cheeks were flushed with colour, which contrasted with his pale skin, and his dark eyes were shining.

It was then that Eldairc noticed something strange. The young man cast no shadow. No wait, there it was: a thin, watery shadow, it fell shakily across the floor behind him. It faded, blurring, then became dark again like any true, self-respecting shadow would. Eldairc drew up his brows and blinked a few times, then shook his head. Must be the flickering candles, he thought to himself. And the cider. He put down his empty mug with a decisive thump. That was it. He was going to bed.

Eleven
Haunted

Rom travelled in a whirl of colours, of pale pinks and sunny orange, when he became aware of a presence in the distance. It was a woman with long, midnight hair and warm, laughing eyes. She held out her arms in an inviting gesture. He hurried towards her, longing for her embrace. He did not know her, yet she was as familiar to him as the mother who had never wanted him.

Suddenly, it dawned on him who she was. His *Tzanatzi* mother, the one who had raised the man he had never been. Riórdirým's mother. The realization stilled the longing in his heart and he stopped to look at her.

It was then that he became aware of something dark that was rising from the ground. It was horribly cold and persistent, and crept up his legs, feeding on his life. He fought to get away, but the cold had leeched onto him like a creeping vine. An acrid smoke filled his nostrils. He clawed at his throat, trying to loose the darkness' hold. He was faintly aware of the woman's voice in the background. She was screaming.

Someone shook him and he opened his eyes, struggling to wake up, like a drowning man fighting his way to the surface. Maetis was yelling in his ear. 'Wake up. Rom, wake up.'

He sat up suddenly, gasping for breath.

'The *Tahiéra*. It has come.'

It was early morning. The watery sun was just pouring out its faint light over the snowy fields. Markel paused from his work to relieve himself against one of the trees at the edge of camp. He undid his trousers, released a small sigh of relief, and started humming a crude tune that had once been popular in certain taverns and brothels in Érskitha. He became aware of a movement behind him. A strange shiver crept along his back.

'Did that harlot of a mother of yours never tell you not to sneak up on people?' He turned his head to glare at whichever rider was behind him. His trousers dropped to the ground as he stood staring wide-eyed in the black eyes and haggard faces of three *Tzanatzi* warriors. In the frozen instant before the sword slashed his throat, he dimly noticed the absence of breath plumes in the air.

Rom was in the washroom, wiping the traces of sleep from his face with ice-cold water from the bucket, when something, a movement in the corner of his eye, made him look up. There was something strange about his reflection. It blurred. His eyes widened as he stared in the dark eyes that looked back at him. A ripple went over the burnished metal of the mirror like the surface of a still lake being stirred by the wind.

Rom gasped in surprise. Shadows began filling the mirror. The young man's features changed. Darkness ate away at his cheeks, his eyes, which hollowed out with silent despair. Rom suppressed a scream. He turned around and fled.

As he hastened through the corridor to Yldich's chamber, he was overcome by the unnerving sensation that he was somewhere else entirely. He stood still, one hand against the wall, concentrating on the grain of the wood beneath his fingertips. Another wave of dizziness went through him. For a moment shadows filled his vision and he felt the cold, hard surface of living rock. The air became dank and cold. A dark mist swirled around him. His hand went to the crystal he wore around his neck day and night.

'Na'Héach,' he breathed. He held it so tightly he could feel the hard edges of the stone digging into his palm. The pain helped clear his vision. 'Na'Héach.' He could see the stone tiles of the corridor under his feet again. He frowned with concentration. When he was reasonably sure he was back in the plane of everyday reality, he began to run.

'Something's wrong,' Rom blurted out as he burst into Yldich's study.

Yldich grumbled. 'You don't say.' He pointed at the window. The Southerner's camp was blurred by hazy, indistinct figures. Rom stared at them open-mouthed. When he looked a little longer, he could discern the helmets and spears of *Einache* warriors. Ghost warriors. A shiver ran over his back. 'They were first spotted this morning,' Yldich said. 'They scared the wits out of the kitchen girl who was throwing out the slops.'

'I count at least fifty.' Maetis said. She was frowning.

'This may sound silly,' Eldairc said in a hopeful tone, 'but wouldn't they work with us? They're *Einache*, after all. Even if they've been dead for five hundred years. Couldn't we get them to fight on our side?'

Yldich smiled grimly and shook his head. 'They are locked in the past. The only enemy they would recognize would be the *Tzanatzi*. I doubt they would so much as notice the Southerners, even if they walked right through them.' Rom sat down, shaking his head. Maetis sat down beside him and took his hand. 'You had better stay indoors,' Yldich said. 'You had a narrow escape last time. You may not be that lucky again.'

A shadow stalked King Farhardt's camp. It slew quietly, and left no trace of its passing but the dead bodies of soldiers, stable lads and kitchen wenches, their eyes glassy and wide with horror, their bodies distorted as if frozen in the throes of death. No-one knew whence it came, and when it would strike the next time. When the sixth body of a man was discovered at the edge of the wood, not smothered, but lying in a pool of his own blood, Farhardt ordered the nobles and captains to his tent for a council.

'There is a killer among us,' Farhardt said, as he warmed his hands on a cup of heated wine. In these isolated, out-of-the-way lands, he was always cold, no matter how many layers of wool he put on under his fur-trimmed cloak. The nobles murmured amongst themselves uneasily. Their sense of superiority was already being gnawed upon by the freak occurrences that had chased them from the *Einache* stronghold twice. It was unheard of. It made them edgy.

'Ghosts,' one of them muttered under his breath. His neighbour nodded in superstitious assent. Farhardt was a practical man, but this could not be said for all of his nobles. They knew next to nothing about the supernatural, but feared it the more. Farhardt caught the remark.

'Nonsense,' he said in a gruff voice, 'ghosts do not smother people or slash their throats. If they exist at all, which I very much doubt.' He smartly put down his cup. His brow was furrowed with annoyance. 'What we have here, my lords, is a threat to morale. The sooner we root it out, the better. Now. Have you any idea who this murderer may be? It must be someone who can move about freely without being seen, by day and by night.'

'Why, my lord,' said Lord Erckhardt, a noble in his late thirties with brown hair and sharp blue eyes, 'would anyone start killing soldiers and kitchen wenches at random? It doesn't make sense.'

Feyir sat staring at the King, his amber eyes narrowed like a cat's. His thoughts circled the *Tzanatzi* woman and her spells, the dark, swirling cold she had conjured up at more than one occasion, the disembodied voices, and her nightly visits to the *Einache* House.

And who knows what else she is up to, he thought with a sense of unease. He trusted her like he trusted his men, which was to say, as far as he could see her. Although she was in liege with him, she had no reason to love the Southerners. He fidgeted with his cup of wine.

'Do you have anything to add, Feyir?' Farhardt asked, noticing his tension. Feyir winced inwardly at the familiar use of his name. Farhardt would not reinstate him to his rightful position as a noble until the Northern territories had been subdued.

'No, my lord,' he said quietly.

'Maybe,' Lord Weldr proposed, 'the killer is a traitor, someone who is being paid by the barbarian clans to sow confusion.'

Erckhardt drew up a brow. 'A Southern soldier who risks torture and death just to supplement his wages? There are easier ways to make money.'

'Whatever the case may be,' Farhardt concluded, 'I want every House to set a continuous watch at their tents. We have to be vigilant day and night. Whatever reason this person may have for undermining our cause, we shall be ready for him.'

Later that morning Rom was sitting in a corner of the kitchen discussing the possibilities of fire magic with Eldairc, when Yldich strode in. 'You had better come with me,' Yldich said. 'It appears we have visitors.'

'Visitors?' Rom stared at him in surprise. 'Who?'

Yldich smiled grimly. 'Your people.'

'What—where did they com from? When did they appear?' Rom sputtered, white-faced and wide-eyed. Yldich pulled him through the corridor by his arm, closely followed by Eldairc, who quickly grabbed their cloaks from the chair where they hung to dry.

'My *Yaever* students spotted them,' Yldich said. 'Odún, to be precise.' He shook his head. 'The boy had the fright of his life.'

They went through the doors and donned their cloaks. As they stepped outside, Rom and Eldairc were about to go left, in the direction of the Northern camp.

Yldich shook his head. 'Not that way,' he said, and motioned to their right, in the direction of the Forest. 'Over there.' They climbed the palisades and looked out over the fields. Rom gazed at the snow-clad grassy slopes and fields, the bare trees, and saw the familiar profile of the Cliffs in the distance. It was the direction of Gardeth Battle Plain.

They could not possibly have been mistaken for mortal men. Eldairc stared at the dark figures that stood watching the House in silence. A low mist was curling at their feet; their pale, haggard faces were so translucent you could see the branches of the trees through them. Their black hair trailed around their heads, although there was no breeze to lift up the midnight strands. Their eyes were dark pits, conveying nothing. Rom put a hand to his mouth.

'There're so many of them,' he whispered. The dark, eerie figures at the edge of the Forest provoked a sense of deep sadness, rather than fear. He wondered in silence how many of them he had known, when his shadow self fought for them. He wondered how many had died in ambushes alone in the woods, or together on the battle field. Somehow he felt his heart go out to the dark, silent figures.

'I wonder what will happen once they get wind of the *Einache* Dead,' Eldairc's dry voice sounded behind him. He was talking to Yldich.

'I'd rather not be in the way, once they've laid eyes on each other,' Yldich said.

'Couldn't you spirit them away or something? Kill them?' Eldairc's voice continued. 'If it's possible to kill those who are already dead... can't the *Yaever* sing them to the Underworld or something?'

'No!' Rom whirled around. He lowered his voice as he saw the surprise in their faces at his vehemence. 'You can't,' he said quietly. 'They're—they're still my people.'

'Well now.' Yldich pensively tugged at his short beard. 'This presents us with an interesting problem—'

You. Tzanatzi. A sharp voice went through Rom's head. He turned around and saw the familiar figure of the *Tzanatzi* woman standing in the snow before the palisades, ahead of the silent, waiting shadows. She was the only one who had left any footprints. He shuddered.

'Iryna,' he said sharply. Yldich and Eldairc leaned over the edge to get a better view. Yldich sucked in his breath at the sight of the slender figure.

'Sorceress,' he breathed. He cursed himself. He had left his *Yaever* attributes on the table in his study, including the large double-terminated crystal.

'The time has come for you to choose,' the dark girl cried with her voice, so the others would hear as well. She held up her left hand, and the sun glinted on a silver dagger. 'I have studied the ancient scrolls, and dreamwalked my way into the past. I have gained knowledge you and your *Einache* wizards would shrink from in fear. It has given me much. It has given me control of the Dead, and of the Entity that was bound to them at their passing.'

She drew a symbol in the air with the dagger, and cried a word that rung painfully in their ears. The low mist grew, as the ghostly figures grew more palpable. It loomed over them and ominously leaned over in the direction of the *Einache* House.

'The *Tahiéra*,' Rom breathed. Eldairc and Yldich stared at it. Their faces were drawn. Yldich felt his lungs constrict and clenched his hands into fists. He had already had first-hand contact with the entity, when they were travelling through the Forest, and Rom had pulled him out of its deadly stranglehold. To see it hover right before his eyes, like a monstrous black snake about to strike, was extremely disconcerting.

'How much longer will you deny your legacy? How much longer will you deny the power of your true name?' the girl cried. 'The power you aroused last night was visible on all planes. Your people have recognized you. How can you desert them? Will you not join us and help us regain our rightful position?'

'I can't help you,' Rom said. He felt strangely guilty. Somehow, the girl had touched a nerve. 'You would wield the power of fire as a tool for destruction. I can't help you.'

'This is the second time you have denied me,' the girl said in a low voice. Despite its tone, her voice easily carried across the field that divided her from the House. Somehow she communicated with more than her mortal voice, Rom guessed. He shuddered. 'I will give you one day and one night to reconsider,' the girl said. 'If you refuse me a third time, the Dead will invade the House.'

'How did a girl that young gain control over such an ancient and powerful entity like the *Tahiéra*?' Yealda wondered out loud. She had joined Yldich and Rom in Yldich's study.

'She appears to be unusually talented,' Yldich said. 'She has dreamwalked her way into the House and our chambers, and even our dreams. She may be young, but I surmise the way she has been using her power, and the contact she has had with the *Tahiéra* has corrupted her.' He rested his chin in his hand. 'Now, she may think she controls the entity. But I wonder if it's not the other way round.'

Rom stared at him. 'What do you mean?'

Yldich pensively stared at the fields in the distance. 'Well. If what you found out about the *Tahiéra* is true, then it is still bound to the Unnamed One. It would surprise me if a magical entity like this, that once summoned, remains for five hundred years, will serve two masters. It follows that unwittingly, the girl might be doing the Unnamed one's bidding.'

'But to what end?' Rom said. He felt cold.

'Well, whatever his purpose might be,' Yldich said, 'I doubt it entails the well-being of the *Einache* people.'

The remainder of that day, all talk in the House of the Deer was of ghosts and spirits. Many of the inhabitants had already caught a glimpse of the eerie figures at the edge of the Forest, or the grim *Einache* ghosts on the other side of the fields. They talked about it in hushed voices in the hallways, to avoid scaring the children. Most of them had already taken a peek while their parents weren't looking, and scared each other with ghost stories.

The clan leaders and their men were in the Great Hall. They drank watered-down beer, and ate their rations of bread with pickled onions and thin slices of cheese.

'What's the fuss all about—they're ghosts, aren't they?' A young warrior of Yldich's house said. 'They're dead. What are they going to do—frighten us to death?'

Morven scowled. 'We've seen what these ghosts are capable of.' Two of his men paled at the memory. They hastily rearranged their weapons and fussed at their clothing. One of them took a deep draught of beer to hide his unease in.

'Not to mention the dark whatsit that sucked the life out of my men,' Ullwich said in a low voice.

'The *Tahiéra*.' Eldairc sat down beside him.

'That's what I said,' Ullwich grumbled, and gulped down his beer.

In the afternoon, word went round that there would be another council of the clan heads. They made their way to Yldich's council room with mounting curiosity. Rom was invited as well. He had taken a seat at the other end of the table, opposite Yldich. He was still thinking of the *Tzanatzi* wraiths, waiting on the edge of the Forest. An uneasy sadness was lodged under his heart. Once everybody was seated, Yldich began.

'The situation is grave,' Yldich said. He stood up and faced the clan leaders one by one, as was his wont at formal meetings. Lastly, he gazed at Rom. 'We are caught between the hammer and the anvil. On the one hand, we have Farhardt and his army, demanding our complete submission. We have managed to hold his army back twice. But we will not be able to hold them back forever.' He paused, looking around the table.

'On the other hand,' Yldich continued, 'we have the restless Dead and the rising darkness. We have found it is the *Tahiéra*, the ancient entity the Unnamed One summoned to conquer our lands. As Rom has found the thing has no will of its own, it must still be bound to the will of the one who called it forth. The will of the Unnamed One.' They stared at him, their faces drawn.

'Are you saying... he is still alive?' Morven said in a husky voice.

'In a way,' Yldich said, his face grim. 'Rom has true-dreamed his way to the Other World. When the mage was subdued, the *Yaever* not only banned his spirit to the Underworld, but cursed his people as well. As long as the Unnamed One remains bound, they can never have peace. As long as the Unnamed One is in the Underworld, his people adrift, the *Tahiéra* remains. It would seem, my friends, that our own curse has turned on us.' They sat staring at him as they digested this piece of information.

'Do you mean... we brought this on ourselves?' Olwen said, his brows bristling ominously.

'It's not that simple,' Yldich said, shaking his head. 'What I mean to say is that both sides are responsible here. And they will need to join forces if they are to resolve it.'

'What are you saying?' Morven said.

'While I hold the House against the Southern forces and the restless Dead with my *Yaever* pupils, someone will have to go to the source of the trouble.'

Rom stared at Yldich. A shiver ran along his spine. 'What do you mean?'

'Someone will need to find the *Tzanatzi* mage, and end this curse once and for all,' Yldich said. 'Someone will need to descend into the Underworld.' There was a deep silence as they all stared at him. Yldich looked down at his hands. He seemed to be deliberating. Finally, he looked up. He looked straight into Rom's eyes. 'I think that someone should be you.'

A murmur rose around the table as all the clan leaders began talking at once. Yldich didn't heed them. In the midst of the gesturing, arguing *Einache* leaders, Yldich sat looking calmly at Rom. Rom felt as if he was sinking, as if he were falling and there was nothing to hold him back from plummeting down a black abyss. He stared back into the calm grey eyes.

'You—you knew it would come to this. You knew all along,' he whispered.

'You can't ask the boy to go to the Underworld, Yldich,' Morven boomed over the uproar. 'It would be the death of him. Look at him. He's a mere child—'

'*Let* him go,' Ullwich countered. His eyes were hard. 'Let him go and clean up the mess his people brought upon us—or perish in the attempt....' Morven shot him an indignant glance. Yldich didn't heed them. He sat looking at Rom in silence, waiting, like an eagle riding the storm.

Rom looked around the table at the gesticulating clan leaders. A few months ago, his sceptical Southern upbringing would have had him question even the existence of such a place as the Underworld. But seeing the clear and distinct fear in the eyes of the big-boned, rugged men at the mere mention of it made him drop his scepticism.

He thought of the snatches of stories he had heard in his childhood, about demons and monsters, none of them very reassuring. Then he thought of what Yldich had told him. It was equally disturbing.

His thoughts went to the gathering army outside the walls, row upon row of tents, and well-equipped soldiers, lying in wait like a great beast of prey, biding its time for a chance to snap its jaws shut and crush them all.

He thought of Maetis, of Eald, and Eldairc, of all the *Einache* he had gotten to know, the cooks, the warriors, the serving girls, caught between the threat of Southern violence and slavery, and the looming presence of the *Tahiéra*, preying on their lives. It was only a matter of time before they were annihilated by one or the other. There was no way out.

He saw in his mind's eye the little villages of the *Einache*, strewn through the hills like little flowers in a wasteland of rocks, where five hundred years ago, they had bloomed in their hundreds. He envisaged the people of the House, the men and women at their tasks, the children roaming free, running barefoot through the fields. A great love for them filled his heart. Even the gruff, bearded warriors quarrelling amongst themselves were precious to him, and he felt a great longing to keep them all safe. But there was no way. Unless it led through darkness.

He swallowed. For a moment, he felt his heart expand. It was as if he was growing, expanding in awareness, his senses stretching wider and wider until he felt he could envelop them all, hold them in his hand to keep them from harm. For a moment, it felt as if it could be done. Then he came back, and was Rom again. He suddenly felt very small. He took a deep breath to steady himself.

'I'll do it,' he said.

Though it seemed he had hardly spoken loud enough to be heard over the din, the clan leaders fell silent one by one and turned their heads to stare at him in shock. Yldich stood up. There was a strange expression in his eyes, one Rom hadn't seen there before. It reminded him of something ancient, and patient, something older than the roots of the oldest tree, weary beyond exhaustion, that suddenly caught a glimpse of long-awaited release. He saw it only for an instant. Then a broad smile lit up Yldich's face.

'*Kalantíri ya hwerdi Sanáyah,*' he said in a clear voice that rang across the room. He came up to Rom and embraced him so forcefully he felt the air being pushed out of his lungs.

When he finally let him go, Rom peered up at him. 'So—how do I get there?'

'There is only one way. And that is through *ayúrdimae.*'

They were back in Yldich's study. Yldich rummaged through his chests, gathering little bags of herbs, and bundles of soft leather of various sizes. Rom wondered what they held.

'Do you mean—I can just *dream* my way to the Underworld?' he said in an airy tone. He felt strangely relieved. For some reason, he had imagined the passage into the Underworld to be a much more difficult undertaking, involving dank and dangerous tunnels guarded by demons and other, less defined and even more gruesome beings.

Yldich turned around and gripped his arms with force. 'You have to be very careful.' He fixed Rom with a stern gaze. 'The only way to the Underworld leads through deep *ayúrdimae*. As I taught you, in deep *ayúrdimae*, you'll be liable to forget that your body is in fact here, lying on the bed. If you forget, and start believing you're wholly *there*, you're vulnerable. It's dangerous, Rom. If you're hurt, or killed in that state, your body will believe it and make it so; and if you get into trouble, there's nothing I can do to help you.' Rom swallowed.

'But there's something I can give you to help you along the way.' Yldich released him and turned back to his *Yaever* things. He opened a leather pouch and took out an object that was partially rounded, like a globe. He set it on the table. 'This is a scrying crystal, such as my *Yaever* pupils use. It can contain and transform energy. Now I know that I'm not training you to become a *Yaever*.' He smiled. 'Still, the abilities you unwittingly seem to have, resemble those of *Yaever* pupils close enough, and in need, you should be able to use it.'

He turned the globe until it caught a ray of light. Rom came a little closer so he could see. The light seemed to be caught in the centre of the crystal. He held his breath in amazement. Yldich turned the globe while muttering something under his breath, and suddenly, the crystal threw back the light in a thousand tiny brilliant beams.

Rom gasped and narrowed his eyes against the light that suddenly flooded the room. 'How did you do that?'

Yldich smiled. 'The crystal will respond to energy that is concentrated by purpose. Words can do it. A *Yaever* song can do it. Even a subconscious desire might do it. But instead of leaving your use of this crystal to chance, I'd rather you learned an *Einache* phrase that might come in handy while journeying through the Underworld.' Rom looked up and nodded.

'Good. Now, the one I'll teach you will help you make use of any source of light, even the memory of sunlight. It will also hide you from prying eyes. Hold it in your hands, turn it until it catches the light, and repeat this word three times: *Ílumae*.'

'*Ílumae,*' Rom muttered, while he turned the dome around on the table. He found the light of the sun and kept it still. '*Ílumae. Ílumae.*' His eyes widened as the crystal took the light and blazed like a second sun. The air changed before his eyes. It rippled and swayed, until he could hardy see Yldich's face.

'Remember, it is not the words the crystal responds to,' he heard Yldich say from the other side of the glassy curtain of rippling air. 'It's the energy. The words help you concentrate on your purpose. The crystal merely responds to your *intention*. The crystal will illuminate even if there's no light source to work with. Simply concentrate on the memory of sunlight.' Rom released the crystal and the light faded.

'Now, there is an important thing you must know about the Underworld,' Yldich said. 'As I told you, in deep *ayúrdimae*, you will take so much of your essence with you, that in fact, more of you will be down there, than over here. Now, the same is true for any object you take with you on your journey, at least, the ones that contain energy.'

'What objects would that be?' Rom's interest was raised.

Yldich motioned at the sword at his side. 'Objects like your *Einache* sword, for instance. It has an energy and purpose all of its own. The crystal you have carried around your neck all this time. And, of course, this scrying crystal here.'

'So, I can take anything that has any meaning for me with me to the Underworld?'

'Anything that has sufficient energy.' Yldich took the crystal dome and put it back in the pouch. 'Oh, and by the way,' he said over his shoulder, 'on your way into the Underworld, you might encounter some dragons.' His tone was airy.

Rom stared at him with wide eyes. 'What?'

'Dragons,' Yldich said, as if Rom hadn't understood the word. 'You might encounter some.'

'You can't be serious.' Rom stared at him open-mouthed.

'I can, when I need to be.' Yldich grinned. 'And you'll still meet some dragons. Two of them, to be exact.'

Rom's brow furrowed as he attempted to digest the idea. 'Why—why didn't you tell me this before?'

Yldich snorted faintly. 'No use worrying about something you can't change. Just stay calm, hold your ground, and everything will be fine.' He gathered his bundles of herbs.

'That's easy for you to say,' Rom muttered. 'You're not the one who's going to come face to face with dragons.'

'Oh, and another thing,' Yldich said without looking up from his work. 'Don't worry about finding your way. You don't need to search for a path. The path will find *you*.'

Rom raised his brows. 'How do you mean?'

Yldich tied the leather string of a bundle. 'You'll see.'

Early that evening, Yldich was in his study measuring the exact amount of herbs he needed for Rom's journey. His brow was furrowed with concentration, his grey eyes narrowed to slits. Yealda sat at the table and watched him work with a pensive expression in her eyes.

'I have to be very careful,' Yldich muttered. He took the small stem of a herb and crushed the golden leaves over a stone mortar. 'Too little *alderae*, and he will not go down deep enough to be able to let go of his body. Too much *darchvar*,' he took a bundle of powdered root and added a tiny spoonful, 'and his heart will stop beating altogether.'

Yealda stared at his hands. 'All this because of my curse... now that I do know him, I would hate for his death to be on my head.'

'Look at it this way,' Yldich said in a gentle tone. 'You have also given him the one chance to free himself. To finally release the guilt and claim his own life.'

'But at what cost?' she said softly.

'You're sending him to the Underworld?' Eldairc said, his green eyes wide with dismay. They had gathered around the hearth in Yldich's study. 'Alone?'

'Of course not. I'll go with him,' Maetis said. There was a wilful curve to her mouth.

'No, you won't,' Yldich said. He sat on the hearthstones, his back to the fire. Maetis stared at him. She was not used to being opposed by her father. Neither was she used to not getting her way.

'What do you mean, *Dáydach*? You can't let him go by himself.' She straightened as if she readied herself for a fight.

Yldich looked at her. 'You'll be needed here, where battle might flare up at any time. You are my heir. People will except you to lead them in battle should anything happen to me.'

'Nothing could happen to you,' she whispered with wide eyes. 'You've always been here for us...'

Yldich smiled. 'I'm not invincible, Maetis. I may not always be here. You have to be ready to lead the *Einache* in case the time comes when I'm no longer here.'

'But that's no reason to send Rom off on his own,' Eald said. He sat cross-legged on a cushion on the floor, his elbows on his knees, his narrow face serious. 'I'll go with him.' He saw Yldich slowly shake his head. 'I'm the only other really talented true-dreamer there is,' Eald added without a trace of false modesty. 'He might need my help.' Yldich suppressed a smile. As Eald saw him waver, a look of triumph began to form on his face.

'You're not coming,' Rom said forcefully.

'Rom—' Yldich began.

'He's too young. I won't have you risk his life again.'

'He wasn't too young to be taken by Feyir's riders,' Yldich said softly. 'He won't be too young to perish when the Dead come or Farhardt's troops overpower us.'

Rom stared at him, his eyes black. 'No.' His tone of voice was unusually determined. 'It's too dangerous. I will go alone.'

Yldich sat thinking for a while. He turned to Eald. 'I'm sorry lad,' he said softly. 'I think Rom's right. You'd better stay here, and help us keep an eye on the Southern army.' Eald pursed his lips and nodded, his face a picture of reluctant compliance.

Later that evening there would be a gathering in the Great Hall to mark Rom's departure. Rom found his usual anxiety about *Einache* social gatherings dwindle into nothing now he was faced with the enormity of descending into the Underworld. He was early; the kitchen lads and girls were still busy clearing tables and lighting fresh candles. He went to one of the hearths and lowered himself in a big seat. He stared thoughtlessly into the flames.

A large shape moved between him and the fire. He looked up. Morven stood before him. The big clan leader lowered himself gingerly and sat on the hearthstones.

'I was thinking,' Morven said. 'You're going on a dangerous journey tonight.' Rom nodded, wondering what was coming. Morven released a breath and pulled at his beard. 'When the call came from Yldich, saying the *Einache* should gather in the face of danger, I knew some of us might not be getting back.' He reached inside his tunic and took out a small object. 'When the *Einache* go on such a journey, they take a piece of home with them.' He opened a big hand. On the calloused palm there lay a single white, smoothly polished stone.

'This pebble is from the river that runs near my House. I always carry it with me on my travels. Now you,' he said as he gazed at Rom, 'strike me as something of a wanderer.' Rom swallowed and nodded. 'You may not have a piece of home to take with you,' Morven continued. 'So I thought I'd give you mine.' He held out his hand and laid the pebble in Rom's. As his fingers closed around the smooth, round stone, Rom lifted his face and blinked at the clan leader, searching for words with which to thank him.

Morven laid a hand on his shoulder. 'May it bring you home, wherever you go.'

As the evening progressed, more and more *Einache* came to join Rom in the Great Hall. They were unusually quiet; when they talked amongst each other it was in hushed voices, and even their gestures were less expressive than usual. It gave the atmosphere a strange solemn feel.

He noticed people look at him from time to time, talk under their breath to their neighbours, and look back at him, with a silent nod. Many warriors would press his shoulder in passing, or nod at him in silence. It moved him and unnerved him at the same time.

It's like attending my own funeral, he thought grimly to himself. He pushed the thought away quickly as he accepted a cup of mead from Eldairc. Rom dimly noticed the young *Einache* had brushed his hair for the occasion. It nearly made him laugh.

I guess there are only two occasions on which anyone could get him to do that. His wedding, and my wake.

Élora joined them. She slipped an arm through Eldairc's. The slender girl was dressed in a simple long gown of creamy wool, her copper hair tied back in long braids. Her round cheeks were blushing as always, but her eyes were serious.

'Eldairc told me what you're going to do for us.' He nodded. 'I think it's very brave of you. Especially, since—because of—what you are....' Rom swallowed, not knowing what to say. Eldairc saved him.

'I don't think it is so much bravery, as total ignorance,' he said in a dry tone. 'He's from the South, you know. The man has no idea what to expect. He doesn't even believe in mountain trolls.'

The girl gave him a slight push. 'You can never take anything seriously, can you?' To Rom's relief, they started a friendly squabble. He looked around the Hall and wondered at Maetis' absence. He hadn't seen her since the gathering in Yldich's study. He wondered uneasily if she kept away out of anger, because Yldich had forbidden her to follow him on his journey.

Suddenly he felt Yldich's familiar presence at his right. The man had come up beside him, and Rom hadn't even noticed.

He moves as soundlessly as a cat. How does he do it? he thought, and not for the first time. Yldich pressed his shoulder much as the warriors had done.

'How are you, now?' he said.

Rom nodded. 'Fine.' He fidgeted with his drink. 'Yldich, where is Maetis? Isn't she coming?' Yldich took a cup of mead from a table.

'There was something she needed to do,' he said softly. 'She'll join us shortly.' He finished his drink. 'Meanwhile, I will speak a few words in your honour. I promise I'll keep it brief,' he said with a grin, and left Rom's side to go and stand in the middle of the Great Hall. People were so unusually quiet he hardly needed to raise his voice to make himself heard.

'*Ya mérweda.* We have come together,' he began, 'in honour of Rom's journey.' He took a deep breath and looked out over the gathered *Einache* who looked at him attentively. 'These are strange and trying times. We are faced with two challenges. Outside, we have the Southern army, threatening our way of life. On the other plane, we have the rising dark that has plagued us for years.

It has finally shown its true face. It is the past, which haunts us. It's our own curse, that many years ago, has chained us to hatred and condemnation, much as it has chained our enemy to the Underworld, the mage who brought his army to Gardeth Battle Plain. Tonight, Rom will travel to the Underworld to end the curse once and for all, so we can live our lives in peace.'

'I thought he was going to keep it brief,' Eldairc whispered to Élora. She chuckled and gave him another thump on the arm.

But how does he think I am going to do it? Rom found himself wonder.

'Tonight in front of you all, I say goodbye to my foster son, and hope we will meet again in the clear light of day, when all battles have been fought and peace has been restored.' Yldich motioned for Rom to come forward. '*Encalimae faire éntme,*' he said, and embraced him.

'*Encalimae,*' Rom whispered, as Yldich let him go. It was then that he saw Maetis approach them in the middle of the Hall. She wore a loose shawl over her head, like a cowl that was draped over her shoulders and back. It made her look like a woman in mourning, Rom thought uneasily. He took her hands. She smiled at him, though her face was pale.

'*Dáydach* has taught me somewhat of energy,' she said. 'Objects of power, as well as things of the body have their own power. As he will not have me accompany you to the Underworld, I decided to give you this.' She laid something in his hands that was soft, and woven of a light, shining material. It was braided into an intricate knot.

'Maetis,' he whispered, recognizing its colour. He pulled back the scarf from her head, revealing a mass of springy copper curls. They had nearly reached to her knees. Now they curled around her shoulders like a halo of red gold. He softly smoothed back a loose curl that had fallen over her brow.

'It's an *Ayéldi Eärwéa*, an...*infinity loop*, I think you would call it in your language,' she said. 'It has been braided into a knot that curves back into itself. *Einache* women weave them for their lovers, and only they know how to make them. It is said it will always bring the bearer home, no matter how far he travels.' He reached out his arms and pulled her towards him. He kissed her in front of the clan leaders and their people, the warriors and the *Yaever*, and didn't care what anyone might think. A surprised murmur went up from the gathered *Einache*.

Maetis' voice whispered in his ear. 'Please come back to me safely.'

The fire in Yldich's hearth produced eerie shadows on the walls of the study. Hours before, he had arranged for a cot and some bedding to be brought to his chambers for Rom's journey.

'I want to be able to keep an eye on you at all times,' he said to Rom, who stared at the blankets and sheepskins with some trepidation. 'In this room, I have all the *Yaever* attributes I might need.' He motioned at the bed and Rom went and sat on its edge. He felt oddly reluctant to lie down.

'Yldich,' he said, as he watched the other man gather his *Yaever* things. 'Will you promise me something?' Yldich turned and looked at him. He set a cup and a glass vial, holding an amber liquid, on the table.

'Of course,' he said. 'If it is within my power,' he added carefully.

'If I don't come back...will you do for me what you did for Eald's people?'

Yldich stared at him. 'What do you mean?'

'If I die, will you come and release my spirit?'

Yldich looked into the eyes that were dark with an indeterminate fear. He shook his head. 'You'll be fine,' he said in a cheerful tone. 'In a few days, maybe even a few hours, you will be back—'

Rom shook his head, refusing to budge. 'But if I'm not...will you come and release me, so I don't have to wander in the Underworld?' Yldich released a breath. He laid a hand on Rom's shoulder.

'I promise,' he said.

Yldich carefully poured the exact amount of liquid from the vial in the cup. There was a soft knock on the door and Maetis came in. She sat down beside Rom and took his hand. They sat holding hands in silence. They had said everything they had needed to say earlier, alone in Maetis' room. Rom felt a persistent lump of sadness in his throat. He brought up Maetis' hand and kissed it.

'*Aye sûa*,' he whispered, but the sadness weighed down his heart, and as he spoke the words he felt as if he was grasping at straws.

'It's ready,' he heard Yldich's voice behind him. Yldich came over to the bed and handed him a cup.

Rom sat staring at him and Maetis. He took a deep breath and steadied himself. 'Well, *ey lénte*,' he said, and raised the cup. Yldich's mouth twitched. The words were a cheery *Einache* toast Rom must have heard at the clan fest. Rom brought the cup to his mouth and drained it. He shuddered at the bitter taste. 'So—what happens now?' he said.

'It won't take long for the herbs to start working,' Yldich said. 'It's a powerful mixture. Lie down and make yourself comfortable. I'll get some more blankets.' As he turned, Rom felt a chill creep up his feet, a numbing cold no blankets or fires would warm. It travelled upwards and reached his knees. He blinked.

'What—what's happening?' he said. The deathly chill reached his loins, his belly. He started to breathe quickly, his eyes wide with fear. 'I know this—this feeling....' he fell back into the cushions, shaking, his face pale as the snow outside. His breath came in shallow gasps. Yldich leaned over him.

'Rom. It's all right. It's just the effect of the herbs. Don't fight it, now....' Rom was shaking convulsively, his hands trembling as he tried to fight off the chill that overwhelmed him, resisting it with all his strength. He was taken by an awful thought.

I'm dying. He lied to me. He has never truly forgiven me. His heart was racing. Panic closed his throat. He wanted to move his arms but they were limp, weighed down by the numbing chill. His hands twitched helplessly.

Yldich took them and held them in his own. They were already cold to the touch. 'Don't fight it, Rom,' he said. 'Trust me. It's just like sleep. You'll be fine, I promise....'

Rom's eyelids fluttered, and then they closed of their own accord. A shudder passed through his body and he cried out without making a sound as he was torn away by darkness. Maetis stared at the bed in horror. Rom's face was waxen like a dead man's, his body stiff and lifeless. She turned to Yldich.

'What have you done?' she whispered. She grabbed the front of his tunic. 'You've killed him,' she cried, her voice sharp with panic. Yldich shook his head.

'Look,' he said, and took her by the arm. He sat her down on the blankets. 'Look. He's alive.' He motioned at Rom's throat. Maetis stared at it. Then she saw a tiny heartthrob, the movement of blood beneath the skin. She released a breath, her hands at her mouth.

'I told you,' Yldich said, and pressed her arm. 'He's going to be all right.'

'How do you know?' she whispered through her fingers. 'He was terrified. He thought he was going to die.'

'Because I know him,' Yldich said, his grey eyes stern under the straight line of his brows. 'He survived a Southern dungeon, Feyir and his riders, the

Einache Dead, and the Northern frost. He's stronger than he looks. He'll survive this, too.'

He released her and sat down beside her. 'Now. This sleep resembles death, but it is not death. It's like the sleep some creatures sleep when the earth is too cold to sustain them. His body shuts down and only functions at the most basic level. While his body is in such a state of deep *ayúrdimae*, like death but not dead, his spirit is free to walk the other world.' Maetis stared at him. 'We'll have to take it in turns to watch him,' Yldich continued, 'for any sign of trouble.'

Rom was falling, screaming, desperately trying to find something to hold onto. Suddenly there was solid ground under his feet. He fell over and his fingers touched bare rock. He gasped with surprise.

'Now, now,' a dry voice sounded next to his ear and he whirled around, ready to attack any demon that dared touch him. To his utter surprise, he looked straight into the face of an old woman. She was small, and bent with age, her skin creased by a myriad of wrinkles, and soft like old leather. She was dressed in simple brown robes of an indeterminate style. Wisps of silver-grey had escaped the brown cowl and fallen around her face. Rom blinked at her.

'You don't have to make such a racket, young man,' the old woman said, shaking her head at him. 'I heard you coming from miles away.'

'Who—who are you?' he said, still breathless and shaken by his journey.

'I am the Warden of the Path to the Underworld,' the old woman said. She held out a wrinkled hand to help him up. After a moment's hesitation, he grabbed it. She pulled him from the stone floor. He blinked at her unexpected strength. 'I receive anyone who dares pass this way. My name is Selena. You may think of me as the, uh... receptionist.'

He stared at her. 'The... what?'

She shook her head. 'Ay, me... I keep forgetting. Time and space do not exist in this place. It's at the centre of all time and space. Or rather,' she added with a grin, showing small, blunt teeth, yellowed with age, '*under* it. Some people call it Hell, you know. Or Hades. Naraka. The Astral Plane. It goes by a lot of different names.' Rom stared at her. He had no idea what she was talking about.

'Anyway,' the old woman said, noting his confusion, 'enough chitchat. I am here to show you the way to the Gates. I gather you're here of your own free will?'

'I—I suppose so,' Rom said with a hint of doubt. 'Yes.'

'Right. Just have to check. Well, finding your way around here is easy. You don't have to search for a path. Just start walking, and the path will find *you*.'

He stared at her in surprise. 'That's just what Yldich said.'

She raised her brows. 'Yldich sent you, eh? Well, well. I wonder what he's up to. Well, off you go. Can't stand here chatting all day.' She gave him a gentle push.

'But... how do I get back?' Rom's voice rose in anxiety.

'Ah. Well, the way back is a different matter. Did the *Yaever* not explain it to you?' He shook his head. 'Then I'd best not meddle. Just go find your way. With any luck, the path will just circle back on itself and bring you back home.'

Rom wanted to ask her how she knew Yldich, but between one blink of an eye and the next, the Warden had gone. He was alone in the dark.

He patted his clothes without thinking, trying to find anything that might give him some sort of comfort. The first object he encountered was his *Einache* sword. Touching the hilt reassured him. He wondered a moment how he could still be carrying his sword, while its real counterpart was with his body in Yldich's room, upstairs. He grinned at himself for the expression. Then he remembered what Yldich had said about energy. He felt around in his clothes and found Morven's stone and the braided knot Maetis had given him. The braid shone with a subtle golden light. He put it back in his shirt with care. He straightened his clothes and took a deep breath.

'Well, here we go,' he said out loud, and took a step forward.

Rom found Yldich and the Warden were right. Though he could see no path, a path rolled from under his feet as soon as he started to move, away into the distance, where all was dark. It was strange. He could not follow the path, because the path followed him, it seemed, just under his feet. For the sake of experiment, he stopped moving. The path disappeared. He put one foot forward, then the other. The path reappeared under his feet. After a while he let go of trying to figure out how it worked and determinately stepped into the darkness.

When he had walked for some time, Rom found he was able to discern shapes in the darkness. A dim light illuminated his surroundings. He couldn't identify the source of the light, but the longer he walked, and the more he was aware of it, the brighter it became. The path led him through a green, wooded area, with old trees and low hills. He wondered faintly what would happen if he left the path to explore the woods, but dropped the idea immediately. The idea of losing his way in the Underworld didn't appeal to him.

He had just stopped for a rest, the path curling around his feet like a dog, waiting patiently for him to resume his journey, when he heard a voice.

'Psst.'

He jumped, turning his head left and right to find the owner of the voice. He saw no-one. 'Over here....' The voice came from somewhere down below, near the roots of an old, gnarly oak. Rom tried hard to see anyone, frowning and squinting, but failed utterly.

'Where are you?' he cried to the air around him in exasperation.

'You silly human,' a small voice said testily. 'Blind to anything but yourselves, aren't you. I'm over *here*.' Rom stared at the tree in bewilderment and focused his eyes. A face materialized from the rough bark of the tree. A small, broad face with dark, beady eyes and a wide mouth. Rom gasped in surprise. The mouth pulled into a broad grin, too broad to be entirely reassuring. The beady eyes glittered.

'Who—who are you?' Rom said. He'd never seen a creature like this before, and wondered if it was real.

'Ha,' the creature said, 'don't think I would give my true name to just anybody, do you?' It was about the size of a toddler, and wore clothes in various shades of brown, that made him melt away into the bark of the tree unless Rom looked at him directly. He wore a pointy hat on his head, which was a little too broad and round to make him look truly human. The same could be said for his pointy ears. 'You wouldn't be able to pronounce it, anyway,' the creature continued, and grinned. 'You may call me *Cheeky*.' Rom stared at him. 'It's a rough translation of my name,' the creature said. 'Now. What name do you go by, human?'

'It's Rom.'

The creature called Cheeky lifted a brow. 'Rom, is it? Hum. Now why does that ring a bell...?'

'What are you?' Rom interrupted his chain of thought. 'If you don't mind my asking....'

Cheeky looked up. 'Not at all. Don't your people have a name for my kind?' Rom searched his mind, sifting through stories his Southern mother had told him when he was little, but didn't come up with anything resembling the creature before him. Then he thought of Yldich's tales.

'You're—you're not a mountain troll, are you?'

'A troll! Pah. Certainly not.' Cheeky shook his head in disapproval. 'It's sad, really. Only the young of your race appreciate the existence of other beings in the world around them. Or *under* them,' he added with a malicious grin. 'We are Merkin,' he continued, 'but different kinds of humans call us different names. We live at the edge of the worlds. The Upper and the Lower worlds.'

'Do you mean—you're beings of the Underworld?' Despite the strangeness of the situation, Rom found he felt really quite at ease, talking to the strange little man, and not afraid at all.

'Not exactly. We live at the *edge*. We are neither of this World, nor of the Other. We live at the edge of both. That's why we are hardly ever noticed by your kind, I suppose... some of us pop up occasionally, and have a little fun teasing you humans.' The Merkin grinned. 'It's so deliciously easy. Just a little pinch here, a whisper there, and they're all upset, running from their houses and calling for the priest.' He chuckled. 'Most of it's just harmless fun. Although there have been cases where Merkin have gone a bit bad, I believe. Pulling nasty tricks. Regrettable business.'

'So... this is not the Underworld?'

'You're wanting to go there, then?' Cheeky said, his head cocked to one side, his eyes slightly narrowed.

'Well, that was the idea when I set out,' Rom said. 'I thought this was it.' Cheeky chuckled again.

'This is just the beginning of the path. If you truly want to enter the Underworld, you have to pass through the Gates.'

'And where are they?'

'Just follow the path,' Cheeky said. 'It will bring you where you need to go.'

Of course. I should have known.

'Now, if you don't mind my asking,' the creature said. He peered up in Rom's face. 'Did you know you cast a very dark shadow?' He sounded like a child, innocently inquiring about something curious hanging from Rom's nose.

Rom's eyes widened. 'What?'

'Your shadow,' Cheeky said. 'It's very dark, and, if I may say so, particularly long. Did you know that?'

Rom stared at him. 'I thought all shadows were more or less the same.'

Cheeky stuck his chin in the air. 'Certainly not. Up there, maybe. But down here, where the true nature of things is easier to see, they come in all shapes and sizes. But I've never seen one as dark as this.' His voice lowered an octave. 'You sure it's yours?'

Rom felt a shiver along his spine. 'Whose else would it be?'

The little man shrugged. 'You're the one who's lugging it around, not me.'

Rom resisted the urge to glance at his feet. Instead, he plucked at a torn thumbnail. 'So... do you always talk to travellers on their way to the Gates to the Underworld? I can't imagine there being many.'

Cheeky grinned. 'You would be surprised. But not all of them come willingly, like you. Anyway, we *Merkin* are inquisitive by nature. That's what draws us Above from time to time. So when I saw you coming this way, a young human with an old, dark shadow, I was curious. It reminds me of something, but I just can't put my finger on it... oh well, it'll come back to me. In the meantime, have a safe journey. And be aware of the Dragons.'

'What dragons?'

'The ones that guard the Gates.'

'I—I was hoping they were a myth....'

'A myth! Ha! Just like me, I suppose?' Rom hastened to deny he thought the little man was a myth. 'All right, all right. Just rattling your chain,' Cheeky said. 'Still, it can't hurt to know how to approach the old worms... you have to be firm with them. State your purpose, and be clear about it. Don't let them intimidate you.'

'That's just what Yldich said,' Rom muttered. The prospect of meeting real dragons made his stomach sink. He swallowed and wondered if it could be avoided.

'Yldich, eh?' Cheeky said, his brows arched high. 'Well, well. I knew there was more to you than meets the eye. My blessing on your head and may you return safely by the same path you came.'

Eldairc sat in the kitchen wolfing down a late meal of bread and watered-down beer, when Yldich joined him. It was still the deep of night. Yldich had been relieved from his watch by Yealda, and he had noticed he was hungry. He sat down next to Eldairc while Yárah set a bowl of soup and some bread rolls on the table.

'So... what happens when you travel through the Underworld?' Eldairc yawned and rubbed his eyes. His turn to watch Rom was next.

'You meet your fears,' Yldich said. 'Every one of them.'

Twelve
The Underworld

The path took Rom through endless low hills, through fields with strange, ever-blooming flowers. Sometimes he thought he saw something move in the corner of his eye, in the fields or between the trees, but he didn't dare leave the path to go and investigate. Instead, he looked around, and kept a firm pace on the path.

It was a strange place. It was neither day nor night, neither winter nor summer. The light was dim, but bright enough to see clearly, without the shine of sun or moon. He could see no bare branches on the trees, and there was no carpet of last year's leaves. Neither were there saplings between the trees or buds still to open between the flowers. Instead, the trees and flowers had a dusty look, as if they had stood for years, for centuries. Rom looked around for a break in the scenery, but everywhere he looked it was the same.

It's as if nothing ever changes. There's no death, but neither is there life. It's in between, as the Merkin said.

Compared to this unchanging atmosphere, the world above in his memory seemed fresh and lively. The knowledge, tucked away in some corner of every creature's mind that death was ever present, added an intensity and vitality to life like the edge of a new sword.

His thoughts drifted to the mage, and he tried to imagine what it must be like, locked away in a dark place somewhere in these un-living lands for ages, alone and with no glimpse of release.

It must be worse than death.

He had been making his way through the landscape for some time, although he had no idea how to measure time in the unchanging gloom, when he noticed his surroundings were changing. There were less and less trees, and the ones that he saw were stunted and gnarled; they held on to their un-life with graceless tenacity. There were no more flowers, and the grass made way for dry flatlands of dusty red. Rocks and boulders lined the path, and there seemed to be ever more of them.

There was no source of water anywhere that he could see, and Rom wondered briefly whether it might get him into trouble. Then he slapped his head.

You fool. Remember what Yldich told you. You're not really here. It's when you start believing you're here, you'll get into trouble.

The trees had dwindled into nothing, leaving only dusty earth and rocks, when Rom noticed a large stone structure in the distance. The path would take him straight to it, so he kept on walking. When he got closer, he could see it was a large open gateway made of big blocks of carved grey stone, and doors of heavy blackened wood. They were open, and behind it he saw an impenetrable darkness. The path went straight through the Gates, meandering for a while until it disappeared from view. Although there were no walls that he could see, he was convinced that the only way forward was through the doors, into darkness.

As he stood contemplating the way ahead with some trepidation, Rom felt movement in the air around him. A hot, dry wind was rising. It plastered his clothes to his back, and blew his hair across his face. Rom looked up, swept dark strands out of his eyes and looked straight into the face of an enormous dragon that swooped past him and landed on top of the Gates.

Rom stared up into the large, yellow eyes of the creature. Each eye was as big as his own head, with vertical slits for pupils, like a cat's. They had a disconcerting intelligence to them. In fact, there was something about them that made him feel as if they knew exactly who he was, what he was thinking, and what he'd had for breakfast that morning. Another dragon, as big and impressive as the first, landed on the other side of the Gate, folded its great, leathery wings and stared at him in silence. Rom laid his hand on the hilt of his sword and took a deep breath.

'I have come to pass the Gates of the Underworld,' he cried. He waited breathlessly, wondering if he would have to fight the creatures, like in the old tales. The idea was laughable. They would erase him within a heartbeat, crush him against the rock floor, maybe leave a smear of blood on it to mark his passing. He shuddered and vehemently reminded himself once more that he wasn't really there. Faced with a pair of very real-looking dragons with dull bronze scales, their acrid smell in his nostrils, it was getting rather hard.

The dragons stared at him in silence, their eyes partly lidded. He had no idea what, if anything, they were thinking.

'I will prove my intentions to you if you so desire,' Rom cried. He laboured to keep his voice steady. One of the great beasts moved. To Rom's horror, it dived off its perch on the left hand side of the Gates. Three beats of its powerful wings brought it up to Rom. He landed right in front of him. The dust whirled up at Rom's feet and he coughed. He looked up, dwarfed by the immense creature before him. It stretched its heavy neck, and brought its great head forward. It was now so close Rom could see his own reflection in its eyes. The dragon sniffed and opened its mouth.

'Who are you, to demand passage at the Gates of the Underworld, which we have guarded for centuries?' the dragon boomed. Its smell reminded Rom of sulphur, the dust of smashed stones, and the breath of hot furnaces.

'I am Rom, whose name was Riórdirým,' he called. He wondered at himself for the use of the name. Somehow, in this place it seemed appropriate.

The dragon cocked its head. The yellow eyes glinted. A little puff of smoke escaped its left nostril. Rom held his breath. 'All right. Off you go, then.'

Rom stared at the dragon. 'But—don't I have to prove myself, or something?'

'No need.' The dragon grinned a cat-like grin. 'We knew you were coming.'

'The Underworld is *that* way,' the dragon on the Gate said, pointing a large claw at the darkness behind him.

Rom hesitated. He wondered if it was a trap. 'You mean... I can just go through?'

'Of course,' the first dragon said. 'No reason why you shouldn't,' and opened its mouth set with dagger-sized teeth, as if it were smiling.

After what seemed like an eternity of walking through darkness, Rom heard sounds in the distance. They sounded a little to the right. He wondered what to do. Should he continue in the direction the path seemed to indicate? Weren't the noises just a distraction, even a deliberate one, to lure him off the path?

A muffled scream sent a shiver along his skin and he veered off to the right. Tendrils of grey mist whirled and suddenly there was light around him. It was like sunlight filtered through thick layers of fog. He frowned and peered through the gloom.

He saw a group of people standing in a rough semicircle. They looked like the kind of people he might have met on the streets of a Southern town. They were shouting and laughing, but he couldn't make out the words. He came a little closer, his hand on the hilt of his sword, just in case. But they didn't take any notice of him. All their attention was focused on something that crouched in the corner.

Rom pushed through the small crowd to try and get a glimpse of the thing they were shouting at. Finally he got an unobstructed view and nausea closed up his throat. It was a creature the size of a large dog. It was dark, and strangely formless, although it roughly resembled a human body. There was a horrible deformity to the creature he couldn't quite define. Maybe it was the way it crouched there that repelled him, its head low, its limbs bent in awkward angles, low to the ground, as if it were grovelling. Rom felt the little hairs in his neck stand on end.

'Kill it, the rancid thing,' a man cried. 'It's probably diseased.'

'Crush it, bury it, quickly,' a woman's voice called. She turned away her face. 'I can't stand the sight of it.' Rom was inclined to agree with her. The sight of the creature was so distasteful it sent waves of nausea through him. Its skin, what he could see of it, was shrivelled and blackened as if it had been scorched. He caught a glimpse of the creature's narrow, pallid face, the gleam of eyes, sunken deep into their sockets, with a nameless hunger at the bottom that made his skin crawl. He wondered if it was a kind of demon, some wretched creature from the depths of the Underworld. He turned away, glad to be rid of the sight of the ungainly thing.

He had taken a few steps when someone in the crowd picked up a stone and threw it. The creature yelped like a dog and crouched even deeper. It was like a signal for the people to follow the man's example. They picked up pebbles, stones, and rocks, and began stoning the creature in earnest.

A low howl came from its throat. It reminded Rom of the horrible sound of a dying hound he had heard at a hunting party of Lord Aldr's. Its belly had been ripped open by the powerful tusks of a boar. The low cry resonated through his bones. He stopped and swallowed. He turned back.

'Stop it,' he cried, as he pushed his way through the crowd. They had really warmed up now, and were enjoying their sport. The men looked around, frowning with annoyance. Why did that young man interfere? What business was it of his if they got rid of the vermin and had some fun into the bargain? They were doing everyone a favour. The thing had to be destroyed. Even he should be able to see that. Even someone slightly outlandish like him.

Now they thought of it, he looked extremely outlandish and strange, with his long dark locks and strange clothes, not at all a reputable citizen like themselves. They turned on him, scowling, their hands clenched into fists, or grabbing at belt knives and daggers.

When he saw the tide of outraged revulsion turn on him, Rom stiffened and recoiled. There was a muffled cry. One of the men at the back had commenced kicking the black creature. It whimpered softly. Rom felt a surge of anger run through his veins. He drew the *Einache* sword. It screamed, a high note of white metal. The tide of outrage threw itself upon him. He closed his eyes and hurled himself at it, hewing and wheeling the sword as if he had become an armed human whirlwind.

After a while he became aware of a strange thing. He met with no resistance. He stood still and opened his eyes. He lowered the sword. There was not a speck of blood on it. The men had disappeared. He sighed with surprise. Then he heard a soft sound. The creature was still alive. Reluctantly, he walked over to the corner where it was trying to get up. It felt his approach and turned its head to stare at him with its hollow eyes. It was bleeding, and looked even more deformed than before. Rom swallowed away revulsion and pity and raised the sword.

'Better this way,' he muttered. There was a voice in his ear.

'I wouldn't do that, if I were you.'

He blinked, and lowered the sword. 'Lakíthra?' he said to the whirling mist.

'If you kill him, you'll kill a part of yourself.'

Rom stared at the creature in horror. It had managed to crawl into a kneeling position and sat staring back at him. 'That? A part of me?'

There was no answer, though the silence seemed to have an odd quality of amusement. Rom put away the sword and took a deep breath. He advanced a few steps, slowly and carefully. The creature sat as if frozen, not taking its eyes from his face. Rom kneeled so their faces were level. He looked into the hungry eyes.

The creature stared back. It raised a dark hand and slowly reached out to Rom. The hand looked pitifully crooked, and somehow the feeling of pity began to resolve the sense of cold disgust, like the sun dispersing the morning mist. A sense of warmth filled his heart and the revulsion melted away.

Rom carefully took the creature's hand. Despite its appearance it was warm, and soft, not coarse at all. He blinked, and looked again. It was a human hand. A child's hand. Startled, he looked up, into the face of a little boy, who sat gazing at him, his dark eyes wide. He uncannily resembled the little *Tzanatzi* boy Rom had seen in *ayúrdimae*. He looked even more like a smaller version of himself. There was a wordless plea in the boy's eyes, and without thinking, Rom drew him to him, and held him. The boy shuddered. He released a long sigh, and then he lay still, his little arms wound tightly around Rom's chest, his cheek against Rom's heart.

For a long time, they sat there, and after a while, Rom found he had softly begun to sing to the boy, a song with words he didn't recognize. Finally he opened his eyes again. The child was gone. But somehow, it felt as if his energy was still with him. He stood up and dusted off his clothes.

'Well now,' he said, and was suddenly reminded of Yldich. At some point in time, he had apparently picked up some of the big man's singularities. He chuckled at the thought. It was oddly reassuring, as if part of him was still with him.

After he had made his way through the twilight for some time, the way became dark again. Rom wondered about it, but the path still rolled away under his feet, and lead him directly through the darkest area.

He had walked through it for some time, his hands outstretched before him to feel his way, when he encountered an obstruction. It felt like a wall, cold and moist. The stones were rough under his fingertips. He held his breath. He felt strangely anxious. He turned a little to the left and resumed his journey, when another dank wall obstructed him. Unbidden, the image of a rat in a trap came to his mind. A cold sense of fear groped for his heart and he quickly swallowed it down.

Don't panic. The path will show the way. Just go on walking.

He turned the other way and went forward again, his pace slowed a little in anticipation and just as he feared, after a few paces he bumped into an unpleasantly cold and dank wall yet again.

He resisted the urge to bang on it with his fists and rummaged around in his pockets instead. His fingers closed on the crystal Yldich had given him the night before. It seemed ages ago. He held it cupped in his hands and closed his eyes, concentrating on the image of the sun, shining though his hands, filling the crystal with the warm light of summer. '*Ílumae,*' he muttered, like Yldich had instructed him. '*Ílumae.*' In his mind's eye, he saw a spark begin to grow. '*Ílumae.*' The crystal started to glow. The light grew until it shone like a small fire. He opened his eyes.

The mellow light illuminated the walls of a large cell. It reminded him unpleasantly of a dungeon. He stared at the walls, trying to find a way out with his eyes, but he could see none. His fear fed the fire until the hard surface of the crystal grew hot in his hands. He dropped it with a curse. It fell on the floor, unscratched, and strangely enough, when the light died, the walls remained visible. Rom turned around to find the source of the light, but it seemed to come from nowhere. He could see no doors, no windows.

'There's no way out,' he muttered.

It was during Eldairc's watch, when Yldich went in for a moment to check on Rom, that the young *Einache* suddenly pulled at his sleeve.

'Yldich,' Eldairc said under his breath.

'What is it?'

'Come, come over here. Look,' he whispered, and held a candle up to Rom's face. 'He doesn't cast a shadow.' Yldich stared at the young man who lay motionless on the bed. He looked strangely unreal, a pale figure in a room filled with shadows thrown about by the flickering light of the candles. 'I noticed it before,' Eldairc said. 'Two or three nights ago. His shadow was disappearing. I thought there was something wrong with my eyes. But it seems to have gotten worse.'

'I don't like this,' Yldich muttered. 'I don't like this at all.'

Rom jumped when he heard footsteps, the clank of metal, and the rattling sound of keys on a chain. It seemed to come from the other side of the wall. The sound was horribly familiar.

'You still in there, you little bastard?' a rough voice sounded. It had a nasty undertone of amusement. 'Just make good use of your time. In the morning Aldr will have you executed.' The heavy footsteps passed by and disappeared in the distance. Rom gasped and looked around. He lay on his side on a low bench. Light came from a slit window. It fell on the walls of a cell. It was his cell in the dungeons of Lord Aldr's Keep.

'No,' he whispered. 'This can't be true. Oh, no.'

Yes, a voice said inside his head. *Oh yes. Is the truth finally dawning on you?*

'No,' Rom whispered. 'I can't be here. I got away. The inn-keeper took me in.' The voice seemed to laugh. It was not a pleasant sound.

You never left this cell. You made it all up.

'That can't be,' Rom said hoarsely. 'I got away. I outsmarted them. I survived, travelling on my own for years.'

Stories. Stories you made up to comfort yourself while you were in this cell, waiting for your execution. Have you finally woken up?

Rom frantically searched his mind for arguments to counter the horrible truth the voice seemed to force on him. 'What about Yldich? And Eald, and Eldairc.'

You made them up, the voice said. *You made them all up.* It laughed softly, a horrible, self-satisfied laugh. *Do you really believe there could be such a thing as an age old Einache wizard, travelling for years to find a lone Tzanatzi bastard?* Rom winced.

'Maetis,' he breathed. 'She's real. I can't have made her up. She's too alive to be made up.' His hand searched for the braid she had given him, lying against his heart, but it was gone. An icy fear crept up his body.

The best proof of all, the voice continued. *When, in your wildest dreams, do you think a girl like that would love a low-life half-breed like you? I mean, look at yourself.*

Rom looked down at his body. The *Einache* clothes he had gotten used to were gone. He wore his Southern page's clothes, the leggings made from course, dark fabric, the white shirt. They looked horribly familiar, ragged and dirty as they were. There were bloodstains on the shirt; a remnant of Aldr's lashing the day before. He held up his hands and gasped. They were small and slender, a boy's hands, stained with dirt and dried blood, the nails worn down to the skin. He became acutely aware of the cold. There was no source of heat in the cell, and he shivered. His back, however, was burning.

I'm only telling you this for your own good you know, the voice continued smoothly. It seemed to sense it was gaining the upper hand. *I'm the voice of reason after all. Wouldn't want to die living a lie, would we?*

'I'm not listening to you.' Rom's voice was shrill. He put his hands over his ears. 'You're lying. I'm not listening anymore.'

You stupid boy. You can't shut me out. I'm inside your head. I'm the voice of your own mind.

Rom looked around the cell to distract himself from the horrid things the voice was telling him. The picture it painted seared his brain. He wondered whether the things it said could be true. They did seem to make much more sense to his confused mind than what he thought was the truth.

He noticed a mouse on the stone floor to his right. It was washing itself with its little paws, delicately brushing one ear, then the other. Rom stared at it as if studying the simple creature could reconnect him with the truth, with all that was normal. The mouse looked up and looked straight into his face with its beady little eyes.

'Do you mind?' it said. 'I don't feel comfortable being stared at when I'm bathing, thank you very much.'

Rom's mouth fell open. 'Can you speak?'

'Can you squeak?' the creature countered. It chuckled at itself. 'Can you squeak, he he he. That's a good one. Got to remember to tell Bevis tonight. "Can you squeak." He he. Humans....' Rom stared at the mouse open-mouthed. It lifted what looked like a brow and Rom shut his mouth again quickly.

'Now I know I must be going mad,' he muttered.

'Mad, eh? Mad's a state of mind,' the mouse said in a good-humoured tone. 'My brother Nevis got mad. Thought he was invincible. Went dancing on the tables to prove he was.'

'What happened to him?' Rom asked, despite himself.

'Cat got 'm.'

'I'm sorry.'

'Don't be,' the mouse said. 'He was a right wanker.' Rom shook his head, lost for words. 'Now,' the mouse continued. 'What's your problem then? What were you moaning about just now?'

'I got out of this dungeon years ago. At least, I thought I did. Yet here I am, and there's no way out, and this voice in my head keeps telling me I made everything up. My escape, my journey north, Yldich, everything.'

The mouse pricked up its ears. 'Who's Yldich?'

Well. Finally a creature who doesn't know Yldich. Then he realized why that might be and he went cold. He swallowed away anxiety and continued.

'He's a *Yaever*. A healer. A very old one. He—he teaches and he travels, he teaches the children of his people to dream, and to heal, and all sorts of *Einache* magic....' The mouse cocked its head.

'Well, what did he teach *you* then? This Yldich?' It noticed its whiskers and began to twirl them between its paws. Rom hesitated, thinking.

'Well, he taught me to face my fears,' he said slowly. 'He told me why the *Einache* warriors of old knew no fear. They knew *Eärwe*, the... the All-encompassing. First-hand, I mean. They knew they were part of everything. He had me go there.'

The mouse gave a final polishing twist to its whiskers. 'So what's stopping you then?'

Rom stared at it. 'What?'

'Well,' the mouse said, and sat up on its hind legs. 'If this Yldich taught you how to be part of everything, why don't you do it now? Seems to me you're making things unnecessarily difficult, sitting here and moaning, waiting 'till they chop off your head.'

'But what if it isn't true?' Rom whispered. 'What if I made it all up? Maybe I'm going mad.'

'Sooner you find out, the better,' the mouse said. 'At least you'll know where you stand.' Rom shook his head.

I'm discussing my sanity with a talking mouse. Now what should that tell me? He closed his eyes and concentrated all the same. He heard the voice laugh at him from a corner of his mind.

All nonsense, it said. *Stop fooling yourself and face the facts. You're having a fever-dream. And in the morning you'll be executed.* Rom set his teeth and shut it out.

He wondered how to find *Eärwe* without Yldich's help. The first time, in the woods, the man had used his herbs and an *Einache* song to help him leave his body. He envisaged the clearing where they had been seated in the grass, the crystal heavy and cold in his hands, while the smoke from Yldich's herbs filled his head. Just before the song had pulled him out of his body, there had been a moment of choice. Then he had rushed towards the stars, wheeling like a great spiral galaxy, of which his heart was the centre.

The stars. I remember.

Their light flooded his heart and he smiled, filled with a sense of timeless, peaceful joy.

This is what I am. Yldich was right. It doesn't matter whether they kill me or not. This is the truth.

The walls of the dungeon fell away and he found himself standing on the path, once more a grown up man, in his familiar *Einache* clothes, the sword at his side. He sighed with relief. He looked around for the mouse, but all he saw, or thought he saw, was the flicker of a tail disappearing at the edge of his vision. It was followed by a high-pitched chuckle. Then all was silent.

Now I wonder what would have happened if I'd stayed there, thinking it was all real? And do I really want to know?

He shook his head to rid it of fearful imaginings and resumed his journey. He did not notice his shadow behind him. It was getting longer and darker every step of the way.

Yldich had just retired to his bedroom when Eald burst into the room.

'Yldich,' the boy cried. 'Come quick. He's disappearing.'

'What?' Yldich followed him through the corridor and threw open the door to his study. Yealda motioned at Rom's body on the bed. Rom was pale, so pale he seemed almost translucent. Impossibly, he seemed to be blurring.

Yldich stared at him in alarm. He could see the folds of the blanket through Rom's right hand. 'That's it. I'm going after him.'

'But—who will speak to the Southern Lords for the *Einache* people?' Yealda said. 'Who will lead us into battle?'

'If he is lost to us, that question will soon mean nothing.' Yldich rose abruptly and went over to his desk. He took the vial of amber liquid and measured it against the light of the candle. There was still enough for another journey. He took a large double-terminated crystal and seated himself in the chair beside Rom's bed. 'Tell Maetis she's in charge of the House. I'll come back as soon as I can.'

The way was getting ever darker and narrower. Rom had to move carefully to avoid stumbling on stones or cutting himself on the sharp edges of the rocks. It was like moving through an underground passage, roughly hewn from living rock.

He thought he saw strange shadows in the gloom. His gaze jumped nervously from one to the other. Every now and then he thought he heard strange noises, like muffled screams or moans, and the shuffling of feet on stone. He tried to get an impression of the direction they were coming from, but they seemed to be coming from all around, echoing through the passageway until it was impossible to tell what the source was.

It's like the voices of the Dead... as if their cries have echoed for centuries, bouncing off these walls, unable to escape.

In the dark it was easy to imagine the twisted shapes of tortured souls, hidden in nooks and crannies, bound to the Underworld for ever. He kept one hand on the hilt of his sword. He set his teeth, and doggedly kept going.

After a while, the passage widened, and he found himself in a large cavern. It looked empty, save for the large stalactites and boulders. Yldich's crystal threw grotesque shadows on the granite walls.

Something moved in the corner of his eye. He whirled around, and found himself face to face with a man. Rom stared in a pale face framed by hair, dark as night. Startled, he quickly drew his sword, only to recognize his own mirror image in a large, reflecting sheet of glassy substance, like black ice, that was wedged between the rocks. He chuckled softly to himself.

A good thing Yldich isn't here. I can imagine what he would have to say about this. Probably accuse me of being afraid of my own shadow.

As he turned away, the mirror image did not move as he did, but remained still, staring at Rom with dark, burning eyes. The sword in his hand was not an *Einache* sword. It was a great, ancient sword with a dragon-shaped hilt.

Yldich hastily made his way through the gloom. Soon he had reached the dark Gates.

'*Yaever*,' the dragons said in unison, with an almost imperceptible bow of their heads.

'The hatchling went *that* way.' The dragon on his left hand motioned with its wing.

'You're speaking of an old and experienced sorcerer,' Yldich said, amused despite his concern. 'You can hardly call him a hatchling.'

'His shadow is old, older than the hills, powerful beyond measure,' the dragon on the right said. 'But *he* is still a hatchling. His eyes have barely opened. You had better watch out for him.'

'I intend to,' Yldich said. He passed through the Gates into darkness.

As Rom walked away, his shadow shortened, shuddering, until it had completely disappeared. Something, a vague sound perhaps, made him turn around. His breath stuck in his throat. It was not his mirror image, this man, the one who held out his left hand to him, an arm that was clothed in ragged shreds of midnight mist. His face was deathly pale, his eyes like caverns, eyes that had seen too much, yet had not seen daylight in hundreds of years. Rom shuddered as they turned on his face.

'I knew this moment would come.' His voice was cold. Rom stared at the man. The language was *Tzanatzi*, but strangely enough, he understood every word. Suddenly he knew why. The man did not use his lips and throat. He had none. The voice was inside Rom's head.

'I knew the time would come when you would come back to me. It was as inevitable as the tide, as inevitable as death—at least, for most. They did not grant it to *me*.' A hint of pain slid beneath the dark surface of the eyes, a flicker of hatred. Then they stilled. The dark eyes narrowed in appraisal. 'You have fulfilled your purpose well.' Rom stared at him.

'Purpose?' he whispered. His throat was dry. 'What... purpose?' The mage lifted a brow.

'It is not for a tool to question his purpose.' His voice was cold and authoritative. 'You have fulfilled your task. Now come back to me.'

'What?' Rom's eyes widened. A chill ran along his skin. The image of a dark path, and a rolling mist forced itself on his mind and he shivered as he remembered. The path his mother had walked, the night she met the stranger who had overwhelmed her. He took a faltering step backwards, then another. 'No,' he whispered. 'No.' Strength left him with every step. The mage seemed to grow taller as the anger grew in him.

'You have no will of your own,' he said. 'You belong to me. You *are* me. Now, come to me. *Lercia ayaz*,' he spoke, with a commanding motion of his hand, and Rom felt his strength dissipate completely.

He fell on his knees on the cold stone floor, gasping for air. He could see his life flow away with his breath. His vision dimmed. He grabbed the crystal that was around his neck, but his hand was already cold, the crystal dull and lifeless. He groped for the infinity loop in his tunic, but its light had grown dim. He couldn't even feel it in his hand.

His life flowed out of him like the blood from a mortal wound. It flowed towards the dark presence, while the cold blackness grew, and filled his lungs, his heart, until there was only a last little spark of consciousness left. He collapsed on the rock floor, his body as cold as the ancient stones themselves. A convulsive shudder ran through him.

'Yldich,' he whispered. Then he lay still.

Yldich felt a pervading sense of alarm and stopped short. There was a tug at his heart. It was as if a string that had been attached to it for as long as he could remember was suddenly loosening, and a feeling of deep sadness rose to his eyes.

He began to run. He followed the string that was ever loosening. As he turned around some large rocks, the thread dropped. He clutched at his chest, his breath taken away by the emptiness of a lost connection. He looked up and saw Rom's body on the stone floor.

There was a horrible finality to the way he lay sprawling on the rock. He lay completely still. His lips were greyish blue. Yldich's heart was crying out to him to run, to get to him as quickly as possible, and search for signs of life. But his *Yaever* self knew there was no longer any need for haste.

He swallowed and kneeled beside the body. He touched the face. It was pale and cold, a faint purple hue around the eyes, as if they were bruised. The body was like an empty thing, bereft of the spirit it had housed, devoid of energy.

Yldich slid one arm under the back and lifted the upper body from the rock floor. He cradled it like a sick child. He pushed away the hair that had fallen across Rom's face and sighed, shaking his head.

'Now why did you have to go and get yourself killed?' He swallowed away a dull pain in his throat. His gaze fell on the infinity loop that was still in Rom's hand. 'What am I going to tell Maetis?' He bowed his head and closed his eyes. Tears ran over his face.

'*Yaever*,' a cold voice reverberated inside his head. Yldich felt a presence behind him. He lifted his head and slowly started to turn around. His eyes widened as he took in the dark shape looming behind him. 'I did not,' the cold voice whispered, 'expect to see *you*.'

Yldich swallowed. The dark figure was tall and gaunt, his cheeks hollowed out, his youth and beauty eaten away by centuries of despair and loneliness in the dark. He was clothed in rags of ink black mist and held a heavy dragon-headed sword in his hand.

'I have come for *him*,' Yldich said heavily, with a motion of his chin at Rom's body.

'Why?' The mage's dark eyes widened. He seemed genuinely surprised. 'He is nothing but a tool, a means to an end.' He took a step forward. 'He was made to be your undoing.' Yldich stared at him.

'What do you mean?' he said huskily. The mage smiled a cold smile.

'After your kind cursed me,' he said, and his eyes were like black holes, 'after centuries of darkness and despair, I sensed an opening. A tiny fissure, a crack in the earth, through which I could send something of my essence. There was a path to the south. A young woman walked the path alone. She was young and beautiful. She was the perfect vessel.' Yldich widened his eyes. The tale was hauntingly familiar.

'I merged with her,' the mage continued, 'and I poured into her everything that was weak, and useless. The pain, the grief, the fear. I poured it all into her. She hated me for it. And she would birth me a son. He would carry everything that I had discarded. He would grow up into my likeness. It would be only a matter of time before the *Tahiéra* came to his call.

Because of your curse, trouble would find him, and trouble would follow him, all the way up to the North. To the undoing of the *Einache* people.' He smiled a slow, joyless smile that did not light up his black eyes. 'The Earth tells me he has succeeded. I have felt the drum of marching feet, and the whispering of the restless Dead. The *Tahiéra* has risen. And now he has come back to me.'

His smile slowly faded as he became aware of an unexpected sound. Yldich was softly laughing. The mage turned his smouldering gaze on him. 'Why,' he said, 'are you laughing?'

'You fool.' Yldich slowly shook his head. His eyes were sad. 'You thought you relinquished what was useless, what made you vulnerable, what was expendable.' His gaze unfocused, as if he were staring straight into the mage's heart. 'The pain that would have taught you compassion. The grief that made you human.' The mage stared at him, a little uncertain. 'You never realized what you poured into this boy was the best and most powerful part of you.' Yldich looked up into the mage's face.

'I have searched for him for years, because I know he is the only one who can reconcile us. He is not your tool, to use as you please. He is your second chance at life. And I have come to love him as a son.' He drew himself up. 'He is young. He deserves a chance at happiness. Give him back his life. I will give you anything you wish, if it is in my power to give it.'

Riórdirým stared at the heavily built *Einache* who kneeled on the rock floor with the young man who wore his own face in his arms. The *Einache* looked uncannily like the warrior he had fought on the cliff at Gardeth Battle Plain. There was something strangely tender about the way he held the young man, as if he held something vulnerable and precious.

Something changed in the mage's face. His eyes lost something of their haunted look. He spoke. 'I will give him back his life,' he said hoarsely, 'if you will grant me one wish.'

'Name it.'

'Let me go.' A formless hunger shone in his eyes, like a light at the bottom of a deep, dark well. 'Release me from this place.' Yldich looked at him, his head slightly to one side.

'Where,' he said carefully, 'would you go?' A deep sadness seemed to well up in Riórdirým's black eyes.

'I don't know,' he breathed. 'I don't think there is a place for me between this world and the other. I have nowhere left to go.' Yldich felt the atmosphere around the mage begin to lighten. Particles of light started to swirl around the dark presence. He smiled.

'I think,' he said softly, 'that you may be mistaken.' He stood up carefully, leaving Rom's body lying on the rock behind him. He approached the mage. 'Hand me your sword.'

'Why?'

Yldich smiled. 'Because I will need it to undo the curse.' Riórdirým looked at him with an expression of mistrust. He seemed to be deliberating. Then he made a decision. He held out the sword. Yldich took it from him and held it up. He touched the mage's breast with the tip of the sword, so gently that it might have felt like a butterfly, mistaking it for a flower. The mage's eyes widened.

'I release you,' Yldich said, 'from the curse of hatred that has haunted you and your people for five hundred years, and has locked my people in the past just as it has yours.' He lifted the sword from the mage's breast. 'May we finally have peace.'

A deep sigh whispered through the air. The mage gasped and started to sway. The lights swirled around, knitting together, taking form. They became twinkling little lights, growing until Yldich thought he could see the shapes of people. The lights were reflected in Riórdirým's dark eyes. They lit up. A slow smile started on his face, smoothing out the bitter lines and lifting the shadows of anguish. Before it became translucent, he looked remarkably like an older version of Rom.

'Ciórdynn,' he said. Then he was gone.

Yldich heard a whisper of breath beside him. He looked down. Rom's still face was different. Some colour had returned to it. Yldich kneeled down and quickly felt for his pulse. Rom's body was different too, no longer the dead weight of a lifeless corpse, it felt warm, and alive. He stirred and opened his eyes.

'Rom,' Yldich said.

'*Ya'hey*,' Rom whispered. His voice was like rustling leaves. It became stronger as he spoke. He coughed. 'Did I have to come back? I was somewhere... peaceful. I think I was happy.'

'Well, I know of at least one person who would be very happy to see you again,' Yldich said. 'Apart from me, that is.'

Rom smiled slowly. 'Maetis. I think... we're going to have a child.'

Yldich stared at him. 'What? What makes you say that?'

Rom sighed. 'Where I was, I could see many things... I could see a thread running between us, and from it sprang another... I followed it and saw a little boy, with hair of dark copper and eyes just like mine....'

Yldich raised his brows. 'Well now... you two didn't waste much time, did you?' Rom grinned and ended up coughing painfully. He tried to sit up. Yldich helped him up. 'Come on. Let's go home.'

It was like surfacing from a deep, dark lake. Suddenly, Rom emerged from the cool water. 'He's gone,' he whispered. 'He's gone. I can feel it.' He wrestled the heavy blankets to sit up. 'It's as if a weight has been lifted.' His face was lit with wonder; his eyes glittered as if he had a fever.

He stumbled out of bed before anyone could stop him. His legs were unsteady and he swayed, vaguely grabbing a chair for support. He laughed, unconcerned by the strange weakness that made even the simplest movement seem hard.

'Easy now, lad,' Yldich said, and took hold of his arms. 'You've been under for hours.' He sat him back on the bed. 'Take your time.' Rom looked up.

'All my life,' he said, 'all my life it was like a dark cloud hanging over me. And now it's gone.' He accepted a cup of water and drank thirstily. He drew a hand across his face to brush away the hair that fell into his eyes.

'You should really do something about that hair,' Eldairc said suddenly. 'Why don't you have it cut?'

'I am *Tzanatzi*,' Rom said with unusual conviction. 'We do not cut our hair short, like little boys.'

Eldairc snorted and turned to Yldich. 'I can see we have to keep him on a tight leash from now on,' he said. 'He's already getting *Tzanatzi* airs.' Yldich chuckled and looked at Rom. Rom was smiling. Lights of amusement danced in his dark eyes.

Fireflies in the dark. A warm glow filled Yldichs heart and he felt something loosen within himself. A thought drifted past.

It is done. A strange weightlessness came over him and he felt himself fade away.

Not just yet. He shook his head, and forced himself to stay. 'Let's have breakfast,' he said.

The sun was just rising and painted the snow clad fields in soft hues of pink. Maetis helped Rom to the washroom, where he stood before the mirror being pleased to see the only face there was his own. After he had washed they joined the others in the kitchen. They had a round of tea and honey cakes, and another, while they listened to Rom's account of his journey. The colour of the fields turned from soft gold to white.

There was a whistling sound. It was followed by a loud crash that shook the House to the core.

'What—what was that?' Eldairc cried.

Yldich was up and at the windows before anyone could move. 'It's the Southern army.' His voice was harsh. 'They've breached the palisades.'

Thirteen
The Tahiéra

The *Einache* left their rooms and passed through the corridors in surprising quiet. They walked quickly and in orderly rows, carrying only the most necessary of goods. They had been drilled well. They had been preparing for the eventuality of sudden flight under the supervision of Maetis and Yealda for days.

Rom hastily returned from his room armed and fully dressed against the winter cold. He met with Maetis and Eldairc in the corridor. He noticed with dim surprise how chunky the refugees looked. Big-boned *Einache* sheepherders looked even bigger than before. Usually lanky children looked like chubby little bears. He realized it must be because they were wearing as many clothes as they possibly could, layer over layer of thick wool, fur and leather.

The older children's faces were pale and set, like their parent's. But many of the younger ones seemed unaware of the seriousness of the situation. They babbled in excited little voices like puppies taken out for a walk. Rom looked aside at Maetis.

'They're playing *hide the treasure*,' she said. 'I've been playing it with them these last few days. Just in case this day would come. They think it's a game.'

He saw Yárah herd her kitchen girls through the corridor with as many food baskets as they could carry. Kitchen boys followed with heavy sacks slung over their shoulders. Rom guessed they carried the most indispensable of kitchen implements and supplies, like water skins, and salt, and copper kettles for boiling.

While the refugees were gathered by Yealda, the clan leaders and warriors gathered in the Great Hall. They had grabbed their weapons and thrown on their heavy cloaks and skins in haste. In the distance loud pounding could already be heard, and the disturbing sound of ancient wood being split asunder.

'They have yet to breach the doors,' Yldich said. His face was grim. 'They will hold for a while. Maybe just long enough to get everyone out. In the meantime, we'll have to keep them occupied. Get their attention away from the House so the people have time to flee and hide in the Forest.'

'What do you propose?' Morven said. He girded on a heavy double-handed sword that to Rom's eyes looked disproportionately large. Morven was neither a small nor slender man, but the sword seemed to have been fashioned for an even bigger *Einache* forefather. He felt Rom's gaze and looked up.

'My grandfather's sword,' he said with a grin. 'He was a giant of a man. Boasted this sword had been used by a forefather on Gardeth Battle Plain, and had brought him home unscathed.'

'Really.' Rom looked at it with slight unease.

'So, what's the plan?' Morven addressed Yldich.

'We attack them in the flank.'

Rom stared at Yldich. 'We're going to attack the Southern army? On their own turf?'

Yldich nodded. His face was set. 'It's the only way.'

'But—how are we going to get out without them noticing us leave?'

Yldich grinned. 'You'll see. Follow me.'

He led them through the back door of the Great Hall, through a series of passages that became ever smaller and darker, until the warriors had to walk in singe file to be able to pass through. The taller ones had to hunch over to avoid bumping their heads on the beams of the ceiling. Yldich, who had grabbed an oil lamp from the wall and had motioned for Rom to do the same, stopped before a heavy door and held up the lamp.

'The beer cellar,' he said, and opened the door. Rom looked around in awe. The cellar was big, big enough to house an entire *Einache* clan, and filled with barrels, casks, and dried goods hanging from the ceiling. 'It was made by one of the *Hárrad* before me, a long time ago,' Yldich told him as they walked through.

Rom drew up his brows. 'In other words, by you.' He spoke softly, so none of the others would hear.

Yldich chuckled softly. 'Luckily he had the good sense, or foresight, to put in a back door. It opens to the field right beside the House. That way, hunters could skin their kill and hang it to dry without having to drag the carcasses all through the House. Also, it saved the kitchen boys many a trip with empty beer barrels.'

Yldich and the clan leaders were moving on ahead when Rom noticed a small figure run along at his right hand. He looked down and recognized Eald's face with a sense of dismay.

He stopped him with a cry. 'Eald!' The boy had slung the bow he had made in Woodbury over his shoulder, and a quiver filled with newly cut arrows on his back.

'I'm coming with you.' Eald looked up at him, his pale face set. 'Don't try and talk me out of it.' Rom kneeled before him and grabbed his arms while warriors and refugees moved around them like a mountain stream around rocks and boulders. Earlier, Rom had fervently opposed any involvement of the boy in the fighting. He noted his experience in the Underworld had changed his view.

He wants to die a warrior. We'll probably perish anyway. Why deny him the death of his choosing? He took the bow out of Eald's hands and looked sharply at him. 'Before you use this weapon,' he said, 'you might want to think about what you're going to use it for.' Eald looked intently at the bow in his hands. 'In the old days, before they were granted the right to use a weapon, *Einache* warriors consecrated their weapons to a worthy cause. So to what purpose,' he said, 'would you dedicate this bow?'

Eald looked up. His eyes were earnest. 'Courage,' he said in a small but steady voice. Rom moved his finger over the boy's wrist in a pattern much like the one Yldich had cut into his skin.

'*Eyespragae Faraër*,' he said in a solemn tone. 'Behold the Bearer of the Mark.' Eald stared at his wrist, then shifted his gaze to Rom's face.

'Shouldn't you,' he said, somewhat doubtful, 'write it in my own blood?'

'No time for that,' Rom said. 'If we survive this, I promise I'll have Yldich give you the Mark properly. Or I'll do it myself. In the meantime, this will have to do. Now come with us. And *be careful*.' Eald looked up, his grey eyes shining. A smile lit up his face. Rom sighed inaudibly. 'Let's go,' he said.

They slipped out of the cellar. It opened to a field behind the House, on the other side of the palisades. People spilled from the opening in silence like ants from a hole in the ground.

Yealda and her maids led the refugees in the direction of the Forest. They were accompanied by young warriors, youths of twelve, thirteen years old that had been taught by Maetis. They were mostly boys, but Rom noticed a girl or two in fighting gear, their hair braided and tied in buns, their faces set.

Maetis and Aeldic brought up the rear. Maetis turned and looked back. The wind blew a loose curl across her eyes and he was suddenly reminded of the first time he had seen her, in his true-dream, a tall girl in a green field dotted with ancient *Einache* dwellings. The image filled him with hope, sweet and bitter at the same time. Maetis held her hand before her heart and extended it to him, a warrior's farewell. Her lips moved, but he couldn't hear the words. He didn't need to.

'*Ti'héldae*,' he whispered. Strangely, it was as if for a moment, they were facing each other, close and quite alone in the field, their eyes locked, two sides of the same coin. He could almost touch her face. Then the moment was gone. He gazed at her as she turned away, the last one to disappear between the trees. He turned and joined Yldich and the other clan leaders. A loud cry tore the air.

Ullwich spat out a curse. 'The Southerners. They've spotted us.'

Yldich drew his heavy double-handed sword. His eyes were an ominous dark grey. 'Close ranks,' he called out to the warriors, who stood staring at the army that was approaching fast. 'Now is the time to show them what we're made of. We are the only ones standing between them and our kindred. Now we have to stand as one. *Eyléa kanáchon.*'

'*Eyléarana kanáchon*,' they gave the traditional response.

It all comes down to this. Here. This battlefield. This battle. I wonder how long I will last. Strangely enough, Rom didn't feel panic, just a melancholy sadness, and beneath it, a sense of fearful excitement. He wondered about it as he drew his *Einache* sword. It sang as it left the sheath; a high, pure note cleft the chill morning air and made his skin prickle. The little hairs on his arms stood on end. He gripped the hilt firmly in both hands and waited.

This is it, Eldairc thought. A belated realization came to him. *Maybe I would have been better off staying at home.* The image of his elderly mother came to his mind, of the smithy in Woodbury where he had worked most of his life, happily chattering with Teldric, or flirting with the girls that came in to admire his work. Then he thought of the children holding their parent's hands, fleeing into the Forest, and he knew he was where he wanted to be. Resolution created a warm glow in his stomach. He drew the replica of Rom's sword. It sang with a clear note, a little lower in tone, but perfectly in tune with Rom's. '*Na'Héach*,' Eldairc breathed. He stood and waited.

Eald notched an arrow to the string of his bow. *Steady.* He set his teeth. *Steady.*

All over the snow-covered field, *Einache* warriors and clan leaders did the same, readying themselves in their own way for the imminent clash. It was like an endless moment of respite, an ever-stretching heartbeat of silence. Rom heard several young warriors murmur in their own language and wondered if they were praying. Their breath plumed in the morning air. The silence stretched to its utmost limit. Then the Southerners were upon them.

There was no time to think. No time to do anything but react to each threat as it presented itself. The circle of awareness stretched for ten feet around him. Ten feet of flashing steel, whistling arrows, and shouting men.

He was the eye of a storm; calm and detached, he was all eyes, all reflexes. One movement of his arm deflected an arrow aimed at his head. He ducked under the sword arm of a Southern soldier and turned, just in time to hew him down before the man could kill Eldairc. The tall Einache had slipped and fallen on his elbow in the slush, which was already turning a pale shade of pink.

He whirled around again, and turned another sword aimed at his back. He didn't think. He wasn't afraid. His face was serene as he wheeled and turned, feeling his way through the battle. Like an extension of the *Einache* sword, he was the dance once more. He was one with its movements, parry and thrust, deflect, thrust and parry, until he felt he could move freely between the gaps of time. It gave him an odd sense of freedom. A sudden laugh burst out of him. Soldiers in his vicinity stiffened and stepped back.

'*Witch*,' he heard one whisper. '*Tzanatzi* witch.' He didn't care. He was the dance. The words bounced off him like hailstones.

The battle was shifting, moving backwards step by step, unnoticed by everyone because every warrior, every soldier was occupied with his own fight, his own adversary, his own death. Unheeded by all, it gradually moved arrow by arrow, spear thrust by spear thrust, to the west, to the edge of Gardeth Battle Field.

Yldich found it was practically impossible to keep his people together. He laboured hard to maintain contact with the *Einache* clan leaders, but it proved hopeless. As the battle raged on Morven, the clan leader of the Red Fox clan got separated from his men and he stood for a while alone, keeping two, three Southern soldiers at sword's length with his ancient blade. One moment of inattentiveness and a sword thrust through his defence. His cry cut through the clamour and reached Rom's ears.

The reality of where he was and what he was doing returned to him and he froze, the sword pointing to the earth, dripping blood in the snow. 'Morven,' he said. He threw himself in the direction of the cry, fighting himself a way through the battle until he finally came upon the body of the fallen clan leader. His breath stuck in his throat. Morven's grey eyes were open. He stared expressionless into the sky. Tears rose to Roms eyes and blinded him. He kneeled in the snow next to Morven's body and took his bloodstained head in his hands. Southern soldiers were closing in, but he didn't heed them. Eldairc saw the danger. He was too far away to intervene.

'Rom! Behind you. Look out,' he cried, but his voice was drowned in the clamour. A heavy battle-axe was raised behind Rom's back. Yldich turned around and saw. He shouted a warning. Rom didn't seem to hear. Yldich threw himself into a run. Eald, who had spent all his arrows, grabbed at a lost one that lay half hidden in the snow and notched it to the string with stiff fingers.

'*Calamêntiré.*'

A clear voice carried across the field and froze them all. All movement ceased. The battlefield became deathly quiet. Yldich stared at Rom in dismay, but he had turned his head like everyone else, and stared as frozen in the direction the voice had come from.

Eldairc spat out a curse. '*Kanáchie*... we'd completely forgotten about *her.*'

The woods were eerily quiet. It was still early morning, but as the refugees went deeper into the heart of the Forest their surroundings became steadily darker. The trees were older and bigger, their trunks closer together the further they went. The virgin snow crunched under their feet.

Maetis and Aeldic had moved to the front of the group. Maetis had sent the youngest warriors back to bring up the rear. The others walked alongside the group, keeping an eye on the surroundings, ready to whistle or shout if they caught a glimpse of anything suspicious.

She wondered about the silence as she walked, her hand on the hilt of her sword, the other in her tunic to keep warm. There were no sounds of birds or of any other creatures. She studied the snow-covered forest floor before her. It was unmarked by the hooves of deer or boar. It was strange. There were no signs of animal life anywhere.

It feels like death, Maetis thought with a shudder. *Like living death. I wonder if this is how it feels to enter the Underworld? Or has the Underworld finally come up to swallow us all?* She shuddered at the thought, and tightened the grip on the hilt of her sword.

Something fluttered at the edge of her vision. The image of a bat came to her mind and she held her arm before her face in a reflex to ward it off. The shadow flew straight over her head and was gone. The light of the sun was cut off. Coldness filled the air around them, a coldness that had nothing to do with the morning frost. It chilled the refugees to the bone.

They halted and huddled together. The children made little frightened sounds; their parents moved the smallest to the middle of the group and shielded them with their bodies. The darkness in front of them whirled and twisted. It took shape. Maetis stood and stared as if frozen, doubting her eyes. Just a few feet away, darkness shaped itself into the night-clad figures of slender *Tzanatzi* warriors. Their eyes were dark pits in their haggard faces. Their swords gleamed like silver in the gloom, sharp and deadly. She had to shake herself to break the spell of motionlessness that had come upon her.

'Run,' Maetis cried over her shoulder to the refugees. 'Try and reach the nearest shelter. We'll keep them busy as long as we can.' The young warrior beside her stared at the dark figures that began their approach without making a sound. Darkness had fallen around them as if it were the deep of night.

'It's hopeless,' he whispered. 'We cannot fight the Dead....'

'Well, you can skin me like a rabbit if I'm not going to try.' Maetis took a deep breath and drew her sword. There was an answering ring of metal as her companions did the same.

It approached from the Southerners' side of the battlefield, like a monstrous black snake, a gigantic whirlwind of darkest smoke.

'*Calamêntiré, ti eyíldi, Tahiéra,*' the clear voice sounded again, and Rom could see the figure of Iryna, the *Tzanatzi* woman, small as an infant beside the massive cloud that swayed before her. In the cloud's wake, soldiers clawed at their throats, and fell to the ground writhing in agony. The air had become oppressive and heavy, until breathing became an effort. Rom felt his breath stick in his throat as the thing approached slowly but surely in their direction. He felt Yldich's presence beside him.

'I thought... it would disappear, once the mage was gone,' Rom said.

Yldich shook his head. His face was grim. 'An entity like this, once summoned, does not go lightly. Nor does it go of its own accord.' He did not have to raise his voice for Rom to hear him. The battlefield had become eerily silent. Every *Einache* warrior, every Southern soldier that was still on his feet stood rooted to the earth, staring up at the monstrous black cloud that swayed over their heads, leaning over those that had fallen.

'But—with the mage gone, what tie can it possibly have to this world?' Rom said. Yldich slowly turned his head and looked at him. Rom's eyes widened. 'You don't mean—'

'I think it is tied to *you.*'

Rom put his hands to his mouth and stood staring at the black cloud that towered over the battle field. It was swaying lightly, as if it were sensing, *smelling* for his prey, Rom thought uneasily, a sickening feeling in the pit of his stomach. No longer a hidden menace, the thing loomed over them like a huge ghostly snake, bloated with the energy of its victims. *But it's still hungry for more. It's always hungry.*

'What's more,' Rom heard Yldich's voice continue beside him, 'you may be the only one who has any true measure of power over it.'

'Now you may think me unfeeling,' Eldairc said, 'but shouldn't we be grateful this thing is doing our work for us?' Yldich turned to face him.

'What,' he said, 'makes you think it will stop at them?'

'It won't stop,' Rom said. 'It will never stop.' He took a step forward.

Eldairc gripped his arm. 'Wait,' he said. 'What are you doing?'

'Let him go,' Yldich said softly. 'This is what he was born for.' Eldairc's hand fell away from Rom's arm and he stepped back.

'I've brought this into the world,' Rom said. He took a slow step forward, then another. He kept on walking until he had reached the Southerners' side of the battlefield. Iryna stood gazing at him with an unfathomable expression; her dark hair moved around her as if of its own volition. When he reached her, he stood still and looked up at the *Tahiéra*.

It was like fighting water, or ice. *Hopeless,* the thought resonated in Maetis' mind. *Hopeless.* Each time she lashed out, each time her sword cut through the rags of midnight mist, her sword arm became a little colder. The whispering all around her indicated the presence of many more Dead. The chill crept up her arm, her shoulder. The cold sapped her of strength.

What when it reaches my heart? She pushed away the thought and set her teeth. Although her efforts to strike at the ghostly warriors proved ineffective, they were not so the other way around. Maetis heard a hoarse cry of a young warrior to her right. It ended in a horrible smothered gurgle and she realized his throat had been cut. She redoubled her efforts, wheeling her sword in a large silver arc to keep three dark-haired wraiths at a distance.

'Na'Héach,' she cried. Her voice cut a clear path through the gloom. 'Herdánte éya,' and the dark shapes wavered slightly upon hearing her voice. *It's not swords that will keep the dead away.* 'Odún! Elwéya,' she cried. She fervently wished the *Yaever* pupils were still in hearing range. 'Help us,' and then she had to focus all her attention on the fight at hand.

Odún heard her. He stopped and turned around. He wrestled for a moment with his desire to run. Then he cursed and ran towards the darkness, fumbling in his pocket for the crystal he still carried with him. He grabbed it in both trembling hands as he started to murmur, concentrating as Yldich had taught him. He sent out his call to the clouds, invisible in the gloom above. They started to whirl slightly in response. He could feel it. His song gained in strength. *Please. Come to me. Please.*

A flash of lighting lit up the clearing. A crackling sound ripped through the air as if it was split by an invisible giant's hammer. There was another boom. Odún stared at the scene in horror. Maetis fell back under the force of the ghostly warriors. All sensation in her arm had gone. Her sword fell from her lifeless grip as a *Tzanatzi* blade was raised over her head. The boy's scream rang in her ears.

The thing was more horrifying than the thought of dying on the battlefield. It had a voice. Rom heard it in his head. Strangely inhuman and void of intonation, it burned a way through his mind like acid. He resisted the urge to cover his ears. He dug his nails in the palms of his hands instead.

You. I know you, the voice said. *You are like the other one. The one who called me.* The *Tahiéra* swayed lightly, leaning over Rom as if to savour his scent. Rom shuddered. He clenched his hands into fists.

'Go,' he said. His voice was hoarse. 'Go back to where you came from. The one who called you is gone. You cannot linger.' There was a soft, horrible screeching sound, like metal grating against metal. Rom realized with a shudder the creature was laughing.

Do you think, the voice said, *I would want to leave now? Look around you.* The battlefield was eerily quiet, a silent picture of death and destruction.

'He's gone,' Rom said in desperation. 'The one who called you is gone. You cannot stay.'

He fed me, the voice seared through his brain. *He fed me well. And then, for years uncounted, I was in the dark. Until you called me again. I like this place. I feed as I please. What do I care if he's gone? I do as I will.*

Iryna spoke to him. 'Release yourself to me. Relinquish your power to me, and I will call it back. You have only to say you will.'

There were voices, hidden in the *Tahiéra's* whisper. He could almost make them out. Suddenly, Rom realized. It was all still there. The anguish and the terror, all the lives the entity had preyed upon from the beginning. From the moment he had summoned it on the ship, all those years ago. The *Tahiéra* had fed off them, drawn its strength from them, and taken on a life of its own. Rom swallowed. Then he drew himself up.

'Give them to me.'

'What?' Iryna's dark eyes widened in alarm. 'What are you doing?'

'Give them to me,' he said. 'All the lives you fed upon. Their fear, their anguish. Give it to me.'

'This is madness. You can't do that. You can't do that and live....' Iryna's alarm grew into fear.

Rom looked at her. His thoughts inadvertently turned to the Underworld dungeon whose walls had fallen away just a few hours before. He felt strangely light of heart. A laugh burst out of him; a clear, joyous laugh, it made Iryna step back incredulously.

'I died one and a half times already,' Rom said. Lights danced in his eyes. 'It's not dying you should be afraid of.' He turned back to the *Tahiéra*. He spoke to the black form in a clear voice that carried across the battlefield. 'Remember who it was who summoned you. See me. Know me. By his name, by Riórdirým, I tell you to release them to me.'

The *Tahiéra* shuddered. It began to quiver. It brought forth an awful low, groaning sound that made the earth tremble and had *Einache* warriors and Southern soldiers bow down and put their hands over their ears. Then it fell apart into a thousand tiny particles.

Little black seeds of terror, they began to swirl, moving like a cloud of flies searching for a direction. It swarmed this way and that. Then the black cloud found Rom. It regrouped, recoiling for an instant, and then moved forward purposefully like a striking snake. The black seeds entered his nostrils, his eyes; they streamed into his open mouth as he cried out in horror.

Images invaded his mind.

The low, bleak winter sun blinded his eyes. A young woman with tangled ash-blond hair crawled behind some bear cloaks, a knife hidden behind the child's back. It whimpered softly. 'Shush, Eldri,' the woman whispered desperately. She stared at the snow outside, hoping the demon riders would pass them by.

'*Ecceloz*,' a voice cried. They had nearly reached the hut. *Quickly*, she thought. *First her, then me. Before they can touch us. Quickly, now.*

'*Ti'héldae*,' the woman whispered. She raised the knife. Then the dark horror trailed into the hut, and closed her throat.

Before he could avert his eyes in dismay, another image forced itself upon him. A dark-haired archer steered his horse through the bare trees and snow-covered hills, when it stumbled into a pit that was hidden in the snow. It was filled with branches honed to the cruel sharpness of knives. The horse screamed as it frantically struggled to get away from the sudden pain. The archer threw himself forward and managed to scramble to safety. He looked up into the dirt-streaked faces of three light-haired barbarians.

'*K'álestre*,' he heard them grumble, their voices hoarse with hatred. He tried to struggle away from their grip, but they only held him more firmly. He was dragged to the edge of another, larger, pit. They still held him as he teetered at the edge. He looked down.

'No,' he cried. 'No.' Just as they pushed him over the edge, the dark mist rose behind them. He heard their muffled screams just before he was impaled on the sharpened trunks of the trees.

One after the other, the images of war seared through his mind as the anguish burned itself a way through his body. He saw the roofs of *Einache* huts burn as villagers were strangled by the creeping horror, and he was filled with their outrage and despair. He heard the cries of young *Tzanatzi* scouts as they were ripped apart by deadly traps in the Forest, and the darkness washed over them all, and fed on their agony. He sank on his knees and held his head in his hands, and still the voices, the raw emotions burned through his heart and mind.

How can one man feel all that and live? He choked on tears that were not his. Despair howled through his bones like an autumn storm.

Iryna gasped as she stared at the young man who was so like her he could have been her brother, bowed down under the weight of the *Tahiéra*. She had never realized how much she relied on it, how her power depended on it. The dark cloak that hid her true self was fading. She began to feel very small, and very vulnerable. She took a step backwards, then another. She turned around and fled. She did not notice the shadowy figure of a man slipping away from the Southern host, unnoticed by anyone, following in her footsteps.

Iryna was in Feyir's tent, hastily gathering her possessions, when she heard a sound behind her. The tent flap was pulled back.

'You.' Feyir's smooth voice sounded in her ears. It was cold with hatred. 'You despicable witch with your magic tricks. Your presence has made a mockery of me.' She turned around to face him, the silver dagger she had just picked up hidden in the folds of her skirts.

'*Câladirce*,' she muttered, but, like in a nightmare, she already knew. The word had become devoid of power. The *Tahiéra* did not come to her call. The dark cloak she had always pulled up effortlessly now eluded her grasp. She remained who she was: Iryna, small, helpless, and afraid. '*Câladirce, eccêloz*,' she cried.

'Have I ever told you,' Feyir said, and his voice, that was unnaturally calm, frightened her more than anything in her life had ever done, 'what Southern nobles used to do with *Tzanatzi* witches?'

The last thing she saw was Feyir's handsome face, a mask of hatred. He moved with the speed of a striking cat. She had no time to use her dagger. Useless, it fell to the ground.

There're so many of them. Rom hadn't noticed the girl leave. *So many.* The screams of men and women roared through his body until he felt he could contain them no more. Without knowing why, his hand went to the hilt of the *Einache* sword. It was whispering. Its blade began to quiver. Rom was shaking convulsively.

An impulse came from somewhere beyond the voices. He felt compelled to follow it. He grabbed the hilt firmly in both hands and held the sword up into the sky. When he could bear it no more, he drove the blade into the earth with all the strength he could bring forth. The voices, the screaming, the pain and despair streamed into the earth. Shuddering, he released it all into the dark, barren soil. A thought sighed through his head.

It needed to be witnessed. Now they are free. After what seemed like an eternity the screaming gave way to silence. The *Tahiéra* was gone. All that was to be seen on Gardeth Battlefield was the clean, crisp snow on the fields in the distance, the bare lines of the trees against the empty sky. Rom let go of the sword and fell over in the snow. He stared up into the air; the blue sky filled his eyes and the sun burned away the shreds of tortured memories, until he drifted away into a pleasant sense of nothingness.

Maetis gasped as the *Tzanatzi* who was about to cut her down shuddered, sighed, and fell away into a thousand tiny particles. The dark dissipated like a cloud of mist before the fiery face of the sun. Beams of sunlight shone through the naked boughs of the trees, changing the atmosphere completely. The ghostly warriors were gone.

The *Einache* refugees became aware of the twittering of birds above their heads. The cooing of a pair of woodpigeons sounded nearby. It was such an unexpected homey sound it made Maetis laugh out loud. It felt as if an oppressive cloud had fallen away. She stood up and sheathed her sword. She brushed the snow from her clothes. 'Well, now,' she said.

The battlefield was quiet. The call of two marsh birds flying overhead broke the eerie silence. Men of both sides stood gazing around with dazed expressions on their faces, as they were trying to remember what they were doing there in the first place. No-one seemed inclined to pick up the fighting again.

Einache warriors wiped their hair out of their eyes and started to murmur amongst each other. Southern soldiers began to call the names of their comrades across the field.

'Hey, Emerick, you still alive?'

'What'd you think, you ugly bastard.' A laugh rang out over the field. The nobles fidgeted with the reigns of their horses, looking down at their troops in vague perplexity. The fighting spirit seemed to have left them completely. It was unprecedented. They wondered what to do.

The first thing Rom noticed when he opened his eyes again, was the sight of two large boots right in front of his nose. They were tilted sideways, which seemed strange. Then he realized he must be lying on the ground. Before he could move, he was grabbed by the collar of his tunic and pulled up unceremoniously. He stared right into Feyir's amber eyes.

He noted without thinking they had changed. Whereas before, they had been cold and calculating, now they had a wild and detached quality. He wondered whether the man was still entirely sane.

'You,' Feyir breathed. Rom tried to struggle from his grasp, but the hiss of a dagger withheld him. 'Finally, I've got you where I want you. Justice will prevail.' Feyir lifted the dagger. A deep voice stayed his hand.

'May I remind you, Feyir,' King Farhardt said in an even voice, 'that you have no jurisdiction here. You cannot dispense justice as you see fit. You have yet to be reinstated as a noble.' He looked at Rom, who stared at him with wide eyes. He had recognized the King immediately. 'Besides,' Farhardt added, 'this young man doesn't look like one of your vassals to me.'

'I am not, my lord,' Rom said in a husky voice. Feyir had him in a rather tight grip. He indicated the *Einache* House in the distance with a motion of his head. 'I belong with them.' Somehow, coming face to face with the Southern King had his entire Southern upbringing rise back up. The page in him felt an urgent need to kneel on one knee and sweep off his cap in a reverential bow. Of course, the last time he had worn a cap was when he was about thirteen years old.

Farhardt drew up his brows. 'I was wondering about that... what drives a *Tzanatzi* to side with the barbarians....' As he shot Feyir another warning glance Rom was released from his grip.

'Half-*Tzanatzi*,' Rom muttered as he tried to find his footing. He didn't think it would do to collapse at the feet of the King.

'I know him,' one of the nobles said. It was lord Erckhardt. He stared at Rom in wonder. 'He's that half-blood boy lord Aldr used to have as a page. I remember him. Aldr beat that boy up every chance he had. I thought he was dead....'

'A page in a Southern court?' Farhardt looked perplexed at the dark young *Tzanatzi*, incongruously dressed in barbarian leather, thick wool, and fur. He deliberated a moment. 'I want to hear all about this.' He reached out an arm towards Rom. 'Come this way.' He motioned at the camp in the distance. Feyir was horrified.

'My King, he is a criminal, a dangerous sorcerer,' he said. Outrage put a ragged edge to his voice. 'You cannot let him accompany you unbound, without the safety of your guards....'

Farhardt turned and looked at the strange young man. He drew up his brows. 'He doesn't look very dangerous to me.' He addressed Rom. 'Have you any violence in mind?'

Rom shook his head. 'No, my lord.'

'Good. And if you make one suspicious move, I'll have you in irons. Do you understand?' Rom nodded. 'Then come with me.' He motioned one of the soldiers to come over and keep an eye on the stranger.

'My lord, what of the battle?' one of the nobles said. He looked slightly vexed.

'Let it be proclaimed I'm calling a truce. No soldier is to make another move until I know exactly what is going on here.'

'They're retreating,' Yldich said in slight amazement. He stood gazing over the field, his eyes narrowed against the sun. 'They're drawing back. Eldairc, can you see what's happened to Rom?'

Eldairc strained to span the distance with his eyes and cursed. 'They're taking him with them. Now what are we going to do?'

Maetis sat at the side of a fallen warrior. The refugees had gathered in a wide circle around the dead. A soft murmur was rising. Maetis closed the eyes of the lad whose throat had been cut, as she sang softly under her breath, an *Einache* song for the fallen brave. She folded his hands on his breast. She laid his sword at his feet. All around her, *Einache* warriors were doing the same for the dead. There were twelve.

'We'll give them a proper burial later,' Maetis said softly to Aeldic. She sighed and stood up. 'First, I want to know what's going on back home. Something has changed. I can feel it. You had better take the refugees to the nearest shelter. Anyone who wants to come with me, make ready now.' A tall figure in flowing robes, her white hair spilling over her fur-lined cloak, disengaged from the crowd.

'I'm coming with you.' Yealda's voice was low. 'I've a feeling I might be needed soon.'

Yldich stood staring out over the field, torn between his *Yaever* self, urging him to take care of the many wounded, and his heart, that told him to go after Rom. He raked his fingers through his ginger curls. He looked up into the sky, where a few wisps of cloud were hurried along by the northern winds.

I shouldn't have to choose between responsibility and love, he thought with uncharacteristic vehemence. He closed his eyes and let out a sigh. He breathed in the clear, brisk air and let his anxiety flow out with it. His mind became still and silent once more, like the sky swept clear by the winds. A thought occurred to him and he sent out a silent call, like a thread that unrolled from his heart.

Yealda.

The group that accompanied Maetis and Yealda grew bigger and bigger. Élora and several of Yealda's maids decided to come, as well as a few *Yaever* pupils, Odún and a girl called Laeta among them. Several warrior youths joined them. Aeldic and the remaining warriors accompanied the larger group, the children, the elderly and the sick, to an old temple ruin in the woods.

When they had reached the battlefield, Yealda and her girls wasted no time but began their work immediately. Maetis stood at the edge of the field and gazed in bafflement at the silent signs of destruction. She turned and kneeled next to one of Ullwich's warriors who was being helped by Élora.

He grit his teeth as the young girl set his leg. The bone had been splintered by a spearhead. She worked deftly and surely, and without so much as moving an eyelash. The warrior blanched as she pulled his leg straight and hissed out his breath through his teeth.

'What happened here?' Maetis said. 'Where's my father?'

He swallowed and looked up. 'The dark... horror came and nearly killed us all. It—it came from their side, and I saw the soldiers fall—' He winced and groaned as Élora pulled the bandage tight. 'Everyone stood as frozen. And then the *K'álestre* lad went and fought it.'

Maetis paled. '*K'álestre?* Do you mean Rom?'

'I'm sorry.' The warrior coughed painfully. 'I know you like him.'

Sorry about the insult or sorry that he's dead? Something tightened in the pit of her stomach. 'What happened to him? Tell me.'

'I don't know... it looked as if he was speaking to it. And then—it devoured him.'

She widened her eyes. 'What?'

'He was completely surrounded by the blackness, as if it—it *ate* him. And then... he drew his sword, and... I think he slew it.' He closed his eyes, drifting away.

Maetis shook him gently. 'What happened to him? And where's my father?'

'The Southerners took them,' he breathed, and passed out.

Rom studied Farhardt as they made their way through the snow. He had to make an effort to keep up with the man. The King was giving orders left and right in a calm, commanding voice as he walked. Soldiers and messengers took off without a word with orders concerning troops, supplies, and the care of the wounded. Feyir kept at their heels, trying to stay within hearing distance, his teeth clenched, his face taut.

Rom had never seen the Southern King up close, although he had seen him from afar on occasion, when he was a child, in the South. He was different than he had expected. Though authoritarian and direct, he had none of the arrogance or bloated self-importance of the Southern noble. His clothes were surprisingly plain and he looked as if he hadn't trimmed his beard in days. Rom wondered about the King's sober appearance as he laboured to keep up, the guard at his side ready to intervene if the *Tzanatzi* stranger made so much as an unexpected move.

'Now. About you,' the King said as he had given his last order. 'I never would have thought I'd see a *Tzanatzi* fighting on the side of the barbarians. Not to mention what you did with that odd thundercloud, over there. I have never seen weather behave like that, and I hope I never will again. I'm clueless as to what you did to stop it.' A puzzled frown creased his brow. 'Tell me, what is your name?'

'Rom, my lord. And I'm half-*Tzanatzi*. My mother was a Southern woman.'

'Really.' Farhardt looked aside at him with growing interest. 'So what drove you all the way up here? And what of Feyir's accusations?'

'It's... a long story.'

'We have time. We have yet to reach camp. You can start telling me on the way.'

'What are we going to do once we get there?' Eldairc was trudging alongside Yldich, who took large strides through the snow. In some places it had been blown knee-high by the wind. The field was lined by trees, the heralds of Gardeth Forest.

Yldich shook his head. 'I'll know once we get there.'

'You don't have a plan?' Eldairc's green eyes widened in consternation.

Yldich grinned. 'Once the situation presents itself to us, I'll know what to do. Or not to do. As of now, we have no idea what we'll find once we get there.'

'Lots of Southern soldiers, and Rom in a whole lot of trouble,' Eldairc said with a grimace. 'And no idea how to get him out.'

Yldich felt a tingle run across his back. There were eyes, watching them intently, from the trees. He did not speak of it to Eldairc.

Maetis stood looking out over the battlefield, her hands clenched inside her heavy cloak. She was weighing the possible courses of action. She found it impossible to choose. She sighed and brought her attention inward. There was something, a growing sensation inside her belly urging her to move forward, to go swiftly. She went to find Yealda.

The old *Yaeve* sat beside one of Morven's warriors. She was humming, her hand on his brow. The warrior moaned, his hands twitching. A shudder went through him and he lay still. Yealda sighed and spoke some words in *Einache*. She closed his eyes and looked up. 'Maetis?'

'Rom and my father have been taken by the Southerners. I'm going after them.'

Yealda folded the warrior's hands over his chest. She took a deep breath and rose carefully. 'Very well. I will accompany you.' As Maetis and Yealda started trudging through the bloodied snow of the battlefield, their departure was noted by several *Einache*.

Odún came running up to them. 'Where are you going?'

'To the King's encampment. Yldich and Rom have been taken prisoner.'

The boy's eyes widened. 'I'm coming with you.'

Maetis was about to protest, when something in Yealda's eyes stopped her. *Why not,* the thought passed through her mind. *If they're lost to us, we're doomed anyway.* 'All right. Come with us,' she said. Several *Yaever* pupils and young warriors joined them. When Élora heard Eldairc had disappeared as well, her bright eyes darkened. She deliberated a moment, then instructed another girl to take over her tasks.

By the time they reached the edge of the Forest, the group had grown into a minor *Einache* clan.

Rom recounted his tale as best as he could. He left out anything that reeked of the supernatural, knowing full well any suspicion of magic would jeopardize his credibility.

When he told Farhardt how he met Yldich and travelled north with him, the King frowned with scepticism. 'Why would you seek the company of one of the people that are your oldest enemy? And for that matter, why would he?'

Rom grimaced. 'To tell you the truth, my lord, I had no idea the *Einache* were the enemy. And Yldich, well, he's—he's different. He's the *Hárrad* of the *Einache*. He's a healer. He wants to heal the past, not perpetuate it. He doesn't desire war.'

'Really.' Farhardt narrowed his eyes in disbelief. 'The sacking of Elbury proves otherwise.'

'My lord, the *Einache* weren't responsible for that. Didn't you get the scroll we sent with your messenger? Woodbury and Elbury were attacked by riders....'

Yldich became aware of a presence behind them. He stopped and looked back, his hand on the hilt of his sword. Then he laid eyes on the group that was on their trail. Before he could utter a word, Maetis had thrown her arms tightly around his neck. 'Maetis—' he said.

'Where's Rom?'

'They've taken him. Now, Maetis—' She shook her head.

'We're coming with you. Don't try and stop us. We'll follow you anyway.' He gazed at her face, the wilful curve of her mouth. He sighed and nodded.

'The youngest have to get back, though,' he said, and waved back their protests, wondering how on earth he would get the *Yaever* pupils to comply when he couldn't get his own daughter to. A sharp cry rose in the air followed by a whistling sound.

Eldairc spat out a curse. 'The Southerners. They've seen us.' Within moments they were surrounded by soldiers, advancing with swords drawn.

Yldich drew his sword. 'Stand back. Get the children to the middle.' The youths stood waiting with swords drawn and arrows notched to the bowstring, their faces grim.

'Now, what in the name of all demons is going on here?' A deep voice boomed through the air. 'I thought I just called for a truce.' A sturdy man in heavy travel gear strode towards them. His blue eyes flashed under his heavy brows.

'I think it's their King,' Odún whispered to Laeta. 'You can tell by his eyebrows.'

The King took in the youths with their fell eyes, their narrow hands tightened on swords, belt knives, and bows. He looked in amazement at Maetis in her warrior gear, her slender hands around the hilt of her sword, at Élora in her apprentice's robes, and at Yealda who gazed at him calmly with her disconcerting lavender eyes.

He shook his head in bafflement. *By all gods. Do barbarians take their women and children along into battle? I've never heard of such a thing.*

Rom pushed his way through the row of soldiers. 'My lord, please don't hurt them. Let them come with us. They're harmless.'

'They're bloody well not,' one of the soldiers muttered, with an eye on the sharp blade of a tall warrior youth. It by no means resembled a toy.

Feyir came forward. 'My lord, you cannot trust these barbarians. They should be slain like the savages they are....'

Yldich looked sharply at the Southern King with his clear grey eyes, as if he were measuring him. 'To receive trust, one sometimes has to give it. I am the *Hárrad* of the *Einache*. I would like to negotiate with you. I'm willing to come unarmed.' He dropped his sword in the snow between them. Farhardt studied him with a pensive expression, his head slightly to one side.

'Very well,' he said finally. 'You will accompany us to camp. And you will come unarmed. All of you. Anyone who disagrees can have it out with my soldiers.' Yldich nodded, and motioned for the others to put down their weapons. One by one, the youths reluctantly dropped their swords and bows on the ground. Their faces were tense with mistrust. 'As for you,' the King said to Feyir, 'I will not have you tell me what I can or cannot do. It is time you should know your place.' Feyir blanched with anger.

'Yes, my lord,' he said.

As the company started moving towards the Southerners' camp, a small figure followed them unseen. It kept to the trees, melting into the shadows, and moved without making a sound.

The King's return caused a slight stir in the encampment. A whisper travelled through the tents and had people gaze up from their work. Children appeared from everywhere and hid behind stacks of firewood so they could take a peek at the savages.

'Your... *Tzanatzi* companion was just telling me the *Einache* are innocent of the sacking of Elbury,' Farhardt said to Yldich as they passed the first tents. The men were separated by a guard, and another one kept an eye on Rom, who walked beside them. Unarmed or no, Farhardt took no chances. 'Why did you not communicate this to me?'

'We sent a scroll with your Messenger,' Yldich said. 'We were willing to have a council and suspend hostilities.'

Farhardt drew up a brow. 'If what you're saying is true, then why did you kill my Messenger? His body was never found.'

Yldich's eyes darkened. 'My lord, we have had no hand in the disappearance of your Messenger. When the boy left us, he was alive and well.'

Meera peered at the strangers from behind the flap of the kitchen tent. The little kitchen girl held her breath at the sight of the fierce barbarians, their fell eyes and fiery hair. She stared wistfully at the strange and beautiful girl that was with them. She was tall and had the audacity to dress like a man. But her face, which was framed by shoulder-length curls, and her slender frame gave her away. Meera looked in wonder at the dark young man who walked next to the King. Unnervingly pale and dark like a *Tzanatzi*, he was dressed in the same garb as the barbarian warriors.

Then her eyes found Feyir's face and she gasped, even though she knew he couldn't see her. He was talking to the King. Her fingers tightened on the tent pole until her knuckles whitened. She strained her ears to hear what he was saying.

'No doubt the barbarians killed our Messenger, as soon as he had turned his back on their stronghold, just as he thought he was safe,' Feyir said. 'And now they are in danger of being overrun, they're changing their story to suit their needs.' Two or three nobles nodded in assent. It just sounded like something the savages would do. 'I'm sorry to say it probably was his own fault,' Feyir continued. 'The boy was vain and careless. If he'd been more careful, he wouldn't have let himself be killed....'

Indignation rose in the little girl's belly. She envisioned the Messenger, his handsome face white as death, his lovely clothes drenched with his own blood as Feyir's henchman searched his body. She gathered all that was left of her courage, and slipped away from the tent. Unnoticed by everyone, a mousy girl in dirty rags, she pushed through the growing crowd and walked up to the King. He only noticed her when she stood right in front of him.

'*He* killed him,' she said in a clear voice, and pointed at Feyir. 'He did it. I saw it. He had a man cut his throat, and then he took that round thing from him.' She shuddered as Feyir's eyes found her face. The hatred in them was almost palpable. She swallowed and involuntary stepped back. Fear made her eyes water.

Feyir took a step towards her. 'You dirty little wench....' Farhardt looked at Feyir. His face stilled. His eyes turned dark under the straight line of his brows. He became icily calm.

'Guards,' he said. 'Apprehend this man. And search his tent. If you find anything resembling a scroll, bring it to me.' Two soldiers took off in the direction of the rider's tents. Two others moved towards Feyir. Feyir's eyes rolled about to find a way of escape, like the eyes of a trapped boar. His gaze found Rom.

'You. This has all been your doing.' His voice was raw with hatred. Before anyone could stop him, he had drawn his sword. He aimed a heavy blow at Rom's head.

It all happened too swiftly. Rom moved his hand to his hip, at the same time realizing he was unarmed. He heard Eldairc gasp. He heard Yldich's warning cry behind him, and the deep voice of Farhardt, ordering his soldiers to apprehend the traitor. They would never stay Feyir in time.

Rom threw himself sideways to prevent Feyir's blade splitting his skull. He landed on the frozen earth with a shock that made his teeth chatter. His thoughts desperately went to the *Einache* sword. It still stood stuck in the earth on Gardeth Battle Plain. He could see it in his mind's eye, so clear and sharp, he felt he could almost touch it. In his desperation, he stretched out his hand. His fingers closed on something solid and when Feyir's second blow came down, he instinctively made a movement to ward it off. He closed his eyes, expecting to feel the cruel touch of cold steel. Two swords collided with a resounding clang.

Farhardt drew up a brow and looked aside at the soldier who had been supposed to disarm the *Tzanatzi* stranger. The man eyed the King guiltily.

'He was unarmed when I brought him in, my lord. I swear.'

'Well, he's not now.'

People hastily stepped back to give the fighters room and avoid being hit by the wheeling sharp steel themselves. Feyir's third blow went wide as Rom had scrambled to his feet and gained enough clarity to see it coming. The fourth he could parry. But not the fifth. Feyir changed his stance and managed a quick forward thrust that scored Rom's underarm. Rom cried out in pain and fell on one knee, labouring to keep his balance. Bright red drops of blood fell in the snow.

Eldairc moved forward in alarm, but Yldich stopped him with a hand against his breast.

'Let them have it out,' he said softly. 'It will have to end sometime.'

The pain seared through Rom's arm and into his brain like lighting. In a strange way, it cleared his head. His awareness was drawn inwards, where all was quiet. He became strangely calm. He stood up and tightened the grip on his sword. He felt for the right moment. Seemingly heedless of Feyir's advance, he started a turning motion, whirling around his axis. He swept the *Einache* sword in a wide arc; the finely sharpened blade cut through the particles of air until it started to sing.

He had completed a full turn when he met Feyir's sword. The swords clashed with a high-pitched screech that had some soldiers wince and put their hands over their ears. Feyir's blade shook in his hands. He stared at it in shock. The metal vibrated with a dull sound, like a cracked bell that had been forcefully struck. Its consistency was stretched to its utmost limit. Then it fell to pieces.

Feyir stepped back, staring at the hilt in disbelief. Rom lowered his sword to the earth, panting, the tip leaning in the frozen snow.

'Enough,' he said hoarsely. 'I've had just about enough.' The memory of the fight in the Forest came to his mind and a weary smile lit his face. 'I'm getting bored. If this is all you can come up with, fighting over and over until we're sick of it—I'm not doing this any more.' He sheathed his sword and turned his back on Feyir. A flicker of hatred flashed in Feyir's eyes.

'Rom!' Maetis cried out. A silver dagger flashed in Feyir's hand. Everything happened at once. Rom turned his head in alarm. Yldich threw himself forward, but he was too far away. Farhardt shouted an order, but the soldiers were too late to intervene. Rom stared at Feyir's face as the man moved his arm back in a throw that would have the dagger fly straight through his heart.

There was a sharp twang and a thud. An arrow was sticking through Feyir's throat. The look on his face was one of pure surprise. He made a gasping sound. Blood spilled from a corner of his mouth. The dagger fell from his hand. Then he dropped at Rom's feet in the snow. A small figure stood behind him. It was Eald. His narrow face was pale.

'That one's for my family.' He dropped his bow, sat down in the snow and started to cry.

Rom sank down before Feyir's body in the snow. Maetis dropped beside him. As he raised his arm to hold her, she noticed the growing stain of blood. She took hold of his arm and sucked in her breath through her teeth at the sight of the wound.

'It's not so bad, I hardly feel a thing,' Rom said. Maetis shook her head.

'You'll feel different in a while, believe me.' She quickly tore a piece of cloth from her tunic and bound his arm tightly. Yldich stood looking down at Feyir's body with a pensive expression.

'He came all this way to find his end,' he said softly. 'I doubt he imagined it would be like this.'

Rom's gaze fell on the dagger that lay next to Feyir's outstretched hand. There was something familiar about it. It bore an uncanny resemblance to the *Tzanatzi* dagger he had seen in his true-dreams. A shiver ran along his spine.

Iryna.

Two soldiers returned from Feyir's tent at a run. Their faces were set. One of them handed a scroll to the King. 'We found something else as well, my lord,' the soldier said. 'The dead body of a woman.'

Farhardt lifted his brows in surprise. 'I hadn't thought Feyir the kind of man to bring prostitutes to his lodgings.'

'This was no street girl, my lord,' the other man said. 'She was like—like the *Tzanatzi*, over there,' and he pointed at Rom.

'Show me,' Rom said. The soldier was about to comply when he realized he had no business following orders from a black-eyed half blood *Tzanatzi*. He looked at the King. When he saw Farhardt give a slight nod, the man turned and ran back to the tent, with Rom at his heels.

Feyir's tent had been pitched at the edge of the encampment, where the Forest had been cut back to provide fuel for cooking and the machinery of war. It was the only thing that could be associated with a Southern noble. Riders with ragged clothing and weathered faces were being herded together by the King's guards. When they laid eyes on Rom some of them cursed and spat on the ground. Rom turned to the guard.

'In there,' the man said. 'But you're not going to like it.'

Rom moved aside the tent flap and entered warily. He waited for his eyes to adjust to the gloom. There was no source of light apart from the sunlight that fell through the narrow opening behind him. He discerned a dark shape that lay crumpled on the floor, a life-sized doll that had been thrown to the ground by a petulant child. His breath stuck in his throat.

'Iryna,' he whispered. Her clothes were drenched with blood. Her face was deathly pale. There was something odd about it. Rom came a little closer. As his eyes adjusted to the dark, he recoiled in horror. He turned and quickly left the tent.

He kneeled retching in the snow, tears running over his face, when the others arrived. Before Rom could speak, Yldich had entered the tent. Maetis made a movement in his direction.

'Don't,' Rom said. His voice was hoarse. 'Don't look. You don't want that image to haunt you at night.'

Yldich returned from the tent. His face was grim. 'He took her eyes.' Maetis' hands went to her mouth.

'She nearly cost Eald his life,' Rom said huskily. He moved his sleeve over his face. 'So why do I feel like I've lost one of my own?'

Yldich shook his head. His eyes were sad. 'She made her choice a long time ago.'

'Well,' Farhardt said. 'Apparently I had a viper nesting among my people.' He spat in the snow, as if to rid his mouth of a foul taste. It was such an uncommon gesture for a member of the nobility Rom nearly laughed. He realized he was on the verge of breaking down. His arm burned.

'Now,' Farhardt said, 'I know who's been responsible for the killing spree in my camp. Although the reason still eludes me. After all, he did his best to convince me to go to the North in the first place. And why would a *Tzanatzi* woman side with him?' He looked at Rom as if he, being of the same kind, had an answer.

'She must have had her reasons,' Rom said wearily. Darkness was closing in. Maetis put her arm around him to support him. Eald came up beside Yldich.

'Are you all right, Rom?' His high voice cut through the murmuring of the onlookers. Yldich lifted the boy up as if he were still a toddler.

'Time to go home,' he said.

Farhardt looked at them. A vague longing tugged at his heart. He shifted his feet. They were getting cold again inside his fur-lined boots. Wet snow seeped in through the stitches despite all his efforts to keep it out. His leggings were getting soaked again as well. His stomach rumbled.

His thoughts were pulled irresistibly in the direction of home, of light, sparkling Southern beer, and freshly baked bread. He found himself longing for his youngest child's sturdy little body in his arms, the giggling of a helpless toddler tossed into the air by his big, grinning father. There were affairs to be settled. There was a young stallion that he had wanted to break in. And there was his wife, Elana, with her barley-coloured braids and her warm, tender hands.

She had a way of tilting her head and looking at him that made him feel... made him feel... well nothing like the bloody wet snow and the emasculating cold in this inhospitable, miserable excuse for a country. He'd had enough. Let the Northern clans keep their frozen territory, and good luck to them. He was going home.

'You there,' he cried, and a messenger boy came running, his eyes filled with surprise. 'Have the men strike the tents and load our things. We're going home.' The lad's face lit up. He started to run towards camp, crying out his message to everyone who would hear.

Rom turned his head to look at Yealda. There was something in the way she stood there, looking at the King, her long hair floating on the wind that was familiar. Suddenly he knew why. 'Yealda.'

She turned to face him, a laugh hidden in her eyes. 'What is it, Rom?'

'Will you promise me one thing?'

She looked at him a moment. 'Of course.'

'Promise me you'll never do that to me. Ever.' She grinned mischievously and suddenly he could see what she must have been like when she was young, many years ago, before the bitterness. She must have been beautiful. Her exuberance reminded him of Maetis.

'I only reinforced what was already in his mind,' she said with a nonchalant flick of her hand. 'But, very well. I promise.'

Farhardt was already busy giving orders to pages and soldiers. They turned upon receiving them and hastened away to carry them out. The look on most faces was one of relief, although some young nobles grumbled in dissent, their hopes for the future scattered and tossed away like chaff to the winds.

The King felt Yldich's eyes on his back and turned, his attention momentarily pulled away from the practicalities of moving three thousand people and their luggage back to the South.

'Ah, yes.' He rubbed his hands to keep them warm. 'What to do with you. Well.' He stood eyeing them for a while. He realized full well that to set the wheels of justice in motion would oblige him to stay in the North even longer. He deliberated a moment.

'It seems clear to me who is responsible for the wrongs that compelled me to come here in the first place,' he said. 'Feyir's men will pay the price for their treason. As for you,' he looked at Rom, 'Feyir's accusations of treason now seem to me the ramblings of a man on the verge of insanity. Any allegations of sorcery on your part are surely the product of said insane mind. Have you anything to add to that?'

'No, my lord,' Rom muttered. He dared hardly breathe for fear Farhardt would change his mind.

'Good. Though I warn you now,' he said in a stern voice, 'if any complaints of sorcery in these parts reach my ears again, I will not hesitate to send my troops to restore the peace. Do I make myself clear?' His gaze held both Yldich and Rom.

'Very clear, King Farhardt,' Yldich said, his *Einache* accent more marked than usual.

'Very well,' Farhardt said. 'Then I bid you good journey, and may you reach your home in peace.' He started to turn away.

Eldairc fidgeted. He raked his fingers through his shaggy hair. 'Just one thing your, uh, your highness, before we go. When do we get our weapons back?'

Farhardt turned and looked at the tall *Einache*, his eyes an ominous indigo. 'I don't believe I heard that. Consider yourself lucky I'm getting a little hard of hearing.' Rom suddenly remembered the *Einache* were officially forbidden to bear arms, on pain of death. Farhardt nodded almost imperceptibly at Yldich and pulled his heavy cloak about him. 'I bid you good day,' he said, and walked away.

'*Neachspragae*,' Yldich said softly. He took Eldairc's arm in a strong grip and began to pull him away. 'And you keep quiet, if you know what's good for you. Come along now,' he addressed the others. 'We're going home.'

They left camp quietly, walking in double file. The youths gazed at the Southern soldiers and guards with eyes hard with caution. But no Southerner seemed inclined to stop them, and nobody harassed them on the way.

They took the path back along the fringe of the Forest, wading through the snow, when they met a group of *Einache* warriors coming in their direction. Rom heard a clear voice call his name. He looked up, and looked straight in the grinning face of a redhead *Einache* youth.

'Réydin!' he exclaimed, glad to see the boy still among the living. His right hand was bandaged and he had a fiery cut on his forehead which he appeared to wear with pride, like a badge of honour.

Réydin clapped his good hand on Rom's shoulder in the warrior's way. 'So you slew the monster! Everybody's talking about it. *Ya'érsi.*' His eyes glittered with excitement.

Rom shook his head. 'Well, not quite... it wasn't really a monster, it was—' Someone behind Réydin called his name and he turned.

'I'm coming!' He gripped Rom's arm once more. 'It was wonderful. Really wonderful,' and shot away. Rom was shaking his head.

'I didn't slay anything,' he muttered. 'I only undid my own spell....'

Yldich chuckled. 'But this sounds so much more interesting. My guess is, by nightfall, the story of how you slew the monster will have grown into a Midwinter Fest ballad.'

Eldairc, who had been talking to Élora further down the line, rejoined them. He handed them slices of bread with big chunks of cheese. Apparently someone had had the presence of mind to run back to the House and bring back food for the survivors.

'Pity about our weapons,' Eldairc mumbled with his mouth full. He addressed Yldich. 'Although you must feel the loss more keenly than any of us. Your sword looked as if it was hundreds of years old....' Yldich smiled.

'That's why it is fortunate I've found the opportunity to retrieve it.' He laid his hand on the hilt of the ancient blade. Eldairc and Rom stared at it with their eyes wide.

'How—how did you do that?' Eldairc said. Yldich grinned.

'Rom is not the only one who can bend the rules of reality when he needs to.' He chuckled, obviously taken with himself.

Rom shook his head. 'I should have known. A *Yaever* who lives for five hundred years doesn't let a simple inconvenience like a Southern King and his army get in his way.'

Eldairc grunted. 'Meanwhile, I'll have to forge a new one. Three days' worth of hard work in the ditch.'

'Consider yourself lucky that's all you lost,' Yldich said softly, his eyes on the prone body of a warrior, dragged along by his comrades on a makeshift sleigh.

When their journey took them along the edge of Gardeth Battlefield, Rom looked at the frozen ground where he had plunged his sword in the earth. Something stirred deep within him. A warm glow rose from his belly and he was moved by an impulse he couldn't ignore. He motioned at the ground. The glow travelled through his arm. He uttered a word he didn't know.

'*Ciále.*'

The word sent ripples of warmth through the air, like the circles on the water when you throw in a pebble. Yldich stared at the ground where tiny shoots of green pushed their way through the snow. Leaves unfurled, and tiny white flowers, like little bells, lifted their heads. They were snowdrops.

'Not the explosion of colour you dreamed of,' he heard Rom remark beside him. 'But for now it will have to do.'

They were almost in sight of the House when they overtook a party of warriors who made their way through the snow at a slow pace. They were burdened with the bodies of the dead. One of them was a warrior who had been so tall and heavy in life his body had to be dragged by three men. Rom looked at the blood-drenched cloak that covered the bier, the ancient sword that had been laid at the dead warrior's feet and felt his throat constrict.

'Yldich,' he said. 'It's Morven.' Yldich stopped the bier with a word. Rom kneeled before it and studied the clan leader's face. For an instant, he thought of urging Yldich to try and bring the man back, the way he had pulled Rom back from death twice already. But there was something about the clan leader's face that stopped him. He looked calm, and peaceful, and... *determined*, Rom thought, for want of a better word. The man might actually be cross with them if they would be so disrespectful as to disturb him in his dignified sleep.

His gaze fell on the clan leader's folded hands. Rough and calloused, a warrior's hands, they had brought him nothing but kindness. As he took them in his own, a heavy sense of loss welled up in him and shaped itself into *Tzanatzi* words. '*Ayáa a eréaz àymire*,' he cried, and did not know what they meant. Tears ran down his face. Yldich laid a hand on his shoulder.

'He died an honourable death,' he said. 'A warrior's death. It's what he would have chosen.'

A little further down the path, Maetis stood still and held in her breath in surprise. She laid a hand on her belly. The fluttering of energy had been slight, but unmistakable.

'It's our son,' Rom said softly, without turning his head.

'What?' She turned to look at him. 'How would you know?'

He blinked and straightened, as if she had aroused him from a waking dream. 'Well, when I was d—when I was in the Underworld, I felt this string between us, and from us sprang a third... when I looked, I saw a little boy. He had eyes like mine, and hair of darkest copper.' She stared at his face as if she had not seen it before.

'I don't know how I feel about a husband who knows these things before I do.' He pressed her hand.

'I'm sorry... I guess you'll just have to get used to it.' He let go of her hand and she walked beside him in silence for a while, gazing at the snow, deep in thought.

'Are you then—are you not glad?' She heard his voice beside her, a hint of worry in it he could not hide. She laid her hands on the soft curve of her belly, where deep within she could feel the little spark of life. Brought to life by the merging of their energy, it nestled drowsily in the cradle of her womb, safe and warm. Her hands filled with a warm glow. It travelled to her heart. She smiled and turned to him once more. She held his head in her hands and kissed him. 'I *am* glad.'

When they had reached the House of the Deer, Maetis felt a lump in her throat that she could not swallow away.

'The doors,' she whispered. It had already been a shock to see the palisades torn down as if a giant had stepped on them in spite. To see the familiar ancient doors wrecked to bits, the heavy wood in splinters somehow brought it all home to her: the battle, the horrid things that could have happened, and those that had. Tears rose to her eyes. 'They stood for over a thousand years...they stood for as long as I can remember. As long as those doors were there, nothing could ever happen to me....'

'They couldn't keep the outside world out for ever,' Rom said softly. 'Even if the *Einache* could convince themselves it didn't exist.' He laid an arm around her shoulders. 'We'll build new ones.'

She snorted and wiped away her tears with her hand. 'You're starting to sound like Yldich.'

He grinned. 'What do you expect, after tramping around with the man for months....'

'I guess I'll just have to get used to it.'

'I guess you do.'

They entered the Hall smiling, hand in hand, while outside the signs of destruction were already being cleared away by warriors, kitchen girls, and clan leaders.

Epilogue

Rom and Maetis were joined together in a traditional outdoor *Einache* ceremony in early July, when the air was filled with the smells of summer and innumerable daisies dotted the grass. Maetis' dress gracefully curved along the line of her growing belly. She made no effort to hide it discreetly, as any Southern girl would have done.

Contrary to what Eldairc had told him, and much to Rom's relief, the marriage ceremony did not involve drinking the blood of a freshly killed boar. Maetis laughed out loud when he told her.

'Let me guess,' Rom said. 'That hasn't been done for—'

'At least three hundred years,' Maetis said. She chuckled.

After the ceremony was over and the guests were gathering in the Great Hall for the feast, Yldich came up to Rom and laid his hands on his shoulders.

'I'm leaving now,' he said.

Rom blinked at him in confusion. 'What? What do you mean?'

'It is time. I'm going.'

Rom widened his eyes. 'But—where are you going? You can't go!'

Yldich sighed softly. 'You have grown up now, Rom. My task is done. You don't need me any more.'

Rom shook his head in dismay. 'Please don't leave....'

'I will always be there. When the wind is in the north, go to the hill south of Gardeth Plain. If your heart and mind are open, you'll meet me there.'

Yldich stepped forward and embraced him. Rom felt a kiss on his brow as light as the brush of an owl's feather. A gust of wind went through the air and made the candles flutter. Then he stood alone in the middle of the hall. A sigh of amazement went through the gathered *Einache*. Rom stood in a whirlwind of consternation, his eyes closed, while the sound of amazed chatter rose up around him.

The first days after Yldich's departure, Rom went up the hill every time the wind was in the north. He sat there and stared in the distance, weeping without being aware of it, and the wind dried the tears on his face. Nothing happened.

After a few weeks he one day went home to find Maetis in labour. She gave birth to a healthy boy with auburn hair and eyes as dark as night. They named him Danayel. When Rom looked into his eyes for the first time, a fierce love for the tiny creature that was his son flared up, and made everything else drop away.

Three days after Danayel's birth Rom went up the hill again. He did not expect anything to happen. He just sat in the grass and listened to the droning of the bees. They were drowsy with the heat of the last days of summer.

Rom found himself telling Yldich of Danayel's birth, about how beautiful he was, and how perfect, even when his little face was screwed up with angry crying and his tiny hands clenched into fists.

'I expected nothing less from my grandson,' an amused, familiar voice remarked. Rom looked up. Yldich was standing straight before him.

'How—how can this be?' Rom stared at the man in amazement. He looked perfectly real, and large as life, with his familiar broad frame, the bright grey eyes that glinted with amusement.

'I've been here every time,' Yldich said. 'You just didn't notice me.'

'But—I wanted to see you so badly. How can it be I didn't see you?'

Yldich chuckled. 'Because you didn't think you could. Remember how the limitations you put on the world are stronger than its inherent magic.'

He went straight into *Yaever* mode again, Rom thought, wavering between happiness and indignation. 'How could you not be there when your grandson was born?'

'But I *was* there. I've seen him already. I'll be there for him when he needs me, just as I'm here for you.'

Rom eyed Yldich darkly from under the straight line of his brows. 'I'm not sure how I feel about my son having to contend with such an elusive grandfather.'

Yldich grinned. 'He'll be just fine. And so will you.'

Acknowledgments

When I started writing Curse of the Tahiéra I entertained two misconceptions about what it meant to write a novel.

The first was that I would have to make the story up. Nothing proved further from the truth. When I had surrendered to the process, the book, to my utter astonishment, wrote itself. The characters, real people with their own energy and personality, had their own ideas about what they were going to do and how they were going to go about it. It felt like being transported in an adventure of the spirit, a movie I only had to step into. The task I was subsequently confronted with was to put my adventures into language.

The second misconception I had was that writing is a lonely profession. On the eve of the birth of 'Curse of the Tahiéra' I am astounded at how many people have helped bring my 'baby' into the world. I would like to take this opportunity to thank them.

First and foremost my tireless editor, my mother and the grandmother of this book, Anneke Marijs. Her natural language skills and perfect sense of rhythm were an invaluable asset when streamlining the text. The many cups of coffee, late night telephone calls and home cooked meals helped too. Without her this book would not have come into the world!

Furthermore, I would like to thank my parents for taking me to the Celtic and Anglo-Saxon world, with its old castle ruins, elves and spirits, at such a young age. It's probably no coincidence that the name they gave me, Gwendolyn, is an old Celtic name.

I want to thank Pamela Kribbe, Wendy Strik, Claudia Bijlhout, Lieve Claes and Martin Langenberger for their invaluable feedback and helping me hunt down the printer gremlins. I would also like to thank Pamela and Gerrit Gielen for their support, tips and encouragement.

My fair(l)y godmother, Francien Fransen, I want to thank for helping me face my own demons.

Everyone who read this book prior to publication: Michelle McLeary, Anita Verbeij, Silvana Klerk, Cindy Gaal and everyone else: thank you so much for your support and enthusiasm!

And last but not least I want to thank Yldich and all my visible and invisible helpers, in this World and the Other, for their guidance, friendly meddling and support: you know who you are!

About Wendy Gillissen

Wendy Gillissen (Delft, 1969) has always been fascinated by dreams and the supernatural.

After graduating as a Clinical Psychologist, she specialized in dreamwork and past life therapy. She taught her first course in dreamwork in 1998. Since 2002 Wendy works as a licensed past life therapist.

The urge to write and her love for the world of castles, elves and ghosts stem from the time she was five years old and her parents first took her to the ancient hills of England, Scotland and Wales.

After an inspiring visit to the Greek island of Cephalonia in 2005, Wendy began writing Curse of the Tahiéra.

Initially, Curse of the Tahiéra started life as a short story but when Yldich walked into the tale of his own accord, it became clear Wendy had something else on her hands altogether.

For months, Rom and Yldich kept her busy with their adventures, springing scenes from the story on her at the oddest times, and soon it felt as if she was actually sharing her house with them.

Although a little overwhelming, the process of writing proved amazingly fulfilling and inspiring and as she was completing the first book, ideas for a sequel already came flooding in.

Creative inspiration also sparked in other areas and since 2006 Wendy creates handmade jewellery inspired by ancient symbols and cultures. In her spare time Wendy plays the Celtic harp.

Websites

Curse of the Tahiéra
www.wendygillissen.com

Practice for Past Life Therapy
www.reincarnatietherapie.com

Inspired by Legend jewellery
www.inspiredbylegend.com

The Search for Tzanáta

Seven years after his sudden disappearance Yldich has a disturbing dream which brings him back to the House of the Deer. Slender ships are appearing at the coast, and they seem eerily familiar.

Meanwhile Rom leads a tranquil existence among the Einache *of the high North. But all is not what it seems. While he still struggles with his* Tzanatzi *magic, disturbing tidings come from the South.*

The last Tzanatzi *are disappearing, and nothing remains except their bones...*

Excerpt

They had searched the vicinity of the *Sparrow's Nest* for hours. They had left Árya asleep in their room upstairs. When they finally got back at the inn, the common room was empty. Eald slumped in his chair and took a gulp of stale beer.

'Now what?' Yldich sat down. His face was strained. He raked his fingers through his hair and sighed.

'We knew the South had become hazardous for *Tzanatzi*. But I hadn't expected him to disappear as soon as we'd arrived....' Eldairc stared at him

'You think... he's gone the way of the *Tzanatzi* the merchant told us about?' Yldich's face was grim.

'It's not exactly like him to go walking off like that for no good reason....' The landlord appeared at their table. He uncorked a jug of mead and put it on the table.

'Gone is he? Your Wanderer friend? Afraid that might happen.' Eldairc pulled up a brow.

'What are you talking about?' The landlord sighed. He pulled a hand over his face, which was blank as ever.

'Well. I should probably mind my own business. But seeing as you people saved it anyway, I'd better tell you....' He seemed to have forgotten his barbarian guests had been the instigators of the trouble in his establishment in the first place. He bowed over his mead and eyed them from under his mousy brows. 'I should probably not be telling you this... and you didn't hear it from me, you understand.'

'Naturally,' Yldich said in a calm voice. 'Didn't hear what?'

'The Castle,' the landlord whispered. 'People have claimed to see *Tzanatzi* taken to the old Castle, at the foot of the hill. Lord Melcher's keep. And they didn't come out again.'

The Search for Tzanáta is scheduled for publication at the end of 2009!

Einache words and expressions

Aguéri	Divinely inspired, esp. of *Náeriae (see Náeria)*
'Aléyante éya'	'Take him away'
'Alyúrimae erdántwe Tzanatzi'	'Tzanatzi are beyond comprehension'
Ayéldi Eärwéa	Infinity knot
Ayúrdimae	Dreamwalking: lucid dreaming and /or leaving the body while asleep or in trance
Ayurië	Spirit
Conache	Troll
Dáydach	Father
Durga	Sword
Eärwe	The All-Encompassing; the state of Unity that transcends Duality
Einache (1)	Ancient *Einache* council, led by the *Hárrad* of the *Einache* (see *Hárrad*)
Einache (2)	'They who are of the Earth / They who guard the Earth'
'Elderána k'álestre Tzanatzi'	'Finish off those demon Tzanatzi'
'Encalimae fayïre éntme'	'Farewell my beloved family' (archaic)
Énthemae	True dreams, dreams in which one learns something important
Érstwae	Personal power symbol
'Eyespragae Faraër, entewé ya élorae'	'I am Faraër, I am beholden to thee' (archaic)
'Eyléa kanáchon'	'I will do battle'
'Eyléarana	

kanáchon'	'We will do battle'
'Ey lénte'	'All good things' *(Einache* toast*)*
Eylérwe	To skip, skipping
(sign of) *Farae*	Archaic *Einache* initiation sign given to aspiring young warriors and novice *Yaever*
Faraër	One who bears the mark of *Farae*
Fírte	Fire
Flestrérer	*Yaever* song that builds awareness of one's surroundings
Hárrad	Spiritual leader of the *Einache*
'Herdánte éya'	'Keep away'
Hwérwoden	Family
Kalantíri fayïre hwérwoden'	'Behold my beloved family' (archaic)
'Kalantíri hwérwoden érda'	'We behold thy family' (archaic)
'Kalantíri ya hwerdi Sanáyah'	'Behold the perfection that is *Sanáyah'* (archaic)
'Kalantíri kenéchie chamera'	'Behold the spear of separation' (archaic)
K'álestre	Demon
Kanáchie	Shit
Lachéia	To make love
Lágea	Everyday dreams, wish-fulfilling dreams
Neachspragae	'Until we meet again'
Nâstréhi ea	'Sleep well'
Na'Héach	'Joyful death', archaic *Einache* battle cry
Náeria	*Einache* harpist *(pl. Náeriae)*
'Ni érsi'	'Don't'
Ohênstriër	Undead (*Einache* obscenity)
Ruan	Manhood
Sanáyah	The inherent nature of things; the 'Way the World wants to unfold'; divine order
Sha'neagh d' Ea	The Wheel of Life; the cycle of death and rebirth
Skélgae	Rat, Rats
'Ti 'héldae'	'I love you'
Ulérstwe	Vermin
Ulúme	The ghostlike appearance of someone at the threshold

	of death
Yaeve	*Einache* shaman (f, pl. *Yaever)*
Yaever	*Einache* shaman (m, pl. *Yaever*)
'Ya'elemni	
aerwascht'e?'	'Who are you?'
Ya'elérwe	'You there'
'Ya élorae	
Faraër'	'Thou art Faraër' (archaic)
'Ya'erwé?'	'Is that you?'
Ya'érsi	Well done
Ya'haeve	Good day / good morning / afternoon / evening
Ya'hey	Hi / hello (informal)
Ya'herwe	
sá eldérwera	'Enjoy the hospitality of my House in peace'
Ya'kalánte	Indeed
Ya mérweda	Welcome all

Tzanatzi words and expressions

Alcánte	Kinsman
'*Altheíra calavéno*'	'The barbarians are coming'
'*Atáre*'	'Break' (*Tzanatzi* spell)
'*Ayáa a eréaz àymire*'	'Behold the passing of a great man'
'*Ayáa elcailië*'	'Behold the light' (*Tzanatzi* spell)
'*Ayàdi eymíraz*'	'Keep away from me'
'*Áya ecúrima moréaz*'	'Take the life from the living' (*Tzanatzi* spell)
'*Aye sûa*'	'I love you'
'*Aymíraz*'	'Good luck'
'*Câladirce*'	'The Cold come to me' *(Tzanatzi* spell that evokes fear*)*
'*Calamêntiré*'	'The cold take you' (*Tzanatzi* spell that raises the *Tahiéra*)
'*Caleërte*'	Well met
'*Calênte áyoroz*'	'The gods help me'
'*Ciále*'	'Live' *(Tzanatzi* spell*)*
Daemo	Totem animal
'*Ecceloz*'	'Take them'
Elcánte	Cursed
'*Élderoz me?*'	'Do you hear me?'
'*Elérimaz io, Éldere*'	'I see them right there, they are here'
'*Enteroz*'	'Come'
'*Ílde me*'	'Listen to me'
'*Ilderae me*'	'I said'
Íte	Now
Laôtha	Here
'*Lercia ayaz*'	'Merge with me' (*Tzanatzi* spell)

'*Oyente sá*'   'Stay there'
'*Oyéntere*
calatíroz, êlcme.'   'I can't bear this anymore, help me.'

Taôre   Here
'*Taz Aléir?*'   'Who are you?'
Ti eyíldi   Hear me
Óyirtaz   Obey me

Pronunciation

Einache 'y'
(Yldich, Yealda, Yaever) :   as the 'y' in 'yes'
Einache 'ich' (Yldich, Meldritch) :   as 'itch'
Einache 'ae' (ayúrdimae, Maetis) :   as the 'ey' in 'hey'
Einache 'ea' (Eald) :   as 'ey-eld'
Tzanatzi 'c' (Ciórdynn, ciále) :   as the ch in 'chess'

'Rom'   Wendy Gillissen, 2006

LaVergne, TN USA
25 November 2009
165278LV00005B/8/P